THE WAR OF IMMENSITIES

Barry Klemm

RUNDOG
PUBLISHING

ISBN 978-0-9807343-5-5

www.barryklemm.com

THE WAR OF IMMENSITIES

"I think the planet is in trouble and it's screaming out for help. I believe you are the first to hear the voice of Gaia."

The Earth is shaking itself apart. Volcanic eruptions of escalating magnitude and frequency threaten to collapse the planet within two years. Norwegian-American **Harley Thyssen**, the aging *enfant terrible* of the Earth Sciences, heads up *Project Earthshaker*, aided by his volcano-chasing student Jami Shastri and seven innocent bystanders drafted because of their personal experience of the mysterious *Shastri Effect*.Six of his team are all miraculous survivors of the first eruption in the series, sharing eight days in a New Zealand hospital in a strange coma apparently unrelated to their injuries They recover and return to their normal lives, but a few months later, they are drawn together again, to meet up in the middle of the Australian bush for no accountable reason, and realise that it is *not* a remarkable coincidence.

Kevin Wagner, American businessman, is sure a new, more advanced species of human has evolved and he is their logical leader;

Andromeda Starlight, second-rate entertainer from Trinidad, evolves into the very personification of the Goddess Gaia;

Brian Carrick, truck driver from Melbourne, whose simple *Science Fiction* approach to the effect allows him to explain the inexplicable to a desperate world;

Lorna Simmons, Irish born receptionist from Auckland, a passionate girl who believes *the Shastri Effect* is a higher expression of love, and so falls in love with an entire planet and it with her;

Chrissie Rice, French-Vietnamese skier, knows it is the hand of God at work and threatens to become the first modern non-Catholic saint;

Joe Solomon was a trustworthy Greek Lawyer, until his belief that it is all a big government cover-up causes him to defraud the US taxpayers of millions of dollars to fund the project;

And with them, **Dr Felicity Campbell**, a humble GP from Wellington, who originally treated the six and has inadvertently become the world's leading expert on the *Shastri Effect*, if only because everyone else knows even less about it than she does.

Slowly they are drawn into Harley Thyssen's web, to become warriors in a battle against forces at the very limits of human comprehension. For if Thyssen is right, then there is a war raging throughout the cosmos that began with the birth of the universe and will continue until the end of time, and now it's humanity's turn to enter the conflict.

CONTENTS

1
THE VOLCANOES OF TONGARIRO

For Andromeda Starlight, as she chose to call herself, there was an amazing sensation that she was flying. What was remarkable about it was that she was both straight and sober at the time and sitting in her bath which, she was absolutely certain, was firmly bolted to the floor of the bathroom. In that she was quite mistaken—it was really flying through the air. Andromeda had dropped enough tabs and sniffed sufficient lines to recognise the sensation immediately—the only trouble was that there had been no tabs for a year, no coke for a month and no booze since last night. Nevertheless, it was one hell of a trip.

She had been lying back, wallowing in the self-indulgence of the hot, steaming water laced with lavender and patchouli, when suddenly she noticed that the water was rippling—the surface was quivering slightly. She frowned. Had she made some movement she would have understood, but she was quite inactive at the time. Then her buttocks informed her that this was because the bath itself was vibrating, and at a rapidly increasing rate.

Even that was not really surprising—the whole north island of New Zealand was prone to shaking frequently and here, near Mt Ruapehu, more so than anywhere. But it would be so *bloody* inconvenient for there to be a major earthquake right now, just when she was settled into her bath... then the lights went out.

Now she knew that was definitely strange, because the light that went out so suddenly was daylight, provided entirely by the sun, shining brightly through the opaque window to her right. It was as if she suddenly went blind... not quite blind. There were all sorts of spots and ghost images floating in the blackness that said she was still seeing—there just wasn't anything to see anymore.

And it was in that time, when she knew she was still conscious, that she had the very distinct impression that the bathtub had sprouted wings and taken to the sky.

*

Someone struck Chrissie Rice with a rabbit-chop to the back of the neck. In the last instant before unconsciousness enveloped her, she realised that no one could have because there was no one back there, for she was sitting in the rearmost seat of the helicopter. What had actually happened was that her head, thrust back by the impact, hit the bulkhead and knocked her out. She remembered that she had just heard Lorna saying urgently. "Shit, look at that!" and was turning to look when the blow occurred.

Lorna Simmons, sitting beside Chrissie, had a moment longer. She had been looking out the window at the plateau below, trying to catch a prospect of the three snow-capped volcanoes in a line as the helicopter banked around the slopes of Mount Ruapehu.

They had flown up to the crater rim of Ruapehu three days earlier and then ski-ed down—Chrissie, who boasted that she had skied everywhere, regarded it as one of her best experiences. Now, they were returning from a sight-seeing flight across Tongariro National Park—this chap from Western Australia named Joe Solomon was footing the bill for the helicopter so the girls went along for the ride.

Lorna tried to pinpoint the Mt Ruapehu Chateau which, she was sure, had to be at the foot of the volcanic cone over which they flew. It wasn't there, and neither was the rest of the snowfield over which they had just passed. What she saw instead was a huge grey cloud billowing toward them from behind. She spoke and then immediately felt the helicopter jerk violently as the cloud overtook it. Everything went black and then even blacker as she too lost all sensibility.

For Joe Solomon, sitting beside his wife Melina in the forward seats, there was just a little more time still, for when he heard

Lorna's cry, he turned and saw the towering black billows of ash overtake the helicopter and engulf it completely and there was a sense of the helicopter flipping onto its back before his vision vanished. Joe Solomon, lawyer and union man, was fifty and overweight and tired of life, of his wife, of conferences and briefs and boozy lunches and scowling judges. He was a Rumpole-like man with no poetry and he came to New Zealand for a holiday that Melina and his high blood pressure insisted upon. Only to be killed in a freak helicopter crash, he thought, before there was nothing else.

In the same instant that Andromeda Starlight's bathtub flew, the tourist helicopter hired by the Solomons of Perth and the two young women from Auckland fell out of the sky with melting rotors, ploughed into a snow drift, and began to skid down the slopes of the mountain.

*

Kevin Wagner was another flyer and in even more improbable circumstances since he was three fathoms underwater at the time. At the edge of the plateau between the peaks was a small pond filling an old volcanic vent. Supposedly bottomless, the pool was a strangely intense blue coloration that changed at this time every year to a sort of murky green. No one knew why—certainly geologists and chemists had long since given up trying to explain it.

Wagner, an avid fisherman from San Diego, came up to dive and try to enjoy the good fortune of catching the change from under the water. He had left Sally and the kids at the Chateau and made his way down to the pond. At this time of the year, the surface ice was melted but the water was still freezing and Wagner had insulated every part of his body against the cold.

He went as deep as he could, peering through the special coating on his visor that prevented the condensation caused by his body temperature. The water was clear and the impression of intense blueness diminished unless you looked upward toward the sunlit surface, and Wagner was doing that at the time.

Suddenly, it went completely dark, as if someone had switched off the sun. Then, oddly, he started to sweat inside his wetsuit in the moment before a fierce turbulence gripped him. He knew nothing else, which he later found regrettable.

Boiling water surged up out of the vent and spilled over the edge of the plateau, creating a new waterfall into the Whakapapa River below. It bore the unconscious Kevin Wagner along with it, straight out over the cataract. It was a thrilling ride that he would have loved to have experienced conscious.

There was a group of four trout fishermen working the river in the valley below. They heard the deep roar above them and looked up in time to see the waterfall come cascading over the rim and with it a flying object that seemed to be a man. He hit the water fifty metres away from them and two of the men plunged over to rescue him. They were astonished to find he was still alive—in fact had they not rescued him so promptly he would certainly have drowned—a doubly miraculous survival.

The two men dragged him ashore amid the violent surging of that normally tranquil waterway and they, in turn, had to be rescued by their companions. Although no one complained about the dousing—the men discovered that they were being engulfed by a fine stinging hot ash that was billowing down upon them from the sky. Their eardrums were still ringing from the roar and the earth shook under their feet and then settled. In the forest trees fell, leaves floated in the ashen atmosphere everywhere. The men grabbed their gear and the rescued man, jumped in their Land cruisers and wildly took to the road, adding a storm of gravel to the drifting fog of ash.

"What's happening?" they asked each other frantically.

One of them had experienced something similar before and was able to guess accurately.

"The friggin' volcano's gone up," he declared.

They raced down the road through the valley, dodging falling trees and flying debris, peering through the sudden premature night, pursued by a massive black cloud of seething superheated ash.

*

Brian Carrick, a truck driver from Melbourne, had a mate down the footy club whose brother had made a packet and bought this Chateau at the base of Mt Ruapehu. A skiing holiday at the lodge was first prize in the footy sweep that year and Brian had won.

He did the right thing and offered to take the wife, but Judy opted to remain at home and look after the kids. Although they were getting along as well as usual, each was probably equally pleased to be free of the other. Brian undoubtedly got the better end of the deal but he worked very hard, Judy knew, and needed a holiday far more than she did. So Brian went alone, to try his hand at skiing.

The result was, as he put it in the one scrawled letter he wrote the family, that he'd never fallen over so many times in his life, not even when pissed to the eyeballs. But Lou and Terri, who owned the place, welcomed him and made him feel at home. It seemed like a nice place and the view was terrific although Brian had already begun to wonder just how he would fill in the time for two weeks. After all, once you learned to ski and got used to the spectacular views, there didn't seem to be much else to do.

It might not have been so bad if the Kiwi beer wasn't weak as piss. Lou politely suggested that they explore the wine cellar before dinner and Brian was about to say how he never drank plonk when he remembered how to be polite and said. "Sure. Love ta."

Still, he took a can of beer with him as they went down to the cellar and Lou proudly took him amidst the rows of bottles on the cobwebbed shelves in the dim musky interior and Brian tried to appear to be fascinated by the gabble about vintages and bouquets.

Suddenly, the walls shifted by about thirty degrees and all the racks fell over. Everything shook and dust blinded him. The room became a blizzard of broken glass raining with red wine.

At that moment, Brian was standing against the wall and, with Lou facing him, was shielded from most of the glass and debris, but that did not prevent the effect of someone belting him with a hammer in both ear holes simultaneously. He remembered the showers of sparks as the light bulbs exploded in the last moment before everything disappeared.

*

Jami Shastri had a dream—it was the dream of all volcanologists—to be right there at the instant an eruption began. But you needed to know the right people to get that sort of opportunity.

She had applied for innumerable field research projects, in those places where volcanoes grumbled threateningly, but she had never been successful. Instead she was put on loan to Auckland University, doing modelling on Mt Tongariro.

There were three active volcanoes in the group, Tongariro to the north, Ngauruhoe in the middle and Ruapehu to the south, all within 5 km of each other. Once a month, she visited the remote station on the plateau below Mt Ruapehu to collect the data and check the maintenance of the monitoring equipment.

The full array of sensing equipment had been installed years ago—seismometers to measure the shaking of the earth; geodometers to check for ground swelling; tilt meters; stream gauges to record water temperature, pH level and concentration of suspended minerals in the nearby waterways; gas sensors to search out changes in escaping hydrogen, CO_2 and SO_2 that might signal movement of magma below the surface.

Ruapehu had erupted briefly in 1995, Ngauruhoe not since 1975 when most of this equipment had been installed and Jami dreamed of being the one who was right there when the first minimal deviations began to occur in the instruments, to be the one to make the calculations that would confirm the oncoming eruption and—more deeply immersed in the same fantasy—be the one to make the predictions concerning what was about to happen.

It would be dark soon and she had a long drive back. She was wearily wandering from console to console, gathering paper, switching check-switches, when suddenly everything switched off. Or seemed to...

A nausea gripped her stomach as her head cleared from what seemed to be a moment of unconsciousness and she was sweating and shaking all over. In the room, for that vital second, everything remained quiet. She stood in utter disbelief—the moment had passed and it was as if it had never happened—and then suddenly the instruments went completely berserk.

Jami stared. There wasn't any measurement of anything going on, just meters waving needles madly, digital numerals flickering incoherently and the chatter of the printers rushing to a crescendo. It was as if the whole system went crazy for a moment, rather than registering anything in particular.

She was a short, slim girl of twenty-eight with the honey-coloured skin and jet black hair that typified the Delhi region. She had initially escaped village life and the dead city of Agra with its hordes of beggars, one of which she might have been had she not won that scholarship that got her to school in New Delhi. Then she won the Jarayan Prize to university in America. She chose Geology because she had never seen a mountain, much less an interesting rock. The terrain of her childhood had been utterly flat and made entirely of dust. And people... far too many people. Geology offered the promise of eternal solitude.

Ten years later, it seemed that she had used up all her good luck in that initial burst. The solitude she found was not the type she wanted, and she was weary of rocks and mountains too. Nothing ever happened. Not when she was around. She had begun to believe that nothing ever would.

So she stared, unable to grasp the fact that she was right there, at the right time. It became even more unbelievable when everything returned to normal one second later. Like it had never happened, like an aberration, like maybe she was fantasizing. The consoles hummed on, almost apologetically.

Her slow reaction, her bewilderment, prevented her from taking the obvious step. The machines were meant to achieve their purpose without human intervention and did so. She was irrelevant. The obvious reaction occurred to her slower than it would have to a person who was not a trained researcher. Instead of continuing to try and make sense of readings that did not make sense, what she needed to do was go to the window and have a bloody look.

And she turned and ran through to the next room where a wide window faced toward the three peaks. What she saw took her breath away. An enormous black smoke plume was hurling itself thousands of feet into the sky from Ruapehu right above her. Similar palls were launched from the two smaller mountains beyond. *It was really happening!*

Already the ground ash cloud was sweeping toward her at terrific speed. One second after she witnessed the vision she had always dreamed of, it was gone. The dust and ash hit the window explosively, splattering night into the middle of the day. The impact caused the wall to abruptly tilt at the ceiling level, and the whole room, befogged with dust, seemed to move several feet to the South.

The building started to shake. A roar rose in her ears until it caused her such pain that she was forced to clamp her hands over them.

Jami staggered back toward a corner and huddled in it. Death, she knew, would have already occurred or it would not. She was still alive and therefore safe, but that knowledge did not make it any less terrifying.

She was a shivering bundle in the corner, trapped in a death-like night of thunder and lightning and heat, and yet her mind was still working. The lights began to flicker as the emergency power kicked in and the fluorescence drew her out of her state of shock. She shook her head, striving to overcome her fear, but frowning too, and beginning to think again.

Her glimpse of the eruption was only momentary but its impression was deeply burned into her memory. The hail of rocks on the roof began to rise toward a crescendo. It seemed that at any minute the structure might collapse but the building was reinforced and could stand up to this and a lot more. She was safe and there were things to do. Important things to do. She was on her feet and made her way unsteadily back into the console room.

The instruments hummed on as if nothing was happening when plainly everything was. The printers had stopped. All the dials were reading normally. Three volcanoes were in full eruption, one of them was massive and less than two kilometres away and the most sophisticated monitoring system in the world didn't seem to know it. Ridiculous.

Jami forced her way to the table and chair at the centre where a yellow telephone reminded her of the next obvious step. She picked it up and was automatically connected to a switchboard. Right now, she knew, the alarms would be going off at the University, at the Bureau of Meteorology, at the National Parks Emergency Service, police, fire stations, hospitals, all around. The initial burst of activity in the equipment would have done that but now they would be waiting for some sort of confirmation, especially since everything had apparently returned to normal. Power surge, they would be thinking.

"Central monitoring," came the voice—a real human female voice, not a tape.

"Ruapehu. She's blown," Jami replied breathlessly.

"Which services are you requiring?"

"All services," she said, trying to remember the right codes. "Level 5, Red alert."

"State your name and location please."

"Jami Shastri. Whakapapa Monitoring Station. Number 3788810. Confirm. We have a Level 5 Volcanic event going on here..."

2
UNCONSCIOUS COLLECTIVE

The cloud had already extended beyond the blown-down zone, beyond the monitoring station, beyond the valley and the lake, beyond the mountain range itself. A black snowfall, fiercely hot, centimetres deep, began to pockmark the landscape. The debris that tumbled into the many rivers and innumerable creeks that flowed from the Tongariro National Park rushed downstream in all directions with ferocious turbulence until it was blocked by the dams it formed itself.

From the three craters on the plateau, a black pall of fiery rock, lava and ash soared far into the sky. Casualties occurred up to ten kilometres away although mostly due to peripheral accidents—cars running off roads in the sudden black fog, people crushed by falling objects or caught in the flooding as the mud surged down the mountain sides. Within a kilometre, people, animals and trees simply vanished, scorched out of existence. The fiery, hot ash blanketed the terrain, suffocating everything, and with it a hail of boulders and mud rained down upon the shocked world below the mountains.

In the nearby town of National Park, the end of a sunny day suddenly turned totally black, as the towering cloud, billowing and flat-topped, deepened the gloom that spread across the land. Lightning burst from the cloud continually as the ground was veiled in the fallout from the pall. Its hurricane wave of scalding gases and fire-hot debris travelled at 200 kilometres per hour as it swept down upon Ohakune. The pillar plumed eastward into a widening dark cloud.

At Napier, 150 kilometres away to the east, a spectacular

sunset was suddenly obliterated by unrealistic blackness and with that unscheduled night came a fog of choking ash. A third of the North Island of New Zealand was brought to a complete stand-still by the ash fall. Days later, the silt would reach the ocean via the rivers after causing devastating floods, closing the waterways to deep-draft ships. The cloud crossed the Pacific to South America in four days.

*

Within an hour, the rescue teams were moving in—by road, by helicopter, on foot. Up to a kilometre from the craters, the 1000 degree ash and the atmospheric heat made the air unbreathable. On the first night they could get no closer but there was more than enough for them to handle at that distance. Dozens of people, injured by fallen buildings or trees or crashed vehicles, were picked up and conveyed to nearby hospitals. Dazed and injured people walked out of the fog of ash into the hands of rescue teams. They knew that over fifty people remained in the critical quadrant, most of whom would surely be dead. Deaths already amounted to thirty on the periphery of the blast area, and injuries over a hundred.

Jami Shastri was found, dazed but unharmed, at the monitoring station two hours after the eruption. She thrust a satchel containing the print-outs and data disks into her rescuers' arms, refused to leave, refused medical assistance, and demanded her data be taken directly to Auckland University where it could be analyzed. Her demand proved impossible for the moment since Auckland was coincidentally fogbound at the time and all traffic was being directed south. Soon the white cold fog from the north collided with the black hot fog sweeping up from the south and a black rain began to fall constantly on the towns right around the Bay of Plenty to North Cape.

In a deep coma and suffering multiple broken bones, Kevin Wagner arrived at the emergency medical centre being established in the town of Turangi on neighbouring Lake Taupo, brought in five hours after the blast by the men who rescued him from the surging river that had once been a trickling stream. Theirs had been a terrifying journey through a smoke-filled night on treacherous roads. The flood waters from the rising river had forced them to divert and they found the road broken by landslides and fallen trees. Along the way, they had picked up four other casualties as they forced their way through a chaotic and unfamiliar landscape.

Wagner's condition was critical but stable, and he was soon dispatched by helicopter to Wellington which, lying south-west of the thermal zone, escaped all of the worst effects of both the meteorological white fog and the volcanic black one.

By morning, the ash pall that veiled the ground from the air began to dissipate and fall to earth. The rescue helicopters probed deeper into the zone, searching for survivors. Beneath them now was a world that only knew the colour grey. All along the plateau between the three peaks, felled trees lay in sweeping rows like scattered straw, stripped completely of their leaves and branches. The entire plateau was a desert of grey mud.

Wayne Higgins was flying a Hughes 500 four-seater helicopter that he used to provide joy-flights for the tourists, but now the seats had been dragged out. Air Rescue had allocated him a crewman, Jim Rogan, who squatted in the doorway, the yellow helmet on his head his sole protection from the downdraft, his visor failing to keep the dust out of his eyes. As they swept around the steaming slopes of Ruapehu, Rogan spotted the glimpse of colour far to the left.

"Over there. Turn 60 degrees left," he shouted into the intercom over the constant crackle of interference.

The colour was gold and green metal protruding from the broad pool of ash and as soon as he saw it, Rogan guessed it was a helicopter. As the chopper banked in toward it, Rogan could see it was a section of fuselage, but there was no evidence of rotors or tail as he might have expected. There was no other wreckage visible that he could see, the rest was swamped in the grey layer of ash that had settled upon the snow.

"It looks soft," he said to Wiggins. "Better not land."

It had snowed the night before, and the effect of the layer of hot grey ash on top of the powder snow was likely to cause all manner of strange effects. Officially, there had been eleven centimetres of snow and about five centimetres of ash, but in a drift ravine like this, there was no telling how deep either might be. The effect of heat on cold might have melted the surface briefly then refrozen it as ice creating an illusion of firm footing when in fact you could slip ten metres below the surface and be lost.

Rogan hooked himself to the winch cable as Wiggins brought them in to a point where he hovered without quite touching the ground. The rotors set off a blizzard of black snow, blotting out all visibility. Into the midst of it, Rogan stepped out onto the landing strut and then jumped blind.

His landing was unreasonably soft, as if jumping into a bed of feathers. He righted himself but still couldn't see anything— had no idea which direction the wreckage lay.

"Okay, take it up slow, Wayne."

He waited while the chopper moved away, carefully ensuring that he had plenty of slack on the cable. The ash was heavier than most dust or snow and settled immediately the wind was off it.

Rogan, wading almost knee deep in the ash, plunged toward the wreckage unsteadily, the cable dragging behind him like a long tail. It was a section of the side of the fuselage that he could see—beyond he could make out a furrow where the wreck had slid almost a hundred metres downhill since impact. The rest of the helicopter might be anywhere. Rogan pushed his way forward, shovelling ash with his hand, in the direction in which the fuselage seemed to widen, and where he hoped he might find a door.

Eventually, he had to clamber up onto the body, where he discovered that the door handle had been melted. He had a screwdriver hanging from his belt and levered in a place where the door had buckled, and finally wrenched it open.

He maneuvered around and peered in, grabbed his torch and directed the beam inside. There was an almighty tangle of seats and people. Five people he guessed, twisted and bloodied. He pulled off his glove and reached for the nearest flesh he could see, the arm of an over-weight woman of fifty or more. The coldness was that special kind he knew only too well.

He was obliged to stretch further in, knowing there was no hope. The warmer air inside the mangled cabin was escaping. A fog was settling in there. His own breath, coming in blasts of whiteness, was enough to obscure his view. Then he realised—it wasn't just his own breath. There were other puffs of whiteness appearing momentarily. Rogan reared back and looked toward the hovering helicopter.

"Jesus, Wayne! Drum up some help! There's people alive in here!"

*

Only with the coming of daylight, more than twelve hours after the eruption, did the various rescue teams begin to penetrate the main area of devastation. The fifty or so rescue workers who had already arrived on the scene were divided into teams of a dozen and equipped with whatever was to hand.

A group of firemen wearing heat-proof suits and with breathing equipment were attempting to make their way up the ridge to the Ruapehu Chateau where they knew the greater number of victims in the quadrant of destruction would be found. At one kilometre from the epicentre, there was over a metre of ash in low places, forcing them onto higher ground.

Soon, they passed beyond the newly created edge of the forest—even there the trees were stripped of their leaves and twisted and laden with ash. Ahead, the logs lay in a weirdly orderly fashion, as if felled by human hands. As far as they could see, the rows of denuded trunks carpeted the earth, and they could make their way forward only by traversing the logs like lumberjacks.

On the low ridge ahead, they should have been able to see the chateau but there was no trace of it, not even the chimneys that usually stood after fires. Beyond that, the smoke pall from the crater still ascended skyward even though there had been no more eruptions. The firemen, led by Del Shannon, worked their way up until they came to the bottom of the ski-slope that led directly to the chateau, but there the logs ran out and they were faced with snow and ash drifts metres thick. That might have been the end of their attempt, had not Jerker Teasdale spotted a strange shape away to their right.

"What's that?" he asked in puzzlement.

It was a curved metal shape about two metres long with four short feet sticking upward, like a dead cow chopped off just below the shoulders. Shannon laughed.

"It's a bathtub. Lou had them old type ones installed right through the chateau. Cost him a bloody fortune."

Because they didn't want to think where Lou might be now, they made their way across to the object. Anyway, they needed to go sideways to see if they could find some way of climbing closer to the chateau. At least that was how Shannon justified it in his mind.

The bath, its enamel belly painted duck-egg blue, had obviously tobogganed all the way down the ski-slope to this point, over-turning at the end of its run and the ash was heavy enough to slip away from most of its surface.

"Maybe there's someone in it," Jerker laughed. "Let's turn it over."

Shannon surveyed the scene—there wasn't really time for this nonsense.

"We'll keep moving this way. Maybe we can make our way up along the ridge over there."

But the irrepressible Jerker and two cronies were heaving on the short steel legs of the bath and tilting it.

The smooth dark brown arm flopped through the opening.

They all stared.

"Shit, don't drop it!" Shannon ordered.

Barely recovering themselves, Jerker and the others heaved the bath clear. The men stood around, spellbound by what they saw. Andromeda Starlight's flesh contrasted stunningly with the area of white snow where the bath had prevented the ash from falling.

"Shit," Jerker gasped. "She's burned to a crisp."

"No she ain't, you fucking dickhead," Shannon snapped. "She already was black. Don't you know a darkie when yer see one?"

"Never seen one in a bath before," Jerker blubbered. "But I always wanted ta."

The men chuckled, not so much at Jerker's sadistic humour as from an hysteria to which none of them would have wanted to admit. They were all possessed by a paralysis, the vision before them seemed to have arrested them completely.

"Well, don't just stand there gawking," Shannon snapped at them. But he was still standing and gawking himself.

It was finally left to Jerker to reach and delicately touch her, seeking vital signs. He pulled his hand back as if bitten.

"Fuckin' hell," he breathed. "I got a pulse."

*

"Chopper coming in!"

The orderly appeared only momentarily at the door, and Felicity Campbell's senses were not up to identifying him. She was moving before she was thinking. Her body seemed to know the right way to weave around the clutter of ICU beds in the room such that she did not trip on cables nor upset consoles. Instincts carried her out into the corridor and into the lift before she really knew she was there.

She switched to the service lift on Level N, running with that shuffling, oriental gait of legs too tired to fully raise her feet off the floor. Earlier, she remembered instructing an orderly to mop up the blood splattered all the way along here—it had not been done. The helicopters kept coming and there was no time, not even for basic hygiene, not to mention safety.

As the lift doors breathed open to the rooftop, she was surprised by the bright light that savaged her eyes. At first, she thought it was the landing lights of the helicopter—only vaguely did she realise it was daylight. Throughout the night, she had done this more than a dozen times, and still they came. The hospital was filled beyond capacity, but the helicopters kept coming and coming.

Desperately, she strove to pull her exhausted brain into order. She ploughed out into the chill of morning before she realised she had gone too far. It was totally exposed up here on the roof of the clinical services tower, and the view was stunning for those who had time to look. The stiff wind off Wellington Harbour—blue and serene beyond the city skyline—grabbed her and shook her. She had passed the nominated examination point in the rooftop hut where the waiting medical teams could shelter from the constant wind; where she had idiotically observed the blood but seemed to have forgotten why it was there.

The helicopter was still way up in the air, on approach to the pad. Felicity Campbell pressed her inner pause button and halted in the middle of the tower roof. A herd of orderlies came by her like a rugby team, racing to meet the helicopter. Felicity gulped the air and it refreshed her and got her brain going again.

The helicopter wobbled down onto the pad, and the crewman jumped into the pack of waiting orderlies and they had the first patient on a trolley and rolling toward her with blinding speed. Felicity backed off into the hut, where another collection of nurses and orderlies were gathering to heed her orders.

All through the night, the helicopters kept coming and coming and Felicity had met them all. She had placed herself at the first line of assault and now carried a knowledge of the overall situation at Wellington Hospital that was so complex and fluid that it could not be passed on to anyone else. She was here to stay until the last helicopter came.

The chatter of the rotors had come to haunt her, and as she heard each approaching helicopter, she abandoned whatever she was doing and raced upward to the helipad. As each victim was rolled in and the paramedics gabbled out what was known of their condition, Felicity made hasty assessments and barked sharp destinations to the orderlies.

"This one straight to theatre 64... Run her up to ward 29... Okay, get him into radiology... Can't do anything here without a cat scan—stick him in the queue."

With each instruction, her picture of the chaos within the hospital expanded. They were under extreme pressure at every level, but the staff, she had observed, remained calm. Just do the work in front of you and treat it like a normal day, had been the general instruction. Felicity had been on her feet for twenty hours and there was no end in sight.

The galloping mob propelling the trolley drew to a halt beside her and she lifted the cover. They had to shout above the wind and chatter of the rotors. "What have we got?"

"Female, black, unidentified, comatose, all vital signs, no apparent injuries."

Felicity gazed down at the face of Andromeda Starlight and saw an incongruous picture of absolute calm. The woman might have been sleeping peacefully. If so it was the first peace Felicity had seen for many hours.

She looked back at the harried face of the paramedic, a young man, splattered with blood, pallid with exhaustion. The helicopter had carried this one victim alone, and now waited impatiently to return. Bewildered orderlies hung about the helipad, unable to believe there weren't three or four more casualties as had been the case on every other helicopter throughout the night.

"What were her circumstances?" she asked, returning her attention to the patient, as if she doubted there was nothing to look for.

"Not sure. There was some yarn that she was in a bath which protected her from everything."

"Exposure?"

"About twelve hours. But she was apparently sheltered throughout. No frostbite. The ash kept the bathtub warm. No burns. No contusions that I could find."

"Okay," Felicity breathed, and turned her attention to the orderlies. "Comatose. Down to CT. Start with a scan for head injuries. Go."

The orderlies whisked the trolley away, and the paramedic was striding back toward his impatient helicopter. Felicity had to run to keep up with him. She did not want to allow her body nor mind to rest until she was sure the initial chaos was passed.

"How's it looking up there?"

The paramedic paused, realising her anxiety, and why. Theirs had been one of the first helicopters on the scene—this was their sixth or seventh trip—he had lost count.

"Hard to say. The damage is so widespread—casualties keep seeping in everywhere. But it has slowed down this morning."

"So the pressure might be off."

"I'd get some rest now, if I were you. They haven't reached the chateau yet—it's too hot up there. They don't expect to get in there until tomorrow. There's still forty people known to be missing, at least."

"Surely there won't be anyone left alive at this stage?"

"Who knows? There's been several miraculous survivals that we know of. That woman would have been dead for sure if the bath hadn't shielded her. There was a helicopter that melted in midair but three people survived the crash. Who knows what lies ahead? But I think it might slow down for a few hours now."

"Thanks," Felicity smiled.

He ran to the helicopter and Felicity walked back, ignoring the downdraft of the rotors, stripping off the rubber gloves as she rode down to Level N and crossed to the public lifts. Sure, time to rest.

All they'd done so far was get the patients in the door. Their treatment had hardly begun. Still, she did need something... Coffee. One quick coffee and then a complete tour of the hospital, to update her mental picture of the madness that reigned in there.

Still, it *was* odd that the black woman was so deeply comatose and yet exhibited no injuries at all...

*

Glen Palenski strolled in and dumped his backpack in the middle of the floor where, Jami knew from long experience, it would remain until she told him to move it. He put on a big grin and struck a macho pose.

"The cavalry has arrived."

"Too late as usual," Jami replied languidly. It had been only two days since she left him in Auckland, but it seemed like years ago. In any case, her days of offering him excited welcomes were long past.

"So, you actually eyeballed it," he said, beginning to move around the room, checking the monitors.

All was calm, there was nothing for him to see, the three volcanoes had been quiet since yesterday morning. But she didn't bother to tell him that.

"I did indeed. One of the privileged few."

"One of the very few indeed that did so and survived. Not many *vulcans* can claim that."

"The image shall remain burned indelibly on my corneas forever. You took your goddamned time getting here."

"Rough journey," he said with a shrug. "It's as if all Kiwiland has been laid waste by the event."

"I bet you were being laid all right."

"Now, now, Jami. One eruption in the vicinity is enough for this season."

In fact she was happy to see him, if only because it gave her someone to talk to. In the two days since the eruption, she had become the unnominated head of a considerable team with an astonishingly international flavour.

First two Geologists came over from Christchurch; one was Maori and the other Samoan and she quickly sent them out with replacement sensors and charts indicating where they should be placed. Then two team members arrived from Rotorua— an Englishman with a Scots accent and a Frenchman who was Algerian, and finally a pair from Macquarie Uni in Sydney who declared themselves Australian when they were plainly Cambodian.

Jami, a mere PhD student, remained in charge mostly because she didn't tell anyone her lowly status, because she was there when it happened, and because she was American despite her Indian heritage, from MIT, and could speak the name Harley Thyssen with authority.

"So how are you coping?" Glen asked.

Jami knew it was really Harley asking. *"Get your ass down there and see she don't fuck up completely,"* Harley would have thundered down the telephone line. Little else would have got Glen Palenski into motion.

"Fully under control. I've got a team of six out there and they've replaced the sensors all the way up to the edge of the hot zone. We have everything on the Net. I've duped all the CDs and mailed them to Auckland. I've faxed all the hardcopy to Harley. And now I'm working on my report."

"Of the big sighting."

"Twenty twenty eyeball."

"Let's have a look."

"You'll see it when Harley sends you a copy. For his eyes only."

"Hallelujah Harley."

"You get some rest, Glen. There's plenty for you to do later."

"Is that an order, ma'am?"

"Does it need to be? What did Harley say?"

"You know what he said. And he wants you to ring him straight away. He's been calling hourly and got zip."

"I haven't been inside any more than I needed to. You know the north side building is leaning fifteen degrees off perpendicular. You can start the repairs over there."

"How much equipment fizzled?"

"Fifty percent."

"And you got a full breakdown already from the rest?"

"Yep. Along with some interesting anomalies."

"Harley will love you."

"Harley will hate me just a little less than he hates everyone else. And I will call him, when I've finished my report."

"My, my, how tough and authoritarian you've become, Jami. A full-on experience seems to do you the world of good."

"Watching a volcano blow a hundred people away does that to you, Glen. Especially when you were six millimetres of plasterboard and a pane of glass from being the hundred and first."

"Hit hard, huh?"

"I have been, of necessity, born again."

There was a time when she idolised Glen Palenski. Watching him now as he ferreted in his pack, giving her a perfect view of his splendid backside, she could understand why.

They went through college together, he the all American boy, she a skinny little Indian girl who followed him around everywhere like a faithful retriever. He had her and dumped her a dozen times and she kept coming back for more. Finally they graduated and bummed their way here—to her moment of destiny but not his, which was a rather refreshing change.

She tried to diminish him in her mind as she did in her intellect, but there was always his perfect, tanned body, which he exposed proudly to the world at every opportunity. It was ten degrees outside and here he was in shorts and sleeveless shirt, showing off. But this wasn't the moment and she averted her eyes. Jami realised that she was still as alone now as she was before he arrived.

*

The young man with his thick spectacles and cherubic cheeks tried his hardest to look serious but was in every way unconvincing. Felicity Campbell poured herself an instant coffee and ran her mind through the case history. Christine Rice, Asian in appearance, French according to her passport, resident of Auckland on an extended tourist visa, aged 22, one of the two young women to survive the crashed helicopter, severe contusion to legs and abdomen, minor facial lacerations, three broken fingers, comatose. No head injury evident. It was just a matter of healing time.

But Barbara Crane, the Chief Administrator, brought this young man who insisted on talking to the doctor-in-charge. John Burton. Wrong name.

"You are related to Miss Rice?" Felicity asked him.

He looked guilty and nervous.

"I'm her fiancée. We are to be married on the 25th of next month."

"I see," Felicity said wearily.

"The thing is, they won't tell me what's happening."

"Who won't?" Barbara had to ask, because Felicity didn't bother.

"The other doctors. I keep asking them about Chrissie's condition and they keep saying it's too early to tell."

"That's because it's too early to tell," Felicity offered. As she sipped her coffee again, she saw Barbara's frown and so, with a mighty effort, continued. "You'll just have to be patient with us, Mr. Burton."

Barbara's eyebrows said that was another wrong answer. John Burton shivered all over with exasperation. "You must have some idea of her condition at this stage. Is she going to die?"

"No, Mr. Burton. She will not die. Her injuries in fact are relatively minor and after a few weeks convalescence, I would expect her to make a full recovery."

That was the sort of thing Barbara Crane liked to hear— stuff she could use later in evidence to the Medical Board if it all went wrong.

"But why is she still in intensive care?"

Persistent little bugger... But, forced to think about it, the answer only occurred to Felicity herself when she said it. "It's the coma, you see, Mr. Burton. Shock, or something. We aren't sure. Really, nothing about her injuries suggests a comatose state, but that happens sometimes. We are monitoring her condition. As soon as she regains consciousness, if she remains stable, you can take her home."

"But what is this coma?"

"We don't know. But she's responding normally in all other ways..."

"That isn't good enough, doctor."

"Damn it, Mr. Burton! She got blown up by a volcano and survived a bloody helicopter crash! She's damned lucky to be alive at all!"

The young man reared back in shock and Barbara Crane had an arm around him, leading him away while offering angry little glances back at Felicity. "Just bear with us, Mr. Burton, and I'm sure everything will be fine."

Her thoughtful hand propelled him out the door but Barbara did not follow. Instead she turned and walked back toward Felicity, frowning deeply. "Nice bit of client relations, Fee."

"Oh, shut up, Barbara."

That wasn't really intended either. She was thinking about something else. "That makes three of them."

"Three of what?" Barbara asked in a fine display of calm.

"That girl—Christine Rice—and the other girl from the helicopter crash and the black woman. All three are comatose when their injuries don't justify it."

"Whereas plainly your own condition almost does, Fee. I don't know how you keep going."

"It doesn't make sense..."

"It will in time. You're wasting your energy trying to solve something like this in your present condition."

"It's not my condition that's important."

"Come on, Fee. You know the score. You're losing your temperament. Next your efficiency."

"Yes, all right. I suppose I was a bit over the top."

"Go home. Sleep. Do not set the alarm. Have two full meals. Spend at least three quality hours with your husband and each of your children. This will all still be here when you get back."

*

When the telephone rang, Jami Shastri lifted the receiver with some trepidation. It had been just six minutes since she emailed her report to MIT.

"What in the name of the four and twenty virgins is this nonsense, Miss Shastri!"

"It's only a prelim..." Jami began. She held the receiver several inches from her ear as the thundering voice boomed at her.

"It's not a preliminary anything, young lady. It is mature garbage."

"Professor, please listen."

"Why? Don't you think you've made enough idiotic statements for one day?"

"That is what the data..."

"Fuck the data. This is garbage. You ought to be thankful that no one has seen it except me, for which I am anything but thankful. Did every word of my hard-wrought lectures pass straight through your aural passages untouched by neuronal stimulation?"

"I do know how strange it looks, Professor..."

"Thank God for that!"

In these circumstances, Jami found it hard to work out if the usual first name basis applied. If she was Miss Shastri, he was Professor Thyssen, she supposed.

"Will you please calm down and listen to me, Prof...?"

"No. I will not. Let me shout a few things first, if only to restore my sense of proportion. Honestly, Jamila, how could you make these sorts of errors?"

"There are no errors, Harley. I checked and double checked. Glen checked and double checked."

"Glen let you send this?"

"No. He suggested I smash the machines and pretend there was no data available."

"Wise of him."

"It isn't my fault if the data doesn't add up, Harley."

"You do realise that you managed to place three unrelated epicentres within five kilometres of each other, occurring simultaneously."

"That's right."

"And you suggest that these three independent earthquakes each measured exactly 6.3 on the scale and caused all three volcanoes to erupt simultaneously."

"That's how it happened."

"Which means there has to be a god-damned mutual epicentre!"

"There wasn't, Harley. All systems agree. The thermals and seismos and shifters all indicate the same locations on both systems that were operating at the time."

"Ridiculous!"

"Tell that to the fucking geosystem."

"It is the Governing Board of the Earth Science Academy that I'm going to have to tell it to, Jami, and they'll laugh me out of the place. They'll strip my professorship and reassign me to Junior High if I try to put this over them. And what about the prelims?"

"No preliminary warning whatsoever."

"Jami, might I remind you that there has never been a volcanic incident in all recorded history where there weren't substantial pre-eruption indicators."

"There has now. The monitoring equipment was all in fine condition and firmly recorded that there was no indication of oncoming activity whatsoever."

"Then the equipment must be faulty!"

"Glen is going over it. Of course, it's all knocked around a bit by the percussion but half of it is undamaged..."

"Pity it all didn't get blown away and..."

"...and me with it?"

"No, I need you despite your obvious shortcomings as a researcher. You drag your ass back here, now!"

"It'll take me days to fly to Boston."

"Now, young lady! We have to get this gibberish into a condition that will allow our colleagues to read it without mirthful convulsions."

"There's too much to do..."

"Glen can handle it. You.. get.. here.. now!"

"If you say so."

There was, finally, a pause. When Thyssen spoke again, his tone had softened considerably. "You were actually in the building when this went down, Jami?"

"I was right here."

"Rather an epiphany, I should think."

"It was that all right. I should imagine that if the plane to Boston falls out of the sky, I'll know what to expect when it hits the ground."

"An enviable experience you know."

"Not nearly as bad as one of your tirades, Harley."

This was as close as Harley Thyssen ever got to expressing concern, for anyone, ever. Jami felt honoured, and decided to push her luck.

"There was something else."

"There couldn't be."

"Something that even I, for all my apparent naivety, didn't dare put in the report."

"Do you have any idea how close I am to a coronary infarction at this moment?"

"Not as close as I was, if I read the physiology correctly."

"Meaning?"

"Something else happened. It's hard to describe. But it was just an instant *before* the eruption. There was a sensation, like a shock wave or something. I almost passed out. My whole body seemed to... I don't know. It was as if I exploded internally. I recovered immediately. There was nausea and a minor state of shock, but whatever it was passed through me in an instant and was gone. And it was *after* that the instrumentation became active."

"After... after what?"

"I don't know. What I described. Some sort of shock wave that the instruments couldn't record hit me first. Then it started."

"More gibberish, Jami."

"But even I knew I couldn't put something like that in the report."

"All right, maybe you're not as naive as I thought. Get on the plane."

"It all really happened, Harley."

"Sure. What you are saying, in reality, is that some sort of mysterious physiological episode distorted your perceptions and impaired your judgment, and thereby we have all these improbable results. How does that sound?"

"Like bullshit, Harley."

"But it is a reasonable explanation, provided, of course, that you are able to offer proof that this mysterious force exists."

"I'm not using it as an excuse."

"No, but I will, to explain your insanity, if I have to. Time's wasting. Go catch a plane."

"See you in a day or two, Harley."

*

The nurses had allowed two middle-aged people into the ICU ward where they stood looking down at the girl within the spider-web of tubes and wires, while walled-eye George Hanley, her senior intern, stood by. Felicity, totally refreshed by just two hours sleep and a quick shower, paused at the door to listen.

"We aren't sure why the coma is persisting," George was saying. "A shock condition probably—but as soon as she revives, she ought to be able to go home."

Felicity might have been listening to herself except it wasn't the same patient. The couple had flown in from Norfolk Island and were the parents of the other girl from the helicopter crash, Lorna Simmons, who had just a few cuts and abrasions. And unexplained coma...

Shirley Benson, the Head Nurse, was going by and Felicity caught her arm.

"I thought you went home," Shirley said in a not very friendly way.

"Not yet. Just a couple of things I want to sort first. Tell me, how many of the comatose patients are not under sedation."

Shirley scowled and consulted the list in her mind. "A few."

"Which ones exactly."

"Oh, um... Miss Simmons, and Miss Rice. And Mr Solomon who was with them in the helicopter but he has serious injuries..."

"..but no head injuries..."

"CT was negative."

"Who else?"

"Mr. Wagner—the American chap—multiple fractures to the lower limbs..."

"But not his skull."

"Yes, again CT negative."

"Keep going."

"Miss Starlight."

"Is that really her name?"

"Apparently. Um—Mr. Rogerson—the pilot of the helicopter. But he's on a respirator and not expected..."

"Any others?"

"What are you looking for? We still have thirty-one ICU casualties in the building."

"CT scan negative—no head contusion or other injury that justifies coma."

"I see. Well, I think that's all."

By this time, George had broken away from the couple and come to join the discussion.

"I want those cases isolated to a single ward. Full quarantine," Felicity was saying.

"You sure that's justified?" George asked.

"No. But all of these people are comatose and there isn't any identifiable reason why they should be. Maybe its some gas or some bacteria thrown up by the volcano. I don't know, but I think we'd better isolate them until we do."

*

They reached the chateau on the third morning after the eruption. There were still hot spots everywhere and bubbling mud pools in the midst of the grey moonscape. An eerie, acrid steam drifted across the whole mountainside.

The rescue team looked at the chateau and saw what they already expected from aerial photographs—that the building was completely flattened with most of the debris scattered over a wide area and the whole lot buried under several centimetres of mud that was the result of the ash combining with the melted snow.

There was no hope of survivors by then—it became the morbid task of digging out the forty or so bodies that they knew to be in amongst the dripping wreckage. Twin-rotor helicopters lowered in excavation equipment and the gruesome job began. The machines gnawed at the ever-hardening wall of ash and the men came in behind, removing the remaining fragments by hand. Within a few days, those bodies not removed would be entombed in stone forever.

The bodies they found were charred, fragile remnants: it soon became apparent that nothing recognisable was going to be recovered. They directed the mechanical claw in ahead of them to hurry the job, but after about an hour, a new tragedy almost occurred when the machine and its driver broke through the surface and crashed into a hole. The driver broke a leg and was evacuated and the machine had been towed out only with great difficulty. As the men stood around the dark chasm they had inadvertently opened, an unexpected odour reached their nostrils.

"Shit," the leader said. "We've broken through to the wine cellar."

Two men in fireproof suits and breathing apparatus entered the hole, flashing brilliant torches. They saw the cellar roof remained intact even though the shelving had collapsed and the floor was a swamp of wine and broken glass. They searched for a time and then came upon a corpse. And then came the cry.

"We got a live one here!"

Paramedics went in and carefully brought the injured man

out on a stretcher. He was unconscious and someone even dared joke about that being the result of two days and nights immersed in fine vintage wine. But in fact he had been lying on a raised bench with the corpse of another man on top of him. They found a few minor lacerations and a great deal of contusion; he had serious respiratory problems and something similar to scurvy had glued his clothing to his flesh. But he was alive.

Eighty-five people had died, two hundred and thirty-three were rescued from the ravaged area, forty-two were admitted to hospital needing intensive care, eleven were missing never to be found. Brian Carrick was the last miraculous survivor of the triple eruption on Tongariro plateau.

*

Gavin served breakfast on the patio—it was a rare treat. He enlisted the aid of the girls as waitresses while Wendell scanned the newspaper.

"They've unearthed another survivor," he announced, perhaps not realising the cruelty of his words.

Felicity tried not to care. She had obeyed Barbara's orders. Long sleep, two meals, time with the family. Gavin should have been at school, she knew, and the girls at childcare, and Wendell at his rooms. They all took the morning off because mum was finally awake. Breakfast was at ten that morning.

Melissa spilled the grapefruit juice on her dressing gown, Megan slopped too much skimmed milk into the muesli, Gavin had boiled the egg thirty seconds too long, and the croissant was cold by the time Wendell filled it with blackberry jam. In other words, it was the most perfect breakfast she could ever remember. And the freshly brewed coffee, after gallons of the muck at the hospital, was a joy in itself.

"Amazing after all this time," Felicity murmured.

"Ah," Wendell grinned. "Am I to assume that your lack of interest indicates the crisis is over?"

"What makes you think I'm not interested?"

"You let me read the paper first. Didn't jump up and rush off to the hospital when you heard about your new patient. I regard all this as indicative of your recovery."

"I'll get there soon enough."

"Well, at least it banished politics from the front page for a few days," Wendell mused.

"There wasn't much lava," Gavin protested.

"What happens to the people when their toes are coma-ed?" Melissa asked.

"Your mother doesn't wish to talk about that," Wendell scolded gently.

"You didn't come home for three days," Megan said, crawling into her lap.

"Meegs, mum is tired," Melissa said bossily.

"She's all right," Felicity smiled. Her knees, like her back, were still very stiff. She had pushed it all right. Still, she was rested and feeling good. Then the telephone rang.

Wendell went and answered it, and returned immediately. "Possibility one," he said sourly.

With a groan, Felicity set Megan back on her feet and found her own and hurried through the house.

"Dr Campbell here."

"Oh, Dr Campbell," Shirley Benson blubbered on the other end. "We had a new IC patient come in overnight..."

"Yes, Shirley. I heard."

"CT was clear, but he's in a coma—like the others. Can't really justify it from his condition."

"What major traumas do we have?"

"None really, except his epidermis is falling off..."

"Truly?"

"He was pickled in wine, apparently."

"Lucky bugger. I wish I was."

"I really shouldn't have rung you at home but..."

"What's your problem, Shirley?"

"Do you want him isolated, like the others?"

"Yes. Have any of them showed signs of consciousness?"

"No."

"Okay. Yes, isolate him too. I'll be there in a couple of hours anyway."

"Fine..."

"Is everything else okay?"

"Umm... Oh yes. Yes. Everything's fine."

When she hung up, Felicity stood by the telephone for a few minutes. It wasn't like Shirley Benson to make such a call. She had already known the answer to her own question anyway. Felicity could not help thinking that there was some other reason why she rang—something that, once on the telephone, Shirley could not bring herself to express. Felicity returned to the patio, smiling at her family.

"I have to go," she said.

"You should really rest a little while yet..." Wendell scowled.

"No. I have to go now," Felicity insisted.

*

Shirley Benson had suffered a rare fright. The truth was that the new patient—Mr. Carrick—was already in the isolation ward and had been since he arrived that evening. Shirley was on night duty and should have gone off in the morning but she waited for Doctor Campbell to arrive. She would wait—no matter how long it took.

In the night she had visited the isolation ward and stood amidst the beds, the lights were dimmed but for the monitoring equipment with its screens of tracings busily indicating that everything was normal. The lights flickered, and the room was abuzz with a faint sound, and it was probably only Shirley's long experience with such equipment that caused her to sense something was wrong.

She busied herself, trying to ignore what was an irrational sensation. These people were all *ones* across the board on the Glasgow Scale—yet there was full EEG, ECG, respiration normal. Every four hours, they needed *liquifilm* to keep their unblinking eyes moist but otherwise nothing happened. There was no decerebrate rigidity—their limbs remained flexible, skin texture good except poor Mr. Carrick. For all intents and purposes, they might have been asleep. Electrolyte balance good, respiratory and circulatory status good. Nothing was wrong, except she could sense at the core of her being that something was different. Something weird.

At first it was impossible to say what. She walked over to Mr. Solomon's console and considered it for a time. All readings normal. EEG, ECC pulse rate, blood flow, normal, normal.

"You seem fine, Joe. Everything ticking along perfectly," she told the unconscious man.

Joe Solomon's spine was broken and no one had told him yet. No one had told him that his wife was dead either. You could never tell just how aware comatose patients were. For Joe Solomon, it might be better if he never woke up.

Worse still was the American gentleman, Kevin Wagner, who didn't yet know that he had lost his whole family. Alone and far from home—but he was a fit and healthy young man who, unlike Joe Solomon, would eventually make a full recovery. Chrissie Rice had some nasty abdominal injuries, and there was Brian Carrick's pickled skin—best not to drive after being too close to him. Lorna and Andromeda were in perfect health. Only sleeping. Strange in itself. But there was something else.

She crossed to Lorna Simmons' monitor and thought about that. Normal, normal. All normal, even Mr. Carrick. And then it struck her. It was all just a little *too* normal.

For a time she moved about the monitors, not quite sure of what she was doing but doing it anyway. She switched switches, individualising the screens and sequences until she found what she wanted. And when she did, she jolted with shock. She almost screamed. She did run out of the room.

She took herself to the cafeteria and had a cup of coffee. Her hands were still shaking. The equipment was faulty. That had to be it. She would call maintenance in the morning and have them sort it out. Only it wasn't an equipment fault. She had checked each monitor and knew the absurdity it indicated so clearly was the truth.

For it had been when she cut out the input from all sources except the EEG on all six monitors that she understood what had bothered her. *They were all the same.* All six patients had precisely the same alpha waves. It was as if only all of the monitors were reading the output from just one patient.

She went back, calmer now, and tried the experiment again. It wasn't a maintenance problem. They hadn't foolishly hooked all the EEGs into just one patient. All six people were experiencing exactly the same brain activity. There was no doubt. The fact that it couldn't possibly happen was rapidly becoming irrelevant.

*

Felicity stood in the ward with Barbara Crane, Roy Bannister the Maintenance chief, and George Hanley, as they considered the machines. Shirley Benson had been sent home with a sedative.

"Perhaps they were all switched on at the same instant," Barbara suggested to show how little she knew about it.

"Doesn't matter," Roy Bannister said. "Each monitor would immediately pick up on the waves of the individual brain it was monitoring."

"Then how do you explain it?" Barbara wanted to know.

"I can't. It's kinda like they all got the same brain."

"A sort of collective unconsciousness," George suggested.

"That's right," Roy thought. "You know. They reckon we all share the same sub-conscious mind."

"Let's leave Freud out of this, shall we?" Barbara scowled, knowing a dirty word when she heard one.

"I don't know if we can," Felicity murmured, looking around as if Sigmund was standing right behind her.

"Well, the patients all seem to be surviving it, whatever it is," Barbara said irritably. "And we do have a lot of other sick people to deal with. Can't afford to waste time over this."

Barbara hurried off as if she had patients needing her

attention, rather than paperwork, and Roy wandered away, scratching his head but then he often did.

"Well, at least now we know why the comas don't relate to their injuries," George said thoughtfully. "They're all in the same coma, literally."

"I doubt that. It has to be in the equipment somewhere," Felicity knew. "Computers behave like this. People don't."

"As far as we know."

"You have a better idea for me, George?"

"Maybe this does have something to do with the collective unconscious."

"Well," Felicity smiled. "They're an unconscious collective, at least. The rest is psycho-babble, George."

*

There was an annoying young man who wore a black silk shirt, lurid checked pants, a tweed jacket and dark glasses even indoors. His hair was all greasy curls and the tatters of a failed beard clung to his acned chin. He strutted about making demands in his abrasive English shop-steward accent, pouting with resolution.

"She's got commitments, you know. I gotta to know when she'll be available."

"We can't possibly know that, Mr. Tierney."

"I've already cancelled engagements right round the South Island. A lot of bloody disappointed people. Andromeda Starlight is a big name in show biz, you know."

Felicity had never heard of her. "We just have to wait, Mr. Tierney," she said wearily.

"I gotta to book her in Oz. There's contracts and all sorts of arrangements. King's Cross, Surfers, big time!"

"I'm sure that when they hear she was blown up by a volcano, they'll understand, Mr. Tierney."

"We really didn't need this right now. Her career was peaking. Gold dust is slippin' through our fingers here."

"You must be patient..."

"But how come you keep sayin' there's nothing wrong with her."

"Apart from a lack of consciousness, there isn't."

"You must have some idea. Come on. Give me your best shot."

"We have no idea. People have remained in unexplained comatose conditions like this for all their lives, although not usually. A few hours or days is much more common. It really is quite unpredictable."

"How many days, average? Give me somethin' to work with."

"We have no idea."

"Can't you give her somethin' to wake her up?"

"No. No such inducement exists and there would be no moral basis for using it if it did."

"But what the hell is she doing, just lying there!"

"Just lying there," Felicity said.

*

Looking like a Viking Chieftain who had just wandered in from a distant century, Harley Thyssen inhabited his office the way a bear inhabits a cave. The whole place was an abominable mess of books and charts despite Brenda's constant efforts to maintain some sort of order.

Of Norwegian origin, Thyssen was a massive man in all directions with wild red hair and beard beneath a weather-beaten balding crown. His narrow eyes looked straight through you. He looked like a man who had spent most of his life too close to the rim of erupting volcanoes and had a voice like an earthquake as well. He sat behind his desk with rounded shoulders and his elbows up and hands placed flat, like a gorilla poised to spring over the laminate and tear his visitor limb from limb.

"You look awful, Jamila," he said gruffly.

It wasn't the lack of welcoming compliment that surprised Jami but the fact that he noticed her appearance at all.

"I got in late last night. Had to book into a cheap hotel. I spent the morning trying to arrange accommodation at one of the colleges."

"You should have called," Thyssen said. "Brenda already arranged a room for you on the campus. See her on the way out."

The office suddenly yawned before her like a trap.

"Thank you," she said properly.

Unlike most student-professor relationships, the longer Jami had known Thyssen the more she had become intimidated by him. It gave her little comfort to know that he scared the living daylights out of everyone else on the campus as well. He was her mentor and intimate colleague and she was terrified of him.

"I spent thirty years trying to get into a position to see a mountain blow its top and never made it," Thyssen was saying. "You ought to feel privileged."

"Perhaps I will when the jet-lag wears off."

In fact she was growing appreciative of her numbed senses. She was preparing herself for a classic Thyssen roasting from a man who learned everything he knew from Etna and Stromboli.

"No time for jet-lag," Thyssen said, smiling, although his smile was always a threat. "While you were lounging in the luxury of modern flight, I was saving your ass."

"Really?"

"Have a look at this," he said, searching under a pile of papers to find his keyboard. She got up and walked around to his side of the desk to observe the computer screen.

"I got Pascoe to model your data from Ruapehu," he said, thumping keys as if he was making a stone hammer. "Three simultaneous epicentres, each 6.3."

"Wow."

"That's not all. We got data in from Auckland and Canberra and Ross Base. Their seismic readings indicated no preliminary activity whatsoever."

"I told you."

"You telling me is of no consequence when unsupported by impartial data," Thyssen said ruthlessly. This, Jami realised, was another of those Thyssen near apologies.

"You know I wouldn't dare bullshit you, Harley," she said in triumph.

He ignored that, searching his desk and coming up with the video remote control. He virtually shoved her out of the way to move across the room where they could watch the television, thumping it on as he walked. He had a tape in and prepared—he had been waiting for her. "This is edited from various news reports on the general media."

A battered woman appeared, dishevelled and troubled as much by wind as the microphone poked at her face. "...there was some sort of shock wave before it happened. I felt it all through my body. It nearly knocked me off my feet..."

"But the explosion came after that?" the reporter asked.

"I felt real crook afterwards..."

The image cut with a crude edit to a fat little man at a different location.

"It was like a punch in the guts. I near blacked out. Then, suddenly, there's this god-almighty bang and up she went..."

Thyssen pressed the pause. "We got six more of them on the tape and they all say the same thing you did."

"I was beginning to wonder if I'd got mixed up and imagined it."

Thyssen lumbered back to his desk and flopped down.

"Well, armed with that stuff and with a bit of re-writing, at least your report will become acceptable upstairs."

"You want me to fix it, huh?"

"No, I don't. I'll fix it. I'll put my name on it—just in case it proves to be worth a Nobel."

"Do I get a mention?"

"The actual purpose will be to try and screw some funding out of them to support you while you do the research, so I guess I can't avoid mentioning you completely."

"What research?"

"You get down the lab now and you study every eruption in recorded history and see if there's any sign of any of these anomalies having happened before."

"Oh God, do I have to?"

"No. But I can justify using an inexperienced student like you to do the work while I maintain control of the project. Otherwise, I'd have to farm it out to a funded research unit and that way we both miss out on the Nobel."

"Do you really think it's that important?"

"Only if you can demonstrate that it might happen again and that its effects are of some importance. So, probably not. And if it is a one off, we'll have only wasted money on one low-grade student. The board will like that argument."

"What if I refuse?"

"You can't. Anyway, if this does amount to something, it'll be called *The Shastri Effect*. Immortality beckons, child. Get outa here and earn it."

*

"You silly, silly man, look what you've done to yourself," Judy Carrick was saying, trying to talk normally to the awful visage of her husband, the way the nurse had told her to. The skin discolouration was not as bad is it looked. Quite superficial in fact, the nurse said. Well, he was getting a little blotchy anyway, with all that drinking down the footy club. His nose especially. Now his whole body looked like his nose. She was glad she had left the children outside as the nurse suggested.

"Brian. It's me, Judy. We've come all the way from Melbourne. I had to use the house payments to pay for the airfare but they say there'll be some compensation. We had a lovely flight. The kids were so excited. They're here with me. They've given us a room in the nurses' quarters and its a bit small but very nice. I'll bring the kids in in a minute and they can have a talk to you. Larry's arranged a driver for the truck and he says he's okay, but, well, who knows what sort of bludger he is and I don't know how we're going to make ends meet. But don't you worry about that. You just worry about getting better. Oh look, here comes the doctor now..."

Red with embarrassment, Judy broke off as the doctor made her way over. Doctor Felicity Campbell, the name tag said. She was a woman of about forty with blonde hair above her smiling ruddy face and a very nice slim figure, just like Judy used to have herself before Leo came along.

"Hi, Mrs. Carrick. I'm Doctor Campbell. Are those your littlies out there?"

"Yes, poor little darlings. They had a sleep after they got here but it's very tiring for them, all that travelling."

"Yes, of course. Why don't you bring them in, Mrs. Carrick?"

"Oh please, call me Judy. I hardly know who Mrs. Carrick is, when you say it like that. And I was worried what they'd think, with Brian being in such a state."

"Children adjust to these things better than we adults, as a rule, Judy."

"I'll just give them some idea of what to expect first."

Judy made her way out into the corridor and along to the waiting room where a young nurse had Leo and Sheila under control as much as possible. Leo was pulling the girl's pager to bits while Sheila restyled her hair.

"No, children. Leave the nurse alone. Thank you miss. I hope they weren't a bother. Now Leo, put those batteries back. You can't have them. How will the lady know when she's wanted if you nicked her batteries? There you go."

The harried nurse hurried away to other duties. Judy sat the children on seats and straightened them and sat beside them herself. Felicity Campbell sat on the other side.

"Now kids, this is Doctor Campbell. She's looking after Daddy while he's here. Say hello to Dr Campbell."

"Hello, Doctor Campbell," Leo said, extending a hand to be shaken.

"Hello," said Sheila, suddenly shy and quiet.

"When can we see Daddy?" Leo demanded.

"In a minute. Daddy is asleep, but you can talk to him. We won't mind if you wake him. He looks a bit funny. He has this big bruise all over his skin but don't be scared because it doesn't hurt him at all, it just looks very strange and it will go away soon, okay?"

"Why is he asleep?" Leo asked.

"Is he very tired?" Sheila wondered.

"No. He's just resting for a while, until he gets better."

"Can we go now?" Leo asked.

They each took a child's hand and made their way forward. Judy lead them to the side of the bed. Leo stood on tip toe, but Sheila needed to be stood on a chair.

"Oh, yuk."

"Has he been sunburned, Mummy?" Sheila asked.

"It's not even as serious as sunburn, Sheila," Doctor Campbell said helpfully.

"He ain't asleep," Leo was sure. "He's just fakin' it."

"What makes you think so, Leo?" the doctor asked carefully.

"He ain't snorin'."

"It's a special kind of sleep," Judy said, trying to hide her chuckling. Dr Campbell had a hand pressed over her mouth as well.

"We put that tube in his nose so he wouldn't snore," Felicity Campbell lied.

"You can talk to him," Judy prompted. "Go on, tell him you're here."

"What if he wakes up?" Sheila whispered.

"We want him to wake up," Felicity smiled.

"Well, okay then," Leo decided and leaned as close to his father's ear as the plastic cocoon would permit.

"Hey Dad! Wake up!" he bellowed.

"Go back to bloody bed, son," Brian Carrick replied.

*

One hour later, all hell broke loose in the isolation ward. Joe Solomon started screaming in agony and with that bells rang all through casualty. The nurses came rushing with crash carts and after a few desperate moments, the interns sedated him again.

"What's going on?" Lorna Simmons demanded, sitting up on her bed. Beside her, Chrissie Rice was murmuring and twisting. Brian Carrick, with full vital signs restored, had already been sedated.

They settled Lorna and sedated Chrissie, and the panic was over. Felicity Campbell looked at the astonished face of Shirley Benson and could only assume a similar expression occupied her own countenance. Almost instinctively, they both went over to Andromeda Starlight. Felicity determined a flicker from the eyes and Shirley took the patient's hand and spoke in a loud voice.

"Andromeda. If you can hear me, squeeze my hand!"

"Go away, Honey. I'm tired. Let me sleep," Andromeda Starlight murmured.

It remained only to check on Kevin Wagner, the American, and Felicity shone a light in his eye. It flickered.

"Better get a sedative course running right away."

Felicity stood in the centre of the room and gazed around. A nurse was just about to start removing the electrodes from Lorna Simmons' forehead.

"Wait a minute nurse," she called, remembering.

"What's up."

"Bring up the ECG on all of them."

Orderlies moved to obey. After a moment, all five screens showed only the alpha waves and each emitted its regular beep. And no two of them at the same time.

3
EXACTLY NOWHERE

When Lorna hit the water, the cold and wet slapped her entire body with a devastating shock, bursting her back to some sort of reality. It was like a nightmare—no, like someone had thrown a bucket of water over her while she slept. A very big bucket of water. She was completely immersed in it and sinking fast. At first she could not comprehend what had happened, but the water was bloody freezing and the panic came with saltiness that attempted to flood her nostrils and throat as she sank. No bloody doubt about it. *She'd fallen in!*

Reflexes took over, her body remembering the innumerable times she had dived into the ocean and rivers and swimming pools. At least she had gasped a full quota of air before she hit and forced it out now, trying to keep the water out of her lungs. It helped when she closed her mouth, which had been wide open with amazement as her whole world suddenly turned aquatic. Maybe the office had been hit by a tidal wave! Then her body automatically righted itself, lighter water above, murkier stuff below. Her dress was up around her ears as she sank—she hoped there weren't any scuba divers around to see this. *Kick! Kick!* she told herself. When she kicked, she fretted as one of her shoes came off. This was unbelievable. She was going to drown. What on earth was happening?

The kick carried her neatly to the surface. She bobbed up, spluttering water, her hair pasted all over her face like a sea anemone. She rubbed the fluid from her eyes, coughed and spluttered a few times, and then trod water, looking around. There was a big pier right by her that she had obviously fallen off—this was ridiculous. Up on the pier, the fishermen had gathered at the spot where plainly she went in, and one young bloke was stripping off his shirt to come to the rescue.

"It's okay," she blubbered. "I can swim."

Her handbag—miraculously still over her shoulder—bumped against her belly as she did the necessary three strokes to reach the low boarding platform. She got hold of the rough timber and hauled herself up and one of the older fishermen, a Maori who had lapsed completely into his native language, took her hand and hauled her up onto the platform.

She sat on the edge of the platform, dragging her dress down to some level of decency, and smiled weakly at the old Maori. "I'm okay. Just give me a minute to gather my wits, okay?"

It was going to take more than a minute.

She had been in the office, and it was lunchtime—was that really the last thing she remembered? She gazed at the more distant surroundings to get her bearings. She had been here before, lots of times, on sunny afternoons. This was one of those spots on the inner harbour—Herne Bay by the look of it—miles from the office. How the hell did she get here? And why? The sun was still high. It was still lunchtime, but she had never come anywhere like this for lunch before. It made no sense. Get a grip, Lorna! Try and remember!

Lunchtime. She recalled that the sense of agitation that had been growing in her since yesterday was slowly overwhelming her—it was like constantly wanting to go to the loo except in her brain rather than her bladder. It was Wednesday when she usually had lunch with Chrissie but she had rung and Chrissie wasn't at work—that was no surprise.

At eleven, she had rung Chrissie at home and shouted at the answering machine until Chrissie finally answered. "I feel terrible. I can't cope."

"Come to lunch."

"No. I just can't. I want to go away somewhere. I want to go now."

"Okay. We'll go away at the weekend. Over to Whakatane. Been planning to for ages."

"No. I have to go now!"

"I'll come over straight after work and we'll plan the trip."

"It's the wrong way!"

"What do you mean, wrong way?"

"Don't know. It just is."

"Oh come on. You'll love it. Just think about it and have a sleep and I'll be there in no time."

"I can't sleep."

She went on for some time, whimpering pathetically but Lorna hardly heard any of it. The words Chrissie had spoken stuck in her brain and she couldn't clear them. *It's the wrong way!* It was too. There wasn't any possible reason why it should be the wrong way but it was. Ridiculous.

So, no lunch with Chrissie. What then? It had all gone blank. There was a bus she needed to catch from outside the railway station to get here, to Waitamata Harbour. She must have caught that bus, or else a taxi, for no sensible reason, nor even a senseless one. Except it was the right way.

Now as she sat on the edge of the boat platform with the rough timber wrecking what was left of her pantihose, she was still facing out across the water. Thataway. Where she wanted to go. Over there, across the bay. Had she really planned to swim the distance? What nonsense. But it was a straight line, she realised. From the office to the railway station, the bus journey, the bus stop back up there somewhere to the end of the pier and into the drink—to over there somewhere. Where she wanted so badly to go. For no possible reason. Jesus Christ, she was becoming as nutty as Chrissie.

Last night Chrissie had called her in tears. She'd had a big fight with John, about nothing as usual, and Lorna had driven over to comfort her.

Chrissie was in a terrible state, pacing about the room, thumping on the walls, so over-excited that she was unbearable. No wonder John had become irritated with her and walked out. There had been a lot of this going on lately, as the wedding plans drew towards a climax. They had always been such a compatible couple but now they seemed to fight over every little thing—it was going to be a great marriage, Lorna sighed.

She knew, as only an intimate outside observer could, that Chrissie was entirely the problem. She truly had not been able to put Ruapehu behind her, as Lorna had, and was becoming a nervous wreck.

Her asthma troubled her and she burst into tears at the slightest provocation. She had migraines almost constantly, and fits of temper that were completely contrary to her previous gentle nature. Lorna wouldn't have married her either, the way she was. And the silly girl was getting worse.

In the three months since Ruapehu, she had changed shrinks three times, attended all manner of counselling and self-help groups—was obsessed completely with all that 'improve yourself' nonsense—and it was only deepening her trauma. Lorna, who showed no indication of traumatic stress, had submitted for a while and often went along to Chrissie's sessions and saw how little good it was doing. The poor girl was going out of her mind and now it was breaking up her relationship as well. John Burton was a wimp and the most tolerant of boys, but even he had run out of patience with her.

Last night Lorna gave Chrissie some sleeping pills and put her to bed, then went home, deeply troubled herself. It was as if whatever troubled Chrissie was contagious and she had caught it too. She didn't sleep and was late for work for the first time in years. And now this.

Okay, looney or not, she had regained her breath and a skerrick or two of sanity—time to sort out her more immediate problems.

She had skinned her knee and holed her pantihose, and got the one shoe she still possessed off so that she could stand. She had almost drowned, but right away her biggest concern was that her little green dress had gone completely see-through—the pervs were having a big day and the fishermen stood in a line along the pier above her, loving it. She took the old man's hand and allowed him to haul her to her feet, and then leaned on his shoulder for a moment to steady herself—but then she was fine. Soaked to the skin, deeply ashamed, totally indecent, very embarrassed, but fine.

As she climbed the steps up to the pier, she was able to take in a clearer view of the landward side of her surroundings. Herne Bay, no doubt about it. She could only shake her head in dismay. Around her the men were growing very excited and all talking to her at once. They wanted to carry her off to hospitals or ambulances but she ducked them with a neat double-baulk and then backed away from them. Policemen would never believe that it wasn't a suicide attempt; medical staff would know that there had to be psychological problems with people who walked off piers.

"I'm fine, really," she insisted, waving her one shoe at them to keep them at bay. Then, finally, everyone calmed down and began to laugh about it.

"It's silly. I just... fell in."

"You're all wet. You'll catch cold," the old Maori was saying—only he dared advance now.

"I'll be fine," she insisted, still holding her shoe as if the stiletto heel was a sword.

She looked at the place where she had fallen. It was too silly to believe, but she knew she had to believe it. She smiled at the old Maori, and then raised her arm, pointing.

"Tell me, which direction is that?"

"West. Sun sets over here. That way is due west."

"Bit over west," corrected the young bloke who obviously regretted having missing his chance to rescue her. "Maybe West Nor West."

"No. West," the old man said.

She looked West. That was where she had been going all right.

"But what's over there?"

"Te Atatu," one said.

"Kumeu Motorway," said another.

"Further than that," she asked, *because she knew it was!*

"West coast," the young wouldbe hero said.

"The sea," the old Maori added.

"There must be something else," she demanded, because she knew there had to be.

"Nope. Tasman Sea, all the way to Australia."

"Australia," she echoed, wrinkling her nose distastefully.

It was time to get out of there, and with a last thankful expression, she decided to turn and walk, giving them their final thrill for the day. She actually heard the collective intake of breath and stopped, turning sideways, grinning, waggling a finger at them. They all smiled back as well they might.

She paused one moment more, to complete the scene. In her hand, she still held her shoe and she regarded it now, and then threw it out into the water.

"Why'd you do that?" the old Maori asked.

"Well, if someone finds the other one, now they'll have a pair," she grinned.

*

Fairhaven Hospital inhabited one of the finest old mansions along the escarpment that overlooked the wide estuary of the Swan River and the metropolis of Perth on the other side. It was used as a convalescent home for those who could pay and was considered to possess the best facilities available in Western Australia. Around the building—classified A by the National Trust—was a tall iron fence and at the front heavy gates, although these days they operated automatically from both inside the building and a small guard post where a hired security guard was always on duty.

After all, within the premises were more than thirty people who were well worth the efforts of a kidnapper or terrorist. A former Prime Minister, a world famous author, a distinguished British General and an aged film star were to be numbered amongst the inmates, in a hospital where the staff behaved more like butlers and maids than the medical teams of most hospitals.

No terrorist, nor kidnapper, nor even assassin—as a potential murderer of one of the patients might have been regarded—had ever attempted to penetrate Fairhaven's walls, but still the security remained vigilant and efficient. Even if, for the period of about a week, their most critical duty seemed to be the interception of a noted lawyer trying to escape the grounds in his motorised wheelchair. He tried it three or four times a day, and never once got past the gate. But that did not deter him in the slightest.

"But really, Mr Solomon. Where do you think you're going?"

"Somewhere else," Joe Solomon said grimly as they wheeled him back inside.

*

Slowly, methodically, as was his way, he began to piece it all together. At first it seemed that it had not happened at all—he remembered none of it—but then, when he concentrated and worked it over in his brain, it began to come back to him. Still it did not seem real, and in fact the only way he could be sure that he had made the journey at all was because here he was at the end of it, even though the destination obviously wasn't anywhere at all.

When he pulled out of the driveway, Brian Carrick had known only that he was going further than he could walk. He had swung the tail out, the engine of the big Scania prime mover chuffing and gruffing at this unexpected activity, and he was surprised to realise that he had known which way to turn. The truck was without a trailer, and Larry had loaned it to them because their car had a flat battery—as if to ensure he got to work. Well he hadn't fixed the battery and he wasn't going to work. One of the many things forgotten or abandoned these days, and now he was taking off as if escaping his whole life. Where the hell was he going?

It was three months since New Zealand and the volcano—his skin had healed although it left him rather botchy, and he was sure that he was all right. He had started back to work—light duties only—and was glad the tedious round of rehabilitation and councillors was ended. If it was.

He remembered with a sickening sensation having glimpsed Judy in the rear vision mirror as he drove away—he had promised to take her shopping but instead left her for dead on the driveway, clutching her handbag and shrieking after him, but he carried on anyway. It didn't occur to him until he reached the shopping centre that he might have at least been decent enough to drop her off along the way. To where? It seemed to Brian that he knew the answer, only it wouldn't come to mind. He was going this way, for some distance and if he didn't yet know where this way led to, still he knew he was going the right way.

"There will be nightmares, there will be unexpected behaviour, there will be a certain listlessness, a lack of concern for important issues. Often, they have a lot of trouble getting their priorities right."

Post Traumatic Stress Disorder, they called it, at least on the forms for Accident Compensation and Sickness Benefits that he had to fill in. In fact the government had been very good about it although now their patience was beginning to wear thin. They had paid the return trip to Wellington for Judy and the kids, the hospital costs there, and the expenses involved in bringing him home. They put him in Monash Hospital until they sorted out that difficulty with his skin, and he seemed fine, keen to get back to work, back into his life. But nothing like that happened.

"He will be very nervous. He may be troubled by claustrophobia. He will sweat a great deal, especially in confined spaces. Loud noises will be a great trouble to him."

He talked to the counsellor about it. Mary Ashwood was a young middle-class girl with a degree and a theory to go with it. "Maybe it isn't because of what you saw but what you didn't. There you were in the middle of a massive disaster, and you were in a cellar and then unconscious. You didn't experience any of it. Maybe that's what's troubling you."

So fucking what?

Onward he had thundered into the evening, leaving the freeways and sprawling suburbs of Melbourne far behind, up the Hume and onto the Northern Highway that would take him eventually to Bendigo and he had some friends there—maybe it was their company he was seeking? But once he got beyond Kilmore, the highway began to swing slowly north-west and he grew increasingly agitated. Yes, it was all coming back to him now, constructed from vague flashes and faint impressions, but definitely assembling itself in his mind. He had pressed on, for the roadmap in his brain told him there was no road that went the way he wanted until he reached Heathcote.

There the highway divided, left to Bendigo, right to Echuca and he chose the latter option and immediately grew more at ease. There was no doubt that it was somehow more correct, and so no choice but to drive on. Eventually, he arrived at an insignificant place called Corop and the road divided—left to Rochester, right to Stanhope and nothing much else. But that was the way to go, no doubt about it.

In Stanhope he stopped and found only a milk bar open but he was able to get a hamburger and coffee, trying to force himself to take an hour. It wasn't much of a town, and noted only for a recent outbreak of anthrax. He regarded the hamburger ruefully but such dangers weren't what bothered him. His system hated the lack of motion. On the one hand he was almost falling asleep, on the other he was frantic to get back on the road. After just twenty minutes he was back behind the wheel and moving on, following the road toward Shepparton, which lay east, but he didn't get far before he knew he must turn north again. The new road led toward Kyabram and he sensed that the corridor of contentment that guided him was growing narrower.

And then he was slowing down and stopped. He was ten kilometres beyond Stanhope and about eight short of Kyabram and had been on the road five hours. At first he thought it was exhaustion and he contemplated taking a non-doze but then he realised he had passed the spot. He turned back, drove three kilometres and then pulled off the road. There was a track of sorts and the gate through the barbed wire was not locked. In the half-moonlight, he could see only that there was nothing to see. He bounced along the track for about a kilometre then swung off onto grassland and ploughed through. The terrain was flat as a dinner table and there were only a few clumps of trees in the distance here and there. He stopped and stepped down from the truck, walking a few yards wide. He was way out in the middle of a completely empty field—not even a sheep to be seen. He had arrived. This was the place. But where was it?

Right in the bloody middle of nowhere.

*

Andromeda awoke with Jim Morrison pounding in her brain—it was the worst kind of hangover.

> *We gotta get outa this place.*
> *If it's the last thing I ever do;*
> *Girl there's a better life for me and you.*

Yo! what a shocker, and all the worse because it was entirely inside her head—out there in the real world, insects hummed and only birds sang. And there was sunlight—wicked and mean and incinerating her eyeballs right out of their sockets. Her nose was hurting unmercifully and had spotted blood on the pillow, she saw. That last line she snorted near blew the sinuses right out the back of her head and there was nothing after that. Wow, what a way to go!

There was a dream too, a nightmare, stuck in the mire of her brain somewhere. She had been standing naked, surrounded by a sea of little boys all of whom were no taller than her mid-thighs. They were reaching with their hands to touch her as high on her body as they could, and although they could reach no higher than her buttocks and abdomen, every one of the thousands of them seemed able to touch her with grubby, pawing hands. There was nothing erotic in it—it was menacing, those little boys were all evil gnomes…. What would the shrinks make of that! Guilt, maybe, for cradle-snatching all those young musicians… She squeezed her eyes closed, to try and force the memory of the dream out of her brain.

Have a damned look at yourself, woman. Just have a goddamned look. Go on, turn the light on and show yourself, you mantis. The fluorescent flickered macabrely and she looked *dead!* Holy Shit. Only thirty-seven and decomposing already. Sure, the body was in good shape—the work-outs and diets took care of that—but the *face!* It gave the game away completely.

She dragged her fingers on her cheeks, to make the wrinkles smooth, like Joan Collins. Still looked god-damned awful. Those eyes, so hideously bloodshot. Bags under that you could pack your entire wardrobe in and go down home.

Yeah, sure. Home. But where's home? For sure not hot and dusty barefoot days in Trinidad—Ma and Pa were long since dead and no one was left to remember her. Nor the even worse poverty of Soho and all those fog-bound years of trying to break into musicals. Not plastic Hollywood with plastic throw-away careers in television and the movies that never happened anyway. Not sleazy King's Cross nightclubs where all the best looking girls were guys. She didn't have a home to go to. No place to go. But she knew she had to go there anyway, and right now!

Get dressed. She hauled her drooping ass into jeans, dragged a shirt over her sagging tits, stuffed a handful of tabs in her pocket—didn't matter which. Forget the rest. Go, go, go.

The heat outside made her reel back against the door-jamb. The god-damned sun was in her eyes no matter which way she turned. Where the hell am I anyway? Whitsunday? Oh yeah. Whitsunday Passage, wherever that was. Go. Hitch a ride and get moving. But where?

Thataway. That was it. South, to judge from the sun. Down Dixie? No, wrong country. So what's south? Not silly-bloody Sinny—hate the god-awful place. Tasmania? Antarctica? Can't go south. Can't go any where because you're on an island, silly bitch. Gotta get out of the sun at least. Coffee. Go to the cafe and get coffee.

When she glanced around, she saw there were some small boys—real ones—over there, in the bushes, watching her. Shit! And all around, the tourists stopped to stare at her and whisper to each other. Okay, so now she was completely paranoid. No reason to be surprised about that.

She struck out across the nicely manicured lawns with tables under the palms, the suburban folks' idea of paradise. People were everywhere, and all gaping at her. Well, look on it as good publicity for her act. The club, *The Golden Dolphin*—her present four week gig—was in the lounge bar of the pub and she went that way, although only because the coffee shop was in the same tourist complex. She marched up the steps into the lobby, and there stood a life-size cardboard cutout of Andromeda Starlight, Superstarlight, in glittering gown and full song. Andromeda Fuck-anything-in-sight Starlight, star of the show, hot from Hollywood and London and Sydney, the Windies Revenge.

No one would have recognised the sorry shabby individual who gave the effigy the finger as she stalked by.

Joel Tierney, her agent, was there, sucking coffee. "Ho, there Andy. Back in the land of the living."

"I gotta get out of this place."

In reply, Joel snapped his fingers in front of her face. "Hey, come on Babe, wake up!"

"I'm awake."

"You sure? I just come from explaining to the resort management how you been under a lot of pressure and it won't happen again."

"I never ... What won't happen again?"

"Don't remember, huh?"

"Remember? What?"

"You were sleepwalking..."

"I never sleepwalk..."

"You did this afternoon. There you were, bollock naked, marching down to the beach. You did it twice. I had to grab you and drag you back to the room both times. Caused a huge sensation."

"Are you serious?"

"Great publicity. The bookings have doubled since...."

At the window of the café, young boys were staring in at her in wonder.

"Sleepwalking. In the buff...?"

"Extraordinary sight, Andy."

"Holy shit."

"That's what most people that saw you said."

She was shaking her head in utter disbelief, but then the new sensation flooded her body again. "Joel, I gotta get out of here."

"Don't worry about it. Everyone's hoping you'll do it again..."

"I'm serious. I want to go. Right now."

"Can't. Booked for a month. Got 'em queuing out to the reef."

The radiantly smiling waitress hovered.

"Gimme coffee."

"Certainly, Miss Starlight. Black or white?"

"I don't give a fuck. Just give me coffee."

"She takes it black with cream, sweetheart," Tierney sleazed at the waitress. Next victim of his despicable charm.

"Will there be anything else, Miss Starlight?"

"Yeah. How the hell do I get out of here?"

"There's flight schedules on the rack by the counter..."

"Just get the coffee, sweetie," Tierney smiled. "She ain't going no place."

"Joel, please! I gotta go."

"Why? Come on, you're big here. Biggest you've ever been."

"I don't know. But I got this big urge to go. Thataway. Outa here."

"Thataway?"

"Yes. That way. I want to go there, now."

"Why?"

"I gotta."

"Here, take this and forget it."

He stuffed a tab straight in her open mouth and she nearly choked on it. But then the waitress brought the coffee and she gulped it down, heedless of burnt lips. It's tentacles immediately began to move through her intestines and into the blood stream.

"Better?"

"I guess."

"This is an island, Andy. There's no place to go."

"Jesus, Joel. You don't know how I feel."

"Get this in yer. Then tell me how you feel."

"I dunno. I just got this wicked urge to move, to go. I feel like I'll die if I don't."

"But go where?"

"That way."

"But there's nothing there except miles of reef."

"That's where I've gotta go."

"Just take it easy. The tab will help calm you. Sleep. Get ready for the show. It'll be all right."

"Yeah, Joel, sure."

*

Remember Xanadu. Harley Thyssen got up with slow arthritic movements and went to the door. Coleridge had begun the epic poem, then someone knocked at the door and by the time he returned to the task, all but the first hundred lines already written had gone right out of his head. Not much chance of that in this case, but still Thyssen approached the door with irritation.

"Are you all right, Harley?" Joanie, his neighbour, asked nervously.

No, he was not alright. "Of course. What can I do for you?"

"Oh, nothing. Albert saw the lights on. We thought we should check..."

Nosy bitch. And she knew it too, as her sentence ran out of words.

"Just had some work to do and wanted to go where I wouldn't be disturbed," Thyssen said heartlessly. The truth was always cruel.

"Oh, I see. I'm sorry. It's just that it was so unusual..."

Joanie, like many gossips, had a habit of embarking upon statements that they didn't know how to finish. He ought to invite her in, ravage her on the couch while her husband stood on the porch across the road, meditating on the Ancient Mariner and not at all wondering why his wife was taking so long. That would give them something to talk about, except of course they never talked about themselves.

She was a sturdy, good-looking woman and heaven knows what was left of his libido needed it. But he didn't have the energy, the risk to his health would be excessive, and anyway, what he had told her was true. He had work to do and did not want to be disturbed. For the first time in about a decade.

"Yes, Joanie. I realise it is quite out of the ordinary for me to be at home at this hour of the evening. Here, smell my breath. Not a trace of alcohol will you find. Do you want to come in and verify that there are no young women hiding under the bed?"

"Oh, Harley, really," Joanie laughed—you could never insult people like her—and then she glanced back toward her own house as if she just remembered she had left something on the stove. "Well, you get back to work, Harley. And remember, we are still here for you if you want anything."

There was little chance he would forget.

"You tell them I've finally decided to get a life," Thyssen said quietly.

Once he got the door closed on her, he knew that her concern was probably genuine. He always worked late and then went to campus bar for dinner and had a few drinks with anyone interesting who might be there. If no one engaged his interest, he made his way into town to visit the strip joints and live out the death throes of his youth and obliterate the reality of his life. This house terrified him and he was never in it except to sleep from whatever hour he staggered in until dawn. He did his ablutions at the gym after exercise sessions of diminishing length and breakfasted in the cafe. This regime existed seven days a week. Though it had not always been so. It was just a phase he was going through. And going through.

There was a time when this house rang with joy and laughter and it would have been the last place where he would have sought solitude. That was before the cancer devoured Karla, and the kids were home. Now Elmore who was doing transport systems at the University of London, and Anna doing anthropology in the wilds of the Andes. All gone now—not even their ghosts remained to haunt him.

Thyssen sat at his desk in what had become unfamiliar surroundings. The house was bare—he had sold off everything he didn't need. He didn't even have a computer and had brought this notepad home to work on. He turned off the lights—Joanie wasn't the only busybody in the street—and the small screen became the only illumination by which he worked.

He did not pause to read what he had been writing—that train of thought was broken and he was sure he had not got where he was going anyway. Although it was hard to tell, because he didn't really know where he was going, and wasn't sure he would recognise it when he arrived anyway.

What he was supposed to be doing was writing his funding submission to the board, to get some money to pay for Jami Shastri's research. But every time he started he knew he was lying—telling them things they might want to hear instead of the truth. That was common enough—what occurred to him then was that he didn't know what the truth was.

And so he began to play this little game with himself—just sitting and writing whatever came into his head and then seeing if there was anything of interest there. It was a useful tool at such times, provided he remembered to delete it later, before anyone saw it. It opened up his thoughts, allowing them to bound freely, unrestrained by the usual faculty politics and the need to maintain some credibility amongst his colleagues.

Where his free-range thoughts took him was alarming.

He found he was thinking about impossibilities. About things that could not happen, and could not be proven if they did. He was thinking about things that men could not know.

To comprehend the incomprehensible. That was the challenge before him.

How to research into matters that lie beyond our ability to understand them, even if we could detect them?

It wasn't the simultaneous eruptions that bothered him. That was feasible. The three volcanoes might have been three vents from a single magma chamber—in fact probably were. Moreover, he discovered that two of those three mountains had been in eruption at the same time in the past. All quite likely.

The lack of forewarning was harder to explain. Volcanoes erupted as the consequence of geological events. This time there was no evidence of any such occurrence. No build up—and just the single blast, albeit huge. There were aftershocks but they were minor surface tremors—the earth resettling as a result of the disturbance, and not actually part of the disturbance itself. The volcanoes had erupted for no apparent reason. Or at least, none that anyone could find.

Still, if unprecedented, it was imaginable. You could conceive how, in certain extra-ordinary circumstances, something of the sort might occur, however unlikely. He was okay with that.

What really bothered him was the shock-wave, or whatever it was, that had preceded the eruption and produced a definite physiological episode in those people near the zone. It had preceded everything—it had made them ill—then the eruption had occurred.

Now that was inconceivable. But Jami had reported it and then the others, independently. So it had to be real. But what could it be?

It was rendered ridiculous by the matter of scale. This force gave people a slight attack of nausea, and could disturb a giant magma chamber under their feet, and yet affect nothing else and be completely undetectable by state-of-the-art instruments. The answer was simple—nothing could. Or perhaps, nothing known could.

Hearsay evidence, the board would declare. No possible connection between the two matters, they would be sure. He would look stupid, trying to present something like that.

Not that he couldn't bullshit them—in fact he often did.

But you could only bullshit effectively when you had some idea of what the truth was. And he had no idea.

On and on into the night he wrote, searching his mind for a concept, an idea, anything at all, in which to sow the germ of his research. He wrote—

The imaginable universe is mysterious enough, but although we lack many answers, there has never been a mystery for which our minds have been unable to account, however inadequately. Moreover, all scientific mysteries possess calculable answers, even though some may be wrong. But what of the unimaginable—even a divine entity and his works can be fantasised. But are there forces that lie truly beyond our imagination, perhaps which touch us all the time, but which our senses ignore because they are completely incomprehensible to us? Or if the senses are engaged, the brain ignores because it can make no sense of the data—nor even conjure a foolish fantasy on the subject.

Such fantasies are the basis of all religions—answers provided by our minds at a stage in our development when we lacked the data and wit to even approach the truth. Our scope to imagine impossible answers has always seemed infinitely broad, but from our lowly remote position on Earth we cannot possibly perceive it all. There must indeed be other, greater forces out there, that lie beyond that scope.

And perhaps such forces within ourselves as well…

In the dark lonely house, Thyssen leaned back and lit a cigarette. Yes, that was what he was looking for. Something truly supernatural—not the foolish stuff of ghosts or demons or aliens in flying saucers, but something that could be proven to exist with all scientific rigour and yet defy all possibility of an answer. And was this the Shastri Effect? Had that cheeky Indian girl accidentally stumbled upon the gateway to the new universe? Thyssen was unsure, but what he did know was that his former life was ended, that phase passed through, and his new existence was underway. The ghosts of Karla and the children had vanished from the house—finally he was able to come home.

*

She awoke being lightly shaken and joggled and gazing at the grey sky through the window. She was upside down and her neck was hurting—it was that pain that dragged her back to consciousness. In a car, the sky rushing overhead, she assessed. Dull day. It was

Lorna's car, she realised and she was lying in the back seat. In her pyjamas and dressing gown with a travel-rug thrown over her. She groaned.

"Ho, back in the land of the living, are we?" came a cheery voice from the front seat.

They hit a bump and Chrissie's neck almost snapped. Moving her head to a more comfortable position was seemingly dangerous. It felt as if the skull bone was paper thin and would crack like an egg shell.

"Lorna, what's going on?" she attempted to say—her thick tongue would not form the words properly.

"We're nearly there," Lorna replied.

Nearly where? It was plain that she would not get any sense out of Lorna and was going to have to look for herself. She gripped the seatback and hauled and her arms found enough strength to drag her body into a sitting position. She was so bloody stiff. Had they had an accident? Had she fallen? Her eyes slowly focused and she looked all around. They were out in the country, for God's sake, and she was still dressed for bed.

"Lorna? Where are we?"

"The coast is just ahead. When we get there, we'll have coffee. I did a thermos. Then you'll be fine."

She would *never* be fine.

"I'm sick, Lorna. What have you done to me?"

"It's just the sleeping pills wearing off, Chrissie. Coffee, a sandwich, a bit of a walk around and you'll be feeling terrific."

Almost everything Lorna said was unbelievable.

"Walk around. In daylight. In my *jim-jams?*"

"I packed your clothes, and everything."

"Did you? Where?"

"They're in the boot."

"Lorna. You told me to sleep. I remember this distinctly. You gave me sleeping pills. Now you kidnap me and drag me way out here in the provinces."

"You said you wanted to go."

"That was... whenever it was."

"Come on, you were bumping into the walls in your desperation to go places."

"Yes, okay. But you could have waited until I woke up first."

"Oh yeah? Wait til you hear what *I* did."

"You mean before you took to kidnapping invalids?"

"I went out to lunch and started walking blindly. West. Remember what you said about wrong directions?"

"Yes, but..."

"So now we're going west. Right direction. Okay?"

"West where?"

"We're through Waimauku. Coast coming up. You can get glimpses of the sea out there now."

"Yes, I can see it. I can't imagine why I'm so surprised."

"So you were right. We had to go places. Right away. And west is the way to go."

"Oh, I get it. So it's all *my* fault."

"Of course not. Here we are. Look at this. Perfect."

Chrissie looked. She supposed, in the right circumstances, it might have been perfect. The sea. The surf rolling in onto a wide beach. A parking area with toilet facilities. Anyway, before she had time to protest, Lorna was out of the car and fussing.

Chrissie crept forth. Fortunately, there was no one else around. She rummaged in her suitcase in the boot and ducked into the toilet to get dressed and by the time she returned, Lorna had coffee and sandwiches spread out on the bonnet of the car.

"Isn't this great?" Lorna enthused.

"No," Chrissie sighed. "But it is nice, I suppose."

The sandwiches were good—Lorna sure had gone to a lot of trouble over this.

"Feeling better now?"

"Slightly. But I also feel very upset."

"Yes, I know. So do I. It's just this overwhelming feeling that you've got to go and this is the way to go."

Now that the effects of heavy sleep were wearing off, Chrissie had to admit her state of agitation was returning. "Yes, okay then. But consider—it's nearly sunset. What plans have you concerning where we will stay?"

"There'll be somewhere."

They sipped and munched. The breakers roared and the sea gulls swooped and called to them, beckoning them out to sea. The gentle breeze tantalised their hair. Chrissie chuckled and shook her head but then got serious and eyed her friend, so called. "So you feel it too?"

"Oh, yes. I guess I'm not as sensitive as you, but, yes, it got to me as well. I just had to go. That's all. I was telling you what happened to me."

"You mean there's *more?*"

"Is there ever. I caught the bus down to Herne Bay and went out on the pier and walked right off the end of it."

"Really?"

"Honestly. I was so oblivious to the surroundings that I went off the end and into the water before I knew what was happening."

"Oh my God. Tell me you didn't really. Did anyone see?"

"Did they ever. A bunch of blokes, fishing. When they pulled me out, my clothes had gone completely see-through. They got a big eyeful of everything I have."

"Oh Lorna, how awful. So what happened then?"

"I got a taxi home. You should have seen the look on the driver's face when he saw me. And then I had to empty the water out of my handbag before I could pay him. Everything was soaked."

"You'll catch pneumonia, swimming at this time of year."

"I took a handful of Vitamin C as soon as I got home. Then I knew what I had to do. I rang them at work and told them I was sick. Packed, drove over and grabbed you and here we are."

By then, Chrissie was so full of giggles she could hardly speak. Finally, she got herself under control enough to look around and ask. "Okay. So we are here, after many adventures, but where are we?"

Lorna too, needed to survey the scene. She balled her sandwich wrapped and threw it in the nearby bin, and looked again. "We're not there yet, are we?" she said solemnly.

"No," Chrissie said. "I don't know how I know that but I do.

We're not even close."

"Well, this is as far as we can go in this direction without getting wet and one dunking a day is enough for me, thank you very much."

"But we must to go on," Chrissie said and even as she did she sensed the agitation growing, her whole body agreeing with her. "What can we do? Get a boat?"

"I think it's further than that," Lorna said thoughtfully. "I think we have to go over to Australia."

*

Felicity Campbell stood by the glass, regarding Barbara Crane and Dr James Turley with quiet dismay. In the room, they could observe the figure of Kevin Wagner, with both arms and legs in traction.

"We've had to strap him down," Turley was saying.

"Yes. He's obviously very agitated," Felicity said. She didn't need to read any monitors or charts to see that. Kevin Wagner shook and squirmed those parts of his body still capable of it.

"Poor man," Barbara Crane was saying. "He's lost everything."

Felicity frowned. "And no one has claimed him?"

"We even had the Minister for Foreign Affairs involved for a little while, stirring up action in the States," Barbara Crane said methodically. "But so far, we haven't been able to turn up anyone who wants to take responsibility for him. He was an only child, both parents dead, and his wife's family had their own bereavements to contend with. Three lovely little children, apparently, all gone."

"Surely his wife's family has some responsibility..." Felicity murmured.

"I get the impression they didn't like our Kevin much," Barbara said. "I gather he was a bit of an adventurer and away from home a lot."

"What sort of adventurer?"

"Well, I understand he was selling diving and salvage equipment..."

"What about his employer?"

"He'd left his job to come here."

"So we're stuck with him."

"For the moment. Anyway, he seemed happy here, until this started yesterday."

"Yes," Felicity said. "But under the circumstances, an extensive traumatic reaction to his tragedy and his condition is to be expected."

"Agreed," Dr Turley said, and looked apologetically. "I'm sorry to have bothered you."

"Oh no, Dr Turley," Felicity smiled. "You did the right thing. But I can't offer any suggestions that you haven't already tried. Nevertheless, I *am* interested. Do let me know if his condition changes."

*

The sign in the foyer of *The Golden Dolphin* declared that Andromeda Starlight's performances were cancelled due to illness.

"I guess she just ain't recovered from that volcano that got her," Joel Tierney explained to the management. It was true in as many ways as it was a lie. He kept her in her room where she sometimes thrashed so violently that he feared she was suffering an OD. When he thought about hospitals, he thought about cops. Joel sat at the bedside mostly, sweating as much as she did.

*

First they took his battery away, but that only meant he tried to roll himself away by hand, which he was just simply not able to do at that stage of his convalescence. He didn't make it much further than out into the corridor.

"Joe, where the hell do you think you can go?" the nurse asked in exasperation.

"I can't stay," he said. "I have to go."

When they took away the wheelchair as well, still he tried to get out of bed, and presumably make his escape by rolling on the floor. In the end, even Joe agreed that it might be for the best if they sedated him.

*

The drive back was a nightmare. Lorna fought her way forward, against nausea and her every instinct insisting she turn the car around and go they other way. But they had been the other way and there was only the ocean. Now her wilfulness alone forced her onward.

"Please turn around," Chrissie had wept beside her. "Please go back the other way."

But Lorna continued east, against every palpable sensation, every imaginable omen, even a mortal dread, determined to make it to the airport. It was only an hour's drive and she was sure she could do it, but the hour went on and on and Lorna leaned into the forces against her as if they were a stiff wind, maintaining a white-knuckled grip on the wheel.

"Not too much further now," Lorna continually told Chrissie, or perhaps herself, again and again, through gritted teeth. Chrissie by then had given into it and curled on the seat beside her, sobbing silently. It was so cruel, to torture her best friend this way, but there was no other alternative. They had to reach the airport—then it would be fine.

They had been friends for only a year but it seemed like forever. She and Chrissie met at a ski lodge below the Remarkables in the South Island. Lorna was born in New Zealand shortly after her father arrived from Limerick—an engineer who came to work on a hydro-electric scheme. But he had been invalided in an industrial accident when she was fourteen and retired with mum to Norfolk Island.

Lorna had never really worked out whether she was Irish or a Kiwi—certainly her red hair, freckled complexion, accent and determined preference for green clothing, made her seem the former; in fact she had never been to Ireland.

But if she thought she was of confused origins, it was nothing compared to Chrissie who, apparently, had first appeared on Planet Earth in an orphanage in Lyon. Nothing was known of her parentage except that they were probably Vietnamese refugees. She was called Christine because a crucifix was her only worldly good, and Rice because that was all they could get her to eat at first.

Chrissie's aptitude for languages got her through and spoke several fluently. French, English, Italian, several Germanic variants and Old French but oddly—perhaps because she had never experienced nor felt her Asian origins—she had never bothered with oriental languages. She did not know a single word of Vietnamese.

Chrissie had come to New Zealand for a ski-ing holiday and met John Burton and decided to stay. She soon got a job with a Government Interpreter Agency and was fully prepared to settle down to married life when she took the fateful trip to Ruapehu.

But it was actually Lorna and Chrissie who were the instant mix, for they found they had everything in common—except anything in particular, Chrissie liked to joke. Sisters of contradiction, was the way Lorna put it. Anyhow, they had done everything together since—did the rounds of pubs and parties together, met for lunch most days, they experienced a volcanic eruption and a helicopter crash together, died together and came back to life together. Together they originally met John Burton who worked in Lorna's office. They were getting married together, Lorna joked.

And now sharing an abominable nightmare together, although it was plain that Chrissie was getting the worst of it. Finally the airport signs swept overhead and they were there when it seemed they never would be, and Lorna dragged Chrissie from the car, gasping with anxiety as much as effort. But—fortunately—the car park lay to the east of the terminal and almost as soon as they started to walk toward the welcoming lights, both began to be restored.

"God, what are we doing to ourselves?" Chrissie murmured. She looked a wreck and no doubt Lorna did too.

"It's okay," Lorna breathed. "We made it."

But she knew it wasn't over yet.

Inside the terminal, they were recovered enough to go to the loo and wash the awfulness they felt away, hide their pallid faces behind make-up, brush their hair and generally make themselves presentable again.

"This is crazy," Chrissie was saying, fiddling with her hair, chewing the end. "Maybe we should have stayed at the beach,"

"No. It wasn't far enough," Lorna insisted.

"But we can't just fly off anywhere."

"Why not? Where's your spontaneity? Just bung it on the plastic fantastic and it'll be terrific."

"I was saving for the honeymoon."

"If you don't take a holiday right now, there won't be any honeymoon."

Out on the concourse, Lorna was all charm and sweetness as she boldly approached a man in a uniform that suggested he was a pilot. The man immediately forgot whatever he was rushing off to. "Can you tell me which direction—exactly—in degrees—this is."

She indicated the direction very precisely. The man frowned playfully as he consulted his mental compass. "Oooo, that looks like about 275—maybe 280 to me."

"Good. Real good. Can you show us on the map?"

There was a map of the world over the cocktail bar and they looked that way.

"Over to Australia. Towards Melbourne, I should think. Maybe a little above Melbourne but below Canberra. Yes, definitely below Canberra."

"Good. That's wonderful," Lorna radiated.

The man knew how to handle flirts. "Do you mind if I ask why you want to know?"

"We don't know..." Lorna said dubiously.

"It was a bet," Chrissie came up with in desperation.

"Yes, that's right. A bet. I thought maybe Sydney but Chrissie said..."

The maybe pilot remembered where he was hurrying to and hurried off toward it.

Lorna stood before the Departures Board. "Qantas 505. Leaving in fifty minutes. Direct to Melbourne. That'll be perfect."

"What do we do when we get to Melbourne, Lorna?"

"Beats me. Know anyone there?"

"John has friends at Bondi."

"Half the population of New Zealand lives at Bondi. That isn't Melbourne."

"This is really silly, Lorna. I've never heard of anyone who just up and offed to Australia."

"We'll be the first. Wait until everyone hears about it. They'll all say 'wow!'"

"What a pair of loonies, you mean."

*

After he put the billy on the campfire, Brian Carrick rolled a cigarette and squatted by the fire, smoking it to the end and throwing it down. The wide brim hat and squatting posture made him look like a character from a Lawson story, the ultimate bushman. For a night and a full day he had camped here, sleeping overnight in the cabin of the truck. Nothing had happened. No one had come. Not even a farmer to inquire about this stranger camped in the middle of his paddock.

It was silly really. He had waited because there was nothing to do but wait—patient, wandering about, taking great time over his meals, reading from a browned and tattered paperback book one of which he always carried in his back pocket—usually science fiction. The truck had a full array of camping gear and the casual observer might have thought he planned his stay carefully—no such thing had happened and there was no casual observer either. From time to time, he had felt another presence, he suspected, and would shiver and study the horizon and the sky. Nothing at all. He settled down to wait it out, sure that sooner or later, something must happen.

He sat with his back propped up against the only tree in this section of the paddock—not really a tree but the ghost of a dead gum, its only branches two snapped limbs that rose out of the top of the leaning trunk in the shape of a man who had just been shot.

He was reading what had somehow become his favourite book— not science fiction although Isaac Asimov wrote it. *A Choice of Catastrophes*, it was called, describing and assessing the likelihood of all the possible disasters the planet faced, starting with the gigantic—cosmic catastrophes like entropy and Armageddon, ranging downward through lesser disasters like the death of the Sun or the collapse of the galaxy, through collisions with asteroids or other free-range malevolencies, to man-made disasters like Global Warming and Nuclear Winters. There was something in this that fascinated him and it was the third time he had read it since his rehabilitation began. There was something about it that continually enticed him back to its pages—something that perhaps he had missed or forgotten—something that mattered.

He settled down to read, knowing that it would come eventually, that it was just a matter of being patient, that he had all the time in the world.

*

It had come down to the cockroach—a creature so simple in its anatomy and habits that even nuclear war would not affect it. Jami was beginning to feel a bit like one herself, scuttling into the shadows when the light came on, hiding forever in dark corners and basements.

Well, they had put her in a corner of the basement in the Earth Sciences Building which, Harley had said, would keep her nice and inconspicuous for a while. He didn't want anyone asking her what she was doing until the funding came through.

She broke the task down. The effect, she knew, happened in advance of the eruption and therefore the first body of research she needed to explore was the business of predicting volcanoes and earthquakes. And, as Harley punned, a shaky business it was.

The interesting thing was that volcanoes and quakes were always predictable, the movement of tectonic plates in subduction zones effected the volcanoes along the andesite line and told geologists what to expect. When the water suddenly disappeared from the wells, the peasants in earthquake prone regions knew it was time to pack up and get out. Volcanoes invariably bubbled and shook for months before they erupted.

Satellites scanned with infra-red and could detect new hot spots below the surface of the earth. The presence of changes in regional magnetic fields or radioactivity or chemicals in the lakes and rivers warned that trouble was on the way.

The only time that volcanoes ever erupted unexpectedly was as a result of a massive earthquake, one momentous enough to disturb their magma chambers. But even then, the changes in the geostructure that precipitated such a huge quake was sure to activate any nearby volcanoes in advance as the internal pressures and tensions built toward their climax.

Upheavals had been successfully predicted, but more often scientists had failed to do so when in fact there had been sufficient evidence to say, with hindsight, that they should have known. The most persistent and reliable predictions were made not by humans but animals, who, folklore at least had it, seemed to know disaster was impending when none of the other signs were present.

Here, Jami decided, her first real parallel lay. Was the momentary warning she received something similar to the sensation that caused dogs to howl and chickens to go off laying and fish to jump out of the water and cows to refuse to enter the barn in the way that farmers and peasants had reported they did a day or two in advance of the first tremors.

All of this was unsubstantiated evidence—the stuff of legends and myths—but it was so universal that several major research teams were heavily involved in exploring the behaviour of animals in unsteady environments. And so it came down to cockroaches.

Here was the most successful creature in evolution, unchanged for 250 million years, which with its elementary nervous system and simple, well known habits, was at the centre of such research. It was also the cheapest laboratory animal imaginable both to feed and keep, and they did seem to be able to detect earthquakes in advance. Not that they needed to, for they usually survived them anyway, as they did all other ecological disasters. Jami explored the cockroach research until she came to a dead end. They still didn't know how the cockroaches—nor other animals—did it, but at least it proved it could be done somehow. They would keep her posted.

She was thinking that at the very moment when the e-mail indicator flashed on her screen. Desperate for any distraction, she checked immediately—the red indicator said it was urgent anyway. The message was from the laboratory upstairs and from Pepe, who was on duty.

"We got a hit! Canary Islands. 1342 hours. Single shock at 6.5. Details follow."

The details never followed. Jami was already out the door and bolting up the stairs.

*

Beneath the cliffs on the western side of Isla Gran Canaria, the fishing fleet wheeled in wide arcs as they hunted for the shoals of pilchard swept southward on the current. At Las Palmas, the capital, there was a large trawler fleet that hunted Hake and bulk catches of Sardines, but here on the rugged west coast of the island the villages went out trailing nets from their small sailboats as they had before the Spanish came, while above the cliffs the women and old men tended the crude vineyards and tomato plantations. In groups of several dozen, these fleets rode the cold waters of the current, hardly ever out of view of the rugged headlands that usually towered above the waves.

Today the sea was calm, flat, and the air breathless, as if waiting for the disaster to come.

Forced to their oars, the fishermen were unhappy, for they had noticed that the flocks of sea gulls that daily escorted their boats were missing, as if there was no air up there to support them. The fishermen looked about anxiously, and some, disturbed by voodoo demons, had refused to sail, and others went back disgruntled. Those that remained watched the signs, unnerved but unable to identify the warning signs. The day was all but over when the sea began to boil.

The turbulence rapidly expanded outward from a single point as if a vast maelstrom was forming and the panicking men turned their boats landward as the huge ripples surged by them. Then the fish that had evaded their nets began to float to the surface belly up, and steam started to waft from the water until they were engulfed in a sauna-like fog. Deep down, some thought they saw the red glow, and then there was no more, then the surging sea was upon them.

Those fishermen further away first noticed the waves rise and then saw the mysterious fog emerging rapidly far out, and they rowed furiously to safety, if safety it was. In the villages along the coast, the earth shook and houses tumbled, landslides blocked roads and then the fog doused them all in black rain.

*

It was like someone had crept into his camp and punched him, in the stomach and the head, and Brian rolled frantically, ignoring the pain and nausea, to strike back and defend himself. But there was no one there.

*

In a room at the Shamrock Hotel in Bendigo, which was as far as the train could take them that night, Chrissie awoke with a scream as a blinding flash struck her eyes so violently that it sent a sharp pain coursing though her bloodstream.

In the bed across the room, Lorna was also doubled up in sudden pain. "Bloody airline food," she muttered.

*

Kevin Wagner's unconscious disturbance came to an end with such a violent convulsion that it set off the alarms and brought the crash cart team running, only to find him normal, and at peace for the first time in thirty-five hours.

*

At Fairhaven, Joe Solomon had been sedated and there was no monitoring equipment to record his disturbance, nor its sudden cessation.

*

And neither was there any telling which of Andromeda Starlight's hallucinatory dreams suddenly stopped being about moving and instead became about being still.

*

Padre Miguel, who ran the mission station in the hills above Playa de la Nieves, felt the tremor and prepared to move the patients outside but already it was over. He walked out and saw the strange cloud rising over the sea. In fact at first he felt relieved—the entire island was a massive extinct volcanic cone but that wasn't the direction from which the cloud arose. It was plainly over there, far out to sea—where there was nothing but the Atlantic Ocean. The sisters flapped about him in a panic but he spoke calming words to them. Sister Anna, his head nurse, came to stand beside him.

"Is it over?" she asked in French because the fear tricked her into using her native language.

"I'm sure it is," the Padre replied in Spanish. "Just a slight tremor."

But he was looking at that cloud of steam climbing steadily upward.

Over the next hour, people with broken limbs or other minor injuries were brought to the mission until it was overcrowded, but apparently no one had been killed. He knew, though, that the disturbance of the water table might cause typhoid or plague if they were not careful and asked each visitor about the wells and rats.

By nightfall, most of the victims had been released and the cloud had turned to rain, a profoundly unseasonable deluge that left dark stains on the clothing. We have known worse, the Padre told himself. But two hours after dark, and three after the tremor, the word came to the mission that most of the fishing fleet from the three villages above the mission had failed to return.

Fear and superstition gripped the villagers, who were now all gathering on the rocks below the cliffs, gazing out into the strange green twilight that hovered over a sea of dead fish. Many of the boats could be seen bobbing on the water out there but it took some time before the braver amongst the fishermen could be persuaded to go and investigate.

"Take me out there," Padre Miguel said to Rogelio, who he regarded as the bravest of the fishermen.

"It is a graveyard of men and fish," Rogelio replied coldly. "You ask me to throw my net on men already in hell."

"Then I will take your boat," the Padre snapped.

"You will make my boat accursed. My net will be empty for eternity," Rogelio complained, but his options were narrowing.

"What does it matter?" Miguel answered cruelly. "As you see, all the fish are dead."

They made their way to the roadstead and took Rogelio's skiff and rowed out of the anchorage where usually two hundred such craft were moored. Rogelio rowed strongly, while the Padre stood in the bow, holding a battery lantern high, calling directions. The smell was indeed the sulphurous odour of hell and the dead fish glowed like evil eyes upon the surface of the dark water.

Soon they came upon the body of a man floating face down,

and the Padre tried to snare the body with the pole and at least turn him and identify him but he lacked the skills.

"It is Pedrico," Rogelio said. "See, there is his boat."

Padre Miguel raised the lantern high and saw the belly of the capsized boat looking like a giant fish, and another further over and two other bodies floating.

But he could also see at least thirty boats floating, apparently empty. Or was that an arm hanging over the side of that one?

"Leave him," Miguel said. "Take me over there."

"You would leave our friends to the sharks?" Rogelio asked mercilessly.

"The sharks are all dead too," Miguel said as if he knew. In reality, he was remembering that he had forgotten the habit of a lifetime—to pray for the dead.

"The ocean itself has died," Rogelio uttered, but he rowed.

They approached the skiff where the arm dangled. Already he could see that the two men were still in the boat, lying in the bottom amid the nets as if they were their own catch.

"It is the boat of Santiago," Rogelio declared.

The Padre reached awkwardly and grabbed the protruding arm of Santiago or perhaps his brother, and immediately, though the skin was chilled by the night air, he could feel the warmth beneath.

"Santa Maria," Padre Miguel gasped. "They are not dead but only sleeping."

*

This was the right place, no doubt about it, except it wasn't anymore. It was gone in a instant, and then this was no longer the place to which he had come, but nowhere, just the middle of an empty paddock.

Brian Carrick knew immediately the waiting was over, although nothing had changed, and it was time to pack up and go home. Mostly he felt a strange sense of freedom, liberated by senses that had forced him to come here, apparently by mistake.

He remained for a while, making coffee and squatting by the

fire, to be sure, but there was nothing left for him here. The sun was preparing to rise. He pissed on the ashes to make sure no fire remained, shouldered his pack—his humpy—and started back toward the truck.

It had been a clear night, almost full moon, the Milky Way prominent, Mars and Jupiter high. He had enjoyed the nighttime best, when he lay, looking at the stars. Next time, if there was a next time—and somehow he sensed there would be—he resolved to know them all. It was the first time in his life that he had ever had the time or been relaxed enough to lie in the dark and study the stars. He was awed.

Now they were dimming out in the lightening sky and he gave them a final glance and a smile as he marched toward the truck. He felt good. He would drive through the morning and be home at lunchtime, and then would come the tricky bit when he tried to explain all this to Judy.

*

After breakfast, they stood in the glorious morning sun outside the Shamrock Hotel in Bendigo and wondered where to go.

"It's gone," Lorna said.

"What's gone?" Chrissie gasped, checking their suitcases.

"We don't have anywhere to go," Lorna said, frowning, looking up and down High Street. The morning traffic was on the move in Bendigo, people and cars and trams hurrying between the drab grey buildings.

"You mean this is where we were going?" Chrissie said in disappointment and disbelief.

"Apparently."

"Can't be."

"No. It isn't either. It's just the feeling has gone."

"Yes. You're right."

In Bendigo, they found the hotel, planning to continue their journey in the morning only now there was nowhere to go. They stood in the busy main street, the tall redheaded girl and the slight

Asian one, frowning at the morning traffic.

"Well, what now?" Chrissie wondered.

"I suppose we go home again," Lorna said with a shrug.

"That's silly. We can't have come all this way just to spend a night in a flea bitten hotel in Bendigo, wherever that is."

"You have to admit it was different."

"Different from what?"

"Imagine how our friends will admire our spontaneity and adventurous spirit."

"I'm not telling anyone about this. They'll have us locked up."

"Maybe we can justify it by doing some shopping in Melbourne."

"Can we?"

"Sure. Best retail therapy in the Southern Hemisphere, they reckon."

"Well, why didn't you say so sooner. Direct me to the train."

*

After breakfast while the kids readied themselves for school, Felicity flicked on the television to check the time and the weather and the news while she got the dishes out of the way. Balance of payments, political anarchy in Eastern Europe, more strikes threatened, more government cut-backs; she yawned as she stripped off the plastic gloves and apron.

Wendell came in from pulling the car out of the garage and began to shuffle through his briefcase, making sure he had everything he needed. She barely noticed where they said the eruption had happened, under the sea anyway and some fishermen somewhere. It was odd the way the word volcano snapped into her attention these days... "...one by one, the rescuers found the fishermen unconscious in their boats. Over sixty islanders remain in a coma at the mission hospital tonight, most of them otherwise uninjured..."

She was looking toward Wendell desperately. "Wennie, did you hear that?"

"Hear what?"

"It's the same damned thing. I'm sure of it."

"Same what?"

"Same thing that happened last time."

"Would you care to make some sense, my love?"

She paused to think. The news report had moved on to other matters. She tried desperately to gather in her head the little she had apprehended. "Canaries? That's what they said. The Canary Islands. Where are they?"

Wendell regarded the small cage in the corner grimly. "I don't know. Why don't you ask the canary?"

4
THE LEMMINGS OF GRAN CANARIA

The chilled hand of God reached out and touched Lorna as she came in from the bright sunshine to the shadowland of the church. She shivered as the holy spirit entered her body, discerned that she was of no interest and passed on, leaving her sullen and alone.

She walked into the church fully conscious of the fact that her body, as well as her mind, exhibited an inappropriate attitude. Her heels clacked on the floor and rang through the chamber about her, defying any attempt she might have made to creep along. The cold touched goosebumps on the flesh above her neckline and made her nipples stick out prominently. Her blue-green skirt was way too short and her blatant young thighs were a clear challenge to the sanctity of the faithful—even St Peter would have been obliged to leer and let her in through the Pearly Gates, despite a life led as sinfully as her circumstances allowed. And the green beret perched on her brilliant red hair was at just the right insolent angle to offend the stained-glass saints gathered in the windows to right and left.

Lorna was letting them have it, right below the belt and she knew it as she pouted sexily and cast her eye about for mischief. But she was as surprised to be here as Jesus would have been to see her, even if it had been arranged for a long time. This was the particular church where Chrissie had planned to be married, on this very day, just one hour ago in fact, and Lorna had always been projected as first bridesmaid.

"If the building doesn't collapse when you walk in," Chrissie had joked.

Well, here she was and it hadn't, but they built these places solidly, perhaps for that very reason. As her eyes accommodated the depths of the vast chamber before her, she could make out the shiny things and silken cloths of the altar at the far end of the long aisle. She would have been standing down there, in the long mauve dress that Chrissie had planned for her, shoes and handbag to match, her hair up and flowers woven into it. The other two bridesmaids—John Burton's sisters—were flat-chested and protested when they saw the designs and how their necklines were planned to plunge, for the dress had been conceived to Lorna's specifications. Now that bit of fun would never be had. It was sad, so sad.

Lorna started to move again, her heels incriminating her, looking to right and left as she went. There was only one other person in the chamber, huddled in prayer right down the front, just a lump of hunched shoulders from Lorna's perspective, but she knew it had to be Chrissie—in the saddest and most unloved moment of her life.

Lorna had been out searching for hours now, at all their friends places and every bar and cafe they frequented and it only occurred to her very belatedly that she would be here. Burton the Bastard—well, you couldn't blame him really: who'd want to marry the fruitcake that Chrissie had become—had called it off two months ago when he got out of hospital after his so-called beloved had bounced a vase off his head in a fit of irrational jealousy.

It was the second time she had hospitalised him—on the first she had run him down in her car when she saw him crossing the road arm in arm with a female that in her blind rage she had failed to recognise as being one of his sisters. But it wasn't just that. Chrissie had worked herself into such a state of nerves with her mad fears that this or that would go wrong and the wedding would be a disaster that, in the end, when it *was* called off, it came as a blessed relief.

Chrissie had lost her driver's licence, she was on a good behaviour bond, she had lost her job and all of her friends except Lorna. All this from Chrissie the Mouse, the quiet thing in the corner whom Lorna had originally befriended on the ski-slopes because her skinniness made Lorna look all the more voluptuous and her quietude emphasised Lorna's smallest moments of outrageousness.

Now there was only Lorna left—the falsest of friends had been the truest in the end. It was she alone who was there to keep count of the pills in the bathroom cabinet and, eventually, to rush Chrissie to hospital when she did, at last, make a complete hack of slashing her wrists.

Lorna made her way forward, closing in on the pathetic heap in the front pew that her friend had become. It was Chrissie, all right, who had never shown pronounced religious leanings in the past, but revealed now that she knew how to get deeply into prayer. A childhood confined to a convent had not been a total loss.

One space had been left as if Chrissie expected her and Lorna sat in it, leaning back, folding her arms, crossing her legs to give God the very best aspect of her thighs.   Chrissie did not respond, on her knees, hands locked under her chin, head retracted into her collar like a turtle, tears dropping from her nose and chin to a not inconsiderable puddle on the polished timber beneath.

This scene Lorna regarded for as long as she could stand it. Eventually, she reached and tapped Chrissie savagely on the shoulder with her clawlike fingernail.

"Lorna, that hurts."

"Pain therapy, my sweet. To burst you out of your melancholy and back into life. Get up before I start kicking you."

"I'm not melancholy," Chrissie said, but she did not move.

"Sure you ain't. Chrissie, I've been looking for you everywhere."

"Yes, I know. I meant to leave you a note but I forgot."

"Chrissie, being here isn't doing you any good, you know."

"I'm at peace here, Lorna. Why don't you try it? Come on, kneel."

"No way. Come on, sit up or I'll drag you."

"Just let me finish this prayer..."

"Not a chance." She grabbed her by the shoulders, pausing only to eye the altar in mock apology. "Sorry to interrupt, Mr God, but I want to talk to her now. You had your chance and you blew it. Now it's my turn."

"*Merde*, Lorna, don't you know anything about going to church."

"Only those few things I haven't managed to blot out of my memory completely. Come on, sit like a person. Tell the deity goodbye and talk to me."

Chrissie managed a few, doubtless more appropriate, parting words with God and then wearily moved back to a sitting position. Lorna immediately saw that the situation was worse than she imagined. Sure, there were tears still streaking her cheeks and her mascara was everywhere and her nostrils flaming and lips blubbery, but none of that was unfamiliar in recent times.

What was strange was her eyes, which had suddenly taken on a far-away look, a weird tranquillity and penetration that Lorna had never seen before. Had the poor girl finally, completely and utterly, tipped right over the brink?

"Okay," Chrissie smiled limply. "What can I do for you?"

"Chrissie, why torture yourself like this?"

"This isn't torture."

"Oh no? Being the only person to turn up for your own wedding sounds like torture to me."

"I'm not alone. You're here. And God is here."

"Maybe, but him and me ain't on speaking terms."

"You can speak to Him through me."

"Cut the crap, Chrissie. And let's get you out in the sunshine and away from this forbidding place."

"Why don't you try opening your heart just a little, Lorna? It can't be all glass. God only needs the tiniest crack to shine through."

"It isn't *my* heart that needs repair, Chrissie."

"It doesn't matter, Lorna. I can do it for both of us."

"Do what?"

Chrissie glanced about. She took a tissue from Lorna and began working as putting her face back together. That, at least, seemed to be a good place to start.

"I didn't mean to come here," Chrissie said, and then she ran an eye over Lorna's appearance and shook her head in dismay. "And I sure didn't mean to drag you into this. But I was thinking about what might have been—you know how I am. Just lying in bed this morning, letting the thoughts flow."

"At present, that is about the most dangerous thing you could do."

"Well, suddenly, it hit me. I knew!"

"You knew what, exactly... or don't I want to hear it?"

"I had this image. You know. Me in my wedding dress, standing before the altar all by myself."

"I'm thankful you left the dress at home."

"All of a sudden, I knew I wasn't alone at all. I might not have been standing in the church for the reason I expected but I was still standing there for a reason."

"You lost me."

"I was here because God called me."

"Oh fuck, you're going back to the bloody nunnery, aren't you?"

"No, silly. After all those years in the convent which made no impression, suddenly it happens now."

"What happened now, exactly?"

"The ... the *feeling*... Whatever it is that sent us running all over like mad things. Don't you see? That's what happened to us."

"It didn't happen to me..."

"That's why we went to Australia. We were called there by God."

Lorna rolled her eyeballs toward Heaven where, she suspected, many other eyeballs were also being rolled upward. "I doubt that God is waiting for anyone in Bendigo."

"It was just like Moses being called upon the mount, and Saul to Jerusalem, and Paul to Rome. We were touched by the hand of God and he drew us along."

"I'll ask God to keep his bloody maulers to himself, thanks very much." But she shivered. She always made her best jokes when completely unnerved.

Chrissie gripped her arm, leaning close, her eyes aflame. "Lorna, be serious for a moment. Wasn't that how it felt?"

Lorna thought about it for a micro-second. Yeah, sure, that was how it felt. *Lorna and Chrissie, goeth down to Bendigo and sayeth unto them, yet forty days and Bondi Beach will be destroyed...* It would have made sense, had it not been so bloody ridiculous.

"What were we supposed to do, Chrissie? Lead the Children of New Zealand back to the land of milk and honey that they broke their necks to get away from?"

"It would help if you would take this seriously, Lorna."

"I'd need to be omnipotent to do that."

"Lorna, whether you believe it or not, we were drawn to Australia and it was obviously for some purpose known only to God."

"That much I believe. So fucking what? God's purpose fizzled."

"No. You said it yourself that morning. We didn't get to wherever we were supposed to go."

"No one ever does."

"We will next time."

"There isn't going to be a next time."

"Oh yes there is. And right away. Lorna, can't you feel it?"

Lorna reared back, no longer mocking as she stared. "Feel what?"

Chrissie tightened the grip on her arm and her eyes with her newfound limpidity stared into those of her horrified friend.

"Lorna, it's happening again."

*

One of the women ran on ahead to raise the alarm at the mission station.

"Demons!" she was shrieking as she rushed about the dusty

courtyard. "The demons are taking our men!"

She might have been possessed by the demons herself, such was her state of hysteria as she finally collapsed in Padre Miguel's arms.

"The demons have turned them into zombies."

Padre Miguel needed no further explanation. He might have come to this island from Morocco and before that Spain but he knew all there was to know about demons, zombies, and throbbing rituals that drove women to a frenzied hysteria.

He rose, giving brief instructions to the sister regarding the sedation of the woman, whom he recognised as one of those from the village directly above the mission. He started walking in the direction of the village—the woman's arms had flailed generally in that direction anyway, but he didn't have to go far before he heard the commotion coming down the path toward him. Female voices, shrieking in terror, pleading in desperation. It was just a few minutes after dawn when the men ought to have been heading down the other path to their skiffs in the roadstead and the day's fishing. Certainly it was far to early for such agitation under any circumstances.

Padre Miguel backed off, returning to the hospital grounds. Plainly the problem, whatever it may be, was coming to him. They were such a skittish lot, right along this coast, full of mysteries and rituals and legends. He called to the sisters, ordering more sedatives, bracing himself with a brief prayer, and stood in the middle of the courtyard and waited. The commotion advanced right to him although what worried him more was a brief moment when the breeze carried voices from farther off, from another of the villages further away, where a similar cackle of women's frantic voices seemed evident.

The first of the men entered the camp. They were, indeed, zombies. Padre Miguel had seen this before, often, but only ever at night when drink and drugs drove the men to this catatonic state during the satanic rituals. They walked steadily, eyes wide and unseeing, offering no response to the women who clawed and buffeted them and shrieked in their ears. There were about thirty men in all, the full complement of fishermen from the upper village, he assessed, and every one of them possessed by the same demons. This was going to take some stopping.

"Don't worry about the women," he shouted to the considerable band of helpers that he accumulated behind him. "Stop the men."

No one moved. They all knew that such demonic possession was contagious and to touch the victim was to expose yourself to the risk that the demons would transfer through the contacting flesh. That the women were seemingly unaffected did not deny this logic—they were assumed to be under attack by their own demons, which they certainly seemed to be.

Padre Miguel tackled the first man to come by, and was immediately repulsed. It was like throwing yourself against a rock, and the man brushed him aside with a sweep of his arm. The sisters rushed to aid Padre Miguel, bravely overriding their fear that he too might now be possessed. By the time he fought off their attentions and got himself to his feet, the procession had already passed by and was leaving the courtyard.

"Where are they going?" he wondered aloud.

"To Hell," an old man on the verandah replied, and put his pipe back between his gums.

Padre Miguel and several of the sisters rushed after them. They were going along the path that went nowhere really except to meander along the cliff tops to the next village. It didn't make sense, but then, perhaps it wasn't supposed to.

They passed several exhausted and overcome women weeping at the edge of the track but the Padre ordered the sisters to ignore them.

"Get the men," he was shouting. He remembered shouting it once before.

It jumped into his mind, just for an instant, that all of these men were those plucked unconscious from their boats three months ago. They had lain, unhurt but unconscious, for eight days while doctors and officials came from the other islands and the mainland to determine what Padre Miguel already knew—

that there was no reason why they slept so deeply. Demonic possession was immediately suspected.

Then on the eighth day, they all revived as if nothing had happened and returned to their villages and their fishing. He remembered that there had been a garbled telephone call from some lady doctor in some other country who spoke no Spanish but finally got the message across that this might happen, that she had seen something similar, that they would probably be all right. So it was. But now this.

It was as if the sea was calling them, its voice on the wind, screaming above that of the women who carried on frantically, trying to restrain their maddened men. Padre Miguel shook off his thoughts as he caught up with the end of the crazy procession. The sounds ahead had intensified and the screaming was on the wind as if the sea itself was remembering its agonising death. He pressed ahead, and the path through the jungle opened to the sky and sea beyond.

Here the cliffs dropped five hundred feet straight onto the rocks and the surf below and the men were disappearing there, dropping from view one by one. The Padre almost went over himself as he reached the edge of the crag and saw the scene below him. The men walked on, straight over the edge and fell silently, shrugging off the women or else taking them over with them. A dozen shattered bodies already surged amongst the rocks down there, and two more fell while he watched, and then three, their stiff unyielding forms in contrast to the flapping gyrating things that were women who refused to let go of her man until it was too late.

"Madness! Madness!" the Padre shrieked, and rushed forward but the first man he tried to stop almost took the father with him. The sisters grabbed him only just in time—he remembered scrambling wildly as stones and branches came away in his hands as his feet swinging helplessly in space and three more men fell by him, and the more, and more.

By the time the sisters dragged the Padre to safety, all of the men were gone. Those women who had survived were huddled and wailing, screaming to God to take revenge on the sea. The Padre, the horror sweeping nausea and bile through his body, looked down the precipice and saw the bodies crashing together amid the rocks and the waves intermittently spraying pink surf. Padre Miguel had again forgotten to pray, instead he wept, and even shook his fist at the heavens.

"Take me. Why didn't you take me instead?" he roared.

The sisters subdued him, one even threatened him with a syringe but he shook his head. And then they pointed and he looked that way. Further around, on the cliffs of the next headland, men were walking off the edge and falling unheedingly into the sea.

*

Just short of Dimboola, Brian Carrick pulled the rig off the road and rolled to a stop. It was all wrong but he could not understand how. There was a wayside stop here, deep in a forest of eucalypts and nothing much around otherwise. The starlines, or whatever it was that guided him, had fucked up and brought him here by mistake—of that he was certain.

Maybe he was tired. He had been on the road three hours now after a troubled morning in the yard—it was four in the afternoon, the sort of time when men dozed. But it wasn't that. He got out of the truck and walked around, boots crunching on the gravel. The day was hot—it was just five days before Christmas—but here in the shade of the gums it was cool and refreshing. No, he wasn't tired. He was in the wrong fucking place.

At first he wasn't surprised that the direction had changed, even if initially it seemed the same. The restlessness had come upon him as the morning progressed and he moved about the yard, checking the loads against the manifests, making jokes, ignoring his senses as long as he could.

He was bored, of course. Larry had been pleased to offer him the job of dispatcher and Judy was delighted to get him out of her hair, but he was a driver, not an office jockey. Judy talked a lot about psychiatrists these days, and padded cells, and the relief from that situation was a blessing in itself. But the work bored him—like *Clancy of the Overflow*, he didn't suit the office.

More and more, since his recent strange experience—or non-experience—up Kyabram way, he had related himself to bushmen, Lawson figures, classic Australians, which he defined as Europeans skewed by the same effects that the Australian landscape had worked to create aboriginal culture. He was proud to be one of them. His suburban life drifted further from him constantly.

The aborigines, they said, travelled the land along the songlines, invisible emotional navigation routes that took them from one waterhole or hunting ground to the next. The Dreamtime was overlayed with a map of the sacred sites and the rhythms of the bush pointed the way. By this means, Brian felt he was being guided even if, at a more rational level, he was rather more convinced that it had something to do with the stars. What ever it was, they had presently brought him to the wrong place.

He wished it was night and he could see the stars—perhaps they would provide some clue or confirmation. He had spent much time studying star maps and reading astronomy books. He had thought about celestial navigation, but it wasn't as simple as that, if such a complex thing could be called simple. The stars did not point the way—like the songlines, they simply nudged and bumped him in the right direction.

By lunchtime, he knew he was going. He was tempted to ring Judy and tell her he was off again, but he supposed she would figure it out soon enough. She would protest no more or less for knowing in advance.

"Larry bent over backwards to get you that job," she would say. "You can't just walk away from it."

He wouldn't be walking away. To get out, he was going to have to steal a truck. Which simply meant that as a final gesture, he would be despatching himself.

The lunch break meant he had the yard to himself. He fuelled up a Kenwood that he knew was in good order but wouldn't be needed for the next few days, signed it out to himself in the most formal manner, turned on the answering machine and drove away, careful to padlock the gate behind him. At least all that would make it plain to Judy, if not Larry, that the nutcase was *gone walkabout* again.

Once more he took the freeway toward the city, and the first inkling came when he did not turn off at Punt Road but continued straight on, around King's Way and Curzon Street and out onto the Tullamarine Freeway. Was he going to the airport? he wondered. No—he went straight on at the Calder Highway and soon after found himself tempted by the Melton exit. Really? He drove on, knowing there were other options ahead.

There wasn't any reason why he should have expected to return to the same place, that empty paddock near Kyabram— after all there wasn't anything there. As he continued toward Bendigo on the Calder Highway, his irritation grew and at Digger's Rest, he did turn off without the slightest doubt in his mind. He crossed on the side roads to the Western Highway and contentment returned to him immediately. Okay, Ballarat, Horsham, Adelaide, Wherever—here I come.

He wondered if maybe he had gone the wrong way on the previous expedition. Perhaps there was nothing at Kyabram because he had failed to read the invisible maps properly. After all, it was his first try. But he knew that wasn't the case. That had been the right place then, this time he was going somewhere different. His sense of adventure grew.

And then, suddenly, beyond Stawell, it was all wrong again. His agitation grew intensely and when he pulled off the road near Dimboola, it was because he had no choice. He sat on the lower rung of the bullbar, rolling a cigarette and allowing his sensations to flow. Okay, he was heading west, but he needed to go north. He did not need a map because he knew these roads. In Dim was the turn-off to Warracknabeal—north-east really—but then on through Donald and Charlton which was fully due east. He stood, drawing on the cigarette, contemplated the position of the sun, facing himself around until he was sure. Yep, and that would point him right back at bloody Kyabram again.

His destination had been the same place all along—he just couldn't understand how this long detour had happened? Perhaps he didn't read these signs as well as he thought. Maybe it would be better, in a couple of hours, when the stars came out...

*

Where the fuck am I now? No-wheresville, that's for sure. Sitting out here in the middle of nothing, squat on the suitcase, showing plenty of leg to any passing motorist only there ain't no motorists, and nothing else much either.

Andromeda Starlight, a figure of tragedy, abandoned at the side of the road. The sun blazed down unmercifully but she at least had a big floppy hat on her head, or else she would have been dead. Ten million flies hung about her, but she had sprayed herself with *Kelvin Kline Exotica* that kept them at bay or at least confused. The more intrepid ones she *maced*.

Her *Raybans* were hardly a match for the glare but they spared her eyes the sprays with which she defended herself and there was fucking nothing to see anyway. Mulga out of sight before and behind her. The road, potholed and straight, disappeared without deviation to left and right. There were some low hills to the right, but no trees at all. What in the name of all that was sacred was she doing here?

She didn't tell Tierney she was going. She had a gig on Great Keppel Island and she wouldn't be there. He'd be furious but that was just bad luck. She'd stolen a fistful of money out of his wallet while he slept by the pool and so the bridges were burned. Except there weren't any bridges, just the ferry right there, all steamed up and ready to go and she just hopped on and was gone.

In Rockhampton, she went shopping, stuffing her purchases into the suitcase and then got out on the road and thumbed it. She'd dropped a tab or two at each stage and hardly knew that she was picked up by a salesman in an air-conditioned Ford.

"Where are you headed to?" he asked.

"Not to, from," she replied.

Far inland anyway, to wherever she was now. When she had passed out from the Bundaberg Rum the salesman offered her continually, he stopped the car and tried to rape her. But she wasn't quite as far out of it as either of them thought and maced him and he drove off and left her. On the whole, when she considered her present situation, rape wasn't such a bad option.

Far out between the low ridgelines, she saw a cloud of dust begin to rise. Three vehicles had already passed her by—a road train that didn't seem to see her, a family of tourists that stared and hurried on, and a bunch of young bucks, probably miners, who called her 'coon' and 'boong' and offered money. Silly buggers thought she was an aborigine—somehow she managed to know that no amount of money would have been worth it. When one jumped out of the car, she maced him too and they raced off, shouting abuse. There was a certain macabre way in which she was enjoying this. It wasn't actually that she was developing some weird sort of morality at this late stage of life—it was mostly because they weren't going the way she wanted to go.

Not that she actually knew where she wanted to go. When they left Rocky, this seemed the right way. Now it didn't. Left was back to Rocky, which was certainly wrong, but right seemed the wrong way too. It was as if the desert had disoriented her.

Amid the growing dust cloud down the road to the right, a speck materialised and took shape and slowly became another road train. Another driver popping pills and seeing nothing, she supposed. She sighed, lighting a cigarette, and watched the approach. The big truck with its three high trailers thundered toward her and she contemplated getting off the road. Nar, let the bastard run over me.

The driver blasted on his clarion as if in warning but then came the squeal of the airbrakes and the massive rig began to slow down. The driver had white hair and beard, all close cropped, and looked far too old to be driving such a monster.

"Anything I can do fer yer, luv?" he called over his elbow that seemed permanently to protrude out the window.

"A beer would be nice, Honey," she smiled.

He rummaged and came up with a can and threw it to her. She caught it deftly—it was remarkably cold. Plainly he had an Esky full of ice in there beside him. She opened it, took a gulp, and rewarded him with her best smile.

"Thanks, Lover. What do I owe you?"

"Nuthin. Where you going?"

She indicated a point directly behind her, at right-angles to the road.

"I wanna go that way."

The driver looked that way, as if to assure himself that the nothing that was out there was out there. It was.

"Can't go that way, luv. You either gotta go where I'm goin' or back where I come from."

"Where in tarnation am I anyway?"

"Ooo, 'bout halfway between Bogantungan and Withersfield."

"Sorry I asked, Sugar. What's that way?"

"Bugger all."

"Well maybe so, that's the way I gotta go."

The driver thought about it.

"South, hey? Well, yer better come with me to the next town. About a hundred kay. There's a turn-off south there, takes yer down through Springsure and Taroom to Brisbane."

She was thinking about it, but she stood and was gathering her things while she did so.

"Brisbane ain't south," she was sure.

"It's where people usually mean when they say south."

"Ain't south enough."

"You wanna *really* go south, you can turn off at Springsure and the highway runs down through Charleville and Cunnamulla and into New South, through Bourke and then on to everything south."

"Bourke, you say, my man. Ain't that where the *Black Stump* is?'

"Sure is."

"Somewhere thataway then, I guess."

*

Police were called to a disturbance inside the Riverdale shopping mall and found a small crowd gathered about a man in a motorised wheelchair. The man was barely conscious, soaked in sweat, breathless and certainly unable to make an account of himself.

An ambulance had already been called and the police would have moved on, had not Senior Constable Belinda Grey decided to check the man's identity. She quickly determined that he was a lawyer named Joseph Solomon.

"I've heard of him," she murmured. "Gets all the fat cats off corruption charges."

She also found a card referring to Fairhaven Hospital and mentioned it when she put the call through to dispatch.

"That's interesting," the dispatcher said thoughtfully. "We had a report of an escaped inmate from Fairhaven a couple of hours ago. Hang on, Belinda, I'll check."

Moments later, the dispatcher informed Senior Grey that Fairhaven were coming to collect him.

"Apparently he has a history of unauthorised departures," the dispatcher added. "But the only risk is to his own health."

By then, the ambulance had arrived and the crew were examining the patient. There were no dangerous signs, but Belinda Grey remained dissatisfied.

"Fairhaven is over ten kilometres away," she frowned. "How the hell did he get here?"

*

A tourist with a video camera had been on hand to film the scene when the *Human Lemmings of Gran Canaria* made their final plunge. The video was just a few shots of indistinct figures falling down the cliff face while others waited their turn at the top, followed by many views of a number of bodies floating in the sea, and it was all out of focus and rather shaky, but it was enough to propel it to headline status by the world's television news producers.

As the shadow line that divided night from day travelled about the circumference of the earth, so those amateur pictures flashed around the world—a tantalising glimpse before the evening news credits, a more detailed showing later in the bulletin depending of the state of local politics and catastrophes.

At twilight in Melbourne, Judy Carrick remarked that the Canary Islanders were plainly as silly as her husband, who had gone walkabout again and stolen a truck to do it. But she was only joking, trying to humour herself out of her shattered nerves.

*

Lorna and Chrissie saw the same video images as they sat in the bar of the Savoy Hotel in Melbourne, as they waited for the departure of their train north from Spencer Street station following another frantic flight from New Zealand. The video images appeared on the TV screen at the end of the bar. Since the sound was turned down, no explanation of the strange scenes was possible, but Lorna was spluttering into her Harvey Wallbanger and pointing. "Hey. That's what I did!" she cried.

"Well, don't tell everybody, Lorna," Chrissie hushed her.

*

Andromeda Starlight saw them in a motel room in Charters Towers to where her erratic hitch-hiking had eventually delivered her. She was so stoned by that stage that that a bunch of humans leaping to their deaths for no reason did not seem at all strange to her.

"I know how they felt," she told the vodka bottle, raising it in a toast and taking the final swig. She threw the bottle aimlessly over her shoulder, and then fell off the bed and was asleep before she hit the floor.

*

Joe Solomon had seen them sitting in the lounge at Fairhaven, an instant in which television wasn't quite as dull as usual, but he thought nothing of it.

*

The penumbra passed right across Asia and Europe and reached the United States where there was a scandal in the Senate, riots in the Bronx and a train wreck in Alabama and the Canary Islands story was committed to the weird and wonderful segment of the news, along with the new baby Panda at Chicago Zoo and the latest shots of modifications to the Hubble Telescope by the space shuttle crew.

The Lemmings item had little story to go with the pictures but the location was enough to draw the attention of Jami Shastri, who almost choked on her veggie burger when she heard it. She was on the telephone to Harley Thyssen before she had fully recovered from her coughing fit.

"It's exactly the same place as the previous eruption occurred, Harley," she was gasping.

"You think there's a connection," he wondered.

"I'm sure there is."

"Well, that oughta up our funding submission."

*

By the time New Zealand descended into the gloaming, the wild speculation that these unfortunate suicidal souls had been apparently affected by a volcanic eruption three months earlier was included with the pictures. A cold chill passed through the body of Felicity Campbell when she heard two nurses talking about the Canary Islands, but she was on her way to an emergency and had no time to ask questions. When she passed the patient through to theatre, the surgeon remarked to his intern about the silly buggers that walked straight off the cliff.

"Which silly buggers?" she asked, trying to keep her voice even.

"Some island off the coast of Africa," he said. "Whole villages of them, just up and walked over the edge and fell into the sea. You oughta see the pictures."

"Which islands?" she demanded. But no one remembered.

As soon as she was sure her patient was settled, she went looking for Kevin Wagner. She found him the first place she looked, on his crutches at reception, arguing frantically with the charge sister as he tried to discharge himself.

"I'm sorry, Mr Wagner. I can't do anything until Dr Campbell signs the release."

"Which I will do at the first available opportunity," Felicity smiled as she walked up. "But that's still a few months away yet, Kevin."

Looking at Kevin Wagner, she could see he had once been a handsome, rugged, well built man, and all the signs suggested that he would be again, but the present figure before her was a grey faced, hunched object that swayed unsteadily on the crutches. The tragedy that his life had become still glazed his eyes and deepened the lines on his face. His hair had turned completely white.

Nevertheless, she knew his rehabilitation results had been excellent so far and the grief and trauma counsellors declared that he was coming to terms with the annihilation of his family. She wondered. She searched his face for pain from non-clinical sources but found none.

A hard man, tough and strong, beaten down but rising again like a phoenix from the ashes of his former life. Such recoveries gave doctors like Felicity the strength to go on.

Even now, when she knew that added to his daily pain and the effects of the drugs was that nerve-shattering agitation that had caused his previous mysterious convulsions—convulsions that had continued for days unabated and then subsided completely. Now, although conscious and more or less ambulatory, he was showing clear signs of that agitation again. He was shaking like a scared rabbit, unable to raise his head properly, plainly near the point of collapse, and yet he could smile and reply in his cool West coast accent. "No chance, hey, Doctor C?"

"No chance, Kev."

"You sure are a tough lady to deal with, Doc."

"With patients like you, I need to be Kev."

"Waal, here's your big chance to get me offa your hands, Felicity my sweet."

"Oh, sure. Just exactly where were you planning to go?"

"Beats me. Ain't got nowhere to go, actually. But I sure as hell wanna go there, and right now."

"Come on. Come with me. Let's talk about this."

"You don't know how badly I want outa here, Doc. Just go. Get movin'."

"Can you manage on the crutches or should I get a wheelchair?"

"Better walk while I can. I know you guys are gonna slip me a mickey at the first available opportunity and then strap me down again so I don't make a run for it."

"Sure we will. For your own good, of course."

"Of course. But Doc, you don't know how badly I wanna get moving."

"I think I do, Kevin. Let's go somewhere quiet and talk about this."

"Hey, is that a pass?"

"Save that stuff for the nurses, okay?"

*

She must have dozed off—when the telephone rang, it startled her. Or perhaps she jumped because she knew it would be Harley. At this stage, no one else would have known the number of the dungeon where he kept her. His voice boomed down the line at her without any greeting or even verification that it was her who had answered. But then, no one else could have.

"You'll be delighted to know that you are now a funded research project. The Board of Governors have approved."

Her heart sank. Had the funding been denied, maybe she could have escaped back into the real world. Now she was trapped forever. "How did you manage that?"

"Swamped them with BS about the possible far-reaching effects of the Shastri Effect and the duty of the university to pursue the project to its ultimate point."

The Shastri Effect—she cringed to hear her own name used that way—it was as if, like certain deities, she had become a swear-word. "We don't even know if there is any such thing as the Shastri Effect, Harley."

"There is now. It says so on the budget documents. The Governors believe it. So you just better get down to work and prove it."

"Harley, you have me trying to prove something that doesn't exist. Just exactly how do you do that?"

"There is a story they tell of how the great Ernest Rutherford postulated that there was more to the atom than had been previously realised. There had to be, he was sure, a neutron, a negatively charged, undetectable particle in there somewhere. But how to find it? To prove it? He went and asked H. G. Wells."

"Yes, I've heard the story, Harley."

He went on, completely undeterred. Once one of his stories began, there was no stopping it. "'Imagine an invisible man walking in Trafalgar Square,' Wells answered, no doubt sublimely. 'How would you know he was there?' Rutherford had little chance to point out that it was, indeed, the very question, for Wells immediately answered it himself. 'Why, by the reactions of the people he bumped into of course? And the scattering of the pigeons before his feet.'"

"All of my sources assure me the story is apocryphal, Harley." Jami interrupted wearily.

Even that would not stop him. "And so it was done. HG wrote an immortal novel called *The Invisible Man*, while Ernest hurried away to discover the neutron."

"I don't see how that is of the slightest help, Harley."

"I just thought it might inspire you in your search for the

impossible."

"As I recall, Harley, the discovery of the neutron would which would prove to be the means by which the atom could be split and a whole new age of power and horrors would be born, was one that Wells had also predicted in *The Shape of Things to Come*. And meanwhile your beloved Rutherford went on the record declaring that anyone who imagined great amounts of energy might be released by splitting the atom was talking *moonshine*."

"I like my version better."

"You would. Yours is fiction and mine is fact."

"Slippery notions, fact and fiction, Jamila. I'd be more careful with them if I were you."

"The fact is that we don't know anything about this, Harley. Not a damned provable thing."

"As Socrates pointed out, true wisdom is to understand your own fallibility. The measure of a worthwhile person is not in terms of what they know, but instead in their awareness of what they don't know. The more you know, the more you discover you need to know. True ignorance is thinking that you know all about it. And the really dangerous people are those who are determined that they are right."

"Okay, so our ignorance puts us on the side of the angels. But no closer to the truth."

"Too many people these days confuse truth with the facts," Thyssen rambled. What was happening? Was he drunk?

"They are mutually dependent..."

"Not at all. A fact is that which you can prove to be so. The truth is what you earnestly believe is how things are. There is no necessary connection between them. Consider a man—I know his name, so do a lot of other people and we all agree on his address, who his friends are, what he wears, his eye and hair colour, what mode of transport he prefers, how his voice sounds—far more than adequate evidence to prove the fact of his existence, but that existence is untrue if he is Santa Claus or Sherlock Holmes. It is true that JFK was killed by more than one assassin, even though the facts assure us Oswald operated alone."

"This conversation isn't about what I thought is was about, is it?" Jami said warily. All of a sudden, it occurred to her that she was receiving an insight into the mind of the true Harley Thyssen—the one he was usually careful to keep well hidden.

"It's a random universe, you see—at least so they would currently have us believe—and in a random universe, no amount of accumulation of facts can ever possibly add up to the truth. All of the facts, and the truth, are totally different things. Science is accumulation of facts. Religion is nonsense. But where is truth? Picasso said: Art is the lie that reveals the truth. So, here we are, both lying and telling the truth. The trick is to believe everything, until you know its a lie. But when you know its a lie, never believe it again."

"I'm not quite willing to abandon the facts at this stage, Harley."

"Neither you should. But remember that Albert Einstein was horrified when he realised that the logical conclusion of his discoveries was that we live in a random universe where there is no order and nothing makes sense. `I cannot believe that God plays dice,' he declared. We cannot believe it either. Things do seem to make sense to us, and we cannot accept that the very idea of something making sense is itself an illusion. And therein lies the answer. Einstein was right: that things can make sense and that humanity strives to make sense of them is the truth—that it is a random universe where nothing makes sense is simply a result of the facts. There's no truth in it at all."

"So how do you explain the fact that the facts work for us, even though they don't exist? How do you explain the fact that there is order everywhere we go, and we never encounter any of this randomness?"

"Maybe because that's the way we make it happen."

"Are you suggesting I should rig the facts and make the Shastri Effect real?"

"Not at all. No, definitely not. I'm suggesting you open your mind to the wider possibilities."

"You think that is what's happening here? That something

truly random is taking place?"

"Just think about it, that's all."

She hung up, realising he was no longer there. At least now she did know one truth. In the night when he was all alone, weird weird things were happening in the mind of Harley Thyssen.

*

Now that they were being guided by the hand of God, things went far smoother. Her newfound sense of purpose placed Chrissie in control and where she took them was directly to the airport without any of the bewildered meandering they had suffered when Lorna had been the prime mover.

"Are you sure about this, Chrissie," Lorna did bother to ask. "I'm not sure our budgets can stand two unnecessary trips to Australia in three months."

"The one good thing cancelling a wedding does, Lorna, is solve all your cash-flow problems."

Bendigo had been off-course—instead they took a train to a place called Shepparton and then a bus to the town of Kyabram, where they realised they had by-passed their mysterious destination. Another bus took them out through open country until, about five kilometres from Kyabram, they came to a place in open country where a dirt road intersected theirs, and Chrissie was tapping the driver on the shoulder.

"What's down that road?" Lorna thought to ask the driver, while Chrissie had already jumped off and was hauling both suitcases.

"Nuthin down there, luv. Just a few properties, then the creek and I think the road runs out after that."

"Okay. Thank you," Lorna said in her disappointment.

The bus pulled away and they stood there, contemplating the dirt road before them. It was really just a gravel track, leading through flat open fields where occasional cattle roamed. Trees lined both side of the track and otherwise dotted the landscape, all individual gums, mostly fifty or so metres away from each other but the horizon was so flat that they created the illusion of a forest way out there in all directions. Behind them, they could see the shining iron of what might have been a large shed, and there did seem to be a farm further down their road, off in a clump of trees.

"Well, do we walk or wait?" Lorna asked.

They were dressed in jeans and light tops, Chrissie in joggers and Lorna in sandals and both had hats and sunglasses. They could walk, or so they thought. The grass was too long to leave the track and anyway, barbed wire fences paralleled them on either side, the dirt of the track was too soft and the gravel in the ruts too rough. They hauled their suitcases about a hundred metres and then stopped and sat on them.

"You sure this is right, Chrissie," Lorna protested. "There doesn't seem to be anyone down here."

"You expect to meet the saviour on a freeway?" Chrissie snapped back.

They should have prepared better, brought water to drink at least. Instead they lit cigarettes.

"Better watch we don't start a fire in this dry grass," Chrissie warned.

"Get rid of the snakes," Lorna sighed.

This place had the most ferocious bushfires and the most deadly snakes in the world, both of them knew. It was hot, dry and alien—a fearful place, unfriendly and forbidding. Neither would admit to the other that they wanted to go home, now. But less definable urges thrust them onward relentlessly.

Instead they walked along the rough track, each trying to keep up the other's enthusiasm.

"Almost there."

"Yeah—I know."

But there was nothing—no farm, no cultivation, nothing at all. And then. "What's that out there?" Chrissie asked. Lorna saw sunlight flashing off something away to their right.

"Dunno," Lorna declared, staring with a hand shading her eyes. "Looks like a truck. Big semi, without it's trailer. What the hell's it doing out there?"

They stood by their suitcases, contemplating the scene.

"I don't see anyone around," Lorna said.

"Right place though," Chrissie smiled. "I know it is."

The shining truck was parked under a solitary tree about a hundred and fifty metres off the track. Plainly, chariots weren't what they used to be, Lorna thought but didn't say.

Chrissie was already heading off that way, hauling the case with two hands, heedless of snakes and everything else. "Come on, Lorna, come on."

They swished through the long grass, following the path flattened by the truck and advanced upon the vehicle boldly. At the foot of the tree, they saw, a man lay sleeping with his hat over his eyes. He was lying on a sleeping bag even though he had a tent and full scale camp set up. He snored.

Lorna looked over the heap of empty cans—Victoria Bitter and a few baked beans, and many empty cigarette packets. Surely God was not going to appear to them as the *Jolly Swagman*. Chrissie stood back, puzzled by the normality of it all, looking around, wondering. But Lorna went forward and lifted the hat from the man's eyes.

"Hello, under there," she said sweetly.

Brian Carrick blinked and stared—of them all, it was only he would have the vision of angels.

"G'day," he said. "Who the fuck are you?"

Lorna smiled, squatting and looking around at Chrissie. Chrissie shook her head sadly. If it was God, surely he would have known who the fuck they were.

*

This was the place where they fell. Sixty-three men and eight women plunged to their deaths from this precipice and two other similar points along the nearby cliffs. Harley Thyssen tried to hold the scene of those dreadful moments in his mind, to experience being there, amongst the victims, to know how they were and what was happening inside them at the time. They walked like zombies, he had been told, possessed by demons. But still it was impossible to conceive, how one man could fall, then the one behind him, then the next with his hysterical wife clinging to his legs. Jonestown, he thought. Or men going up out of the First World War trenches, scrambling over the slain bodies of those ahead of them, or the redcoats marching resolutely without breaking ranks as snipers felled individuals in their ranks. Yes, something like that, but not exactly. His main difficulty was that the Padre did not speak English and Thyssen had to gather his picture through an interpreter.

He turned to the Padre now.

"Did they scream?" he asked.

Munro, the geophysicist from the US Geological Survey, who had taken charge of the site, frowned at the question. He was acting as interpreter. Thyssen needed to raise his eyebrows to get the question passed on.

No. The women screamed but the men did not.

There were no other witnesses to the event. The villages above the mission from where the victims had come were now deserted, exorcised and burned. All the boats were gone from the roadstead below. Things were so quiet around the mission these days that Padre Miguel was thinking of moving on.

"And they were the same men? The same ones who were in the coma three months earlier?"

Yes. They were the same men. It was said the demons possessed them while they slept.

"And none of them survived, and no man who was not in the coma died here."

That is so. Except, of course, the women they dragged over with them.

Munro, a long skinny Southerner with blonde hair and glasses, looked far more convincingly a scientist than Thyssen, who might have more resembled a pioneer mountain man, or the boss of a biker gang. Munro was continually saying things to the Padre that Thyssen did not ask, and mostly they were reassurances that Thyssen was to be respected. Now that the wave of journalists and tourists had passed, the Padre had settled into deep suspicion of all strangers.

"How were the boats arranged when the men were first found in the coma?"

Munro could answer that himself, with a slight irritation.

"They were in a circle as you would expect."

"Expect? Why?"

"The shockwave would have pushed them all outward from the centre."

"All of them?"

"No. But those inside the circle all perished, and those outside it suffered no effects."

"Interesting."

Munro shook his head. "Harley, we've already explored all those possibilities. We tested for bacteria and chemical effects emitted from the caldera during the eruption. As we expected, it was too deep for anything like that to reach the surface."

"But there was turbulence. The shockwave that pushed the boats into a circle."

"True. At eight hundred feet depth, you wouldn't expect that. But it was only very slight."

"Yet severe enough to kill these men three months later."

"We can't be sure there is a connection."

"There has to be. Sixty-three men are knocked unconscious in their boats during the eruption—all of them at the same distance from the epicentre. All sixty-three lie in a coma for eight days, all recover on the same day and eight weeks later, all sixty-three take a casual stroll to Kingdom Come at the same time. How can you imagine there is no connection?"

Munro hissed with exasperation through the gap in his front teeth. "I didn't say there wasn't a connection. They are obviously linked by a common series of experiences. What I mean is that there is no evidence of a common cause. Not a trace."

"You mean, none that you've been able to find."

"Oh, you imagine that you can find something where thirty of your peers failed?"

"No. I don't. Perhaps everyone looked in the wrong places. Or perhaps all trace of the cause had been eradicated before they started looking."

"There's always traces, Harley. You know that."

Thyssen gazed at him severely.

"Under the circumstances, I'm not prepared to be convinced of anything that I *thought* I knew, Munro. And you shouldn't be either."

They stood for a time, in the sun and gentle breeze. Like its cause, there no trace of the tragedy that had happened here. That was only in the minds and memories of men. Then the Padre was speaking.

"It is time for mass. The Padre asks if you have finished with him?"

"One more question," Thyssen said first and then thought of the question second. "Of all of the people he had talked to about this, did the Padre hear of anyone who had experienced anything similar."

The translation took some time and the Padre shook his head at first, but then his face cleared of doubt and he spoke again.

"There was a woman," Munro translated. "A doctor, from New Guinea or somewhere. She telephoned, apparently. Said she had treated patients with a similar condition. She predicted they would recover in seven or eight days with no ill effects. But there were language problems and nothing much is clear."

Thyssen nodded, and then asked very directly. "Are you sure it wasn't New Zealand?"

*

This was the place, there was no doubt about it, even if Chrissie could not see why it might have been. There was no questioning her faith and if it guided them to someplace in the middle of nowhere, then that was the divine plan. Lorna, sweating, unsuitably dressed, swatting at flies, might not have liked it, but that was the way it was. And then there was this truck driver who had parked right where the divinity least wanted him. Some people had no sense of perspective.

They had hung around the campsite while the man stirred himself and then stirred the fire to life and put the billy on. Now he was squatting in front of the fire and although evening was coming on, it was by no means cool. Lorna, exasperated by his gaze, hung back and Chrissie had to go forward.

"Excuse me. Is this your property?"

"Nope," the man grunted.

"Do you live around here?"

"Nope."

"Is there any reason that you're here?"

"Not that I know of."

"Oh," Chrissie said. She had run out of questions. Usually, this was the bit where Lorna babbled out a lot of questions and found out the man's entire history in five minutes, but instead she sat on a jerry can and looked grumpy, swishing at the flies madly.

The man regarded her far too long, before he reached into a pack at his feet and produced a can of insect repellent. He threw it to her. "Give that a bash."

Lorna caught it deftly but it wasn't a brand she liked. She scowled.

"When the sun goes down, the mozzies'll eat yer alive," the man said offhandedly.

Lorna sprayed liberally and then passed the can to Chrissie, who also hesitated. Was it right to kill a few hundred of God's creatures at such a moment? For the moment was close, she could feel it. They had arrived just in time. But then she reasoned that the creatures would not be killed but only repelled. She gave herself a few disdainful blasts, took a couple of paces forward and handed the can back to the man. His hand was very grubby.

In fact she could not work it out. All along she was expecting to meet someone here—this man just wasn't the image she had in mind.

"Just makin' tea," the man said in his gruff tones. "Want some?"

"Yes please," Chrissie smiled, and Lorna scowled but finally nodded.

The man grabbed a handful of tea from the packet and chucked it in the billy. Oh boy. When the water boiled, he stood, picked up the billy by the handle and swung it. That did it.

"Are you for real?" Lorna snarled at him.

"Girlie, I reckon you're the one that don't exactly blend into the landscape."

"Who could?" Lorna snapped.

*

The pager summoned her to the reception desk where an urgent call awaited. In fact it wasn't so much urgent as long distance, the admissions nurse pointed out as she handed the receiver over. "Dr Campbell speaking."

From the other end, the voice boomed so loudly that she had to hold the receiver away from her ear. The admissions nurse needed to put a hand over her smile.

"My name is Harley Thyssen, Professor of Vulcanology, Massachusetts Institute of Technology. I'm sorry to call so precipitously but I think we have something in common, Dr Campbell."

Felicity tried to take it in, but really she was wondering if this was one of her patients that she had forgotten, despite the fact that it could not be. "I'm afraid I don't understand..."

"Allow me to navigate the conversation for a few moments, Dr Campbell. If you can answer a couple of simple questions, the matter might be expedited."

"Sure. Okay," she said, irritated to notice that she was already mimicking his American accent.

"I understand that some time ago you made telephone contact with Father Miguel Sierra of the Magaria Mission on Gran Canaria Island? Is that so?"

"Well... yes..."

"The good father tells me that you wished to discuss the

circumstances of some of your own patients in regard to the medical condition of sixty-three patients previously under his care?"

"That's right. There seemed to be similarities between six people I treated here and those..."

"Yes. And these patients were all victims of the Ruapehu eruption?"

"Yes," Felicity said softly. A mighty sense of relief swept through her. Here, then, was someone who understood.

The voice on the other end, who to Felicity might still have been that of a god, allowed a satisfied pause. "Okay, Dr Campbell. First let me praise your diligence. And add that I, like you, am investigating the connection between the volcanic activity and the comatose conditions of the victims. I'd like it if we can pool our resources."

Felicity baulked. There were, after all, matters of patient confidentiality to consider, not to mention that the hospital would be none too pleased if the matter was not directed through the proper channels. She would have said all that, had she not suddenly realised that she did not even remember the name of the man to whom she was speaking. From the desk she snatched up a pad and pen and asked him to repeat his personal details. Professor, no less. MIT, no less. Thyssen answered patiently.

"Dr Campbell, we cannot hope to achieve much with this call. I am merely attempting to touch base."

"I don't know how I can be of any assistance..." Felicity said helplessly.

"You already have been. You made the connection. However, I must point out that at this stage, there is no evidence to support that connection whatsoever, except that of coincidence."

"Oh."

"Nevertheless, we must proceed."

"What do you want me to do?"

"Have you maintained contact with the six patients?"

"Yes. One of them is still here in Wellington Hospital. His condition is steadily improving and he ought to be able to be released in a few months. I observed unusual behaviour in that patient and then wrote to the medical practitioners responsible for the others. They reported their patients as normal, with respect to their on-going conditions. More recently, two days ago in fact, I tried to contact the patients themselves. None were available to speak to me."

"None of them?"

"One was under sedation, as indeed Mr Wagner is here. The other four had all gone away and no one seemed to be able to tell me where."

"Excellent, Dr Campbell. Fine work indeed. Okay, so obviously we need more details. I wonder if you would be good enough to provide the data you have on the six patients, their condition and progress and present circumstances and send it to me at MIT. To which, I will reciprocate with all the information I have on Gran Canaria and other incidents. Then, each of us will be in a position to know more precisely what we are talking about."

The enormity of it once more shook Felicity to the core and she procrastinated desperately—if only to give herself time to think. "There will be limitations in regard to patient confidentiality..."

"Of course. I too will have to withhold certain information until its security classification is more clearly known. But the more you can tell me and the more I can tell you, the better our chances of determining just what this condition is and what the connection is, if any."

"All right then..." Felicity sighed, knowing that there was no time in her schedule for such a task, but the true concern then came to her. "Do you think they are in danger?"

"Yes, I do," Thyssen said chillingly. "And if we are right, it could be that a great many other people will be in danger in the future. We really need to get on with this, urgently."

"I'll do what I can."

"Thank you doctor. No doubt we'll speak again. Until then, I suggest discretion. This all might amount to nothing. We wouldn't want to make complete fools of ourselves before the public, would we?"

*

They had taken his battery away again, and once more the chase was on through the corridors of Fairhaven as Joe attempted his umpteenth escape by hand. At least, he mused, it was building the strength of his arms. For he had suddenly stopped, and the two nurses in pursuit almost ran into the back of him. They stood to either side, hanging onto the wheelchair grimly, panting desperately. Joe flinched in pain several times and then suddenly became calm.

"Perhaps you'll be good enough to push me back to my room," he smiled up at them.

*

Felicity looked over the monitors grimly. Kevin Wagner, sedated to oblivion, was at peace at last.

"Same as last time," Turley said.

"Yes, I know," Felicity said in quiet bewilderment. "I watched it happen. He just grew more and more agitated until finally he threatened to become violent. But now, all of a sudden, he's calm again. I just don't understand it."

*

Andromeda gave out a few extra snores and that was it. She had passed out on the floor of the motel room, hours ago, her second bottle of Vodka half-drunk, tilted from her hand. In the middle of nowhere, nowhere had been the only place to go.

*

Chrissie could feel the moment was close. She sat on the bull bar of the truck and gazed at the sky away to the east, sipping the tea out of the dirty cup in which it had been offered. Lorna sulked and drank. The man squatted and regarded the fire. It was ridiculous.

And then the sensation came upon them and they sat, stiffening their bodies, bowing their heads, gritting their teeth. The nausea swept up through their feet, erupting through their bodies into their brains. The man sat back on his heels with a grunt, Lorna almost fell off the jerry can as she wrapped her hands across her midriff, Chrissie clutched the bull bar and tried to raise her head. The Angel of Judgement passed by and hurried on toward the west and the moment was over.

Lorna unravelled and stood up, dusting herself off embarrassedly. She had spilled most of her tea and the tin cup hung uselessly from her fingers. The man stood and bent forward, resting his hands on his knees. Chrissie rose and walked unsteadily, studying everything. But it was gone. They had been passed over again.

The man then straightened and looked around.

"Well, I gotta go now. Can I give you girls a ride somewhere?"

*

An unnamed mountain, insignificant amid the neighbouring peaks of the Southern Andes, suddenly exploded. Amid rain and storms, the brilliant flash reached no human eyes, and the tremendous roar no ears, or if it did was mistook for distant thunder. Like the tree that fell in the forest, no one saw or knew it had happened. The massive ash cloud pumped up to be lost amid the swirling hurricane, the shaking of the earth disturbed no feet. Lava burst from the crater and spilled down the slopes and there were a couple of further blasts an hour or so later but then the mountain, even less significant now with its cap blown away and replaced by a rugged crater, began to quieten again and slide back into obscurity.

And anyway, had the eruption been noticed, it would hardly

have been regarded of importance. This was Tierra de Fuego, The Land of Fire, the great island amid thousands below the Strait of Magellan, a disjointed tail of the Andes and snow-bound tundra, eternally under grey clouds or so it seemed. This was the land, they said, where the sun never shone. In fact it did, but always so feebly it could be ignored.

There were people who lived there but on the flat lands further north, eking out an existence in the most inhospitable land on earth. None of them saw the eruption nor felt its tremors, and such events were so common anyway that they would have thought nothing of it in any case.

It was even of little interest to vulcanologists, being so remote, amid so many other greater recent eruptions and mightier mountains, away from all civilisation.

When the seismic readings came through, there was perhaps only one person in the world who took any note of it. Jami Shastri shook her head in dismay.

"Why don't these things happen where someone can get near them?" she murmured.

It briefly crossed her mind that she was asking for the death of multitudes. She shuddered as she made her way to Thyssen's office with the preliminary data hardcopy in her hand. He was still in the Canary Islands, as far as she knew, but wherever he was, he would want to know about this right away.

5
BEYOND COINCIDENCE

She stood in the doorway, watching him pack like a wife who had just kicked out her husband and began to regret it before he got out the door. Kevin Wagner was hurriedly pushing his belongings into an overnight bag—wherever he was going, it wouldn't be for long.

But Felicity already knew that. And he had been good enough to call her and tell her he was leaving.

She had hurried to the rehab centre where he made his home for the present but it was hard to say why she should be concerned. This was what she expected, the way she expected it. Everything was happening normally—still she found she fretted. "Do you have any idea where you're going?" she asked, leaning on the door jamb, her arms folded in front of her.

Kevin Wagner threw a casual wave as he blew the dust off his spare shoes.

"Thataway. West. Australia, I guess."

"How will you get there?"

"Fly. I do possess a current pilot's licence, you know."

"You mean, fly yourself?"

"Sure. I can hire a plane. No problem."

"I don't think your medical condition..."

He stopped her with his winning smile. The deep lines either side of his mouth, the lights in his eyes, the kindness in his voice, all soothed her such as that she could feel it physically.

"My medical condition is absolutely excellent," he was saying, "thanks to your skills, Felicity. And you know it."

It was true. When fully clothed, there was no trace of his

injuries to be seen, except a slight limp and a scar across his chin. And the suddenly white hair. And the deep seated sadness that he subtly exuded despite his bright outlook on life. He was ready for adventure, to test himself out against the world and she knew she should have been delighted.

"I was thinking about the state of agitation that seems to accompany your present condition. Surely it won't sit well with piloting a plane."

"Felicity, I know what to expect. We've been through it, studied it from every direction. I know my limitations and for a pilot, that's the ball game."

The bag was packed, he was gathering wallet and watch and glancing in the mirror with a quick sweep of his hand through his hair. "I'll drive you to the airport," she suddenly proposed.

He picked up the bag and stopped in front of her, moving toward the doorway where she stood, blocking his way. "Don't be silly. I know you're up to your neck with patients as usual. There are cabs waiting at the rank right outside. Don't worry."

He even pecked her cheek. Just like a real husband, except Wendell never kissed her lightly.

Now she backed off to let Kevin Wagner through. "You'll call me and let me know where you are," she insisted.

He waved his mobile phone at her. "Every day. Count on it."

He walked down the steps and went out into the early morning haze.

Felicity remained, leaning on the wall. Her apprehension was immeasurable. But he was right—she did have work to do. Heaps of it. And all the more because of this occurrence. She watched Wagner all the way to the cab—he did not look back or wave. She gave him a bewitching wrinkle of her nose to make him disappear.

She walked slowly back toward the main building, as if deeply contemplative, but in fact she was busy shutting out thoughts and doubts because this was all as planned, and she knew exactly what she had to do next. She passed by casualty to assure herself that chaos had not ensued the moment her back was turned and then took the elevator to Barbara Crane's office. It was after six, Barbara and her staff had sensibly gone home but by prior arrangement, Felicity had a key and let herself in.

She turned on the computer and brought up a special file of names, addresses and telephone numbers that she had prepared in advance for this moment.

She dialled the number for Lorna Simmons and got no answer but that was hardly surprising—it was just after six in Auckland. Christine Rice was not at home either. Wasn't she supposed to be married by now? She would try them again later.

Next, realising it would be after three in Perth, she called Fairhaven Hospital and was informed that Mr Joseph Solomon had been discharged a week ago. There was a number for his brother and she tried that and had her first success. "No, he isn't here, Doctor. I put him on the train to the east coast a couple of hours ago."

"East coast where exactly."

"He said he'd decide that when he got to Adelaide."

"When are you expecting him back?"

"He cleared all his appointments until late next week."

"He's back in his practice then?"

"Oh yes. Got a new ground floor office and put ramps all over the place and he's doing fine."

She left a message for a return call and hung up.

The next contact number was for a Mr Tierney in Brisbane who was Andromeda Starlight's manager. The paging service made the connection to a number further afield.

"Mr Tierney, I am trying to contact Miss Starlight..."

"Sorry, love. Don't handle her no more."

"Oh, I see. Can you give me a number I can call her on?"

"She don't have a phone. She don't live nowhere. She's run out on me one time too many and I've had it with her."

"Do you know where she was going?"

"Don't know and don't care."

And he hung up. Felicity smiled to herself as she dialled the final number.

Judy Carrick remembered her and they could chat freely—it almost came as a blessed relief. "No, I'm sorry doctor. He's gone walkabout again."

"You mustn't worry yourself, Judy. It does seem to be normal for someone in his condition."

She was startled by what she was willing to call normal these days.

"They were going to lock him up. There were charges laid last time because he stole their truck but he just got a bond. First offence. Now he's pinched another truck and gone again."

"He'll be back—within three days if my information proves correct."

"There was talk about putting him in a home."

"A psychiatric institution, you mean?"

"Yes. That's right. What do you think, doctor?"

"I should think that to be completely unnecessary, Judy. Apart from these brief periods of restlessness, he ought to be fine..."

"He isn't."

"I've spoken to his local doctor and rehabilitation officer and they said he was fine."

"Well he isn't."

"Could you explain how..."

"He used to be a good man, hard-working, devoted to his family and thoughtful. Now he's just a layabout and doesn't care about anything."

"Oh. I see. Judy, I'd like to look into this matter, if I may. Can I call you again?"

"If you want."

"Thank you. I'll be in touch. And in the meanwhile, don't worry. There are a number of others with his condition that I know of and none of them have come to any harm. I should think Brian will be fine."

"What is his condition exactly, Doctor?"

"That is what we are trying to work out. I'll be in touch. Thank you for your frankness, Judy. Goodbye."

Felicity Campbell leaned back in Barbara Crane's chair. She had told a lie. She had said that none of them had come to any harm when in fact she knew no such thing. But even at this distance, she could sense Judy Carrick's stressed condition and knew instinctively that a palliative was needed if they were to get through this. There was one more number on her list and she dialled it immediately, without dispensing with her worried look. She had no idea what time it was in America and didn't care.

"Professor Thyssen please."

*

Jami Shastri sat huddled and blinked like a creature unfamiliar with daylight, but that, Harley Thyssen knew, was just his imagination. When he called her and instructed her to report to his office immediately, she asked him: "Is it day or night out there?"

"It's an hour before that great supper I'll buy you at Kandinsky's if you tell me what I want to hear."

"Harley, I only ever tell you what you want to hear. It's faculty policy."

"Make haste, girl. I'm finally giving you your freedom."

"Define freedom."

"You go where I tell you and do what I say. Glen is taking over down there."

"Oh great. I do all the footslogging and just when we're ready to get to the interesting modelling stuff, you take it away from me."

"Glen is better at modelling than you are. But he would never have worked as diligently gathering the data as you have. Why do I need to explain the obvious?"

"I thought somebody said that slavery has been abolished in this country."

"It's not slavery—it's exploitation of unemployed youth. Come on, we're in a hurry here. The way out is down the corridor on your left."

"I've been living the lifestyle of a cockroach, Harley. Freedom will require a period of adjustment."

"Get your cheeky Hindu ass here now. And bring all the data."

"All the data is on the network."

"I know it is. But I want you to bring all the stuff you don't want anyone else to see as well."

He gazed at the window thoughtfully as he hung up. As she trudged across the campus, she would surely notice the darkness and desertion—it was way past midnight and Kandinsky's would be closed.

When she appeared in his office ten minutes later, he had made her coffee as a bribe. She walked in with her hands pressed into the pockets of her jacket, looking like she was just off the set of *West Side Story*. One of those pockets, he hoped desperately, contained scraps of paper on which she had made private notes.

"Black and two sugars. How sweet of you to remember."

Thyssen managed to smile as he gazed across the desk at her dark face. She looked desperately tired. Thyssen remembered the skinny little girl with no friends, shy and bewildered by advanced civilisation, as she was at the time her brilliant intelligence had first caught his attention. She had come a long way from village life since then, and seemed to have taken on all the worst that America had to offer—fast food, substance abuse, alienation, and with no defence except a fierce line of aggressive retorts.

Now, her somewhat blotchy colouring plainly indicated the diet of fast food she had lived on throughout her manic hibernation in his basement. She might have been hopelessly insecure but she was the best student he had ever produced and the way she bluffed and blustered her way through life suggested that she had little grasp on the extent of her own brilliance.

"What have you got for me?" he asked as he sat down.

"It's all there," she said, gesturing toward his computer terminal.

"No it isn't. A prediction of the next occurrence of the Shastri Effect isn't to be found there anywhere."

She pouted and threw a shrug at him. "Insufficient data to

make any such prediction. Christ, Harley, there have only been three instances."

Thyssen nodded. He offered her a cigarette and they both lit up in bland defiance of departmental regulations. But at this time of night all of the departmental toadies had gone home. As had anyone else with any respect for their own wellbeing.

"Naturally. Now make a guess."

"I'm a well trained scientist who would never make such a conjectural leap."

"Assume I have thrown you to the floor and twisted your arm up your back."

"Somewhere about ten thousand miles northwest of here, next week maybe."

"My data says Monday," Thyssen smiled.

That threw her. She gave the sort of frown that he liked best—the moment when the outstanding protege realises that the master is still the master.

Her eyes narrowed. "You can't know that?"

"No. But I can guess it."

"How?"

"I'm the boss. You have to explain your guess first."

From her pocket, she produced the scrap of paper he had been hoping for. "There is a sequence developing of some kind," she said, rotating the tightly folded sheet until it was right way up. "For instance, Ruapehu was 6.3 on the scale, Gran Canaria was 6.5, Terra de Fuego was 6.7, so we could possibly assume 6.9 this time."

"Let's assume. What else?"

"Location is impossible. There is no recognisable relationship between the angles or the distances associated with the three points. All we have is an irregular triangle."

"Which is meaningless."

"True. However, we do have the sequencing relationship Southern Hemisphere, Northern, then Southern again so that possibly narrows us down to the Northern Hemisphere this time."

"The situation improves immeasurably."

"And the fact that all of the incidents occurred on or near islands located in the largest oceans, respectively, the South Pacific, North Atlantic and Southern Oceans, which suggests the North Pacific Ocean this time."

Thyssen gave out a snort which might have been laughter. "Very iffy."

"I know, but its the best we can do until we have a few more instances and Glen can develop the models."

"Okay, and time?"

He was toying with her, and she hated it. He had said Monday. None of the numbers she had conjured could possibly add up to that. With a sigh of defeat, she continued. "The dates have a decreasing pattern. 23rd of June, 28th of September, 23rd of December. Periods of 97 days and 86 days. If the rate of decrease had been maintained, it would have been 75 days, Saturday March 8th, which was yesterday. The average is 91.5 days which is 25th of March. However, the first knowable date is the minimum, 86 days again, which is ten days from now."

"Very good."

"But you said tomorrow."

"I did."

"It's not likely. Two of the three incidents already happened on a Monday. The third was a Wednesday. Another occurrence of a Monday is statistically improbable."

"Let's steer clear of superstition, shall we? It will be Monday."

Jami grinned. Harley Thyssen did not usually commit himself to anything. If he proved to be wrong, her delight would be immeasurable.

"Okay. Your turn."

"Our doctor in New Zealand, the delightful Mrs Campbell, was very thorough. On both prior occasions, her patient became agitated for thirty-three hours and then calmed at the moment of the incident."

"Doesn't prove much."

"No. But the lemmings walked off the cliffs of the Canaries

again thirty-four hours before Terra de Fuego."

"Better."

"And Doctor Campbell cites two instances each regarding two other patients—the one that escaped from the hospital in Perth twice and the chap who keeps stealing trucks in Melbourne. All between thirty and thirty-six hours in advance of an incident."

"It *does* become interesting."

"Indeed, and guess what?"

"They're on the move?"

"All of them. The good doctor checked. All six of them on the move in the past couple of hours. Which means the event occurs in roughly thirty hours. Six in the morning, Monday, our time."

Jami laughed. "Is that all?"

"Not enough for you?"

"We really don't have much, Harley. Just a few vague guesses."

"True, but since that's all we have, let's go with it."

She shrugged a throwaway gesture. "Okay. Consider me persuaded. So what do we do?"

"Our subjects are on the move and so should we be. Pack your bag and grab your passport and be ready to go wherever the hit occurs. Get there, commandeer whatever and whoever you need—use my name for authority, whatever that may be worth—and do whatever is necessary to fill all the gaps in your data."

"And where will you be?"

"I'll be linking up with Felicity Campbell in New Zealand. I want to find out how these people are connected, where they are going, and why."

*

The dun yellow and drab green of the Australian landscape stretched out beneath him, reaching toward a purple-grey haze that obscured the horizon. He shifted the controls lightly, adjusting to the vibration caused as the rotor blades flapped against the thermals.

It was great to be flying again, to be testing himself, showing what the human spirit and body could do if it had to. Initially there had been disappointment when he had been unable to hire a plane in Wellington with the range to fly the Tasman Sea. He had plenty of money, but suitable aircraft simply weren't available at such short notice. He had wasted a great deal of frustrating time arguing with operators and airport officials before finally resorting to the commercial airlines.

Qantas landed him in Sydney—far wide of his destination but there he was able to hire this nifty two-seater helicopter with enough range to get him to Albury where he refuelled. And now he was closing in on his destination—he could feel it in every part of his body.

He felt good. Felicity's fears about his strength were completely unfounded. It was a fabulous sensation. They had smashed him to smithereens but the body fought back with everything it had and restored every part, as good or better than before. Well, almost. There were scars, everywhere. Great chunks gouged from his buttocks and grafted to his chest, right shoulder, back and both thighs. There was a problem with his liver that they had not quite resolved, which caused him to fart rather more often than was socially acceptable and one lung pierced by his shattered ribs would never again attain full function. But all that was minor. Sure, he'd never play football again and might have trouble scaling the higher alps or diving to the greater depths. But really, he was fine.

It was great to be reborn, reinvented, reconstructed, whatever. It made his past life seem as if it had never happened, or was a movie he saw once. He closed his mind with an effort that was almost physical every time the past tried to intrude. "You're in denial," the psychologist said. You bet he was. And he was going to keep it that way.

Occasionally, less frequently now, images of Sally, or the kids, would try to creep in from the periphery. He struck them away with actual physical movements, thrusting his mind into the present, the immediate. At night he dreamed about them but his dreams were all so painful that he awoke, sweating and terrified. Grimly, he would force them from his conscious. Only then would sleep return.

Well, he couldn't do anything about that. But he could deal with his conscious thoughts and it was all a matter of discipline. He prided himself on his willpower in that he couldn't remember the last time he had thought about them. It was almost like they had never existed...

But that wasn't the only reason they kept him in Rehab for so long. It also had to do with the mysterious coma and its periodic effects. Felicity had discussed it with him intimately, explored every aspect of his psychic condition and did so to a depth that the professional psychiatrists, psychologists and counsellors did not even approach. He co-operated because he was as curious as she was. Something quite strange but seemingly quite wonderful was happening to him. It was especially wonderful now as he neared his destination.

The periods of agitation—the aberrations as she called them—carried with them an exquisite sense of strength. It was impossible to define. At three monthly intervals, for a period of three days, he would become grindingly tense and desperate to be on the move. It was really a chronic wanderlust but within it too was a sensation of purpose, of precise need, that was in itself exhilarating.

It was as if some new part of his brain had been opened, admitting senses hitherto blocked to all other humans. There was definitely a sense of superiority attached to it that was hard to explain. It was as if the aberrations were the real moments of his life, and the periods between merely flowed to and from them. Daily he searched his being for the new powers that the aberrations unleashed and if he found none, he was not disappointed. He knew—he didn't know how he knew but he knew it with certainty—that such super-strengths would eventually appear. It was just a matter of looking for them in the right places. He knew that it was just a matter of time.

He had passed the spot. It was knowing something like

that, with such utter certainty even though there was no physical evidence to support it whatsoever, that convinced him all the more of his hidden strength. He swung the helicopter in a wide circle and soon determined the region he was seeking so blindly yet surely.

This was flat country, cattle and some sheep, although in some regions the irrigation channels from the Murray River reached down to touch green rows of orchards and other diverse crops. He passed over a town of medium size that his map identified as Kyabram and going in low swept over the paddocks until he circled again and was over the exact spot.

Someone was already there. A camp fire smouldered, a prime mover *sans* trailer was parked nearby. The man sat in the shade with his back against a solitary tree trunk, his hand shielding his eyes as he regarded the chopper hovering above. Wagner moved wide of the spot, away from the camp and the tree, to nearby open ground for he knew such dry country would throw up a vast amount of dust when he landed and he did not wish it to blow into the man's camp. It was the decent thing to do.

Carefully, he set down in the middle of the paddock. He turned off, unstrapped and looked around. There was nothing else to be seen in any direction. He got out—his right leg was cramped and he needed to walk in a few small circles to get the circulation flowing properly. By then, the tall man in the big bush hat had walked over to him.

"G'day," he called.

"Hi there."

"This your property?" the man asked, before Wagner could ask exactly the same question.

"Nope. Not yours either then."

"No."

They stood facing each other—Wagner could see that this man was as uncertain of his right to be here as he was. He extended his hand. "Kevin Wagner."

"Brian Carrick," the man said and shook firmly.

The name stuck a chord. Wagner was certain he had heard it

before, somewhere… "You from around here?" he asked.

Brian Carrick eyed him suspiciously. All questions seemed a great trouble to him.

"Nar, I come up from Melb'n."

Since he knew Melbourne was a major Australian city but wasn't too sure where it was from here, Wagner nodded and could think of nothing to say.

"I'm just making tea," Brian said.

They had tea, and then Brian provided sausages and eggs for dinner. Finally -about an hour later as night came down and they squatted by the fire—Brian said: "You're a Yank."

"That's right."

"What part?"

"San Diego."

"Long way from home."

"I sure am."

And, exhausted by all that conversation, they soon retired to their respective vehicles and slept.

*

Twenty-three hours after he left the bemused Jami Shastri in his office, Harley Thyssen landed in Wellington. He had flown New York to Los Angeles, and almost immediately by United to Hawaii and then a wait of several hours before the Air New Zealand flight carried him directly into Wellington. He walked off the plane refusing to face his body's demands for rest and re-orientation.

It was 9am, local time and there were only seven hours left if his calculations were right. Customs officials fussed over a passenger with only a small overnight bag and then finally he emerged and approached the information desk. The girl did not have to bother to page Doctor Felicity Campbell—she was standing right beside him.

"Professor Thyssen I presume."

"Doctor Campbell, good of you to respond on such short notice."

They shook hands. Hers was cool and fresh, his was sweating and clammy. He could tell by her bemused expression that he was far from what she expected.

"A long journey, Professor."

"Let's be informal, shall we Felicity? Even my students call me Harley."

"Well, Harley. As a doctor, allow me to recommend immediate rest."

"No time for that. Next time, assuming there is a next time, I'll be better organised, but right now time is running out. What can you tell me?"

"Let's at least sit down and have a cup of coffee, Harley. The next flight to Melbourne doesn't leave for two hours and we are booked on it."

She took his arm and led him off toward the coffee shop. Thyssen was thinking rather more in terms of a couple of quick Bourbons but at such an ungodly hour and in the presence of an MD, he supposed that would be out of the question.

Felicity Campbell, he was beginning to notice, was a cool attractive woman, straw-haired, freckled, beaming smile, fit trim body, efficiently dressed in a purple suit with a skirt was rather shorter than most forty year-old women would have dared wear. Although friendly, she remained cool and businesslike. Thyssen made an effort to subdue his essential loneliness.

They sat and she ordered black coffee without asking his preference. He fumbled in his pocket for saccharine.

"So," he asked, when her fussing over him finally subsided. "What do we know?"

"Not a lot. Judy Carrick reports that Brian said he had been '*up Shep way*' after one such trip and 'same bloody place' after another. '*Up Shep way*' seems to translate into a region in Central Victoria where Shepparton is the major rural city. Lorna Simmons' employer said she 'kept disappearing off to Australia all the time' and I spoke to John Burton, who was but is no longer

Chrissie Rice's fiancee and he thought they went to Bendigo, a big provincial city a hundred kilometres from Shepparton but also in Central Victoria. That's all I was able to find out."

"You haven't heard from Kevin Wagner?"

"No. He promised to call but hasn't. I've arranged for all of my calls to come through on the mobile," she said, waving the instrument at him. "But no luck so far."

"Still, he remains our best chance."

"We could seek the co-operation of the Australian Police. I understand Brian Carrick is, once again, driving a stolen vehicle. Although, since they can reasonably suppose from experience that he'll probably bring it back after three days, this time the owner has decided not to complain."

Thyssen was shaking his head wearily. "I'm reluctant to involve the civil authorities at this stage. The risk that it might start unfounded rumours which in turn could lead to unnecessary panic, not to mention possible future embarrassment, is just too great."

"You didn't seem to have any trouble bringing diplomatic pressure to bear on the hospital," Felicity said provocatively.

"No. I am sorry to drag you away from your patients like this. I know that you have a very busy schedule."

"I needed a holiday anyway," Felicity chuckled. "But I would be interested to know how you did it."

"Friends in high places able to persuade the New Zealand government to turn you over to us on a matter of national security."

"Good Lord, they'll think I'm working for the CIA or something."

"And your family? How will they cope?"

"Oh, fine. They think I'm off to a conference on renal procedures. Nobody asks too many questions about things like that."

"Still, I apologise. I hope it's worthwhile."

"I hope it isn't," Felicity said quietly. "On the whole, I suspect it would be best for everyone if this proved to be a wild goose chase."

*

So here they were again. Same old paddock down the same dirt road. Same bloody truck driver in the same sort of truck but red this time not blue, same journey to nowhere. It was past summer now and although the grass was still yellow, it wasn't as hot, it wasn't as dusty and there were no longer the swarms of flies that drove them mad last time. But this time they were dressed for the occasion in jeans and sneakers, hats and sunglasses and instead of hauling suitcases each had a small pack on her back.

Lorna refused to go at first and Chrissie had to be patient with her.

"It's ridiculous. I can't afford to go running off to Australia every three months for no good reason. I've gone through all my savings. I can't afford it."

It was actually the shopping in Melbourne that she couldn't afford, but Chrissie had plenty of money to pay for them both so it hardly mattered. Lorna had gone to work that morning, and Chrissie, to try and subdue her agitation, went to the local church and prayed and prayed. If it didn't provide any comfort or relief, at least it offered a point for all that suffering. Lorna turned up late in the afternoon, and knew exactly where to go to find her.

"I broke down in tears in the office. They sent me to the hospital, but I knew I had to come here instead," Lorna confessed sulkily.

Chrissie offered the Almighty a small smile of thanks.

They had to stay overnight in Melbourne because there was no train to Shepparton until next day. The hotels in the city were all terribly expensive but they asked around and finally came upon a pub in Carlton that offered cheap overnight accommodation. The rooms were small and the furniture decrepit but the staff was friendly and the food was good.

Lorna set about getting herself thoroughly drunk, so drunk that she failed to pick up one of the locals because she made herself violently ill, and Chrissie needed to help her to bed.

A seedy but unrepentant Lorna rode the train to Shepparton next day, and then the buses to and from Kyabram.

"I still feel bloody randy," she murmured.

The fresh country air did nothing for her and she was a complete wreck by the time they arrived.

"Maybe our friend the truckie will be in the mood," Lorna remarked when their objective was in sight.

"You suppose it's him again?" Chrissie wondered.

"Of course it's bloody him again. Blokes like him are the original bad penny."

"You don't *really* fancy him, do you?"

"Why not?"

"He's a bit old."

"He looks fit and he ain't bad looking, in a rugged sort of way. Lousy conversationalist but who cares? If I don't get a bit soon, I'll turn lesbian and go after you."

"Maybe he isn't so bad after all."

But as they got closer, they began to be able to make out a strange object standing in the paddock some way off from the truck.

"It's a helicopter," Chrissie realised.

"Well, at least it's something different," Lorna sighed.

Finally, they were wading through the grass toward the camp site. The quiet man was sitting back against the usual tree reading a book while the newcomer sat on a log, studying a map. Lorna brightened immediately. "Wow, what a spunk," she breathed.

Chrissie considered the man as he looked up in considerable surprise as they approached and smiled an encouraging smile. He was almost as old as the truckie—Brian, she remembered—and somewhat shorter. But yes, he had a nice smile.

"Hullo there, you guys," Lorna bubbled, all trace of the pallid wreck that she had been all day utterly eradicated.

"You two again," Brian remarked flatly, doing nothing other than looking up from his book.

"Well, hi," the newcomer drawled in his American accent.

"You didn't tell me about this, Brian."

"Didn't think they'd be back," Brian remarked and returned to his reading. "Better put the billy on, mate. They drink a lot of tea."

"Sure, but you better do the bit where you swing it," the man said, tipping water from the jerry can into the billy. "So how about an introduction to your friends."

"Can't. Don't remember their names."

"I'm Lorna and she's Chrissie..." and with extra emphasis, she added. "*Brian.*"

Brian Carrick gave a little twitch and went on reading.

"I'm Kevin Wagner. Damned glad to meet you. Grab a seat. What the hell are you two doing way out here anyway?"

"We were hoping you might know."

"Damned if I do. Hey, where you from anyway?"

"New Zealand," Lorna enthused. "Auckland..."

"Waal, godammit. How about that. I just flew in from Wellington myself."

"Really? I thought you were American."

"Yeah, well, some time back. But how about that. Beautiful place, New Zealand. Love it. You ever been to New Zealand, Brian?"

"Yeah. Once. Hated it."

"How could you hate New Zealand?"

"I had a real bad time there."

"I would have thought you'd have a pretty bad time in most places, Brian," Lorna said sweetly.

"I had an *especially* bad time in New Zealand."

Wagner winced as if he was the victim of the sarcastic exchange, and then continued to try and keep the conversation light and bright.

"You know, I get the feeling I've met you before," he said, referring to both of them but looking at Lorna.

"Maybe we all met in New Zealand," Lorna smiled sweetly.

"No way. If I'd met a girl like you, Lorna, I wouldn't have forgotten it."

Chrissie shook her head in dismay—she heard males say that to Lorna at least twice a week. But it was Brian Carrick who answered, drawling; "Yeah, it's the sharp tongued ones you remember."

Still, for all the difficulty, Kevin's charm battled on. "So, here we are," he soothed. "All been to New Zealand and now all here. What a coincidence."

"Yeah," Brian Carrick muttered. "Bloody big coincidence."

Perhaps they were all saved from disaster, if not embarrassment, when they saw a vehicle coming down the road.

"Waal, will you get an eyeful of that!" Kevin declared and they all looked.

A white stretch limousine gracefully slid along the bumpy road.

"Some people travel in style," Lorna breathed.

"Must be one of them down-at-heel cow-cockies you hear so much about," Brian declared.

But the limo drew along the road until it reached the gap in the fence and stopped. The middle-aged uniformed chauffeur jumped out and opened the rear door, and a tall black woman flashed elegant thighs as she climbed out. She offered a gigantic smile to the chauffeur and thanked him and then looked and waved toward the four astonished onlookers.

Chrissie immediately realised that she knew this woman—a black giantess was hard to forget. She was struggling to place her, as were the two men, but it was Lorna who got there first.

"Andromeda Starlight," Lorna breathed.

"Yeah," Brian Carrick grunted. "I think this just stopped bein' a big coincidence."

6
THE VOICE OF GAIA

Along the shores of Lake Baikal, the rugged Buryat tribesmen lived as they had for a thousand years, tough Mongolians who prided themselves in their horsemanship and their absolute control of their animals. In their small rustic settlements—almost entirely family groups—they followed the teachings of the Dalai Lama, to whom they were returning their devotions since the fall of the Soviet Empire. For this was Soviet Mongolia, where the 300,000 Buryats live in collectives, migrating with their sheep between summer and winter pastures, the latter to which they had just returned.

Then in an instant, everything changed. Their animals went berserk with a universal suddenness that filled them with terror. Along the edge of the rapidly receding lake, steam began to rise and then, only moments after first of these terrors commenced, they knew no more. Right around the southern end of the lake, the people fell into sudden unconsciousness—people and horses and sheep and dogs alike—all dropping in their tracks. The solid wooden houses shook and collapsed on the unconscious inhabitants. There were few survivors in the affected zone—most were killed by the searing steam from the lake, or swallowed as they lay sleeping by the explosive lava flow.

And there was no one left awake to see the great cracks open in the muddy floor along the edge of the lake and fire burst forth, followed by oozing lava spreading out in all directions. Over a thousand died in the affected region and, days later, when the neighbouring tribes overcame their fear of the towering pyroclastic cloud that had swallowed that end of the lake and came to investigate, they found those few who had survived locked in an unresponsive coma.

*

The white stretch limousine had been provided by Tierney, wanting her to make a big impression with the paparazzi when she arrived for her opening night at the Sands in Surfer's Paradise.

"Keep going," Andromeda Starlight had said to the chauffeur as they slid into the Sands' driveway. The doorman in green topper and tails was reaching for the door-handle at that very moment and clean missed as the limo failed to stop. Andromeda glanced back saw the man standing at the end of his stumble, catching his topper as it jarred from his head. She'd also seen Tierney, harried and bewildered, come rushing down the steps. She turned back, smiling with delight. He chased them on foot.

"Hoy! Where you goin'! Where you goin'!"

Gone, Joel, gone.

"Where to, Miss Starlight?" the unflappable driver, who wore a neat uniform and was named John, asked calmly.

"Way we're goin', my man," she smiled.

A thousand kilometres later, he remained calm, unruffled by the unexpected length of the journey, although he had needed to be continually reassured by the use of the credit card she had stolen from Tierney. He remained bemused and tolerant, all the way to the bumpy dirt road, to the place where a truck without its trailer and a bubble helicopter stood incongruously in a paddock and four people stood in a line and stared at them.

"My man, we have arrived," Andromeda grinned. "You just hop in the back here and get some shut-eye. I'll gotta go check out these dudes."

She got out of the car in her still spangled but much crumpled dress, slipped off her high heeled shoes and on her sunglasses, and walked toward them. Two older men, two younger women, all gazing on her with appropriate astonishment. The females looked familiar, somehow.

"Hi there," she called as she approached them.

"Hullo, Andromeda," the red haired girl said with a cheeky tone. Not another fan... no. The name Laura sprang to mind.

"Well, bless my soul, Honey. You were in the hospital in Kiwisville," she said as if it was an accusation.

That had them all looking at each other.

"So was..." Brian began, and stopped.

"I just come from there," Kevin Wagner was saying.

"Good God," Lorna gasped. "*We all were.*"

"Of course," Chrissie cried. "Talk about mysterious ways. Lorna and I were in the intensive care ward and you were there too."

"All comin' back now, Honeychilds," Andromeda said. "This here's the dude in the coma. Exceptin' you had black hair in them days."

Kevin Wagner nodded, touching his hair as if coming to terms with the change. But there was more to come to terms with than that.

Lorna pointed at Brian. "So you must be the chap that woke up before the rest of us."

"That's right," Brian said.

"We were all in that coma. That's what this is all about," Chrissie was gasping with realisation.

They all found somewhere to sit and gather their wits. One or the other babbled some realisation or other without adding to the general knowledge. Then Chrissie went over and sat on the log beside Wagner, and took his hands in hers.

"There was your wife and children," she murmured. "I'm so sorry."

Kevin Wagner's head was already bowed as he strove to fight back the tears.

Suddenly, Chrissie was looking beyond him to the glowing horizon. The land was deep purple, the sky bright orange. She stood, backing off, peering. Then the others were too.

"It's happening," she said. "I can feel it coming."

Almost immediately, Andromeda felt the nausea hit her. She

staggered a little but then straightened. A sensation not unlike an orgasm swept through her body, arising from her bare feet in the soil and out through the top of her head. After a moment, she recovered, and immediately saw all of the others were recovering too. She had experienced it before and so had they, but this time Andromeda realised something she had not noticed before. The sensation seemed to come right out of the ground, entering her body through her feet. It was as if her feet were the points of a power plug, inserted into the electric earth itself.

The others were staggering or sitting, doubled up.

"Happens every time, then it's over," Brian said.

"How do you mean, over?" Lorna asked.

"Don't you suddenly have the feeling that you can go home now?"

Each realised that they did.

Wagner raised his head and looked at them all.

"We gotta to talk to someone who knows about this."

"Sure, but who?" Lorna wondered.

"There ought to be a long range cell phone in that limo of yours," he added. "There's Dr Campbell—Felicity Campbell—in Wellington. I promised to keep her posted. We can start with her."

They rose as one and walked over to the limo. John snored peacefully in the back. Wagner got the phone and dialled the number. The paging system transferred him to a second number. "Felicity Campbell please."

He waited while she was fetched from wherever she was. Finally, he spoke briefly, then listened a lot, saying yes and no. Finally, he put his hand over the receiver and called to Brian Carrick.

"Hey, sport. Your wife wants to speak to you."

A few amusing moments followed while Brian said 'Yes luv" a great deal into the receiver and when that was done, he hung up and Wagner explained.

"Felicity's already in Melbourne, at Brian's home, looking for us. She didn't seem surprised that we were all here. She's got some big-wig scientist from the States with her. She said we are all to go to the biggest hotel in Kyabram and make ourselves comfortable. They'll be here in two or three hours."

"A beer would be nice," Brian said enthusiastically.

"Might even be a decent counter lunch," Andromeda mused.

"Anyone remember a Mr Joe Solomon?" Wagner asked.

"Oh yes," Lorna cried. "He hired the plane for us. A lawyer from Perth."

"He lost his wife in the crash," Chrissie said solemnly. "And he broke his back or something. He was in a terrible way."

"Well," Wagner continued. "We're to have a search for him. They think he's here somewhere too."

They rode to town in the luxury of the limo, and booked a room in the pub in which they put John the exhausted chauffeur to bed. There was a bus due soon after and Lorna and Wagner met it. Indeed, a thick-set swarthy man in a motorised wheelchair emerged down the ramp provided by the bus company. Lorna went and knelt before the man, taking his hands.

"It's me, Lorna Simmons. From New Zealand. Remember, Mr Solomon."

Joe Solomon peered at her and smiled.

"Yes, of course, dear girl. But what are you doing here?"

"Same thing as you, Mr Solomon," Lorna smiled, rubbing his hands warmly. "Come on. The others are waiting."

*

"Mongolia! You got any idea how difficult it is to get somewhere like that?"

Glen shook his head as they walked across the campus in fading sunlight. Autumn leaves lay all about. The air was orange with fine mist. Glen loped along, Jami had to gallop to keep up with him.

"No magic carpet from Harley, then."

"No. Of course the Russians don't want us there. They think their own geologists can handle it."

"They have very good geologists. Remember Tolbachik in 1975?"

"It was just a lucky guess."

"They predicted the eruption, bang on."

"Bully for them."

Glen laughed. Plainly he was enjoying her frustration. She felt like a Pekinese beside him, trying to scare a tiger. "Anyway," he was saying. "Word is that Russian geological pride isn't the problem. The truth is that they suspect they might have some sort of big ecological disaster on their hands and don't want to admit anything until they figure it out."

"It's one of mine. I know it is."

"I know," Glen laughed. "Come to the lab. I've got something to show you."

"Can't. Got to get to Mongolia, somehow."

"You've got plenty of time, Jamikins. The Geo Survey is assembling a team in London to fly in as soon as the Russians permit it. You'll be with them. But they won't be going anywhere for days. So play it cool."

"How can I..."

"Come on. This will amaze you."

They made their way down into the basement lab that had once been hers but now was his. It made her feel all the more a displaced person. He sat her before the screen and tapped the keys over her shoulder, but the intimacy did nothing for her either.

"We got this off the satellite," he said proudly.

"Bloody hell. What is it?"

"Infra-red."

"But I mean..."

What she meant was that such images of erupting volcanoes showed up as white hot spots, surrounded by a spectrum that indicated decreasing temperatures away from the epicentre. But this was a long narrow line running straight as an arrow. It looked like the flare at the base of a rocket.

"Good god. What is it? It must go for miles."

"A single open fissure in the valley floor, twenty kilometres long and just a few metres wide."

"A basalt flood!"

"Looks like it."

"Hasn't been one of those for a hundred years."

"Two hundred."

"No wonder they're confused."

"It gets better."

Jami stared. A whole valley had split open as if sliced with an axe and the lava gushed all along the line, forming fiery rivers and lakes to right and left. A truly stunning event and foolish nationalistic suspicions prevented her from being there.

"How can it get better?"

"Look at this. I took the wrong satellite pictures at first—it was the sweep an hour before the eruption and I couldn't find it anywhere. See."

She looked at what she supposed was the same valley immediately prior to the earth cracking wide open. There was no sign of what was to come.

"Not even a hot spot."

"Nope. Which kinda confirms your effect, doesn't it."

"It can't be right."

"So I thought at first. So I called up the pictures of Terra de Fuego. The satellite passed over there four hours before it blew. Get onto this."

Again, no hot spots.

"Are you sure of these pictures, Glen?"

"Don't you believe your own research, girl? The effect occurs without warning. A single blast, a few aftershocks, and then all over. But no preliminaries. And no particular type of tectonic movement. Ruapehu was a subduction zone; the Canaries is a hot spot and there can't be any tectonic link between them."

"But still there ought to be some sort of indication..."

"None. As you see."

"But even extinct volcanoes have some infra-red signature."

"This mountain wasn't a volcano, extinct or otherwise. There was no history of vulcanism in the region at any time."

"I don't believe it."

"And the same is true of Lake Baikal. No history. Ever."

"So these things just come out of the blue?"

"No. Ruapehu was already active, Gran Canaria was dormant, and these two, nothing. So what it means is that, geologically, there is no connection between them whatsoever."

"Baikal is a rift valley—I'm sure of it."

"Yes. And the innocent mountain in Terra de Fuego lies right at the tip of the Scotia Plate—the very point where the fracture in the South American Plate dwindles to nothing."

"So they are all weak points."

"Yes, but not always the same kind of weak point."

Jami leaned back in the chair, studying it all grimly.

"What the hell is going on?" she asked the world in general.

*

The Kyabram pub was able to offer them a sizable conference room where they sat about a large table in their various attitudes.

Joe Solomon wheeled his chair to what might have been the chairman's position and looked completely in his element in his blue suit and red tie.

Kevin Wagner sat at his right hand and even produced a notebook as if to take the minutes, but in fact it was the log book from the helicopter and he was making his fuel calculations.

By contrast, Lorna Simmons seemed to think she was at a cocktail party, having supplied herself with a long glass of exotic pink stuff which she sipped through a straw while perched on a barstool that ensured her thighs were in clear view above the level of the tabletop.

Chrissie Rice, looking small and skinny even for an Asian, nursed a cup of tea and sat with her chair back against the wall away from the table and would have to be invited to draw it forward when the conference began.

On the other hand, no serious meeting had ever experienced

the likes of Brian Carrick and Andromeda Starlight. They sat at the opposite far corners of the table, both smoking furiously, sharing a jug of beer. Brian, big and weather-beaten, and in his shirt with the sleeves hacked off roughly, was sweating and too loud and would have dominated the room had it not been for Andromeda's plunging neckline which insisted on being the focal point.

Which failed only because Harley Thyssen was there, a man made to intimidate mountains, with his great body, great beard and thundering authoritative voice. Thyssen had placed a smaller table adjacent to the end of the main one, and then sat on it, adopting the high ground.

And, finally, Felicity Campbell who did not sit, but stood in a corner making these observations. She would continually shift to a different part of the room in order to study her patients in detail, although she later admitted that the one she studied most was Harley Thyssen. He had spent a little time interrogating his subjects and now undertook to summarise the results.

"You are all participants in an unexplained phenomenon," Thyssen said loudly, "about which there are some things we know, and a few more things we can guess at, and a great deal that we have no idea of. Let's deal with the things we know first. Each of you, simultaneously, experienced a comatose state for a period of eight days, from which you have apparently recovered. The implication is that the coma was brought on by exposure to a volcanic eruption of an unusual kind which, for the present, we will call the Shastri Effect. There has never been a previous instance of that effect that we know of, but there have been three instances since—one in the Canary Islands, one in Terra de Fuego and one in Russian Mongolia. The events were placed roughly three months apart. The volcanic activity in each instance was entirely dissimilar except that the Shastri Effect was present on each occasion.

"The Canary Islands event produced sixty-three victims who, like you, experienced an eight day coma and then completely recovered. However, three months later, the sixty-three rose as one and walked in a zombie like state and fell from the cliffs into the sea. All were killed. Miss Simmons has reported doing something similar. Miss Starlight too. Thirty-four hours later, the Terra de Fuego event occurred.

"In those hours prior to each event, we understand that each of you were drawn by unknown forces to gather in the paddock outside town. Mr Carrick made it each time. Others variously. Terra de Fuego produced no casualties and we have no information about Mongolia as yet. But Dr Campbell reports that while comatose in Wellington Hospital, there was some sort of linkage between your individual brain wave patterns. A biological impossibility but that doesn't seem to have prevented it from happening anyway. This is something we need to know a great deal more about. Any questions so far?"

"Why us?" Joe Solomon asked.

Thyssen stood up and went to a large folder he had brought with him. He produced the chart he wanted and laid it on the table before them. It showed the Ruapehu site. The three calderas were evident, but wide of them, there was a circle drawn with a diameter of roughly a kilometre from the epicentre of the blast.

"Consider this circle. Everyone inside the circle died at the time of the eruption. Outside it, many casualties survived but none of them suffered the effect. You, Mr Solomon, and the two young ladies, were flying in an aircraft *inside* the circle, but which crashed *outside* the circle. Similarly, Mr Wagner was diving in the pond *inside* the circle but the cascade carried him *outside*. And Miss Starlight's very exciting ride in her bathtub also took her from *inside* to *outside* the circle. Mr Carrick is the exception to the theory, being stationary at the time, but he was right on the line and underground. There was considerable slippage along the fault line at that point, away from the crater. The best theory we can come up with is that the ground movement was just sufficient to carry him too, from inside to outside the zone."

"My gawd, Professor," Kevin Wagner was very impressed. "Whatever made you think of that?"

Even Thyssen looked impressed with himself. "The fishing-boats in Gran Canaria. The shock wave from the underwater eruption pushed the boats outward in a wide circle—we assume that the coma victims drifted from inside to outside the circle."

"So you think that was it," Felicity asked. "Moving from inside to outside the circle."

"I think so, yes. Anyone inside the circle probably suffered the effect but they all died. Survivors outside the circle, whether injured or not, did not suffer the effect."

"So it was just a fluke," Chrissie said in disappointment.

"I think so. The miraculous circumstances under which each of you survived was also why you have suffered the effect. It is interesting to note that a lot of people who were just outside the circle at the time felt a shockwave and experienced nausea and headaches immediately prior to the eruption, but they did not sustain the Shastri Effect. So yes, it is confined to a very finite group."

"Sounds like the same thing that happens when the effect goes away," Lorna said quietly.

"Indeed it does, but we'll come to that in a moment."

"So why here, in that paddock in the middle of nowhere?" Brian Carrick wanted to know.

Thyssen had a chart for that one too—this time encompassing all of Australasia.

"That was much easier to figure out. In fact I'm a little disappointed that you didn't work it out for yourselves. Your paddock in the middle of nowhere is in fact the exact midpoint between Perth and Wellington. Indeed, precisely between Wellington Hospital where Mr Wagner has been residing and Mr Solomon's convalescent home at Fairhaven. All of the rest of you were closer to the midpoint than those two and therefore, apparently, irrelevant."

"Hey, man. I was way up in Queensland," Andromeda Starlight protested.

"True, but nevertheless closer to the midpoint than either Mr Wagner or Mr Solomon."

"Only those people furtherest away count," Wagner considered.

"So it seems. Now, this is interesting. In the second instance, Mr Carrick and Miss Starlight report heading off in a different direction and then suddenly reverting back to the original one. I believe that is because the midpoint then lay between Wellington and the Canary Islands, somewhere in the middle of the Bay of Bengal. But when the Canary Island victims—the so-called lemmings—all died, Mr Solomon once more became the westward limit and the midpoint reverted back here."

"So we can expect to do this every three months?" Lorna was saying. "I'm sorry. My funds aren't up to it."

Thyssen smiled warmly. "This project has a substantial budget. You can expect all further costs to be met by us. You may also make application for compensation for your past costs. We may even extend to providing Mr Carrick with a hire car to curb his disposition toward vehicle larceny."

There were smiles all around, but Andromeda Starlight knew that nothing was for nothing. "Okay, so where's the catch, Smooth Man?" she asked lightly.

Thyssen smiled evilly. "No free lunches, in science nor anywhere else, hmm? To begin with, your co-operation. Most of what we know is unsubstantiated but if made public the danger of unnecessary panic would be very great. Therefore, for as long as possible, discretion. Obviously, if this situation is escalating— and I believe it is—then it won't stay under wraps for long. But we would like to be as sure of our information as we can before placing it before the public."

"Wadda ya mean by escalating?" Kevin Wagner demanded.

"We don't have enough data to be sure, but indications are that the events are increasing in strength, the zone of influence is widening thus threatening increasing numbers of people. And the time span between events appears to be shortening, by about eleven days, per instance. This thing has the potential to get a lot worse."

"How do we keep this from our wives and families?" Brian wanted to know.

"I said discretion, not secrecy. I have neither the desire nor the capacity to coerce you. You must use your own judgement."

"And is that all?" Wagner asked.

Thyssen now settled back on his table—he was getting to the point.

"No. We can assume that in sixty-four days from today—if our calculations are meaningful—which means around the 19th of May, the next event will occur. Therefore, one week prior to the event, on Wednesday the 12th of May, we would like to gather you together and keep you under close observation before and during the period of the event."

"Observation how?" Andromeda asked suspiciously.

"We are unsure at this stage," Thyssen said. "But probably we will locate in Melbourne. I understand that government policy has caused the closure of a number of wards in the public hospitals and we will seek to take over one of those. Hopefully at the one best equipped for our purposes."

"You mean guinea pigs," Chrissie Rice muttered.

Thyssen rocked his head in feigned reaction to the attack. "You are already guinea pigs, but no. We will not be experimenting on you in any way. We will not want to exert any influence on the effect. We will only want to monitor your physiological condition and try to determine the exact nature of the effect on *you*. It is in your own interest as much as ours."

"Can't do it," Joe Solomon said. "I have a law practice to run, you know."

"By the 17th, if we are correct, you'll be on the move anyway. If there are survivors in Mongolia, you'll be heading for some point in the sea off the Philippines. We can help."

"What if we refuse?" Brian demanded.

Thyssen's mighty shoulders raised a shrug. "Then you refuse. I have no way of forcing you and if I had such power I would not use it. But the more you assist us, the sooner we will know how to deal with and perhaps cure the effect, in yourselves and in others.

But it is up to you."

"No pressure, hmmm?" Solomon said coldly.

"Not from me."

"I don't believe it."

Thyssen eyed him sadly. "Tell me, then, Mr Solomon. What do you believe?"

"I can recognise a cover-up when I see one," Solomon said pointedly.

"I thought I was being completely open with you," Thyssen said with an innocent look and a spread of his hands.

"Except for all those other things you are being... discreet about."

"I assure you there are none. But please. I am interested in your impressions."

"I want to know why the American government is involved in this? It happened in New Zealand. Other places, none of them US territory. But here you are, moving in and taking over."

Thyssen gazed at him sadly. "A fair point, Mr Solomon. Given the prior performance of the United States in global matters, you are very wise to be circumspect. In the first place, an American researcher was present at Ruapehu and originally observed the effect. Jami Shastri, for whom the effect is tentatively named, is one of my students and her on-going research is centred in my department at MIT. Right now, she's headed for Mongolia, trying to find out as much as she can about the vulcanism of the effect. It is *her* project—I am merely her head of department. Secondly, I am not an American citizen. I am Norwegian, to which my passport will attest."

"Sure. But who is footing the bill for all this?" Solomon demanded.

"MIT. So yes, US money. But no government agency is involved at this stage."

"Why should we believe you?"

"I have no answer for you," Thyssen sighed. "But I assure you I am a vulcanologist, not a CIA agent. And anyhow, Dr Campbell will be in charge of the medical aspects of the matter, not myself. There will be no direct American involvement."

"But we only have your word for that."

"Indeed. But you mentioned a cover-up. What on earth do you imagine is being covered up?"

"Rest assured, Professor Thyssen, that I will be making every effort to find out."

"Feel at liberty to do so, Mr Solomon," Thyssen said. "Should you find out anything interesting, I'll be as fascinated to hear it as you are."

The impasse brought them to silence, and Felicity Campbell felt she needed to contribute then. "I don't think there is any chemical or other ecological factor at work here, Joe," she said to Solomon. "I've been able to monitor Kevin's condition closely and there is no indication of any viral or other physiological condition involved. I think we are dealing with something altogether new."

"Perhaps some new sort of virus. Brain wave virus, maybe," Wagner offered with a grin.

Felicity frowned at the idea. "I doubt such a thing could exist."

Thyssen took over seamlessly. "Still, we have to keep an open mind about this, and it is that sort of area we will want to explore. We will try to arrange as expert a group of specialists as we can, covering as wide a range as possible, and for the benefit of you, Joe, I'll make sure that none of them are American."

"You approve of this, then, Felicity?" Wagner asked.

"I think it is essential that this research be done, yes. To the best of our ability, yes. As soon as possible, yes."

There was another pause, this time broken by Thyssen.

"Fine. Well, before we go our separate ways, since we are taking opinions, I'd like each of you to express your own views on what you think is happening."

"What does it matter what we think?" Brian asked.

"You are the ones who experienced this," Thyssen said lightly. "You're thoughts on the matter are the best information available. And there's no telling, at this stage, what might or might not be important. So, we have Mr Solomon's view, and Dr Campbell's.

Miss Rice, you're very quiet. What are your thoughts?"

"I think we should not interfere," Chrissie replied, carefully examining her fingernails. "I think we should accept and have faith."

"Faith in what?" Felicity wondered.

"I believe we are being guided by the hand of God," Chrissie said, and she finally looked up shyly.

"To what end, Chrissie?" Felicity asked.

"To His divine purpose," Chrissie said with sudden emotion. "We must let what happens happen."

"But surely we must try to understand..." Felicity tried.

"To try to understand is itself a failure of faith."

Brian Carrick sat with his arms folded before him. "I don't believe in God but I think I know what she means. We are being guided—like the songlines, for instance."

"The songlines?" Thyssen asked.

"Yeah. The paths the aborigines followed through the Dreamtime. Something like that."

"Oh yes," Thyssen nodded as if impressed, "I have heard something of this. Various original North American groups employ similar methods. I don't know how it works—I doubt anybody does but its reality cannot be denied, nor therefore the possibility of its relevance here dismissed. Consider migrating birds, and whales, and many other creatures. And the remarkable ability of the Bedouin to find oases—there's lots of examples that science cannot explain. It all might add up to something relevant."

"It comes on at you right out of the ground," Andromeda said. "It's like I'm plugged into the planet. It comes up through your feet."

"Maybe we should all take off our shoes," Wagner joked.

"You disagree, Kevin."

"Yeah. It ain't from the ground. It's within ourselves. You know how they say we only use part of our brains. Maybe this is a different part kicking in."

"The next step along the road of evolution?" Thyssen suggested.

"Yeah. Like maybe all our brains can be linked only we don't know how. But the volcano caused us to link in."

"An interesting view. Which leaves you, Lorna."

Lorna thought about it for a long time. "I feel I know all of you. I feel close to you, like you do when former lovers become friends. The old intimacy touches something deeper. We are sharing something. We are all very close, even though we hardly know anything about each other."

"The power of love," Felicity suggested.

"Or maybe," Lorna said, "contacting the force within ourselves from which love arises."

"I'm afraid," Thyssen said with a smile, "that on the subject of human emotions, I am completely out of my field. But another good idea. If only some of my students were as imaginative and thoughtful as you people."

"How about you, Professor," Wagner asked. "What do you think?"

"As a scientist, I'm not allowed to speculate from insufficient data," Thyssen grinned.

"We shared our thoughts. It's only fair," Lorna insisted.

"Very well. In the interest of fairness," Thyssen said, and paused. "Speaking as a person, not as a scientist, I'm reminded of Gaia."

"Who's that?"

"The ancient Greek goddess of the earth. Mother Nature, if you wish, but more than that. A rather fanciful but by no means discredited idea that the earth is an organism, a living entity unto itself and we are part of it, as blood cells or bacteria are part of our bodies."

"I heard it was more like the fleas on a dog," Brian Carrick grunted.

Thyssen raised his eyebrows. "Well, don't let its proponents hear you describe it that way but, in any case, it means that whatever happens to the planet, happens to us."

"And this is relevant, how?" Joe Solomon asked suspiciously.

Thyssen shrugged as if it was a small thing he was saying. "I think the planet is in trouble and it's screaming out for help. I think you are hearing the voice of Gaia."

7
NATURAL PROGRESSION

The rock stood like a gigantic rude finger-gesture pointing upward amidst the wide mountainous terrain and Wagner banked the helicopter toward it, making a deft landing, right on the top of the pinnacle. Lorna was, by spine-rippling turns, terrified and thrilled. She had, all the way, been oscillating between doubt and self-assurance in regard to her reasons for being there—the exhilaration of the impromptu touch-down more than made up for her feelings of guilt.

When they finally dispersed from Kyabram that evening, Wagner declared that he had to 'return the crate to Sydney and did anyone want a ride?' He had been looking at Andromeda Starlight, but she shook her head.

"Gotta wake up my man John and do the figuring." the black woman smiled regretfully.

At the same time, Lorna had said 'me', but no one heard her except Chrissie who stared at her with absolute betrayal, to which Lorna shrugged. Chrissie looked away in a huff and Lorna returned her attention to arrangements. There were plenty of rides available to get everyone wherever they wanted to go so she sidled up to Wagner and breathed. "I love helicopters."

Wagner eyed her with a wry smile—his warm handsome features softened by late afternoon light. "Woulda asked you first, Lorna my sweet, but I figured you mighta been spooked by helicopters, after your crash at Ruapehu and all."

"I don't remember anything about it," Lorna breathed.

So it was settled. Dr Felicity seemed to have taken Chrissie under her wing and so, and with a final guilty glance in that direction, Lorna ran hand-in-hand with Wagner to the helicopter.

They flew with the sunset behind them and she babbled on about god knows what as the mountains reared up beneath them. And then this rocky up thrust that seemed an absurd metaphor for the occasion—she pointed it out and declared `I want to go there' and he laughed and obliged.

At the top of the rock was an area about twenty metres square that seemed far larger when they touched down than it had on the dare-devil approach. To the west, a huge boulder jutted out over the precipice and they walked to that, watching the orb of the sun drop toward the distant line of deep purple peaks while the scattered cloud glowed in blood red and mellow orange. The air carried only a slight chill at this height but the rock was still warm beneath her feet—she had removed her shoes beforehand. The rock soothed her as she wiggled her toes upon it. They put arms around each other as the mighty globe touched the first ridge.

"Isn't this wonderful?" she breathed.

And he kissed her neck.

She hastened out of her clothing and lay back on the rock, her flesh felt a strange welcoming caress from the hard stone. He did not undress but simply opened his fly—she did not, at first, realise the mess of scars and grafts to be found on his flesh.

"Only bit of the equipment I haven't really tested yet," he said, as if by way of explanation.

His penis was huge! She stared for a moment and then craned her head back and closed her eyes and indeed his penetration caused her some pain, but the rest of her senses understood it as pleasure. As he thrust, she was forced up the rock until her head and shoulders hung over the edge of a thousand feet of thin air.

Terror replaced the pain—as first she gripped the fabric of his shoulders in desperation but then, strangely, she began to relax. Somehow there was a surety with which the stone gripped her back and buttocks and she knew she would not fall. She released her grip and threw her arms wide over the edge and opened her eyes.

Upside-down, the glorious multi-hued vista opened up to her and the blood rushed to her head in a way not unlike the orgasm shortly to follow. Throughout, it was as if the stone rather than the man was the force that gripped her passionately. "Hey, Honey, where you goin'?" he asked, between panting breaths.

When she was done, he withdrew—she had no idea whether he had come or not, so little attention did she pay him. He grabbed her by the ankles and dragged her back to a more secure position on the stone.

"Thought you were going right over the side," he gasped, once his breathing returned to him.

She did not reply. The stone's rough loving hands cried for more of her and she rolled over onto her belly and pushed herself against it as tightly as she could. She spread her hands and clutched the basalt and pushed her cheek down until it pained and her belly and breasts tried to absorb the rock inside themselves.

Perhaps he mistook it as an invitation but in any case he entered her from behind and began to thrust again, and the more he crushed himself down upon her, the more she was squashed against the stone but her desire to be part of it became all the more unquenchable.

When he finally grunted out his orgasm and departed, she felt completely splattered upon the rock, like an old blob of birdshit or the contents of a dropped bottle, or perhaps even a part of it, like a growth of moss, but certainly not anything separate and discrete.

All the way from her toes to her fingertips, she sought a totality of touch. "I love you, I love you, I love you," she breathed.

It never occurred to her that the man might have thought she was referring to him.

*

They were waiting for him. He returned the truck to the yard and walked home, ambling along hands in pockets, through the chill of the night, along suburban streets where no one ever strolled at night. These nice safe streets with good lighting and good footpaths, nature strips, low fences if any, only a few cars not slipped into garages with automatic doors. There was no one else. In such places, everyone drove and no one walked. You could be murdered or assaulted and no one would know—unless your screams for help were able to carry the distance and overcome the television voices. But no one was ever murdered, nor assaulted. Not here. The only fatal incidents possible were motor accidents and illness. No gangs of kids hung out at the local milk bar and even the packs of domestic dogs that once foraged out here were now locked up at night. Everyone was locked up at night, in brick veneer houses with burglar alarms, thinking themselves safe. While the very planet they lived on was shaking itself to pieces.

As was his life, he realised, when he arrived at his house and saw Larry's car parked on the driveway. He let himself in and tried to slip into his chair in front of the television as if it was just any other evening. *The X-files* was on—bloody perfect. How could he make what he had to say believable under these circumstances? Judy sat at one end of the sofa, Larry at the other. Cups on the coffee table said tea and chocolate cake had been served and a glass for Larry's scotch. He wondered if they had sat so far apart all evening—it was a set-up anyway—he had telephoned to warn them he was coming.

No one spoke. Perhaps they were waiting for an ad. Feeling decidedly like an intruder in his own home, he decided to head off toward the bedrooms instead.

"Where are you going?" Judy asked sharply.

"See the kids."

"They're asleep. Leave them alone."

"I better be going," Larry interjected, slapping his thighs as he stood.

"We'll all stay here and talk about this," Judy demanded. Mulder and Scully were entering a dark building with torches flashing—how could anyone talk about anything at such a time.

"What do you want me to say?" Carrick asked, still standing, still on his way to see the kids.

"Who were those people?" Judy demanded.

Carrick could not help smiling at the way a man like Thyssen might have described himself.

"Who they said they were," he offered.

"They were doctors. Looking for you. They just walk in here and take over and give no explanation. Off they go. What the hell is going on, Brian?"

Carrick shrugged. He would have liked, had he been able, to give Thyssen's explanation right now, but could hardly remember any of it.

"I have a condition. They are studying it."

"What condition?"

"That's what they're trying to find out."

"Well I want to find out too. But I'm using doctors we can trust—not strangers from foreign countries. It's all arranged."

"What's arranged?"

She paused, glancing at Larry who stood with his head bowed, unable to raise his eyes. Judy lowered her own voice and tried to adopt a reasonable tone.

"When you went this time, I said: that's it. You need treatment, right away."

"I don't need treatment. I'm perfectly..."

"Keep your voice down. You'll wake the kids."

He shut up. In his agitation, he knew that everything he said and did now would only serve to prove her contention. Think of the kids, he told himself. Keep it simple. He moved to confront them directly, trying to look as unthreatening as possible.

"What, exactly, have you arranged?" he asked softly.

Again she needed to look to Larry for aid, and this time Good Old Reliable forced himself to meet his responsibilities.

"You gotta understand, mate," Larry said. "You just can't go on like this. Causes all sorts of problems. Tryin' to explain to the kids and the neighbours. Stealing trucks. It's gotta stop."

"I put your bloody truck back!"

"Sure. I ain't worried about that. It's you we're worried about. What's good for you."

"Just leave me alone."

"We gotta think of your wellbeing."

"I'm okay."

"No, mate. No," Larry said and moved to stand directly in front of him, gripping his shoulders. "You ain't even nearly okay, mate. You got a problem and we're all here for you. You gotta believe that's why we done what we done."

Carrick eyed him suspiciously. "Just exactly what have you done?"

"You gotta... You are to report to the local cop shop, mate. That's all."

"Why? Are you having me arrested?"

"Not arrested, no. You gotta be put somewhere where you can get some treatment."

"Like where? The loony bin?"

"Nothing like that. It's called a Trauma Centre..."

"You can't do this."

"It's done, mate. Judy signed the papers and the cops are waiting. Either you go there or they come here and get you."

"This is totally unnecessary. Call Doctor Campbell and ask her."

"I did," Judy put in. "She tried to tell me there was nothing wrong with you. But I also spoke to Dr Mangels and we are following his advice."

Carrick sighed. Was there a way out of this? It was too silly for words, but he knew he needed to keep control now or else it would get right out of hand. He burned to smash Larry's sympathetic face, and Judy's... No. Nothing like that. Stay calm.

"I want to see the kids first."

"You can't." Judy said firmly. "They aren't here. We had them removed when we knew you were on your way."

"What? There's no danger..."

"We can't know that. This is how hostage situations develop. We had to take precautions."

"You think I'm that bad?"

"It wasn't worth the risk."

"There's no risk. None at all. I'm calm. There's nothing wrong with me."

"Then there won't be any problem, Brian," Larry was saying. "Sooner we start, the sooner we finish."

Carrick eyed them, one then the other. Larry was right. The sooner this ended the better. The two people he trusted most had betrayed him completely. There was nothing to be done after that. The numbness of shock had a firm grip on him, enfeebling him in every way.

"What do you want me to do?" he murmured.

*

When a man walked into his office and shot him in the middle of the chest, Joe Solomon was forced to make a determination. The young man had shot him with a paint-ball gun, splashing red dye all over his shirt.

"It's just to show you how slack security is around here," Cecily trumpeted. The `assassin' had been her boyfriend.

"The security isn't slack," Gloria mused. "It doesn't exist."

What did they expect? Since he had become a cripple— `physically challenged' some idiot always chortled when he described himself that way—and they moved the chambers to the ground floor, putting ramps in and opening up spaces to accommodate the wheelchair, the result was easy access, not just for him but for anyone. Although he could not imagine why anyone would want to shoot him, the girls insisted on protection and so he had no choice but to call Barney Touhey. He had won a case for Barney years ago when Touhey Security Systems was feeling the economic pinch and Joe had accepted only slight payment. But Barney was a good bloke and would help out anyway, even if there wasn't an unspoken debt.

"But who'd want to shoot me?" he protested again when Barney arrived.

"Great bloke like you, Joe. Not an enemy in the world, hey?" Barney chuckled.

"Having good friends is the basis of this business," Joe muttered.

"A man is measured by quality of his enemies, Joe. You sure?"

"Yeah, well, in your line of business, you'd have to believe that, wouldn't you."

"Well, Joe, let's see. You got elected to the City Council again, I noticed."

"Fifth time in a row."

"So there's all them crooked traders you defeated and all those who would vote for them, and the opposition in every issue that you fight, and the people that affects. How about all them for starters?"

"I fight for seats at bus stops and unfair dismissal cases—gentle stuff. If I was to take on the larger traders and the corruption in the re-zoning system or stuff like that, I'd understand."

"Why don't you?"

"There'd be no one left on the council, nor trading in the city, except me."

"But they all love you."

"They don't care about me."

"Then there's all those accident compensation cases you fight in the courts for employees against their employers—large corporations mostly—am I right?"

"You don't shoot a bloke because he wins a few Workcare cases."

"You sued the State Government for twenty-five cents, didn't you?"

"It was a matter of principle."

"But they all love you."

"Okay, okay, I'm getting the point."

"And then there's the Union cases against the big corps for illegal dismissals and lock-outs and pay cuts and safety breaches and god knows what. No enemies amongst all them?"

"I said you made your point."

Barney Touhey laughed outright. Joe Solomon wasn't used

to losing arguments—he had been winning them against the best QCs and judges in the business for decades—but he was losing this one. That was what being personally involved did to you. Except, it was said that Joe Solomon got personally involved in all his cases...

"So, what security do I need, Barney?"

"Hardly any. You got two assets. One is that even the cruellest assassin isn't likely to shoot a bloke in a wheelchair."

"That kid did."

"He only loaded tomato sauce. And he was doing you a favour. Which leads us to your second asset. No one gets past that bunch of harridans you keep in the front of the office."

Joe groaned. He was losing an argument against a bloke who contradicted himself.

"That bunch of harridans, as you so decently call them, happen to be some of the best legal minds and administrators in the business."

"Never seen such a bunch of ugly women in all my life."

Joe groaned again. The joke in the business was that his staff had been chosen by his wife, but that wasn't true. The legal profession admitted women aplenty these days, but only if they looked great in a black mini-suit. And for that reason, Joe was able to collect a fine array of talented women who no one else wanted because they didn't have the figures and faces of film stars. He gave them a go because no one else would, and was rewarded with a fierce loyalty and efficiency that had made his firm the top labour legal service in the state. And it had remained so even throughout his long period of his convalescence.

"Look, you do me a submission of what we need and give it to Clarissa. Let the girls decide. Okay?"

"Sure," Barney laughed. "Don't know why I'm botherin' to talk to you anyway."

"Let's call it a courtesy," Joe said and, perhaps only to change the subject, heard himself adding. "There's something else I want you to do for me."

"No worries."

"Have you still got your contacts in the States?"

"Got a few, yeah. Ex FBI blokes mostly. What do you need?"

"There's a man I want to find out about, quietly."

"Sure. What's his name?"

Barney had his pad and pen ready.

"Harley Thyssen. A geologist, he says. I guess he is. Seems to know his stuff. They called him Professor. MIT, I gather. I want to find out who he is really working for."

"Should be easy. Any reason why you doubt him?"

"He looks more like a lumberjack. Remember that bloke Pop-eye was always fighting? Bluto or something, wasn't it?"

"I think so. Anyway, no reason why a geologist can't look like that."

"No. But I also want to know about the latest biological weapons research and that sort of thing. What's being covered up at the moment?"

"Just about all of it."

"This might have something to do with toxic waste being disturbed by volcanic eruptions. Something along that line."

"Wow."

"Of course, I may be way out. But I want to know about Thyssen."

*

Father Gilbert sat with quiet respect while she spoke, sipping the tea they shared, a plate of cream biscuits of which Chrissie had devoured four in her anxiety.

"I know you are going to think I'm insane," she told him.

"I'm here to listen, not to judge," he answered.

He was a young man, earnest-looking, bespectacled, and had a very scholarly way about him. Chrissie supposed he was just the sort of priest she was looking for.

"Do you believe in Judgement Day, father?"

"Naturally."

"I think it's going to be soon."

"I know of no reason why it should be either soon or not soon."

"I'm not really allowed to tell you anything about it."

"Everything you tell me will be held in the strictest confidence."

She eyed him dubiously. He had all the right answers, the right attitude—that was what bothered her. Would he really be able to take her seriously?

"I don't think you'll be able to."

"Able to what?"

"Keep it in confidence. It's too big for that."

It shook him all right—physically—his head, at least.

"I'm sorry, child. I'm not following you. Too big for what?"

"To be kept a secret. You'll have to tell people. Warn people. Make preparations. If you believe me."

"Child, what on earth is it that troubles you so?"

He was probably a year or two older than she, but called her *child*. She decided she needed to shock him.

"They've been saying in the news that there's been a lot of volcanoes erupting recently."

"I have noticed such reports, but..."

"The eruptions are increasing in intensity, and frequency, and I did a little calculation. It all comes together on July 15th, next year."

"I see," he said, and she heard his sigh of relief.

"You don't believe me."

"Who told you this, Christine?"

"I'm not allowed to say but he's one of the top scientists in the world."

"And he said that was the date?"

"Oh no. He supplied the information. I did the calculation myself. I admit I got a `Z' for Maths, but it was very easy. And that was the date that the converging lines came together."

She offered him a sheet of paper with the lists of dates. Chrissie saw he was impressed by her reasoning. She was feeling very proud of herself.

"Then that, I think, will be Judgement Day. It's really going to happen."

He was silent. He took off his glasses and cleaned them with a few huffs of breath but she knew that wouldn't help him see things any more clearly.

"You don't believe me. I knew you wouldn't. That isn't why I'm here anyway. I just thought you'd like to know, so that as the date draws nearer and the disasters become more frequent, you'll know what it means."

"Christine," he said, having finally gathered his wits, "in a frightening sort of way, I do believe you. But what I believe doesn't matter. You believe it, and we must deal with that accordingly."

"Quite so," she smiled. "As it happens, there's more."

"Oh really?"

"Six people appear to have been chosen—I don't know why, but I know that they are. Chosen, I mean. And I'm one of them."

"And the other five?"

"Well, I can't vouch for all of them, but two at least are thorough-going heathens."

"Christine, it really isn't proper to joke about this..."

"I'm not joking. Father, in the middle of this month, the six of us will be put in a special hospital ward where a group of doctors will try to find out why our minds have suddenly become connected. They were linked because we were all at the first of the series of volcanoes I told you about. Of course, the doctors are looking for brain diseases and ESP and psychological effects arising from trauma."

Again Father Gilbert's glasses needed cleaning. This time she waited to see what he thought, if he was able to think anything.

"Christine, you are a rather new member of our congregation and... Why me?"

"I've decided to stay in Melbourne and wait for this. There's nothing back in New Zealand for me anyway. I have no family, and I've lost my job and my fiancee over this. I've taken a nice little flat down the road. This is my local church—and a very nice one too—and you're my local minister."

"If indeed that matter falls within the scope of my ministry, of course I'll do what I can. But what do you want me to do?"

"Just pay attention to whatever happens from here. So if I'm a Looney Tunes who needs to be locked up, I'm sure you'll know what to do when the time comes. No need to discuss that. But what, Father, if Judgement Day is *really* on the way and I am *really* one of the chosen. What on earth are you going to do about that?"

The enormity of it all made it somehow easier to grasp for the man of faith.

"I can't imagine. But I suppose we must seek out the appropriate preparations and implement them."

"Fine. So how do we begin?"

"With a prayer, I should think."

*

Andromeda Starlight sat in her flowing white bath-robe, delicately administering vanish to her nails. Claws, Tierney might have said. She paused to raise a cigarette to her glistening lips but made no attempt to light it. With her eyes, she insisted that he pick the lighter up and do it for her, but silly Tierney failed to get the point for so long that the guard walked over and did it for him, the revolver on his hip swinging under Tierney's nose. Power, Andromeda mused, was a wonderful thing, and just as satisfying when used on a worthless germ like Tierney.

"Now, Joel, sweetie-pie. I'm gonna tell yer how things are gonna be."

"Bitch," he seethed at her. "Fucking two-faced bitch."

"Such language, Sugar." she smiled. "Maybe I ought call Gordon back to cuff your ears, or are you gonna attempt a smidgin of self-control."

Joel Tierney, a weedy little insect of a man, contented himself to sit and sneer. She had, for some time, been telling him how it was going to be.

There had been a long series of telephone calls, followed by a number of visits, which brought them to this meeting. At first he had raged, calling her names and expressing his general regret at allowing the joint access to their wealth.

"You mean, lettin' me spend some of my own hard-earned?" she asked.

"I kept it because you woulda blown it all on dope in five minutes."

"Well sorry to disappoint you, Joel-baby. Ah am off the hook and lovin' it. Bumpy ride, but I'm startin' to get a kick outa bumpy. Whacha think of that?"

It wasn't only Joel who had been amazed. For all that time, he had controlled the flow of uppers and downers and on-ers and off-ers into her system by which means she kept herself alive and able to perform. Now she had kicked the lot. Well, not actually. There were sleepers at night and one upper before performances, just to maintain the balance.

But all the rest, gone for good. It was as if she had replaced the chemical drugs with a stimulant of a new kind, one entirely mental. It was called belief in herself. And it was working.

"Looks like you've blown it on a luxury lifestyle instead."

"No point having success if you don't enjoy it, Joel."

"You got your success from me!"

"No. I got it because I'm a right talented girl, Joel. You just managed the bookings."

"Well, now you're gonna have to manage without me," Tierney had raged. "See how long ya last."

She got herself a gig at the Melbourne Casino and two engagements on television, and booked into this hotel overlooking the Yarra and its ramparts of skyscrapers.

"I've decided to keep you on, Joel. If you learn to behave."

Each time he telephoned, he was arranging bookings in places a little closer to Melbourne. She refused them all. As soon as he resorted to abuse, she hung up. He was learning.

"I told you, Joel. I'm not available between the 10th and 30th of May. You'll have to cancel it."

"But why?"

"Because I'll be in hospital, Sugar. I told you."

"Put it off! This is the Sydney Hilton, god-damn you! Biggest gig in the country."

"Not available, Joel-baby. Sorry."

"You fucking bitch, why..."

She hung up. It was so satisfying.

Finally, he brought himself to Melbourne. Each time he tried to invade her hotel or her latest venue, security threw him out. He was a slow learner. But worth it, she knew. Joel Tierney might have been a lowlife germ and a minor drug pusher, but he was basically honest. It would take her such a long time to train a new manager, and time, of course, was running out.

"All right, bitch. We'll do it your way. What do you want me to do?"

"Behave, Joel. Learn a few manners. And buy yourself some decent rags. Spend some of that brass you've been pimpin' off me on yourself."

All along she had continued to pay him his thirty percent.

When it finally came down to this visit, she had employed Gordon, the security guard, to be present and make sure he behaved. Joel Tierney, a beaten man, looked just as downtrodden and weedy as when he was a winner. But it was going to be a fine arrangement, she was sure of it.

"Look, Joel. I've made all these plans. You're getting thirty percent and I'm doing your job for you."

"What is this shit?" he protested. He hadn't really looked at it.

"My new image, Joel. Great, huh."

It wasn't particularly great just yet. She had done the designs herself on a computer the hotel provided. There was a photo of herself in a glittering dress, in full song with arms wide-spread, and a few stock images of the Earth photographed from outer space on which she had superimposed herself by means of Photoshop and printed it on a nifty little ink-jet. It was rough but it would do the job.

"What's fucking Gay-yah?" he asked. He didn't want to admit

that it wasn't bad.

"Gaia, Joel. Goddess of the Earth. See the list of numbers?"

She had written down the name of every song she could think of that had something to do with extolling the beauties and wonders of the Earth. Only Carol King's: *I feel the earth move under my feet* was in her regular repertoire and even that was really called *Tumblin' down* but soon many others came to mind. Joan Baez songs, Dylan, Kate Bush. Great stuff. She was already practising all of them.

"Jesus, you're turning into a fucking greenie."

"Get with the program, Love-child. It's just the two matters usually go together. Anyway, I'm writing a couple of songs to link them all together."

"Bloody hell. *The Songs of Gaia!* Who's gonna buy 'em when they can't even pronounce the name?"

"It'll be a name on everyone's lips in no time at all, Joel. We're riding the crest of a wave here."

He groaned. The image was good, he could see, and suited her. The songs all had a bit of guts to them and she was at her best when belting 'em out. She looked like a Goddess. To all this, Joel was slowly succumbing, in the manner of sinking into quicksand.

"So where'd you get all this from?"

She didn't want to attempt to explain Thyssen—there were no adequate words to do so anyway. When she had asked, before they departed Kyabram, he had given her a list of books—one on mythology, one on the geological history of the earth, and the one by James Lovelock that carried the whole idea.

"Gaia (Gaea) the mother-goddess, first and oldest of all Greek goddesses, deep-breasted giantess, whose soil nourishes all that exist and whose blessing brings forth the fruits of the earth. The one supreme goddess, worshipped not only by all men but by the gods themselves. Gaia was not just the Goddess of the Earth—she was the Earth itself."

When she read this to him, Joel Tierney nodded. "Giantess, okay. Deep-breasted, yeah you got that. Boss goddess—got it all. So fine, I can see it, but will they? The punters. Sure it ain't too high-falutin' for 'em?"

"They will learn, Honey," Andromeda smiled. "I will show them the way."

"It's a great image," Tierney conceded. "Yeah, it suits you. So, if you want to play at her, okay. Fine."

"I won't be playing at her, Joel," she said determinedly. "I am her."

*

Extreme! The Max! Rip into it! He had to be tested all the way, in every way. Kevin Wagner worked his body furiously, manipulating every muscle daily. It was the only way forward. Use it or lose it. He could allow no part to fail him.

He established himself in King's Cross in Sydney where he knew all the weirdest and most extreme people lived. There he took a flat from which he could range out, trying everything, doing everything. Money was no problem. He had sold off his house and other interests in the States, and of course there was the insurance...

At first Lorna Simmons, that silly girl, tagged along with him rather like a stray dog, but he was already bored with her. She seemed to be taking the relationship at rather a slower pace than he, and was anyway a very conventional girl. She wanted monogamy without the slightest regard for the fact that he was no longer a family man. He had placed pictures of his dead wife and children everywhere for her to see.

"You have to get over it," she told him.

Insensitive little bitch, seeking domestic attachments in a purely sexual relationship.

"I've got over it," he answered. It wasn't really true. He had never for a moment mourned them. It was rather that he had died with them, and reawakened in a new dimension, a new life, from which they were absent. The universe they belonged to went out of existence. He hardly even remembered them, and only thought about them in unguarded moments.

But Lorna was sure he needed to grieve, and that they needed to be replaced. Her persona as a sexual adventuress was a lie. One day she was gone and he hardly even noticed. His daily regime was by then completely established and he was absorbed in it. He needed to prepare himself for what was to come in every way.

Each morning he rose and went to the gym for a three hour workout. He had a map of his body and worked every muscle systematically, discussing himself with the trainers to the most intimate detail. He took himself to the speedway where, he learned, you could pay crews to allow you to take the cars out for training runs. He joined a parachute club and jumped every Sunday. On Mondays he sought out a new peak to scale up and abseil down. On Tuesdays he went sailing on the harbour in every kind of craft in every sort of conditions. On Wednesdays he ran over places—The Razorback and all sorts of rugged places in the Blue Mountains. Thursdays he relaxed with a bit of bungy-jumping from increasingly high places. Friday was diving day, at places further and further up the coast. Saturday he liked to join teams of those people who enjoyed running rapids down through steep chasms with their broiling cascades.

He found a rugby team he could train with on Tuesday and Thursday evenings and although they pleaded, he never turned up on Saturday for the game—there was a limit. It made him feel cowardly for all that body-armour he had worn when he played American football in his youth.

His diet never varied and every calorie and vitamin was carefully counted. Once Lorna was discarded, he soon attracted fit young women to test out his sexual skills. His body grew hard and spectacular and he allowed them to admire it. They traced their fingers along his scars and asked about them. He told them he was injured in various war zones—no one doubted it. He didn't forget his brain—there was a forced two hours every day at the library, reading on the latest scientific and technical subjects, and current US and European politics and social conditions in Third World countries.

He needed to become the perfect man in body and mind, or as near to it as he could humanly manage. If he was participating in the next great step in the chain of evolution, he wanted to give it the best possible circumstances in which to flourish.

"You're crazy, Kevin," Lorna had told him, sometime shortly before she left. "You're absurdly self-obsessed."

So he told her his plan.

"You're just running away from your grief," she deduced as a result.

It was disappointing, but still he told her what he believed.

"Is that all you think this is," she said, shaking her head sadly. "That this is just evolution in action."

"It's all around us, all the time."

"And we are some sort of superior humans in development?" she chided.

"It has to happen sooner or later. And you have to admit..."

"There was a bloke called Adolf with similar delusions, Kevin. They thought they were the Master Race but they were really just stodgy old Germans."

"Not Master Race, Lorna. Master Species."

"The result could be the same. The Germans needed to prove their superiority. They needed to conquer the world and kill off the competition. Really, they were insecure and afraid."

"Forget about goddamned Germans," Kevin muttered grimly, sorry he'd started this. "A superior breed of human wouldn't have to prove a thing. They wouldn't need to conquer the goddamned world. They would have nothing to fear. They would take control simply because they were best people for the job. Just a simple natural progression."

Lorna stood her ground, the flaming hair a match for the fire in her eyes.

"You aren't taking me seriously, Lorna. I knew you wouldn't."

"I don't have anything to prove, Kevin. I don't need to feel superior to anyone. I'm afraid your argument runs up its own arsehole."

Come to think of it, that was the last time he saw her before she left.

*

It was the most amazing thing she had ever seen. To witness the initial eruption of Ruapehu was a remarkable achievement, but the stygian vista that lay stretched out before her now was almost impossible to grasp. Yet grasp it she must. She sat on a boulder on the top of a hill that had no name, her lap-top perched on her knee as she tried to describe the scene to Glen which she would soon dispatch by email, if she could find somewhere in this godforsaken place to plug in her modem.

She was rugged up like an Arctic explorer from behind where a chill wind bit into her but in front she had unbuttoned her parka and jacket and dragged the scarf from her face and neck. The effect was like sitting too close to a fire while a fan blew iced air on your back, goosebumps behind, sweat bubbling at the front and maybe blisters too. Yet that fire was more than three kilometres away.

The valley below was a vision of hell, mostly in varying shades of black. Here was a volcano without a mountain—a rare sight indeed. The lava had spread freely across the valley floor and solidified while still in the form of giant waves such that it reminded her of the lake that had once occupied this place in a moment frozen in time. The actual lake—Oz Baykal, once five hundred kilometres in length although somewhat shorter now—was visible on the horizon, the water black as crude oil, hazy with a fog that was really seething steam. To left and right in the distance, low mountains rose in orderly fashion, their tops and slopes still green with tundra—the blight that had destroyed the valley had not quite reached that far.

But the valley was an astonishing scene. The waves of basalt lava with the crests running in long rows seemed to have polished sections but that was just where the heat had melted it in the form of hot mud. Everywhere, pockets of red glowed but mostly it had encrusted except in three main sections. Each of these were wide bands of lava, flowing outward in fine red and orange ribbons while down the middle, straight as a rail, was a line of fire bursting upward, looking rather like the spines along the back of a dinosaur. The fire seethed up out of the fissure, belching white smoke into the sky which mostly dissipated as the wind carried it off toward the mountains. The crest of each black wave, she knew, was itself a long, straight fissure, newly sealed over as the fire extinguished.

It wasn't Mongolia at all. The border of that country lay about one hundred kilometres to the south and west, but the Buryat people who inhabited this region of the former Soviet Empire were culturally Mongolians. There was once a sizeable town down there somewhere—Slyudysanka on the banks of the southern end of the lake—now not a trace of it remained and the lake had moved ten kilometres away. Through here, the Trans-Siberian railway had passed—now they were already laying new track on the other side of the ridge for it would be a decade or more before the ground here would once more be hard enough to bear the weight of a train.

It was a nightmare scene of destruction, yet there was creation too. The lava that filled the valley would become the finest soil in the world in a few decades, once it cooled and eroded. In total, the lava bed stretched two kilometres across and ten kilometres long, dotted by fire-breathing fissures all the way.

The US Geological Survey sent a team of twenty in, of which she pretended to be a part. She knew this was not a country where it was wise to play at deception. The team busied themselves, setting up to study the effects, and this data Glen would be able to freely access. If she doubted why she was there, Harley made sure such doubt was quickly eliminated.

Bloody Harley. What the hell was he up to? The story made news everywhere, mostly as a novelty item. But Harley offered quotes and interviews and even, holy Moses, made predictions. There will be a new eruption on the 19th of May, give or take a day. Very brave, his colleagues declared. There were about 1500 eruptions on Earth annually, but usually an average of only eight big eruptions each year and they had already had four, before May began. Somewhere in the Indian Ocean or thereabouts, Harley had boldly told the media, although that, unlike his date, was just a guess. He really was an embarrassing man to work for.

But she knew his madness. Obviously, he had made no impression in his mission to Washington and so went public to scare them into funding him. The prediction closed their options—he was the top expert in the world and they could not afford to ignore him, no matter how silly he sounded. And it did explain the lemmings of Gran Canaria.

She was being roasted alive, sitting there, and so turned away, walked away, immediately pulling her warm clothing about her. Off to follow Harley's instructions and seek out the Red Cross folk and ask about *sleepers*, as they had come to be called. No one knew anything, but that was typical of this place.

"People who were in a coma for eight days and then recovered completely?"

The Red Cross people were frantically busy as always and in no mood for idiotic questions, but she had persisted. There were none that anyone knew of. But it was hard to tell.

"Half the population of the region have simply left, and will never return," the Portuguese administrator told her. "And those that intend to stay have gone to the mountains until things quieten down. There's over five hundred people missing for those reasons and most will stay that way."

"But these would have been unconscious for the first eight days."

"It was three weeks before they let us in," the man said helplessly.

He promised he would let her know if he learned anything. But outside, a Turkish nurse caught up with her.

"It's not official but some of the locals think there has been a camp established in the next valley and a lot of people were taken there under guard. But no one seems to know if it's true."

"How many people?"

"Two hundred maybe. But no one knows."

Harley, she knew, hated it most when people didn't know things.

`What made him think of the Indian Ocean?' she typed to Glen.

`Sequential by oceans was your theory, remember?' Glen replied.

`You got any idea how far I am from an ocean right now?'

`That's what you get for making bold predictions.'

`I'm not sure whether I want Harley to be right or wrong.'

`Harley's always right, even when he's wrong.'

*

Psychiatrists were a breed apart—they came from another planet. They seemed like pleasant friendly people but they were not— they were very strange. To begin with, they seemed to listen to what you said—not a common human trait in most circumstances. And, odder still, they always let you finish what you were saying without interrupting, which never happened when real humans conversed.

But he was getting used to it. The important thing, he knew from the outset, was to avoid trying to right the wrong that had brought him here. He raged no rage, put up no fight, tried to remain as docile as possible. The various shrinks talked to him and he chatted as lightly as he could, which wasn't easy when the interlocutor didn't reply in accordance with whatever you said. Instead, they nodded thoughtfully and asked: `Yes, and how do you feel about that, Brian?' or, if he had already told them how he felt, said, `that's interesting, go on'. It was really like a monologue of his entire life and he rather enjoyed being able to talk about himself. It was a pity, though, that the psychiatrists didn't know how to talk back. Once they taught computers to talk, nothing would be quite so easy to replace.

Of course, the one thing he never mentioned was the Shastri Effect and Professor Thyssen. Had he done so, he knew there would have been no hope of proving himself sane and getting out of here.

But otherwise, he was polite and friendly to everyone and co-operated with everything. `What do you think about that, Brian?' they would ask when one of the group had broken new ground and reduced themselves to tears or rage.

"Since I'm sane and here by mistake, I really don't think it would be healthy for me to comment," was the sort of answer he gave.

He told them, all the time, that there was nothing wrong with him, but he never insisted. He just made sure they were informed. No one seems madder than someone trying to convince another that they are sane.

He wondered, always, how they pondered his `condition'. He wondered how long it would take them to catch on to the fact that he really was sane. After two months, there really was no sign of it.

"I think we're making real progress here," the shrink said at the end of his most recent interview.

After a month, he was allowed visitors. Only Judy came and he refused to see her unless she brought the kids, which she refused to do. She didn't want them to see their father like this. The siege was yet to be resolved.

"But why not accept a visit from your wife?"

"Are you kidding? She's the bitch who got me locked up in here."

"Do you often feel this anger, Brian?"

You see? No way out.

Felicity Campbell was waiting in Dr Blackburn's office. Brian entered and they both looked at him. No one said anything. No one dared. Blackburn signed a document and handed it to Felicity who walked out, summoning Brian to follow.

"Do you have anything to bring with you?" was the only thing she said as they walked the corridors toward the light of freedom at the end.

"Nar. They can keep the toothbrush," Brian answered.

They walked right down the steps and out the gate where she had a taxi waiting. Only then did she pause and look at him with sorrowful eyes. "Oh, Brian. I'm so sorry about this."

"Wasn't your fault," Brian replied.

She was a lovely woman, with her straw-blonde hair and bright eyes, standing before him in the sunlight, his hero and rescuer. He had never loved anyone as much as this since his mother when she gave him a train set for his fifth birthday.

"Oh yes it was," Felicity was saying as they got in the backseat of the cab. "I knew that our flying visit to your home must have left your poor wife utterly bewildered by events. Imagine the impression on a simple housewife of having someone like Harley Thyssen barge into your house and out again without any explanation. I planned to go and see her and explain. It was on my list of things to do before I went back to New Zealand, but... well, there was so much on my mind and I clean forgot. This is entirely my fault."

"A doctor admitting she's wrong? That don't happen every day."

"It isn't funny, Brian. I feel so awful."

Brian was tempted to put a comforting arm around her, but supposed he'd better not. "Well, don't worry about it. It gave me a nice rest and it wasn't so bad. It got me away from Judy's nagging and the kids' fighting and all that. Just like a holiday, really."

"Well, I'm glad to see you're taking it so well. Poor Judy is so terribly distraught."

"Might do *her* a bit of good to be locked up for a while."

"Don't be hard on her, Brian. She thought she was doing the right thing."

"Well, maybe this will teach her to have a bit of faith."

"I've talked to her now and she understands. You can go home any time you like."

"Not just yet. Allow me to enjoy my freedom."

"Not much of that, I'm afraid. We're ready to receive all of you at the hospital right away. I just thought you might like to go and see Judy first."

"Bugger Judy. I'm in your hands, woman. Take me and do what you want with me."

Felicity Campbell shook her head and laughed. "Alfred Hospital, thanks," she called to the driver.

*

The Alfred Hospital had a complete ward available to them on the eleventh floor of the North Wing. From its windows it offered a perspective of the broad park across Commercial Road and over the top of the trees, the towers of the metropolis glimmered in the smoggy haze. Bridging the road, they had built a helipad that allowed direct access to the casualty ward and you could actually see the police rescue chopper come and go from the ward—Thyssen would like that. He would have access to the state-of-the-art equipment to be found on the floors below and the smiling co-operativeness of the administrators and technicians. Of course, she knew there had been a letter from the Department of Health in Washington to its equivalent in Canberra that smoothed out the arrangements, but she had found the location and made the initial approach herself.

Thyssen would be pleased, too, with the list of specialists she had arranged once she had returned to New Zealand. Jenkinson, Tuang Giap, Mendelev, Chomolski, Inpasit—neurologist, physiologist, psychologist, haematologist and virologist, had all been delighted to lend their time to the project. No one seemed at all embarrassed by Thyssen's outrageous predictions although they all commented on it. The hospital had a fine array of contract technicians and nursing staff looking for extra hours. She'd been able to arrange all that by telephone from home in New Zealand, and still found time to do the rounds of her neglected regular patients.

Less pleasing was the position regarding Wendell and the children. They had another of their breakfast conferences, since that seemed to be the only time that they were all together these days.

"But why you?" Wendell asked over his newspaper.

"Because I discovered it. Look. It will only be for two weeks out of each three months. I'll just be over in Melbourne. There's always been conferences..."

She didn't want to admit that Thyssen believed they were on a diminishing time scale.

"That is hardly the point," Wendell sighed. "Appearances suggest that that the rest of your life is being sacrificed to this project. And if the publicity is any guide, the man in charge must be regarded as dubious at best."

Harley? Dubious? Not much doubt about that.

"It is very important, Wendell," she persisted. "And, from a medical point of view, that dubious character in charge is me."

"But you admit yourself that you don't know what's going on? Your kids need you. Your patients need you. Not to mention me. You've allowed a top posting at Wellington to go through to the keeper. Really, Fee, the implications are of one hell of a gamble."

She knew it was. She had wondered, all along, what drew her along this course. Maybe the madness had infected her as well.

"It's only tough going now, while I'm setting it up. When we know more about the condition, the specialists will take over and I will be phased out."

That was, she knew, absolutely untrue. The various specialists would depart the project once they had proven that their field was not relevant. But until the cause of the symptoms was fully diagnosed, they would always need a GP broadly experienced in all aspects of the condition. That was why Thyssen had put her in charge of a team of vastly senior personnel. She would be the last to go.

She had departed from New Zealand with the domestic situation very much unresolved. The final position had been Wendell's threat to employ a nanny to replace her, and her plea to him to hold on and see if that was really necessary. She flew to Melbourne knowing her career had taken a big stagger sideways and her status as a good mother a gigantic step backwards. And then she collided head-on with her own fallibility when she went to visit Judy Carrick.

Brian Carrick was a grave error. She should have checked. That she had allowed him to sit it out in that mental home while the situation in the Carrick household ran completely out of control for two months was unforgivable, even if Brian offered no objection.

She had gone to Judy and carefully explained, but she knew she had allowed an irrevocable rift to occur in that marriage, entirely due to her own carelessness.

She arranged for Judy and the kids to come and visit Brian at the Alfred, and if the conversation was stilted and the room temperature icy, still he assured her that he would be home in two weeks. That had to be enough.

Then she settled down to await the arrival of the others, wondering what other disasters she might have caused amongst them. She sat in the ward while the technicians and nurses breezed back and forth, their activities calmer now as the job neared completion. It was like having the house prepared for a party, and the unbearable hours sitting and waiting before the first guest arrived. In those hours, you could persuade yourself that you had offended every friend you had and none of them would come. This time, maybe it would be true.

But throughout the day, they began to appear. Chrissie Rice brought with her a young handsome priest who was at first astonished by everything he saw but eventually wished to bless the proceedings.

"So what she told me is all true?" the priest gasped at Felicity.

"Whatever Chrissie told you, she did so in strictest confidence. But you may judge for yourself the seriousness with which the matter is being taken."

He did, and it floored him. He stuttered through a brief prayer and Felicity, although a lapsed Catholic, allowed some of his blessing to splash in her direction.

Kevin Wagner failed to get permission to land his helicopter on the hospital pad and was diverted to Moorabbin. It was after dark when he got back. He brought with him a set of weights.

"The hospital has a first rate gym," Felicity pointed out.

"These are my own designer type," Wagner explained.

The surprise was Joe Solomon, wheeled in by an over-weight woman named Clarissa who was one of his associates and would allow him to run his business from the hospital. She immediately grabbed the lap-top and went looking for the nearest place to plug in the transformer.

"I must say I'm surprised, Joe," Felicity mused.

Joe Solomon snorted with his customary grumpiness. "Bloody Thyssen outmanoeuvred me."

"As he did all of us."

"Oh yes," Joe grunted with disgust. "He handballed the whole bloody thing to me, that's what he did. He employed my firm to look after the project contracts and accounts. `*That way you'll know just exactly where the funds are coming from and who's ripping off who,*' he said. Bastard."

"Good contract though, Joe. What's your percentage?"

"Mind your own bloody business."

"Still, Joe, it is a comfort to know the man in charge is smarter than everyone else."

"Yeah, I guess so. Except that also includes us."

"Still, he seems to have gone out of his way to secure your trust, Joe."

"That's what worries me. People who say `Trust me' are the only ones you can't rely on."

Lorna Simmons had been shopping all day—just a few things she would need for her stay. A nightie from Country Road, fluffy slippers from Myers, a fabulous Japanese geisha dress for a dressing gown. And a whole reserve supply of make-up... One glance between Lorna and Kevin Wagner informed Felicity that they should be positioned at opposite ends of the ward.

Then Andromeda Starlight swept in, calm and light and serene. There seemed to be an aura of tranquillity surrounding her that made Felicity wonder what she was on at the moment. She had decided deliberately to avoid thinking about possible impact of withdrawal symptoms on their test results. Felicity stayed calm, even though she could not have known that no drugs were involved.

The ward offered no partitioning between patients, with only curtains that could be drawn around for privacy. She watched as they looked over these communal arrangements and was surprised that no one saw fit to complain. Admittedly, six beds in the ward rather than the possible ten allowed greater intervening space than customary, and the excess of monitoring equipment created natural barriers. But Felicity preferred to believe Lorna's view of the matter—that these six strangers were remarkably comfortable in each other's company. Like a family? No. Few families were as harmonious as this.

Except Lorna and Kevin who, although they weren't speaking, were always able to remain far enough apart that it didn't matter.

"They had a big bust up in Sydney," Chrissie informed Felicity softly. "Lorna's been staying with me for a month."

"Well, let's hope they soon get over it," Felicity smiled.

In the evening, they had arranged their beds and televisions and reading matter and were waiting to be fed and settled down. Then, despite the heavy security that had been arranged for the ward, a skinny, dark-skinned young woman wandered in, wearing torn jeans, crumpled shirt hanging out and a leather jacket with badges. With her spiked hair and nose-ring, she looked like a street kid who had been brought in by accident with the garbage bins.

"Can I help you?" the ward nurse demanded.

The urchin retreated and disappeared.

Conversely, the security guards weren't about to allow a Neanderthal like Thyssen through and a chuckling Felicity had to go out and rescue him. He lumbered into the ward, looking bright-eyed and well pleased. "Great work, Fee. Terrific set-up."

"Do you want to have a conference and tell these people the plan?" Felicity asked, trying to get things on a formal note.

"No way," Thyssen said. "You're in charge here. I'm just an observer."

"That'll be the day," said a voice behind them.

The urchin had returned, leaning in the doorway, licking an ice cream.

"What the fuck are you doing here?" Thyssen demanded of her.

"Indian Ocean, you said, Harley," the urchin replied blithely. "Which makes this the perfect spring-board for attack."

"I was rather more thinking of Cape Town," Thyssen muttered.

"Was there any reason why it should be the Indian Ocean, Harley?" the girl demanded as she advanced into the room.

"Hasn't happened there before," Harley murmured lamely.

"Then you'll be delighted to know that Glen came up with the Indian Ocean in five out of thirty-seven model runs."

The girl stopped beside Thyssen, who put his arm around her and dragged her to open ground. "Folks, I want you to meet Jamila Shastri—the discoverer of the Shastri Effect. You won't see much of her because she's our volcano chaser. Always to be found where the eruptions are hottest."

"Why do I suddenly feel so very insecure?" Lorna Simmons said in mock horror.

"So these are the *sleepers*," Jami remarked, looking them over like specimens in a bottle. "I've heard a lot about you guys."

"Whereas we've heard nothing about you, young lady?" Joe Solomon said

"That's because Harley always takes the credit for my work," Jami said cutely.

"That's because I do all the paying and take all the flack," Thyssen defended. "Anyhow, since we're all here, I have something to say. I'll keep this short," he said amid their groans. "I just want to thank you all for coming. And you ought to know that the project now officially has a name. Project Earthshaker."

"Wow man, talk about originality," Kevin Wagner sneered. "How many bureaucratic geniuses did it take to come up with that one?"

"Came from the US State Department, as a matter of fact," Thyssen said. "I thought it rather appropriate myself."

"I thought these names were supposed to obscure, rather than tell everything," Felicity said lightly.

"Maybe they're referring to Harley," Jami grinned.

The next day the patients were hooked up to the monitoring equipment and the detailed observation of their physiology and mental states began. Interest focused on a set of six small monitor screens that were slaves to those placed individually beside each bed. These Felicity positioned at the nurse's station where they could be constantly watched. The six bands of light darting with endless repetition across the screens measured the alpha waves of the patients and their names were tagged below each monitor. Their output was also constantly recorded. As such they represented the only positive external measure of the condition of the group.

"See how they are all different," Felicity pointed out to Thyssen.

"They all look the same to me."

"No. Observe how no two blips are the same point at the same time."

"I suppose."

"Please have a bit of faith, Harley. Since I anticipate being able to show you something that I know is medically impossible and don't even really believe myself, even though I witnessed it, I need just a small degree of indulgence."

"Okay. They're all different."

Thyssen was mostly busy with logistics. Air forces, both Australian and US, were on stand-by with aircraft fitted out to his specifications. Thyssen would have rather avoided involving the military, or even governments, but there wasn't time, nor available skills, to fit out private aircraft. They had a USAF 707 fitted out to duplicate most of the equipment in the ward, and although it would not be completely ready for three months, still it had arrived and stood on the tarmac at Tullamarine, just in case it was needed.

The RAAF was standing by with an Orion, fitted out for weather observation and hunting down lost yachtsmen in the Southern Ocean, which would fly Jami and a vast array of equipment to the scene of the next eruption. In addition, two buses had been fitted out as medical laboratories, residing in the belly of a USAF C-130 Hercules, ready to collect any new sleepers should they occur, and two further wards had been made available in the Alfred to receive them. These arrangements, coordinating the various authorities involved, were what occupied most of Thyssen's time. It was a great deal and all of it based on Harley's speculations. He tried as hard as he could to shrug off the pressure.

His first moment of relief came at ten minutes to eight on the morning the 18th of May, when suddenly Felicity summoned him urgently to the nurse's station.

"It happened three minutes ago," she said. "See how Chrissie and Joe have locked together."

Thyssen watched the ongoing lines streak across the screens for some time before he could see it. Yes, identical. The others were not... Though you really needed an expert eye to detect it.

"Lorna says Chrissie has always been more sensitive to it," Felicity said. Thyssen went with her through the ward. Everything was checked. There was no other indication that anything had changed and even the subjects themselves had not noticed anything.

"I don't even feel it coming on yet," Chrissie said uneasily.

"Well, don't force it. Let it happen of its own accord," Felicity smiled.

There was hardly room around either bedside for all the activity of the nurses and technical equipment, much of which Joe Solomon tried to fight off grumpily. Even while they were there, Andromeda Starlight locked in.

"Did you feel anything at all?" Felicity asked.

"Nothing," the black woman shrugged.

"I was taking her pulse at the time," a nurse added. "I'm sure there was no physical indicator."

The various specialists and their teams busied themselves, each shaking their heads negatively. Somehow, Felicity was not surprised.

Within two hours, all six monitors were reading identical brain waves. Thyssen, Jami and Felicity went to the cafeteria and relaxed over coffee.

"Well, I'm glad that's over," Felicity said, stretching her neck.

"Indeed. I can only hope that *I* can match the precision of your observations, Fee," Thyssen said.

"What's your current guess?" Jami asked in mock awe.

"If my theory is correct, the event will occur tomorrow evening at about five or six, Melbourne time. You'd better be ready to go then."

"I have such faith in you, Harley, I'll be sitting on the aeroplane with my parachute strapped on."

"Are you kidding about the parachute?" Felicity asked.

"Yes."

"But it wouldn't be a bad idea," Thyssen mused.

"It's a *very* bad idea, Harley," Jami said coldly.

Thyssen turned to Felicity.

"At the earliest possible time, I want you to move the group into the bus and get them underway."

"Underway where?"

"Kyabram, we have to assume."

"What if the story of there being sleepers in Mongolia is true?" Jami asked.

"Then the focal point will lie in the Pacific west of the Philippines. But you'd think we'd have heard something positive by now if there were. The damned Ruskies are supposedly not keeping secrets these days."

"Yeah. Like us Americans," Jami said dryly.

"So. Assume Kyabram," Felicity said.

"Well, the airport lies in the same direction. So we can at least make a start."

"I'll check around my team and see how soon they can free the patients."

By the time the test procedures had reached a point where they could be temporarily broken off, it was nearly noon. By then, each of the subjects was beginning to feel seriously agitated.

"We ought to let them sleep," the psychologist said.

"They'll be too agitated," Felicity was sure.

"Sedate them."

"No. Leave them be," Thyssen instructed. "Tell them to get what sleep they can. We'll move them this evening. That'll still give us twenty-four hours before the event. Ought to be enough."

"You should sleep too, Harley," Felicity said.

"I'll sleep on Tuesday. Jami sleeps now."

"Am I supposed to be asleep?" Jami asked.

Thyssen and Jami had been establishing a control room on the same floor as the ward, in which they had installed a full array of monitors. Those from the ward, and others by satellite from Glen, full seismic equipment and monitors and videos from each of their transport vehicles. In the end, it needed two technicians to run it.

"I think that covers everything," Thyssen said.

"We ought to be able to tell if someone down there spills their coffee," Jami remarked.

The evening was foggy and very cold as the group were wheeled in chairs with their attending equipment onto the ambulance bus. Each had a technician, a nurse and one specialist and Felicity overseeing it all. Thyssen sat in his control room and watched them on monitors and communicated directly with Felicity.

As the bus set out along the Tullamarine freeway, Chrissie Rice said. "We're going the wrong way."

"Kyabram is in this direction."

"This way."

The direction she indicated was ten degrees east. Each of the others indicated agreement. Kyabram was slightly west of north—they indicated somewhat east of north.

"Shit," Thyssen snapped. "That means the Russians have got sleepers in Mongolia. The bastards and their fucking secrets."

"So where does that mean we are going?"

"We calculated some place in the Pacific Ocean, just east of the Philippines."

From the bus, there came a collective groan.

"Do we really want to go there?" Felicity asked.

"The plane's waiting. So we just fly you out there and back again. Aim to be over the location at an hour before sunset and you should be right. And your exact location ought to give us a precise location for the Mongolian sleepers. Who, we must assume, are presently heading south."

"Do you suppose we'll meet them?"

"Beats me. Depends on whether the Russians have been taking any notice of me. If not and the poor buggers are on their own, they have to cross the Gobi Desert and all of China from north to south."

"I think I'm just beginning to appreciate you, Thyssen," Brian Carrick chuckled.

Thyssen leaned back and smiled. It wasn't every day that someone said that.

*

The snow-cat ran out across the white land, trundling over flat terrain, beneath an amazing sky. The winter night had just begun and the Aurora Australis—unusually for this time of the year—danced across the entire heavens in every known colour. Great swirls drifted back and forth, the size of the milky way, looking like the bottom of a gaudy curtain rippling in the breeze, intermingled with blinding flashes of light and darting streams of iridescence. The greatest fireworks show in history was underway and the polished orange skin of the cat reflected such an array of colour that it might have been driving under the neon lights of Las Vegas.

And back behind, in the direction that the twin caterpillar tracks had scoured across the snow, another display of pyrotechnics was underway. There a black cloud that thundered skyward, illuminated constantly from underneath by a brilliant red glow. Great bolts of lightning burst continually from the cloud, cracking downward into the white steam cloud beneath. From back that way, bone-rattling roars were heard, as if the clouds hid a gigantic dinosaur, and there were other, deafening cracking sounds as massive fissures opened in the Ross Ice Shelf. It might have been that the cat was fleeing this ice bound inferno, except that it made no haste, rumbling on its way at just twenty kilometres an hour. And never at any time did it deviate from its course.

The cat had trundled on for five hours by the time they located it. True, the terrain here was flat as a table top, yet still it was surprising that it had come so far without dropping into a crevasse and being overturned by one of the upthrusts that dotted the landscape. And still it might, before it ran out of fuel and ground to a halt. The helicopter followed it through the dazzling night, helpless, keeping it under the eye of its landing light, praying that the cat's engine died before the helicopter reached its own maximum fuel range.

Earlier that evening, at 1727 hours, they had felt the earth shake and a few minutes later, the seismic station at Oates confirmed what they already guessed—that the region had been hit by a massive earthquake. From then on, reports came through every few minutes; that the single shock measured 7.1 on the scale—by far the most powerful quake in the admittedly limited recorded history of the Antarctic continent—that the epicentre was located twenty-eight kilometres east of McMurdo Sound; that whereas all of the bases in the Ross Ice Shelf region had suffered damage, there were no casualties. Almost immediately, they were informed that an Orion aircraft was on the way from Australia, bringing a team of geologists and prepared to return any casualties to Melbourne, even though none had been reported. Throughout the Summer, the Americans flew back and forth from New Zealand to their bases all the time, but the Orion was on its way and seeking permission for a risky night landing on the nearest US runway when already in the air.

Then they remembered the survival group. They had been

forgotten because they were not part of any particular scientific team, but instead sponsored by an oil company for a promotional television program. They were camped near McMurdo, and last reported fifteen kilometres from Mt Erebus, which, they had every reason to believe, was probably in full eruption.

The helicopter came out of Roosevelt Base, and Kim Ah Cheung went along as observer. Being a climatologist, she was as near to a geologist as was available at the time, and if able to constantly report on the remarkable aurora, was a little out of her depth with more terrestrial matters.

"There are huge cracks running all over the ice shelf, and colossal ice bergs breaking off. Gee, I think the whole shelf is going to collapse."

A trained geologist would have known better than to say that—still, the largest icebergs in known history were already beginning their long diminishing journey north.

"Erebus is gone," she cried over the radio. "It just isn't there. Oh, hang on. It's obscured by steam. I can see lava flowing onto the ice shelf. Oh wow, you ought to see this. It looks like there's a great big crack opened up in the west side of the mountain and great streams of lava are gushing out. But there's steam everywhere. Jesus, and lightning in the cloud above. Is that usual?"

From the Orion, Jami Shastri, to whom these reports were relayed, reported back that it was not uncommon. She asked an array of technical questions in response, but the poor woman peering out of a helicopter flying in very rough and dangerous conditions, was not really able to understand them. Jami understood. The volcano, the aurora, the shattered ice shelf, in a chopper bouncing from one thermal to another, out over the ice in the endless antarctic night—any one of these things would have made most people babble, all of them would have been devastating.

And Jami was thinking, Mt Erebus—only two thousand kilometres from the nearest point of the Indian Ocean. Guess again, Harley.

In the chopper, they were searching for the survival team,

whose task, plainly, had taken on a meaning far beyond their expectations. They were a young fit group of athletes—four males and four females, all from different countries. Kim Ah Cheung remembered their smiling faces in the press photograph, standing in a line, all in the same splendid ski-suits, Japanese, French, Malaysian, Indian, American, African, Arabian and Swedish versions of the same person.

They crossed and recrossed the terrain east of Erebus but it was plain that their camp was well inside the zone of multi-hued seething steam that had surrounded the mountain. Then one of the pilots spotted the caterpillar tracks. They came out of the steam-ridden zone and went straight out across the plain and the chopper zoomed low as the pilot dived and chased after them.

Only to hover helplessly when they reached the source of the trail. They should have been able to make radio contact with the team but there was no response. They dropped down to a few feet above the ice, running beside cat and trying to shine their lights in the windows, but they had fogged up.

"If they're fogged up, it means there are people breathing in there," Kim was able to tell them.

They could see the green luminescence from the dash board lights. That made them hopeful.

"Put me on the ground and I'll jump on it. It's only going slowly," Kim suggested.   "You can't run at twenty kay on snow, Kim," the pilot snorted over the headset.

"Then drop me on the roof and I'll get in that way."

The roof racks, she could see, were empty and offered plenty of handholds.

They were within five minutes of their fuel range before the pilot agreed to let her try. Kim was chubby, thirty-eight, mother of four, but she was very fit. As soon as she was out, swinging on the cable beneath the chopper, she knew it was a bad idea. The wind howled and hurled her every whichway. No part of her flesh was exposed but suddenly if felt as if her protective clothing was rent in a dozen places. Her goggles seemed to fog up. There was no air that was breathable. She swayed and swirled everywhere, even though the drop was only twenty feet. She was bashed against the side of the cat twice before she finally got a grip on the roof rack, then had to let go three times as the turbulent air wrenched the chopper away. Swinging like a sack of potatoes, she was finally directly over the roof and she closed her eyes and released the cable. Bruised and battered, she lay on the rails of the roof rack for a few minutes.

"That wasn't too bad," she told herself.

In fact she'd cracked two ribs and broken three fingers.

The cat swayed violently and it rumbled along and the slipstream was buffeting her furiously and now pain savaged her lungs as she tried to move. But move she did. From the rack, she was able to get the rear doors open and then, with a frantic, painful and very awkward scramble, got herself in.

The eight young people sat, three on each side in the back, two in the front, as if going on a picnic. Icicles of condensation hung from the roof from their breathing but breathing they still were, in steamy gusts now that Kim had admitted the outside air. They just weren't doing anything else. She scrambled over their feet and leaned past the one in the driver's position and turned the engine off. The cat slowly rumbled to a halt.

"End of the ride, kids," Kim smiled with relief. "You can wake up now."

8
SLEEPERS AND PILGRIMS

She was just getting into her act when she spied him in the audience—usually she ignored them as individuals but there was no avoiding him, sitting alone at a table amid the beautiful people like a gigantic member of Santa's elves. God knows how he got in—dressed as usual in plaid shirt, jeans and hiking boots—although at that time only half the tables were filled. Admittedly she was just the warm up act for the megastars to follow but that didn't mean they didn't give her the works—full orchestra, backing group, dazzling light show that actually met her request to establish a rotating planet earth behind her and she blasted through her routine. And she knew that tonight she gave it a little something extra because Thyssen was out there, watching. Whatever could he be thinking? she constantly wondered.

This was the Melbourne Casino, largest gambling complex in the southern hemisphere they reckoned, and they had invited her—it was by far her biggest gig yet. Amid all the glitter and excitement, the name of Andromeda Starlight was becoming known in all the places where it needed to be.

The unexpected flight to nowhere over the Philippines returned her to Melbourne with only a few days to spare to her opening night, and she was still in the process of settling the act into this larger format. On this the second night, the presence of Thyssen seemed to be the little boost she needed to pull it together. The casino management were very strict in regard to the personal conduct of the performers and so she sent Tierney to collect Thyssen and arrange for them to meet nearby in an obscure bar, an hour later.

"My, my, just look at you," she smiled as she walked in.

"Just keeping my finger on the pulse," Thyssen replied by way of explanation, indicating her into a chair.

"So, how'd I do?"

"Technically, very impressive."

"Take care, Lover. I may swoon."

He arched his big furry eyebrows at her, and looked at her through one eye. "Gaia, huh? Mother to all things. You've incorporated the idea nicely."

She found she was remarkably relaxed with him. He had always been a group experience until now. Even in the half-light, she could see his face splattered with red blood vessels. She knew what that meant. His skin too was pitted all over like a surface of the moon. Sweat bubbled along his brow and upper lip. He was possibly the first man she had ever liked that she didn't want to touch.

"You thinkin' you've created a monster, Harleykins?"

"A beneficial monster, if that's true."

Joel Tierney was catching on, looking from one to the other and figuring things out. "So you're the geezer who fed her all that earth-mother codswallop," he said.

"Are you dissatisfied with your percentage, Joel?" Andromeda said coldly.

"I think I need a piss," Joel said and left them.

Thyssen watched him walk out of sight and then tilted his head and looked sideways at her.

"I like your friends," he said with an ironic smile.

"A sorrowful soul, Harley. But I didn't want you leavin' without a word."

"Are all managers as seedy as that?"

"All the useful ones are."

Thyssen nodded and said no more.

She sipped her drink quietly. She was in no hurry to get to the point of this, whatever that might be. For there had to be a point—with Thyssen there always was. The situation called for light chit-chat but a man like him was hardly likely to be interested in that. Surprisingly, he made an attempt.

"Harrandel Thöensen Heuwenstrepp," he said emphatically, turning to face her directly now.

She frowned.

"That's my real name," he grinned. "I was nine years old before I was able to pronounce it properly. Harley Thyssen was the invention of an unimaginative immigration officer on Ellis Island."

Andromeda smiled and words avoided for a decade suddenly flowed from her with ease. "Edna Krebbs."

"I think we'd both be well advised to stick to our alias'," Thyssen chuckled.

She raised her glass to toast him and he responded.

"How is it that you have an American accent when you aren't American?" he asked pointedly.

"There was a time when I got to thinkin' it would be good for my image. But once I took it on, it stuck. What's your excuse, Lover?"

"Same as yours. Except I didn't plan it. Technically I'm Norse."

"Well, Vikingperson, so now that you know my deepest secrets, what is there left?"

"A deal."

"Deal?"

"Yes," and he paused, looking toward the men's toilet to determine that Tierney was not yet returning. "An arrangement that you may not want your manager to be in on."

"Joel, believe it or not, is an honest man," she pointed out.

"There are some concepts too incomprehensible for even so vast an intelligence as mine."

"Tell me about the deal."

"I want to employ you. That is, take you on as a member of Project Earthshaker."

"And there I was thinkin' I was just another lemming."

She found herself very proud of that, especially because he stopped and chuckled before continuing.

"That's the point. Felicity's medical team have taken over the new sleepers from Antarctica and are keeping them in isolation as a control group. Which means you guys—the original six—are now redundant, from a medical research point of view, that is. You've all been tainted and contaminated by your subsequent experiences."

"I am aghast. Should I be checkin' out my health insurance, Sugar?"

"That may be completely pointless. But you have been living normal lives out in the real world rather than being safely quarantined in an isolation laboratory like you should have been."

"You scientists sure have a funny way of looking at the world."

"Don't I know it. Anyhow, what it all means is that it's likely that your period of usefulness as a research subject is ended or at least minimal. But I want to keep you around. So I'm suggesting we take you on the staff."

"You're offering me a job? Doing what?"

"What you do."

"I don't get it."

"I want to incorporate your act as part of the project."

"Just a moment. The germ is returning."

Joel Tierney's timing was impeccable as usual, for as he made his unsteady way through the tables toward them, it gave her time to think. Unfortunately, thinking it through did not make things any clearer. Perhaps he misunderstood what she did.

"Take a seat over there for a moment, Joel," Andromeda called, and Tierney immediately sat on the chair nearest him.

"You've trained him like a dog," Thyssen mused.

"Explain to me, Harleykins, how a li'l' ol' night club singer like me can possibly be regarded as a component of a scientific project."

"Well, you've already incorporated the project into your act. Why not go the other way?"

"Ain't soundin' reasonable so far, Honey."

Thyssen leaned back, lighting a cigarette, thinking, not

wanting to explain himself so deeply. "We will pay you five thousand US a month. Anything you earn over and above from your performances is yours."

She regarded him as suspiciously as she would any promoter. "For which you get, what?"

Thyssen couldn't look her in the eye—instead he played with the crescent of fluid left on the table by his glass. "I'd like to be able, from time to time, to offer further ideas for you to make use of on stage."

"Do I have a right of veto?"

"No."

So it wasn't a soft-sell then.

"How come I get the feelin' that ain't all of it, Sugar," she was sure.

"It is."

"You want to use my act as some sort of promotional tool for the project."

"Why didn't I think of putting it like that?"

"And that's the deal?"

It wasn't. The tiny puddle before him got another work over. She was realising this was the basis of his charm—being able to swing between Tyrannosaur and naughty child at will.

"I might want to have some power to arrange your venues and locations."

"You can do that?"

"I have some interesting contacts."

It was her turn to think about it. When she did, the answer was fairly obvious, although she hated herself for having to admit it. "Harleykins, there ain't no need for you to pay me for this. Why, I figger it's an honour to work with your ideas, and I'd go anywhere and do anythin' for you."

He looked up. His eyes, at all times, carried a great sadness. "That might not always be the case. I'll have Christine draw up a proper contract."

"Chrissie?"

"I've taken her on as project administrator."

"Oh fine. That I can understand. I just don't see why you need me."

Thyssen was nodding. He gave it a lot of thought and then seemed to suddenly decide to be more candid than he had originally intended. "Okay. Consider this. I believe that the population of Planet Earth is facing a catastrophic disaster. Humanity is going to need to be strong to face the threat. There will need to be the sort of strength that Londoners showed in the blitz, and you will be the Vera Lynn who symbolises that strength. You see?"

She wondered if she should have been shocked. Obviously, he was trying to shock her. But instead she could smile. "I sure ain't never been averse to immortality, Lover."

"Then we better get your man over and start working on the details."

*

Much to his discomfort, everything was running so smoothly that when Barney Touhey rang and said he had the *good dope* on Harley Thyssen, Joe Solomon felt a severe pang of guilt. By that time, about half of his daily workload was taken up with the Project Earthshaker accounts. There was a credit understanding with the Chase Manhattan and he needed only to forward the bills as they arrived and soon cheques returned for his signature and dispatch. All costs, no matter how great, seemed to fall without a murmur into the black hole of that account. Well, not quite. Indeed, it almost came as a relief when one of them came back with a query. Looking it over, Solomon was surprised that he had accepted it himself, even though he had been a participant in the expenditure. Was it true, the bank wondered, that a chartered USAF Boeing 707 had flown Melbourne—Darwin—Melbourne to absolutely no purpose whatsoever. Apparently the crew had grumbled about the pointlessness of the flight.

So had all the others. In fact Darwin had just been a refuelling stop on the way out and the passengers had been allowed no further than a guarded transit lounge. The actual destination had been a point over the Pacific Ocean five hundred kilometres east of the Philippine island of Mindanao, where the plane had circled while its passengers agreed that this was the place.

"It's like a religious trek," Lorna Simmons said. "We'd be pilgrims if we had somewhere to pilgrim to."

But it wasn't funny at the time. A twenty hour flight to nowhere and back was assured to induce grumpy moods and they collectively confronted Thyssen about it when he met them at the airport. It was as effective as all protests were with him—he took the wind out of their sails by admitting that, yes, it was all his fault, that he had known where they were going, that it was a waste of time.

"What bloody drongo came up with this plan," Brian Carrick muttered, looking Thyssen right in the eye.

"I just thought you'd be more comfortable at the focal point," Thyssen said. "We would probably have had to sedate you, had we tried to keep you in Melbourne."

"That's not the thing to say to a bunch of people at their wit's end from lack of sleep," Felicity pointed out.

Thyssen could not have looked more miserable. "Well, let's look on the bright side. We did get the precise co-ordinates of the focal point—that might be useful later on. And we did prove that you all lost interest in the focal point at the very moment Erebus blew. So we gained a great deal."

"Hardly worth a good night's sleep," Lorna grumbled.

Thyssen smiled at her. "Yes, and one other thing. *Pilgrims.* I like that. I think from now on we will call you *pilgrims*, to distinguish you from those *sleepers* who are still comatose."

Lorna beamed a big smile and gave a little bow.

"Better than bein' called fuckin' lemmings," Brian Carrick muttered as they walked away.

But that was Thyssen—always able to charm his way out of anything. Joe Solomon would have preferred to keep an open mind but how could he when the man was so bloody likeable. But, in any case, Barney Touhey who turned up in his office next morning, carrying a video cassette and a thick file of documents.

He dropped the file on Joe's desk with a heavy thump. Joe regarded it grimly.

"I need to read all that?"

"No. That's just the supporting evidence," Barney smiled. "Mostly, we have it all here on video."

He waved the cassette and Joe indicated the video player set in the bookcase opposite his desk.

"You're not going to like it. He's one of the good guys."

"That doesn't exactly make me unhappy."

Barney plugged the cassette in, fast forwarded to the right place, then put it on pause.

"Open the file to the first page. You'll see his real name is completely unpronounceable."

"Harrandel Thöesen Heuwenstrepp," Joe Solomon attempted, with a pause between most syllables. "I can understand why he changed it."

"He didn't, apparently. That was done at a refugee camp in USA when he first arrived there. Born in Holmestrand, Norway, 1941. Mother was Jewish, apparently. Parents fled the Nazis to New York but were interned until the end of the war. They returned in 1947 to a small place named Lavik in the fjords of Norway, but little Harley was entitled to a US passport, which he has never claimed apparently."

"An un-American American?"

Barney ignored the heckler. "Educated in sciences in Bergen and graduated first class honours in geology from University of Oslo, 1965. Post grad in Hawaii, specialising in volcanoes. Wrote some sort of ground-breaking paper on gas pressures in fumaroles, which is in the file if you are interested."

"Was the pun intended?"

Barney looked a little puzzled. He pressed the play button. "He was a tutor at Berkeley in California at the time of the student riots protesting the Vietnam war, but he sided with the students and became very politically active at the time."

"How active?"

"Arrested seven times. Fired from the staff but by then was

travelling as a sort of professional student protester."

"No friend of the CIA, then?"

The video was running. At times, a slim gangly man with flowing hair and beard appeared, looking half-stoned most of the time.

"Apparently not. He got fired from three lectureships at three different universities throughout that time. Even UCLA. Finally, no university would touch him. In 1972, National Geographic took him on to do a series on the world's active volcanoes. The work he did then established his early fame as a vulcanologist—no one else could get so close to eruptions as he did. He seemed to have an uncanny sense of where and when major eruptions would occur."

"A talent that seems to have deserted him now. His predictions have been woeful."

"No man is ever quite as good nor as bad as his reputation," Barney smiled.

On the screen, volcanoes were blasting and lava was flowing, buildings were falling, the earth was opening. Solomon had seen most of it before at various times. They were amongst the great early images of volcanoes.

"All of the film you are watching now was taken by Thyssen at different times. But we don't see the man himself again until 1974, when still no university would touch him and so Greenpeace snapped him up."

Now the scenes were of spray-swept Zodiacs tormenting whaling ships and challenging French destroyers and Thyssen, bulkier but all muscle, hair and beard trimmed along ancient warrior lines, looking fierce, usually in a wetsuit.

"For the next six years, he's one of the top Rainbow Warriors, in where the action is thickest, picking fights with French paratroopers on nuclear bomb sites, riding the bow-wave of US nuclear warships, chained up in front of all sorts of dangerous machinery—that sort of thing."

Muscle-bound, teeth-gritted Harley grappling policemen and shoving whalers around—the Arnold Schwarzenegger of the

Green movement. And then all smiles with his arm about a lovely woman, in matching wet suits on a ship in bleak seas.

"Met and married Karla Ann Somers at the time—fellow Greenpeace hardliner, two children. Elmore lives in France, married, works for the Lyon Transport Authority. Katrina is an Anthropology student, presently working somewhere in Peru."

Now the wild man was replaced by more serene images of a comfortable family in suburban surroundings as the children grew older. The beard became very neat, the muscles diminished and the waistline expanded and the wetsuit was replaced by a suit and tie with aplomb, or else smart casuals.

"They quit Greenpeace in 1980 and settled in Washington where Thyssen became a major lobbyist for the Green movement. No politician dared close their door to him in those days. Every Congressman and Senator wanted to be seen as his friend. With Greenpeace, he made prominent friends right around the world. As a lobbyist, he's owed favours by everyone in Washington. And that is how he gets things done."

"That's Harley. Everybody's friend."

There were a series of pictures of Thyssen with famous people—Jacques Cousteau, Richard Nixon, Jackie O, Carl Sagan, Jane Fonda, Sadam Hussein, Paul Ehrlich, others Joe knew he should have been able to recognise.

"Yep. For all that trouble and conflict and controversy, he seems to be the best buddy of just about everyone who matters and doesn't have an enemy anywhere, outside France."

Joe Solomon laughed. "Yes. If you'd met him, you'd understand why. He has a jovial way of being humble and commanding absolute authority simultaneously. He has an aura of great knowledge and strength and he gives it to you straight and simple, no bullshit. He allows everyone, even lowly underlings, to ridicule him openly, admits his every little mistake, seeks your opinion and makes you feel really important by taking it seriously, no matter how silly it might be, and the result is that you feel desperate to get the chance to do whatever he wants. He's kinda like God if God was a good bloke instead of being a complete arsehole."

"You seem very impressed by him, Joe."

"I would be if I wasn't so bloody scared of him. I just hope to hell we're on the same side."

"Well, according to all this, you are."

"Yeah. That's what bothers me. He's too much a good guy."

"Not completely. We'll come to that. May I continue—there's not much more."

"Go on."

Now on the video, the volcanoes roared again, this time more intense video images.

"Then he got bored with Washington life, whereas his wife was deeply into it. He ran off, chasing volcanoes again, getting closer and closer than anyone had before. He was after chemical changes in the magma itself prior to eruptions with a view to predicting outcomes. Very dangerous. The papers he wrote were all the rage in volcanoland. It took him to the top spot in the discipline and, when he discovered his wife's illness, took the Chair of Earth Sciences at MIT, in 1992, where he still is. Karla died of uterine cancer in 1993, aged 41. He seems to have little contact with his children these days."

The woman in the hospital bed was smiling, and still very beautiful despite the obvious ravages of the disease.

"Wow," Joe Solomon said.

The video began to provide images of Thyssen matching those familiar these days, the shabby lumber-jack outfits, unruly hair, an obesity that ought to have been ponderous carried lightly on massive legs.

"That's the good news over with. Ready for the bad?" Barney said slyly.

"How can there be bad news after that?"

"I have an old CIA contact—John Cornelius—who is very interested in all this. He even wants to come here and suss it all out for himself."

"What does he think?"

"That Thyssen gets whatever he wants from the US Government because his work has weapons applications."

"Oh really? Do you have any evidence of this?"

"I'm just the messenger. But Cornelius is serious. He said he'd like to make contact with you some time in the future to discuss it."

Solomon was surprised to find himself saddened. Within him he felt the spike of a loyalty to Thyssen that he would liked to have denied but could not.

"So?" Barney asked.

"So what?"

"Can I tell Cornelius that you want to talk with him?"

"Are you certain of his credentials?"

"Absolutely. A trustworthy CIA veteran."

"Isn't that an oxymoron?"

But he was stalling, and he knew it. He almost flinched with pain as the spike was withdrawn. It was the sadness he often knew in court, when the fine ideals of justice once more fell to tawdry pragmatism. But the other thing he also knew was that Harley Thyssen was far too good to be true. While Barney was still trying to puzzle out the joke, he said.

"Yes. Tell him it will be okay."

*

Immediately upon their return from the pointless flight to the Philippines, Thyssen had taken Kevin aside for what was obviously a formal chat.

"You used to run a security company in San Diego, Kevin?"

Thyssen, of course, thought he knew everything.

"Not exactly. It was a fire-fighting equipment company. Therefore alarm systems. Security crept in as an optional extra."

"Still, you have some experience of the matter."

"Some."

"I want you to take charge of security for Project Earthshaker."

"Surely the military..."

"That is exactly what I want to avoid. I don't want us to be beholden to government at any level. Which means we must make our own security arrangements."

"Look, it does sound interesting, Prof, but I've just established myself a nice lifestyle in Sydney and I'd like to get back to it."

"It'll pay very well. There will be a formal contract..."

"I don't need money."

Thyssen scratched his nose. Plainly he wasn't expecting to be turned down. It was nice to see him off-guard for a change.

"Give me a chance to interest you," Thyssen said carefully. "If my expectations are even slightly right, Project Earthshaker is going to expand, very rapidly. I anticipate further outbreaks, large numbers of sleepers all around the world, very broad research operations, large scale logistics. All of which needs to be secured against all manner of threats."

"I don't see any threats."

"Immediately, media and government interference are the concerns, but in the future I expect us to be in danger of espionage by other research outfits, direct threats by local authorities and individuals, maybe even terrorist attacks. It will become very big and I want the security system to grow with it, and with the growth, there will be expanded profit for the security company involved. You follow me?"

Wagner followed him all right. He had been ahead of him, in fact. Riding the crest of a rapidly growing organisation to a global level. Yes. It was a great opportunity all right. But he liked to see Thyssen squirm.

"Sure, I understand all that, Prof," Wagner said with false uncertainty. "But you gotta understand the state of my life. All that is behind me now. I don't have to work anymore and I don't think I want to."

If Thyssen had been talking to Felicity—and you could bet he had—then he would have known her belief that the sooner he, Wagner, ceased to take such profound precautions against grief and arranging his life to shore up his denial, the better he would be. Now he expected Thyssen to indulge a plea along those lines.

Instead, the big man nodded, smiled, and thumped his shoulder. "Fair enough. It's your life, buddy. It was just a thought."

And he started to walk away.

Shit! Kevin Wagner thought. He was being outplayed at his own game. Or was it that Thyssen truly meant everything he said. Just a dim scientist who, in his essential honesty, didn't realise how clever he was being.

"Just a minute, Prof," he had to call and Thyssen paused on the tarmac and looked back. Wagner had to try and shrug off the defeat. "I just need a bit of time to think about it."

"Twenty-four hours enough?"

"Sure."

"I want to fly back to the States on Saturday. If you're interested, you'll need a couple of hours briefing before I go."

"I'll let you know."

So he turned up for the briefing on Friday, in this vacant shop near the hospital that had been rented as the temporary headquarters of Project Earthshaker. This office would be his, if he wanted the job. Brian would be organising transport and logistics in the other upstairs room, and downstairs Chrissie was office administrator and Lorna in charge of PR.

When he learned all that, he realised Thyssen's intention of keeping the project in the family.

"Apparently, we've been superseded," Brian explained. "The eight fit healthy young people they picked up in Antarctica make much better subjects than we do. They haven't been contaminated by being exposed to their former lives the way we have. So they become the control group."

"So we became redundant," Wagner said.

"Yes," Chrissie said. "But Harley didn't want to lose track of us, so he's given us all jobs."

"I didn't realise guinea pigs could be promoted," Lorna smiled.

He hadn't troubled to mention that, which meant, to Wagner, that he had been outplayed after all.

"I want you to throw a net over the whole project and the

idea is that the security expands with the project, wherever and however necessary," Harley explained when he arrived for the briefing. "So you will always need to be ready to move fast to cover any new developments."

"What sort of equipment and manpower is available?"

"You obtain whatever you think you need, whenever you think you need it. No limit. I want a monthly report, but you have full responsibility for all decisions."

"And budget?"

"Joe will provide whatever funds you need and Chrissie will do the paperwork and ordering."

"Okay. It's a big ask, you know, Prof. I don't know the local security scene at all."

"Talk to Joe Solomon. He has his own security, a guy named Barney Touhey with a nationwide security company and international contacts. He ought to be a good man for you to get to know."

"Can we be sure of him, Prof?"

"I think so. He's the guy Joe employed to check up on me. His agents were asking questions all over Washington."

Wagner had to laugh despite himself. "Joe Solomon has been spying on you?"

"That's right. I think he found out everything he wanted to know."

"And you don't mind?"

"Never been one to discourage healthy scepticism. And I don't have any secrets."

It was, finally, a challenge that could not be ignored.

*

She was exhausted in every part of her body. The Orion returned to risk a second landing in the dark, and Jami abandoned the Erebus project as impossible to establish before the end of the winter and made a run for it.

They flew to Dunedin and left her Orion and Antarctic crew

there, and made her way on domestic flights to the northern hemisphere and finally Boston which seemed remarkably warm to her.

It was Spring, coming on Summer, and slowly she began to thaw. She cursed the Shastri Effect and all who sailed in her. It had taken her to all the worst places in the world and she shuddered to think of what bleak rat hole would be next. Had it not been for the heroism of the Orion pilots, she would have been stuck in Antarctica for six months. The thought depressed her beyond imagining.

Then Harley arrived from Washington and they gathered in the basement headquarters of Project Earthshaker, while Glen amused them for an hour running his models. He had become very good at it but, like Jami, he too was becoming convinced that there was nothing more to be learned this way.

"There is always more to be learned," Harley said brightly.

"But none of the data means anything," Jami complained. "I froze my butt off down there and I can tell you it was a complete waste of time. Not one new scrap of information was gathered from Erebus."

"I agree," Glen said wearily. "There just doesn't seem to be anything new to find out here."

"Well," Harley said, eyeing them both malignantly. "If we have all the data, then we must be able to find the truth. Okay? So… let's brainstorm?"

"Oh, must we?" Jami moaned with every weary bone in her body. "I need rest. My entire physiology cries out for it."

"I haven't been out of this dungeon for more than two days in the past month," Glen concurred.

Thyssen thought about it for fully ten seconds. He looked fresh and bright and sharp. Life, for him, was just one big vacation. That, at least, put an idea in Jami's head.

"I demand a vacation, or I'll make a complaint to whoever you complain to about things like that," she said as forcefully as she could manage.

"Me," Harley grinned. "You complain to me. And Jamila,

my heroine—have I ever denied you anything since the project began?"

"You mean except freedom?"

"Freedom's just another word for not enough work to do," Harley chuckled. "Okay. A month in Hawaii, on the project."

"Oh no. Too many fucking volcanoes there."

"Okay. Florida? Bahamas? Bermuda? Anywhere you like. You take a month and then come back here and work the models while Glen takes a month, wherever he likes. Okay?"

Even though it was perfectly okay, she hated agreeing with him. "What's the catch?"

"Brainstorm. Now. As a final summation before easy times."

"I hate you Harley."

If he looked pleased with himself, it was only because he won all the arguments, even when he lost.

"Glen," he said now with a wave of his hand. "Give me your wildest explanation. Doesn't matter how silly."

"Harley, what the hell do you think I've been sitting here doing all these months? Any idea I have, no matter how ridiculous, and I come here and model it furiously. I've tried everything," Glen said grimly.

"But have you sat back and tried to grasp the overall?"

"It's too big to grasp that way."

For Glen, it probably was, but to her horror, Jami immediately found ideas coming to mind. "Every so often, the earth changes the tilt of its axis. Maybe something like that is going on."

"No," Glen said. "I checked with the Geographic Survey. No change in tilt."

"Magnetic field?"

"Done all that."

"What about perturbations in the Earth's orbit?"

"There are always perturbations, and the Shastri Effect always causes a small one. But nothing unusual, and nothing regular."

"Collisions with meteors?"

"Done all that. Anyway, it's the wrong side."

Harley's woolly eyebrows raised with ponderous foreboding.

"Wrong side?" he asked, with a profound upward inflection.

Glen gazed at him bleakly. Jami thought furiously about *wrong sides*. Neither dared speak, but Harley's glare forced words into Glen's larynx.

"Umm... You mean you haven't noticed that the Shastri eruptions always occur within an hour of sunset."

Harley was aghast. He began whistling and put his hands in his pockets as if he intended to go for a stroll all over the campus. But he only went three paces, and then turned back. His voice was barely a murmur. "You mean we missed something as obvious as that?"

"I'm sure I pointed it out several times."

"Glen, you've pointed out ten million bits of data in the last few months. Was it underlined and asterixed and whatever?"

"Why should it be? It can't mean anything."

Harley advanced and leaned until his nose was a millimetre from Glen's. "It has to mean something."

Jami thought about sundown. It was ridiculous. Millions of dollars of state of the art technology and they had failed to notice something that would have been obvious to any peasant farmer. Yes, yes, always at sunset.

Admittedly, it had been some time other than sunset in whatever place they were in at the time and you needed to notice that the local times of the eruptions always started with a one. But because it was impossible for volcanic eruptions to be related to the time of day, no one had looked. She even remembered noticing all the ones and thinking nothing of it herself. She was alive now, and looking at Harley Thyssen.

"Yes, it must. But what?"

"Glen said it," Harley said and even gave him a thump on the shoulder. "Never occurred to me because we were looking at it the wrong way. We've been looking into the earth to try and see what's in there. Instead, we've forgotten to look outward."

"You *do* mean meteors," Jami said.

"Not at all," Harley said, unusually serious now. "Consider the Earth as a planet, orbiting the sun, rotating. What is sunset?"

"The trailing edge," Glen pointed out.

"That's right."

"If it was the leading edge," Glen went on, "then we could think about collisions with whatever might lay in the Earth's path as it travels around the sun. But it's the trailing edge."

"The most protected part of the planet," Jami thought.

"Exactly." Harley demanded. "So how come it always occurs at what is theoretically the least probable time?"

Jami tried to think. There had to be something.

"The slipstream," she said.

"Explain."

"Consider a sonic boom. The air is forced above and below the aircraft's wing and collides with itself on the trailing side. Suppose we were hitting unusually intense cosmic rays or something that was divided and did not go through to the surface. The impact would flow around the planet, in the magnetic field or troposphere or wherever, and then all meet up exactly on the other side of the planet and impact with the other half of itself."

"Not bad," Harley said. "But the older less aero-dynamically sound aircraft were always destabilised by the build-up of air in front of the wing before it broke the sound barrier. Similarly, although the real impact might be behind the earth as it travels in its orbit, still there would have to be some indication of the leading side. There must surely be a point of impact at the front initially."

He was pointing at her, like trying to move information by means of a cattle prod. She felt herself clutching furiously, desperate for answers now. "Maybe it's because of something gathering at the rear, like an exhaust. It builds up and then blows."

"Better. But Shastri comes from within. The eruptions are outward, not inward. And with all those satellites up there, someone would be detecting something."

"And none of them are," Glen said bitterly. "Because I've checked the data from every fucking one of them."

"So it has to be in the mantle."

"Yes," Jami was saying. "Some force strikes the leading

edge of the planet, affects the Asthenosphere, the impact flows through the mantle around the core and meets at the back side and it blasts out through the nearest available weak spot in the lithosphere."

"I'm liking that better," Harley was saying. "But I still don't like the idea of the planet running into something that can affect the mantle but have no discernible effect on the crust. We have too much detection stuff out there for that to be possible."

"So, whatever it is must already be in the mantle," Jami realised. "And somehow accumulates at the back and reaches bursting point, egressing on the trailing edge."

"Just like any conventional rocket," Harley said.

Glen was already tapping the keyboard. "Let me run that through all the existing models."

"We're getting somewhere now," Harley was saying. "But we still need to figure out what it is that could affect the mantle this way."

"How are you on fluid dynamics?" Jami asked innocently.

"It must be some sort of bubble, generated by God knows what," Harley was remembering. "It must be able to become less dense as it grows larger—perhaps many small bubbles accumulating—drawn toward the trailing edge by the momentum of the Earth, overcoming gravity as it becomes less dense until it reaches a certain size and it hits the inner side of the crust."

"It blows out through the nearest crack or vent or rift, and then the process starts all over again," Glen was saying. "Look, you can see it here."

"Not quite," Harley said. "Since the time span between each instance is diminishing but the other factors are constants, some part of the bubble must remain. When it blows off steam, denser gases remain, it becomes heavier and gravitation obliges it to fall back toward the core. But each time it is just a little larger, and so takes less time to build up until it hits the crust again. How does that model, Glen?"

"Give me a few thousand nanoseconds, will you?"

"Okay," Jami was saying, mostly to fill the gap while Glen

worked. "So the time and trailing edge theory determines the longitude of the event. How about the latitude?"

"I'm still working on that," Harley shrugged.

"And then why the oscillation between the northern and southern hemispheres?"

"Position of the moon," Glen cut in as he punched keys furiously.

"Hey?"

"If the moon is trailing, it's northern, if leading, southern."

"You might have mentioned that earlier," Harley grumbled.

"It's factored into the models."

"Okay. Lunar gravitation, I suppose, would have some effect on the position of the bubble."

"Why not?" Jami said with a throw-away look.

Harley looked a picture of patience and he smiled and twiddled his thumbs. "I'm pleased with that."

"It's just a theory, Harley," Jami said cautiously.

"But it's a theory that works."

"I'm sure we must be able to shoot holes in it somehow," Jami persisted.

"Fine. But until you do, I will consider it to be the truth."

"And you offer no explanation as to where this bubble came from."

"That is what I'm going to work on next," Harley said. "While Glen runs up models on that basis."

"And what will I be doing?"

"You'll be on vacation."

"You really think I'll be able to get this out of my mind?"

"And otherwise, you'll be doing what you are always doing, Jamila, my brilliant protege."

"Which is?"

"Trying to humiliate me by proving me wrong."

*

Harley Thyssen telephoned Brian Carrick from Moscow—of all

places— and informed him that there was a fax to follow with the dates for the next convergence.

"Make certain you meet all the dates, Brian, bang on. And if it goes wrong even slightly, let me know immediately."

The fax was an itinerary for the next gathering of the pilgrims. It was very detailed and precise and Brian had to sit and work on it for two hours to get the logistics right. By then he had run the pilgrims into a list of priorities according to degree of difficulty.

But first Felicity Campbell. He telephoned her in Wellington. "Thyssen wants the pilgrims on the move a week earlier than expected."

"Yes, Brian. I know. He warned me to expect it."

"The important date, as far as you are concerned, is the 9th of July. He wants us all to fly out then."

"The 9th? But the hit isn't due until the 20th. Why so early?"

"He wants us to have a week's holiday—vacation he called it—in Bali. And you can bring your family if you want. Paid for by the project."

"Won't they get in the way..."

"Not if you put them on a plane home by the 16th."

"I'm not sure if I can organise this, Brian. The kids have school. Wendell has his work..."

"But an all-expenses paid week in Bali at the Kota Sands. How can any Kiwi say no to that in mid-winter?"

"You're right. I'll see what I can do. How are things going there?"

"Oh, Kevin's security men are a little overbearing, but otherwise fine."

"The girls coping all right in the office?"

"Like pigs in shit."

"And how about you?"

"Me. I'm fine. Be a bit busy now this has come through."

"I meant you and Judy."

"Not so fine. I'm out again. But it isn't your fault this time, Fee."

"I still feel guilty."

"Our marriage has needed a work over for a long time. Now it's getting it. Don't worry. It'll sort itself, one way or the other."

"And Harley and Jami—where are they?"

"Harley's in Moscow. Jami's in Bermuda."

"Got to go, Brian. I'll need a week to organise the new sleepers. Ought to see you around about the first. Okay?"

"Okay. I'll book you Wellington-Melbourne on the 1st, your husband plus two Wellington-Bali to meet you there on the 9th. Send you the tickets and details. Hooroo."

Next he rang Joe Solomon, whom he knew would resist every aspect of the plan, so he only told him about Bali.

"I hate holidays, Brian. And what the hell is a bloke in a wheelchair going to do for a week in Bali?"

"Sit on the beach and fish and stuff."

"You ever tried to push a wheelchair through sand?"

"Get pissed and eat yourself stupid."

"I can do that in Perth."

"I can arrange for you to fly direct Perth-Bali on the 9th if you'd prefer that to coming here."

"Bloody Harley. Can you ask him to make it a bit later?"

"No, he's in Moscow."

"He's where???" Joe erupted.

Brian hung up before he said something even more stupid, if that was possible.

It was then evening and he knew he would catch Lorna and Chrissie tomorrow, so he took himself to the pub for a beer and a counter tea and from there he would just make it to the Casino in time to catch the end of Andromeda's show.

"I know. Bali, then Hong Kong," she told him.

She was in her dressing room, sitting at the mirror, taking off her make-up. There was barely room for Brian to stand behind her and the atmosphere of scents and perfumes would have knocked him flat on his back had there been room to fall.

"How could you know? I only found out today."

"Because my man Joel received a couple of mysterious bookings that just had to be arranged by Harley."

She hunted amongst the bottles and tubes on the top of the dresser and came up with a card.

"Kota-Sands, Bali, 8th to the 14th of July but I gotta be there on the 6th for rehearsals. Then the Hong Kong Sheridan from the 22nd for a month."

"Bloody hell."

"The reason Harley is smarter than the rest of us is because he learns from his mistakes," Andromeda smiled.

*

"...the sky split in two, and high above the forest the whole northern part of the sky appeared to be covered in fire. At that moment I felt a great heat as if my shirt had caught fire... I wanted to pull off my shirt and throw it away but at that moment there was a bang in the sky, and a mighty crash was heard. I was thrown to the ground about three sajenes away from the porch and for a moment I lost consciousness. My wife ran out and carried me into the hut. The crash was followed by a noise like stones falling from the sky, or guns firing. The Earth trembled, and when I lay on the ground I covered my head because I was afraid stones might hit it. At that moment when the sky opened, a hot wind, as from a cannon, blew past the huts from the north. It left its mark on the ground..."

Nikolai Singara closed the book on his own fingers to mark the place and gazed serenely across the table, where Thyssen sat, pouting.

"That's all of them," he said, and Thyssen nodded.

"No other eye-witness accounts?"

"No," Nikolai smiled with patience. "So, tell me. Is there to be some explanation of why I am reading to you this admittedly fascinating but nevertheless very ancient piece of our history."

Because it's in Russian, Thyssen somehow managed to avoid saying. You didn't make trite jokes in the presence of any Russian, especially not one of their most eminent scholars.

"I was hoping for something, but I think we have to agree it was a comet," Thyssen said sadly.

"On the face of it, to be sure. But remember, these eyewitness accounts were the translated words of the very primitive Tungus people, and they were making their accounts five years after the event."

"Five years?"

"Alas, the officials of the Czar considered the affairs of court infinitely more important than the mere collision between the Earth and a giant meteor."

"That was what they thought at first?"

"Oh yes. But even so, they knew it was so massive an explosion—it was felt in Moscow, the shock wave circled the earth twice, and they could read at night in the city streets by the scattered light for a week. But it was way out in Siberia and just a bunch of dumb peasants and who cared? When the expedition lead by Kulik finally arrived, they saw the forest flattened in that radiating pattern we've come to know so well for a diameter of ten kilometres from the centre. They expected to find a crater bigger than the one in Arizona. But there was nothing."

"Yes. I know," Thyssen said. "Extraordinary. Are you satisfied by the comet explanation?"

"Those who made it are completely. And you should be too. It is the only way to explain how the object left no trace. The ice, burning up in the upper atmosphere... I don't need to tell you this, Harley. But I do want to know why it tickles your fancy some ninety years after the event."

"Oh, I was just looking at the Oz Baykal region on the map and happened to notice Tunguska nearby. It set me thinking..."

"One thousand kilometres nearby. You think these matters are related, Harley?"

"No reason why they should be..."

"But you wanted to hear the eye-witness accounts from the original Russian to see if there was any mention of people being rendered unconscious and waking up eight days later."

Thyssen laughed. Of course he knew he could never fool this old man and hadn't really been trying. Nikolai loved mind games, and being allowed to show he could read Thyssen's mind was plainly giving the old man the greatest pleasure. It was fun for Thyssen as well.

"I can see it is hopeless to try and keep secrets from you, Nikolai."

"And alas, having found no such reports, does that mean your theory is confounded?"

"I guess."

"You don't sound completely convinced."

Thyssen smiled. "As you say, inarticulate peoples, and long after the event."

"Still, Harley, it is always a difficulty, isn't it, when the evidence refuses to fit the theory."

"It usually means you need a new theory."

"Or better evidence," Nikolai smiled, and snapped the book shut. "I know a place where a most reasonable coffee may be had."

It was a joy to talk to the old man, his mentor from Greenpeace days. Now retired, Nikolai still remained a man of great influence around the Kremlin. He was, after all, one who had tasted the temptations of the West and returned to Russia quite untainted. Although it took a few years of impeccable behaviour in the gulags to prove it.

Thyssen had arrived in Moscow and contacted Nikolai immediately. His only fore-warning had been a one page summary of Project Earthshaker emailed a week beforehand. A desire to speak with the Secretary for the Interior? Within an hour, Singara was able to report that the Secretary would be able to fit them in tomorrow, at two. With time to fill, they had strolled into the Museum of Science, and Thyssen, rather casually, had asked about Tunguska.

On the 30th of June, 1908, something hit the Earth, big enough to flatten 2000 square kilometres of forest and be felt all around the world yet it left no crater, no fragments, no radioactivity, no trace. A touch, it was called, of the finger of God. No human had been killed or injured, although a vast herd of reindeer had been destroyed. The biggest explosion in recorded history and hardly anyone noticed.

Nikolai had, at Thyssen's request, read to him the eye-witness accounts without surprise nor complaint. Thyssen supposed that the old man had already double-guessed him. As he always did. He had not, for instance, bothered yet to ask why Thyssen wanted to see the secretary, nor had the subject been raised. As they made their way through the smoggy streets toward the cafe, Nikolai finally said. "Harley, I do not believe that the Tunguska event was a comet."

"Really? Why not?"

"Because a comet, at any size, would have been visible in the night skies for some weeks or even months before the event. And no such thing was reported."

"So what do you think it was, Nikolai?"

"The same thing you think it was, Harley."

In the warmth of the cafe, they sipped the coffee from big mugs. Nikolai was ready to play the next stage of the game. Without preamble, he said with a mischievous look over his steaming mug. "So, you believe that there are —sleepers, you call them?—at Baykal."

"I know there are. And I know exactly where they are. Precise co-ordinates."

"How many of these unfortunates do you think there are?"

"I have no idea. There may only be one, but I suspect more."

"One hundred and ninety-seven, according to unofficial reports."

"That many?"

"Unofficial reports are always inaccurate."

"Unlike official reports?"

"Official reports are only usually inaccurate. Unofficial ones always are. But the real difference, Harley, is that the degree of inaccuracy of official reports can always be assessed by political analysis, whereas this is not possible with unofficial information."

"Still, I have towards two hundred people in there."

"I understand that is so."

"Interned, I suppose."

"Quarantined. The contagion being presently unknown."

"And is the Secretary likely to accept my assurances that there is no contagion?"

"Hardly."

"Is he aware that—what shall we call it—relapses are likely when they get to the pilgrim stage?"

"They have seen it for themselves. A mass escape was attempted."

"Did any of them actually escape?"

"No."

"Officially no or unofficially no."

"Actual no. We are not complete barbarians, Harley. These people are receiving the best medical care available."

"I see."

"And they are not unaware of Project Earthshaker. They have heard all of the unofficial reports concerning it."

"The trouble with our unofficial reports are that they are always accurate."

"Yes, we know that, Harley. And your official reports never are."

"Will it be effective, do you think, to plead with the Secretary for the release of these people into my custody?"

"I should think not. They are Russian subjects, with no permits to leave the country. It would be most irregular for such permits to be issued to persons in an unstable medical condition."

"Meaning?"

"They don't trust you, Harley. They suspect that the sleepers have suffered an ecological accident which you know about and they don't. They suspect that you might be trying to find some way to blame Russian scientists for your own ecological disaster."

"I though the KGB was all wrapped up."

"It is, but it's mentality remains."

"So, I shouldn't plead for their release."

"It would be fruitless, and, I should think, unwise."

"Then I need a better plan."

"A Rambo-style, single handed rescue, perhaps?"

"Is that what you suggest?"

"No, Harley. It was a joke. I'm sorry. I'm not very good at them."

"Yes you are."

"In any case, I think the plan that you have in mind is the correct one, Harley."

"Which is?"

"You don't want the Secretary to release those people at all. You want him to assure you that they will stay exactly where they are."

*

Chrissie watched in amazement as the two women confronted each other with broad smiles and admiring looks. Lorna, in a smart blue mini-suit and green beret perched on her flowing red hair, and the American woman, in a similar suit, long black hair, about ten years older but not showing it.

"Sit down, Mrs. Tribe," Lorna said. She might have been asking the journalist to sit on a hand grenade.

Stella Tribe perched on the edge of the chair and produced from her crocodile skin handbag a small tape recorder which she switched on and set between them on the desk before she smiled warmly and asked. "Do you mind?"

In reply, Lorna Simmons picked up the tape recorder, switched it off and handed it back to her. "What I have to tell you you'll be able to write by hand."

Without the slightest flicker of protest, Stella Tribe took out her notebook, pen, poised to write, saying. "I really do appreciate this interview, Miss Simmons. You just don't know how much trouble I've had trying to get to speak to one of you people."

"Oh yes I do," Lorna smiled. She wasn't fooled by Stella's show of innocence.

"So, tell me, Miss Simmons, when did you..."

"No questions."

"I need some background..."

"You have all the background you need."

"A statement then?"

"Exactly. I am Lorna Simmons and hereafter I am spokesperson for Project Earthshaker. You want to know something, you talk to me. The project is classified Top Secret by both the US and Australian Governments so you are warned that any attempt to interview other members of the project will be a breach of the official secrets act and I can assure such a breach will be prosecuted to the full extent of the law."

Chrissie was delighted. She had listened to Lorna rehearsing that as she paced the office all afternoon and, as far as she could tell, Lorna had got it word perfect.

"I understand," Stella Tribe said seriously.

"Good. I want you to organise a press conference for me, tomorrow afternoon, anytime, anywhere and make sure all your competitors are there. I will answer any questions that I am able to."

"Will Professor Thyssen be there?"

"No. Just me."

"I wasn't aware you had any training in sciences, Miss Simmons."

"I don't. But I have been carefully instructed in what I can and can't say."

"Well, Miss Simmons, I'll do what I can. But I doubt that you'll get a full press turn-out if you're all that's on offer."

"I know. So I'm going to give you a scoop, Mrs. Tribe, which will make sure they're all be there."

"Oh really?"

"Take this down."

The pen hovered over the paper.

"Shortly before sunset, on the 20th of July, a massive earthquake will occur in Western Europe, at about 7.4 on the moment-magnitude scale. Probably in the Mediterranean region. We expect it to trigger a number of volcanic eruptions in the vicinity."

"I assume Professor Thyssen has made this prediction?"

"He has."

"He's been wrong in the past."

"From which errors he has learned. This one will be right."

"7.4. That's awfully serious, isn't it?"

"Depends on how close the epicentre is to populated areas. In 1993, a 6.2 at Latik in India killed nearly 10,000 people, but a year later in Bolivia, an 8.3 killed only ten."

"Is that part of the statement?"

"That's all of it."

"You really don't give me much to work with."

"You can go now, Mrs. Tribe. Thank you for your attention."

"I have just a few..."

"Are you leaving or do I have to get security to throw you out."

Lorna, clearly, was warming to the task. She was still all smiles as she herded Stella Tribe out the door. Then she turned to Chrissie, and all trace of the smiles were gone.

"How'd I go?"

"You were great, Lorna."

"And tomorrow, I'll have to be even greater."

"If the prediction is right."

"Yes," Lorna said sadly. "It's very good of Harley to make me the one who looks silly if he proves to be wrong. But that's the job."

She was packing her things, ready to make a dash for it. Chrissie realised that she had a question. "If he can predict this event, he can predict all the future ones."

"I guess so. The dates are on a fixed diminishing scale, or so he said."

"Do you have the dates?"

"No. But you can probably work them out for yourself. Gotta go. Bye."

Chrissie was left alone in the office. Brian was out organising their coming expedition, Wagner off guarding something somewhere. Yes, she had calculated the dates, but she would rather have had Harley's official figures.

On the other hand, it might have been better if she had more time, since she had certainly achieved little along the line of what she regarded to be her primary purpose—that of converting her fellow pilgrims in preparation of the Apocalypse. She was fully ready herself. She wore simple dresses that did not follow the line of her form, always white. She no longer wore make-up, nor did she interfere with the natural growth and colour of her hair and nails. She was studying The Book of Revelation assiduously, and looking for clues in the real world. But, apart from the spiritual guidance of Father Gilbert, she was all alone.

Andromeda Starlight wasn't about to believe in any God but herself—Gaia—whose personification she had completely embraced. "Christianity is out of date, Chrissie. You must get with the new religion."

It was discouraging that the one person who had been converted had given herself to a different faith.

Brian Carrick was more thoughtful. "I seem to recall that the Messiah is supposed to turn up, before we can have the Apocalypse."

"And the Anti-Christ," Chrissie murmured.

"Let's assume that's Harley," Brian chuckled. "And is there anything in your bible that says the Messiah can't take the form of a French-Vietnamese female?"

"That is blasphemy, Brian."

"I was trying to be nice."

"And heresy, and sacrilege, and… and…"

"No reason why it can't be so at all."

Lorna was an even more hopeless case.

"I wonder what turns God on? I hope he's a bit of a spunk." she mused.

Kevin Wagner believed only in himself. "The Bible got it wrong, Chris. It's man who made God in his own image."

Joe Solomon was a Communist and knew all about the pernicious effects of the 'opiate of the masses'.

"If bloody Jehovah is behind this business, we're all fucked. He lies about everything and can't be trusted. Read your Old

Testament, you'll see. A megalomaniacal mass-murderer. Give him a chance to destroy a whole planet and he'll jump at it. And no one will be saved if he has anything to do with it."

Jami Shastri she had only got to speak to briefly.

"Put it out on the net, kiddo. All the other god-bothering whackos will think you a wonder."

And as for Harley Thyssen.

"It is as valid a theory as any of the others, at this stage, Chrissie. I'm afraid I can find no argument against it."

Yes, it was going to be a tough job all right, but who ever said it would be easy. Nightly Chrissie worried about them, poor heathens all hell-bound, and there didn't seem to be anything she could do to help them.

But she had gained something. She followed Jami's advice and put herself on the internet using the computer Harley had provided in the office, introducing herself and her message to the world. After a month, she was getting a hundred hits a day and stacks of email. There were some abusive responses but mostly everyone was asking her what they should do next.

"Pray," she told them, following Father Gilbert's advice. "And tell everyone you can about this. We have so little time and so very many souls to save."

She didn't see any wisdom in mentioning that she had not managed to save a single soul herself at this stage, and so doing probably even doomed her own.

*

So they went to Bali, with *Earthshaker Tours*, as Brian Carrick joked. In the end they all went by scheduled flights, the USAF 707 being unavailable because it had been held back to bring the control group and medical team and equipment later. By then it had become conspicuous that they were being kept separated from the survival team from Antarctica.

"Scared we might pollute them with Thyssenism," Lorna said.

They spent the week-end relaxing at Kuta Beach and environs. Andromeda Starlight was already there and in full song at the Paradise Room, but Felicity and her family preferred to head inland to Ubud. Wagner was off looking for rock faces to scale, Brian and Joe Solomon settled into a beachside bar and saw little reason to stray, Lorna was left to frolic on the beaches with no less than three admiring males at any given time while Chrissie sat meditating in the shade. There was no sign of Thyssen himself.

Each day, Brian organised tours in which they could participate if they wished, but on the 13th, which was the Tuesday, a compulsory tour had been organised.

"Why compulsory?" Solomon demanded.

"Because that's they way Thyssen organised it, and he's paying for all this."

They all went, in the end. They flew to Jakarta where a boat waited to take them on the Krakatoa tour. Though there remained little of the island left to see, that was the point and the enormity of it was not lost on them. Next day they roamed Jakarta and then returned to Bali, overflying two active volcanoes—Semeru and Mt Bromo—along the way. It was plainly intended to give them some idea of the sort of forces they were dealing with. They were told tales of the year without a summer in Northern Europe, caused by the explosion of Tambora in 1815.

Until the second weekend they were left to their own devices with the warning that they should be ready to get down to business on Monday. That morning they were gathered in a transit lounge at Denpassar, waiting for the link.

"Why here?" Lorna asked.

"As near as I can figure," Felicity explained. "The control group is on a boat, parked in the ocean about two hundred kilometers south-east of here. Which means the halfway point between them and the Mongolian pilgrims is Hong Kong. Harley is waiting for us there. He's so confident that he's booked us all into the Hong Kong Sheridan."

They sat about the lounge, watching Chrissie for she was always the first to detect anything.

A few minutes before noon, Chrissie smiled and told them she could feel it. Moments later, a telephone report informed them that two members of the control group had linked. Within an hour, all except Joe Solomon and Lorna were linked in.

"Can't we go now," they protested.

"We have to be sure, or all this is for nothing," Felicity persisted. She was nearing her wits end. Plainly a week on holiday with her family had not relaxed her. Lorna linked shortly before two and they all glared at Joe.

"Are you sure your detectors are stuck on properly?" Wagner asked him.

"It's not my fucking fault!" Joe snapped back.

"All that sweating. Maybe they aren't connecting properly."

"I'm holding them down with me fucking fingers, okay?"

At twenty past two, he linked, and they headed for the waiting aircraft.

"We'll be in Hong Kong at sundown," Brian told them.

"Isn't this the time Harley predicted?" Andromeda wondered.

"Yeah," Brian pointed out. "But we're about seven hours behind the time zone at the latitude he named."

They landed in Hong Kong and just after eight, gliding in amidst the mountains and apartment buildings to where Harley Thyssen met them as they came through the aero-bridge.

"Well, is this the place?" he asked them.

They knew it was, almost.

"Just over there a little way," Brian considered. They all agreed.

Just over there a little way was Hong Kong Island with its luxury hotels to which they proceeded on the ferry. When, eventually, they came to rest, they saw they were standing right in the middle of the lobby of the Hong Kong Sheridan and Thyssen bought them all drinks.

"All right, Harley," Andromeda smiled. "You've hit the spot, right on."

"Certainly near enough for my liking," Joe Solomon concurred.

"So, let's see if I understand how you did this," Brian said suspiciously. "By manipulating the position of the control group in their boat, you were able to cause the focal point to be right where we are standing."

"You got it," Harley said proudly.

"Why here?" Chrissie asked.

"Most comfortable place I could think of," Harley grinned. "Anyone disapprove?"

"What a clever little Harley," Lorna grinned and raised her cocktail in a toast to him.

*

In Sicily was twin cratered Mount Etna, at 10,902 feet and climbing, the tallest volcano in Europe, continuously active since the days of Pythagoras. In ancient times its continual bursts of flame and lava and the constant rumblings within the mountain gave rise to the myth of Vulcan, the Roman God of fire, toiling on his forge deep beneath the earth. Here too, Odysseus encountered mad one-eyed Cyclops. In the fertile soil, farmers occupied lava flows only 70 years old and sightseers engulfed the region whenever the word was out that activity was intensifying.

There was a place where the lava flow was so thick and turgid that they had built a concrete platform for the tourists to stand and watch the heated rock creep forward, an inch or so each hour. With the spectacular sunsets that always accompanied volcanoes, the platform was full that evening. And the wall of incandescent lava that had inched along for centuries, suddenly leapt upon them and swallowed them. Vulcan growled in rage and all the new farmers on the lava flow and all the tourists to Etna were vaporised in a final moment of seething terror.

Across the bay from Naples, Vesuvius let fly with one single great ball of cloud, pumped into the clear twilight sky to cast a deep shadow over the ruins of Pompeii and all points south of the city. The three million inhabitants of Naples and environs felt the earth shake briefly and then heard the roar, and when they saw the cloud they dreaded that the apocalyptic moment that had threatened their city for 6000 years had finally come. But then, as the cloud rose and dispersed into the upper atmosphere, the moment was passed and the Queen of Vulcan fell silent again.

Stromboli, the lighthouse of the Mediterranean, an island cone that burps with great regularity every twenty minutes without disturbing the villagers below its slopes, broke its routine to emit a thundering blast that knocked a hundred feet off the top of the mountain and showered it into the sea all about the island.

Across the Lipari Islands, the earth shook and the sea broiled and the black plume brought on nightfall an hour early. Hot muddy rain fell on the villages and the people ran to their boats with their ears covered, such was the impact of the blast. Vulcano and its child Vuncanello roared to life for the first time since 1890.

But it was away from roaring Vesuvius and thundering calderas of the Lipari Islands that the full force of the impact was felt. On mainland Italy, inland from Salerno in Province Lucania, a sudden earthquake struck. Here the villages that had clung to hilltops for centuries tumbled into the valleys below and great fissures opened in the earth, from some of which fire burst forth. A deep cloud enveloped the landscape and the people blundered about, screaming the names of lost loved ones in their blindness. A region twenty kilometres in diameter was completely destroyed and with it 4000 souls. And the damage stretched fifty kilometres from the epicentre, and fires raged amongst the forests and vineyards and olive groves, killing hundreds more and causing untold thousands of injuries.

In a street cafe in Rome, a sudden silence amid the urban cacophony told Jami Shastri something had happened. All about, men—for there were only men—clustered about cars with their radios or televisions in the cafes and bars. Commuters stopped in a stride, their mobile phones or pocket radios clutched to their ears, gasping frantic words and all around them.

An Indian girl amongst Italians, Jami had to ask the waiter to translate what had happened.

"All of the south. She blow up. Boom."

At this news, Jami simply nodded. She paid for her cappuccino, walked to a kerb and hailed a taxi to the airport.

9
CORE PROBLEMS

When the First Secretary spoke her name, she wanted to fall right through the floor. It was no different now, she tried telling herself, than any of the other innumerable medical conferences that she had addressed in her career, but there was no persuading herself of that. In this room of shiny coloured marble and frescoed walls and ceilings by Michelangelo's apprentices, at the head of a huge table of polished mahogany, in plush matching chairs with pure silk liners, was the most powerful gathering of people she had ever seen in one room.

The First Secretary of Italy, the Deputy Secretary General of the United Nations, the European Director of the Red Cross, the European Secretaries for Sciences and Medicine, a Brigadier General in charge of the NATO Central Region, three officials from United Europe, and she—Felicity Campbell, MD. To her shame, she had forgotten all of their names—though not their titles—while everyone one of them knew exactly who she was.

She rose to speak on knees trembling in a way they hadn't since she was a student doing her first medical demonstration. This was both the worst and most important moment of her life, and she feared mightily that she was inadequate in every way.

All along, she had seen herself as seconded on a temporary basis. Already the Earthshaker team possessed nine medical staff more senior and more experienced and better qualified than herself and at any time she expected her position to be usurped by one of them, if not all. She believed that she would be overrun by events and finally left behind to her domestic bliss and a dream of private practice. But unfailingly they had accepted her authority without question, although that was only because they knew that behind her stood the formidable bulk of Harley Thyssen. But still she had been a pretender, waiting to be exposed. Only now she realised that she never would be—or if she was it wouldn't matter. Thyssen had caused her to become recognised as the world's leading authority on the Shastri Effect and now she stood to speak in that capacity, in her own right. Now, the pretence would no longer be sustainable. Nor would her dreams of home and peace.

If she'd had any residual doubts, they had evaporated when the telephone beside her bed in the Sheraton rang and she heard Harley's voice thunder down the line.

"It's happened. Get your skates on. We're meeting in the lobby cafe in twenty minutes."

They were all there. Andromeda was in her performance dress; a dazzling spangled thing that, Felicity realised, bore the colours and patterns of the earth viewed from space. She and Lorna had plainly enjoyed one or two cocktails too many and had entered leaning on each other exchanging fits of giggling. Now, they obediently sipped coffee. So did Kevin and Brian, both wet haired from showers and puffy-eyed from sleep. Joe Solomon rolled his wheelchair up to the table and ordered tea while Chrissie lounged serenely on a couch. And Thyssen, massive, was busily ensuring that they were all ready to listen.

"Okay. The hit was Southern Italy, just inland from Salerno if you know the place. Jami has already flown over the area and reports a wide area of devastation. It's much bigger than expected. Every volcano from Etna to Vesuvius erupted simultaneously, which is newly different and frightening, but the epicentre was away from the mountains and whole towns and villages have been destroyed. The primary impact zone was about twenty kilometres in diameter, and all around the circumference we can expect there to be hundreds of sleepers. If so, it gets deadly serious from now on."

"But we don't know for sure?" Felicity said hopefully.

"It was a definite Shastri event. You can bet on it."

"Shit," Brian muttered and they all nodded agreement to that.

They sat around one table, their coffee and tea ignored now, while Thyssen sat on the top of the next table, his hands pressed together with an uncommon show of anxiety.

"Okay, so now we go into action. First job is to get in there and collect and tag all the sleepers. Fee, when we hit the ground, you will be in command. You just do it any way you can. No doubt you'll have all sorts of difficulties with emergency services and local authorities, not to mention outside agencies, all of whom will be getting under your feet, but you just get in and do it."

"I can't even imagine how," Felicity heard herself say nervously.

"Hopefully, it will become clearer as we proceed," Thyssen sighed. "Kevin. You go in and liaise with Fee and Jami and whoever else you have to and secure the whole situation. The important thing is this. If we lose track of just one of the sleepers, we lose the ability to predict the next pilgrim focal point. You all saw how difficult it was to get six of you to the right place. Next time we might be moving hundreds. Which is where you come in Brian. You have to start figuring out the best and easiest ways of moving these people around. And therefore, in co-ordination with Kevin, how to tag them so you can round them up when you need to."

"Fuckin' hell," Brian gasped.

"I think that a likely prediction," Thyssen agreed. "Plane leaves as soon as we get to the airport. We will take the 707, and the medical team."

"Right," Brian nodded and waved a finger around the room. "What about the others?"

"Andromeda—you can go to bed. Lorna, you're with me so you better hit the black coffee."

"Oh goody," Lorna breathed sleepily. "Where are we going, boss?"

"Rome with the others, then on to Geneva and Brussels and anywhere else we have to go to talk to the top brass and get Felicity, Kevin and Brian the co-operation they need. And you promote the cause all the way."

"Aye, aye, sir."

"Joe and Chrissie—you make your way home in your own time..."

"I want to go to Italy," Chrissie said adamantly.

For the first time in Felicity's memory, Thyssen hesitated. He looked at diminutive French-Vietnamese girl thoughtfully for a long moment, and eventually she continued. "The dying and the injured will need my ministrations." To which Thyssen offered a dubious look. "Anyway," Chrissie added with a faint smile. "You'll need me. I speak Italian."

Thyssen was floored. Felicity could see it took everything he had to restrain himself, but somehow he managed to cave in. You could see this wasn't something that happened to him every day. "All right. But remember, once this gets underway, the paperwork will be piling up in Melbourne."

"Direct it to my office," Joe Solomon said. "I'll take care of it until Christine is back in harness."

Joe Solomon co-operating? Felicity could hardly believe her ears by then.

"Thanks, Joe," Thyssen said with breath-taking sincerity.

"I'll just hang in here a couple of days and make my own way home," Joe added quietly. "And I can organise the control group back to base if you want to get to Italy immediately, Brian."

It was just too much. Thyssen, unresisted, was at a loss. The glance he exchanged with Felicity said so plainly.

"Good on yer, mate," Brian said in vague disbelief.

They were a team, working together as harmonious as any team could, and even the man who had moulded them was astonished. And so it continued as they flew into the disaster zone. There was Jami at her shoulder, making sure she understood the proportions of the disaster; there was Kevin poised to back up her every whim; there was Brian, harried and uncertain, ensuring their every transportation need was met.

They flew over the impact zone, a burned and blackened region and charred chunks of stone and rubble and naked tree trunks, still smouldering and burning freely in places. Jami had a map on which the circle was drawn and they flew that circle, noting the roads and villages and emergency bases.

"How the hell are we going to do this?" Wagner wondered.

"We just start where we land and work our way around the circle," Felicity told them. "And hope we find them all within the eight days."

They bounced the cracked and debris-strewn roads in a land rover, amid frantic Italians. It was total chaos, the emergency services seemed as disorganised as the victims and each little region seemed to have its own entirely different way of going about the evacuations. And no one wanted to understand anything they said. They would have been a total loss had Chrissie not been with them to interpret everything.

And then help arrived. The Red Cross moved in and immediately began to prepare lists of names of the victims, and NATO troops, mainly French and American, came to secure the region. From afar, Thyssen and Lorna had been doing their bit too. On the fourth day after the disaster, she was summoned to this meeting in Naples. A British diplomat named Sanderson was there to advise her on protocol and explain.

"They have all been advised of Project Earthshaker, and received instructions to co-operate and now they want you to tell them what to do."

Good old Harley, Felicity smiled.

So she stood before the table in the opulent marbled room. Before her, the heads of the most powerful organisations and all of them were there to hear her, mere Felicity Campbell, GP, from lowly New Zealand. Now Felicity Earthshaker. She cleared her throat and found it unnecessary. She was calm and clear, despite sleep deprivation, and it was all in her head and ready to flow.

"Gentlemen," she said resonantly. "This is what must be done..."

*

There aren't a lot of parks in a vertical city like Hong Kong where real estate is fabulously costly, and therefore not a lot of park benches. This one was really in the forecourt of a skyscraper owned by an oil company, but there was grass, there were trees, and a fine view of the harbour. Away to his right was the ferry terminal and a bustle of activity to occupy his mind while he waited—the sky was grey but it was warm and the office workers were all about, eating their lunches from bags. The British had gone and the Chinese came but you still sat on the grass and had lunch with your girlfriend. Absolutely everyone he could see— several thousand people he supposed—wore western dress— suits and ties, mini skirts and high heels—the regimental uniform of the world's most numerous army, the forces of commerce.

Joe Solomon did not have his lunch in a plastic bag and brought his own equivalent of a park bench anyway—plainly this Mr. Cornelius didn't know everything. He parked his wheelchair beside the bench, making a personal annex, and waited for the secret rendezvous to occur. His knowledge of such matters was entirely gleaned from Ian Fleming and John Le Carre. They were meeting in a public place, out in the open where they couldn't be overheard, in a noisy place where they could not be bugged; if Cornelius turned up in a trench coat all the clichés would be in place.

Fortunately, it was not so. He proved to be a craggy beanpole of a man, in a creased blue suit, bent at the middle, a week's grey stubble on his chin. In fact, he looked rather more like the park bench was his living room. Joe had dumped his briefcase on the seat to keep a place for him and the young couple who had sat there while he waited now moved on at the convenient time. John Cornelius advanced and if the wheelchair was a surprise, he did not let it show.

"Mr. Solomon, is it?"

"I guess you must be Mr. Cornelius."

"Please, call me John." Joe doubted that he ever would.

The briefcase was moved to the frame attached to the wheelchair which was its customary position and Cornelius suffered to bend his long frame and seat himself. Joe could see he had a bad back and probably piles. He was at least sixty, his face heavily lined, and what was once a fine crop of white hair now thinning.

"Ah," Cornelius breathed. "Nice to get out. It's a lovely view from here, don't you think?"

"Nice to get out of where?" Joe asked. He suspected it might have been a cave or a soft spot under a bridge somewhere.

"Oh, the hotel and all that. I don't get out as much as I would like, and I haven't seen Hong Kong since the handover."

"So where do you usually live?" Joe asked. Had this man really come to Hong Kong, just to see him? No. The location had not been known when the meeting was originally proposed.

"Where the work takes me."

"What work?"

"A book. I'm writing a book. Research, you know."

"What's it about?"

"Oh, the old agency days. All I know really."

"But you don't work for the CIA now."

"Heavens no. Fully retired. Ten years now."

Joe Solomon let that sink in. It certainly fitted the facts well enough, but it didn't explain anything.

"Look," Joe said. "I have to ask you a few questions before I decide whether I want to talk to you or not."

"Oh, indeed. Ask away. I have no secrets. Well, not any more."

"Just exactly what is your interest in this?"

"Personal. Private. But I can help. Let me explain."

"If you would."

"I was data analysis, as most agency men are. Office work. Computers. Hardly ever left Langley. Just a clerk, really. But, well, freedom of information, you know. Decided to write a book about the interesting things that came across my desk over the years, and I realised that I had never been to most of the places I was talking about. So I travel, and I write, filling in the gaps, so to speak. And Thyssen was one of the very interesting things that came across my desk."

"I should imagine."

"I doubt you do. He was one of ours, you see."

"You're pulling my leg."

"No, really. Think about it. A rabble rouser like him—student activist, Greenpeace, all that environmental lobbying. Made waves everywhere he went. Yet the Chair of Geology at a prestigious university was open to him, as was every door in Washington. Limitless funds for his pet project. To an outlaw? I don't think so. No. It's because he was undercover all the way, and now all those favours he is owed for invaluable service to the agency and various presidential executives are to be repaid. You see?"

"Are you speculating or do you know?"

"His inside reports on the Green movement came to me for years."

Joe hated it. It was ridiculous. This man was ridiculous. He wanted to just go away and ignore all this. Here was an Iago, pouring poison in his ear. Unless, of course, there was proof.

"You can prove this, of course."

"Of course," and he reached into his inner jacket pocket and extracted a creased and folded sheet of paper. He handed it over and Joe opened it. It was on CIA stationery. It was stamped TOP SECRET. It was signed Harley Thyssen. Joe read enough to give him the drift. Poison.

"You see," Cornelius was saying. "That it places the Rainbow Warrior in Auckland harbour on the appropriate future date. Information for which the French were most thankful."

Joe folded the document and handed it back. Back in his office in Perth, he could have faked such a document in *Photoshop* in about ten minutes. But perhaps the best plan was to go with the flow.

"There's more, I hope."

"Of course. I can get you all the proof you need."

"Why don't you tell me what you have to say instead," Joe decided. "And we'll deal with proving it later."

"Watch out for Thyssen. He has a hidden agenda. That's all I have to tell you."

Joe considered it. It was spoken with adequate sincerity, there was no doubt about that, but this man just did not add up. He seemed only vaguely outlined, as if he was unsure himself of just exactly why they were sitting there, having this conversation, about this man Thyssen.

"Look, Mr. Cornelius..."

"Oh, John, please."

"Okay, John. Look. I'm a lawyer. I spend my life looking for people's hidden agendas, even when they don't have one. It's a reflex these days. I assume it automatically. Understand?"

"Of course..."

"Thyssen is plainly a dangerous man. He's dangerous if he's a bad guy with a hidden agenda, but even if that isn't so, if he's a good guy with only honourable intentions, he still remains very dangerous. To everyone. To the whole bloody planet."

"I hear that."

"So unless you can be specific. Unless you can provide precise information and back it up with proof, there is no point to this discussion. Indeed, it amounts, as it stands, to no more than gossip."

Cornelius, positively scolded, could not have looked more dismayed. "Obviously, such matters are classified."

"Obviously..." Joe murmured. Inwardly, he was surprised to feel a sense of relief. More sure of his ground now, he decided on a different tack. "When did you meet him?"

"I never did. I told you. I just sat in an office and read reports."

"Which, themselves, might have been faked."

"Oh, I don't think so. But I see you are unwilling to believe me. That too doesn't surprise me. Many people have reported a reluctance to distrust Thyssen. He has that effect on people. They get mesmerised by him. I would, truly, love to meet him one day."

"Give me proof and I'll believe."

Cornelius was nodding and surveying the scene. "You are the proof, Joe. Living proof. They ran some sort of test and it went wrong somehow. And Thyssen has the task of measuring its effects. The Shastri Effect, you see."

"But no proof."

Cornelius slapped his knees and began the laborious task of rising from the seat. "We'll met again, Joe. Talk again. Perhaps by then your faith will be dented somewhat. I see that you are wisely skeptical. For the moment, that is enough."

"Yes, I think it is," Joe Solomon said.

He watched Cornelius until the man had shuffled completely out of sight. While he did he measured every part of his consciousness. He felt like his pocket had been picked only when he checked there was nothing missing. Only, of course, there had to be. He realised that he must have lost something that he never knew he had.

*

When the nurse summoned her to the telephone and said the call was from New Zealand, Felicity had to run through the dark stone corridors to the far side of the ancient building they had been given, a former convent converted into a hospital sometime around the Second World War. There had been few improvements since then, but it was a satisfactory base, even if it had little chance of accepting all of the sleepers, and no hope of accommodating all of their equipment. But it was an improvement over where they had started last week, in bivouac tents in the open.

"I'm sorry," Wendell said. "You must be very busy."

He was referring to the length of time it had taken her to reach the telephone and perhaps the fact that she was out of breath when she got there.

"We have time," she said, still gasping. "The project will pay our telephone bill."

"I wasn't concerned about that..." Wendell said testily.

Emotional matters on the telephone were always so vulnerable to misinterpretation.

"Is there anything wrong?" she asked desperately.

"No, no," Wendell grovelled. "We saw you on television. The girls wanted..."

"But everyone is okay?"

"Melissa has a slight cold and I'm suffering from an ingrown toenail. How about you?"

"I'm fine."

"You *looked* exhausted."

"I'm always fine when I'm exhausted. You know that."

"Megan wants to speak first."

"Put her on."

"Hullo mummy. We saw you on the telly."

They had been invaded by CNN and less conspicuously by other world media. Surprisingly, they had been helpful rather than a hindrance. In a scene of widespread chaos when information was desperately needed, there were few better sources than news camera crews. They had picked up at least a dozen sleepers that everyone else had missed because of prying eyes that seemed to see more clearly through a viewfinder than they did in reality.

"Yes. They interviewed me yesterday."

"Were you at the beach?"

She had to think. Beach? No. They were nowhere near the sea. But the interview had been in the open, in a barren yellow landscape, on a hot day with the wind in her hair and she was burned so very brown by the sun. Yes, she could understand beach.

"No, dear. I'm in Italy. It's a place where the sun shines a lot."

In fact she was having to raise her voice, because of the rain pelting on the roof.

"Are you going to be home for my birthday?"

Oh shit! The fifteenth, but what was today's date? Day Six was all that would come to mind. The hit was the 20th. Three weeks away...

"Oh yes. How could I miss something like that?"

"Daddy said there's lots of people to make better and you might not be able to."

"I'll be there, love. I promise."

"Okay mummy."

Without the slightest doubt about such a promise.

There was a pause and Melissa was next, her voice muffled by her cold.

"Hi mum. Is it dangerous there?"

"Not at all."

"They showed all these volcanoes erupting and earthquakes and fires and floods. Isn't that where you are?"

The rain that was falling was black with ash. The pillars of cloud from both Vesuvius and Stromboli could be seen in the distance on clear days.

"Not quite. Anyway, the volcanoes have quietened and the tremors stopped days ago. It's perfectly safe."

Yesterday a flash flood carried away a village further up the valley when a temporary dam formed by a landslide gave way. The day before, a stationary truck suddenly disappeared underground as the earth adjusted to the impact of the fissures. A nurse had been electrocuted by the inadequate wiring, and another infected when bitten by a rat in the main ward. All perfectly safe.

"They said you were going to raise all these zombies from the dead."

"Oh my god, did they?"

"Yes. Just like in Stephen King."

"Nothing like that, dear. The patients are in a coma, and are expected to regain consciousness soon. That's all."

"Will they be zombies but?"

"No. They will be perfectly normal, once they wake up."

"How do you do it?"

"I don't. I just know, from prior experience of these cases, that it will probably happen. We actually don't know much about the condition at all."

But the telephone was being handed to Gavin.

"It looks like we're going to make the finals."

"Oh well done."

"They start in September..."

"How have you been playing?"

"Won best afield three times this season and you missed all of them."

"I know. I'm sorry."

"And now you won't be here for the finals."

"Maybe not the semis, but I'll be there for the grand final, I promise you."

"If we make it."

"Well, you just better make it, hadn't you."

"Did you see the volcanoes erupt?"

"No. That happened before I got here. And they are miles away from where I am."

"But they said you knew it was going to happen."

"We can predict it to a limited extent."

"Then why can't you prevent it?"

"Can you imagine trying to stop a volcano from erupting?"

"But if you know it's going to happen, why don't you move the people away?"

"Because the prediction isn't accurate enough. Anyway, that's nothing to do with me. I just help the victims afterwards."

"But why do *you* have to do it?"

"Because nobody knows more about it than I do."

"Couldn't you teach someone else?"

"Look, Gav. I don't want to be here. It makes me so sad to be away from you all. Missing out on all the important things. I have to be here. That's how it is."

"Dad wants to speak now."

There was some sort of brief discussion before Wendell took the receiver. She could imagine the huffs and gruffs all too easily. But even the bad moments would have been a joy to her right then.

"So, there, see. We're all coping. Who needs you?"

"That isn't what I want to hear right now, Wen."

"Yes, well, I'm sorry. And you can add to that an extremely large apology for not understanding in the first place."

"I thought you *did* understand."

"Not like I do now. Truth is, we're all enormously proud of

you, now that you're famous. It's a lot easier being able to brag about you instead of being vague and secretive when people ask where you are."

"I guess so."

He lowered his voice. "Okay, so the telly's back on. Now you can tell me about this plague?"

"This what?"

"A new plague threatening all humanity, caused by the ejecta from volcanoes."

"Is *that* what they're saying?"

"No. That's what they're continually denying."

"There is no contagion whatsoever, Wen."

"But what is it?"

"When we know that, I'll be home for good."

"And what of the world blowing up in the middle of next year?"

"Are they denying that too?"

"We see that Vietcong prophetess of doom saying she'll lead the pilgrims to the land of milk and honey."

"That's been on the news?"

"A right little Mother Theresa with a Moses complex and a former refugee to boot. And *French*. Even Joan of Arc would have been under-qualified for the job."

"Jesus, Wen. How much hype are they giving this?"

"The full treatment, as far as I can see. Although the importance might be distorted here. It's not every day three Kiwi lassies make the international news."

"Who's the third?"

"The Irish redhead from Auckland who tells the official lies."

"Oh God, what's she been saying?"

"Don't panic. Make sure you know where your towel is."

The reference meant nothing to Felicity and she was too tired to bother working it out. Lorna, she could imagine, was parroting sensible things word perfect from Thyssen with her easy smile and calm demeanour. She responded with a huge sigh.

"It's all getting out of hand, Wen."

"I'll say it is. You were the sole voice of sanity amid a sea of madness."

"Well, at least that matches reality."

"So when can we expect you?"

"Oh. I ought to be clear from here in a couple of weeks. I must get back for Megan's birthday. And at least one of those semi-finals, I guess."

"The 7th, then the 14th if they win."

"14th for sure."

"For how long."

"Two weeks maybe. Then on to the next one."

"You mean they know where and when it's going to be?"

Felicity felt the chill run through her body. Was this how great secrets began to leak? "If they know they aren't saying."

"If they can predict one, they can predict the rest."

"It isn't that accurate. I think they can work out the when and figure the longitude, but not the latitude. This one could have occurred anywhere between the north pole and central Africa. We had no way of knowing it would be Italy."

"They said Mediterranean."

"I think that was just a lucky guess. Anyway, they don't tell me everything."

"Who is they?"

She found that she had to restrain herself from using the word *Thyssen.*

"The project. Earthshaker, they call it," she said, wondering why she needed to pretend to be vague. Now that she had reached the point of lying to her family, she knew she had to terminate the conversation. "Look, I've got to go. It was great hearing from you. And the kids. You don't know how much I've missed you all."

"Hang in there, kid. We're all behind you."

"Love you. Bye."

She laid the receiver back in the cradle and rested both hands on it for a moment. The black rain made it seem to be night as it thundered on the roof. Nausea swept through her and she closed her eyes until it passed. It was only a small thing but still it mattered. Forced to chose once more, even in this tiny way, between her family and Thyssen, she had made the same choice again. But how much longer could it go on?

*

As the NATO forces and civil guards pulled out, Wagner had been frantically hiring security guards from local Italian companies but they all proved very unsatisfactory. Those who didn't abuse their position by bullying the locals, or extorting money, or just getting drunk and starting brawls, only failed to do so because they were sleeping on the job. Or seducing the local maidens. Or running through the stocks in the vineyards. And crashing his vehicles everywhere. They visited greater disaster on the region than the Shastri Effect, Wagner lamented to Brian. He was airing the idea of employing South African mercenaries.

"Why don't you let the problem solve itself?" Brian responded. "Recruit the guards from within the sleepers and train them to guard themselves. That way they'll have an interest."

It sounded like a good idea at the time. Wagner got hold of the Red Cross list and highlighted all people between eighteen and forty as interview candidates—both male and female—no need to be sexist about this—which ought to save him an earbashing from Lorna, *and* Felicity, *and* Jami, *and* just about everybody else. Fabrini was one of the few useful private men he had engaged, a tall thin man with a gigantic moustache who always wore a peaked cap. Together they went off to do the interviews.

No one would talk to them. When they raised the subject of protection, the interviewee would bow their heads, cross themselves, murmur and edge away. The nearly 700 sleepers were largely old people and children—he only had 118 candidates and he had got halfway through the list without a single volunteer. The offer of good money to these desperate starving peasants made no impression. He began to realise how frustrated Chrissie must have felt about all those souls she wasn't saving.

Then, as they were walking off their frustration, a big black sixties-model Pontiac pulled up beside them and two very large men in suits got out.

"You will come with us," they said.

"We will go with them," Fabrini nervously translated.

They were driven away from the damaged region, out through orange groves and to a vast vineyard where the local baronial villa stood atop a slight rise, all white arches and porticos and ivy hanging from the balconies. You could tell that Romeos had been climbing up to their Juliets on that ivy for centuries. They were led to a patio overlooking the estate this fine sunny day and a spread of antipasto and good wine awaited them. Two women, mother and daughter presumably, chatted with Fabrini with warm smiles.

The reason for their visit presently arrived. Don Severni, tall and elegant, white hair and beard, white suit, big smile and handshake.

"Please forgive my tardiness, gentlemen," he said in perfect English. "I hope my family have not been too tedious."

All family members had faded completely from view.

"Obviously, you know who I am," Wagner said.

"Yes, Mr Wagner. Have you tried the wine. It is one of our finer vintages."

"I'm sorry, signor. I don't drink."

Fabrini was looking around for hiding places.

"A thousand sorrows are visited upon you, as on us all, but for you there is no escape."

"I meditate."

Don Severni smiled graciously. "And work out four hours, every morning, Mr Wagner. But please, allow some slight concession to my hospitality. At least nibble on some antipasto."

Fabrini nodded furious encouragement. Wagner nibbled.

It went on for some time. Fabrini tried to admire the vintage and praise the consumables but the Don dismissed him with a wave of his hand. Instead, the whole estate was pointed out to Wagner from the balcony, and the awfulness of the Shastri disaster discussed and the Don wished to praise the excellent work done by the emergency services before finally they were ready to get to the subject.

"Yes, Mr Wagner. I know who you are. I know what you want. What I don't know is why?"

"Why what, exactly?"

"Why you feel you need protection?"

"I don't. It is the pilgrims collectively whom I wish to protect."

"In these parts, protection is a luxury few can afford. It is the most valuable of all commodities and its bestowment jealously guarded."

"I know that. Most generous payments can be made."

Don Severni nodded with a sincere pouting expression. "Yes. I know that too. Project Earthshaker. The most perfect of titles. We all tremble at the very words. What possible protection could be needed by men who control the very forces of nature?"

"As I say, the pilgrims... your own people..."

"Forgive me, Mr Wagner. I wax lyrical too freely. Tell me, are you a friend of the friends?"

Fabrini choked on his cigarette, but Wagner knew the name of the Mafia was never spoken. "No. I am a complete outsider."

"You understand the difficulties that this presents?"

"Which is why I am speaking to you, signor."

"From whom do they need to be protected? It seems to me all threats are behind them."

"Soon, the pilgrims will depart on the first of their pilgrimages. There will be outsiders who will not understand their peaceful intentions. There will be soldiers and local authorities and perhaps interference by foreign powers and maybe even terrorist groups. And the hounds of the paparazzi must be kept at bay. All manner of dangers lie before these pilgrims. My job is to protect them."

"But it is being misunderstood that you fear most?"

"Exactly. Which is why I want the protection to come from within the pilgrims themselves."

"From within?"

"I wish to take those who are willing and able and train them into a security force. That way, they will be protected at all times, permanently."

"I see. And do you have adequate trainees from within the pilgrims, Mr Wagner?"

"No, signor. I have none. But I believe, were you to give the word, such trainees would be readily forthcoming."

Don Severni laughed, took wine and toasted his fields. "Ah, Mr Wagner. You Earthshaker people speak with such strength. And so you should, with tectonic power at your command. Yes, I see your difficulty now. There seems to be a problem of divided loyalties."

"I think so, yes."

"Is there such a difficulty, Mr Wagner?"

"I don't think so. I believe that my pilgrim guardians could, whether they were friends of the friends or not, be able to carry out the duties I would want of them without the slightest disloyalty to the friends."

"Well put, Mr Wagner," the Don smiled. Fabrini needed to sit and mop his sweating brow. "Two masters but no disloyalty. That would be a most unusual set of circumstances, were it to happen. Explain to me how it would work."

"Because there are no secrets in Project Earthshaker, signor. There are no words of disloyalty that a spy or traitor could speak, therefore no spies nor traitors are possible. Further, the loyalty to Project Earthshaker is of a very precise and limited kind. Specific time periods, clear duties, all very predictable in advance. Beyond the specific duties and timings, no loyalty to the Project is required. They can go anywhere they want, do anything they want, say anything they want."

"How wonderfully idealistic. Do you think you can control this, Mr Wagner?"

"I can't and I don't. The circumstances control it. These people will be participating in the pilgrimage anyway. My plan is simply to train them up so they can protect themselves and the others for the duration of the pilgrimage, and presumably those that follow later. Beyond that, they will have no particular responsibility to us whatsoever."

The Don walked his patio, shaking his head, a huge grin on his face. "It is the most extraordinary proposition."

"We find ourselves in very extraordinary circumstances."

"That we do, Mr Wagner. So tell me, should I be able to do whatever it is you imagine I can do to assist you to achieve your objectives. What then?"

"You mean, what's in it for you?"

"If you must resort to your American colloquialisms, yes."

"A large sum of money."

"Presumably, appropriate financial exchanges will be worked out by our accountants. That is not what I mean. My personal involvement will be in the form of a favour to Project Earthshaker. Perhaps then, at some mutually convenient time, a return favour might be possible."

"If it's possible, I'll do all I can."

"Then tell me, Mr Wagner. How well do you know Miss Lorna Simmons?"

*

The convent formed the top of a hill as they are wont to do in Italy, with the attending village a tiered clutter of rooftops gathered about its skirts. Down a series of narrow lanes with steps worn concave by centuries of the tread of monks and the devoted was a small square in the middle of the village, both horizontally and vertically centred. There was a cafe with a nice local vintage and a good sense of coffee and an array of tables that afforded a wide view of the valley. You could sit there, as they did in the evenings, and contemplate the scene below. This Brian Carrick was doing now, alone and contemplative as he waited for the others to arrive. In his rough hands he held some documents that he seemed to be making a point of not reading.

Out there, you could clearly define a full quarter of the circumference of the circle of destruction that had descended upon the valley a week earlier. Outside the circle, the farmers continued their timeless toil in orange grove, vineyard and corn field, and vehicles and pedestrians did commerce along the roads from settlement to farm. There was an order and sense to that world that had been going on unabated since the time of the Trojan War and still did despite the proximity of the disaster. But within the circle, all was chaos. The whole area was charred, with only yellow blobs of rubble here and there. The trees that still stood were stark and leafless, and everywhere lights flashed to direct the unwary away from the fissures that had opened in the earth. Smoke still rose everywhere even though all fires had been extinguished. The smoke was coming out of the ground itself.

At the edge of the blackened zone, you could see the cleared areas where the bivouac tents had been erected and the casualties and homeless originally gathered. Now the victims had all been moved off to regional hospitals, the homeless temporarily housed and the tents destructed. But you could still see the rough road they had forged that circumnavigated the charred region.

Thirty or forty times, Brian must have bounced over that road in those first desperate days. A tank came in and ran the route, flattening everything in its path—later they got a grader but the continual black rain that had been falling at the time turned it into a quagmire. Gravel had been hastily laid but that only made it bone-shatteringly corrugated. At night it had been illuminated only by the stroboscopic lightning forking the volcanic clouds above, until slowly the NATO troops floodlit the whole area.

Now the lights were gone and natural darkness was allowed to return. Now the rain had stopped and this smoggy humid weather had hardened the ring road into permanence—it might have been the roughest road built since before Roman times, but it had served them well nevertheless. The sleepers had wakened and returned to their homes, and the job was all but done. This would probably be the last night that they would meet in this pleasant little cafe. The lingering ash in the atmosphere ensured that, once again, the sunset would be stunning.

Felicity was next to arrive, looking exhausted as she always did these days, but that didn't mean she didn't spot the papers that Brian attempted to slip into the large envelope before she got there. Brian poured her a glass of wine and ordered more coffee.

"The special is lasagne."

"Sounds great," Felicity said as she flopped in the chair. "Who's suing us this time?"

There was no point denying it. Felicity had long since figured out his trouble.

"Not us. Me. Judy's lawyers. I'm sending it straight on to Joe to take care of."

"Oh, Brian. I'm so sorry."

"Strangely, I'm not. She likes to keep life plain and simple. Larry can do that for her."

"Simple as that? Fix this for me, Joe. End of story?"

"No time to do it any other way."

"She could try being a little patient."

"Nar," Brian heard himself laugh slightly. "I'm not the man she married. Whereas Larry is me one step further up the line. It makes too much sense to argue with."

"And the kids?"

"Work something out when I'm in a position to do it, I guess."

"Brian, you can't just dismiss fifteen years of marriage with a shrug."

"As things stand, that's about all it's worth."

"And you?" the doctor in her had to ask. "How are you coping?"

"Me. I'm all right." It was said so emphatically it had to be a lie.

"Yes, and you look it too. Fit and calm and steady as a rock, that's good old Brian. But sooner or later, it's going to hit you, mate. And hard."

"I know," Brian smiled, appreciating her generosity of spirit. "And no doubt I'll fold like a house of cards. We'll just have to hope it's later rather than sooner, that's all."

"And if it's sooner?"

"Well, a nice restful breakdown with you around to pick up the pieces, Fee. That's almost worth looking forward too."

"Yes. I know what you mean."

Kevin Wagner arrived with a squeal of tyres as he drove his shining land cruiser to a sudden parking spot and jumped out. He wore a para-military outfit these days, with a heavy assortment of equipment attached to his belt, including holstered pistol and emergency flares, and even a peaked cap which he discarded in the front seat of the vehicle to show it was an informal occasion. He marched over and took a chair. His paraphernalia rattled as he sat.

"God these people are a shambles," he exclaimed.

"Earthquakes are prone to make people so," Felicity pointed out coolly.

"Oh, I don't mean them. I've got used to babbling panic-stricken Italians. It's those bloody NATO bigwigs. Full co-operation, they call it. Total obstruction is more like it."

"I've found them pretty helpful," Brian said lightly.

"Very helpful indeed," Felicity concurred.

"You would. They respect what you're doing. But security, they reckon, is their concern. Territorial bastards. They keep giving me the run-around and bogging me down with paperwork."

"The situation does seem secure," Brian ventured. Such grumbles were a nightly event.

"Sure it was. They brought a bloody army with them, didn't they? Now the troops are pulling out and there'll be nothing left to secure."

"Must be very frustrating for you," Felicity mused.

Fortunately, Chrissie was approaching. She seemed to positively glow with divinity these days and walked as if she was not actually touching the ground. She smiled upon them all serenely. Brian signalled to the waiter to supply mineral water.

"And you," Wagner said before Chrissie had the chance to sit. "Do you really believe that you can just go marching off on your pilgrimage to God knows where and expect all these people to wander out of their houses and follow you?"

Chrissie received the words with pious calm. "Well, they will, won't they."

"They won't be following you. They'll be being drawn to the focal point."

"So will I. And I'll be in front of them all, so they'll be following me. All you have to do is direct them after me."

"It's a charade."

Chrissie nodded. "Of course it is. But it will help to explain what's happening and keep it all organised. Where's the problem?"

"What happens when you cross Italy and reach the sea?"

"I'm organising some boats," Brian could not resist saying.

"For which we are all very appreciative," Chrissie said with a radiant smile.

Wagner held his head in his hands, and Brian had to continue. "You'd better be. Finding boats to carry 647 people to an unknown destination is no small task."

"Is that the final number?" Felicity asked.

"Final known number, according to Red Cross numbers. There's still 188 people classed as missing," Brian pointed out.

"Harley promised me Jerusalem," Chrissie added, to increase Wagner's dismay.

"Harley would," Felicity sighed.

Brian had been thinking about it. "I suppose if he places us and the control group accurately, he can make the focal point anywhere he wants. Why not Jerusalem?"

"Why not indeed," Jami Shastri said, for she had arrived in her smart hired Celica and flopped herself down at the table while they were talking. "The Great God Harley can do anything he wants."

The bad climatic conditions had worsened the blotches on her face and she was wearing dirty jeans and a dirtier singlet. The Italian sun had burned her skin darker than they remembered.

Brian indicated the post-pak before him. "Anything else for Joe before I send this?" he thought to ask.

"I sent all the bills to him last night," Chrissie said.

Jami chuckled. "Old Joe has a permanently suspicious mind. He wanted a copy of all the data we have on you sleepers. I think that'll cover it."

"Not completely," Brian said sadly. "He also wanted to know what Harley was up to in Russia."

"Everyone who goes to Moscow is a spy, huh?" Jami mused.

"Joe is very old school," Chrissie pointed out.

"But we know why," Felicity said. "He had to be sure that the Mongolian sleepers would stay where they were."

"Yes," Brian added. "Otherwise he would not have been able to land us all so neatly in the lobby of the Hong Kong Sheraton."

"There was another reason," Jami said sublimely. "He was also investigating the Tunguska event."

At this word, Brian almost jolted out of his chair. It was as if he, rather than Chrissie, was the one having a revelation.

"I know about this," he said excitedly. "Collision between the earth and a comet in Siberia at the turn of the century."

"Right on, Brian. 30th of June, 1908," Jami elaborated. "Bright lights in the sky, biggest bang ever recorded, massive shockwave, forest flattened for miles around, but no impact crater at the middle."

"They thought it a comet entirely made of ice that melted in the atmosphere, causing a huge explosion but no crater," Brian explained, hardly able to control his enthusiasm.

"There are other theories," Jami said with amusement.

"All of which, I understood, were discredited," Brian said with a frown.

"More or less," Jami replied blithely. "But consider a singularity, or mini-black hole as they are sometimes called, for instance."

"If they exist," Brian persisted.

"Exactly," Jami nodded. "This thing would be about the size of a pinhead but weigh as much as Manhattan Island. It would cause such an explosion but leave no crater."

"It might, if it existed," Brian stonewalled.

"Try having an open mind, Brian," Jami sighed. "Black holes are dead matter with the atoms compressed so tightly that if all the matter in the earth was so compressed, it would be reduced to the size of a basketball. An object of such weight would hit the earth and pass straight through."

"And then there would have to be a similar explosion when it came out the other side of the world," Brian was sure. "Which didn't happen."

"Precisely," Jami said with a triumphant smile. "That was why the idea was generally rejected. But suppose it never got out the other side. What if it was captured by the earth's gravity and pulled into orbit while still inside the crust. It would then orbit the earth's core, eating up all the matter in its path, growing larger and heavier. Devouring the inside of the planet like a worm in an apple."

"What a horrifying thought," Felicity gasped.

"If it was getting heavier," Brian considered, "wouldn't that mean its orbit would grow smaller?"

"We would have to suppose so," Jami agreed. "Eventually, it would be the size of an orange and settle at the centre of the earth, still dragging matter from all around it. And then finally, the rest of the earth would collapse into the vacuum at the centre, and that would be the end of everything."

"And you think that's happening?" Chrissie gasped in horror.

"Maybe. It was when Glen, our computer modeller at MIT, started his models off from the 30th of June, 1908, that we then got a fixed longitude for this event. So it fits."

"Jesus," Wagner said. "So that's it. We're all doomed."

"If the theory is right," Jami said.

"And it probably isn't," Brian told them determinedly. "Mini-black holes are only theoretical. They exist only as a mathematical construct."

"Oh good," Felicity said, rising from the table. "So there *isn't* some horror eating the earth out from the middle."

"I'm afraid there possibly is," Jami said. "Just because it doesn't exist in any form that we can understand doesn't mean it isn't there."

"That's enough for me. See you all tomorrow," Felicity said and walked away. "Thanks for the nightmares."

"Gotta get back to it," Wagner said and rose.

"The sheep await the shepherdess," Chrissie smiled serenely and left.

"I have a plane to catch," Jami said. "Goodnight."

"So you think it might be a singularity?" Brian asked, halting her departure.

"Good a theory as any, Brian. But who cares? We've all got enough problems with the things we *do* understand. Goodbye."

Brian Carrick sat at the table alone and poured the last glass of wine from the bottle.

"Now why didn't I think of that?" he said to the empty square before him.

*

It was important, Thyssen knew, that he should not regard these men and women as fools. They were bureaucrats, not one of them trained in sciences, with matters beyond scientific outcomes and humanitarian considerations to take into account.

"You have seen the preliminary report from our investigative committee?" the woman in a dark suit said.

Everyone here spoke English, with varying accents. This one sounded Polish.

"Yes, I have," Thyssen said evenly.

He didn't remember any of their names, didn't care about them enough to find out. Their self-importance might have been somewhat deflated to know that. But their anonymity did not mean they were unimportant. Of the dozens of meetings and discussion groups he had attended in the last three weeks, this was probably the one that mattered most.

"You understand their conclusion, I assume?" the Polish woman asked—she was trying to be kind but her accent was not equipped for it.

"I do," Thyssen said, loud and clear, like a marriage vow.

"No relationship, they say. You saw that conclusion. No relationship whatsoever between the seismic events in question."

"Yes. That is their conclusion," Thyssen assured her.

Apparently, the Polish woman had carried out her function, having established that he was able to read and comprehend a two page report in his own field of expertise. She settled back in a chair. They were very plush chairs, placed behind a long oak table. His own chair was most comfortable, almost an armchair, amid fifty others facing them. He was alone on his side—this was not an occasion at which Lorna would be an asset. He was positioned like a schoolboy in a class of one, facing eight teachers. Except the modern appointments of the room would not have been found at even the most exclusive private school.

A grey haired man in a suit to match took over. His accent was Spanish, perhaps, Latin anyway. Thyssen remembered there was a Chilean amongst them—perhaps this was he.

"Would you care to comment, Professor, on that conclusion?"

"Yes. I believe that it is the correct conclusion, given the data available to the investigative body."

The investigators had been scientists, after all, and from Geology or related fields. He had met with them and answered their questions as honestly as he could. They were all skeptical. They all hated him as they did all of their colleagues who indulged in grandstanding. Thyssen hated such people himself. It was all understandable.

The grey haired man didn't hate him. Probably the grey haired man did not feel anything about him at all.

"Persons of eminence and considerable expertise, Professor."

"No doubt about it. I think you chose the best available personnel for the task."

"So you agree with the conclusion."

"Certainly not."

"How can that be?"

"Had they possessed the data and modelling techniques collected and developed by the members of Project Earthshaker, they would have reached a different conclusion."

Thyssen felt uncomfortable, having said that. The eminences on his side were two research students—Jami and Glen—neither possessing even a doctorate. That they might have been the two most brilliant students on the planet would cut no ice with these people. Thyssen decided not to correct himself.

"It was considered important that the investigation be an independent study."

"The proper technique, to be sure," Thyssen replied. "But it did substantially limit their ability to reach a satisfactory outcome."

"Satisfactory to whom, Professor?"

"To all of the inhabitants of planet Earth," Thyssen replied, biting off the `sir' that seemed to naturally fit at the end of his statement.

"The investigative committee did review your data, once they had reached their independent conclusion."

"That's right."

"The final paragraph of their report outlines their conclusion to that review."

"It does."

"They considered the data to be prejudiced by a predetermined outcome and your techniques radical and inconclusive, Professor."

"That's what they said."

"And do you care to comment on this?"

"Yes," Thyssen said, becoming impressed by the way he was able to keep rancour out of his voice. "I will say to you what I said to them. 155°West, 20°South. 7pm, Central Pacific Time, on Monday the 13th of September."

"And this is, what? A prediction?"

"The next event, yes."

"I'm not sure if that is a valid comment, Professor."

The grey man had reached the extent of his job description and now a tall thin man in a brown suit took over. He was North American—possibly Canadian.

"This... statement... of yours, Harley. You are.. um... you wish us to accept that the next seismic event will occur at this time and that place."

"I am giving you that information. Acceptance is up to you."

"How accurate do consider it to be?"

"The time within an hour either way, the longitude within

five degrees, the latitude more approximate, accurate within several hundred miles."

"I see. You are aware, are you not, that the investigative committee were unable to find any basis whatsoever for the predicting future outcomes in any way."

"I think we've covered that already."

"Yes, of course. Only I'm wondering how you expect us to react to that?"

Thyssen decided to pause to consider his reply. Just because a cause was hopeless did not mean it should be completely surrendered.

"The event will occur about halfway between the Cook Islands and the Society Islands. Volcanoes at both locations can be expected to erupt. Orohena on Tahiti is a danger, as is Raratonga in the Cook Islands. Most of the hundred thousand population of the region live within the danger zone of those mountains. There are five other volcanic mountains that threaten the region. I expect you to arrange for all those people to be evacuated."

"You are certain all those volcanoes will erupt?"

"Not certain. It is highly probable. There may be unknown dormant volcanoes nearer the epicentre but beneath the ocean which, if they exist, will take the pressure off."

"A high probability, at best, of a theory unsupported by independent evidence. I'm sure you can see where we are going here, Professor."

"Yes. And let me say that while I am disappointed, it does not diminish the esteem I hold for the United Nations and all the other bodies involved here. The assistance Project Earthshaker has received from various governmental bodies in the recent crisis has been first rate. I'm sure it will be in the future."

All the right asses appropriately licked, Thyssen thought to himself.

The brown man did look genuinely uncomfortable with the inevitable conclusion that the matter had been brought to.

"I'm sorry, Professor, that we can do no more, but you must understand our position. To evacuate a hundred thousand people unnecessarily would be a disaster in itself."

"It will not be unnecessary."

The brown man retired and now a sharp-looking woman in a green suit cleaned her glasses and cleared her throat. She was Slavic, maybe Russian, more likely from the former Yugoslavian states. But she spoke with the neutral monotone common to psychiatrists.

"Why are you here, Professor?"

"Because you invited me."

"You knew in advance what the finding of the committee would be, did you not?"

"I did."

"Yet you have come and persisted with your discredited claims."

"After the next event, I believe you will be of a different view. I came to give you the opportunity to save a hundred thousand lives."

"Except the best research shows no danger to those people."

"Second best."

"You regard it as a competition, Professor?"

"I regard it as a responsibility. Lives are at stake. I must do all I can to save them. And if that means being subjected to this embarrassing little charade, so be it."

Oops.

But he would have worried about himself had he got all the way through this ordeal without losing control at least once.

"I believe you possess a megalomaniacal desire to transfer the burden of your obsessive guilt onto this committee."

"I don't care how you assess my psychological condition, lady. I'm giving you the opportunity to act in advance. That's all I can do. Just because you won't believe the truth doesn't mean you should be denied it."

"Very generous of you. I think there is no more to say here."

"I could repeat my warning."

"That will definitely be unnecessary."

They were waiting for him to leave. But then the obvious

Englishman at the far end waved for him to stay in his seat.

"One moment, Professor. Let's wait for the smoke to clear and then see what action is to be taken here."

"I understood you were going to take no action."

"Not exactly. What action will you be taking?"

"Myself and my team will proceed and do everything they can to persuade those people to leave those islands."

"Very candid of you, professor. I'm sure the French government, not to mention the New Zealanders, will have opinions on that."

"As I say, I will only do what I can."

"Allow me to express to you the grave dangers involved in creating a panic of this sort. You would be wise to keep your speculations to yourself."

"How would that be wise?"

"It will avoid great destruction to your credibility later on."

"Whereas, ladies and gentlemen, let me assure you that yours will be safe. I will not tell anyone that you were warned of these dangers in advance. And now, good afternoon."

"Please, Professor, try and understand..."

But he did understand, perfectly. He rose and walked from the room, and smiled to himself as he went. Yes, it had gone as expected and he had probably got the best possible result he could have hoped for. Life was always a lot easier when important decisions were taken out of your hands and the way forward obliged by the actions of others. They gave him no choice which meant that there was no further need for consideration. As soon as he was in the corridor outside, Thyssen pulled the mobile telephone out of his pocket, switched it on and jabbed a precoded number.

"Yes?" a female voice inquired.

"Okay, Lorna," he said. "Do it now."

*

Lorna liked best, when enjoying sex, to watch herself on television.

She had set up a large screen at the foot of the bed and had prepared a tape of every video moment of her short but prolific career as a media celebrity, which she replaced with an updated version each day and kept plugged in at the right spot. All she had to do was reach sideways to the bedside table and press the Go button and there she would be in all her glory.

"It's better than a vibrator," she told the man in question candidly.

Since the man ordinarily had his back turned to the screen, it offered him little hindrance.

"Hearing your voice coming from behind gives a bloke that little bit of distraction he needs to avoid shooting his bolt too soon," the man of the moment admitted. She kept the volume just a little louder than necessary, hoping for that very sort of voyeuristic effect.

"The next event will occur on the morning of the 13th of September, at a point halfway between the Society Islands—Tahiti—and the Cook Islands," her video self said gravely.

"How can you be so sure?" one of the disembodied voices beyond the array of microphones before her asked.

"I am sure because the scientists of Project Earthshaker tell me it is so," she replied with a nifty little arch of her eyebrows at the end.

Just because she was the bearer of dire news didn't mean she couldn't be playful. That, after all, was the whole effect. She had a cheeky beret perched on her flowing red hair and always offered a touch of cleavage for the upper body camera shots, and plenty of leg for the full length stuff. Best of all were those sorts of interviews where they placed her in an armchair and she could cross her thighs straight at the camera. The Harbinger of Doom was the sexiest thing on television and the combined effect gained her almost nightly admission into every lounge room in the world.

She wondered how many other women used her image in pursuit of a speedier orgasm.

Already the journalists hated to see her—well, all except

the French and Italians and the gutter press who never tired of finding new angles on her anatomy. But those journalists who took their work seriously knew she was a buffer, a wall that they were never allowed to see behind, the Cerberus, guardian of the jaws of hell, as one of them lugubriously put it.

"But you don't possess any appropriate qualifications to make these statements, do you Miss Simmons?" those earnest sorts of late-night female interviewers accused.

"You don't need a degree to read an autocue, love," Lorna replied slyly. She could match them, bitchy for bitchy, and loved it.

"But you don't have any sort of degree at all?"

"No. But the people who write my script do. And bigger degrees than those who write yours."

And cunning she could meet with cunning.

"So who is the real Lorna Simmons?"

"A Kiwi receptionist lucky enough to land a job fronting for the most important scientific project in the world."

"But you, personally, are not important."

"Oh, I don't know. How long since you last had your picture on the front page of *Time*, Maxine?"

If she wasn't well on the way to her orgasm by then, she never would be.

She knew the reason why she was there and was permitted to be honest about it. Nothing could have been worse than a genuine geologist facing these interviews where their every statement could be twisted and distorted by the media and every sentence taken out of context to create those sensational but false headlines that media moguls were sure they needed. To most serious questions, the ones that really probed the situation, she was able to offer a shrug that enhanced her bosom and a mischievous wrinkle of her nose and admitted she had no idea. No scientist could have got away with that.

The truth was that Harley wanted to make sure that the public clearly understood everything he told them. What Lorna understood, anyone could. Not being burdened with extraneous expert knowledge, she was never able to jump to conclusions, nor add confusing jargon, nor assume a certain base level of knowledge on the part of the audience. Lorna was the model of her own audience—she said everything from the heart and in terms that the lowest common denominator viewing public could easily understand.

"I tell the public what I am told to tell them. No more or less because I don't know any more or less. And you can't bamboozle me into saying more than I should because I don't know any more than I should."

"Unlike your boss," one interviewer said cruelly.

It was, of course, reference to the official condemnation of Harley's public announcement of his predictions. Harley had learned from these misfortunes, which was exactly why he had placed her so firmly between himself and the media. How they would have loved to have got at him and Harley was the first to admit that under pressure he would babble and create chaos. Now, with Lorna telling everything he knew, he was able to dismiss the media out of hand. When they trapped him on the steps of important buildings, Harley could herd his way through them like a half-back going through the pack, grumbling at them to 'fuck off' to make sure his words never went on air in prime time.

"How can you be sure that he is right about this, Lorna?"

"I can't. I don't know any better than you do. We'll all just have to wait and see."

"What would you recommend people do if they are in the designated region?"

"Go somewhere else."

"And if they can't?"

"Hide under the bed."

"Is that what you'd do, Lorna?"

"No. I'd be on top of the bed with my favourite lover. It ought to be a fantastic moment."

Like everyone ever interviewed, all of her best bits ended up on the cutting room floor.

Afterwards, they leaned back on the pillows and shared a cigarette. She ran the tape from the start so he could see what he missed.

"Well, what do you think?"

"Looks to me like he's moulded you into exactly what he wants you to be."

"Yes. It's just me, doing what I used to do locally, suddenly gone global. Do I live up to my media persona?"

"You might be the only person in the world who does."

But of course it wasn't always about her. She considered sex something shared and the man was important, whoever he may be.

"Aren't you allowed to go home anymore, Brian?"

"I guess not."

"Well, I think she doesn't appreciate you. I think you are a truly fine man in every way. Very loving and attentive to a girl's needs, and a strong lover. Good sense of humour. Interesting to talk to. They don't make you men better than that."

"Thanks, Lorna. Coming from you, that is one hell of a recommendation."

10
THE CHAMPAGNE FLOWS

Amid the orderly chaos, dazzling neon and seething heat of Las Vegas, Andromeda felt she had come home even though it was a place she had never been before. When Tierney had told her of their next engagement, she had snorted in faint disgust.

"I might have known Harley would have gangsters for friends," she said.

"You think that's how he does these things?" Joel asked seriously.

"Everyone knows Las Vegas is run by the mob. I guess the connections to Washington are strong."

"That's history. The mob is out of Las Vegas these days."

"Not according to Martin Scorsese."

"What would he know?"

"More than most people," she said, and she believed that too. Great artists told the truth, even when they lied.

But she went to Las Vegas and found it different to her expectations. Oh, it was big and brassy and fake and miserable like every place where the high rollers were the basis of the economy, but there was something about it that suited her and she knew she settled into it like an old shoe. Maybe she was made for the casino world. She had done gigs at casinos in Australia and the Pacific but they were truly sleazy and their criminal basis unmistakable. Las Vegas was more like a businessman's convention in Disneyland. It was like the aristocrat—having risen above its origins and putting on airs. For all its fierce modernity, it was a staid old lady at heart.

There were two engagements, actually, at the Sands and then The Golden Nugget, but for Andromeda there was little difference. Her act fitted in perfectly and was a hit, almost as if it was preordained. Even she could see how appropriate she had become to this world. She flowed through it, seamlessly, and if she could see the mechanical processes in operation, plainly no one else did.

Anyone who tried could blend in here—there was a universality about it that said 'we don't care who you are as long as you play the tables'. She even saw men like Harley looking quite at home, and one night a girl who looked like Jami Shastri, except she was wearing a dress. And thick make-up. And she had done something civilised with her hair. Really, the only reason that this person resembled Jami at all was because it was actually her.

"Jami, darling, you look fabulous."

Jami did a little curtsy and smiled brilliantly. Sure, her thighs were too thin to be on show like this and the dress fitted her like a sack, but there was no need to quibble.

"I didn't know whether it'd be okay to come and see you. Now that you're such a big star and all."

Andromeda gave her a big public hug, just to cure her nervousness. "Of course it is, sweetheart. You people are like family to me these days."

Which was true. She found she hung out for every small fragment of news about the others of Project Earthshaker, from whom she constantly felt estranged. They were always off, doing things elsewhere and together, a team, while she was somewhere else and alone. It was a strange sensation to feel so close to people she hardly knew. And yet it was so. When they were amid the disaster in Italy and nightly they variously appeared on television, she was like a mother with sons and daughters away at a war. And on these rare occasions when one of her fellow earthshakers came her way, she found she was desperately anxious for gossip about the others.

As she was now, with awkward Jami, but she could see that would have to wait. Plainly Jami was unhappy and needed to confide—Andromeda felt the earth mother within her assume immediate ascendancy. She knew a place where they could meet for dinner later and have a good chat. Jami was delighted.

"I'm on my way to Tahiti, but yes, dinner will be terrific."

No flight to Tahiti demanded an overnight stop in Las Vegas that she knew of. Andromeda felt she was right. Jami had a big problem.

And naturally, it turned out to relate to men. Who else could cause a girl such obvious grief and on what subject could Andromeda better give advice? The chap's name was Glen, a colleague on the project. Yes, Andromeda had heard of him. The mysterious extra member of the Earthshaker team, locked up in a dungeon in Boston, being fed on microchips and water, condemned to an eternity doing Harley's sums. She had never met him and imagined some stodgy, cobwebbed fellow until she saw his photograph. Good looking, athletic, all American boy. The nature of the problem was obvious. Just when Jami had begun to dream her dreams once more, Glen dumped her for a water-ballet star.

"We're just friends, Jami. You must understand that." he had told her and she left for Tahiti immediately after that.

"You don't need me to tell you what to do, honey-child," Andromeda said, sadly.

She could see the future easily. Most likely he would abandon her eventually for someone as handsome and clever as himself and Jami would be left to devote herself to her career. Or, should she succeed in trapping him, he would continue to have affairs and she would grow to tolerate it and never allow his infidelity to diminish her devotion. Many attractive men were like that. And just as many foolish women put up with them.

"But I want Glen," Jami insisted tearfully. "I know we're made for each other."

Since it would have been cruel to point out that they almost certainly were not, Andromeda could only sympathise and pacify and advise her to transfer her unbounded love to someone worthy of it. Which she would be the first women in history to achieve, were she to manage it.

But there was far more historical fame going on at present

than anyone could handle. Eventually, they got around to the gossip. Naughty Lorna and cuckold Brian. Felicity Nightingale and Saint Chrissie. Harley the bull in a bureaucratic china shop, suspicious old Joe and his conspiracies, Adolf Wagner.

"Everyone is becoming famous," Jami said, her tears dried for the moment.

"I find it majorly weird, Jami. Remember Kevin and his master race idea?"

"It's nothing like that."

"Are you sure, Jami? If it did happen that a new improved species evolved, wouldn't they all start over-achieving and become celebrities? I mean, how else would they be superior?"

Jami looked at her, beginning to take the idea seriously. "I always imagined that a superior race would excel in sciences. I've never thought media stars superior to anyone."

"But think about it, Jami. Lorna, Chrissie, Brian, Kevin, Joe and me. We were all nobodies when this first happened. Now we are all big successes."

"Joe hasn't changed."

"No, I guess not. But his capacity for change is mighty limited."

"And Felicity has become just as famous even though she wasn't touched by the effect. And my name has become a household word around scientific circles. And Harley, although he was famous in his way all along."

That was the trouble with talking to scientists—they always knew the facts and messed up the loveliest theories.

"Damn. I sure thought I was on to somethin'."

Jami smiled. She was finally beginning to loosen up. "I can't blame you for thinking so, Andromeda. I began to think so myself for a while. Lorna is so utterly brilliant on TV. You ought to see dull old Brian strutting about like a field marshal, organising everything. But, when you think about it, nothing has really changed."

"Hasn't it?"

"You were always a terrific entertainer. You were waiting to be discovered. Earthshaker gave you the break you needed—that's all."

"There's a lot of better performers around than me."

"Sure. And a lot who are better than Elton John and Sharon Stone. Being good gets you to a certain level. Then you need a break. A bit of luck. Your bit of luck was being on Ruapehu when it blew."

"You gotta be in a position to exploit a break when it comes. Yeah, I get it. Harleykins has simply oiled the wheels and let it happen."

"It's the same with the others. Lorna was always a quick-witted sexy thing. Brian is a natural organiser who never had anything to organise before."

"I ain't so sure about that..."

"He was the one who always got to the focal point and did whatever was necessary to get there."

"He had the shortest distance to go."

"But he didn't try public transport or hitch-hiking like the rest of you. He stole a truck and drove straight there."

"Hmm, I guess so...."

"Kevin ran a security company in the past—this is just on a bigger scale. And Chrissie was born to be a martyr. And that explains Joe—he continues doing what he does best."

"Oh all right then."

"They are all doing what they do best. So am I. So is Glen. So is Felicity. And so is Harley. And one of Harley's great talents is arranging for people to do what they are best at."

"So you think it is just a natural progression."

"Extraordinary events are taking place. At such a time, anyone doing what they do best, unhindered by outside forces, are always going to look pretty good."

"And you reckon Harley read us all like that?"

"I think he just opened the opportunities and allowed each of us to flow into them."

"Why?"

"Why what?"

"Why did he take the trouble? Why bother to help us all along like this?"

"I have no idea."

"But do you think Harley has a plan or does he just make it all up as he goes."

"Harley? He doesn't have a spontaneous bone in his body. He plans everything, as meticulously as possible, as far ahead as possible."

"So what's his real agenda?"

"You'll have to ask him that."

"But he sure as hell is up to something, ain't he?"

"Harley wants to be the greatest human being ever. Bigger than Buddha, Caesar, Shakespeare, Einstein. He reckons exploiting Project Earthshaker and us will get him there. He is a complete and utter megalomaniac."

"I thought I had ego problems."

"Not like Harley."

"I thought you liked him."

"I don't care about him or anybody," Jami said adamantly.

*

All through the night before, Chrissie remained in the convent chapel, deep in prayer.

Tomorrow the pilgrimage would begin and everything was ready, and even if she knew it was something of a ploy entirely set up by Thyssen, still she knew it was really the hand of God. For Harley was no exception—God could work through him as readily as any other man, and if it was a certainty that the pilgrims would follow her tomorrow, was it impossible that from time to time, God rigged the odds in his own favour?

But her prayers did not concern such thoughts anymore. She could be realistic about this when appropriate, even join in their jokes at her expense, but now it was the serious time. These people would follow her rather than make their own way to the focal point, and she needed to cleanse her soul and make herself worthy of them. She now must rid herself of all the cynicism that she had tolerated these past weeks, even gone along with, even participated in.

Without the skeptical jokes, they would never have assisted her on her course whereas because they all believed in Harley rather more than they believed in God, so they had co-operated. They took her seriously because it was couched in terms they could accept—for them faith and belief have to follow later.

In the end, they had all helped her. Joe the Communist had happily provided the funding; Lorna the great sinner had promoted her on television; Wagner, the unbeliever in everything except his own superiority, had trained guards from within the ranks of the pilgrims to protect them along the way; as they journeyed they would sing songs made popular by Andromeda the false goddess; they would ride in transportation provided by Brian the atheist. Each of them had risen above their lack of faith to help her. It was of them, too, that she needed to be worthy.

When midday passed, the expected linkage of the pilgrims was only hours away and Chrissie went out and found Brian Carrick waiting by the truck. It was a battered old Fiat tray truck, rusted and noisy, but she had chosen it herself. Brian had offered to have a *Popemobile* built for her, but she knew this was the appropriate way to go. Christ had ridden to the Holy City on a donkey, and this wreck of a truck was certainly the modern equivalent of that.

"We got her running as well as she ever will," Brian said kindly. She knew he had been working on the engine himself, surrounded by a team of Italian mechanics. "Dropped a new donk in her. All new brake system. Reconditioned the transmission. She'll get you there."

"I have no doubt of it, Brian," Chrissie smiled thankfully.

"We also installed a radio and the driver will be in direct contact with Kevin who will be sitting over the top of you in a helicopter."

"A daunting thought, Brian."

"Come and have a gander at the chair."

There was a plain solid wooden chair that they had bolted to the floor of the tray, facing backwards. All about, cushions were scattered for the children, a group of orphans created by the disaster who would travel gathered at her feet. There was a clear plastic tarpaulin that could be pulled over the top of it all if it rained but the sides and back of the tray remained open. Loudspeakers, also facing backwards, had been installed on the roof of the cabin.

"Yer can see the mike attached to the side of the chair. Okay."

"All absolutely wonderful, Brian. I'm so pleased."

There was an experienced driver, also a pilgrim, and another man who Kevin had provided and was called Fabrini, with sorrowful eyes, a drooping moustache and an automatic weapon constantly nestled in his armpit.

"I'd be thankful if you'd keep that out of sight, Mr. Fabrini."

"Yes sister," Fabrini murmured reverently.

The route was carefully planned. They would travel by road in a close convoy across the Apennines to Potenza and then on to Massafra where tracks would allow them to bypass Taranto and into Brindisi. There Brian had arranged for a recently decommissioned ocean-going ferry to convey them, vehicles and all, across the Adriatic Sea to Greece, and into the Gulf of Corinth. They would briefly take to the road again, into Athens after which it was tentatively planned that they would pick up another steamer at Piraeus which would complete the journey to Tel Aviv and inland to Jerusalem.

There were difficulties. They might have flown, but the Israelis had denied them permission to land. They had also prohibited the ship from docking but that didn't matter because the thirty-six hours would have expired long before they reached the Middle East. The bit of the pilgrimage that mattered most was the first stage anyway, and when it was realised that it would be all over somewhere off the coast of Greece, it was decided to land them in Corinth and allow it all to continue into Athens, giving them someplace to arrive. The Greek authorities had reached no opinion on the subject and continued to argue and it was assumed would still be undecided when it was over. Since the pilgrimage could never reach its destination, it was decided that it was better to culminate in a place where there could be local interest and media coverage, rather than some obscure spot in the middle of the Mediterranean.

All of this, Chrissie absorbed stoically. She wasn't about to believe that her pilgrimage had nowhere to go. Something would happen to change things, she was sure. There would be a point to it all—God would see to that. And if not God then Harley, who had plainly gone to a lot of trouble to organise it this way.

Brian had got out his map of the world and showed it to her the night before. There were three points on the globe—Italy where they were, Russia where the still quarantined Buryats remained, and the control group, presently in Melbourne. You drew a circle such that its circumference passed through each point and the centre of that circle was the focal point. Move any one of the groups before the linkage and the focal point changed. A wildcard was Andromeda in Las Vegas but during the night she had flown over them and landed in Athens where she would meet them at the end of the pilgrimage. So all they had to do was reposition the control group so that the direct line from Italy to the focal point passed through Jerusalem.

It wasn't as easy as it sounded. The control group needed to be repositioned far out in the Indian Ocean, 1800 kilometres south of the island of Mauritius, whereby the focal point was caused to be at Meshed, a town in north east Iran. No one could get there, even if they wanted to, but the line from the marshalling point in Italy to Meshed ran straight through Athens and Jerusalem. Not only wouldn't the pilgrims arrive, the Holy City wasn't really where they were going anyway.

"I think I'm asking more questions than I need to know the answers to," Chrissie smiled sadly.

Not far away was a hill beside the road which could be seen from some distance around. They positioned the truck there and waited as the sun rose on the day. Chrissie continued in prayer. Throughout the region, Brian and other men were positioned with buses and vans, ready to pick up those pilgrims who would not be able to provide their own transport, which, beyond a few bicycles and Vespas, was most of them. The orphaned children were brought in and Chrissie led them in prayer and song. The time drew nearer.

"We shoulda got one of them brain monitors so we'd know when to start," Kevin said. He had landed his helicopter nearby.

"I'll know when," Chrissie told him.

And she did. She was deep in prayer and suddenly her mind flowed out into all humanity—it was so intense a sensation that she reacted physically. "It begins now," she told them.

She climbed onto the truck and stood on her chair and below her, everywhere, the people came. Along the road, they formed into a convoy. Along the flanks, helpers rushed with clipboards, checking off names.

"Only about 300 have gathered," Fabrini informed her.

"That's enough," Chrissie said. "We will begin slowly. The others will follow."

She took her seat and fitted the safety belt Brian had thoughtfully provided and they drove down onto the road, took the head of the convoy and started at six kilometres an hour. As they went, people were calling.

"Bless you, sister. Bless you sister."

Inside, Chrissie could feel her heart swelling. The children looked up at her with shining credulous eyes. The logistics and bureaucracy slipped away and she knew only her faith and that the true journey had begun.

*

Pierre Duclos declared himself the boldest pilot in the world, both in person and on the sign that advertised his profession—joy flights over the islands at 530 Francs an hour. He had no idea that his claims were about to be fully tested.

"How much per day?" Jami had asked him—his English was better than her schoolgirl French.

"Ten hours of daylight. How many of them do you actually want to fly?"

"All of them."

"The plane must land every four hours to refuel."

"Sure. As long as we go straight up again."

"But where will we be going?"

Jami, in reply, drew circles in the air. The Frenchman gave a shrug and stated a price. Jami immediately shook his hand in agreement. "You'll fly around the crest of Orohena, just below the height of the summit, as close to the ground as you can get."

"Just around and around."

"That's right."

"When do we start?"

"An hour before sunset. Don't be late."

Duclos eyed her bleakly.

"I will not. Until when?"

"Believe me. You'll know when to stop."

"I need to know when. Other people wish to make bookings to fly with me."

"There won't be any other bookings," Jami told him.

Then she invited him to have lunch with her, but he looked her over and refused in such a blatant way that Jami decided not to explain any further.

Instead she ate with Felicity.

"Evacuated anybody yet?" Jami asked.

Felicity pulled a face and offered feeble gestures. "A few wimps have run away. Some luxury cruisers have sought sheltered harbours. But really, no. The French authorities refuse to co-operate. They won't even put it over the radio."

"But everyone knows."

"And they all think it a joke."

Jami put on a bad French accent. "Madame, none of the volcanoes here have erupted for a thousand years."

"Ignorant pigs. In a sense, I'll be glad when today is over and I won't have to argue with them anymore. I've given up already anyway." Felicity lifted her champagne in a toast. "Until tonight, huh?"

They drank champagne and studied the menu, but it wasn't time to order yet. Jami eyed her companion thoughtfully. "Will you be staying, Felicity?"

"Well, since you gave up your seat in the Orion, I'll grab it and go for a ride. I'll be up there somewhere between here and Raratonga. Unless you want it back?"

Jami shook her head—up in the Orion at 20,000 feet was the safest possible place to be in the region but she had never really considered it a possibility. "There won't be anything to see out there over the ocean. I'll be taking joy flights around Orohena."

Grave concern crossed the face of her companion. "Truly. Is that safe?"

Jami could laugh at her concern. "I think I'll know when to make a run for it."

"Be careful you don't get yourself Shastri-ed."

Jami laughed all the more. "That would be ironic, wouldn't it. But no chance. The zone will be far out in the Pacific."

"If Harley's right…"

"Yeah."

"But what will you see from up there?"

"I'll see it happen," Jami said, sparking with enthusiasm again. "There's nothing else for me to do. My people and those from the Geo Survey have put all the sensors and monitoring equipment all over the volcanic islands, and they won't tell us anything new anyway. I want to actually see a volcano in the first moment of eruption."

"I hope it's not the last thing you see," Felicity said grimly.

"I won't mind if it is," Jami said harshly. Both women shivered at that thought.

As she spoke, she only had to turn in her chair and see the mountain in question. In fact the entire island of Tahiti was the slopes of Orohena, which was at the centre and towered 7000 feet. It was a gigantic, sharp pinnacle of rock, as exotic in form as the Matterhorn, and every river ran through gorges that were steep fissures in its sides to the coral reefs around the island. Here, in this hotel restaurant at Venus Point, Orohena's sabre-point stood out plainly against the red sky of sunset.

"Are you sure it will blow?" Felicity asked.

"Of all the mountains in the affected zone, it is the most likely. It is the most unstable structure of all of them. That pinnacle is really just a volcanic plug, and when the pressure is on, it'll pop."

It was Felicity's turn to try a bad French accent. "And if it pops, the champagne flows, as one French Administrator put it to me."

"And I shall be there to drink it," Jami said, again raising her glass in a toast.

Felicity clinked her dubiously. "How bad will it be, Jami?"

"Hard to say," Jami said grimly. "But that magma will have to come to the surface and it will be moving one hell of a lot of rock to do so. If it gives easily, there will probably only be minor earthquake damage and landslides. But if it resists and holds for a time, it'll go with a hell of a bang, and all the rock you see there will go up in the air and come down on Papeete and all the surrounding terrain. That will be terrible."

"Fools."

"I hate talking like this," Jami said, feeling again that sadness well within her. "You know, there was a time when I wished for this. I got sick of all those remote locations and wanted it to happen somewhere civilised, somewhere exotic. Well, I got my wish in Italy and I'll get it again tomorrow evening. I feel so awful about it."

Felicity reached and patted the back of Jami's hand. "Jami, you can't hold yourself responsible."

But she did. She was. "Why not? It carries my name. These disasters are the way I'll always be remembered."

"These are forces beyond your control. Beyond any control."

"Still, sometimes I think it's me doing it."

"We all feel like that. Everyone does. If I get out of bed on the other side, or avoid black cats, or say my prayers, maybe it won't happen. Foolish superstitions, Jami."

Jami nodded. Even she thought she was becoming too maudlin over this. "Still, like you say, everyone feels it. It's just I feel it a little bit more than most."

"No. You feel it exactly the same as everyone else. It's just human nature. Whatever is the matter with you?"

"Are you asking as a doctor?"

"No. As a friend."

"There's nothing wrong with me."

"Except a sudden strange recklessness."

"It's what Harley would do."

"Most people would think that a poor example to follow."

Jami offered her a smile of encouragement, as if it was Felicity and not herself that was taking the risks. "It'll be safe tomorrow, really. I know the risks."

"Are you sure it's not a death wish?"

"Of course not. I'm just a bit depressed, that's all. I'm not planning to commit suicide."

Felicity looked at her as if she was a specimen under a microscope.

"But you are suffering depression."

"It's just marginal."

"Which is not a good time to be judging risks."

"I know what I'm doing, Fee. Volcanoes I understand. It's men that fuck me up."

"Oh I see. Men."

"Yes, it's just men. You know?"

"Only too well. I could give you something."

"I should think, Fee, that the exhilaration of actually seeing a mountain erupt will be all the tonic I need."

"Yes, that's it. Stick to mountains. Forget about men."

*

They grabbed the last few hours of sleep that they would get for some time, and then as the sun descended toward the Pacific, they shared a taxi to the airport and flew their separate ways. Felicity flew in the Orion with a team of analysts to be ready to fly immediately to wherever new sleepers might be found. None were expected, since the effected area would be entirely in the middle of the Pacific Ocean, but still they wished to be sure, just in case there was an error and one of the islands might be engulfed.

Jami flew with Pierre Duclos, in circles around the towering peak of Orohena.

"The sunset is very beautiful from up here," Pierre suggested.

But Jami didn't answer and didn't look at the sunset.

"I know what you are looking for," Pierre said over the intercom—it was a twin engine plane with a sealed cabin but it was still rather noisy and rattled rather more than Jami was happy with. "You are one of those fools who think Orohena will become a volcano tonight."

"It will," Jami said sharply. "And I am the very fool who said it would."

"This is nonsense. It has been extinct for thousands of years."

"Until tonight."

"Look for yourself. Extinct. Quiet. No earthquakes. Nothing."

"Expert on volcanoes, are you?"

"Enough to know there would be some fore-warning."

"So you really don't think it will erupt?"

"If I did, we would be flying out to sea, not around and around with the trees dusting our bottom."

"There'll be more than trees dusting our respective bottoms in a moment."

"You know, *mon cherie*. You begin to frighten me."

She wasn't frightened herself. She was exhilarated. As they flew, she operated a video camera but that she pointed only vaguely in the right directions. She didn't want to see it through a viewfinder. She wanted to see with her own eyes. She could use the camera to zoom in on relative spots. Still she kept it running, just in case it might pick up something she was missing.

Ten remote automatic cameras on the ground were also recording the scene, spaced equally all around the island, as they were on several other nearby volcanic islands, and in the Cook Islands too. Never had there been such a preparedness for an eruption, but this time she had the hottest seat in town.

Around they went again as the sun crept nearer the horizon. It was twenty-one minutes before official sunset and the light was clear and nothing was happening. Or so it seemed. Then there was the sudden shock ripping through her body, the moment of nausea that was all so familiar and she knew it was about to happen. Her eyes locked on the mountain, straining for signs.

For it took Jami a moment to realise that there was something going on, and then even longer to grasp what it was. At first there was dust kicking up here and there in the forest below. Earth tremors causing landslides? she wondered. Below the cliffs at the foot of the peak, the trees of the forest on the gentler slopes seemed to be shrinking. Startled flocks of birds flew everywhere.

Trees can't shrink, Jami told herself. She focused with the zoom to get a better idea. Trees fall, they don't shrink...

There were some trees that toppled now, but apart from them, the whole forest seemed to be descending into the ground. Then she realised she was perceiving it the wrong way around. The forest on the slopes was staying where it was—it was the cliffs that were rising out of the ground!

She looked at several places at once. Everywhere, the volcanic rock of the steep cliff faces were rising, dragging themselves out of the ground as if by the roots. She could even see, in places, a line of darker rock appearing above the tree line as stone previously underground was exposed to the daylight. She saw it now—the whole upper pinnacle of the mountain was rising upward.

"Merde!" Pierre said.

Jami grabbed his arm as he tried to move the rudder. "Don't go yet. It's still safe."

Pierre could hardly react. He was staring and blank astonishment at the impossible.

Jami knew what was happening. The pinnacle, all of it, was a giant volcanic plug and now the pressures below were forcing it out, indeed exactly like a cork out of a bottle. Clouds of dust were rising everywhere, and soon her view would be obliterated. She wanted to hang on these last few seconds, to see it all. And even as she thought that, the plug began to break up, with giant cracks opening and flame and smoke bursting through. And then the whole top of the mountain was lost in smoke and the cloud rushed toward them.

"We can go now," she told Pierre.

But the pilot was in a paralysis of terror and she needed to belt him about the head. He nearly vomited, wide-eyed and gagging convulsively.

Jami jerked the rudder to swing them away from the blast and then Pierre had it. He opened the throttles and dived low and away they went, with what sounded like rain beginning to pelt on the skin of the plane.

Stones, Jami knew, and then rocks.

There were several severe crashes as boulders bounced off them but somehow they remained airborne. Pierre, a great pilot after all, dived for speed and then swooped upward to get above the igneous hailstorm. The plane bumped and jolted wildly and the windscreen was awash with mud, blinding them. But Pierre was climbing and knew which way out to sea was—he didn't need any visibility.

"Stupid bitch," he was shouting in English. "Stupid stupid bitch."

He seemed to be addressing this to the aeroplane, but Jami supposed that it was more likely her. She didn't care. Long before they had escaped the danger zone, scurrying ahead of a great wall of fire, she flopped back in her seat with a huge smile.

"Wow," she cried. "That was fantastic."

*

Far out to sea, the shockwave hit the Orion as a severe bump.

The technicians were all watching their instruments and only Felicity, looking out a side window, saw the huge cloud rise above the horizon. It was, she observed, exactly like a nuclear mushroom cloud, soaring upward, illuminated from beneath by fire and throughout by bolts of lightning. The technicians babbled jargon, only a little of which she understood. She didn't ask for explanations—she would get all the details she wanted later. For the moment, she picked up what she could from what had become a cacophony of voices and whirring engines and beepers.

Five volcanoes had erupted—three in the Society Islands and two in the Cook Islands, all exactly as predicted. 7.8 on the scale. The epicentre was far from any island but they were checking thirty kilometres outward from the centre for signs of habitable places.

"Shit!" someone shouted. "There's a ship. There's a fucking ship, ten klicks from the epicentre."

That, Felicity knew, was her own cue. She undid her seat belt and moved over to the operator who had spoken, leaning over his shoulder to look at the radar screen before him. She could plainly see the ship within the sweep.

"Any idea what?"

"Looks like a destroyer. Both the Americans and French have warships in the area."

"Yes, I know," Felicity said. You couldn't blame them for wanting to gather their own data, but at what cost? She felt the Orion banking steadily. She picked up a headset and spoke to Captain Taylor, the pilot.

"I assume we are going to overfly that ship."

"Yes," Taylor answered. "We're in contact with Fleet Task Force Command right now."

"Hard to make out," the radio operator reported. "The Yanks seem to have lost contact with one of their ships. USS Barton. Ahh, they're calling us." There was a pause. And then. "They admit loss of contact. They want to know if its safe to approach her."

"Tell them, yes," Felicity said automatically. "There are no contaminants involved here. From a medical point of view, they can approach the ship, and board it, safely. They can expect to find everyone in a state of unconsciousness, from which they'll recover in eight days."

The radio operator gazed at her quizzically. "Do you really want to transmit that?"

"Yes I do."

Within minutes they located the USS Barton, looking remarkably awkward and cumbersome despite its trim lines as it rolled with the turbulent sea. The violence of the sea itself seemed incongruous, under the gentle yellow glow of a twilight suddenly extended. Three tidal waves, of increasing size, had departed the area that they knew of, to batter the coastal communities all the way around the Pacific rim. The waves crashed over Barton's decks and she bobbed about like a cork in a stream. A French frigate, they had been assured, was on the way to take her in tow.

"To where?" Felicity demanded.

"Papeete."

"Is there a dock left to tow her to?"

"Early reports suggest only superficial damage there."

Felicity nodded, moving in the cramped thundering confines of the cluttered tunnel that was the interior of the Orion. Everything was illuminated only by the monitor screens and dial lights. She pulled off the domed helmet they had given her and extracted with considerable effort, a mobile telephone from her pocket and punched out a number. An excited voice answered.

"Jami. Are you okay?"

"Wow, Felicity, you should have seen it."

"I'm rather glad I didn't, kiddo. How are things there?"

"Orohena blew all right, but it all went straight up—the entire top of the mountain. It rained boulders for a while. Hailstones the size of television sets. They'd hit and bounce. I saw one go straight through the roof of a house, out the front door and into the house across the road. I guess there's a lot of people killed or injured, but the town is still standing and its nowhere near as bad as we feared."

"Is it possible for a ship to dock in the harbour?"

"Oh yes. And the runway at the airport is still okay. Everything is working here, more or less. A few fires. Practically no panic. Mostly there are people all around the island standing and watching the show."

"As long as you're okay."

"I'm fine. What happened at your end?"

"We have a ship load of sleepers, compliments of the US Navy."

"You should have seen it, Felicity. The whole top of the mountain rose like a Saturn rocket and then—wham-o."

"Take care of yourself, Jami."

"I will. Bye Fee."

Felicity broke the connection. For a moment, she thought of the serenity of whisking about the polished sterile floors of the hospital, of the warmth of nights on the couch in front of the television, of the gorgeous aroma when Wendell had just mowed the lawn. That was who she really was. Not this unfortunate thing in a hellish dark tin can, all atangle with wiring. She fitted her helmet again, returning to her android self, and spoke to Captain Taylor.

"How many men on a ship like that?"

"About two hundred. Men *and women* in the US Navy these days."

"Instruct them to follow full quarantine procedures. Ask for permission for me to board the ship at the earliest possible opportunity."

"They said not without the appropriate security clearance."

"Tell them those sailors aren't in the US Navy anymore. They now belong to Project Earthshaker."

"I think you better tell them that yourself, Dr Campbell," Taylor said with a chuckle.

11
ELECTROMAGNETIC RODENT GHOSTS

On this radiant Athens evening, Andromeda watched the pilgrims flood into the city. Away to her left were the orange remnants of a glorious sunset, over the right shoulder a tumid full moon was rising, at her back they had turned on the lights that floodlit the Acropolis especially for the occasion. From her high vantage point, she watched for some sign of the convoy advancing through the streets but it was Lorna Simmons, sitting beside her and watching the procession on a video monitor, who would give the signal to begin.

Athens had taken them to her bosom as only Athens could. Originally they had booked the amphitheatre at the foot of the Acropolis for the concert that would follow, expecting only the pilgrims to be there. But soon it became apparent that the whole city was determined to get into the act. As the convoy advanced along the road from Corinth, the people came out of their farmhouses and villages to line the way and watch the procession pass, after which they fell in behind, swelling the numbers to an uncountable host.

Lorna and the governors of the city went into a panic and hastily expanded arrangements. There was a huge scaffold built by the men renovating the Acropolis with a high platform that clung to the cliffs just below the walls on the crest. The giant speakers, as big as shipping containers, had been positioned there and the lights moved and now the crowd could gather on the broad slope below, and back into the excavations of the Agora, and down through the throats of the streets that led to those places from the body of the city beyond.

It was expected by the general public that the procession would pass straight through the city and carry on, presumably to Jerusalem. But it would not. It would end here. Early that morning—twelve hours ago now, Andromeda had felt the tremor through her body and, with a glance sideways at Lorna, acknowledged that the time of the pilgrimage had passed.

"Do you think they'll still come?" Lorna wondered.

Out on the road, Brian Carrick had reported that while a great cry had arisen from the travellers and there was some brief panic, they were too much caught up in the momentum of the event to deviate from their course.

Lorna and Andromeda sat in the communications tent, awaiting news of friends.

"Sure is a strange sensation, Babe. When it ends," Andromeda said.

"Something like it must have been to have our umbilical cords cut," Lorna supposed.

"I don't remember that, Sugar. I'm thinkin' it's more like when a love affair ends."

"I never felt that good when someone walked out on me," Lorna said grimly.

"Uh-uh. It's like the way you feel when *you* walk out on *them*. You got that moment of doubt when you're sayin' to yourself—maybe I oughta go back and make it up—but then you say, hell no! And you walk on Baby. You got a stab of pain, a moment of sadness, and then comes the flood of relief that all that shit is over."

Through the speech, she saw Lorna watching her quizzically. "I wouldn't know, Andy. I always went back."

Soon, word was relayed that Felicity and Jami were both okay and the moment of relief and jubilation was followed by sadness as information about the devastation in the Society Islands came through.

"Now that was the same sort of feeling going backwards," Lorna remarked.

"No. Those are real emotions. The Shastri thing is different," Andromeda was sure.

But things were happening and it was time to get on the move.

"Are you going to be alright to go on straight after all this emotional trauma?" Lorna asked with serious concern—it was a technical question.

"You bet, sweetheart," Andromeda grinned. "I never felt so exhilarated in all my life."

And it was true. In her time she had been possessed of every sort of self-doubt and stage-fright and for a long time she needed to be stoned just to get out on the stage. But all that was behind her now. She walked to her spot on the stage, in the darkness with the lights of the entire city before her, and she knew she was going to be fantastic, that this would be her greatest performance ever. In a moment they would hit the flood lights and the music and her voice would carry out over the city, and everyone who was in the streets would hear her. And in Athens on such a warm clear evening, the streets were invariably crowded. She had a full orchestra and a rock band—the Tum-thumpers—hottest in the business right now. But mostly, she had herself. This would be Andromeda Starlight's greatest performance—what do you think of that, Edna Krebbs of Trinidad?

Down there she could see right along an arterial road, and away in the distance, she saw Chrissie. Saint Christine. A pristine white figure on the back of a truck with her arms raised to the heavens. Behind her, all manner of moving lights and pandemonium seemed to be going on. Anxiously, she turned toward Lorna, hidden away behind and at the same moment, Lorna said. "Hit it!"

The lights came on blindingly and Andromeda threw her arms wide and went into *The Age of Aquarius* from *Hair* and she could feel the earth stand still and every face turn toward her in her dazzling brilliance. She sang with her mightiest voice and behind her the thirteen ladies of the backing group seemed insignificant by comparison. She went straight on with several other popular songs designed to draw people toward her and although she could see little with the dazzling lights in her eyes, she sensed them gathering below her.

Now she went into her full repertoire of gospel songs, bouncing back and forth between herself and the backing group, and while that happened, she saw Chrissie climbing the hill, moving through the gathering crowd with a big Italian chap clearing her way. Chrissie, the lights making her white robes glow mystically, ascended the steps—it was almost surprising that she didn't simply levitate herself onto the stage, such was her aura of spirituality. She took her place beside Andromeda on the stage, thumping on a tambourine of all things, and completely off the beat. By then, an enormous crowd had gathered all around and police and soldiers were struggling to control them and Andromeda sang *Amazing Grace* to quiet them and bring Amazing Chrissie to centre stage.

Andromeda, exhausted, soaked in sweat, utterly triumphant, flopped in the seat beside Lorna, away in a dark part of the stage. Lorna handed her a flask of athletic juice.

"I hope there's some scotch in this," Andromeda said with a gasp.

"Aren't you going to ask me how it went?" Lorna asked with a grin.

"I know how it went."

"Then consider the unfortunate lot of the humble PR girl. You've upstaged my wildest promotional exaggerations."

Out there before her now silent audience, Chrissie led them in prayer and then spoke to them of the Hand of God and how it had brought them here and how to prepare themselves for the Apocalypse.

"Only nine months to go," Andromeda remarked ruefully.

"Harley says most of us will be dead some time before then," Lorna said quietly.

Soon she would go into her second bracket—her Earthshaker performance complete with the dazzling light show, hot from Vas Vegas. But for the moment, there was the tranquility of Saint

Chrissie, guiding the devoted along the path to paradise.

"I wonder where Harley is. He ought to be here," Andromeda realised.

"Oh. He rang. While you were on stage. He's in Washington and—get this—watching you live on television."

"Really?"

"Yes. The networks dumped their regular programs and took you live. You're the biggest hit in history."

"Well, that's how it feels," Andromeda admitted and then jerked her head toward Chrissie. "Only is it me or is it her."

"For all our sakes," Lorna said grimly. "It better be you."

*

Glen would have been a pushover, for anyone except poor Jami Shastri, Lorna was thinking. She sat opposite him in the cafe, watching his eye roam as he talked about himself and his importance to the project. Lorna listened to none of it. He was a good looking bloke and far too aware of it, athletic and proud of his successes, intelligent but unable to allow that to shine through his conversation.

A weird sort of loyalty to Jami had caused Lorna to decide to hate him and she was pleased to discover that it was no difficult task. It would have been akin to white-anting one of Chrissie's rare boyfriends, to which she had never succumbed despite many temptations. It was a joy, to sit and listen to Glen trying to 'hit on her' as the yanks put it. This was going to be the biggest fresh-air shot in history and the thought pleased her deeply.

But Glen would not give in. He was so sure of himself. By then you would have got the impression that he was Project Earthshaker and Thyssen merely a figurehead. And Jami non-existent. Her name had not even been mentioned. But the truth, if it needed revealing, was made plain just an hour before when Thyssen brought her for the first time to the dungeon that was the headquarters of Project Earthshaker.

This really was a basement. Air ducts and water pipes

snaked about beneath the ceiling everywhere and you could hear the pumps humming through the thin partitions. The stairs descended from ground level and ended at the car park, where a door marked Strictly No Entry admitted them to a steel stairway and they plunged down to the janitor's quarters. Long corridors carried them away from the elevator (she was enjoying her knowledge of American idiom) and through dark places with exposed fluorescent lighting to the door of the office they inhabited.

There were five computer screens, each with their own seating spaces, but the chairs were a hotchpotch obviously scavenged. The file cabinets showed streaks of rust. Every bit of vertical space had printouts and notes and maps and photographs stuck on it, often tiers of over sticking. Each of the computers and all of the electrical equipment had been deprived of cabinets and from them disembowelled components clung to their function by bunches of wires. Heaped boxes of additional components littered the floor.

"What did you say our budget was?" Lorna asked when she saw it.

Thyssen smiled. "It all functions, and it's away from prying eyes."

"Unless you include the rats," Lorna said with a shudder.

"Any rat that came in here would be electrocuted in thirty seconds," Glen grinned. "So watch where you step."

That idea stuck in Lorna's mind and kept her rooted to the spot.

Thyssen introduced them—until then she had assumed Glen to be a technician's apprentice.

"How we doing?"

"Sixty-nine percent on the Japan trench region."

Thyssen grabbed handfuls of print-outs and shuffled through them and the two men spoke ten minutes of solid jargon, not one word of which Lorna understood. It made her realise just how much they simplified their thoughts for her benefit on other occasions.

"I hope you don't expect me to remember any of this," she interrupted at one stage.

Both looked at her in annoyance.

"You're not supposed to remember any of it," Thyssen said grimly.

"Then what am I doing here?"

Thyssen ran his eye around his domain. "I just thought you might like to see the throbbing heart of our operation."

"Yes, I thought I might have too."

"We'll be finished in a few minutes," Thyssen gruffed at her. "Why don't you make us all coffee?"

The last hundred times some male had said that to her, they had been met with the most vehement refusal—this time it sounded like an excellent option. She looked around with a frown.

"You mean one of these contraptions makes coffee?"

"Over behind the door."

She found a sink and a bench, stained beyond reason, and three jugs all with their electrical innards hanging out. One of them was plugged into a power point that was hanging from a hole in the wall, but the red light was on and she bravely made assumptions. There was a coffee plunger stained the colour of beer bottles and some mugs all suspiciously coffee coloured that she suspected might have originally been white. Into this lot, she was required to add the most expensive Brazilian coffee on the market. No one could accuse them of lacking class.

They sat on chairs amid the jumble of wiring and gadgets and Thyssen studied the monitor screen, Glen occasionally pointing things out, Lorna still looking for electromagnetic rodent ghosts.

"Yeah, I got it," Thyssen finally said. "Now you two piss off for an hour and let me get into this."

So they went, Lorna and Jami's fantasy, to the cafe where he tried to chat her up at ten o'clock in the morning. But there was something occurring to her.

"What's he doing? Right now, I mean?"

"Working out the final position."

Lorna arched her eyebrows at the obvious contradiction. "I thought you did that?"

"No. I work up the models. This time, with the data from Tahiti, I've run 602 models and they all have slightly different answers. But most of them point to a region of about a thousand square kilometres. Harley then takes over and works out which is the right one."

"How?"

Now that they had got down to scientific facts instead of seduction, he was able to be quite candid. "I don't know. Theoretically, he can't know any more about it than I do. But somehow he does."

"Intuition?"

"Not the way he'd put it."

"But is he guessing?"

"Only if he's wrong."

"But he was right last time."

"He sure was. With the data I had, I was able to place it accurately within about a thousand miles. With the same data, he was able to place it within a hundred."

"Which is why he's the boss and you're a humble student?"

"That's it exactly."

Lorna thought about it. There was only one possible answer. "He must know something that you don't know."

"No. You're missing the point, Lorna. He knows *everything* that I don't know."

Then Thyssen was there. He walked up to the table in a great hurry, jerking his thumb over his shoulder.

"It's all set for you, sonny. You got two hours to prove me wrong."

"You know I can't," Glen grumbled.

He rose from the table and left.

"Right, lassie. Our cab awaits."

"The big announcement?"

"That's right."

"Whose turn this time?"

"NBC."

He handed her a slip of paper. On it he had written '38 north 140 west'- longitude and latitude.

"Where's that?" Lorna asked.

"Right smack in the middle of Honshu, which is the main island of Japan. This is gonna make Italy look like a marshmallow roast."

*

By the time the pilgrims had been loaded on the ship—which had come around the peninsula to meet them at Piraeus—Kevin Wagner and Brian Carrick were there to see them off.

"By the way," Brian said, "I got a message from Joe."

Wagner hoped that he knew what it would be about. They were standing on the wharf watching the ship sail, two men both a long way from home.

"A fourteen million dollar message," Brian elaborated with an inscrutable smile.

Wagner hated it. He was being played with. "Why did the message go to you?" he demanded.

"Because Joe wanted someone to check it out and see if you plan to spend the project's money wisely."

"How would you know what was wise and what wasn't?"

"I wouldn't. I just report back to Joe and presumably to Thyssen. They make the decisions. I'm just their eyes and ears."

"I'd rather wait until Thyssen gets here."

"He won't be here. He's gone to Washington to chat with the President."

"It'll wait until he gets back," Wagner persisted. He truly did not want Brian Carrick or anyone else prying into his affairs.

"No it won't," Brian grinned. "That was the other part of the message. Report back by Wednesday."

"Why Wednesday?"

"Joe, like Thyssen and that other bloke, moves in mysterious ways. But aren't you, like me, just a little surprised that such funds might be available?"

"Nothing surprises me anymore," Wagner sighed.

Left little alternative, Wagner decided that he ought to explain. He suspected that the time limit was a real one, and anyway, Joe Solomon was not the type to panic nor make jokes. He hated the idea of Brian checking up on him, but it might have been worse. In fact, when he thought about it, he realised almost anyone else might be worse.

"We need a base," Wagner said flatly.

"Do we? I thought we were based in Melbourne."

"Not suitable. Too far away."

"How can it be too far away from anywhere, when we are dealing with random global events. Everywhere is too far away in those circumstances."

"We need our own airfield, and a place to house the pilgrims. And somewhere to set up a nerve centre for our operations."

"It all sounds disgustingly military to me, Kev."

Wagner could shrug that off. The idea, he knew, was to keep it as simple as possible. "It happens that our needs for the present and those for the foreseeable future can be met immediately, if we move quickly enough. I'm talking about the existing arrangements in Italy. The convent which can continue to be used as a hospital, the village, the damaged area, the airstrip the Americans built there and their facilities. Everything we need and if we don't claim it immediately it will be broken up and redistributed. You understand?"

"You want to buy the whole lot up."

"Sure I do. Of course, the locals can stay to keep the infrastructure running—they'll just have a new landlord—us."

"Sounds like a hell of a complicated thing to do."

"It is, unless you know the right people. It happens I have an acquaintance who can arrange it all for us, immediately. He owns a great part of it already, and has good relations with the other owners."

"I though the Catholic Church still owned the monastery?"

"They do. But my friend can arrange for us to make use

of it as we presently do, and keep the nun's running the place otherwise. It's a very good deal."

"A snap for a mere fourteen million."

"That's the deal. And Joe knows that. I don't know why he is hesitating."

"I do," Brian said quietly. "I can understand why we need the hospital and the airstrip. I don't understand about the other military facility."

They stood on the dock the day before, two men with their hands in their pockets, looking around, standing just a little further apart than might have been expected. Wagner directed his gaze toward the departing ship as he spoke.

"What I need is a base, to train and house my security people," Wagner explained.

"It'll do that all right," Brian said, also squinting off into the distance. "You could base the Red Army there."

"Before long, I believe I can expect a couple of hundred personnel seconded from the US Navy."

"Somehow I can't see the US Navy giving them up so easily."

"I think they won't have any choice. In any case, Thyssen said to prepare for a steadily expanding force. They need to be trained and to keep their training up. And they need a base somewhere nice and central to everywhere."

"Fine," Brian agreed. "Although I'm still having some trouble with the idea of being central to a global event."

"Central to the largest population centres, where, presumably, the greatest need for security will be required."

"And we house all stray sleepers in the local hotels, right?"

"Sure. And we can add prefab housing for greater numbers at will."

"And all for a mere fourteen million."

"A fantastic bargain, Brian."

"Fantastic is right."

"Come on, Carrick. Look beyond the end of your nose."

"Keep your shirt on, Kev. I can see certain advantages in the situation, assuming the project escalates."

"It will."

"It might. There are no certainties."

"Give the idea a chance, sport."

"Haven't you noticed how I'm not laughing. This character you're doing deals with. He's the local Mafia don, isn't he."

"Something like that."

"You sure that's the sort of folk we ought to be doing deals with, Kev? They have a very extreme way of closing deals in their favour."

"All the more reason why we use the money to buy them out of it completely."

"Deals with the devil, Kev. They never come out the way you plan."

Wagner groaned. There plainly wasn't anywhere to go in this direction. Brian Carrick could be so damned stubborn. Why couldn't he see how this mattered?

"All right, Brian. So tell me. What do you suggest?"

"Wait and see what happens."

"It'll be too late then."

"Too late for what?"

"Can't you see how we need to be organised. This thing is starting to get right out of hand."

"I'll say it is."

"And that's what you're going to tell Joe?"

"Nar, I'll keep my opinions to myself. I'll tell him it's a bargain. But it doesn't matter much what I say because you aren't going to get this sort of money anyhow."

"Sooner or later, something like this is going to need to be done."

"Then let's do it later, and only when it's necessary."

"Not much on forward planning, are you Brian?"

"Do you really believe you can plan something like this? You got no idea what's going to happen next."

But neither did Brian Carrick, because as it happened, Joe Solomon provided the funds and Wagner got his base.

*

The Oval Office was a masterful illusion for it drew the eyes inward from both sides to the man behind the desk at the middle. Not that Eugene Grayson needed such assistance—he was a startlingly charismatic man, boyishly handsome, tall and elegant of movement, his black skin like polished mahogany. No man in history had travelled further from slavery than he, and yet neither did any man more closely resemble Jack Kennedy, despite the difference in skin coloration. He was living proof of the ignorance of racial discrimination, both in his appearance and the screams of betrayal from the rioting Afro-Americans in the southern states.

President Grayson rose from behind the chair and walked around the desk with a huge smile and an extended hand of welcome. Thyssen wondered if he knew the circumstances under which his visitor had arrived, politely arrested by a team of FBI agents, body searched and interviewed in a fashion that seemed mostly intended assure him that he was vulnerable to serious unspecified charges and test his views on patriotism. They were plainly none too happy with what they heard, even though Thyssen tried to co-operate and reassure them of his good intentions. He had guessed where it was all leading. When he saw that Lorna Simmons did not appear on the evening news as anticipated, he knew he could expect rather more than a reprimand from the Board of Governors. There weren't many people in the country with the power to persuade NBC to pull a news segment for which they had paid an exorbitant sum for exclusive rights.

But Eugene Grayson, consummate political animal, could don his campaign smile and still manage the last of two hundred handshakes that day.

"Professor Thyssen, you don't know what an honour it is to meet you at last. Come, sit here. I hope you are not inconvenienced by the late hour."

Thyssen's brain all but failed him. In the first place, he had no idea what time it might have been. The pretence by Grayson was so overwhelming that Thyssen was unable to believe that he must have known the circumstances of his visitor's arrival. He wanted to say the most cynical and hurtful thing possible but all he could think of was to say `I didn't vote for you' which would not only have been childish but ridiculous since Thyssen had never voted for any politician in his life. He could only remain silent and shuffle into the chair. His body absorbed the comfort desperately.

Grayson remained standing, continued smiling, and walked away from the desk to stand by the window in a classic presidential pose.

"It's a beautiful night, Professor. Don't you think?"

"I wouldn't know," Thyssen replied. "I spent most of it in your basement."

The President turned from the window to eye him coldly. All trace of the friendly smile was gone now, just when kindness entered his tone of voice.

"Now Professor, you must not be hostile. We have important matters to discuss and I hope we can do so in an amicable manner."

"Do you have any idea what's happened to me tonight?"

At this, Eugene Grayson was able to laugh. Perhaps he was not so far from the cruelties of slavery as Thyssen had imagined.

"I'm sure you understand that certain precautions and procedures must be followed before an interview with the President can be granted."

"I don't remember requesting any such interview."

"You have a reputation as a very dangerous man, Professor."

"I'm a sedentary academic nudging sixty. I shudder to think what my blood pressure is right now."

Grayson advanced to Thyssen's side of the desk and leaned on it. Thyssen could have head butted him in the balls if he'd had the strength.

"I'm sorry. It was my idea that I talk to you alone. Those people responsible for my safety insisted on certain precautions. But I'm sure you understand that already."

It was true. He understood it only too well. He even began

to feel pathetic, as if he was protesting too much. Feeling guilty about being mistreated? The verbal manipulative skill of this man was awesome.

"It's odd you'd want to talk to a man you've gone to so much trouble to muzzle."

"Not a lot of trouble really," Grayson said as he drifted back behind the desk and sat, leaning on his forearms, hands clasped before him, ready to be reasonable. "Surely you can see how we cannot allow an individual like yourself to make such far-reaching announcements unhindered."

"I'm just telling them what's going to happen. That's my job."

"No, Professor, it is not. Your job is to gather data and draw conclusions and pass your recommendations on to the relevant authorities. Our job is to decide who tells who what."

"And your natural response is to secrecy on the basis that the less the public knows, the better you can control them."

Grayson laughed, reaching for a more personal tone. "You really are still the naive under-graduate at heart, Harley. Look, all we want is time to study your data and conclusions and make a broad-based decision regarding the announcement. Perhaps we will decide that your action is correct, but first we must study all aspects of the effects of any announcement."

"The more time you have to evacuate the region, the more lives you will save."

"You cannot just evacuate a million people without a clear idea of what you are doing. Suppose there is an error and you evacuate them into the path of the disaster—the death toll will be increased manyfold, quite unnecessarily."

"There is no error."

"Harley, surely you must see that we cannot take any one man's word for this, no matter how skilful and well qualified he is. We must at least have the opportunity to consider your data and draw independent conclusions. You must also see that."

Thyssen nodded in agreement. He was beginning to get the run of it now.

"Yes, I see that. Which is exactly why I went ahead on my own. No two scientists are going to agree on this. Only someone who knows the subject as intimately as I do can possibly reach the correct conclusion."

"I think you underestimate your colleagues..."

"I was precisely correct last time. No one agreed with me."

"Because no one else possessed your data. Now we do."

It was a slip. Thyssen could see it plainly. Not a flicker of a grimace showed in Grayson's face, but you could feel it ripple through his aura.

"Do you now?" Thyssen said provocatively.

Grayson sighed and bowed his head and when he looked up, his eyes flashed with anger.

"Yes. The facilities of Project Earthshaker have been seized and everyone involved placed under house arrest."

"Then why are you bothering with this pleasant little chat?"

"Because we wish to retain the project and we wish to retain your input..."

Thyssen could feel the anger rising in him like bile. "But on your terms, to your agenda. I don't think so."

"Then the project funds will have to be withdrawn..."

"That would be idiotic," Thyssen snapped.

"You will not raise your voice in this room!"

"You have no sensible reason for doing this. It isn't even in your own best interests. But there's some power to be had and you just can't stand the idea that you don't control it. You'll do anything, take any risk, just to make sure that all of the power is in your hands."

"You cannot speak to the President of the United Sates in that fashion, Professor Thyssen. Get out!" Grayson demanded. The secret service men had mysteriously appeared in the room.

Thyssen was on his feet anyway. "Well this time it won't run for you, *Mr.* President! I have always distrusted governments and I have always been vindicated in doing so. This time you are out of your depth, as you will soon find to your loss and to that of thousands of others. You're up against forces so far beyond your control that you can't get your head around them and yet you try to dictate terms. Well you can rot in your folly for all I care!"

Nothing happened for a moment. When Thyssen was prepared to be dragged from the room, heels bumping over the carpet, shouting all the way, the secret service men had not seized him. They stood beside and behind him, ready to play their game of stacks on the mill if Thyssen made the slightest threatening gesture, but Grayson had signalled them to wait. It took some time for the President to bring himself under control—as for Thyssen, he had lost it completely and would have continued to rave had the President not roared back at him. "Please, Professor Thyssen! Listen to me!"

"You have nothing to say that I want to hear!" Thyssen thundered back.

Grayson let another pause pass, then tried again for a calmer tone. "Suppose I said you can just walk out of here."

"I don't believe it."

"You can go. After you've heard what I have to say."

"And the project?"

"It can be fully restored at any time."

"At what cost?"

"Only that you withhold your statements regarding the time and location of..."

"Not a chance!"

"Please listen... the location of the next eruption, just long enough to allow us to examine your data."

"Not possible."

"You must be reasonable, Harley. Thousands of lives are at stake."

"Precisely. And I will not allow the political priorities of the government of the United States nor any other country to override my duty to the population of the earth as a whole. They have the right to know everything I know, as soon as I know it."

They were heating up again, standing toe to toe now, each with his nose within inches of the others. "No individual can be permitted to dictate terms to the planet in the manner you describe!" Grayson positively yelled.

"It isn't me dictating terms. The planet is doing that. My position is just a simple case of honesty. No secrets. Just plain honesty!" Thyssen shouted back.

"Such ill-considered honesty can be very dangerous."

"Only to people who live by lies."

Grayson turned away, shaking with anger. Thyssen was sweating like a horse and weak at the knees. The secret service men fidgeted and glanced desperately from one to the other. Once more, Grayson had forced a calm into his voice. His will power was formidable.

"I had hoped to avoid this, Harley, but I'm afraid we must detain you."

"That won't stop the information from getting out."

"It will give us the breathing space we need, and maybe give you a bit of time to come down from your absurdly high moral ground. Once we decide to make our announcement, you will be released and allowed to continue."

"You can't stop the truth. Hundreds, maybe thousands, of people already know."

"Yes. You put it on the Net. We know that. We've put two hundred identical alternative predictions into the system alongside it."

"You can't keep something as big as this under wraps," Thyssen told him.

"I can keep you and your friends under wraps," Grayson said quietly. "That will just have to be enough."

"There's only me. The others can't harm you."

"No. But maybe some pressure on your loyal little team might just help you see reason."

"You have no right to do this!"

"I was elected to protect the best interests of this nation, Harley. Who elected you?"

"I serve no interests. I'm just doing my job."

"Your job is to do what I tell you!"

"My job is to present the facts in a completely disinterested manner, which I have done, and will continue to do and there isn't a damned thing you can do to stop me."

"Don't be so sure."

"Is that a threat, Mr. President?"

"Get out of here, Thyssen. Take him away and lock him up."

"You'll have to kill me to stop me, Grayson," Thyssen raged, completely out of control now. As the secret service men closed in, gripped his biceps and set about removing him from the room, he yelled back over his shoulder, "Think about the political cost of that when the Shastri Effect hits California!"

That brought everything to a standstill. Grayson stood, clenching and unclenching his fists, but his look caused the secret servicemen to freeze. Thyssen, the secret servicemen holding him roughly by the arms, gazed back at the President and smiled faintly.

Grayson raised his head, his eyes shinning defiantly, his brow glistening with beads of sweat. "You're bluffing."

Thyssen shook his head sadly, a grim smile stretched on his face, his narrow eyes squinted as if facing bright light. "The concept of truth is really alien to you isn't it? You just don't understand it at all."

Grayson was right at the end of his tether. "I am the President of the United States! You can't talk to me in this tone."

"Which only makes you a bigger fool that everybody else!" And they were roaring like a pair of combatant dinosaurs again.

"I won't play your game, Thyssen! I won't call your bluff!"

"Data doesn't bluff!"

Grayson sighed. The secret service men had Thyssen by the arms but they remained, waiting for the dismissal that never came. The President had his head bowed, his face strained with what might have been physical pain. Gradually, that effort of will forced him back under control and when he finally raised his head, he was calm again.

"Tell me about California," he said quietly.

Thyssen grinned. "No. You cannot be trusted with that information."

"You bastard," Grayson thundered erratically. "So what was all that crap about the public's right to know."

"I tell everybody or I tell nobody. No compromise."

Grayson sagged. He slid into his chair, his head in his hands. When he spoke it was to the security men. "It's too late to go on with this. Take him back to the hotel. Keep him under guard."

"That's another advantage in always telling the truth, Eugene. You never have to make difficult decisions."

Thyssen was walking to the door, the secret service men trailing behind. He heard Grayson's voice pursuing him.

"Don't let anybody talk to him. Don't allow any harm to come to him. Don't let anything happen concerning him, whatsoever."

As he went through the door, Thyssen was grinning as widely as he could.

*

Joe Solomon sat behind his desk in his wheelchair that day, which he never usually did. Ordinarily, there was the well-practiced action in which he transferred himself into his executive chair which he performed without thinking these days. But that morning, it had slipped his mind and the thought amused him—a definite Freudian slip, he knew. He was staying in his wheelchair in case he needed a fast getaway, as any criminal should. Ridiculous, of course, but somehow the idea persisted as he waited for Barney Touhey to arrive. The picture of himself trundling through the office with policemen in hot pursuit was just too funny for words.

Barney arrived and didn't notice the difference. But he did notice the worried look on Joe's face and commented immediately on that.

"I think I'm going to be arrested," Joe said.

"How exciting," Barney said. "Did you do it?"

"Unfortunately, yes."

"If you are about to confess to a crime, perhaps I ought to have my lawyer present."

"Very funny."

"Will I get to be an accessory after the fact or whatever it is?"

"You watch too much television. And I think you'd better take this seriously."

Barney took a deep breath, forced the smile off his face, and sat ready to be serious.

Joe Solomon eyed his friend strangely. It was good to have friends who accepted you without question, even if you were wrong. That was the sort of friend he needed now.

"First," Joe began. "You will not be implicated in any way because this conversation will never have taken place. I'll never admit I told you and you will deny all knowledge."

"Does that mean I leave now?"

"Lissie will take over the business here, should I get into hot water, but I don't want him to know anything about this. I want to keep the firm's normal business and my dubious extra-curricular activities completely separate."

Barney nodded. He was growing very red in the face as he sat, hunched, ready for whatever horror lay ahead.

"Okay," Joe went on. "I'm telling you because I think someone ought to know... in case something that doesn't bear thinking about happens to me. You understand?"

"Not at all."

"I got a call from that sinister John Cornelius character, late at night, in whispers, the full melodramatic bit. He told me that Project Earthshaker was just about to be scrapped and that Thyssen was arrested, everyone else could expect to be, and generally we were to be taken out of existence."

"That ought to be a great relief to you."

"Well, I didn't believe it, of course. But I checked. Thyssen has this set-up at MIT—some of his students on computers doing his sums for him—and I called there. I got a gruff voice demanding to know who I was."

"I see," Barney said. "So you reckon they've been nabbed."

"Exactly. And I assumed that the funds would be seized."

"No doubt. How much are we talking about here?"

"Over ten million."

Barney choked on his cup of tea. "That much?"

"Yes. Well, it is a very big project. And there was income. From short term investments and television rights and Andromeda's concerts make a huge profit. I kept all that in a sort of slush fund."

"Ten million dollar slush funds boggle the mind. I can't imagine it."

"There it is there," Joe said, pointing across the office.

Barney turned in his seat and stared. Beside the shredder was a huge pile of strips. "That is the ten million?"

"More like fifteen. And no, that is the proof of the existence of the fifteen million."

Barney gave a little shudder. In fact, Joe could see his hands were shaking.

"Do I have to ask the obvious question?"

"Well, that whole Tahiti business reminded me that there was a client of mine who died some years back but he included me as silent partner in a little off-shore deal. Quite honest. The deal ended but the array of little companies with their head office in the Christmas Islands remained. I was supposed to wipe it all out but, as I say, the guy died and I forgot."

"So you just dropped the fifteen million in there."

"That's right."

"Is there a project connected to this arrangement?"

"As fate would have it, yes. I bought a chunk of Italy for development."

"I've been to Tuscany. Went there with Margo and the kids in 1984. Beautiful place."

"This is in the south. But it apparently has a village and a convent."

"Will you be Mother Superior?"

"Kevin Wagner is running it. He needs a base to operate and look after the sleepers and train his guards. It has an airstrip."

"Sounds fabulous. When do we leave?"

"When I get out of prison, I suspect."

"Is it illegal?"

"Of course. It's embezzlement."

"Are you sure?"

"The money does legally belong to the US Government."

"Okay."

They both sat for a time now, thinking about it. Clarissa poked her head in and they ordered more desperately needed tea. Neither wanted to speak as they thought through the story so far. In the end, Barney found the right question. "So why did you do this?"

"I don't know," Joe said with a sorrowful shrug. "I can't believe I've done it. I don't see the point of it nor the sense. But it somehow seemed like the right move. It still does, in fact."

"So we can claim deprivation of the balance of your mind."

"I knew exactly what I was doing."

"We can claim that Thyssen had some demonic power over you."

"I retain all of my doubts about that man. I distrust him and his motives. I'm sure he has his own agenda. But nevertheless it seems I felt I owed him this gigantic favour."

Barney raised his eyebrows and offered a sly smile. "So that's what it is. A favour."

"I don't know. I can't say that my actions will be of any benefit to Thyssen nor anybody else. Maybe I've dumped him in the shit. It's impossible to say."

"But you can't withdraw."

"There is no proof that I ever had any such money. How can I claim it back?"

"That was silly of you."

"Except this?'

From his drawer, Joe lifted a compact disk and dangled it before Barney's eyes. It was marked 'Fire and Security Maintenance Contracts'.

"A copy."

"Yes. A complete copy of the accounts. Put it somewhere safe, will you?"

"Won't that implicate me?"

"Not if you think it has our security contracts on it."

"But you don't want to know where."

"Nope."

"I'll visit you every Sunday."

"I'll appreciate that."

Deep within him, Joe was feeling sad, but he was also feeling good. He was feeling clever. Only he wasn't sure what he felt so clever about. Barney eyed him dubiously.

"So, what's the wash-up?"

"They'll never be able to take Project Earthshaker out of existence."

"Is that good?"

"I thought about all those pilgrims, Barney, and how there is likely to be so many more of them. They seemed like the lost tribes to me. So I gave them somewhere to go."

*

"Mr. Carrick, I wonder if you would be good enough to step in here?" the customs official said with a warm friendly Tahitian smile. Two large gentlemen in military uniforms and machine-pistols slung implied the consequences of non-acceptance of this kind offer. He went quietly, exhausted from his long journey, exasperated mostly by the possibility that it was all in vain.

With the Italian pilgrims safely returned to their homes, he had flown to Tahiti to try and assist Felicity in her dealings with the US Navy, but he got no further than this. He was directed into this featureless room with no windows and one door that the man locked as he left. His meagre luggage was placed neatly in the corner. There was a washbasin and mirror and behind the only other door was a toilet. The colours were soft, and lighting subtle, it was hard to recognise the room as what it was—a prison cell. The only real clue was the TV camera, watching him from high up in the corner of the room.

There was a couch on which he could recline and, on the assumption that he would be here for some time, he lay on it and fell sleep immediately. When he awoke three hours later, he was still alone. He used the facilities, shaved and washed and was just about to begin to think of what to do next when there was a knock on the door. A pleasant woman brought coffee and breakfast—bacon and eggs—and she smiled as asked if there was anything else he wanted. The large soldier standing in the doorway suggested that any remark concerning freedom could at best be regarded as a joke.

He ate his breakfast, changed his clothes, dug a paperback out of his pack and lay on the couch to read. It was, after all, a random universe where the laws of mathematics and physics had no meaning, except as good descriptions of the way our minds worked. In such circumstances, was it reasonable for him to expect his own miserable life to make any sense?

So he mulled his way along until there was again the polite knock on the door. They entered, all smiles and deference, and collected him and his luggage and took him out to a transit lounge where he found Felicity Campbell waiting. She sat serenely in the lounge wearing her nice travelling clothes, her suitcases at her feet.

"What's happening?" he asked with a warm smile.

To his astonishment, Felicity gave him a hug. Then she handed him a letter.

"I got one of these too," she said.

Brian tore the envelope open and read. It was signed by the General Secretary of the United Nations, and informed him that Project Earthshaker had been discontinued, and that he was to place himself under house arrest and make himself continuously available to the Special Investigative Committee formed to look into the project and its activities. He was banned from speaking to the media or anyone concerning the project, every part of which was now classified as Top Secret—failure to comply would result in charges being laid under the Official Secrets Act and, more immediately, confinement to a state institution.

It was a very polite letter, on fine paper and with the UN crest at the top but no address for reply. Brian folded it and stuffed it into his pocket. "Tricky to put myself under house arrest when I don't have a home to go to."

"You're welcome at the humble Campbell home in Wellington if you wish, Brian," Felicity said.

Somehow, Brian suspected his rough domestic standards would not quite measure up there, but still he could smile with appreciation at her gesture.

"Nar. I gotta get back to Melbourne and do some sorting out. Custody of the kids and all that. Ain't seen 'em for months."

"If you need any help, just call."

"Sure. How'd you go with the Navy?"

Felicity snorted and threw her hands in the air. "I never got near them. The sailors all awoke from the coma on schedule, completed medical checks successfully of course, and the USS Barton sailed for Pearl Harbour yesterday."

"It must be nice to be able to believe your problems will just go away," Brian said.

"Ours have," Felicity smiled. "I must say, it'll be nice to have a rest. I'm looking forward to this."

"Where's Jami?"

"Oh, she skipped out of here days ago. Didn't discuss her plans."

"And the others?"

"Thyssen is apparently under guard in a suite at the Washington Hilton and Lorna, always the opportunist, got herself confined to a room in a different part of the same hotel. You can imagine what house arrest means to her."

"Andromeda is in London, I know," Brian said. "She's got a big concert there next week."

"I wonder if the muzzle will extend to her songs."

"She's a big sell-out everywhere. A lot of disappointed people if they try and cancel her."

"And Wagner?"

"Well, I think I know where he is but I'd better not say."

"I heard something about the convent in Italy," Felicity said, leaning and whispering in his ear.

"Joe bought it for him."

"Good old Joe. Can he get me one?"

"I don't know how it happened. But it did. Just shows how little I know."

"We are all learning how little we know, Brian."

"You can say that again," Brian laughed.

*

You could lose anything in New York, especially if it wanted to stay lost. People, their whole lives, even complete cultures, had vanished there without a trace. Along with vast sums of money and vast quantities of drugs, and millions of careers and disconnected fragments of creative talent. Such a talent was Val Dennis, who was rich enough to do whatever he liked and chose Astrophysics, of all things, and related disciplines. He had been abducted, so he said, by aliens when young and therefore believed every known conspiracy theory, and since there wasn't a lot of work in his trade outside government projects, he had set up his own private laboratory in a tenement in The Bronx where he gathered other brilliant outcasts and any black market equipment available and was available to do any scientific projects that the government banned or refused to take seriously.

Jami had suffered through the freakiest night of her life when she met him at a UFO conference and they indulged in a one night stand that got lost sniffing coke. It was unclear whether they had actually had sex. But, importantly, Val was a friend that no one knew she had, because it would not have offered the slightest benefit to anyone's career in sciences to have Val Dennis appear on their credentials. She only realised the value of that as a secondary line of thought—she had intended to consult him over Earthshaker anyway and events simply added an imperative of immediacy.

Fate, plainly, was on her side, delaying her arrival at the Earth Sciences Building by means of a flat tyre. When she arrived, a removals van was parked outside the building and men in black suits were loading equipment. She halted in the car park, watching, sure the scene did not fit somehow. Glen saved her by putting up a fight and she saw him brought out, handcuffed, still shouting abuse and struggling and they put him in a black Lincoln with tinted windows and drove him away.

She got back in her car, a ball of nerves, and drove off the campus, stopping at the first telephone box she came to. She rang Harley and got no response. She rang the dungeon and a strange voice answered. She drove back to her apartment building and saw two men standing by another black Lincoln in the street outside. Instinct, and maybe too may conspiracy thrillers, warned her to keep driving. She went to an Internet Cafe and made use of the web. There was email from Wagner. *'You will be arrested,'* his message, plainly directed to all project members went, *'effective immediately. Thyssen directs you to surrender without a fight and tell them anything they want to know.'*

Not fucking likely.

Not without a trill of excitement, she immediately formulated a plan. They would be able to trace her car—she drove downtown and parked it deep in an underground car park and walked around to the station. She waited until the buses deposited a large crowd in the station, put on her overcoat and sun glasses and a woollen beanie, and went in, mingling with the travellers, and bought a ticket to New York. She travelled all the way to The Bronx on public transport—cab destinations could be traced and she didn't want to risk that—and walked the last distance constantly stopping to check if she was being followed. By then it was after midnight, and these streets were not safe, but she slunk along in the shadows and arrived.

Val, straggly and undernourished as ever, was delighted to see her.

"Hey, Jami, Hey. Yo, baby. Who let you loose in the Big Apple?" and such like went down. He offered every known drug of abuse before he thought of coffee.

"You know the one about government agents hunting down the innocent lab assistant because she is the only one left alive that knows the secret formula?" she asked him.

"Does that make me Cary Grant?"

"As near as you'll ever get, Val."

"Hey, whoa there. I sure hope Hitch's directin'."

"Alfred Hitchcock is dead. And so is Cary Grant. And so will I be if it gets known I'm here."

"Babe, welcome to the other side of the event horizon."

It wasn't at all clear whether they had sex that night either, but in the morning she made him the sort of breakfast that only sexually contented women can, and then put him to work.

"Consider a black hole. How would you detect it?"

"Ain't none been detected, so who knows?"

"How do they try?"

"There's a scream, they say. Registers small on the spectro. X-rays from the stuff fallin' in. Get it?"

"Perfectly."

"Like the water goin' down the gurgler. Matter being eaten spins, faster than light before it pops in and goes out of existence. Synchrotronic radiation they call it."

"Suppose there was a black hole inside the earth's core. What then?"

"Direct me to the next shuttle to Mars. One way ticket, Babe."

"But how would we detect it?"

"Get real? Terra don't swallow black holes. Black holes gulp galaxies."

"A mini black hole."

"Singularity. Oh yeah, I get it. Whacko idea."

"Eating the earth out from the middle, like a worm in an apple."

"Heard it before, Babe. Asimov. Sci Fi. That's his gospel."

"If it did exist, and it was there, how would we know?"

"By noticing our non-existence."

"Before that. Early stages."

"X-ray. Wheel the whole planet into radiology and zap her. It'd show as long bright streaks with no apparent energy source."

"Does such technology exist?"

"No way, Babe. Getoutahere!"

"Could it be made to exist?"

"You bet. Fifty satellites spaced evenly, shooting X-rays at each other. Cat scan the whole planet. Can have it hot to trot in the millennium after next."

"How about next week?"

"I got appointments next week."

"Can you do it for me, Val?"

"Got a hundred million Georgie Porgies and I'll see what I can do. Hey Babe, you're talking post-Slartibartfast."

"We need a way of proving it's there, and then a way of tracking it."

"You're talkin' Earthshaker, Babe. You're talkin' Thyssen."

"It's just one theory."

"No way. Big Harls won't go for shit like that, Babe."

"He's mellowed out. It was his idea."

"He knows it ain't so."

"But it is the best he's been able to come up with."

"Make the theory fit the data, huh?"

"Find it for me, Val."

"Hey Babe, for you, anything. These guys on your tail—they wear white coats?"

"First time you've ever been short of a plan, Val."

"Can't be bigger than microbe size or the planet would have already collapsed, Babe. Travelling at maybe half light speed. In 260 billion cubic miles of hot stuff. Hey Babe, that's the ittiest needle in the gargatuanest haystack."

"There's got to be a way."

"Drill a hole to China and wait a million years for it to pass by."

"Well that's something."

"Build a moon sized power station and shoot an X-ray bullet to a catcher on the other side."

"Go on."

"Wait through a thousand years of evolution until we can

understand what it really is."

"Meaning?"

"I know, and Big Man Harley knows, and you know if you use your greystuff—that there ain't nothin' of the kind down there. Black holes are just a best guess based on limited knowledge based on mathematics that are meaningless."

"God dammit, Val. Don't give up on me."

"Babe, I can die now. I've had my last idea."

*

The continual intrusiveness of the media had obliged the Campbell family to take extreme defensive precautions. It was just too difficult to get in and out of the house, even though Kevin had provided a roster of security guards who stood permanently at the front and rear doors. Wendell had taken to sleeping at his surgery, Gavin and Melissa were both staying with friends and Megan had been sent on an unscheduled holiday at Granny's.

Eventually, Felicity had offered to go elsewhere but her family saw their absence as proof of their determination to stand behind her—as contradictory as that sounded—and anyway, the officials pointed out that there was a legal requirement that a person under house arrest remain in their normal place of residence.

By turns, one of her brood would stay in the house with her, prepared to run the gauntlet of the microphones and lens to gain access to their normal lives. She wanted, anyway, to be where she could be easily contacted, especially as the time of the linkage drew nearer.

To her surprise, at first, she found she was free to maintain communication with the others of Project Earthshaker. It became less of a surprise when Brian had pointed out that it was probably because her telephone was tapped.

"I don't care. I don't have any secrets," she told him. But it still made her flesh crawl, every time she picked up the receiver.

All of their cell phones seemed to be off the air, but after a while, she began to open lines of communication. She needed something to do anyway—there was little hope of making arrangements to see patients when they had that mob of jackals at the front gate to fight their way through.

Chrissie had been confined to the convent in Italy, where she spent her time in prayer. There was a continual problem of both reporters and devotees jumping the convent wall and invading the grounds, but the chapel door was kept locked and the nuns brought her food and comfort through the secret passages that such places contained as a matter of course. She sounded well and happy and naturally very relaxed, even though she expressed genuine anxiety concerning how the pilgrims would manage without her.

"They've done it before," Felicity assured her. "They can probably manage all right by themselves."

She didn't want to think of where they might go, without Thyssen rigging the focal point. She had no idea whether the people who had taken charge knew about that or not—she had tried explaining it to every official she had spoken to but none seemed to grasp the idea.

The riots that followed the last minute cancellation of Andromeda's London concert had led her to the singer, who was confined to a posh hotel in Mayfair. She rang and left her number and, a day later, Andromeda called back. She was still very distressed—the riots had led to deaths and many injuries and she was condemned by the establishment as a danger to society.

"The same people said the same thing of the Beatles, Andromeda," Felicity assured her. Andromeda had called again several times, when she needed a sane voice to talk to. Her hotel remained picketed by thousands of her fans and there was on-going trouble.

Somehow too, her colour had made it a racial issue and there had been other riots in Memphis, Cape Town and other places in her support. She might have been the first political prisoner in history that the human rights movement wished to liberate from a luxury hotel.

With Brian, contact was almost daily until it suddenly stopped, but she knew why. He had been staying in a pub in Melbourne and trying to arrange for a lawyer to set a case in motion for the custody of his children but no one would help. A homeless man with a history of violence and criminal acts, not long before released from a mental institution, involved with undesirables and foreign radical fringe groups—there really wasn't any hope. It was amazing how these things could be described.

In the end he made the news as far away as New Zealand when he took the media on, hospitalising two reporters and a cameraman. Under arrest in Melbourne, he made his one permitted telephone call to Felicity. "You can't imagine how much better I feel," Brian laughed.

Felicity could. In the past month there had been many times when she might have envied a violent nature. "You must have done wonders for your custody case, Brian."

"It was hopeless anyway. And since the media invented the stories about my violent nature, I decided to make it a wish fulfilling prophecy."

"Do you have a history of violence?"

"Snotted one or two blokes in pubs and on the footy field. Of course, the way they say it, you'd reckon I'd been laying into Judy every night, but I've never hit anyone that didn't have a fair chance of fighting back on equal terms."

"Should I try and get on to Joe, Brian?"

"You won't be able to. He's dropped out of sight."

"Yes. I know. But someone from his office might be able to help."

"No. I got lawyers if I need them. Anyhow, it ain't so bad here. The way things were out there, a bloke's better off in the slot."

"I'd better go. I suppose they'll be annoyed if they realise you've made a long distance call."

"Fuck 'em."

"Take care of yourself, Brian. Remember the next link is due on the evening of the 29th."

"Yeah. The coppers here understand that and they know

what to expect. She'll be right."

Joe had dropped out of sight. Kevin too. Rumour had it he was building a private army on some secret base somewhere. Jami had vanished completely but you could bet she was making her way to wherever the next prediction suggested somehow. The surprise was one evening when Lorna rang.

"I wish they'd let the media get near me," she protested. "I'm comfortable but under close guard. They won't let me out at all."

"Have you seen Thyssen?"

"No. But I know they've got him here in this hotel somewhere. You know they changed his prediction. He said it would be the middle of Honshu but they've moved it..."

The call was immediately cut off.

Felicity sat for a long time with her arms locked between her knees and her head down. The location of the next eruption had been announced a week ago and the public was assured that all the affected populations had been moved to safer ground. They had said it would occur in the Pacific Ocean, at the northern extremity of the Marianas Trench, a thousand kilometres south of Japan. In the region there were just a few small islands that had been evacuated. But that wasn't Harley's prediction apparently.

She felt ill. Then her head cleared and she knew what she had to do. She found an atlas in Gavin's room and quickly looked it up, got her geography straight and rehearsed the names.

Then she walked straight out of the house, signalling the security man to follow and strode down the driveway to where the media folk, caught completely off guard, dived for their cameras and tape recorders. She stood patiently while they gathered before her, the guard thrusting them back a pace. They babbled a thousand questions but she said nothing, raising her hands above her head in a gesture demanding silence.

Finally they fell silent and allowed her to speak. "The location of the next eruption is not Professor Thyssen's prediction. Apparently, he placed the event a thousand kilometres from the one officially released. It will be right in the middle of Honshu— the main island of Japan." As their questions assailed her, she turned on her heel and walked back into the house.

Still, she was surprised to see herself dominating the images that made up the television news that evening. She stood tall and proud, her hand pushing at her windswept hair, once more speaking the gospel according to Harley Thyssen. Once more she had found herself coming down on his side. Her loyalty, she suspected by then, was almost an obsession.

"How on earth could you do that?" Wendell demanded of her when he saw his wife's picture dominating the front pages of the newspapers. He was speaking by phone from his surgery, of course. "What in the name of all that is holy do you owe this man?"

"I owe him nothing. But he's been right every time. My loyalty is to truth, Wendell."

"You can't know this is truth. You can't know he's right."

"If he ever fails me, Wennie, I'll agree with you. But he hasn't yet. They suppressed that information, Wen. If he's right, thousands of lives will be lost that could have been saved if they'd listened to him."

"Some of the world's top geophysicists dispute his ideas. It is to these eminences that you are according error. Certainty cannot be possible?"

She had seen it. Every current affairs program had offered its experts discussing the controversy. The sensible, eloquent scientists were all the ones that disagreed with Harley—his supporters, who received far less time and were always placed between the opinions of the sages, all looked like ratbags and spoke poorly. If it hadn't happened every time, she might have doubted it herself. But she knew a PR job when she saw one.

That every media outlet used the same format and images and style of expert was the clue. "Professor Thyssen seeks to sensationalise his prediction and has chosen a location designed to draw the biggest media impact," they said. How likely was it that four different scientists from four different countries would say precisely that?

"I'm sorry, Wen. If he is right and I had not spoken up, I'd never have been able to live with myself. I had to do it."

"If I might venture to say so, your sense of obligation seems seriously misplaced. As I understand it, your project has been discontinued."

"Sadly, it isn't."

"It becomes increasingly difficult to proceed."

"Please, Wen, don't say that."

"So... my threats and protestations are to no avail, hmm?"

"I'm afraid not."

After a long pause, Wendell said softly. "Well, such being the case, best I swallow my pride and displace my jealousy and show my heroic but foolish wife some absolute blind loyalty, as a good husband should."

"Are you jealous of Thyssen, Wennie?"

"I despise him with every microbe in my body. I'm so green I'm surprised that some horticulturalist hasn't potted me."

"You don't need to worry about that."

"Still, I perceive my rightful action is to come home this evening and show some family solidarity."

"I don't give a damn about solidarity, Wen. But I'd love to see you."

*

At some time she was unaware of, a man came and knelt beside her. He knelt too close, and slowly she emerged from her transcendental state to glance toward him nervously. The air of tension he had brought with him was palpable.

"Come with me, Sister," Fabrini said softly. "You are needed."

"There is nothing I can do that God has not already decided," she replied serenely.

"The pilgrims are in grave danger," he said adamantly. "Without you at their head, they have gone the wrong way."

"The Hand of God guides them. It cannot be the wrong way."

"They have taken the road to the north and we cannot turn

them from it," Fabrini said desperately. "We tried everything. We pleaded. We prayed. We put false road signs. We lied. We made many threats. Nothing will turn them to the right road."

"The road they follow is the right road, Mr. Fabrini," Chrissie said, shaking her head at his naivety.

"But they are going to the north, and there are no boats there."

It was plain the time of her peace was over. The daylight poured in through the newly opened doors. Without Harley to organise the movement of the pilgrims, who knew where the focal point might be. North was as likely as any other way.

"They must go as they go, Mr. Fabrini."

"But that way is very dangerous."

"You and your guards must do what you can to protect them."

"There is no order without you at the head of the convoy, Sister. They stray and straggle like sheep. They get lost. They get bogged. There have been many accidents. Please believe me. I would have proudly led them, had it proven possible. It hurts my pride deeply to come here and plead with you like this."

"Yes, I see that, Mr. Fabrini. I'm sorry to have put you through such an ordeal."

She rose then, brushing her robes straight, bowing deeply to the alter, clasping her hands before her. "Anyway," she continued. "Now that my meditation is broken, I also must go the way that they've gone, or else I'll go mad and you'll have to shoot me."

"Never, Sister!"

"Oh, *please*, Mr. Fabrini. Lighten up."

They walked out into the chill of a beautiful Autumn evening. She was less than half his size and felt odd in her pristine robes beside this big rough-looking gangster with his huge drooping moustache. At least he was keeping his weapons out of sight. The sisters had gathered by a smart red BMW. They clasped their hands and bowed to her and she responded.

They regarded her as if she was one of them now, and it struck Chrissie as peculiar that no one ever commented on nor seemed to notice her distinctly Asiatic appearance. Most of the time, she felt as Italian as Fabrini.

"I have obtained the best car to be had locally. We must hurry to catch them."

"And where is Mr. Wagner and his helicopter?"

"No one knows. He has not been here. The Carabinieri have a helicopter but they are busy rescuing our people from frozen rivers and snow-filled ravines."

Chrissie took time to thank the sisters before settling herself into the BMW, and with a blast of tyres on gravel, they were away.

"It would be best if we got there late, Mr. Fabrini, rather than not at all."

As he drove, Fabrini offered her a map to spread on her lap, at which he pointed between bends. Added to his expressive hand gestures, there was far too little handling of the steering wheel for her liking. But Fabrini was anxious to explain.

"They set off along the side roads, many different roads were used and it was night and no one knew what was happening. But all of them went north or as near to it as they could manage. Next morning, they began to come out on the coast road, at Termoli, most of them, but some as far up as Pescara. You see. Most of them turned along the coast road, but some tried to go into the sea. Some walked into the sea, some drove. There were many rescues. But no one died."

"For which we must be thankful, Mr. Fabrini."

"The water is very cold at this time of the year, Sister. I assure you. But now they carried on, all strung out along the road, but all pushing up the coast through Ancona, where I tried to hold up the leaders and allow the rest to gather behind but they broke through and four of my people were injured and one of my women shot a man. It was chaos. But they went on."

"Yes, they must go on."

"They went through Rimini and Ravenna and then toward Padua and suddenly I realised what lay before us. By nightfall, they would reach the foothills of the Dolomites, and the first blizzard of the season is filling the valleys with snow. And they will go into these valleys and be lost."

"And at what time does the pilgrimage come to an end."

"Not until nine tomorrow morning, according to the news reports. That is when the eruption is expected, translated to local time."

"So they will spend the night trapped in the snow."

"These are southern people. They are inexperienced with snow."

"And how long is it before darkness falls?"

"Sunset is just over two hours from now, but the bad weather in the north means darkness will come early."

"Then what can we do?"

"The authorities have arranged an aeroplane. We can fly to Padua and then try and make our way to the head of the line and turn them back."

"They cannot be turned back, Mr. Fabrini."

"Still we must try."

*

The two men from the US Embassy came shortly after Wendell left home for work next morning. The evening had been tense, but that was because it was also the time for the linkage. It was odd how she felt it, as if in sympathy for the others. Wendell had been attentive and sympathetic, but she knew the pilgrims were on the move out there and fretted at the lack of information.

The two gentlemen from the American Embassy could not have looked more uncomfortable. After a month with the media camped on her front lawn, Felicity had no reason to be friendly, but she invited them in and offered them tea. They looked sheepishly at each other as they took up seats on the couch.

"I'll make it," said Melissa said, hoping that if she played a role she would not be left out, as had happened on the occasions of previous discussions between her mother and officialdom. This troubled time, Felicity reflected, had not been completely wasted.

"We need your assistance, Dr Campbell," the taller American official said.

"I'll do anything to help, if I'm able to believe it really will help."

They promptly destroyed any possibility of trust by informing her (yet again) of her obligations under the Official Secrets Act.

"I promise nothing," she responded coldly.

The two men looked at each other, plainly each hoped the other might do the talking. By sheer intimidation, the short one lost out. "Last night, the crew of USS Barton mutinied."

Felicity stared at them incredulously. "You kept the crew together?"

"There was no reason not to. They seemed perfectly normal."

"But you were warned of what to expect."

The two men gazed at each other with accusative expressions. "You expected this, Doctor?"

"They are *Pilgrims*, gentlemen. The link has occurred. They have no choice but to proceed to the focal point by whatever means are expedient or available."

"They did that, all right, Doctor. They hi-jacked the ship..."

"You left them all on the same ship?"

"The Barton. Yes."

"Then, yes, if they had control of the ship at the time of the link, they could hardly have been expected to do otherwise."

"USS Barton is a nuclear armed destroyer, Doctor."

"You can only blame yourselves for that. The Shastri Effect is well documented. I personally issued warnings to American government officials."

"The best medical experts advised us that there was no indication of any such effect."

"The best medical experts, gentlemen, are those best paid by the biggest vested interests. Did anyone trouble to ask any of the medical experts who were involved in Project Earthshaker and therefore knew what they were talking about?"

"Eventually. They each referred us to you."

"Did they really?"

"The Joint Chiefs need an assessment fairly immediately."

The Joint Chiefs of Staff might have been a bunch of pre-school children, gathered about her ankles with expectant eyes. "No doubt they do. Tell me. Are the crew of the Barton handling the ship competently?"

"From a seamanship point of view, I guess so. They sailed the ship out of Pearl without hitting anything. Why?"

"Some pilgrims have exhibited a zombie like effect. But most behave perfectly capably, as long as they are headed in the right direction. If impeded, disorientation may occur, after which anything might happen."

"But what dangers can we expect?"

"There is no danger, gentlemen. The pilgrims will head directly for the focal point for thirty six hours after the linkage occurred and then stop. Cessation coincides with the next volcanic event."

"Thirty six hours from when they took the ship?"

"Presumably. After which, I would expect them to give your ship back with all due apology for their behaviour."

"And meanwhile."

"I should imagine they will proceed, full steam ahead, toward the focal point."

There was more hesitation, and then the taller one offered. "They are headed north. Toward the Bering Strait."

"North?"

"That's right."

Felicity felt again the sweep of nausea as she realised what it meant.

"My god. That means the focal point is leading them over the pole."

*

In Tokyo, it hit with intensity 6.3 on the old Richter scale but that wasn't enough to stop the traffic. The walls shook back and forth and the pavement bounced up and down but the pedestrians hardly paused as they bustled about their business, hurrying from commerce to relaxation venues. The buildings rolled on their foundations designed to withstand such earthquakes and shelves arranged to prevent the crockery from falling did their job. The lights blinked but the shockproof power stations withstood the tremors. Some people, tourists probably, looked out windows and grabbed parking meters for stability but for the locals in Tokyo it was just another day and another quake and they took it in their stride.

Some wondered though. It seemed a rather strong shake for one with an epicentre a thousand kilometres out to sea. For this, they knew, was the one that had been predicted by some American crackpot. There was, officials had warned, some danger of tsunami, but the city was prepared for that as well.

Mt Fuji, that most perfect of mountains, a shrine in itself in a land of shrines, with its gleaming snowcap and symmetrical sides, suddenly disappeared in a dense black cloud. Five other volcanoes roared to life at the same time in the mountains of central Honshu and three more out to sea off Cape Omae, but all of these were to be numbered amongst Japan's fifty active volcanoes. Mt Fuji was supposed to be dormant, but it slept no more.

In the towns and villages and the farms along the south-east coast and inland almost to Kofu—where the population density was 500 persons per square kilometre—there was no one to see the last perfect moments of Fujiyama. In the seconds before the mountain awoke from its long sleep, the people fell to earth in a slumber of their own. Some died, some were injured, but most simply slept where they fell.

*

Somewhere north and east of Midway Island, USS Barton turned its bows to face the oncoming tsunami, its bewildered crew individually fretting regrets regarding their recent actions and wondering why they had come here, nowhere really, for no reason at all. The captain had already spoken to the crew and they had agreed with his intentions. He advised Naval Headquarters that once the tsunami danger was past, they would put about and return to Pearl where they wished to surrender their ship and themselves.

*

Kevin Wagner had placed himself in Paris and bought a pushbike, racing style, the very model that won the last Tour de France. In fact he was there because he heard that the French Government had two Hercules C-130 aircraft for sale and wanted to open negotiations. He also knew that the French would not bother to comply with the UN order for his arrest. When the link came, he went with the flow. He got on the bike and rode and was a little startled at first to discover he was heading north, toward Brussels although of course he never got that far. He was just short of St Quentin when the link ceased a day and a half later. He ordered breakfast in the small hotel where he had spent the night and asked about nearby car hire places, and did they know anyone who might like to buy his bike.

*

Andromeda Starlight also went with the flow, but she did it once again in chauffeur driven style. She easily charmed her two police guards into allowing her to hire the car and they went along too, sharing her chicken and champagne. They drove out of London heading north heading for Nottingham and Sheffield and into Scotland, the officers interchanging at the wheel. They were all the way to Inverness when at midnight she declared the journey ended.

"Where now, Miss Starlight?"

"Back again, I guess."

"Just as well, luv. Not a good time for swimming in the North Sea."

"Is there ever?"

*

Lorna Simmons was escorted to the airport by a squad of US Marines and put on a plane that she discovered to be the old Project Earthshaker 707. The pilot introduced her to the team of technicians and then directed her to a seat in the cramped body of the aircraft, for it was filled with computers and other monitoring equipment. The navigator sat beside her and awaited her instructions.

"That way," Lorna said with an indicatory hand.

"Are you sure. That's almost due north. They said..."

"It's that way," Lorna assured him.

So they flew north, to Anchorage in Alaska where they refuelled and wasted some time then flew on over the ice cap and landed in Reykjavik, Iceland, with Lorna furious because they had passed the spot. She was pacified only when they flew again and as the deadline drew near and were circling over a spot off Cape Richards, in the Queen Elizabeth Islands, 700 kilometres from the North Pole when it was agreed the journey ended.

"I'm glad we didn't have to walk," Lorna snapped at the pilot. "Harley used to organise it better than this."

"Not all he organised, apparently," the pilot said grimly. "There's been a big earthquake right in the middle of Japan."

*

The problem had been Joe Solomon who, as he had expected, was arrested and handed over to US Treasury Officials and eventually flown to New York where gentlemen from the United Nations Investigative Committee wanted to talk with him. No one realised the effect it would have. When the link came, Joe raged and was hospitalised and sedated.

*

Not far away, also in New York, Jami Shastri and Val Dennis were capturing seismic waves and trying to get them to read out on a spectroscope.

"So your man was right, Jami-kins," Val smiled. "Honshu, bang on, 8.2. Outstanding."

"I'm getting nothing here," Jami protested, offering the palms of her hands in frustration to the computer screen.

"Don't chill me, Babe. It's rock-a-billy right around the geosphere. We're an all shook up and shaking all over, shimmy-shimmy planet. You gotta be gettin' something."

"Not a sausage."

"Well bite my ass."

"How can you be picking them up and I'm not?"

"The spectros fucked out."

"It reads the same on the back-ups."

"Well, then, if our hardware is fine and it reads weird, then it's weird."

"You are picking up seismic waves coming around through the crust but I'm not getting any coming through the mantle. How can that be?"

"A disco at the Moho."

"The Mohorovicic Discontinuity can't be a factor. Seismic waves have always travelled through the mantle in the past. Why not this time?"

"Core distension."

"Not to this degree, surely."

"Figure it assupwards, dodo. Where can't seismos go?"

"Where there's no solid matter."

"Which means somewhere between here and Nipland, as the gopher burrows, there's a lack of solidarity."

"Harley's bubble!" Jami shrieked.

"I guess it ain't burst after all, hey Babe?"

*

In his cell at the Remand Centre in Melbourne, Brian Carrick emerged from a haze of sedation. Outside he could hear excited voices.

"D'ya hear? Big earthquake in Japan."

He tried to pick up the remote control and switched the television on but discovered he was strapped to his bunk. He felt like hell.

"Hey, out there," he called throatily. "Bung the telly on, will ya. It's almost time for the six o'clock news."

*

In the pouring rain at the side of the road, Chrissie knelt in prayer. All along the road behind her, the jumbled outlines of the stalled convoy flashed as people walked past vehicles with shining headlights. But most were no longer walking but also out on the road, and praying. A police official had come down the line and explained to Fabrini that about ten frozen bodies had been recovered from the passes above and wanted to know how many more might be expected.

"They were wet and not appropriately dressed. When their vehicles stopped, they got out and walked. They died in a few minutes."

"We have no idea how many got past us. But most seem to be here," Fabrini said, shivering but not from the cold.

"It was lucky," the police chief said, "that the sister was able to stop them in time."

"I didn't stop them," Chrissie said. "They just stopped."

*

Harley Thyssen sat quietly in his room, the curtains drawn, no lights on, quietly waiting in the dimness. There was a knock at the door, but he ignored it. They had keys and he did not but, being well trained in politeness as all FBI men should be, they always knocked before they let themselves in. This time, he noticed, the knocking lacked its usual authoritative tone. He allowed himself a sad little smile.

12
THE GRAVEYARD OF GALAXIES

On the morning of the day following the Japanese event, Lorna discovered that the guard was gone from the door. There had been three of them on a rostered shift, and the morning chap was a rather cute guy named Elmer whom she had several times tried to lure into her room for coffee... and whatever...

"Sorry Miss Simmons. Against regulations."

Elmer and each of his colleagues were required to stand at her door for eight hours, and they were all young and very polite in their nice suits with the bulge of the gun in the shoulder holster. Secret Service—the same lads who guarded the President. She was very impressed by that.

That morning, she was too hung-over to bother with seduction and gathered her breakfast and the paper from the hall in her green-with-shamrocks flannel pajamas and it was only when she decided to shoot Elmer a smile anyway that she noticed he was gone. Maybe he went somewhere for a pee? No. Such desertion of their post for any reason had not occurred before. She suspected Elmer and his associates had perfect control over their bladders and every other bodily function.

She considered immediate escape. Perhaps this was only a momentary window of opportunity. But no—not a chance. The image of the front page of the popular press, with photo of Lorna Simmons, fleeing through the streets of Washington in her pajamas, barefoot, hair like a Condor's nest. No way. She went back in, nibbled toast and drank the coffee and then peeked out the door again. Elmer was nowhere to be seen. Okay—so if it was to be an escape, let's do it with a bit of style. Lorna headed for the shower.

Forty-five minutes later, she was dressed to face the rainy November weather in Washington, sporting a long yellow scarf overflowed by her red hair, a green beret, an ankle-length black coat from which her black-nylon legs protruded below the mini-skirt as she walked on her highest heels. Classiest jailbreak in history, she murmured to her mirror-image. Handbag swinging from her shoulder, she strode the corridor to the lift and went up to the thirty-third floor. Although she had never been there before, the number was easy to remember—3333—and she saw there were no Secret Service men there either and knocked. A ruffled, weary Thyssen answered the door, walking away with a motion for her to enter.

"Has all been forgiven?" she asked as she wandered in.

"The arrest order has been withdrawn, if that's what you mean," Thyssen said in a thick grumble as he flopped into the chair before the computer screen.

Five floors lower, Lorna had been occupying a room that would have been identical to this one a month ago, but now there was hardly any point of comparison. Once she collected her suitcase, there would be as little trace of her occupation as any other relatively tidy guest, but Thyssen's room had been utterly engulfed in Harleyness. Gutted computers and other machines with exposed wires hanging all around, dozens of books with pages marked with scraps of paper, every newspaper published in the world during the last month, each left open at relative pages or dumped in disorderly heaps, many pizza and other takeaway containers, innumerable Styrofoam coffee mugs. Maps and charts were plastered all over the walls. Harley's clothes and personal belongings were jumbled into the midst of it—it all stank to high heaven. Harley himself looked ill and unwashed, as much a wreck as the room. It was perhaps the shaggy toothbrush protruding from a Coke bottle, standing in the middle of the coffee table like a misguided flower arrangement, that stuck in her mind most.

"How'd you get all this stuff in here?" Lorna gasped. She had been confined to videos and newspapers and her request to visit a library or bookshop had been denied.

"They let me have anything I wanted. All properly fitted with bugs and homing devices no doubt. I bet they even go through my garbage every night. I know they had people in here going through stuff when I was sleeping. I got to play with every pet project that crossed my mind over the last decade. It was great fun. And it'll take them years to figure out what it all means."

"You're going to leave it all?"

"You bet," and he walked over and addressed a mirror behind which you could only assume there was a hidden camera. "And yes, you guys, what you want to know *is* in here somewhere."

Lorna was looking over everything, the staggering clutter about her, and something caught her eye. Under the circumstances, something had to. It was a sheet of paper on the table on which Harley had scrawled in large red letters—everything else was output from the printer. She picked it up and looked at it aimlessly—CONSIDER ENTROPY, it said. Immediately, Harley was standing before her, extracting the sheet from her fingers and balling it up, throwing it onto the heap of similar balled papers on the corner buried under which, she supposed, there was probably a waste paper bin.

"Mustn't pry," he said, giving her fingers a playful slap.

"What, exactly, is Entropy?"

"The graveyard of the galaxies," Thyssen replied as he collected his wallet and cigarettes and herded her toward the door. She supposed it was a silly question.

"Come on. Let's walk," Harley said. "There's a lot to do."

They went through the lobby to the elevator, and still Lorna was thinking that perhaps they ought to be making a run for it, just in case someone changed their mind and decided they ought to be confined again. As it happened, she was very nearly running to keep up with Harley's long strides—it was just so hard for a girl to be elegant beside such a rough and rampant man.

"Can we pause for a moment to enjoy our freedom or are we making a fast getaway?" she asked as they waited before the lifts.

"Neither. But they have, for the most part, admitted that

they were wrong and I was right, and the pilgrimages fucked up completely without the rest of you guys organising them."

"So is the project to be restored?"

"No. Not yet, anyway."

"Not yet?"

"They've offered me a consultancy, which I declined."

"Why?"

The elevator arrived and they entered, and Lorna was wondering if they should be talking so frankly in places that could harbour listening devices. But that was just her being paranoid, she realised, since they weren't saying anything Harley didn't want them to hear.

"Their trouble is, they think I know something they don't, but they don't realise that I get it right and they don't for the same reason the rest of you do your jobs better than anyone else can. Because we were all in on the ground floor and learned how to do these things when it was simple and easy to learn. Now everything's become too complex to comprehend properly. But for all of us, our best guess is better than anything they can learn from the data."

"Not very scientific, Harley."

The truth was, she didn't believe him. She had been there when he had worked alone for an hour to come up with his prediction. It was a strange moment. She waited for a sense of betrayal or disloyalty to hit her but it didn't. Apparently, it was quite natural to distrust him. She'd never thought of that.

"Not everything is scientific, Lorna."

"Heresy, surely."

"Computers, and mathematics, suffer as perceptions do, from occasional distortions. In any case, I have told them that its no deal unless Project Earthshaker is fully restored."

"And what did they say to that?"

"No one has dared answer at this stage."

"Are we all reinstated?"

"Project Earthshaker continues, with or without official sanction. Okay, let's walk. Joe is here in Washington. Apparently he's secreted all our funds in mysterious investments and they have been trying to persuade him to tell them where." He handed her a business card. "He's been turned over to my lawyer at this address. You go fetch him and deliver him to Wagner at San Carboni. Felicity is in San Diego, dealing with the Navy. Andromeda is in London, hitting the big time and moving on to Paris next week. Chrissie is at San Carboni, in the convent playing nuns. They all know the situation well enough that they'll know what to do without help from me. I know where Jami is and you don't want to know. Fuck knows where Brian is—find him and tell him I want him in Japan. He is going to have to figure out how to move 16,000 people and he only has six weeks to do it. Got all that?"

"Yep. What about the prediction?"

"I don't know yet. But Jami has set up a secret lab somewhere and that's where I'll be."

"So now we are some sort of underground movement."

"If you must be romantic about it. The truth is, we have to go on. We will do what we can, and governments can help or hinder as is their wont. But the Project continues."

"Long live the Project."

"I'd forgotten your weird sense of humour. You'll be calling me King Harley next."

"I can't imagine how I avoided it so long."

Suddenly he rushed into the street and hailed a cab. As it squealed to a halt beside them, he smiled briefly.

"Don't worry about checking out. The US Treasury will have to worry about the hotel bill. Just round up the team and get them moving. I'll get the details of the next event to you as soon as I know it. You'll have to use your celebrity status to get yourself on air and tell it to the world."

"All by myself?"

"We are, each of us, all on our own from now on. We do what we do, the best way we can."

"You run a pretty loose ship, Harley."

"When will you realise that I'm not in charge of anything. I just do my part for the project, same as everyone else."

He jumped in the cab and was whisked away into the traffic, and she stood, truncating a wave. She was a young girl in a strange city, alone and abandoned and far from home. And she knew just exactly what she had to do.

*

Cardinal Valerno was a much younger man than she expected, maybe forty-something but with the general appearance of an Italian businessman—black-haired, strong-jawed, ruggedly handsome features. He arrived dressed in a simple cassock and the sisters fussed as they brought him through to the small garden courtyard where Chrissie sat on the fountain in a white robe and bareheaded, just to make sure than no one mistook her for a nun.

Outwardly, she offered her most serene mode—inwardly, she was a ball of nerves. She had never encountered anyone as important as a cardinal before, and the word around the convent was that he was some sort of envoy from the Pope himself. Hence the younger man, someone she could almost regard as a contemporary, was a grave disappointment. She expected to be overawed, instead she wondered how appropriate it might be to ask him for a date.

"It's good of you to see me, sister," Valerno said in English with a fulsome bow.

"I don't think it's right to call me that," Chrissie replied in Italian. "I'm not one of the Sisters, nor anything else officially."

"So we have noticed," the cardinal smiled. His English was just the way they spoke it in Oxford, without trace of accent, cool and assured. She wondered if his Italian and Latin were as good. "We have decided that *Sister* would be the best form of address only after much discussion— at a very high level, I might add."

If he was surprised at her Oriental appearance, or even at her command of Italian, he gave no sign of it. Undoubtedly he had been well briefed. It made her almost desperate to shock him.

"Well we can ditch the protocol for starters," Chrissie said aggressively, settling them into English. "My name is Christine. You should call me that. If we get to be friends, you call me Chrissie."

Cardinal Valerno smiled and bowed—next he'd be grovelling on his knees. "I would sincerely hope that we do become friends, Christine."

"Well that isn't going to happen if I have to call you Your Holiness or Your Eminence or whatever the right term is. What's your first name?"

"Luigi."

"Okay, Luigi. Sit yourself on whatever stone you like and for God's sake, stop all that bowing and scraping."

She knew what this was all about—the Mother Superior had warned her. When the pilgrimage began, three cardinals had been sent, along with other lesser dignitaries, to try and take command of the convoy. Their failure to stop it, or redirect it, or even slow it down, was a matter of record. Then Chrissie arrived by helicopter and walked out in front of the first truck and the whole procession halted, seemingly at her command. Of course they thought it a miracle and the press described it that way to the great embarrassment of the Vatican, but the truth was that, as she advanced through the rain toward the convoy, she knew the sun was setting at that very moment in Japan.

Cardinal Luigi sat on a stone bench facing her and looked as awkward as is permitted for a man of the cloth. He nodded his approval at everything she said. But she could see beads of sweat across his brow. The day was cool and pleasant. She decided the conversation should be as well. But not just yet.

"You are not one for formalities, then, Christine," Luigi said lightly.

"The Apocalypse is eight months away. There's no time for formality."

"My thinking exactly."

"And that of your masters, presumably, or else they wouldn't have sent *you*," Chrissie said jubilantly.

"The matter of which of us was likely to be able to

communicate with you most effectively was the basis of their choice, I understand."

"Well I think they made a very good choice," Chrissie grinned.

Luigi Valerno was not so deeply engrossed in the faith that he did not recognise the fact that she had made a pass at him. "It's very good of you to say so," he said, but she could tell he was flustered.

Chrissie smiled jubilantly. It amazed even her to realise how good she was at this sort of thing. "Explain to me precisely the nature of your mission."

"Liaison. Between yourself and the Holy See."

"I'll accept any help I can get. In case you haven't noticed, we have an escalating situation going on. Or don't heathen Japanese count."

"There are many Catholics in Japan, as everywhere else, Christine," Luigi said, beginning to relax a little. "And, in any case, let me assure you that the Vatican is not so narrow minded that it imagines it needs to serve only the faithful. We wish to offer whatever help you need, to whomsoever needs it, as best we can."

"On what terms?" Chrissie asked slyly.

"I should imagine that you would be dictating the terms," he said with bland generosity.

"I don't. The circumstances do that."

As he absorbed that, the cardinal lowered his tone. "Of course. Tell me, this matter of the Apocalypse..?"

"Yes."

Valerno was not sure how to proceed. Plainly they were getting down to the point before he was quite ready for it. "Needless to say, His Holiness has expressed some concern..."

"As well he might."

"I'm sure you can see the difficulty confronting His Holiness. There is a question of the basis upon which the date was chosen."

"Oh Luigi, come on. It's a matter of faith."

That perplexed him. He paused twice as he searched out the appropriate reply. "As are all things. But in this case, we were wondering about the data upon which the idea is based."

"You'll need to talk to Professor Thyssen about that."

Luigi Valerno plainly did not want to talk to such a pagan. "Did he verify the date?"

"He hasn't questioned it."

"That's hardly the same thing..."

"It is for a man like Harley. He questions everything. He is going along with my work. If he had doubts, I'm sure he would have expressed them."

Valerno, through this, was contemplating the sea gulls that lined the roof at this time of day. To them, he explained. "Still, surely you understand how our independent experts might wish to make their own study of the data."

"You only have to ask."

Now he turned to look her right in the eye. "I'm asking you."

"You must ask the professor. It is his data."

Luigi was stumped. His face contorted with the effort of finding the right words as he continued. "Professor Thyssen is... I understand... not an easy man to deal with."

"Rubbish. He'll talk to anyone willing to give him the opportunity. Even His Holiness."

"His Holiness, on the other hand, has matters of protocol and ... other matters... to take into consideration."

"And an audience with a renegade like Harley would not go down well with the faithful, hmm?"

Valerno flinched. "It is the matter not of what actually takes place but how it might be perceived. You must understand—the slightest suggestion of Papal approval of Professor Thyssen will create an ill-balance in the situation..."

He tailed off, unsure how the sentence ended, if it did.

"The data is there to be had. All His Holiness has to do is ask."

Valerno took a very deep breath before going on. The whole conversation seemed to be becoming increasingly painful to him. "To do so would give a credence to the prediction that... without having had the opportunity to study the data... the Papacy would find... it could not accommodate with comfort..."

"I'm sure it can all be arranged in a manner which is comfortable for His Holiness."

Valerno's face lit up and he raised a declamatory finger. "Ah. Now we are to the nub of it."

"Are we indeed?"

"Obviously, His Holiness would not, in all conscience, be able to offer whole hearted public support for Professor Thyssen."

"Hardly."

"But perhaps the right word in the right official ear might go a long way to restoring Professor Thyssen to his former position within the project."

She wanted to laugh. This silly stuffy man was so polite, even when broaching Papal corruption. But he was rather sexy, for all that...

"In return for which, the Vatican gets full disclosure," she said, only to assure him she understood and was not anywhere near as shocked as she should have been.

"Exactly."

"You might tell his Holiness that the idea seems most satisfactory."

"Then I will see what can be done. After all, time is short."

"Indeed it is. Just two hundred and forty days, in fact."

*

It was when Lieutenant Jackovitch made reference to hostages that Felicity was suddenly possessed of a profound enlightenment—a moment of clarity, as someone once said. They had flown her to San Diego as an expert witness in a preliminary hearing to determine what charges be laid in regard to the 'unsanctioned and inappropriate use of USS Barton' as Jackovitch termed it. Apparently, Captain Maynard had taken full responsibility for all of the actions of his crew and faced Court Martial on an array of charges but of course it wasn't as simple as that. Every one of the crew had breached regulations in some way or other, and the trial of each individually was not an impossible outcome.

But that was the US Navy's problem—hers was that no one listened when she tried to explain that she actually had no qualification and no expertise to offer as a witness.

"We need you to help us understand what happened, ma'am," Lt Jackovitch explained in his initial telephone call. Felicity wearily packed her bags and went.

"We all expected you to rush off to Japan anyway," Wendell said, no less wearily.

"And who did you imagine would pay for it?" she asked.

"Who *is* paying for it?"

"The US Navy, as it happens."

"A Supermum's work is never done," Gavin remarked dryly.

"Oh stop it, you lot," she grumbled generally at her far too perfectly understanding family. "I already feel such a fake."

She flew to San Diego, a hot ugly city although since all she saw of it was the Air Force and then Navy Bases, maybe she was judging harshly. Lieutenant Ryan Jackovitch was a handsome young man, too handsome to take seriously, too young to possibly defend any case competently. She had always thought casting actors like Tom Cruise in such roles was just Hollywood marketing—now she realised it was factual. He collected her from the plane and they rode in a chauffeur-driven Navy limousine, sitting a mile apart in the back seat as could be done only in American cars.

"I really don't see how I can help," Felicity insisted. "Everything I know is well documented. I'm just a Physician with no specialist field. No one will take me seriously."

"I was assured that you are the *only* specialist in the field of the Shastri Effect, Ma'am."

"I can give you the names of a number of real specialists who are all far more qualified than me."

It turned out that Jackovitch already had the names of her former team of specialists and several of them had already agreed to give evidence. They were readily available, being currently based in Hawaii because that was where the former Project Earthshaker control group were currently stationed.

"They wanted to study the crew of USS Barton in relation to the control group, in order to assure themselves that there would be no ill effects," Jackovitch said.

"Then they must have expected the pilgrimage."

"They did. They just didn't expect them to hijack their own ship."

"The Pilgrims will always make their way to the focal point by the best means of travel available."

"There!" Jackovitch cried jubilantly. "You see? Expert knowledge. If the hospital staff and security forces had known that in advance, the ship could never have been stolen."

Felicity groaned. "Surely one of the medical team knew that."

"They are each experts in their own fields. It's you who has the overall picture. That's why we need your evidence."

"No one will believe me. I don't even quite believe what I know myself."

It was true, Right then, she was wondering just exactly how she knew that the Pilgrims chose the best means of transport available. No one had ever said so. It was just... well... obvious. If so, her so-called expert knowledge was no more than a bunch of unfounded guesses. There had been no study of how the Pilgrims arranged their transportation, there was no proof that her statement was correct. She had just said it, as if it was a profound truth, but really it was all her own speculation and hearsay, based mostly on Brian Carrick's propensity for stealing trucks. She shuddered to think what a good prosecutor might do with *evidence* like that.

"But everyone says you are the one who understands it best," Jackovitch persisted.

"Everyone being my former medical team?"

"Yes ma'am. Them, and the hostages," Jackovitch added.

For a moment, Felicity searched her memory to assure herself that no one had said anything about *hostages* before. They had not. There was an inexplicable cold chill running about in her bloodstream as she sat staring at him. "What hostages?"

"The hostages... I'm sorry, ma'am. I didn't realise you hadn't time to see the official report on the incident. The crew took hostages on the ship with them. Civilian hostages. In fact, the control group."

Felicity pressed down an invisible force between them with the palms of her hands. "Go slower. You're confusing me."

"The former Project Earthshaker control group were in the same hospital as the crew of the Barton in Pearl, although on a different floor. They were, of course, properly quarantined. The crew took the control group as hostages, on to the ship with them. That's the worst offence—not just hijacking the ship but worse, taking civilian hostages along for the voyage."

"But they were all going the same way anyway."

"The Navy doesn't like unauthorised civilians on their warships."

"But don't you understand. The control group weren't hostages. They just all went together, because they were all pilgrims."

"That's what we need you to explain..." Jackovitch was saying.

But he stopped when he saw the way she rocked back in the seat, as if she had been shot. A bullet was impossible since they were surrounded by bulletproof glass but nevertheless her brain seemed to explode internally but the projectile that struck her was purely one of enlightenment.

Suddenly, she was thumping on the glass at the point directly behind the driver's head. "Stop the car! Here! Now!"

Her agitation caused Jackovitch to respond immediately on the intercom and then as the car slowed, he asked if she was ill. But she waved him off. "Stay here. I just need a moment alone," she gasped and was out of the car before it fully stopped moving.

As she stumbled on the rough edge of the road, she barely took in the surroundings. They were certainly not worth stopping for. Rubble and possibly garbage littered the scene with flocks of screeching seagulls, and the place smelled to high heaven with rotting weed and dumped fuel. Beyond the cyclone wire fence, a huge aircraft carrier was moored out across the stretch of water along with several other warships—one of them perhaps the delinquent USS Barton.

Felicity walked a little way from the car, rubbing her eyes and cheeks, her head bowed. Behind, Jackovitch remained, watching from the car, willing to allow her some dignity for he assumed she was discomforted by her rushed journey. But she wasn't. It was all because her brain was screaming at her. *Stop. Think this through. Work it out.*

She was smiling when she finally returned. Jackovitch climbed out of the car to meet her. "Are you okay, ma'am," he asked with genuine concern. Perhaps he wasn't sure that he hadn't offended her in some way.

"I'm sorry. It just came to me and I wanted to get it clear in my head before we said or did anything else."

"Get what clear?"

"Something I didn't understand," she said and pressed her fingers on his lapels. "Now listen. I want to make sure we get this straight. The so-called hostages weren't hostages at all. The control group took the sailors to the ship."

"Pardon, ma'am," Jackovitch gasped, sticking to his more formal mode until he got a better grasp of this mad woman.

"You've got it the wrong way around. The control group kidnapped the sailors."

Jackovitch blanched at the thought of how this was going to go over in the court room. "You can't be serious. How could..?"

"Shut up and listen," Felicity snapped. Anything to stop him calling her ma'am again, but she knew she must concentrate and get it right. "When the linkage occurs for the first time, after the sleepers wake, they go into an ambulatory catatonic state. They just head off blindly in the direction of the focal point. You remember the human lemmings in the Canary Islands."

"Yes, ma'am. We thought that was an exception case..."

"Yes I know. So did I. We white supremacists will never be entirely free of our racism. We all assumed it was a bunch of dumb native fishermen, sucked in by their voodoo or some such primitive nonsense. But it wasn't. Lorna Simmons did exactly the same thing. She walked straight off a pier and fell in Auckland harbour."

"She doesn't admit *that* on television," Jackovitch grinned.

"The truth is, on the occasion of their first linkage, each of them wandered off blindly, zombie-fied or whatever you want to call it. If they don't get run over by a bus or fall off a cliff, it's just plain lucky."

"And you think the crew of the Barton did too?"

"I know they did. But, you see, at the second post sleeper linkage, there's no zombie effect. The pilgrim now knows where they are going and why, and they lead the first timers."

"Are you sure of this?"

"That's why the Italian pilgrims *all* followed Christine Rice. *All* of them. Even the ones that weren't Catholics. They *all* went with her. But the second time they *all* went without her."

"Some of them still died—in the snow."

"I know. But that was because they were caught in the blizzard. So there's your defence, Lieutenant. The sailors didn't hijack the Barton. The control group did."

"Well, I'll be god-damned... Oh, excuse me, Ma'am."

"You call me *Ma'am* one more time, I'll belt you one."

Jackovitch needed a moment or two to recover, at all levels. He went to his most commonly used line, just to be sure he was on safe ground. "But can you prove it?"

"I think so. If there had been just one experienced pilgrim present, the Canary Island fishermen wouldn't have gone off the cliffs. They would have followed him or her down the path to their boats instead."

"I just don't see how we are gonna convince the Court Martial of this."

"That isn't the problem. The proof will come eventually. Right now the worry is how to get enough pilgrims into Japan to stop 16,000 sleepers from walking into the sea."

Jackovitch was leaning on the car, shaking his head in

disbelief. "Well, ma'... um, I mean, Doctor Campbell. I don't know whether this is gonna help our defence or not, but it sure as hell proves one thing. You *do* know a damned lot more about this than everyone else."

*

The interrogations had been polite and respectful at all times, much to his surprise. Joe Solomon must have been one of the few people who could be edified by a hands-on tour of several of the world's major correctional facilities. The worst had been in East Perth lock-up, where he had been taken initially to await the arrival of FBI agents from America. That had been a barbaric place, brutal and full of drunks and thugs but because he was in a wheelchair, no one bothered him. He made a court appearance in which the FBI asked for extradition to assist them with their inquiries and this was immediately granted because Joe instructed his QC to say that he agreed and was willing to assist in any way possible.

Within a week, they flew him to Washington. There they kept him in sparse rooms within the FBI building and rolled him out most days to one of several conference rooms where government officials questioned him, usually in an informal manner. At first he denied everything and then took the 5th Amendment and they argued for two weeks whether that was valid. It wasn't, since Australia has no Bill of Rights attached to it's constitution.

But the FBI was hamstrung from the start—once they went through those records he had allowed to continue to exist, they discovered he had accounted for every cent of the funding that the project had received officially, and there was no trace of the covert funds, nor of the slush funds that had evolved from money the project made itself.

"You keep very fine books, Mr. Solomon," the judicator said at one point. "It's a pleasure to investigate you."

Throughout it all, bureaucrats mulled over what to admit to

and possibilities and consequences and it was probably a great relief to them when Harley sent a lawyer to organise his release. There were no charges at all, in the end. To prove something stolen, first you needed to prove its existence.

As Lorna wheeled him out into a rare day of winter sun, Joe knew that his commitment to the project was complete.

"Harley said to send you wherever you want to go. So, where do you want to go, Joe?" Lorna asked him lightly.

"Italy. To the convent."

"You planning to become Chrissie's first real convert?"

"No. Despite the fact that I think it's a miracle that I didn't end up doing decades in Sing-sing, it's Wagner who interests me now."

"You think you'll need his protection."

"No. That isn't at all what I have in mind."

*

He got out of the cab in the Bronx, huddled against the wind and pouring rain. It was four in the morning and there was no one about.

"You better watch yourself in this neighbourhood, buddy," the taxi driver warned and he searched out the change.

"Keep it. Any mugger who comes out in this weather deserves what he gets."

"If you say so, buddy."

Thyssen watched the cab until it disappeared from sight. He was wrapped in a yellow raincoat with the hood pulled right over his head. The driver might remember him but would never be able to make a positive identification. He turned then and surveyed the street—the ruined tenements towered all about and the gutters spread to lakes as the garbage blocked up the drains. With his hands in his pockets and his head down, he started to walk along a carefully planned route through streets and alleys until eventually he came to a wide square that he crossed. He did not know the area and had no idea where he was—he was tracing his course on a map secluded in the folds of the raincoat. At every possible corner, he halted and looked back to ensure no one was following. But he knew that a professional tail would never be caught by that method.

At the next corner, a man sat in a car, lighting a cigarette as Thyssen passed on the other side of the road. Neither acknowledged the existence of the other. Thyssen walked on and the man in the car, who was Val Dennis, waited ten minutes without moving, watching for signs of life, contented himself there was none, and then drove off. Thyssen meanwhile was two blocks away, and stepped into a doorway and made a call on his cell phone.

"All clear," Jami responded. "You go in the steel door in the alley across from you and up to the top floor in the goods lift."

When he got to the lift, Val Dennis was standing there, grinning and smoking. "Yo, Prof. Remember me?"

"I seem to remember kicking you out of one of my tutorials about ten years ago, Val."

"Hey man, big favour. I was so pissed, I assholed Geology and took Astrophysics in a rage of vengeance. It's much more fun looking up than looking down."

"Pleased to oblige."

"So, are we at the end of the exercise in paranoia?" Val asked with a grin.

"Yeah. I was sure I lost them at the airport. They'll still be watching my luggage waiting for me to collect it. But I didn't want to take any chances."

"Cool, Daddio. I surely don't wanna get tumbled at this stage."

"Unless, of course, they didn't need to follow me because they've tumbled your little set-up already."

"No way, bro. They been tryin' to bust me for years. I got so many anti-counter-measures installed that Deep Thought will need another Earthlife to find me."

"Well, we'll soon know if that's true. Is there somewhere warm around here?"

They rattled their way up in the elevator to where Jami awaited them on the top floor.

"Welcome to Hole-In-The-Wall, Butch," she grinned.

"Gawd," Thyssen grinned back. "You could hide the Titanic in here."

"It's in the room out the back," Jami laughed.

There they shed rain coats and she handed them towels to dry the peripherals as they made their way into Val's amazing clutter of equipment.

"What is all this stuff?" Thyssen asked in amazement.

"What falls, I catch," Val said with a shrug.

Thyssen saw a bathysphere, and a jet engine, and what seemed to be a communications satellite.

"Got outmoded before it got launched," Dennis explained when he saw Thyssen staring.

"You wouldn't have a nice, standard Pentium around someplace, would you?"

"Thisaway."

It was in fact the sort of place where Thyssen was at home, the machines reduced to their components and reconnected by exposed wiring. Jami sat at the screen. "We tried to duplicate Glen's set up as near as possible. How is the blue-eyed boy, anyway?"

"Gone over to the other side, I fear."

"Bastard."

"Taken you far too long to realise that, honoured student. But Glen's a practical lad. Either he works for them or he doesn't work. Eventually, he'll see reason and return to the fold and when he does we'll know everything they know."

"But doesn't that mean that right now they know everything we know?"

"They know everything *he* knows. But I managed to pump a few vital bits into the net."

Jami opened the page. "User name?"

"Drongo."

"*Oh boy*. Isn't it some sort of bird?"

Thyssen leaned over her shoulder and typed in the password

with one emphatic finger. "Yes. It's also a word I picked up from Brian Carrick. Australian for someone who knows less than they ought to."

"Isn't that everyone?"

"No. Only the undeluded. You got it?"

"Yep."

"Okay. Dump it into the models."

"Just like that?"

"Indeed. Set 'em running."

"How long will it take?"

"About ten minutes."

"And it'll come up with the answer?"

"It will come up with an array of statistical possibilities that will need to be analysed."

"What answer are we expecting?"

"Indian Ocean."

"You always say that, Harley, and you're always wrong."

"African side."

"But hang on. If we can do it this easily, why can't they?"

"We're smarter than they are."

"Getoutahere! This is really simple."

"If you get the right answer. It will require my magic touch afterwards."

"What now?"

"Delete Drongo."

"But it hasn't done anything yet."

Jami watched the models flashing on the screen and the columns of figures building in the window in the corner. And suddenly she knew.

"You've done something to it."

"Oh?"

"Drongo is readjusting the figures. I can see it happening."

"What a sharp eyed little student you are."

"You've put a virus in the models so that they'll always come up with the wrong answer unless they run Drongo."

"The data must be safeguarded."

"You bastard!"

"You seem to hang that descriptive on all the men in your life, Jami."

*

They walked out into the sunlight, the first that Brian Carrick had enjoyed for some time.

"I seem to be making a habit of being rescued from these places by beautiful women," Brian mused.

Lorna's eyes darted brightly. "It's hard to know which of your bad habits to criticise first, Brian."

"Still, it was good of you to think of me," Brian grinned.

"I was ordered to come and fetch you. I didn't realise you were still in gaol."

"It was the best way of keeping myself out of trouble."

They walked across the road and into the Flagstaff Gardens, both of them absorbing the fabulous Melbourne sunshine through their pores. It was an equal delight—after a gaol cell or a Northern Hemisphere winter.

"That's the worry, Brian. The rest of us are all going from strength to strength while you go down and down. We all feel a bit guilty."

"Life's a bitch, then you die."

"Life can improve, if you let it."

"Is it too early for a beer?" Brian asked.

"Far too late, I suspect."

"There's a nice pub down the hill with a beer garden."

"Lead me. But please, no more trouble."

"I promise."

They found the beer garden and sat, he with a beer and she a frightening cocktail.

"So the Harley Thyssen show is on again," Brian said. "You just can't keep a good man down."

"As far as I know, we are very unofficial. Almost covert. But yes. You're needed in Japan. The Japanese government even asked especially for you. That's the only reason we'll be able to get you out of the country with all these charges pending."

"But he sure showed 'em, our Harley. Didn't he?"

"He surely did. Tell me, what's Entropy?"

That raised his eyebrows. He knew the answer—he was simply surprised that someone like Lorna might bother to ask the question. Usually she was the first to glaze over when he went into one of his raves.

"Heat death of the Universe," he said as if it occurred every day.

"Yeah," Lorna said with a roll of her eyeballs. "Harley said something like that. Now explain it so a dumb bum like me can understand."

"Not so easy. Tell me why you want to know?"

"Aren't I allowed to know?"

"Usually, when I talk about such things, you nod off in five seconds."

"This time I'm interested."

"Which makes me wonder why?"

"Something that caught my eye amongst Harley's papers. He was evasive about it. Harley is never evasive about anything."

Wasn't he? Brian could not agree. If he read the right books for a thousand years, he would never know as much as Thyssen, but millimetre by millimetre he was gaining ground. He knew enough now to be sure that Harley Thyssen had all the answers. He was only telling people what they needed to know. For there were things that were obvious that he seemed surprised by, and it was impossible to believe that Thyssen's surprise at anything was genuine.

"No need to be evasive about this. It ain't no sort of secret. And I can't imagine what it has to do with anything. And I can't imagine you'll last more than twenty seconds before you switch off anyway."

"Try me. And I'll reward you with the hottest send-off to Japan in history."

Brian got himself another beer and lit a cigarette and when

he was settled, gave it his best shot. "The driving force of the universe is energy, and the most basic law of nature is the Law of Conservation of Energy. What that means is that the reason why the universe is not a stagnant solid ball of dead matter is because bits of energy flow from one place to another, sometimes changing in form as they do so."

"I haven't glazed over yet. Is there an English translation?"

"It's all about electrons and other elementary particles. The particles move from atom to atom, always tryin' to simplify things. Inside you. Inside stars. Everywhere. No energy moving and all you got is dead matter."

"Like my brain, huh?"

"Okay, so all this to-ing and fro-ing of subatomic particles all over the universe is called energy. The movement gives off heat and light and radiation and that is the engine that runs everything."

"Why does it move?"

"The energy is unevenly distributed throughout the universe—because it began randomly with a big explosion, you see? Ever since, its been flowin' to try and even up the distribution. Light, nuclear reactions, electricity, the neurons firing in your brain, is all transferred between elementary particles in their various forms, and that movement increasingly occurs spontaneously, they reckon, and always from uneven distribution toward even distribution. Still with me?"

"Hanging in there."

"This transformation of particles creates heat and energy, and as they even out and slow down and eventually stop, energy, and therefore life, is no longer possible."

"They get a nice rest at the end of the day."

"Right. Almost all studies of energy involve heat flow and temperature change, and this science of energy change, energy flow and conversation of energy into work is described by the Greek word for 'heat movement'—Thermodynamics."

"I am almost understanding this. Go on."

"Somewhere around 1850, a German Physicist named Rudolf Clausius came up with a Second Law of Thermodynamics, which necessarily lead to the invention of the First Law of Thermodynamics: the first law stated that the universe is immortal, the second that it is doomed."

"I'm sure I detected a contradiction in that."

"Absolutely. Black and white. Listen: The First Law of Thermodynamics says the energy content of the universe is constant. The Second Law of Thermodynamics says the energy flow of the universe is steadily decreasing."

"Really?"

"Really. Big contradiction. Big trouble for Physics. So, they get themselves out of it like this. The First Law says that the universe will last forever—everything that exists will continue to exist in some form or other constantly and ceaselessly."

"A comforting thought."

"The Second Law states that the universe is dying, that because the energy flow is always from uneven to even distribution and that it can only spontaneously flow that way, eventually everything will be evened out. The energy will still be there, locked up in dead matter, and motion, life, work and change will cease to be possible."

"I've known blokes like that..."

"When it reaches that point, when everything in the universe is at exactly the same temperature and no further activity is possible, it is the Heat-Death of the universe. And the process by which it occurs is Entropy."

"Right."

"You got all that?"

"I think so."

"Does it help?"

"Well, how could that possibly be of immediate interest to Harley?"

"I can't imagine. But it'll be interesting to try and find out."

*

Give a man too much money and too much power and too high

an opinion of himself, and the result was inevitable. Joe Solomon watched in dismay as Kevin Wagner gave his briefing for the next Shastri Event. There wasn't any problem with the briefing—it was clear and lucid and a spectacular bit of showmanship, only it wasn't about earth bound disasters. It was just another petty king of just another Fiefdom, strutting his self-importance. Joe supposed they should have seen it coming.

"The target area is the African state of Malawi," Wagner was saying from the rostrum, resplendent in military green, and he carried a pointer although he didn't need it for high over his head, video images projected on a huge screen indicated the location on the map of South East Africa. "Here, right along the western shore of Lake Nyasa, where about 6 million people live an almost entirely subsistence existence. It is the highest population density in Africa and they've had a miserable time of it—no external economy whatsoever, subject to continual droughts and flood, and their only claim to fame is that they were a rich source of raw materials for the slave trade, and their land is the home of the tsetse fly. The place is run by a dictator named Banda who sold out to South Africa and developed the most one sided capitalist system in the world. But, believe it or not, their luck is about to get worse."

You might have thought he cared, but Wagner showed no emotion. The speech, anyway, was written for him by Joe himself, based on raw material that came by e-mail from Thyssen with no return address.

"The zone of influence is expected to be about 100 square kilometres in the region at the middle western edge of the lake where it's all dense forest, thousands of tiny villages, unbearable heat, poverty and disease. And the lake is full of crocodiles, the jungle has Black Mambas and the region boasts the fattest vultures in the world. Nasty place. There are no volcanoes in the immediate vicinity but there's a big dormant one at the north end of the lake called Mbeya, about a two hundred kilometres away and it may erupt, and dozens more volcanoes a thousand kilometres away in Kenya that probably won't be effected, but might. In any case, we will have two hot spots, but the lake itself sits between two fault lines which may break open. Whatever happens, it's gonna be one hell of a mess."

They were in the main dining hall of the convent, and Wagner's audience—only two hundred when plainly the occasion justified several hundred more—sat at the long tables. Stained-glass windows which, primarily depicting the heroisms of the crusades, looked far more appropriate to the occasion that they might have to dinnertime. Joe had wheeled himself into a position behind, where he could survey the entire scene. Wagner strutted, chest thrust out, king of the convent, although his American accent fitted badly with the circumstances. It needed British officer class, or perhaps German, to give proper weight to the event.

"The restrictions placed on Professor Thyssen by various authorities have caused the data to come through too late to be of any use. There is no hope of getting these people out of the area in time, and nowhere to take them anyway. Mozambique, Zambia and Tanzania have been receiving refugees and work gangs from the region for decades and resent them, and we could start a war if we tried to get them out. But in any case, it's too late for that."

Wagner's mini-army, most of them mercenaries primarily recruited during his Italian operations, had busied themselves for the past two months repairing the airstrip and one of the hangars in which the two old C-130's were housed. Joe had been able to secure a team and deploy them to the task of building ramps all about the convent and his possible range of movement expanded daily. He could see all about him how the money was being spent and had to admit that there were few luxury items. The mercenaries had been divided into teams long before, and trained as well as they could be for their role in the forthcoming event, and almost all expenditure had been devoted to that.

"The *official* prediction, by the way, is here, north of Malagasy, in the Indian Ocean almost on the equator. They expect little damage and few serious effects. But we will proceed with the *unofficial* version. Thyssen has been right every time in the past and there's no reason to think it will be different this time. We will establish our main base in Salisbury, which I know is a long way away, but Zimbabwe is about the only place where we can expect reasonably modern facilities and cooperation from the government. A task force base will be established at either Lilongwe or Zomba, which are the main population centres near the zone. In fact, either but not both are likely to be inside the zone. That will be decided immediately we know how it comes down.

"We turn now to the focal point of the pilgrimages," Wagner said and on the screen above his head, the earth rotated to what might have been a space ship view, observed from some point over the Arctic Circle and rotating slowly around its line. Red indicators showed the locations of the pilgrims. Their own position in Italy, Chrissie thankfully still in Rome where she could not see this going down, Andromeda in Paris, the USS Barton sailors in the brig in San Diego, the Japanese back in their fields but apparently all tagged by Brian Carrick.

The control group—their medical usefulness now outlived and their legal status very much in question—had been released into Felicity Campbell's custody and she handed them over to the project. Presently they were all in this room, ready to be dispersed to where-ever they could help out. The Buryats were either in a camp or returned to their fields but in any case could not have gone far. Lorna Simmons was doing television appearances in New York. From each point, the red lines converged.

"These are the present locations of the pilgrims and since Japan is roughly the same distance as Lake Balkai from the previous focal point, it will be in much the same place as last time. Latitude 84.6 degrees North, Longitude 118.3 degrees West. About 150 miles West-Nor-West of Cape Richards. Just a little closer to the North Pole in fact. But since our plan is for no one to go there, that should not be a problem. The Italians will follow the same route as last time, though perhaps a little more carefully under the guidance of Sister Christine. Those of us affected, including myself, will by then be in Japan where the greatest difficulties will arise. The decision has been taken to abandon vehicles there and move the 16,000 pilgrims by foot, which means after thirty-six hours, they will still be travelling the roads on the Honshu Island."

Sixteen thousand Japanese peasants walking the road to nowhere, and after the 11th of December, perhaps more than 100,000 Bantus, abandoning their subsistence crops to take to the road. Where did it end, Joe wondered. The Apocalypse was coming but that was hardly likely to make any difference. More people involved each time, the time gap shortening, he'd done a little calculation that said the end of the world would be the 22nd June, which was just over six months away.

At the present rate of decrease, that would be when the two events came so close together that they occurred on the same day. Each would have a zone of influence would cover 5 million square kilometres, about the land area of the United States of America, or the average tectonic plate. By then, pilgrims would probably outnumber the unaffected on a global basis. Just nine months and an area the size of Africa would find nothing holding it up and fall into the core of the earth. If the Shastri Effect had not wiped out all humanity and destroyed the Earth by then, there would be three more events next day, each double the size of the one before. Why were they bothering?

Because it couldn't happen, that was why. Because it was all too gigantic and catastrophic to contemplate. Because it was completely beyond comprehension. Admittedly, he was no scientist and his figures were rough as guts, but the progression at the present rates went something like that. Perhaps there would be some upper limit that a Shastri Event could not exceed, or maybe next time the bubble would blast an extra moon into orbit around the earth, incidentally drowning all life. The return of Noah and no one he knew was thinking of building an ark. Except maybe Kevin Wagner.

*

Mount Fuji was all but restored. Only the most avid admirer would have noticed a large chunk missing from the crater rim that had collapsed during the eruption. It was quiet again and had been since the Shastri Event of the 1st of November had burst it to thundering life. Only the usual white mist drifted from the caldera now, and the snows had returned, covering the black stain of ash on the slopes. Once more the symmetry of the most perfect mountain in the world was restored, and so by appearance had been the rural scenes on the plains below. But that, Wagner knew, was an illusion.

There was a house atop a hill with rippling ponds amid the landscape garden and those paper sliding doors and even some geishas provided by the government to keep the guests happy. The girls, and the visiting Japanese officials, had smiled warmly and bowed and called them honoured guests. They were rested, they had eaten well, they had been looked after to the highest degree of the fabled Japanese hospitality. All they couldn't do was leave, and constantly out of sight but always present were soldiers with machine guns to ensure it remained so. They called it *The House of the Golden Carp*. In these perfect surroundings, they had nevertheless been prisoners.

"It's become my natural state these days," Brian Carrick remarked.

Well he might joke but Wagner saw nothing funny in it. They, Wagner and the four members of the control group he brought with him from the base, had been picked up when they arrived at Tokyo airport and brought here. The other four had gone to join Felicity in Malawi. Brian Carrick had flown in two days earlier and was waiting for him.

"I got a message to Felicity telling her to stay away," Brian had assured him when he arrived.

"Why didn't you warn me?" Wagner bit back.

"Why didn't you tell me you were coming?" Brian smiled in reply.

Wagner's chagrin was all the worse that Brian seemed so completely at home in *The House of the Golden Carp*.

"I've looked in all the ponds in the garden," Brian said sadly. "There are no carp, golden or otherwise."

"I don't think the number of fish in the garden is the hot issue here, cobber," Wagner seethed.

"No, you're right. I should have bought more books," Brian said. "I'm through all the stuff in my luggage."

"Are you going to take this situation seriously or what?" Wagner often found Brian's casual attitude annoying, but never more so than now.

"Why? There's nothing we can do. They'll let us go on the thirteenth when the event has passed."

"And how are we going to cope with the thirty-six hours of the linkage?"

"As irritably as you're behaving now, I suspect."

"It is only three days away."

"The stock of Saki should see us through," Brian said.

But Brian was right. The Red Cross and the UN Emergency Corps had dealt properly with the sleepers and they were all tagged and prepared. Brian said he had been no more than an observer and that the locals seemed to have matters under control.

"We are not officially involved," Brian pointed out.

"Do they realise that without us they are going to have sixteen thousand zombies roaming the countryside?"

"They know it, but I don't think they believe it. They've told the local population that there's to be a festival at Shibata on the north coast and that they're to go on foot from their homes to make offerings to the shrine there. It sounds like a perfect plan to me."

"Oh yeah. And maybe we oughta get Saint Chrissie to lead them?"

"The Nips take their festivals and shrines very seriously, Kev. They'll all go, nice and quiet, as far as anyone can figure."

"So what the hell are we doing here?"

"The Japs aren't masters of the world for no reason, Kev. They want to do it without involving us, but still keep us around in case it goes wrong."

"Why didn't I stay in Italy?" Wagner muttered in disgust.

But because their cell phones and all other outside communication had been confiscated, there was no way of knowing how the others were faring.

The link was due at midnight on the 11th and by dawn next day, three senior officers of the Imperial Army were on their doorstep. Wagner was roused and went unsteadily to the central room where the officers paced. Brian was already there, and Kenitsu, who was their translator and also a pilgrim from the control group. Each of them was agitated, but still dulled by their tranquilliser of choice.

"We'll see what happens when they wear off," Brian had said. His had been Saki.

"It is a great disaster. You must come and help us," General Matusu, who spoke some English, declared.

"I was just beginning to feel the urge to mosey along," Wagner replied dreamily.

The bus had been provided and within minutes, the six pilgrims from *The House of the Golden Carp* were in it, dressed and bewildered, drinking coffee with great care as the bus jolted them down the road. The General and his officers, and the Chief of Police and his men, and the three government gentlemen who had been so officious earlier and now were humble beyond words.

"They came out of everywhere and just started walking," the story went, mostly through translation. "They ignored roads and orders from our soldiers. They just walked, blindly, all going in the same direction but spread across a front of about three kilometres. They walked straight into people's houses and some were assaulted. They fell in rivers and some drowned. They walked straight in front of traffic and some have been injured. There is no ordering them."

"It's too late for us to do it now," Brian said.

Wagner knew it was true. This was the effect Felicity had warned them about.

"They would have followed us, had we been allowed to lead them," Wagner said bitterly. "But they needed to know that in advance. Now, Brian is right. There is nothing we can do."

"The soldiers have had to shoot some of them, when they refused to deviate from their course even slightly."

"All your men can do," Brian said, "is work on clearing the path in front of them."

"There are problems there too. In towns lying in the path of the pilgrims, the word has come that the human locusts, as they are called, are advancing. Gangs of armed men are coming out to meet them."

"Your soldiers must clear the armed men from their path."

"And at Shibata, the local population has formed a human barricade to protect their shrine."

"But the shrine was an invention, wasn't it?"

"Still, now that they know it exists, they are determined to defend it."

Wagner was studying the map at the time, realising it was important.

"In any case, they won't go to Shibata now. They would only have gone there if we had led them. Now they will head toward a point just a few degrees west of due north from each person's original starting point. I'll get an exact fix for you in a moment, but it looks like the vicinity of Takada. The path must be cleared to that point, right away."

"What happens when they get there?"

"It's two hundred kilometres. They can't walk that far in a day and a half."

"They are stealing cars, and bicycles. Any sort of vehicle they can find."

"Yes," Brian put in. "Felicity said they will go by whatever is the best transport means to hand."

"Boats must be provided for those who make it to the coast, or else they will just walk into the sea," Wagner was saying, getting into his stride now.

Already, traces of the event were beginning to show. There were fires burning up ahead, and ambulances and police rushed along the roads. In some places, injured people were being treated at the road side. When they arrived, they were near a town that fiercely defended itself from the invaders. There was a great commotion of voices and dust rose everywhere. Young men mostly, threw themselves into a pitched brawl with great frenzy while riot police tried to control them.

"This isn't the way," Brian shouted at the generals. "The soldiers must not try to stop them. They must clear the path."

And Wagner, angered by the scenes before them, of bloodied bodies and huddles of weeping people, turned to General Matusu and said. "And you must tell them that this would not have happened, had we been allowed to lead them."

Even as they watched, a gang of men came out of a village on the rise before them, and the riot police were gathered in a line to meet them. There was no hesitation, the two forces clashed without breaking stride. At that moment, rocks and other objects began to crash against the side of the bus and riot troops were forced back by the mob.

The rock hit the window and everyone in the bus went for cover, diving down below the level of the backs of the seats. Wagner already hated himself for doing it—it was an unavoidable reflex but that didn't make it any less a blow to his self-image. He bobbed up again so fast that no one could possibly have noticed, except the only person who mattered. Brian raised his eyes from the cushion of the seat opposite and was chuckling.

"Nerves of steel," he murmured ironically.

Wagner was reasonably sure Brian was referring to his own reaction, but the joke was not funny across the aisle. Wagner had already twisted his head and saw the jagged hole with his spiderweb of cracks. Not a bullethole, to be sure and anyway, there was no way the skin and seating of the bus would offer the slightest protection if it was. In the other seats, the occupants all began poking their heads up like a meerkat colony.

Now, Wagner shouted an order which the language barrier could not defeat clear comprehension. 'Get us out of here,' he roared and the driver—a Japanese Corporal—looked several different ways at once as she crashed through the gears, revved the engine and blasted on the horn. But they weren't going anywhere, except possibly onto their roof. The heavy thud of bodies against the front and side of the bus rocked them violently. Out there, most of the scene was now lost in a furious fog of dust, but when he risked pressing his cheek against the glass, Wagner could see the black uniforms, shining helmets and Perspex shields of the riot police as they were back up against the side of the bus, fighting the mob furiously.

"I think we need to revise the plan," Brian said, eternally seeking humour where there wasn't any.

Wagner was moving toward the back of the bus where, conventionally he hoped, the rear window served as an emergency exit. Not that he was planning to go out there unless he had to, but it might be handy if they went over. He saw the way was open and turned, shouting. "It's clear back here."

From halfway down the aisle, Brian relayed the message to the driver. "Bung her in reverse and go like fuck, luv."

One of the Japanese managed a translation, the girl ground the gears and they lurched backwards. The riot police, deprived of the wall their backs had been against, spilled across the dust shrouded scene out the front and sides. The girl reversed them wildly across the square and then swung into a blind turn and the passengers were thrown this way and that as she lurched them around and finally they were heading back down the road they had come, climbing the hill out of the valley where, behind, wild scenes of confusion continued unabated.

At the top of the hill, they came to a halt and it was time to let the panic subside.

"You see it is as I said," the Japanese official said, not quite proudly.

"You see it is all completely out of hand,' General Matusu added dismally.

"We see," Brian murmured.

They stepped out of the bus to survey the scene and regather their wits, and each of them made some gesture or remark of appreciation to the driver as they passed. The girl remained behind the wheel, knowing she had found her vocation.

From this point, they could see right across the valley and at five different places they could see the dust rising, signifying trouble. In the village they had just escaped, the police seemed to be getting the rioters in hand but still there were momentary images of frenzied action as bodies hurled this way and that. From this point was offered a splendid view of Mount Fuji, not as good as the one from the *House of the Golden Carp*, but not bad either. They might as well take in the scenery, Wagner knew, for all the good they could do otherwise. As the man said, it had all got out of hand, but that was their own goddamned fault. In this defeat, there was also victory, for Wagner at least.

"This wouldn't have happened if you put us in charge," he snapped at General Matusu, and the soldier cowered, knowing it was so.

"We were not informed it would be like this," the general glowered at the Chief of Police.

But Wagner knew who to blame—not those who followed orders but the three gentlemen from the government who each already had their heads bowed in shame, as if waiting for the emperor to have them chopped off.

"We did, and we warned you, and instead of listening you locked us up in that bloody brothel."

If the abuse was justified, the offence was not. Brian placed himself in front of Wagner and placed hands on both of his shoulders.

"Cool it, Kev. Can't be helped now."

Wagner felt the peak of his anger slip by, but still irritably shrugged off Brian and turned away, looking back toward Fujiyama.

"This must not happen again," Wagner uttered bitterly.

*

The sun dropped toward the horizon, building up for another spectacular African sunset, only this one was going to beat them all. It was the perfect spot, to be standing on the tallest mountain in the range with a three-sixty degree view of the dusty world below. To the south the cruel capitalist state of Malawi where for thirty years a crazy dictator with an allegiance to South Africa had built skyscrapers and super-highways and railways to please the rich minority and created the poorest population in all of Africa. Though what Jami could see of it from her vantage point was only the shimmering beauty of Lake Nyasa, stretching away three hundred miles to the south.

At the other end of the lake, Felicity strove to prepare the locals for the disaster to come, but at last information, had not even managed to get admitted to the country yet. Malawi, under a brutal and rigid bureaucracy, considered itself a perfect state and would not admit the possibility of trouble in their so-called paradise.

The lake itself was a tributary of the Great Rift Valley, but this was the nearest decent volcano to the expected zone—Mt Mbeya—a solitary cone amid a wild wide plateau that was in fact in Tanzania, where no one cared where she went and what she did. She had located a private helicopter firm and arranged to be brought here—the mountain was virtually inaccessible otherwise. A cheery Zambian named Bono flew her up here, and landed her right on the rim.

"You stay here?" he said, looking around.

"Yes. Unpack my equipment please. Then you can go."

"Go? And leave you here?"

"That's right. Pick me up tomorrow morning, as early as you can, if you can."

"It's not safe to stay up here all night. Alone..."

He tailed off.

Jami knew what he was thinking. Young women like herself constantly worked to maneuver young men like Bono into the right position to enjoy them as part of their 'African experience', and he plainly expected that now. AIDS infection in the region was about 85% but that did not deter the rich American women from fulfilling their sexual fantasies. But Jami had other things on her mind. She didn't want to tell him that he had only an hour to get clear of the mountain or else he never would. She just wanted him to unpack the stuff and leave.

"Just dump all the stuff there," she said flatly.

She surveyed the location while he did so.

It had been a long time since Mbeya's last eruption, centuries, but the crater was deep, at least a thousand feet straight down and all solid lava and cinder. It crunched underfoot as she walked, and nothing grew here. Nothing to obstruct her view. From here she would be able to see and record everything that happened in that crater. All she had to do was get rid of silly Bono.

"Okay, now go."

"A woman, all alone. Who knows what can happen?" he was babbling.

"Nothing can happen. No wild animals or humans can get up here. The weather is perfect. I'll be fine. Now go. Come back tomorrow."

Eventually, he saw her point. It was, perhaps, the safest place in Africa, in normal circumstances. She needed to herd him along but finally he went. She watched the little helicopter fly away across the mountains until it was out of sight. She expected a pang of regret or something but she was too excited. Time was running out and she had a lot to do.

First a box of seismos and other detectors, all fitted to a little transmitter to a monitor she had placed in the town of Mbeya below, which in turn would feed via the net to Val's lab. The data would probably tell them nothing, but it did also provide her with an early warning device, if she needed it.

Next the two video cameras housed in a solid fireproof cases, one of which she set up right on the rim, so it could film the depths of the crater. That settled, she turned the other until it pointed at a director's chair, placed beneath an umbrella.

Next a yellow, padded, fireproof overall, into which she fitted herself and a domed helmet that she left off for the moment. Now she was set. She turned the camera on and sat in the chair. She hoped she looked good—the light was turning orange and the slight breeze mussed her hair, but it was her show and she was the star, for the moment.

"I am sitting on the edge of the crater of Mt Mbeya, which, in a few minutes, I expect to erupt. I am here to observe that eruption from closer than anyone has ever been. I'm doing this for my own satisfaction, but I brought this camera and some data gatherers along, for what it's worth. The box of tricks will record data for as long as it lasts, the camera will record the eruption for as long is it lasts, and I was stand on the edge and observe it for as long as I last. This is going to be the best thing I've ever done."

That sounded good. She was sure her voice was level and she was calm and looked happy, which was also the way she felt. There was exhilaration, and if she was also apprehensive, she wasn't anywhere near as troubled as someone ought to have been when they were within moments of being blown to smithereens.

She had allowed herself minimum time so there was as little opportunity for her emotions and survival instincts to overwhelm her as possible. And anyway, whenever the fear snatched at her, she thought of Harley. *This will show you, big fella. Even you have never been this close.*

"It might sound suicidal, but it isn't really. All the data is being transmitted and in sealed containers so it has a good chance of lasting as long as possible. The camera is fitted with a special steel case and padding and it probably won't survive but think of the footage if it does. They reckon it can survive being dropped from a hundred feet, so maybe there will be something to show for it. But if not, bad luck. All that is secondary anyway. I'm here for me. I have this special suit and helmet but of course I can't predict what will happen to me and I don't care. This is worth it. I always wanted to stand on the edge of one of these things and watching it happen and now I will. It's worth it."

It was also stupid, but that was what she had been. Stupid, stupid, to chase after blokes like Glen and believe in men like Harley Thyssen. They put it over her, every time and it had to stop and this was the only way to stop it. If she died, she died, but think of the respect she would gain if she survived. It was worth it.

"That's all," she said with a smile. "Enjoy the show."

She got up and swivelled the camera on its tripod to point into the crater. Perfect. She quickly checked the other equipment and then walked to the edge of the crater and looked down. Nothing was happening.

For the moment, she kept the helmet tucked under her arm like a spare head. She would put it on when necessary, but she wanted to see this with the naked eye, for as long as she could, rather than through a visor. This was going to be fantastic.

Harley had lied. He had lied to her. He had lied to the world. He was setting himself up to be the only man who could get it right, the top man, king of the world, but he had rigged the results to do so. Just another megalomaniac, convinced that what was right for him was right for everyone. He probably had his reasons but she didn't care. She had placed her faith foolishly once more and it would never, never happen again. That was all.

Something was happening... First she felt the grip of nausea that she remembered from that first time, and she seemed to lose consciousness for an instant. She dropped onto one knee and almost pitched headfirst into the crater. Her senses had shut down for an instant, then recovered, and she knew it wasn't fear and doubt. It was the effect. Every instinct screamed at her now to run but she knew there was nowhere to run to. Stay, her mind ordered, stay and do this right.

She felt the ground begin to shake under her feet and down in the crater, cracks appeared. There was the illusion suddenly that she had fallen in and was dropping toward the bottom of the chasm but it wasn't so—the depths were moving up to meet her. Through the cracks, she saw glimpses of the fiery lava beneath and then the gases and smoke and dust suddenly burst through and instantly filled the crater and her world. She frantically got her head into the helmet and snapped it into place, and by then was blinded by the cloud as it burst by her. Then everything was a blur, and then it was gone. The final sensation was flying through the air... It seemed she was spinning like a top, around and around or over and over, and through her visor she glimpsed the red hot ash cloud pursuing her down the slope as her body tumbled just out of its searing grasp.

And her mind screaming. "What do you think of this one, Harley!"

13
GOODBYE CALIFORNIA

Like the first amphibian crawling onto land, so she emerged into consciousness in a slow uncertain fashion, with images and fragments that slowly coalesced over what she understood to be a considerable length of time.

Mostly, the images were faces leaning close to hers, and white jackets, and tubes, and silver instruments, and little flashing lights.

And all along, the visage of Harley Thyssen appeared again and again and she wanted to have a few words to him. 'See what you made me do, Harley, you lying bastard,' she wanted to tell him. And maybe she said it too, because when finally she snapped out of it, he was there.

"Nurse, you better have a look at this," his gruff voice commanded from somewhere outside her limited range of vision.

"Oh, yes, Professor. I think she's finally back with us."

The nurse leaned over and looked into her eyes.

"Gllllurrreck," Jami said to her.

"That's right, dear. You just take it easy. Do you have any pain?"

She remembered that she had a body, but it didn't seem to be there at the moment. She was just a dismembered head on the pillow, looking upward. But, because the nurse obviously understood gobbledygook perfectly, she thought she'd better mention it.

"Nobble bobbie," she declared informatively..

"Yes. That's just effect of the painkillers. If you feel any pain, I can give you something."

"Nopin," she said. Nothing at all really. Obviously she was

much worse than she thought.

Then Thyssen leaned over her. She would have spat in his eye but her mouth was devoid of moisture.

"Dim wit," Thyssen said.

"Assole," she replied.

The clairvoyant nurse immediately provided a plastic cup of pink fluid and it refreshed her and she tried to keep from gulping it all down but couldn't... and Harley had moved out of range anyway.

She indulged her exhausted eyelids a slow blink in which a long time must have passed because Harley had transmuted into Felicity Campbell.

"How am I?" she asked.

"Don't ask me. This is my day off. I'm just a visitor."

But Felicity couldn't help herself—Jami felt pressure on her wrist and a cool hand on her cheek. "Give it to me straight, doc."

"There's only two hours of visiting left. Nowhere near enough time to tell you all of it."

"That bad, huh?"

"You did quite a job on yourself, if that's what you mean. But you do have some bones that *aren't* broken, and one or two organs that *are* still working properly. You'll live to regret your foolishness."

"It wasn't foolish, Fee. It was fucking great."

Plainly Doctor Felicity knew how to ignore nonsense when she heard it. "The good news is that everything that's wrong with you will mend eventually. Which makes you one of the luckiest people on the planet."

She already knew that. "What about the equipment?"

Felicity was shaking her head in dismay. "Oh, I see. So your insanity is completely incurable. Perhaps we shouldn't bother with a million dollars worth of medical science to make you well again. Maybe we just ought to turn you over to some witch doctor and have him sacrifice you to the volcano god and be done with it."

Promising idea... "Did the film come out?"

"It did. We've got it here in the video—you can have a look when you're able to turn your head enough to see the television screen. You'll also be the last person on Earth to see it. It's been shown on every news program and everyone in the world sat in their lounge rooms and said *Wow!* They also all said *What a stupid person.*"

So what was the bad news? Maybe that it hurt her lips when she tried to smile. "It was worth it, Fee. My God it was worth it. What about the data?"

"Harley said the data is fantastic."

She remembered. Bloody Harley. *Asshole.* "He was here..."

"Yes. He haunted the place for three days until they assured him you would be all right. He left when I arrived."

"Bastard!"

"So he said. Apparently, this was all his fault." Felicity's pout doubted it.

"It was," Jami insisted, like a child who knew in advance that the adults would not believe her.

Felicity obviously caught the same metaphor. "Sooner or later, the student must stop blaming the teacher for their shortcomings and take responsibility for themselves."

Bastards. They were all in it together... "No, Fee. Really. He lied. He lied to me. He lied to all of us. The bastard."

Somehow Felicity was able to shrug that off. "Okay, so he lied. Everyone lies. Was that any reason to have yourself blown from Tanzania to Malawi?"

"He lied about the data, Fee. He rigged it so that everyone else would come to the wrong conclusions."

Incredibly, Felicity was even patting her on the back of the hand. "You must stop thinking about that for now, Jami. It's making you too excited. Your anger is registering on all the monitors."

Indeed, it brought the nurse with a worried look.

"But he..."

"Jami. Stop thinking about this or they'll have to tranquillise you again. I mean it."

She calmed. The nurse stood, looking dubious and frowning as Felicity waved her away. "It'll be all right now. She's calming."

And Jami finally felt something. Sensation at last. Something tickling her on the cheek. Felicity reached with a tissue and wiped the tear away. The nurse finally backed off.

"We can talk about those sorts of things later, when you're stronger. But put it out of your mind for the moment, okay?"

"I guess..."

"Have you seen your flowers?"

There were bright coloured blobs at the periphery of her vision. Felicity walked around and moved them so she could see them more clearly.

"Did you bring them?"

"No. A lovely little black man named Bono."

She supposed the dials must have gone berserk if the thrill that passed through her system was any guide. "He came back for me!"

"Indeed he did. He couldn't stay but I spoke to him. He..."

Her memory was filled with his huge toothy smile and shining black face. "He was so worried about leaving me there."

Felicity was seated again and nodding. "He told me about it, Jami. His country was blown to hell and he hadn't slept for days but every chance he went back and flew across the slopes and saw something yellow. It was just your arm sticking out of the ashfall. He landed on a thirty degree slope of hot ash halfway down the mountain and dragged you into his helicopter and saw your camera and grabbed that too. He thought you were dead, of course. He was so excited when he learned you had survived."

Her emotions were really out of control in a way they had never been before, not even over Glen. "My hero. Will he be coming back?"

"He, and his helicopter, are still badly needed. It's chaos out there. But yes, he'll be coming back. He found time to bring the flowers, didn't he?"

"Wonderful man. I'll marry him."

"The planet is full of wonderful people, Jami. It really is

worth saving. And we need you to help save it."

It flooded back again. "He lied to us, Felicity. I believed in that man so much and he lied."

"But we need him too, Jami. Personally, I find it rather gratifying to discover that Harley Thyssen is just another flawed human being like the rest of us."

"I never want to see him again."

"The readings are going off the scale, Jami. Calm down. Stop thinking about it."

And the nurse was there.

"Yes, I know," Felicity said to the authoritarian scowl and then, as she stood, smiled down on Jami. "Put Harley out of your mind. Think about Bono. And how he came back for you."

*

Lorna Simmons dumped her briefcase on the polished top of the mahogany table, flipped it open, removed her cell phone, closed the case, and sat leaning her elbows on it. Four men and six women sitting around the table all watched her every move. She presumed she was wearing her expectant expression. They were executives, producers, managers—it didn't matter who they were really and Lorna had not bothered to learn any of their names properly. The big boss-cocky was named Roy, and dangerous woman executive producer was named Katrina, and the rest were generally lackeys and brown-tongues. All they were to her were the people that called that shots at CNN.

"Okay, let me tell you what we want?" Lorna smile blithely.

"By 'we', you are referring to, who exactly?" Katrina asked, in case Lorna failed to notice that she had an equal rival in the mini-power struggle to follow immediately.

"The Unofficial Project Earthshaker, for which I am merely the humble spokesperson," Lorna said with a coy bow and a nervous hand to her throat.

"But who do you speak for exactly?" Katrina persisted.

"The Project is a collective. Media is my responsibility."

"I see. I had hoped you might be speaking for Harley Thyssen."

"In part, yes."

"And I was wondering why Professor Thyssen doesn't speak for himself."

"He doesn't because he has me to speak for him. And he is much too busy trying to save the world to bother with television interviews. And he isn't pretty."

"Why does he feel he needs to be so defensive?"

It was war, then. "Do your questions always inherently harbour their own answers?"

"Ladies, ladies, please..." Roy was saying placatingly.

But since both sides believed they had won, the war was temporarily suspended.

Lorna had been thinking a lot about Harley, and she had begun, amongst other things, to wonder why he hid so resolutely behind her. Admittedly, he was not the television celebrity type, but he seemed to handle his words with care at all times and if so, why did he fear that he might let the cat out of the bag when confronted with a professional interviewer? And what particular cat was that, anyway? The question was, as the likes of Katrina suspected, that if Harley really did harbour secrets so terrible that he feared to speak publicly, just in case such secrets slipped out? And if so, given what was known, how much more terrible could those secrets be?

Lorna had determined, some time ago, that she must use all of her powers to seduce Harley Thyssen and see what could be learned on the pillow. That little matter began to become extremely overdue.

"Okay, can we begin?" Lorna asked, innocently.

"Please do."

"We wish to prepare a documentary program to go to air on Sunday night, at prime time, and be immediately available for syndication on all networks right around the world within twenty-four hours."

"Prime time Sunday—in competition with the network

movies, no doubt," Katrina savaged.

"No. Beforehand. 7.30."

"Against Sixty Minutes. Are you kidding?"

"I think Thirty-eight Minutes are about to get creamed, Katrina," Lorna smiled. "I believe that when you hear the content of the program, there will be no problem with the timeslot demand."

"Oh why not. Are you sure you don't want to go up against The Simpsons?"

Lorna stayed calm, where Katrina was losing it completely. It was a joy to watch. "The production will be hosted by myself and Andromeda Starlight jointly, and will be provided to you as a package. The intention is to explain to the world in general just exactly what is going on, what we know about the Shastri Effect, dispel all the myths and rumours and generally put the whole matter straight."

"This is with a view to—what?" Katrina demanded with a frown and a shake of her head—as if someone had kicked her in it. But Roy stepped in quietly—he was a blessed relief. "I presume we are looking at a build-up to the Apocalypse..."

"Quite so," Lorna said. "Including details on what we can expect, and when."

"Won't we look rather silly if the dates are wrong?"

"That is another of the issues. People do seem to keep worrying about how they'll cope *after* the end of the world."

"Is that what you'll be talking about? The end of the world?" Roy gasped.

"Not entirely. Just the facts on the Shastri Effect as they are known at this stage."

"Well I hardly..." Katrina began.

But Lorna cut her off sharply. "That's just the build up, of course."

"To the next prediction?" Roy guessed.

"Exactly."

"By which you mean," Katrina burst in, wounded but far from incapacitated. "Professor Thyssen's prediction, as opposed to the official one."

"I do indeed."

"But surely the customary news release will be the more appropriate outlet," Roy was saying grimly.

"You haven't heard the prediction yet," Lorna said.

"You mean you know it?" Roy gasped.

"I know Professor Thyssen's preliminary guess. The confirmation will occur before Sunday."

"You mean you intend to keep something like this secret until Sunday night?" Roy said—he was beginning to sound as shrill as Katrina.

"The President of the United States has known the preliminary guess for two months and has seen no reason to make it public. However, the full assessment of the data will take until the weekend, after which, Sunday is the most appropriate release date."

"If the release is approved by the White House?" Katrina spluttered.

"Whether it is or not."

"But, for the moment, we are going on the basis of the guess?" Roy worried.

"He's been right every time so far, remember?"

"But what is this... this guess?" Katrina cried in outrage.

"Are you sure you want to know?"

"Of course we do!" Katrina hated it.

"Surely you see, Miss Simmons," Roy said with an edge to his voice. "That we would need some idea in order to justify the prime time demand."

"Right now, only the Professor, the President and myself know about it. I'm happy to pass it on but think of the threat that a leak would be to your exclusivity."

"But we cannot offer exclusivity unless you give us some idea."

"And," Katrina had to add. "Obviously, that would affect the price of exclusive rights..."

"It will be a fixed price, whether exclusive or not."

"I'm afraid we cannot deal on that basis, Miss Simmons," Katrina was sure.

But Lorna could see she had them. Roy was regarding her now with grave concern. He knew there would be a deal, that they would have no choice, and he knew that Lorna would know that. Lorna was enjoying her moment of supreme power.

"Just exactly what sort of ballpark figure are we talking about here?" Roy asked in that quieter, slightly embarrassed tone that people always adopted when it came down to the bottom line.

"I should think the largest sum of money ever paid by any network for any one-hour, one-off program in the short but spectacular history of television," Lorna said blithely.

"Which is how much?" Katrina demanded.

"I don't know. Check the records and you tell me."

"I'm not standing for any more of this," Katrina said and she was standing too. "It's a con..."

"Exclusive rights always are," Lorna said quietly. "But, do bear in mind that all such moneys will be poured directly into the project and devoted entirely to the purpose of saving lives."

"Oh my God, now she's the Salvation Army..."

"Project Earthshaker, Katrina, is a non-profit organisation."

"Miss Simmons, you cannot..." but Katrina got no further.

"And we will refund every penny if you're disappointed."

The silence grew in the room like a nuclear mushroom cloud, and one by one they turned and stared.

"It's that big?" Roy gasped with sudden realisation.

"Yes, it is."

"It's *the* big one," he cried as the knowledge firmed like concrete within him.

"Do we have a deal?" Lorna asked with eyebrows raised benignly.

"We do."

"Believe me. We need the money. There is no possibility that you'll be disappointed."

*

For two days they were marched along the ridgelines and through the valleys of the mountains to the west of Lake Nyasa. Even Wagner, and certainly Fabrini, struggled in the oppressive heat while the locals lost none of the spring from their stride. The lengthy and arduous trek, Wagner was certain, was a meandering one designed to obscure the actual location of the camp, poised as it was above the capital, preparing for the final assault. Twice they were ambushed by government troops but the leader of the march had the wisdom to run most of his force to the flanks of the central group, and the contacts were soon forced wide and away from them.

They had finally entered Malawi without official permission, by helicopter and landed in the town of Kasungu, the nearest settlement, they had been assured, to the main rebel camp. There they made it known they wished to speak to the rebel leader, Mombatu. No one had ever heard of him in Kasungu. Then, in the night as they left the only tavern in town where plainly Carlsberg had the beer monopoly, they were accosted by men with machineguns who made it plain they should follow.

They were taken in trucks at first, and then on foot through dense forest. Fabrini ran out of patience on the first day and by the second was too exhausted to continue his grumbling. He had nasty blisters on his feet to keep him quiet. Wagner strode on, but even he was becoming no less blistered and frustrated.

Then they were in the camp, and the only real way of knowing was that the population of men in rags with shining new Kalashnikov's slowly began to increase until they were all around, watching quietly with suspicious eyes. Mombatu was just another man in rags, although he was a little fatter than the rest, and could offer flamboyant gestures in comparison to his sullen, taciturn troops. He spoke in the sort of perfect rhythmic English that only blacks can achieve.

"Ahh, Mr. Wagner, welcome to our humble headquarters."

"A pleasure to arrive," Wagner replied.

"Nevertheless, do please forgive us the runaround. There are security measures that need to be taken, of the sort of which I am sure you are well acquainted."

Wagner was determined not to admit anything. "I suppose you *are* Mr. Mombatu."

"Please. Colonel is my official rank. You should adopt one for yourself." Mombatu said and looked appropriately proud of himself.

"I am a civilian, Colonel. Just a tourist, really. At least that's what my passport says."

The truth was, Mombatu was no different to the lethargic and officious border guards who seemed to make their own rules when stamping the visas and searching the luggage. The rebel leader might have been embarrassed on their behalf.

"Such formalities mean little here. My goodness, Mr. Fabrini, you do look most unwell. A chair in the shade and a drink for our visitors. Handsomely, now."

Mombatu snapped his fingers, and men even more lethargic than Fabrini responded. They were seated and Carlsberg was provided, and Mombatu sat before them, in the sun, his hands on his knees they way schoolboys do in class photographs.

"You declare yourself a tourist, Mr. Wagner, and yet you come to my country with troops and combat equipment of the most sophisticated kind."

Wagner jerked his head toward the plain below. "Since the earthquake, it's chaos down there, Colonel, as you well know. The rioters have already overthrown the government on your behalf and the government troops have been driven out of the city and most of the major towns. Those troops lie between you and the seat of government, fighting for their lives because they know they'll be butchered to a man if they surrender. Now both sides are gathering into their tribal groups and taking on all others. There is wholesale slaughter everywhere."

"Ah, and since, as you say, the government has fallen, you must switch your allegiance from them to us."

"We are on neither side, and want to make with you exactly the same arrangement that we have with the government, without fear or favour."

"A barbed wire fence cannot be the most comfortable kind to sit on, Mr. Wagner."

"We have to be able to work with whichever side wins this conflict, and with both sides while the conflict remains unresolved."

"A most audacious demand, Mr. Wagner. In this state of total propaganda, how can we be sure of your intentions?"

"You must listen to the foreign radio broadcasts?"

Mombatu offered a look of mock horror. "Against the law, as you know."

"Will it remain against the law when you have the power, Colonel?" Wagner asked slyly.

"I do not seek power. I seek to free my people," Mombatu declared with assurance.

No doubt, Wagner knew, after all of his opponents had been properly tortured and purged.

And maybe, Wagner considered, it was a natural law that brutal and barbaric men like this one were the only kind capable of overthrowing tyrannical governments. Certainly, for all his cheery manner, Mombatu looked the part.

"So do we," Wagner was saying. "But we want to free your people from forces far more powerful than the government troops you fight against."

"So it is said. Even I have the sense to fear your Professor Earthshaker, and his ability to control volcanoes. You would be dead already, were it not the case."

"Perhaps half a million people have been snared by the Shastri Effect, Colonel. You must help us help them."

Mombatu gave a helpless shrug. "The people have scattered. As you say, it is chaos down there. What you ask may not be possible in the circumstances."

"Possible or not, it must be achieved," Wagner said emphatically. In truth he wanted nothing more than to use his superior firepower to step on vermin like Mombatu, but knew he must not let his revulsion show. As with a savage dog, you needed to be firm and sure.

"And there is another little difficulty," Mombatu said with another helpless expression.

Now we are coming to it, Wagner knew. After the impossible was accomplished, there were the strategic considerations to be dealt with.

"Which is?"

"The eruption of the volcano and the disappearance of the lake struck great fear into the hearts of my people, and many thousands of them fell into a sleep and did not awaken for many days."

Wagner nodded as if such were everyday events. "These are the people we want to protect."

"But this remarkable event was a sign from the gods. It was the instruction to rise up and overthrow their tyrannical masters, once and for all."

"Yeah. The interesting thing about a propaganda press is that it can be made to work both ways," Wagner said with fraying patience.

"The people you seek therefore lie at the heart of this popular revolution."

"And they'll remain that way," Wagner said, and leaned forward with his elbows on his knees, lowering his voice as if about to share a secret. "In just twelve days from now, all of those people will rise up and begin a pilgrimage. They will go as one, in a single direction."

Mombatu frowned dubiously. "How do you know this?"

"Believe me," Wagner said, nodding emphatically. "I *can* prove it to you, if I must."

"I have seen the pictures and heard the words of these marches of the masses," Mombatu admitted. "You think it will happen here too?"

"It will definitely happen here too. As I say, in twelve days time. We know the exact moment they will begin and the exact direction they will follow. And there will be half a million of them."

"It will be a miracle," Mombatu cried excitedly.

Wagner continued keeping his voice level and adamant. "When they go, the path before them must be declared a no man's land. Before then, it must be cleared. Before then, the pilgrims must all be gathered such that when they move they do not stray outside the demilitarised zone."

Mombatu's mouth was open and he gazed all around, as if the right words might be captured like flies. "What you ask is preposterous..."

"You miss the point. All these things *will* happen. All I ask of you is that you cooperate and go along with it when it happens. I'm giving you the opportunity to exploit it to your advantage.. All you have to do is get your men to cooperate."

Mombatu looked glum. He was sure that someone was trying to saw off a small branch of his power. And, when he thought about, he knew who, or thought he did. "My soldiers will do what I tell them... But why should I cooperate with an American, whose mysterious forces shall must come only under orders of the President of the U. S. A."

It was a blind, to try and allow time for the rebel to think. But it was always hard for such men to think when the letters CIA were flashing before their eyes.

"You know I'm nothing of the kind," Wagner declared with a lowered brow. "And I can control the path the pilgrims will follow. Think of it, half a million people, rebels and government troops alike, marching in a direct line to the capital. I can order the government troops to stop fighting and offer them an escape route, all you have to do is allow them to escape. I can make the pilgrims march directly to the palace, and all you have to do is walk in front of them."

That was a better image. Mombatu smiled at the thought, savoured it, bathed in it. "How can you do this?"

"When at night the people have listened to the foreign radio and after the news programs have ended, isn't there a single voice amongst the thousands of voices that they hear which reaches right into their hearts."

"Is there?"

"You know there is."

"Do I?"

Okay, we'll do it the long slow way, Wagner was smiling to himself. He dangled the bait and the fish was eyeing it with growing hunger. "It is the voice that will call them all together and tell them which way to go. And they will follow, whether you help or not."

"Tell me of this voice?" Mombatu gasped, as if he hardly dared think it.

"Andromeda Starlight."

There was a massive intake of air from all in earshot, and that seemed to include Fabrini. Wagner sat back, looking delighted with himself.

"She would come here and lead these people?" Mombatu spluttered.

"If you guarantee her safety, yes she will."

"She is of the Maravi?" Mombatu frowned.

"She is the spiritual leader of all Maravi, in their hearts, as you know."

Mombatu did know. He did listen to the foreign broadcasts after all. "Yes, I do know. So she is."

Wagner could only smile. (*'Bullshit!' Andromeda Starlight had raged when the idea was put to her three days earlier. 'I'm from fucking Trinidad.'*

'But your ancestors. Surely they... The slave trade...'

'No, fuck it. They emigrated from Sierra Leone.')

But he looked Mombatu right in the eye and said. "Yes, she'll be here to lead them, if that's what you want."

*

Now that he had embarked upon a life of crime, there seemed to be little reason why he did not follow his snout into the trough for a thoroughgoing wallow. After all, that had been the fashion amongst the rich and powerful for centuries.

Joe Solomon had always regarded himself as an honest man,

the sort of lawyer that one could allow to attend to trusts or wills with confidence. He was the sort of man who paid his traffic fines promptly, who walked back into shops because the salesclerk had offered him a few cents more change than he was due, who guarded the financial affairs of all sorts of people, rich and poor, honest or the reverse, never overcharged for his services and didn't charge at all if the client couldn't afford to pay. A lifetime devoted to impeccable honesty. Thus he was just a little shocked to discover that he had swindled the US taxpayers out of many millions of dollars.

Yet it was so. Of course, he could justify it all. The money had come from suspect sources in any case, and he had not been required to lie at any time throughout the long weeks of interrogation. They had investigated him up and down and around and around and no charges had been laid. There was a suggestion that there might be charges later, but that was just one of those threats that petty officialdom makes as an admission that it was wrong.

No one had proven anything against him. No one could call him thief without the serious risk of litigation for slander. No one, that was, except Joe himself, who made the accusation every time he looked in the mirror, and saw the guilt in the suspect's eyes. But he knew the solution to that problem. He needed to stop looking in mirrors.

The truth was, as a man with failed kidneys and a dicey liver and being overweight, high blood pressured and sedentary in his wheelchaired ways, he wasn't going to last. Moreover, the planet was on an even shorter life expectancy. *Seven months tops*. There just wasn't going to be time to get him into a courtroom, even if they nailed him dead to rights. That was the first justification.

The second came from Lorna. 'It isn't as if you're stealing their money for personal gain, Joe. You're using it for the benefit of all humanity. That makes it different.' Sure it did. Al Capone and Adolf Hitler would have made the same argument. Al supplied moonshine to a nation crippled by evil prohibition, and there would certainly have been a peaceful planet, free of racial and religious wars, if everyone left alive was a blonde, blue-eyed heathen Nazi. You could justify anything that way if you were sufficiently deluded.

After all, Lorna's argument harboured the rather dubious assumption that Project Earthshaker—that was, the *Unofficial* Project Earthshaker since apparently the official one lacked the imagination to think of another name—was indeed a great benefit to humanity. Certainly not if humanity was blown to smithereens before the year was out. Certainly not if Thyssen was in error. And grave doubts were arising from all quarters concerning the big man.

Joe had been suspicious all along. Others weren't sure but he had never been in any doubt. Thyssen was too good to be true, organised the impossible too easily, had dubious friends. Maybe the CIA connection and the sinister Mr. Cornelius were nonsensical but you simply could not take a man like Thyssen at face value. He was too powerful, and too complex. Like a tame grisly bear—just because he hugged you affectionately today didn't mean he might not crush the life out of you tomorrow.

Thyssen knew that Joe had buried the slush fund and made no objection. A man you could trust would have at least commented. Thyssen was dishonest to that degree, and told lies about his data or so he had heard. Not a man to be trusted. And Thyssen was Joe's third and biggest justification of his own actions.

'Grab all the money you can get hold of, Joe, but any means you can,' Thyssen had told him. 'We are going to need every penny you can raise.' 'Any means?' Joe had asked. 'Any means your conscience can handle,' Thyssen replied pointedly. Fine, and the money was rolling in. Andromeda's concerts and Lorna's soaring media career and donations from the followers of Christine Rice and just general public generosity from true believers. There was plenty of money, enough to bankroll the private war Kevin Wagner was waging in Africa. Heaps of the stuff.

And now, Joe had a new project, for Thyssen had passed the message down the line and as soon as he heard it, Joe knew what to do. He rolled his way through the convent and got on the Internet and faxed every property dealer he could find in California and Nevada. His request was simple. He had a client who was interested in buying up any property available on the eastern side of the San Andreas fault.

*

Then, as the first days of the new year began, Chrissie discovered that she had lost her faith. It was hard to say how it happened— maybe it had not been there all along, only presumed, and she had failed to notice. She had been to Rome for an audience with the Pope, a man from the Jurassic period whose hand, when she kissed his ring, was cold and reptilian. He had murmured a few words in Latin that everyone later translated differently and gave her a blessing and she walked away from what was plainly another failed attempt at the greatest moment in her life.

He was just an old man, senile and incapable, who could barely sit on his throne. Her sense of disappointment, despite the pomp and media coverage of the occasion, could not have been more pronounced.

All along, she knew she was playing a role, keeping up appearances, faking it. Perhaps that was when her faith began to dissolve.

No, not really. She'd never really been much of a Catholic anyway, disgusted by the church's money grabbing ways and its general failure to uphold the fundamentals of Christ. She had known it was all bullshit all along—her experience in Rome did not change anything.

In an attempt to get real, she rushed off to Africa to try and help but never even got close. Malawi and the neighbouring regions were in utter chaos and the disaster had precipitated a full-scale war with several sides and even the news reports had little idea of just exactly what was happening in there. The borders were all closed, even to her, and she got no closer than Salisbury.

Although she could have. Kevin Wagner had arrived in full force, his two huge transport planes full of men and equipment.

They would be going in the next week if she wanted to wait. But she looked at the combat ready troops and their guns and fierce expressions and decided that it was not the sort of company she wanted to keep. Felicity Campbell, who had been there before her and been similarly frustrated, had already headed for home.

The only truly Christian thing Chrissie found to do there was visit Jami in the hospital. It meant she also had to visit all the other patients and chat with them, followed around by the media crews, but the price for that was that she got to talk to Jami in private.

It was immediately apparent that while she might have suffered extensive physical injuries, Jami was undiminished. Admittedly, her hair was ungreased and unspiked because 'you need two hands for that' and the ring through her nostril—and presumably any others she wore—had been removed for fear of infection. Her greatest trouble seemed to be that her favourite tattoo had been obliterated by third degree burns—it was the one on her bum. Jami, all in all, looked strangely normal.

"Sometimes there's something you've just got to do, Chrissie," Jami said by way of explanation. "It doesn't matter if its silly or dangerous. You gotta do it. If you don't, the rest of your life will be wasted regretting that you passed up the chance."

"Yes, I understand that," Chrissie smiled, trying to get into benign mode. "It probably explains why most women undergo the horrors of pregnancy and childbirth."

"Yes. That's it. I just had to do it, just once, to see what it was like."

"Even if it killed you."

"If it did, it did. But if I got away with it, then Wow!"

"So this is the joyous state of 'Wow!' Laid up in hospital wearing more plaster than the walls?"

"It'll come off. I'm doing wheelchair practice already and I'm out of here in two days. Kev is going to fly me to his convent. His planes have to go back to get more equipment anyway."

"What do you want to go there for?"

"First because Joe has a fulltime nurse who can also look

after me. Second because a full set of Earthshaker monitoring equipment has been established there. Third because with the way the tourists are flooding New York for the last New Year's Eve, I'd rather not go back there just yet. And fourth, because I want to avoid Harley until I'm ready for him."

Chrissie blinked. "I missed on that last point."

"He lied to us, Chrissie. God damned Harley, he rigged the data so only he could make the proper sense of it."

"Are you sure?"

"Yes. He's got something called Drongo buried away under a ton of electronic safeguards and Drongo is some sort of system which is the reason why his predictions are right and everyone else is just guessing."

"Drongo?"

"It's Carrickspeak for fuckwit."

"Yes. We have the expression in New Zealand. But why?"

"I don't know why. To prove he's smarter than everyone else or something... To maintain his power over us and the project..."

"But what is it?"

"I don't know, but when I get to the convent I'll be hacking furiously until I find out."

It was too much to take in at one gulp. Chrissie backed off, thinking it through and trying to get to the more essential aspects.

"You say, everyone else is just guessing. Explain that."

"Perturbations in the movements of the Earth, and the Sun and Moon, mean that the configuration is never quite right. We can get the longitude reasonably—because the time period between each event is the same number of days, less about ten percent, each time. Trouble is that they can only get the ten percent bit accurate within one hour—but that hour means 1670 kilometres as the earth spins. Drongo eliminates that hour of give or take. The latitude is always in the quadrant opposite the previous event and then its a configuration of the positions of the Earth, Sun and Moon, taking any major bumps and wobbles in their orbits into account. Again, Drongo can do that more accurately than anyone else can."

"So the data is useless without Harley."

"Yes, because there's some other factor that only Harley has thought of. Anyone can work out the zone of influence within an area about 1500 kilometres by 5000 kilometres. After that, they look at the fault lines and such like and guess. Harley can get it to an area a few hundred kilometres each way."

"And he won't tell anyone how he does it?"

"No. The bastard. But I'll find out."

Perhaps it was all the fault of Jami, whose loss of faith in her god—Harley—had contaminated Chrissie's faith in her own God. Although that was hardly likely—her own faith was slipping before she knew of Jami's apostasy. And anyhow, Harley had provided her with a CD that she carried to Rome which she was eventually able, in a plush office in the Vatican with Valerno and several other red robed cardinals peering over her shoulder, to plug into a computer and show them the way to the Project Earthshaker data.

"There it is. Best of luck."

Of course, she hadn't known about Drongo.

She returned to the tranquility and sanctity of the convent and the small chapel that had, more or less, become her own, and as the world began counting down to the end of human history, she knelt and tried to pray. But her faith was gone and she could not catch God's attention. Instead she began to weep and, as far as she knew, she knelt there, sobbing, all night.

So they had come to the final New Year's Eve. And simply because it would have been so appropriate, an inordinately large number of people decided that this might well be the end of the world. Chrissie knew better, but she spent the long night in prayer, just in case. And when the rising sunlight stretched long hazy fingers of light through the stained glass windows, she dried her tears and rose, staggering on ruined knees, and made her shuffling way to the door and threw it open. She walked out onto the steps, pale and shaking and deathlike in her pallor. The beautiful, radiant, magnificent planet she lived on was still there in all its glory. There just wasn't any way that she could believe that it would ever be any different.

*

In the café in Paris as the sun rose, and the staff were packing up and hosing down the footpath, Lorna lowered the boom on Brian Carrick. It might have been a sad occasion, had Brian not been so bloody stoic about it.

"And there I was thinkin' we'd be together until the end of the earth," Brian chuckled.

"It isn't funny, Brian. I feel like such a bitch."

"Well, don't. If I'd got the chance, I'd of shot back to Judy and left you in the lurch without a second thought."

"I know," Lorna said, smiling but forced to dab a tear from her eye while she did so. "But I did think I might have stuck it out until that happened."

"Oh I see. You wanted to be the one who got dumped."

"It is my usual role."

"Okay, you're dumped."

"You just can't take this the least bit seriously, can you?"

"No hope. Look, Lorna, you are a truly wonderful young woman. I had the time of my life with you. And I am sad it's over, but you gotta face reality. You're an international superstar. I'm a solid family man. While you hit the high spots, I'd rather be at home in front of the telly with a beer and the wife cookin' in the kitchen and the kids playin' in the yard. There was no future in this. We were the original odd couple."

"I'm not the high flyer you think I am, Brian. I'm just a simple suburban girl at heart."

"Yeah, sure. But one who has managed to turn her simple suburbanness into a global icon. There's no going back from there."

And, for the first time in their relationship, they had run out of things to say. Then the obvious occurred to Lorna. "So how are things with Judy, anyway."

"I rung her on New Year's Eve. To speak to the kids. After which, unusually, she wanted to speak to me."

"What about?"

"Nothing at all, which I think was the point. Apparently, Larry was out getting drunk with his mates and left her abandoned with the kids, just the way I usta. I reckon there's a bit of reality being faced down that way at the moment."

"Kids good?"

"They still call me Daddy. Although Larry seems to have graduated from uncle to 'pop'."

Again there seemed to be nothing to add to that, but Lorna was brightening, and finally the obvious did occur to her. "Don't you want to know why?"

"Why what?"

"Why I'm dumping you."

"You mean there's a reason."

"Yes, there's a reason."

"Somehow I knew I couldn't have been getting it right the way I thought I was."

"No, silly. You were the perfect man. If only they were all like you. The reason has nothing to do with you at all."

"So why tell me?"

Lorna bowed her head in dismay. "Do you have to be so fucking practical all the time?"

"Sure. After all, I am twenty years older than you. It's my job to be the practical one."

"Older doesn't matter."

"Maybe not, but it probably is time you played with someone your own age."

"That isn't quite what I've got in mind…"

"Okay. So you can tell me, if you really must."

"Well," Lorna said, finding the words hard the way she rarely did these days. "I wanted you to know in advance. It was only fair."

"Know what."

"I'm going after Harley," Lorna murmured embarrassedly.

"Oh I see. So impressed with us forty year olds, you thought you might up it another twenty."

"He isn't that old!"

"Alright, only about fifteen. Still, I can't say I'm not losing out to a better man."

"I am enormously attracted to him."

"Aren't we all. Has he suggested any reciprocal feelings?"

"No. I have tested the water from time to time…"

"And?"

"Zero response. He treats me like a daughter."

"Grand-daughter?"

She poked her tongue out at him. "In any case, I'm going to have to make it happen."

"You sure ain't lacking in ambition, Lorna."

"It isn't really ambition. I think it's necessary—for all of us."

"You're doing it for us?"

"We need to know this man. We have got to get to the bottom of him. I believe the only way to really know a man is to sleep with him, and I need to know—and we all need to know—all we can about Harley."

"Maybe he's bottomless."

"Oh very funny. But seriously. I'll need all the help I can get with this one."

"You surely know how to create a challenge, sweetheart" Brian laughed. "Are you sure Harley does normal things like sex?"

"You mean, maybe it's below his dignity?"

"Or maybe he's just too old," Brian said.

"You're not being helpful."

"That's because I can't imagine how it can be done."

"You must be able to offer some suggestions. Something I might say to grab his attention."

"Ask him about the Uncertainty Principle."

"The what?"

"Look it up. Ask him about Schrodinger's Cat."

"Cat?"

"The wave-particle conundrum."

"Can we have a nice simple version that I can slip in over a glass of champers?"

"What all these things amount to is this: the experimenter is, of necessity, a part of the experiment."

"I'm still not getting it."

"You cannot open the box and see exactly what is inside without disturbing the contents."

"Well, at least I understood the words that time. Why is it important?"

"It's a random universe. The laws of physics and mathematics are meaningless in reality. Yet, whenever we humans apply those laws, they always work for us. Everything we do obeys those laws. And what's more, if we fuck up and break the laws, what we do won't work. The bridge falls down, the spaceship blows up, the aeroplane crashes. How can that be?"

"Magic?"

"Sort of. If it is true that the laws of physics and maths don't work in reality but always work for us, there is only one possible explanation."

"We make them work."

"More than that. Those laws describe our minds and how they function. And what it means, therefore, is that when all those random elementary particles and quanta and suchlike, fall within the influence of our intelligence or collective consciousness or whatever, they conform."

"They fall into line with our perception of how things are? How very obliging of them."

"So that's what we are really. Chaos destroying machines. We force order into the randomness."

"Wow!"

"Wow indeed. You tell that to Harley and watch what's left of his hair stand on end."

"I almost understand it. Is it true?"

"No one knows. But that's what I reckon Harley thinks is happening. That's the Shastri Effect."

*

How the hell had they talked her into this? When Wagner's plane landed her in the middle of a war zone, all of Andromeda's illusions about a concert tour honouring her African origins and aiding a crippled nation were annihilated. Fires burned all about the airfield, and troops ran this way and that, ordered by their hotfaced leaders. Wagner's commanders were the only white men to be seen anywhere. She heard sporadic gunfire coming in from all directions, and occasional explosions further out. She wanted to get right back in the plane again.

"It's okay," Captain Maynard of the US Navy said. "This area is secure now."

The captain, who insisted he was a sailor, was dressed like a combat soldier in camouflage fatigues with the sleeves torn out, and he was filthy and his clothing ripped. On his muscular shoulders, blood showed, running with the sweat down his arms. He had a US army netted helmet from under the shadowed rim of which his dark eyes peered fiercely, but despite the disguise, Andromeda knew who he was. Not only had she been told who would meet her, but she might have recognised him from his media image anyway, for she had followed the case with great interest. This was the captain of the ship that Felicity had defended so remarkably in San Diego, and the other *soldiers* scattered about were his crew.

"Looks a bit rough, I know. But it's safe," he said to assure her as he gripped her arm in a very gentlemanly fashion and nudged her toward a jeep.

They set off, Maynard driving, and a truckload of US soldiers who were probably also sailors following. Andromeda pointed a playfully accusative finger at him.

"You're the one who stole the ship," she told him.

"That's right, ma'am," he grinned, seeming very at ease for a sailor in a landlocked war zone.

"You don't meet a lot of pirates in this century. Did you also steal the jeep?"

Maynard relaxed, the stiffness and formality but not the urgency draining out of him. He seemed very relieved to discover that this woman, a global celebrity, a full head taller than he was, had a sense of humour. He knew she was going to need it. "As a matter of fact, we did, ma'am. It belongs to the government troops. But they don't care for it anymore."

"Wait till I tell Felicity."

"Finest woman I ever met, ma'am."

"She's that all right. And this, I suppose, is punishment for your sins."

"No, ma'am. Dr Campbell got the admirals at the court martial so bewildered they couldn't reach a conclusion. This is what the navy does with people they just want to go away."

"Turn them into soldiers, you mean?"

"Something like that. Better than the brig, no matter how you add it up."

"Well, captain. I don't like it much here. Let's do some further going away."

"Ma'am, this is one of the prettier places to be found in Malawi right now."

He was not mistaken. After a very short distance, they drove into a village that had been shot to pieces. Bodies lay all about in the street and town square. All the walls were chipped by bullet holes. Burned out vehicles were everywhere. Few of the corpses wore any sort of military garb.

"Stop here," Andromeda ordered.

"We can't, ma'am. The Red Cross has all this under control."

"Stop, I tell you."

Maynard sighed and stopped. She got out and walked amongst the corpses, the swarms of flies made most of them hard to see distinctly. Maynard was right at her side, with his machinegun levelled this way and then that.

"These are mostly women and children," Andromeda said bitterly.

"Yes. The government troops went through here as they fled."

She looked about. There were some medical people but mostly they seemed engaged in driving the vultures away. Men were busy at the other end of town, collecting the bodies and loading them into trucks.

"Is this typical?"

"In some places, unfortunately. We just couldn't cover everywhere. Mr. Wagner has only a thousand troops at his command. It wasn't anywhere near enough."

"And the rebels? Are they any better behaved than the government troops?"

"Not really. But mostly, the people abandoned the villages and hid in the jungle. They're waiting for you."

"Me?"

"Yes. Everyone knows that you are coming to lead them to the place of peace."

"Oh good. And where, exactly, is this place of peace I'm supposed to lead them to?"

"Wherever you go, but Mr. Wagner has placed his camp so that when you go, it will be into the capital."

"I'd like to talk to Kev baby, right now."

"That's where I was taking you, ma'am. There's nothing you can do here."

"So I see."

They drove on and, only hours before the linkage was due to occur, they arrived at the camp. It was really a village that looked exactly like the first one—and several others along the way—only this time the bodies had been removed. But still it smelled of death. Kevin Wagner was dressed just like Maynard, except he wore a peaked cap instead of a helmet.

"Good of you to come, Andy," Wagner said. They were in the tavern. Carlsberg would keep their beer monopoly no matter who won the war.

"Did I have a choice?"

"Not everyone gets to stop a war, Andy."

"Cut the crap and tell me the plan, Kev."

"In a few hours, you start out from here to the capital, which is the right direction for the pilgrimage. They'll follow you, right into the capital, and the war will be over."

"And you'll be claiming victory?"

"The rebels have already claimed victory. Once it was known the pilgrimage was on, the government troops all ran away. The rumour that you would be here did the job. Now, it's just a formality."

"So, I'm doing nothing really."

"You're doing what Chrissie did in Italy. Leading the pilgrims to safety."

"And into the hands of the rebels."

"It was a popular revolution, truly."

"Yeah, I know. A whole lot of dead women and children back there told me how popular it was."

Wagner looked tired. He rubbed his eyes. There was no point talking about this. It was going to happen and nothing could change it. But Andromeda needed to make someone pay for this, and Kevin Wagner, with his own little private war, was the only one available to received her anger.

"How do you know they'll follow?"

"There's about 600,000 pilgrims, out there in the bush, mostly south of here. Shortly, they'll be heading north. So will you. So will I. And when they go, everyone else will follow."

"I don't like this, Generalissimo. It's a put up job and you know it."

"No. It's genuine. These people see you as a spiritual leader. I made use of that, I admit, but only because it was there to be done."

"Are you telling me they play all my records here?"

"Practically nothing else. They love it. You are the greatest. Bigger than basketball players even."

"Damn you, Wagner. Damn you. What I did was clean and honest. You've dirtied it somehow."

"The war will have stopped. Thousands of lives will have been saved. You can't argue with that."

"That's the same justification that you lot used for dropping atom bombs on Japan. You Yankees just don't learn, do you?"

"Either you walk or thousands more will die, Andy. That's all there is."

And so, when the time came, she walked, and the people came out of everywhere in their thousands, tens of thousands, to tramp the road amid the soaring dust, ragged and thin with malnutrition, their bony legs seeming unable to hold them up yet they walked boldly, striding on with bare feet on the hot dust. As she walked, they crowded about her, called her name and called her Marava, which seemed to mean Messiah. Andromeda opened her arms and her heart and walked tall amidst them and carried on down the road to the capital and they followed, coming out of the bush on all sides. Ahead, Wagner rode atop a tank and troops lined the way, looking grimfaced and battleworn but determined, sharp-eyed, ready for trouble but there would be no trouble. Andromeda knew the time of danger was past and so did the population accumulating behind her. The people came out of hiding and walked the roads everywhere, and the war was dumbfounded and stopped.

She walked on, and the people kept coming, their tramping feet on the road throwing up enough dust to turn the sun orange. The Shastri Effect was no longer a factor—not for the moment at least—they were following her because they could not go home and had nowhere else to go, and because they believed she had somewhere to lead them to, but most of all because she was who she was. And she regretted her words then, because she knew Wagner was right. These people did see her as their spiritual leader. They worshipped her with a simple reverence that no words could describe. She walked and they followed, and Andromeda knew that although she had never been here before, still she had come home.

*

From every available vantage point, they came to watch the

greatest show on earth. Every peak in the Santa Monica Hills and the San Gabriel Mountains was foolishly crowded by those who had not paid sufficient attention to the warnings and thought themselves safe, but further out, more prudent and only slightly less foolish soles crowded the peaks of the San Bernardino Mountains, and the southern extremities of the Coastal Range and Sierra Nevadas.

As they flew in the Orion along the coastline offshore from Long Beach, Felicity Campbell gazed out the window in continuing astonishment and shook her head in dismay. Everyone had been warned—the Lorna/Andromeda show had been the highest rating program since the moonwalk. There had been time, she knew, and every possible warning had been offered, to ensure the entire evacuation of the endangered area, but in its last moments of existence, Los Angeles remained the mad thriving metropolis that it had always been since the movie moguls first came to town, a hundred years ago.

All along the coast, from San Raphael to Tijuana, the people had generally heeded the warnings of the President and packed up their belongings and headed inland. A lot of diehards remained in San Francisco but even they had moved across the fault line and those parts of the city south and west of the Bay area were virtually deserted, as were most towns in Monterey and all down the coast, and San Diego. *Cross the San Andreas fault and go at least twenty miles inland,* President Grayson warned them. Most people had done just that. And this despite the official Project Earthshaker assurances that the disaster would occur offshore from Mexico and there would be no danger. The Unofficial Project Earthshaker, in the bright-eyed form of Lorna Simmons, had said goodbye to California, and the President added that although he believed the Official outcome would prevail, Harley Thyssen was not a man to be ignored if you valued your life.

The population of Los Angeles, it seemed, had generally viewed the matter one of three ways and seemed fairly evenly divided in those classes. There were those who took Lorna, Grayson and Thyssen at their word and packed up and fled to the east, causing the greatest traffic jam in history. People were spending three days or more, camped in the gridlock, just to get into Nevada. But really, most people who feared 'The Big One' had moved away from the southern California coast years before, scared off by the Northridge, Landers and Loma Prieta shocks.

The second group were those had heard the warnings too many times before and weren't any more likely to believe it now and determined to stay and get on with their business. The third class shared the beliefs of the second, and then changed their minds at the last minute. There was little chance of escape from Los Angeles for those who left it to the final twenty-four hours—every road and track, not to mention freeway, was solidly gridlocked, every plane had been flown away and every boat had sailed off or else, more heartlessly, had long since been hauled onto a trailer and driven away by the owner. As they flew by the airport, Felicity could see huge crowds moving amid the fires of several crashed planes, offshore were only the navy vessels, plucking desperate souls off the beaches.

Helicopters buzzed everywhere, as if a swarm of giant bees had invaded the city. They were snatching people off the rooftops and out of the open land of football fields and parks and desperately hurrying them to the giant camps established in the Mojave Desert and the hills above Bakersfield—anywhere at all as long as it wasn't near the White Wolf Fault, on which Harley had also offered grave pronouncements. Every volcanic cone, even those extinct, from the Salton Sea to Yosemite, could be expected to erupt and the region around them should be avoided.

And what, Felicity and many others had wondered, of those people safe from fault lines and calderas but within the zone of influence and subject to the Shastri Effect. Of this Thyssen had offered little information. The zone could not be known with certainty, it would be huge and probably unavoidable, and anyway, the task was to save lives whereas the Shastri Effect was not likely to kill anyone. That, Felicity Campbell knew, was a very dubious proposition.

Harley offered a circle of six hundred miles diameter centred roughly on the Grand Canyon, which took in half of Baja California, stretched into Oregon and Idaho, east to the borders of Kansas and Oklahoma, south to Chihuahua, and somewhere in that vast area, a region of perhaps two hundred square miles would fall into the Zone of Influence of the Shastri Effect. It was just simply far too great an area to clear, or even consider seriously. Felicity wondered. She was sure that in the past, Harley had pinpointed it closer than that. Indeed, he had assured the pilot of the Orion that 'if you stay offshore, you'll be alright.' That placed them two hundred miles inside the western extent of the possible affected zone—how the hell did he know that?

But her mind was shaken back to more immediate matters when all of the alarms in the cluttered belly of the Orion went off and a frenzy of activity began. It was happening, and she turned with a sickened feeling in her belly to watch the death throes of Tinsel town. By media outlets and scientists alike, no event in history was more precisely nor copiously recorded, and yet for all that, it was rather hard to say exactly what happened. For in an instant, the entire metropolitan area was completely lost in a haze of dust.

Down in the city, the few miraculous survivors subsequently reported that the first effect was the rolling and jolting of the earth and then they were blinded by a hail of dust. This was because the impact of the earthquake caused the sedimentary soil on which the city stood to liquefy and virtually turn into quicksand, and all around, buildings and vehicles and people disappeared underground. Los Angeles began to sink into the earth before it began to sink into the sea. Then, as the masonry began to fall, there was a great roar and geysers of water erupted out of every drain, often hurling the grates high into the air. Vast fissures opened in every street and steam gushed out, adding its searing horror to the pandemonium. Now the buildings were collapsing all about with the noise with continuous thunder. And then it stopped—the geysers, the shaking, the thunder and everything was still for a moment.

In the Orion, Felicity had seen the city simply vanish in a

yellow dust cloud and thought that was the end, but then it seemed that a great wind suddenly blew the dust and smoke away, and Los Angeles, looking decidedly jagged and uneven but still possessing its proud towers, reappeared for an encore performance. It lasted only a moment and then the veil of steam and dust and smoke engulfed it again, but that magical lull was extraordinary, and from her position, Felicity could see why. The water had drained out of Santa Monica Bay and welled up in a giant bulge about the Channel Islands, parallel to the coast, and now the swell turned and rushed back toward the city. A tsunami, maybe two hundred feet high, raced up the newly exposed beach and crashed over the docklands as if it was tripped, cascading down upon the doomed city.

The great wave swept away the people on the Santa Monica and San Gabriel Hills, such was its enormity. It forked and cascaded up the San Fernando and San Bernardino valleys, swallowing all the towns and landscape beyond. All along the coast, the rivers, even the mighty Colorado, flowed backwards for a while and flooded all the lowlands about them. The wave roared northward and drowned Santa Barbara and hit the San Raphael Mountains and to the west, it began to crash against an indomitable cliff. Mighty jagged escarpments had appeared, all long the horizon line and the sea struck there and surged back, thick with mud. All of the waters over their newly claimed land churned dark and muddy as currents and whirlpools surged everywhere. Again and again, the greedy sea hurled itself at the cliffs, demanding more and more land but it was to be denied. From Palm Springs to Tejon Pass, the San Andreas fault was the craggy new coast of California and the high ground west of that line was distributed as islands. And only about a thousand survivors were awash, clinging to debris as the helicopters rushed in to begin plucking them from the water.

Perhaps the most startling image, certainly the one the TV news people most favoured as symbolic of the whole event, was the one that passed under the Orion as they crossed onto the land. The great Route 5 Freeway from the north of the state, sliced through the landscape relentlessly until it reached a point just below the town of Gorman, where it came to an abrupt end at the edge of a sheer precipice that dropped vertically into the surging waves of the Pacific Ocean.

Three new long peninsulas formed between Santa Barbara and Salinas as the sections in between fell beneath the sea, and all along the new towering coast, great chunks of earth and rock broke off and plunged into the jubilant ocean, dark versions of the way icebergs fall from the face of glaciers. San Diego, although wrecked, remained above the waterline but now stood at the end of a peninsula that ran back as far as the place where the Salton Sea had vanished but four small volcanoes now erupted furiously. North of the new cape, the Gulf of Catalina had now doubled in size, and into it the Colorado River now flowed.

The Orion banked across the place where Ventura used to be and flew towards two large islands that were once Reyes Peak and Mt Pinos, and he radioed ahead to Bakersfield airport and got no reply. This he reported to Felicity.

"The flood couldn't have gone that far," she called back. The navigator was able to assure her she was right. The pilot could see that far ahead himself.

"The city's still there. I just can't raise anybody."

Felicity went forward to watch from between the two pilots as they approached the city and then the airfield. There had been some flooding along the Kern River, but not enough to have any major effect. Fires blazed at several locations, but none of them were large enough to suggest wide area damage. Three such fires were on the airfield itself, one plane and two helicopters had crashed there.

"Oh my God," Felicity breathed with suddenly realisation. "I think you've managed to bring me to the exact place I want to go."

"You think they're all sleeping down there?" the pilot said in astonishment.

"Yep. If you want to talk to them, come back in eight day's time."

They checked the runway and it seemed undamaged and then flew on for a while before attempting to land, and in that time the radio operator searched his network and by determining who he could and could not contact, was able to draw Felicity a rough map of the Zone of Influence. It swallowed the cities and towns from Fresno to Mojave and the new coastline to King's Canyon, and all of Bakersfield along with it, and those colossal temporary camps to which those Los Angelians who had fled along US99 had gone. There were almost one million sleepers in the zone.

"Harley, what have you done?" Felicity breathed as the cold reality closed about her.

14
EVERLOVIN' BOSONS

So it had come to this. Thyssen had known it would, sooner or later, and the fact that it was sooner impressed him. They gathered in what had become called the control room, in the convent on San Carboni, ten days after the destruction of California. The location of the disaster meant other authorities got involved sooner than usual, and allowed them time to converge here, for what he presumed was to be a Council of War.

It was the first time they had all been together since Melbourne—just over a year ago which meant it was long overdue—and some things had changed and some had not. He looked them over now, with his memory firmly locked on the images of that gathering. Then he had been king, the master, the boss man who knew it all and would take them in hand and guide them through the nightmare that confronted them. Now they were his equals, or betters, each of them as powerful as himself, a force to be reckoned with individually, greater still in unity. His little hotchpotch team of galactic warriors were ready to go into battle. And the next thing to be done was to resolve what even Thyssen agreed was a growing crisis of confidence in their leader.

Felicity Campbell, who had called them all to this meeting, perched on the far end of the long layout bench with her arms folded below her breasts, dressed in a neat business skirt and blouse. Gone forever was the harried yet cool medico from Wellington, now her lanky blonde curls had been pulled back severely into a small tight bun at the back of her head. Her gentle features had all disappeared and been replaced with sterner lines—perhaps a slight flabbiness had gone from her cheeks leaving them gaunt and sharply defined. The overall effect was that she looked her forty-three years of age, whereas before she'd seemed much younger. She was the Queen who had lost faith in her King.

Behind her, Brian Carrick leaned casually against the chart cabinet, also with his arms folded, but he was utterly unchanged by his experiences. If Thyssen's memory served, he was even still wearing the same clothes, as if it was the only outfit he possessed when his wife kicked him out. Flopped on the top of the cabinet was the Akubra hat that had been stiff and new in those days but now was battered and full of character. It was the only sign of the several hells he'd been through since then. The permanent smile still fixed his lips and his eyes still darted around, eternally seeking mischief. Plainly he was not prepared to take this matter seriously because he knew that no meeting in history had ever solved anything serious. Nor was his loyalty likely to be swayed by anything less than absolute betrayal.

At the centre of the bench, Joe Solomon had wheeled himself, resplendent in his best lawyer blue pinstripe suit, and flopped before him a huge stack of documents—the file on Harley Thyssen presumably—to make sure everyone got the facts straight. The Greek looked sleek and alive, as any man who had made many millions in the past year ought to, but he was also sharp-eyed and ready for anything that might portend his inevitable downfall. And nothing was more likely to bring that about than doubt over Thyssen's leadership. He would remain impartial until someone presented him with irrefutable evidence of something. Which, in this case, wasn't likely. Two votes to one...

Jami Shastri had rolled her own wheelchair to the end of the bench and glared at Thyssen with utter resentment. Her bones would mend but she looked thinner and her face was all the blotchier from burn spots. Thyssen looked at her and could not avoid a pang of guilt that surged through his body and pumped blood into his ear lobes and other extremities. She was the very manifestation of his errors—as if, Dorian Gray style—she took on wounds and scars that he did not allow himself to feel. The challenge, the only challenge really, for Thyssen that mattered was the task of winning her back to his side and that, he knew, would be hardest of all. The worst mistake he had made to date was to underestimate her devotion to him, and the depths to which she would plunge when her belief in him faltered.

Back in the corner, a picture of pure menace, Kevin Wagner was all but unrecognisable in his military outfit all brass buttons and straight creases. He stood with his feet apart and his hands clasped behind his back but he was anything but at ease. The product of another grave underestimation, Thyssen knew, but who could have predicted the way a man who had lost his family and his existence at one blow would react. The old charmer was outmoded and replaced by this Hollywood hero figure, waiting to receive his orders for the next mission impossible from whoever made the strongest show of giving the orders. And ready to take complete control if that show of strength didn't happen, for such a man was utterly loyal to whoever was in charge for only so long as they maintained absolute authority.

Chrissie Rice sat on the window sill, in faded jeans and a light top, bare feet despite the cold stone floors of the convent. Her hair was cropped short and her head was permanently bowed, as if she had resumed her former, shy, self. Gone was the saintly robes and celestial glow, and she clasped her hands in front of her but rested them on her knees. It was impossible to know what she might have been thinking.

Lorna Simmons sat sideways on the other window sill with her shoes kicked off and feet up, offering a fine show of leg and absolute disrespect for her short skirt. Her hair was down and her head flopped against the window glass but when Harley entered she raised it and offered him a warm reassuring smile. That smile would have been impossible had she known what he had in mind for her.

And Andromeda Starlight, now arrayed in African robe and a floral cotton headband, dozens of bangles and necklaces and dark glasses despite the dimness of the room, as if she didn't want to see what was happening. Of them all, she had voiced the greatest protest at beginning brought here, for the Malawi pilgrims had passed straight through the capital and continued marching, northward generally, and so Andromeda had been obliged to continue leading them. Daily Wagner's supply planes parachuted food to that vast swarm of humanity advancing through Tanzania toward the Congo Republic, while on the ground Maynard had taken command of the trek. Andromeda had refused to leave, but Felicity had insisted and so she allowed herself to be borne off by helicopter and jet to attend the meeting, and when it ended she would be going right back again. She allowed her annoyance to show, but still Thyssen was sure he could count on her support. Not that he needed it because he knew he had the numbers anyway.

He walked in and every eye was on him. They had arrived at various times during the night before but he had deliberately avoided contact with any of them, remaining in a separate part of the convent, just to be sure no one could accuse him to trying to influence the outcome. He took two steps and flopped in a chair, rolling on the castors a few feet and leaning back, smiling. He was seated lower than everyone in the room, just to give them every chance. And he spoke immediately because he knew he needed to.

"Before we begin," he said. "you should all know that the word 'Unofficial' has been dropped from our name and we are once again the one and only Project Earthshaker. The UN Security Council voted on it this morning, their time and we got eighty-two percent support. President Grayson himself telephoned to tell me."

All of them laughed except Jami, whose head swivelled violently as she glared from one laughing face to another with growing horror. Even the rigidity of Kevin Wagner cracked, even Felicity Campbell had to smile crookedly and bow her head and turn away, therefore looking at Brian Carrick who was chuckling behind her.

"Clean bowled first ball for a duck, luv," Brian said.

Solomon slapped his files closed. "Meeting over. We can all go home."

"You can't..." Jami gasped, overcoming her initial shock enough to finally find speech.

"No, Jami's right," Thyssen said. "You each have grievances. Let's get them out in the open where we can get a good look at them."

"I assume what you say is true," Felicity asked, superbly disguising her disappointment.

"I wouldn't lie to you," Thyssen said pointedly.

"Yes you would!" Jami Shastri shrieked.

"No," Thyssen said, turning to look at her directly. "No, my beloved and very heroic student, I would not."

"Explain Drongo."

"You've been studying it for two weeks and know as much about it as I do."

"It's just a bunch of statistics."

"That's right. A little statistical tool I use which seems to work better than anyone else's. But it still comes down to an informed guess."

"But how can you be so accurate, if that's the case," Felicity asked.

"I'm not. It's an illusion. I didn't expect Bakersfield and Fresno to fall within the Zone—I expected something further out in the Nevada desert—but it did fall at the limits of my margin of error. And the consequences for California would have been the same, either way."

"But why can't anyone else predict as accurately as you do?" Wagner said bluntly.

"Three reasons, Kevin," Thyssen said, wondering if indeed there were three. "First, as much as my name might be discredited these days, I am still the top man in the field. My intuition is pretty likely to be better than anyone else's. Two, there were other geophysicists who got it right and agreed with me but they didn't get any publicity. The publicity went to those with alternative points of view and axes to grind—those who wanted to prove me wrong. Three, I always knew the volcanism and earthquakes were collateral damage. Only the Zone of Influence counted. From the viewpoint of the project, the recent event did not take place in Los Angeles nor along the San Andreas Fault. It happened in Bakersfield. Few people would be able to see it that way. And you, Jami, were the first to do so."

"That's not enough," Jami said flatly. "It doesn't explain it at all."

"Then perhaps there are other reasons that even I don't understand," Thyssen said, losing his calm he noticed now, in his desperation to win her back. "You people have always imagined that I knew more about this than I did. Every scientist, every person, working on this, has a point of view. They are going from a certain angle. Geophysicists see it as a geophysical problem. Volcanologists as vulcanism. Seismologists look at the Tectonic plates. Spiritualists see it as divine intervention. Each of you see it differently, from your own point of view. But I see it entirely as a function of all of you, as a whole, with none of the outside angles. And that simply places me closer than anyone else."

"Harley," Chrissie Rice asked quietly from her corner, "do *you* know when and where the next events are going to happen?"

"Yes. Within a scale with a rapidly escalating error possibility, I do."

"Then why aren't you telling anyone?"

"Because of the danger involved in someone like me engaging in speculation. Suppose I make statement A and then tomorrow get better data and realise that it's B instead. Given the way the media and the world behaves, there will be no withdrawing A. The consequences of the reaction to A would be so great that there would be no changing it."

"God must have similar difficulties," Brian remarked.

"Precisely. All of my pronouncements have become Godlike, which meant I needed to avoid making public statements and had Lorna reading carefully prepared announcements. Only those things I could be sure of."

"Okay," Joe said. "But you can trust us, Harley-boy. Tell us, where and when for the next, say, five events."

"Jami can do that."

"Can you?" Felicity asked abruptly.

Jami ruefully nodded her head.

Thyssen pulled a scrape of paper from his pocket, opened it out and handed it to her. "You agree with these?"

They all waited while a flushed Jami read it through. There were tears appearing in her eyes and she had to pause to wipe them away with the back of her bandaged hand. She passed the sheet back and swung her wheels to face away from them all.

Thyssen read from the list although he hardly needed to look at it—it was firmly impressed in his memory. "Java, 20 Feb, magnitude 10.1, 3 percent error margin; Middle East, with all that bloody oil it ought to be the biggest bang ever, 20 March, magnitude 10.6, ten percent error margin; somewhere in Brazil, 12 April, magnitude over 11, twenty percent accurate but it ought to be a real horror; then the Pacific maybe around Hawaii, 2nd of May, biggest magnitude ever at probably 11.5, forty percent error margin and it ought to cover something like 6000 square kilometres; then the mid-Atlantic Ocean on the 20th of May maybe around the Caribbean someplace but after that the error margin grows too large to be realistic."

Felicity Campbell stood now, planting her feet and facing him with her hands on her hips. "Harley, we call a meeting at which you are to explain your actions. You walk in with a megaton announcement and floor everybody. And *that's* the problem. All the time, you seem to be one step in front of us."

"Whereas, in fact, I'm redundant," Thyssen pointed out.

"I don't think so," Felicity said, riding the switches and changes deftly.

"Oh no. Think about it. Each of you has a crucial role to play in the project. But Lorna does all my talking for me, and Jami all my research. And now that I've directed her to Drongo, she can make the same predictions I do. I am the only one who no longer serves any purpose."

"If you disregard being our exulted leader who gets direct

phone calls from President Grayson," Brian pointed out.

"Figurehead leader only."

"I know how you feel, Honey," Andromeda chuckled.

"Okay," Felicity put in. "For the moment let's accept that you have reduced yourself to mere ornamental value. Why?"

"Because I was always the weakest link in the chain. At all times I was vulnerable to being attacked and discredited by the media or my peers. I was even in danger of being rolled at this meeting. Those circumstances are likely to get worse. I had to arrange things so that the project could precede without me. Which I believe I've done."

They all needed a moment to take that in and he allowed them that. It sounded frightening when he spelled it out in such blunt terms, but now, at least, it was done.

"I guess," Jami said finally, with a huge sigh. "But I still don't understand it."

"Nevertheless, it does make a mess of your arguments of megalomania."

"Yeah," Brian said. "We all shoulda known better than to try and argue with you, mate."

"Look," Thyssen said, letting go now and he could feel the pressure draining out of himself. "I admit I did some ducking and dodging, but it was all with a single purpose and that was to keep you people in charge of the Project."

"Why must we be in charge?"

"Because everyone else is either a scientist with a theory to prove or a politician with insatiable power lust or a fanatic with a blind faith to fulfill or someone with something to sell, and if we are to see this through, it needed to be kept out of the hands of national leaders and generals and media barons and people with a research grant to defend. It is just too big for any of them to deal with. It is a global problem to be handled globally, and only you guys have the experience and knowledge to do that."

"Fine," Felicity said, able to recognise a snow job when she heard one. "So while we are doing all the work, what will you be doing with your redundancy?"

"Trying to free myself up and get my mind above everything and see if I can come up with an answer to this."

"An answer to what, exactly?" Jami demanded, her emotions still raw.

"A way to overcome the Shastri Effect."

"Won't that be impossible?" Brian asked.

Thyssen shrugged his great shoulders. "We can sit back, assume that the earth is going to destroy itself and wait for it to happen, or else we can proceed on the assumption that there is something we can do, however hopeless it might seem. I favour the latter plan."

"Don't we all, Sugar," Andromeda said. "But jest how do we go about tacklin' something so big and inevitable?"

Thyssen rolled on his casters to the table and spread his hands there as he got it straight in his mind. It seemed for a moment that all the air had gone out of the room. He began slowly, making sure of it in his mind as he proceeded. "Look. Let's assume there is something going wrong at the Earth's core. There isn't a damned thing we can do about that. The theory that it's a singularity devouring us from the middle outwards like a rotting apple is as good as any, but we can't prove it. It fits the known facts best within our very limited knowledge. But it might equally be a normal change to the core of some kind, or maybe a change to the earth's magnetic field or god-knows what. We have no way of knowing and we aren't going to find out. We do not possess the technical means to look and see the nature of the internal structure of the Earth. The truth is we know more about galaxies and stars millions of light years away on the far side of the universe than we do about the stuff that's anything over ten miles under our feet. Even the concepts suggesting there's an iron-nickel core, surrounded by hot rock called the mantle—which is the accepted wisdom concerning the inner structure of the Earth—as all just the best available guess. There is no proof of any of it.

"So even if we did know what the problem was in there, we do not have the technology to invent a super laser or suchlike device and neutralise the thing. We are never going to be able to identify the cause of the problem nor do anything about it if we could. So we might as well forget it and let nature take its course."

"So it's hopeless," Chrissie groaned.

"Not completely," Thyssen said, knowing he was playing his last card. "There is the matter of the pilgrims, the linkage, the sleepers. That happens inside our heads and *that* we can explore. And it *has* to have something to do with it."

"Solve the question of the linkage, and you can solve the problem," Jami supposed.

"Yes. Or maybe it's the other way around," Thyssen said, for it occurred to him only as he said it.

"What other way around?" Felicity asked.

"Maybe you pilgrims aren't the question. Maybe you're the answer."

"How do you mean, answer?" Wagner asked. It was almost as if Thyssen had compelled him to ask the question.

"I mean that, either the sleepers and pilgrims are just a meaningless aberration which means there's nothing we can do and therefore no sense in doing anything, or else there is some underlying purpose to them, whereby we must explore the phenomenon and try and discover how it works and what it is for."

"Are you suggesting some sort of divine purpose?" Chrissie Rice asked with amused eyes.

"No," Thyssen said flatly. "I don't think so, but I don't know everything, and I'm not prepared to ignore the possibility no matter how strongly I disbelieve it. Which is why you are an essential function in the project, Chrissie. It's vital that you continue to explore down those roads that my skepticism denies me."

"Break out the Holy Water," Brian muttered from the background.

"I mean that no line of thought should be disregarded, no matter how improbable I or any of us think it to be. And you ought to know that better than anyone, Brian Carrick, with your science fiction fantasies."

Brian flattened against the wall and raised protective hands. "Too true, great white father, too true."

Thyssen had swivelled to face Brian and there he stayed, folding his arms across his massive chest and continuing to stare Brian down. Brian was, after all, a man who seemed to quit long before he gave up. But Thyssen now spoke in his more general tone.

"You all may have noticed, at the last event, that the focal point moved somewhat, dragged as it were away from the northernmost extremities of Canada across the ice cap to a point in Barents Sea, just above North Cape in Norway. Not a lot of difference as far as the pilgrims were concerned, but it was the presence of the new pilgrims in Malawi that caused it. The addition of all those Californians will drag it further south next time, to a point in the Norwegian Sea, about halfway between Iceland and Scotland. Still a pretty inhospitable spot, I agree."

"Sure," Felicity Campbell said in subdued tones. "But since no one ever makes it to the focal point anymore, why does that matter?"

Thyssen dismissed it with a faint shrug. "It would make life a lot easier for you all if you were at the focal point to begin with."

"North Sea," Joe Solomon said with a shudder. "No thank you."

"I agree," Thyssen said.

"But we can move it somewhere more hospitable," Thyssen went on. "All we have to do, for instance, is move the Japanese pilgrims inside the circle and, with a slight adjustment, we can drop it right on Ireland. Very nice place, Ireland."

"To be sure it tis the luvliest of places," Lorna beamed like a fine Colleen.

"And just exactly how do you propose to move 16,000 Japanese pilgrims inside the circle?" Brian asked with a vague air.

"I was hoping you'd tell me..." Thyssen smiled at him.

"Actually, the Japanese government will be glad to be rid of them," Brian shrugged. "It might be possible. Where do you want them to go?"

"Brazil, I think, would be best."

"Brazil?"

"Yes. With the Japanese pilgrims repositioned, they could counterbalance the Buryats, whom we cannot move, on a line which will bisect that between the Californians and Andromeda's Malawis, the intersection being straight over Ireland. Now, we'll need to work out the precise location in Brazil that will have that effect but I suspect it to be on the Matto Grasso, a sparsely inhabited region in the south west of the country."

"And what are we to suppose the Brazilians will think when the Yellow Peril come over the horizon?" Brian wondered.

"That's the sort of thing we're here to solve," Thyssen said lightly. "Joe, I want you to obtain for us a nice big chunk of Brazil."

"Sure," Joe said, a bemused smile on his lips but not in his eyes. "How big a chunk?"

"Say, twice the size of this base."

"Ought to be a cinch," Joe said, and his eyes twinkled toward Brian as he said it. "Lots of big Ranchos down that way, and for sure some of them are going broke and on the market at a bargain price. Give us plenty of room to move around."

"I gather you want all this done before the next linkage?" Felicity wondered, her face going vague.

"If possible."

"With a leg in the air," Brian said flatly.

"Pushover," Joe confirmed, equally flatly.

*

After a splendid dinner put together amid an unpromising cacophony of giggles by Lorna, Chrissie and Felicity, they drank wine and told each other exciting stories of their adventures in a broad room of couches and coffee tables. More than once, they remarked upon their closeness as a team, of their remarkable unity, of their deep caring for each of the others. Even in crisis, the resentment of Jami Shastri soon melted and the stiffness of Kevin Wagner dissolved.

"I've worked with a lot of teams," Wagner said at one point. "I've never been part of one as harmonious as this outfit."

"I think you'd find that if any of the other pilgrims were present, you would each feel the same toward them," Thyssen said to try and shatter the mood.

"Certainly that's what I feel in the presence of my Italian pilgrims," Chrissie said thoughtfully.

"But you're not a pilgrim, Harley," Andromeda pointed out. "Fee and Jami ain't either. But we got all them warm snugglies toward you too, no matter how badly you fuck up."

"Perhaps we stand too closely in your aura," Felicity said with a smile.

"And maybe we're just a bunch of folks who would have got along no matter what happened," Lorna supposed.

"No," Jami put in firmly. "It's more than that. I really resent you for what you did, Harley. I still do. But that doesn't change my admiration for you as a scientist. It just means I no longer think you're infallible."

Joe Solomon said. "I've always prided myself on my professional detachment from people I've worked with. But that's out of the question in this case. Fuck it all, I—after thirty unblemished years of handling other people's money without the slightest temptation—and some of my clients were very careless with their trusts and suchlike but I never even contemplated taking advantage of them—and suddenly, I misappropriate millions of dollars for you people, without even thinking about it. I'm still waiting for the first twinge of conscience. In normal circumstances, I dissolve with guilt when I don't have enough change to tip the taxi driver. This is something truly strange."

"You gotta face it," Lorna said. "We all love each other."

"Yes. And with absolute blind loyalty," Felicity said. "It's family stuff. We might fight and squabble over everything, but no misdeed damages the depth of feeling between us."

"Or combat units," Wagner put in. "Guys that snarl at each

other all day long but would gladly die to protect each other any time. It is a glimpse, I think, of that state of harmony that we will all know in the future."

"Or maybe it's just an excess of Bosons," Brian Carrick said.

They all groaned, but only because it had become a habit when he said something like that. For at least two of them knew exactly what he meant.

Andromeda Starlight wasn't one of them. "Don't tell me, let me guess. Bosons are some kind of kangaroos with an insatiable sexual appetite."

"No. They're elementary particles. Quanta," Brian said. "Right Harley?"

"Right Brian," Harley grinned. "But perhaps you might demonstrate your inestimable skills by explaining the theory in a way everyone can understand."

"Oh, please do," Felicity sighed.

"Sure thing. The elementary particles from which everything in the universe is made, come in all sorts of weird shapes and forms, but the most basic types are bosons and fermions."

"Named after blokes named Boson and Fermion, I bet," Lorna chuckled.

"Satyendra Nath Bose, and Enrico Fermi, who helped describe them," Harley put in. "Carry on, Brian."

"Bosons are hyperactive dudes, attracted to each other and are the basis of all energy, such as heat and light and gravity. Fermions, mostly electrons, are shy retiring types, avoid contact, forming the rigid structures that everyone calls matter. Originally, everything was bosons. The Big Bang was a godalmighty scattering of bosons, but then the nasty old fermions began the task of converting the boson energy into stodgy old matter. Entropy, the heat death of the universe, is a final victory of fermions over bosons, right Harley?"

"Not the way I would have put it, but I have no argument."

"Okay. So you need both. Fermions provide substance, bosons movement and ultimately life, since the firing neurones in your brain are bosons, which means that thought and consciousness are bosons—the same stuff that everything was made of before matter began to take over. Our thoughts are the stuff that the universe is made of."

"You mean we made it all up?" Andromeda gasped.

"No. It made us up. The universe thought itself into existence, and it thought us into existence."

"And now," Joe Solomon said. "It seems to be thinking us out of existence again."

"Would anyone care to explain," Chrissie said quietly but resoundingly. "The difference between a thinking universe and God?"

"None," Brian said with a shrug. "Except you waste your time praying and leading an unsinful life because the universe does not give a stuff about us or any of its other creations. And anyway, it's got enough problems of its own."

"What sort of problems?" Chrissie wondered—not completely willing to let go of that point.

"Like entropy, for instance."

"Heat death and Hell sound like pretty much the same place to me."

"They're not. At heat death, everything is utterly cold and nothing happens there at all. And we're all going there, no matter what."

"I don't know about that," Jami interrupted. "It's never where we are going that's important. It's the fact that we are on the way that matters."

"Yeah," Wagner said. "Humanity has always had an expansionist way about it, and with no regard at all for the outcomes."

"After all," Felicity said. "Whenever we go somewhere new, the first thing we do is try and change it to suit ourselves."

"And so here we are, on a journey to the end of the universe," Brian grinned. "And when we get there, the first thing we've gonna do is try and stop it from happening."

One by one, they faded away and drifted off to bed, until only the hardcore drinkers remained, Lorna nodding off on the couch but hanging in, Harley and Brian locked in increasingly speculative and incoherent conversation.

On the couch, Lorna Simmons stirred. "On the subject of all those ever-loving bosons flying around the place, Brian, don't you have a plane to catch to Japan?"

"Up at sparrow's fart. No doubt about it. Better get some kip, right away," Brian stuttered. He started groping around for the door, but then paused, looking back. "And you want all them 16,000 Japanese in Brazil, mate. Just like that."

"If it's possible, Brian."

"She'll be right, mate. Don't you worry about it."

"I appreciate your thoughts on these things, Brian," Thyssen said quietly. "It does give me things to think about."

"Piss in the other pocket. That one's full."

It took a little time but finally he found his way out of the room.

Lorna uncurled on the couch and braced herself. It was now or never, she knew. Surely he must be drunk, even if he didn't show it. Certainly, she was properly primed. He turned his head and looked at her quizzically—she searched his face for something faintly resembling a leer but was unrewarded. If there was a demeanour to be observed, it was that of a father looking upon a daughter. She needed to change that fast. But it was Thyssen who spoke first.

"Lorna, I want you to do something for me," he said.

"Sure. Anything," she said with a shrug.

"It will be very dangerous," he said.

"Whatever," she shrugged again.

"The next event will be in Java and I want you to be there. I want you to place yourself right in the middle of the Zone."

"Really? Why?"

"Because someone has to do it. A pilgrim. Someone I can be sure of. The others all have important tasks to perform but since we're now the top news story, the media stuff can manage itself for the moment."

"Oh I get it. It's really me who is redundant."

"No. This is very important."

"Why?"

"Because we need data. We need to know what happens when a pilgrim gets a double dose."

Lorna thought about it. In fact she couldn't see what harm it might do, nor why it mattered. But there was a severity in Harley's tone that worried her.

"Sure, fine, what's the problem?" she said blithely.

"It may kill you. Also, depending on the relationship of the Zone and the seismic activity, the earthquakes or volcanoes might get you. You may be out there unconscious for some time—we just have no idea what will happen to you. And we need to know."

"So I just go there and find a nice soft place to fall and wait for it to happen."

"It'll be a little more complicated than that. We'll have your telemetry fully wired."

"So you'll know whether I'm dead or alive before I do."

"If you must put it like that."

He sat, leaning forward on the sofa, his hands clasped before him and if he wasn't wearing a pleading expression, it was at least implied. For a final time she shrugged.

"Okay," she said. "And now there's something I want you to do for me."

"It will be a pleasure," he smiled.

She smiled back. He truly had no idea how close to the truth he was.

*

Captain Maynard had traded his helmet for a baseball cap with US Navy emblazoned thereon, but otherwise he was still dressed as a fully equipped combat soldier.

"They scattered pretty badly while you were away, Andromeda."

"Weren't no alternative, Cap'n," she said grimly.

They met on this barren hilltop with a commanding view

of the surrounding countryside. The thing to do was to make herself as prominent as possible, now that she was back. That meant a lot of standing in the open back of vehicles, choking in the dust, and otherwise positioning herself in prominent places like this, where she could be seen and reported to be seen.

"The flanking units report that they are turning inward. Apparently word of your re-appearance has begun to spread."

"There been a lot of trouble?"

Maynard shook his head. "No. They're all happy to keep moving and leave their former lives behind them. And the locals remain so awed that they don't interfere as our people pass by."

"And the direction?"

"Just off north."

"Which takes us where?"

"Into Tanzania. They'll walk straight into Lake Victoria if they keep going this way."

They had a map spread out on the bonnet of his jeep. Andromeda had only glanced at it before spying out the surroundings. Still to the left lay the steamy remnants of Lake Nyasa, and otherwise the flatlands reaching to the mountains on the right. Everywhere, in the lightly forested terrain below, she could see evidence of people moving toward her. Somehow she felt the need to explain.

"I'm sorry you got dumped with all this. But it was a big deal."

"I'm sure it was." Plainly Maynard was still not happy about it. "What happened?"

"We had a meeting to cut off our leader's head, but he chopped us off at the knees instead."

"I guess you're meaning Professor Thyssen?"

"Yep. When the link occurs, they'll swing West."

"That will run us into Lake Tanganyika instead."

Andromeda groaned and walked over to the map. Maynard had drawn a line to indicate the path the pilgrims had generally followed, from the capital in the south of the country, to the north, almost two hundred miles since the trek began. But the supplies kept flowing, and there was plenty of water. In fact, there was too much water. The long lakes formed natural barricades all the way along the route.

"Well, can we get to here?" she asked, pointing at the spot to the southern extremity of Lake Tanganyika.

"That's almost due west of our present position."

"The next linkage ain't til the 17th. Right now we can lead them anywaywhichway we like. We jest stand me someplace, have the supplies dumped there, and they will follow. Ain't that so?"

"It will also take us into Zambia."

"Just sneak along the edge of it—below the lake. I don't reckon the Zambians will mind."

"And then into the Republic of the Congo."

"But on course. And no more lakes or major rivers to worry about, leastwise for the moment."

"The government in the Congo is not going to like it."

"Otherwise we push north, risk running them into the lake when they link, and then have to get through Rwanda, where I hear tell there's a lot of trouble."

"But at least the population there is familiar with mass migrations."

"Sure, and they got rebels who know how to hold whole nations hostage. I think it wise to avoid them."

"Yes ma'am, they surely will. Maybe we could get some boats and sail them right up the middle of the lake?"

Andromeda had to laugh. Maynard was not one to hide his true motivations. "Yeah, I can see how you sailors might fancy that, but I'm sure it ain't practical. And remember what happened on those crowded trains in Rwanda. No, I reckon they're better off doing what they do best—walking."

"If you say so ma'am."

"Whatever way we go, we eventually gotta cross the Congo Republic from one side to the other. We deal with that when we come to it."

"You're the boss."

She paused and looked him in the eye with a wry smile. "Still think this job is better than the brig, Captain?"

"Yes, ma'am."

"Okay, Sailor. Let's get them past Lake Tanganyika. Then we worry about the rest."

*

As they flew in the Orion, Felicity insisted on doing Lorna's physio-telemetry herself, and the girl brazenly stripped off her blouse right there and then and, since she wasn't wearing a bra, seriously compromised the technical team's ability to concentrate. Felicity pushed her into a seat behind the meteorological monitors which offered basic modesty and some chance of the seismic data making sense. There, as she began to stick on the patches with their micro-transmitters, Felicity saw that those breasts—amongst the top ten of the most admired in the world if you read the trashy women's mags—were in fact somewhat small, and very perky, and splattered all over with freckles. She shook her head to get it back into her almost forgotten detached medico mode, but Lorna had seen the look and was grinning at her. Even faced with crisis, she couldn't help being a tease.

"Now look, Lorna, one more time..."

"I know. I know," Lorna sighed, the those breasts heaved up and down far more than the occasion demanded. "I don't have to do this. I know. But really, Fee, if you disapprove so strongly, why not let someone else do this?"

"Because I want to make damned sure it all works perfectly," Felicity said doggedly.

"It always does, and it will this time."

"Your blood pressure is dangerously high for someone of your age and fitness," Felicity said coldly. "Admit it, Lorna. You're scared witless."

"Well, what to you expect, Fee?" Lorna laughed. "I am, after all, as Chrissie put it, about to walk straight into the valley of death."

"But why are you doing it?"

"Because somebody has to, and I'm the right person for the job."

"He's using you as a guinea pig for..."

"Eeekkk!"

Felicity rolled her eyeballs toward the ceiling and said through gritted teeth. "Was that supposed to be a guinea pig sound?"

"No. I always squeal when someone touches me there."

Felicity groaned, and sat with her head bowed. It was all just too exasperating. Amazingly, Lorna slipped her bare arms about her head and pressed her to her bosom.

"Fee, Fee, don't worry so much. It'll be alright, really. You're being far too emotional about this."

Felicity allowed the moment, then gently disengaged herself—not only because no patient had ever done *that* before, but because one of the transmitters was sticking into her cheek.

It was probably true. She was plainly feeling the strain and all her bodily signs assured her it was so. It was like being constantly at the weepy stage just before menstruation. She had visited her family, and they were as thoughtful as ever, but Wendell especially seemed frayed. They had at no time discussed the subject that had dominated their lives this past year—when it would end and she would come home. Wendell, plainly, had grasped the fact that the planet would be destroyed sometime before that would be possible. Instead they had been tender with each other, in a way they never had been before, as if both of them were made of some exquisite and extremely fragile glass. For the first time since it began, the family departed tearfully as the Orion warmed its engines at Wellington airport.

They picked Lorna up in Auckland where she had been visiting family and friends—farewelling? Not according to Lorna. But now they had hopped to Darwin and Denpassar, where the Orion had taken on maximum fuel. When they landed in Makasar in the Sulawesi Islands, they would be a hundred miles inside the expected Zone with the linkage only hours away.

There, Harley would be waiting with an especially modified Land cruiser and a jet helicopter. The Orion would drop Lorna off and return to Denpassar until dawn approached on the following, fatal day. It would be airborne, as usual, when the Effect occurred, and just outside the Zone with the usual margin of safety. The Zone was expected to swallow the southern half of Sulawesi, but there were no active volcanoes within it. However just to the south, along the main spine of Indonesia, there were a hundred volcanoes waiting to erupt and destroy their surroundings.

Against which the Indonesian government had taken no precautions whatsoever, for the government was composed of hard-line Islamics who weren't about to believe anything the Americans or the United Nations told them. On Sulawesi, there were six million people—about four million of whom were likely to become new Sleepers. And along the volcanic line from Timor to Sumatra, a hundred million people would face the devastation of the volcanoes. Felicity's mind could not cope with such massive figures. In reality, the Indonesian government was right to take no precautions, for both sets of victims had nowhere to go and would have had to take their chances where they stood anyway.

Into this hell, Lorna was to walk like a lamb to the slaughter and Felicity found the prospect unbearable. She despised Harley for making it so, and for choosing this wonderful healthy young woman as his victim, but most of all, that he had the power to make Lorna go so willingly.

Now, as the Orion made its approach toward Makasa and Lorna buttoned her blouse, Felicity had run out of arguments. Lorna could smile for her.

"You just don't understand, do you Fee."

"Why you need to do this? No. I don't."

Lorna cocked her head on one side and gave a sparkling smile. "I'm doing it for the only reason I ever do anything, Fee. I'm doing it for love."

"Love?"

"Yes, Fee. Remember you heard it here first."

*

Logistically, it was a very difficult thing to organise, for although there were no volcanoes within the expected Zone, the region would be subjected to severe earthquakes. 10.1 on the moment-magnitude scale was anticipated—with the potential to kill far more millions than in California. The main catastrophe would be in the very active volcanic regions lying outside the Zone, but still the dangers from falling buildings and trees, earth fissures and uncontrolled vehicles and animals, flooding and explosions—the list went on, and Lorna was to take herself right into it all, and presumably find a place were she could safely lie unconscious until help arrived. Then they had to find her again, before the ants ate out her eyes.

For this, Harley had obtained a big solid four-wheel drive with extra fuel tank, reinforced on all sides, airtight, unbreakable glass, stuffed with transmitting equipment. Lorna would drive northwest along what seemed to be a reasonable road out of Makasa, moving as the lure of the focal point directed. Of course, no one could go with her. The place had been chosen because there was a good road heading in the right direction, arrowing the anticipated focal point.

They had made a bed for her in the back of the vehicle where she would lie herself down as sunset approached, hooked up to the array of monitors and wait for it to happen. Several different types of homing devices would direct rescuers to the spot—in fact Harley himself would be airborne in the jet-helicopter positioned just outside the Zone and race to collect her as soon as the Shastri moment had passed.

"The plan is perfect," Lorna insisted. "Nothing can go wrong."

Underground gas chambers might explode, the sedimentary soil could liquefy and swallow the vehicle whole, boulders and snakes might fall out of the sky.

"The snakes will all be Shastri-ed too," Lorna said stoically. "Bring a shovel."

She drove along the bumpy road with dense jungle to either side. There were people and villages all the way, and all of them stopped doing what they were doing to watch her go by.

"Keep looking for the turn off on your left," Harley was saying on the radio.

"I don't see no turn off. Nor any hill for that matter."

"It's there. Just keep looking.."

She found her hill. The sun was already below the treetops and she knew from experience how suddenly night fell in the tropics, but she found the right road. It went through three crowded villages in less than a kilometre and was not made for motor vehicles. She bumped and jolted her way forward, soothed along by Harley's deep controlling voice and then the upward incline and she broke up into sunlight again.

"Good hill," she reported faithfully. "No doubt about it."

The land around was relatively flat, a swampy plain between the sea and the mountains and there was a village in visual distance just below the barren crest of the hill.

"You there, darling?" she asked.

He always was. Harley remained in radio contact for every moment of her journey.

"Don't you ever go to the toilet or anything, Harley? You don't need to nursemaid me. I'm fine."

"Your blood-sugar is down. You need to eat something now," he replied.

She was doing it for love, she had told Felicity. Well that was true enough. Felicity had stared, and did so all the more when they were on the tarmac in Makasa and Harley directed her to the vehicle, offering unnecessary final instructions. Lorna had kissed him full on the lips, mostly to shut him up. She glanced over at where Felicity stood not actually wringing her hands but looking like she wanted to, and saw her jaw drop. It was worth the whole damn thing, just for that moment.

"This is your last chance to back out," Harley said, to prove he didn't have a romantic bone in his body.

"My life is now entirely in your hands, Harley," she said softly. "And that is just exactly where I want it to be."

And she climbed in the vehicle and drove away.

True, they had slept together only once and no one had actually said anything to anyone about love. Nor anything else much for that matter. But she was on a mission and bundled him along, and to her complete astonishment, although none of it went according to plan, still she had learned everything about him that she might ever hope to know.

At first, he had been rather shy and embarrassed. "It's been too long. I'm not sure I can do it anymore."

"They tell me you never forget how."

Determinedly she led him by the hand toward the bedroom, and if he didn't actually dig his heels in, still he made a chore of it. "Oh, I remember all right. It's just that the physical side isn't what it ought to be anymore."

"I do the physical stuff," Lorna said grimly. "You just lie back and take it."

Nothing like that happened.

They stood in the dimness of the bedroom and tried to be romantic. But she needed something to stand on to kiss him and he didn't seem to know how to stoop.

"I just don't think I can take seduction seriously anymore," he admitted, though only when that was ridiculously obvious.

"Look," she said, getting irritated. "Let's just take our clothes off quickly and jump into bed and fumble about and do what comes naturally, okay?"

There was no fumbling.

He went at her the very moment their flesh contacted, and seemed to want to devour her completely. It was more like a bear tearing its prey apart in a cave than making love. Never in her life had she experienced a man so completely overcome by rampant passion and it frightened her at first. All attempts to slow him down were futile—the biggest and most powerful man of her sexual experience was completely out of control and she was thrashed this way and that in the bed without relenting. He was eating her, snorting and grunting furiously and he seemed to come twice before he even entered her and three more times before she knew what was happening. She calmed her panic while he pawed and mauled every part of her body simultaneously and finally she managed to go with the flow. The sheer power of the moment brought on her own orgasms, not by any conventional means but because suddenly she too was caught up in the animalistic rampage. Then suddenly their passion went screaming into the night and it was over.

He had collapsed on top of her, his body still between her legs though at about the chest region, his head on her breasts. *Oh god he's dead* she thought at first, but then her inner thighs told her of the tremors that periodically racked his body. He convulsed, cried out, settled again, and something wet dripped onto her right breast. To her complete amazement, she realised he was crying.

Now this had never happened before, and she truly didn't know what to do. This massive man was weeping in her arms and didn't seem able to stop. But slowly it came to her and she relaxed with it and still his convulsions went on. In fact they continued unabated for over an hour and she wrapped her arms and legs about him as tightly and protectively as she could and stroked his wet hair and made soothing noises. Eventually, every muscle in her limbs was aching with strain and some were crushed to numbness by his weight but still she held on, as if to a life-raft. And finally he eased off her and slept beside her and she lay, caressing him, until her own sleep came. He snored thunderously but she was so drained and emotionally and physically exhausted by then that she didn't care...

In the morning when she awoke, he was gone. Her body had scratches and bruises everywhere and when she tried to rise, her legs had trouble co-operating. Inwardly too, she was numbed by the shock of the experience. He had wept in her arms, more profoundly that anyone in her experience. It was a staggering emotional trauma shared, even though only one of them had any idea what it was all about. With shaking hands, she located her cell phone and pressed out his number and he answered immediately, from wherever he was, near or far, she never bothered to ask.

"Okay, Harley," she said. "I'll die for you."

And now that the moment of dying had come, she was

astonished to find she remained without doubt. Of course, she knew that she wasn't going to die really—every precaution had been taken and her faith in Harley was unshatterable. In any case, she would be in a coma, for eight days or forever, what did it matter? That Harley himself was unable to assume the obvious and needed to conduct this experiment was just his exacting empirical scientific mind at work. Science was never about obvious truths. It was about what you could prove by experimentation and so the experiment needed to be done. There was no doubt. A double dose of the Shastri Effect. Maybe she'd sleep sixteen days this time. In any case, it was worth it. But even had she thought it wasn't, still she would have done it for him.

"I do wish you were here, Harley. It'd be so much easier if I could hold you in my arms."

"You do realise," Harley muttered, "that about twenty other people are tuned in to this."

"I don't care about the others. I only care about you."

"This is supposed to be a serious scientific experiment, Lorna."

"Your adoring guinea pig drools at the sound of your voice."

The sun was setting. She'd slipped out into the nearby jungle and cleansed her inner self, as Chrissie might have put it. She did so with great trepidation, snakes or spiders or scorpions might easily have bit her on the bum but she persisted until it was all done. After all, her Prince Charming was coming to find his Sleeping Beauty and she didn't want him to have to give her the kiss of life while she lay in a puddle of excreta. A girl needed to offer her best at such moments, when so helpless.

"Where the bloody hell were you?" Harley demanded over the radio.

"I'm here, Harley. Don't yell at me or I'll turn you off."

"We should do one last instrument check."

"The instruments are just dandy, Harles. Why don't you tell me how much you love me instead."

"This is being taped for posterity, Lorna."

"All the more reason why."

She'd dressed for the occasion, as if she was an Ancient Egyptian Queen expecting her sarcophagus to be opened in some future paradise. A good strong halter to make sure her breasts stayed up front as she lay on her back, tight shorts, her favourite beret on the hair that she had just spent an hour brushing assiduously.

"How are you feeling?" he demanded of her.

"Deliriously happy, my sweet."

"Good luck, kid."

"Just the thought that the next thing I'll see will be your smiling face sustains me still, darling."

"Jesus, Lorna. Try taking this a little bit seriously."

"Would you prefer I fretted as badly as you are?"

"I'm not fretting!"

She sat on the mattress in the back of the vehicle—temperature controlled until the auxiliary battery ran out—took off her boots and lay back, carefully arranging her hair so that it cascaded across the pillow. She held a mirror up, to ensure everything was in its right place.

"Are you in position? It'll be any moment now."

"All set for the missionary position, lover, should you be in a hurry."

Her pendant—a gold Project Earthshaker badge—on a chain around her neck, had slipped sideways—she picked it up and dropped it so that it fell neatly into her cleavage. All ready. She lay there waiting.

"Anything happening?"

"Just my bosom rising and swelling with love, dear one. Otherwise nothing..."

Nothing happened for far too long. She began to sweat where her flesh contacted the mattress. Of course she had scented herself everywhere but think of the smell if it took them days to find her! Maybe she should...

"Any minute now. Hang in there."

"I'm not a bat. I'm taking it lying down like always and ..."

The pain was like her entire body was crushed flat instantly.

A tremor ran through her and she opened her mouth to scream but held it back, knowing he would be hearing it—and in the last instant of consciousness, she was irritated that she would be found wearing a dreadfully contorted facial expression.

*

But he did not hear her scream. The radio went dead and Thyssen was left shouting her name into infinity. The chopper swung wildly in the sky as the shockwave hit them from behind, and the turbulence shuddered the rotors violently. The pilots struggled to maintain control of the wildly lurching aircraft and Thyssen was thrown this way and that such that the jerking of his head almost caused him to lose consciousness. Then came the detonation, so profound that he would not have been able to hear her, had there been anything to hear. It slammed into their eardrums and they were instantly deafened, and the chopper whirled downward toward the sea as both pilots clutched their helmets in agony. The explosion, in fact series of explosions so close together that they sounded like one continuous burst, was heard in Tasmania, in Cape Town, in Tokyo, in Honolulu. Over half the globe, people stopped and looked at the sky, expecting to see thunderheads.

Thyssen jolted forward in his seat and stared from the dome of one pilot to the other, to assure himself they were still conscious. The co-pilot lolled for a moment but then regained control—the pilot opened his mouth a bellowed a rage that none of them could hear and worked frantically at the controls. Below, the Timor Sea spiraled up toward them and Thyssen fought back bile, as indeed the pilots did. The water, deep blue when he last looked, had now turned a dirty green, and the wave crests all clashed together, having lost their current as completely as the pilot had lost control of his machine. The chopper shuddered fiercely again as the engines surged and then they levelled out, only a few hundred feet from the erratically broiling sea.

"Can anybody hear me?" Thyssen was bellowing into the microphone.

"Yes, we can hear you, Harley," Felicity Campbell said from a vast distance away. "Turn your volume down. You're too loud."

Thyssen fought for self control, every bit as much as the pilot had. His ears were ringing now and a dulling pain replaced the numbness, but he didn't touch the volume—he knew he was loud because he was bellowing.

"We've lost everything here," Harley was saying. "What's your status?"

"Bit shook up, but we're fine. We've lost all contact with Lorna though. And there's only static coming through from all land stations."

It was not surprising that the Orion had come through unscathed; it was a remarkably stable flying platform; that was why they had chosen it.

"You've lost her completely?" he asked, his lips pressed firmly together.

"We lost everything for a moment. There must have been some sort of pulse. But some of it is coming back up now."

"Anything of... any indication..." but he just couldn't get the words out.

"Harley, I'll let you know as soon as I have something. Anyway, you know where she is."

Thyssen nodded. The pilot knew her last known position and had already plotted his course and now, hearing Felicity's words, turned in his seat and gave Thyssen a smile and a thumb's up sign. Meanwhile, the list of panicky co-pilot priorities had worked down to internal communications and he got that on.

"You read me, Prof?"

"I do," Thyssen said, his ability to get a grip on his surroundings expanding all the time. "And you're bleeding from the right ear, Bill."

"Yeah. I reckon I perforated an eardrum. Hurts like hell. I'll switch earphones when I get a minute. Meanwhile, I'd appreciate it if you guys whispered."

"That sure was one hell of a bang," the pilot said. "You didn't warn us about that."

"I thought we were far enough away," Thyssen said.

"We ought to be at Lorna's location in just under two hours," Gordon the pilot was saying—relaxed now into that typical calm pilot mode.

"And we'll be on the ground at Makasar by then," Felicity chimed in. "Providing the runway is still useable. Meanwhile, have a look to the south."

Since they were flying due north, rear vision was not easy. Gordon diverted briefly, allowing them a southern perspective.

"Holy shit look at that!" Bill gasped, and then groaned as he hurt his ear.

Right along the horizon, a huge black cloud was building, billowing furiously as it advanced. It stretched the whole distance, from east to west.

"Gordon. Whatever you do, don't let that cloud catch up to us," Thyssen said menacingly.

"Sure thing. How fast you reckon it's approaching?"

"Six hundred miles per hour is average for them."

"We can't go that fast."

"Put your foot down. It's already come hundreds of miles offshore. No telling how much further before it dissolves."

"What is it?"

"Flying mud at about a thousand degrees."

"Holy shit!"

"Yeah, that's exactly what it's like."

The nose of the helicopter dipped as Gordon laid on the acceleration.

"Felicity," Thyssen asked. "You get that?"

"We are scurrying north as fast as we can go, Harley."

"What sort of ground readings are you getting back there?"

"Thommo has just picked up a satellite image. It's mostly a big black smudge but he says there are plumes running from dozens of sites, from the middle of Sumatra, right along Java, all the way through the other islands to Timor. Krakatoa's disappeared again and places like Lombok and some other smaller islands have vanished altogether. And you'll be glad to know the ashcloud is slowing down."

"Anything on Lorna?"

"No. All the transmitters are out. I think she'll be okay, Harley."

They flew on and as time passed, Harley fretted and Felicity added data provided by the technicians in the Orion. Bali was now a crescent shaped island, half its former size, at least six small islands had vanished completely, Lombok was now three small islands, each of them a thundering volcanic peak. But the main devastation had hit Java where it was unlikely that any part of the island had escaped destruction. Jakarta was wrecked completely, although along the south coast of the island, the damage seemed minimal. But all the middle and north of the island lay under searing ash and lava flows that spilled into the sea, raising vast clouds of steam.

Gordon located Makasar first. In the dust-filled night it was impossible to see the lights of the city below, and Thyssen realised they were not lights, but fires. They flew on along the coast.

"I think we're over the spot now," Bill announced and they circled, but the brilliant spotlights of the chopper only reflected back at them from the fog. Gordon eased them lower and until treetops came into view and then began a grid search. It took forty minutes before the shining skin of the land cruiser flashed back at them.

"There she is!" Harley shrieked, unleashing the last of his anxieties, for now the truth, whether good or bad, would stride into its place.

He bounded from the chopper before it quite touched the ground and raced forward, the lights of the chopper behind him dazzled when they hit the dust but he blundered forward and found the vehicle. Hastily he unlocked and opened the rear door. There was no sign of Lorna in there.

15
THE THIRD LAW OF THERMODYNAMICS

Joe Solomon, a free man at last, planned ahead. He flew to New Orleans and waited for the linkage to take hold of him, then made the long slow journey by rail back to Washington on what he suppose to be the Chattanooga Choo-Choo. In fact it went a little quicker than he planned and he arrived too soon and had to keep on going, all the way to New York. But that was okay. Through Lorna, Thyssen had provided him with an address in The Bronx, which was supposedly their secret base, and while the news broadcasts made their initial reports of the disaster in Indonesia, he rode the final stage in a taxi. He supposed, in the end, it was perfect timing.

The whole journey took over a day and the final taxi ride almost an hour but Joe didn't mind. A time of relative peace, after two weeks of wheeling and dealing over ranches for sale in the Matto Grasso. Yet it was here, not Brazil, where such deals were to be done and he was getting there. It was just a matter of time. The driver had the temerity to sneer at the miserly tip and roared away in disgust. Joe checked the street both ways before he approached the building.

They weren't following him. At least, not that he was able to observe. He had listened for extra clicks on his telephone and heard none. Of course, there were no charges pending and he wasn't really wanted for anything, but they might at least have had the decency to keep an eye on him. As it was, he felt lonely, cut off from the world, as if he barely existed. So too, as he approached the building, did he realise that he had no idea where his colleagues of Earthshaker were nor what dangers they faced, no idea of how his business in Perth was faring, hadn't heard from his brother in five weeks.

He pressed the special code into the intercom and, while he waited to go through Val's complex security procedure, saw instead that the door simply opened. Val Dennis, the most antisocial man in New York, had ramps for people in wheelchairs, all the way to the goods lift and there everything was within reach, as if it was designed for him. There was no button to press for Val's floor, but a code that Joe didn't know. But when he closed the grille, the lift set off without any instructions.

It stopped at Val's level—Joe recognised it immediately from the vast array of electronic and other junk piled everywhere. It was such a tangle that it took Joe a few minutes to realise that the place had been wrecked. Everything he could see was smashed. His wheels crunched over shattered glass. He had to push his way through a forest of hanging cables. Once again the idea of carrying a gun seemed sensible. On a couch over by the window, he saw the figure of Val Dennis lying and as he neared it, he saw the blood all about.

Val Dennis, his eyes closed by swelling, blood running from his spilt lips and nose, lay on his belly with an arm that was plainly broken dangling over the side of the couch. Joe could see he was still breathing, though he showed no other sign of life. He looked around and spotted the telephone and picked it up. It might had been the only thing in the place still working. He called an ambulance and hung up and then advanced to see what he could do to help Val. Not much really.

Then astonishingly, Val spoke, though without moving his jaw. "Who's there?"

"It's Joe Solomon, Val. What happened here?"

"Joe? Ah, yeah. Joe. Thyssen's creative accountant."

"That's me all right. What happened here?"

"They came, man. Took all the Earthshaker stuff. Wrecked the rest. Wrecked me too."

"Who came?"

"Suits, man. Government dudes. Bastards."

"Our side?"

"Bad guys wouldn't be this nasty. Left me here to bleed to death. Can you believe that?"

"I've called for an ambulance."

"Ain't paid me subscription..."

"I'll pay for it. Do you know what they wanted?"

"Kill Earthshaker. If they ain't got it, no one else can have it. You know how they think."

"You just take it easy."

"Hey man, listen. You gotta get onto Harley. Jami went to Lombok."

"Where's Lombok?"

"Java, man. Near there anyway. Said she wasn't gonna miss the biggest explosion in history."

"She went there. How?"

"On crutches. I couldn't talk her out of it. You get Harley to pick her up before it's too late."

"It's already too late, Val. Most of Indonesia has just been blown off the face of the earth."

*

She awoke in utter darkness—perhaps this was what it was like to be dead. Or maybe she had gone blind, and deaf. When she had been knocked out, the sun had set and the very sudden night of the tropics had been coming down, but there were lights, and sounds, all around her. The interior of the vehicle had glowed with red and yellow lights on the control panels, and two computer screens, and green digital figures, all of which whirred and buzzed lightly. And the static on the radio. Now all of it seemed to be gone.

She hurt everywhere, as if she had been completely crushed. Her head throbbed, every muscle ached, her stomach was terribly upset. Had she lain here, she wondered, for all eight days? So where was fucking Harley? Where was everyone and everything.

The moon and stars seemed to have gone out. Painfully, she forced herself into a sitting position. She was starting to sweat—it was very hot and stuffy in the vehicle, now that its air conditioning system had stopped. But she could move. In fact, nothing seemed broken or severely damaged when moments ago she could have assumed many injuries. She was just sore. And it was so very dark. And quiet.

Then, slowly, her senses began to kick in and start working— it was as if they had been stunned into dysfunction and needed a moment to find their start button again. It wasn't quite as dark as before—so she wasn't blind. There seemed to be a faint glow illuminating the interior of the cabin, coming from behind her. And sounds. Faint crackling sounds. In a way, that emphasised the darkness and silence—only in these conditions could such faint emanations be so prominent.

She got herself onto her knees. She was so stiff and sore but still it was apparent to her that she had *not* been lying here for anything like eight days. Her mouth wasn't even dry—it couldn't have been more than a few minutes, but in those minutes, an eternity had passed. Something tickled her upper lips and she wiped it—she realised her nose was bleeding. But almost as soon as she knew it, it stopped. In the faint glow, the interior of the cabin was beginning to take shape. She found the radio switch— the only one really familiar to her—and flicked it. Nothing happened. She flicked it back and forth but still there was no static in the headphones. She took them off and threw them away in disgust. He hadn't come, the bastard. Like every other man in her life, Harley too had let her down. Then she remembered the auxiliary power switch and flicked that a few times. She wasn't dead, but the technology certainly was.

There was the glow that was her only source of light. She slid across to the rear windows but it was just a foggy glow. Then she realised that was on the inside, her breathing on the window. She gave it a wipe and things became clearer. There was a fire, which also accounted for the crackling sound. Down in the village, one of the huts was well alight. Now that gave her something to think about. The fire could spread and, if the wind direction was right, could come this way. Something needed to be done.

Fire. Light. Her instincts were kicking in and she remembered she desperately needed a smoke. Which lead her to her lighter and a moment or two of illumination. Enough to see the blood on her hand from her nose. She flicked the lighter off and sat, smoking. And as it calmed her, her brain began to work. There was a fire extinguisher in here somewhere. She went forward and discovered it attached under the dashboard. Along the way, she remembered there was a torch clipped to the window frame. Battery powered—should work. She found it and it did. Fine. Let's go fight the fire.

She opened the rear door and immediately the outside air hit her. It was pretty hot and stuffy inside but out there it was even hotter. There was a strong wind coming from, if she was right, the south. For sure if she didn't put that fire out, it might come her way. But it just didn't seem right, to go and fight a fire while smoking a cigarette. She leaned on the back of the vehicle and smoked, and then realised that she didn't want a pee.

Which meant that not a great deal of time could have passed. Maybe she had only been unconscious for minutes, or even seconds. No. There was the afterglow of sunset when she last saw anything, but not this utter blackness. She raised the torch. The sky seemed so close overhead that she might have been able to touch it. Smoke from the fire—some of that for sure but there seemed to be some denser, darker, cloud up there, heavy and ponderous. Dust thrown up by the earthquakes that she might have gladly slept through? She reminded herself to watch out for fissures.

Now she was ready. She was pushing thoughts of snakes and spiders and scorpions out of her mind, not to mention all manner of other dangers, but the cigarette had provided courage and she stamped it out with thanks. She started off, and immediately saw little bundles littering the ground. Dead birds. Not dead, just KO-ed. As all the snakes, spiders, scorpions and all other dangers would be. Feeling even braver, she headed down the hill.

The hut was completely destroyed when she arrived, and she could smell pork chops cooking. When she realised what that was, she wanted to run right back up the hill and hide in the cruiser. Instead, she steeled herself and attacked the perimeter of the fire, in the places where it threatened to spread. Soon the hut was just a heap of charred wood, under control she assessed from no knowledge or experience whatsoever. Now the village had become deathly quiet. Earlier, there had been noise everywhere. Voices, birdcalls, things rattling. Now nothing. She held the torch high. Several bodies lay in the street—all of them men. She went to each in turn, found a pulse, rolled them over and straightened them out. Harley's comments about the ants eating out their eyes worried her briefly, until she remembered there wouldn't be any ants. The last man she found had fallen in a puddle, face down, and had drowned. She backed away. Yes, there remained dangers. Now she could see what she had to do.

One of the more substantial huts had collapsed and she soon found several people trapped in there. She set the torch on a post and dragged the bodies out. All alive but one youth had a terrible open wound. She tore the boy's shirt off and used it to bind the wound and staunch the flow. Left here, he would surely have bled to death. Her sense of importance soared. She started to check out the huts one by one and soon made a shocking discovery. A mother had thrown her body over her children to protect them and now they were suffocating under her. She hauled the woman aside and the gasping children immediately regained normal breathing.

Now she had a mission. She rushed from hut to hut, and found three other places where misguided attempts to protect the innocent had backfired, on one occasion fatally but Lorna reckoned she had saved four young lives. At a table, she found a man whose face had turned blue in the midst of his meal. She belted him on the back until he vomited and resumed normal breathing. A lot of people had fallen on sharp objects or awkwardly—she extracted them and bound the wounds as best she could, and straightened out everyone she encountered. She was running toward exhaustion and was aware of the sound of the helicopter for some time before its significance occurred to her.

She raced outside, shouting and waving the torch but the chopper was only a glow of landing lights amid the dense overhead haze. It passed right over her, very low, and still she could not make out its shape. Then it was landing, on the hill by the vehicle. Frantically, stumbling and falling twice, she ran that way, shouting and screaming like a mad thing lest they go away before they found her. Then the pilot shut down the engine, and she stumbled breathless into Harley's arms.

"Where the bloody hell were you?" he demanded with annoyance. "Didn't I tell you to stay with the vehicle..."

He hadn't. She was sure of it. But she had no breath to fight back. "There were people... needed help... I was saving... lives..."

Harley looked toward the village, and then held her tighter as his anxiety passed away. "Yeah. We expect to lose a lot of sleepers before we can get to them."

Her breath was coming back. She looked up at him. "You yelled at me."

"I'm sorry. You weren't here and it gave me a fright."

"I thought you stood me up."

"No. I'm on time. You woke up early."

"Did I?"

"Eight days early, in fact."

"Oh yes," she said, the significance of it only occurring to her slowly. "I was only unconscious for a few minutes, I think."

"Well, we'll have to wait and see how you behave at the next event," Harley said benignly, "but my guess is that you're no longer a pilgrim."

She thought about it. Did she feel different? Or was it just that she was able to feel at all. "You mean I'm cured?" she asked, wondering aloud really.

"Well, yes," Harley smiled. "That is, if we are to assume you were ever sick."

*

Sulawesi, at the best of times, was not a place where a person could expect to lie unconscious for eight days and survive; the climate was too hot, the air too fetid, the terrain too rugged, the earth too damp, the insect life too rampant.

Felicity set up operations at Makasa Airport since that was the place where she first touched down, and started gathering the nearby victims, attempting to control the circumstances as best she could. She stayed at the airport because from all around the world, people and supplies from government and private aid agencies began pouring in.

She went on television, and was able to transmit the situation on all news outlets.

"The country is littered with comatose people," she said, her hand constantly pushing her hair off her brow as she spoke, urgently and unapologetically. "We estimate four million people spread over an area of 160,000 square kilometres. The terrain is mostly mountainous, dense jungle, there is no organised transport, few roads, no railways, one decent airport. You reach most places by the rivers, then you walk. Getting to the victims will be the hardest part. Once they are located, they have to be lifted onto a stretcher or a bunk or table or anything at all, to get them off the ground where they are very vulnerable. Then they have to be hooked up to a glucose drip, tagged for identification, and examined for injuries. Any unattended wounds, no matter how minor, could be fatal in a day or so here. We need helicopters and pilots, medical staff, bedding of any kind, glucose, catheters and stands, blankets, bandages, disinfectant, in short we don't have enough of anything. We need it all, right away. Tomorrow will be too late. We expect people to die at a rate of 100,000 a day. Come to Makasa Airport and we'll direct you from there."

She was not overstating the situation. Possibly half the sleepers were doomed never to wake. The response was immediate—the UN teams were on stand-by anyway but most had gone to Java and the other islands devastated by the volcanoes, where there were millions of rescues awaiting them, and tens of millions of lives to save. Armies from all of the surrounding countries— Thailand, Australia, Malaya, friend and foe of Indonesia like— landed and took over under UN direction. There was no longer any government in Jakarta to object. Felicity and her sleepers were regarded as the secondary problem.

Still, they began to flow in and she supplied them, briefed them and dispatched them in accordance with a huge gridmap of the Zone that she had set up on the wall of the terminal building. Mostly they were from private agencies, some of them decidedly shonky, but Felicity welcomed them irrespective. Many demanded to be paid up-front and she had found a safe in which to place several sacks of money in various currencies from Joe, surrounded by a team of Wagner's men, menacing the jungle with machineguns. Out there, looters and bandits rampaged.

In those moments when she allowed herself to pause for a cup of tea, she realised that she was presently the dictator of a small country, where all of her subjects were asleep. Kevin Wagner would have found the experience exhilarating, she only found it an appalling responsibility and utterly exhausting.

Her teams radio-ed in whenever they had anything to say. They had been able to take over the control tower to facilitate communication. She had several people receiving messages and compiling statistics and huge charts. The reports indicated one in five sleepers were dead or dying. Almost a million people. But that was a good result, compared to the thirty million who had died in the islands to the south.

She wept every time she thought of Jami. Over a hundred members of the International Geological Survey had been down there to observe the eruptions at the time and more than half of them had been killed. Jami had apparently slipped herself in amongst them, although there was no confirmation available. They couldn't even prove she had arrived. Flight manifests established that she had flown to Hong Kong, but since all traffic into the endangered area had been fully restricted, there was no record of where she went from there. No doubt she had talked her way onto a military or UN plane, using her US Geological Survey status to do so, but no one knew that for sure.

Except people like Felicity who were only too aware of Jami Shastri's determination to get where she was going. The silly girl should never have been out of hospital...

Still, Felicity always terminated such moments of melancholy with the thought that the `missing' status meant that Jami might come wandering in at any time, suddenly materialising, leaning on a doorjamb taking big munches out of an apple, looking like a street kid checking out the joint to see if there was anything worth stealing.

At night Felicity wandered in the hanger which, like all other accessible buildings, had been turned into a temporary hospital. The main lighting had failed, and all illumination was from light stands below eyelevel. It cast gigantic shadows, her own was a monster fifty feet high that rippled along the galvanised iron of the structure, massive and terrifying, following her everywhere. Her despair was like that monster now, dwarfing her but just behind, waiting to pounce and devour her.

She wondered why she was bothering most of the time that she allowed herself to wonder anything. Why not let these people die now, while they were at peace? Why trouble to save them for the even more appalling disasters that lay ahead of them? Hoping for the miracle that Jami might have survived was little different to hoping for the one that somehow the destruction of the planet might be averted. And now Harley reckoned he had the cure for the Shastri Effect. The double dose. Could she really, in any medical conscience, allow him to subject these people to this a second time? And that only to die anyway when the planet collapsed under their feet.

On the television in the Orion, she had seen Lorna on the screen, on a tape that Harley had sent her. Lorna spoke with great excitement of her adventure, of how she had gone into the Zone and emerged awake and unharmed. No longer a sleeper, no longer a pilgrim. Just another media superstar ordinary person, healthy and unaffected. At the bottom of the screen her words were mimicked in Arabic subtitles, and then, on another appearance, with Italian subtitles. Now she was off to California to spread the word. Hear ye! Hear ye! Follow me and I will free you of the burden of the pilgrims. Like some mad evangelist. Did Harley truly plan to stand them in the middle of the Matto Grasso, where the next Zone of Influence was expected to fall, and zap 'em all again? And for what?

"That seems to be the way to go," Thyssen had said with a faint smile before he left.

"But you don't know the long term effects."

"In the circumstances, long term effects are the least of our troubles."

"You can't be sure, from one instance, that they'll all come through it the way Lorna did."

"You examined her and passed her fully fit yourself."

"But she'd had a hell of a shock."

Thyssen gave a big sigh of exasperation at her persistence and explored the distant mountains as he continued in a deliberately controlled voice. "Felicity, I believe this is the answer. No other suggestions are offering. Are you seriously proposing I ignore it?"

"These are people's lives your playing with, Harley."

"Yeah, I know. I'm not God. So I'll just have to fake it."

The truth was, in her grimmer moments, that she knew she had lost her faith in Harley Thyssen completely. Even when she knew he was probably right, still she was unable to believe him.

*

Beginning from the town of Chitipa, there was a road they could follow approximately that led them along the border between Zambia and Tanzania, directly toward the southernmost tip of Lake Tanganyika. Sometimes the bulk of the pilgrims travelled in one country, sometimes the other, and sometimes Maynard wasn't at all sure where most of them were. But every day the two C-130s flew overhead and parachuted supplies into the intended path and would report what they could see of the migration from the air. Mostly, they reported a vast cloud of dust from the tramping of a million feet.

The planes reloaded primarily at Wilson Airport in Nairobi, when the incoming stores were accumulated, but would usually make refuelling stops in Tanzania, with the result that the Tanzanian officialdom knew what was happening and chose to ignore a problem that they could be sure would soon go away. Zambian officials, however, were of a different attitude. Almost daily, individual or groups of officials would arrive and seek out Andromeda Starlight, ask for her autograph for their children and the children of friends and then inform her that the pilgrims were not allowed to enter Zambia.

"They are not," Andromeda told them. "They are in Tanzania."

She gave the same answer, even though sometimes they were as much as twenty miles inside Zambia.

There were always many forms to be filled in and instructions concerning any matter the gentlemen from Immigration could think of.

"You need a permit to parachute in Zambian airspace," was the sort of thing they were told. Andromeda walked at the head of her flock, filling in the forms on a clipboard without reading them, signing the CDs and photographs of herself, always pressing on.

Then one morning, a helicopter landed and Harley Thyssen stepped off. Captain Maynard lowered his weapon and extended his hand. It was their first meeting, but each was so familiar with the other that they did not bother with introductions.

"Sorry to drag you so far from the sea, Captain."

"Most days, my men and I climb a mountain and we can see one lake or another. That sustains us."

"How are your men standing up, Captain?"

"They are standing up very well, Professor, considering the constant difficulties of the trek. One dead in a vehicle accident. Two seriously injured in a food stampede..."

"Food stampede?"

"They don't happen anymore, now that the pilgrims understand the food drops are regular events."

"It's been a long tour of continuous duty for your men, Captain, and in unfamiliar circumstances. I can arrange for you to be relieved by some of Wagner's men if you wish."

"We've already had a meeting and canvassed that idea, Professor. My men decided by unanimous vote that we'd like to go all the way. If that's okay."

Andromeda Starlight emerged with a broad smile and a welcoming hug for the big man. "Harley, what a delight. Are you staying for tea?"

"No. I just dropped in to hand you this," Thyssen said and handed her a large envelope in heavy paper. "It's a right of passage from the President of the Republic of The Congo."

"Another friend of yours, Harley?"

"No. But acquaintances of mine did study with him in Paris."

"Fine. But we're not in The Congo yet. And we are having enough of trouble with the Zambians to keep us on our toes."

"It's just practice for The Congo, I assure you," Thyssen told her. "There, every petty official will hold you up by force of arms if necessary, until appropriate bribes are paid."

"We've already paid out a fortune in bribes to the Zambians."

"Stop doing it. It only encourages them."

"They make a pretence that it is some official tax or duty."

"If they ask for it in US dollars, it's a bribe. The best policy is never pay. In The Congo, the officials will literally queue up with their hands out if you do."

"So how do we handle them?"

"That document will help with the real officials. But most are conmen and bandits and with them, concede nothing."

"And if they make a fight of it?" Maynard asked.

"Use your discretion, Captain. One shot in the leg, I'm told, ought to get rid of most of them. But, whatever you do, do not let them get the upper hand. Take any action necessary to prevent that."

"And the government of The Congo..."

"Is very unpredictable. However, The Congo Republic is a big place and most of the military power is concentrated at the centre, protecting the President. You will always be a long way away from there and their transport and communications are woeful. Everything favours you, Captain."

"I think I understand."

"However, to be on the safe side, the President has offered a little toy that might help. It will be delivered with the first drop when you reach the border."

"Harley, where are we going, exactly?" Andromeda had to ask.

"Every bit of ground you make to the west helps us with adjusting the focal point," Harley said and he pulled out a small map, folded in preparation for this moment. "See this road? From Kalemie, it goes north-west, given a few staggers, all the way to the Congo at Bogbonga. Stay on that road. Otherwise, you'll get trapped by the rivers."

"And then what?"

"And then it'll be June and if we all still exist, we'll need a new plan."

Within the hour, Harley was back in his helicopter and gone.

"Always inspirational when the commander-in-chief drops by," Maynard remarked.

*

The two gentlemen—agents of the US Treasury—sat with their hands clasped before them. They might have been waiting for the teacher to ask them the next question. The younger one was a very handsome, neat fellow, in a designer suit and wearing cufflinks embossed with the American Eagle. The older man was exactly what the younger man would become when he went bald in twenty years time, frequented the same tailor and wore the same cufflinks. Maybe they were a departmental job lot. Maybe they were a uniform. Joe Solomon had never met two such polite and obliging gentlemen in all his life. The very improbability of finding two such considerate souls in one American city made them suspicious in itself. They made you want to confess everything, just because they were so nice.

"I want to confess everything," Joe Solomon said cheerily.

They even took him to the hospital where he lured them into the morgue to watch while he identified the body. Val Dennis had no known relatives—apparently Joe's dubious status as 'colleague' was the nearest thing he could manage to a friend. Or at least, a friend who would willingly expose themselves to official channels. Joe considered the fact that he was under arrest and escorted by two US Treasury Agents at the time was most appropriate.

"He died of a cerebral haemorrhage, but you can see plainly how they beat him to a pulp," Joe said grimly. "A brilliant young man, top scientist, but he was a radical and independent soul who didn't want to devote his talents to making weapons. But that wasn't why they killed him. They killed him because they wanted Project Earthshaker. They wanted to control it. There was nothing he could tell them that they didn't already know. It was just that they didn't control the source of the data. They beat him to the point where he would be paralysed for life. If the haemorrhage hadn't killed him, he'd have been an permanent invalid. This is how we treat our brilliant young minds."

The two Treasury agents were as respectful of the dead as they were of the living. They stood by without comment while Joe Solomon delivered the eulogy of Val Dennis. He did so there, in the morgue at the hospital, because he knew there would be no chance at any graveside. Val Dennis had donated all of his body to medical science and insisted there be no funeral. The sad thing was that so few of his body parts would be of any use.

"We have to go now, Mr Solomon," the older agent said.

"I just wanted you blokes to be sure you know who you're working for," Joe said coldly as he spun his wheelchair around and led them out.

And so he continued to lead, for there were two other sets of agents, identical to these, who would accompany him everywhere he went from now on. And he could go anywhere he wanted.

At least there would always be someone to push the wheelchair, which was their own fault since they had deprived him of his motorised one.

"Take me to your offices," Joe insisted. "It'll save us all a lot of trouble."

They didn't interrogate him, not as such. There was no nice cop, nasty cop routine nor any of those techniques. They sat him down and gave him tea. The room was plush leather couches and coffee tables and they all sat about informally. No one took any notes, but there was a video surveillance camera on the wall with the red light on.

"There are just some broad questions we wish to put to you, Mr Solomon. You are under no obligation to answer them. Since you have not been formally arrested, nor warned of your rights, this interview cannot be used in evidence. The video recording is for reference only and is not considered admissible evidence in court."

"I want to confess everything," Joe insisted.

"You'll need to do that in writing, Mr Solomon."

"Bring me pen. Bring me paper."

"Perhaps it would be better if you answered our questions first, Mr Solomon."

"Ask away."

"We are interested in certain extensive properties you purchased on behalf of yourself or others in California and Nevada during the period from the 15th of December last year until the 19th of January this year."

"I bought every bit of land I could lay my hands on."

"And what have you paid for it so far?"

"Nothing. It's only been a month or so since purchase was arranged. The first payments aren't due yet."

"But, on the 15th of next month, the first payments will begin to fall due."

"Yes. Arrangements have been made for payment as they fall due."

"What arrangements?"

"There's a numbered account in a Swiss Bank."

"Are you prepared to provide us with details of that account?"

"Don't be bloody silly."

"Have you any idea what funds are available in that account?"

"No idea. But plenty."

"We find that hard to believe."

"There was too much money. I got tired of counting it."

"So you refuse to answer."

"No. I don't know the answer. And the account is arranged such that it can only be accessed by the claimants, for the sum claimed, for ten days after the date due."

"A curious arrangement, Mr Solomon. How was it made?"

"The bank's agents handled it. I know nothing."

"I see. Now. You seem to have arranged for all those properties to be divided into allotments and made available to certain persons."

"That's right. Anyone who lost property in the 19th of January disaster is entitled to an allotment, free of charge. The allotment of their choice, on a first come first served basis."

"You've given them the land."

"That's right. All persons whose property fell into the sea are entitled to an allotment."

"And what plans do you have for development of the allotments?"

"None. The government has provided reconstruction funding. I'm providing land for them to do that reconstruction on."

"Yes. So we understand. But... Mr Solomon, if you'll forgive me, we can't quite see how you intend to profit from these arrangements."

"There's a wide margin for profit. Built in is an agreement that if any of the allotments are exploited for profit, we own ten percent of it. It's likely to amount to a great deal."

"But if they just build a house and live there..."

"No charge."

"Well, there are matters of land tax and other charges..."

"It's up to the government to collect those, when and where and how it thinks appropriate."

"This is a very strange arrangement, Mr Solomon."

"Strange circumstances require strange arrangements."

"But, since the January 19 subsidence, the value of these properties has increased a hundred fold and more."

"That's right."

"Yet you claim to give them away."

"I do. I have."

"Still, you see how our suspicions are aroused."

"You Treasury blokes will always have a problem with generosity."

"Generosity. Yes. But tell me, in consideration of the increase of value of the properties, were they bought with prior knowledge of the increase?"

"Certainly."

"From what source was this knowledge obtained?"

"General press releases from Project Earthshaker."

"Project Earthshaker being Professor Harley Thyssen?"

"Project Earthshaker being Project Earthshaker."

"But Project Earthshaker did not exist at the time."

"Oh yes it did. It was just that the government tried to pretend it didn't exist."

"Nevertheless, it must be regarded that Project Earthshaker was embodied wholly or in part in the person of Professor Thyssen."

And finally, finally, Joe could see where they were going. It was almost disappointing to him. It wasn't him they were after at all. He was just a small fish. He was just the bait.

"Professor Thyssen played no part in nor had any knowledge of these transactions," Joe said coldly.

"Surely you were acting on his behalf?"

"Nope. Completely autonomous."

"Or with his permission."

"Professor Thyssen has no control or interest in my activities whatsoever."

"I see."

"No you don't. Professor Thyssen has never had any authority over me. He has never directed my activities in any way. He has never sought any information regarding my activities nor sought to guide them in any way. He has no idea about this still."

"He doesn't know that you are giving his property away?"

"Not his property. Never was."

"It was purchased for or on behalf of Project Earthshaker of which he is regarded as the executive authority."

"No. The Project is leaderless. All parts of it are autonomous. Professor Thyssen has no executive authority in the Project nor any authority over me or anyone else in the project whatsoever."

"A very improbable arrangement, Mr Solomon."

"We live in improbable times."

"All right then. Now, if we may, there are some interesting facts concerning your purchase of extensive properties in Brazil..."

*

They had been stopped continually throughout Zambia. The march had continued relentlessly at around seven miles a day by Maynard's calculations, and it had been ninety days since it began at the fall of the Malawian capital Lilongwe. At first they had travelled within their own country, roughly following the road that ran north parallel to Lake Nyasa, until Andromeda had returned from her conference with the Earthshaker group and turned them west, or at least slightly north of west.

On the day following Thyssen's impromptu visit, two very officious Zambian gentlemen arrived. They brought with them a huge stack of outstanding fines and duties to be paid. Such payment was to be made in US dollars.

"In Zambia, only bribes are to be paid in US dollars," Andromeda Starlight told them.

"You accuse us of taking bribes. This is outrageous. There will be further fines..."

"Captain!…" Andromeda called over their heads.

The immediate response was that Captain Maynard turned out twenty of his most heavily armed men, clumping into a line directly behind the two officials but they were not to be so easily intimidated.

"Lock and load," Maynard ordered, and his men responded with well drilled skill. The two officials turned now to confront the soldiers, while Andromeda towered over them behind. And then she saw the solution to the confrontation with a clarity that shocked her—after all, despite Thyssen's warnings, she was sure that it would not be right to fire upon these men, however corrupt they might be. The right answer was so obvious that she carried it out in the same instant she thought of it. All she had to do was reach forward, and with a grand sweep of her hands, cracked the heads of the two officials together.

They went down, both of them, in a rather awkward embrace. Andromeda stood over them triumphantly. Captain Maynard was staring at her in complete disbelief.

"I can't believe you did that," he murmured.

"Well, captain," Andromeda said with an assurance that she definitely didn't feel. "It sure was better than shooting them. In this part of the world, people get shot all the time, but how often does something like this happen?"

Maynard, still shaking his head in disbelief, called to a medic and between them they got the two dazed officials back onto their feet. Hastily, they rushed them off to their cars. Their drivers and attendants looked on in utter bewilderment. Then the cars were gone.

Maynard dismissed his men and walked over to Andromeda. She could shrug it off.

"I just did it on impulse. And maybe, when word of this little humiliation gets around, some of these jokers will be a little more reluctant to harass us."

"Oh yes," Maynard smiled. "I should imagine a lot of people will find this incident quite unforgettable."

"Being unforgettable is what they pay me for, Cap'n,"

Andromeda smiled.

But she proved to be right. There were no further Zambian officials after that.

*

And so it was back to the *House of the Golden Carp* where they could sit on the wide verandah and survey the countryside in the evening glow, served saki by the geishas in their colourful kimonos and lament upon the hardship of their lives.

"We never even went close to meeting the deadline," Brian said grimly.

Why did he bother? Wagner was wondering, looking at him sideways. They all did the same thing. Miracles immediately—the impossible takes a little longer. Harley asked and they tried to deliver, against all odds.

"Trouble with the government?" Wagner asked conversationally. He presumed that Brian would get around to explaining why he had been summoned here eventually. You just had to be patient with him.

"Not at all—well, you know how the Japanese are—it's all bowing and scraping and exchanging compliments but they need all that ritual to be polite because underneath they are just as inefficient as any bureaucracy," Brian said without the slightest consideration that it might have been a racist generalisation. "Anyhow, as I suspected, they were dead keen to get rid of the pilgrims. They've had to guard them day and night to protect them from gangs of hooligans anyway. Then, when Lorna went on the telly and did her magic cure routine, they were hooked. Y'know, she even learned her lines in Japanese. That impressed 'em."

"Always was a smart girl, that Lorna." Wagner said begrudgingly.

"Too smart for you and me," Brian said with a grin.

"What you gotta ask yourself is, will she be too smart for Harley too?" Wagner said with a sly grin.

"Yeah, I heard about that. Now that she's got to the top, where does she go from here?"

"Well, one day she'll be old and ugly and us guys will stop falling for her charms," Wagner laughed.

"Assuming, of course, that any of us get to be much older and uglier."

Okay, enough jocularity. Back to the serious stuff. Brian was so predictable.

"You don't believe, then, that Thyssen has a miracle up his sleeve?"

"Oh no," Brian laughed. "I know he does. The problem is, even if it does work, it's gonna be bloody nearly impossible to pull off."

"Tell me about this miracle," Wagner said, knowing fully what he was letting himself in for.

"It has to do with the Third Law of Thermodynamics."

"I thought there were only two."

"There were. Well, there are. It's only me and Harley who reckon there's a third one."

"Refresh my memory on the first two."

"The first one says the universe will remain constant forever. But there's small print, which says that what it really means is that the amount of material, or elementary particles, that make up the universe will remain the same. What it doesn't say is that those particles can change, from matter to energy or vice versa, and that the balance will not stay the same. There'll just be the same quantity of them. Then there's the second law, which says that eventually all particles will be converted into matter and there won't be any left as energy and the universe will become entirely dead matter. The Heat Death of the Universe. Entropy."

"Yeah, right," Wagner said. "Got all that."

"Okay. So, in very general terms, the stars continually produce Bosons and the Black Holes continually swallow stars. But every star is slowly dying, producing less Bosons, while black holes continually grow larger and more numerous. Every day, there are more Fermions and less Bosons, and that's been happening since the Big Bang."

"So it's inevitable."

"So it seems, except, there is one exception. Of course, the evidence is slight and we have only one sample planet to work with, but it seems one source of Bosons that is continually expanding, and that is *thought*."

"Thought?"

"Yes, well, call it what you like. Intelligence, sentience, cognisance. But I prefer to call it just plain *thought*. You see the neurons firing in your brain and every other brain are Bosons. Thought, whatever it is, generates Bosons."

"So you figure that one day we'll grow up to be big enough and nasty enough to take on black holes?"

"Precisely. Not soon, of course. But we can assume that wherever there are life forms and evolution is taking place, Bosons are being generated. And one day, us and all the billions of other beings from inhabited planets out there will be so numerous and widespread about the universe that the effect will be to reverse entropy."

"Holy Jesus. We're failing to save a planet and you're plotting to save the universe."

"Exactly. So that's the Third Law of Thermodynamics. Thought runs contrary to the Second Law and can overcome entropy."

Wagner, goggle-eyed, took one more saki than he might earlier have needed. "Now come on, Brian. Just exactly how much evidence is there to support this theory?"

"Not a lot. But, some scientists think there might be something in it somehow. And we do have absolutely no idea what thought is and how it functions. This is the best theory going around."

"And Harley thinks all this somehow has something to do with the Shastri Effect?"

"Harley is a sensible man with a strong scientific reputation to protect and he is admitting no such thing. But he's letting me get away with believing it."

"Well, I'll wait until Harley says so, if you don't mind."

"Suit yourself."

"Let's get back to the subject in hand, shall we?"

"Which subject was that?"

"About moving these difficult Japs."

"Oh, right. So *you* think the fact that Harley plans to move as many pilgrims as possible into the path of the Brazilian Shastri Event isn't the same subject."

"He's doing it because it'll cure them."

"I believe he has another reason."

"Like what?"

"Look, it's a random universe, right? Except here on Planet Earth where the laws of physics and maths work for us, despite the fact that they don't work in reality. There is only one possible explanation for that."

"That, somehow, we make those laws work."

"That's right. Whenever those random elementary particles fall under the influence of our collective consciousness, they conform to the rules by which our minds operate."

"You're kidding me, right?"

"Take it as serious as you like, mate. But I reckon Harley's idea is that, down there in the earth's core, there's a chunk of the random universe on the rampage. And he figures that if he can get enough people, with linked brains, all directing the same thought toward the singularity at the moment when it is most vulnerable and closest to us, we'll hit it with Bosons and force it to conform."

"Good God."

"And how will he get them all to think the same thing at the same time?"

"Because at this last instant, they'll all be feeling exactly the same thing at exactly the same time. Pain."

"Carrick, you are crazy."

"Yeah, maybe. Only I reckon I'm slowly becoming crazy in just the same way Harley is."

"If all this is so and Thyssen knows it, why doesn't he just come out and say so?"

"Because most people will react as sceptically as you are now, and right now he cannot afford to have people not taking him seriously."

"And you think that's his hidden agenda?"

"Yep. I reckon he figured all that out a long time ago and he's been working steadily towards it ever since."

Wagner groaned. Did this truly matter? All this shoving populations around like chess pieces. There was part of him that wanted to believe what Carrick told him. But the rest of him was bloody determined to keep the situation earthbound and manageable.

"Okay. So let's leave Harley to his fantasies and deal with the problem in front of us. What about the Brazilian end? How do they feel about copping all these Japanese immigrants?"

"Not a problem. They're all on tourist visas, off to Joe's El Rancho resorts. All them tourist dollars. Brazil said fine and dandy."

"Tourist resorts?"

"Well, mostly they'll actually be building the resort complex when they get there. But, anyhow, most of them are there already. They went like lambs, believing their troubles would be over. Of course, there were all sorts of religious rituals that they had to put themselves through and a hell of a lot of bureaucratic bullshit, but all that was just as well because the Japanese kept accurate records on them and at the end of the day, there were 1467 missing."

"Missing how?"

"Missing any way they could. All the ones that didn't want to go. Hiding under their beds, disguising themselves as someone else, or just taking off to the hills."

"And we gotta round up every one of them?"

"That's right. Just one gets left behind and the whole scheme turns to shit."

"Surely, if we get most of them...?"

"No way. The random universe isn't a democracy, Kev. We're dealing with some sort of collective consciousness here. So if there's just one bloke in a different place to all the rest, no matter how numerous the rest of them are, the focal point with fall halfway between the one bloke and the rest. The only way to control the position of the focal point is to get them all —every last one of them—to the same place."

"Shit."

"So every day, a few more are converted to the word of Lorna Simmons and turn themselves in, and there's an army of riot police out there rounding up a few dozen each day. There's down to eight hundred and something now, but its going too slow."

"Which is where I come in, I suppose."

"Yes, Kev. I've done all I can with my soft touch. Harsher and more direct methods are required now."

"How much co-operation can I expect from the locals?"

"It'll help if you can put the frighteners on them a bit. But anyhow, they have to be found and processed and shipped to Brazil by the 10th of April."

"That gives us a month. And there'll be another link before then, won't there?"

"Yep. But the Zone will be in Iran, which no one fancied as a good place to gather pilgrims."

"Still, it might have been interesting."

"I think you'll find you have enough on your hands here to keep you amused, Kev."

Wagner was beginning to understand the point of all this. "Do I detect that you are saying me and not we? I thought I came to help you out."

Brian thought that very funny. "I just wouldn't be comfortable giving you orders, Kev. No. You're in charge here. I'm pissing off."

"Pissing off where, exactly?"

"Italy. I'm going to help Chrissie move the Italian pilgrims to Brazil."

"Does she need help?"

"She might. Now that the Pope has said they can't go."

*

The wine tasted bitter in her mouth. She knelt before the icons and symbols of a religion that she no longer believed and Cardinal Luigi Valerno gave her the sacrament while speaking in Latin, not one word of which she understood. That had never seemed so appropriate before. She wasn't at all sure why she was doing this, carrying out this pagan ritual for the benefit of a soul that had made its commitment to another God. But Valerno had insisted.

"It would be improper for you to leave here, after all that has passed here, without taking the Holy Sacrament before you go," he said.

"But it no longer means anything to me," Chrissie protested.

"It will mean much to me, and the sisters here. They would be very disappointed if they hear that I let you go without our final blessing."

Anything to get out of here, she was thinking.

The wine tasted like poison to her, but she gulped it down and clasped her hands and bowed her head as if in prayer, and he placed his hand upon her skull. His hand seemed surprisingly warm and even sweaty. He spoke more Latin—she felt like a dog trying to comprehend spoken instructions. But all she was thinking was that in a few moments she would be able to leave this place, and Valerno, and all he stood for behind.

He had arrived in his red robes, full of reverent joy. "His Holiness is concerned about the Pilgrims, and believes they are in need of a strengthening of their faith."

"Their faith needs no strengthening..."

"But it does, Christine. A great temptation has been placed before them."

Chrissie chewed on her lower lip. In a weird way, she understood exactly what he was talking about. But she wasn't about to admit that. "There is no temptation."

"Look, I know Miss Simmons is a friend of yours..."

"A very good friend, Luigi, and more reliable than most."

"A woman who walks in sin, I'm told."

"That's the trouble with you, Luigi. You believe everything you're told..."

"But she has made false promises."

"How do you know they are false?"

"They contradict Scripture. What makes you think otherwise?"

"Because Lorna, unlike certain popes and cardinals, wouldn't lie."

"You can't be sure..."

"I can be sure. It's one of the few things I can still be sure of."

"But what she claims is ridiculous," Valerno spluttered. Plainly he had not expected this level of resistance.

"It worked. The result of a properly conducted scientific experiment."

"But what is being suggested here is the reversal of a miracle..."

"There was never any miracle, Luigi. The Shastri Effect was acquired. Now it can be unacquired."

"Miraculously acquired, Chrissie. You told the pilgrims that yourself."

"I changed my mind."

"Which you are at liberty to do. But you are also implying that God has changed his mind, which is untenable."

"Stuff and nonsense. Read Exodus, Luigi. And Jonah. God changes his mind more often than you change your knickers."

"The quotation of Scripture is not your domain."

"No, Luigi, that's true. My job is to lead the pilgrims and that's what I'll be doing. All the way to Brazil."

"Brazil."

"That's right."

"To take the cure."

"That's right."

"It will not be permitted."

"You can't stop it. Once the link occurs they'll be going that way anyway."

"I cannot allow this."

"*You* can't allow it?"

"The pilgrims must remain. They have become a symbol of... of..."

"Papal power, Luigi? That's just exactly why I'm getting them out of here."

"That isn't what I mean. You will be exposing these people to great danger, and all for a supposed experimental cure..."

"I'll be freeing them of the burden of these monthly pilgrimages."

"I see. And what happens after that?"

"They'll return here and continue their lives."

"There is a rumour that attempts will be made to convert them to a new pagan faith."

"Implying that Catholicism is not a pagan faith, I assume."

"A faith to which it is suspected you have been converted yourself."

"You mean Gaia?"

"If that is what the abomination is called."

"It isn't a religion. Just a rebalance of the facts..."

"That is not what we have heard. In Zambia, they tell me, millions of natives are following the false goddess Andromeda in a trek across the continent."

"Andromeda is a goddess only in the sense that showgirls usually are."

"You say it isn't so?"

"What I say doesn't matter."

"How can I dissuade you from this folly?"

"You can't Luigi. I may or may not be undergoing some sort of conversion to a new, more appropriate form of religious belief. I don't know. Maybe Andromeda does fancy herself as a goddess. That's up to her. But I do know one thing. I no longer have faith in you, Luigi, nor in your Pope. You have become meaningless and irrelevant to me."

"I see. And when will you depart?"

"From here. Now."

"Then you must allow me to offer you my blessing before you go."

"Oh really?"

"And that of His Holiness."

"I consider myself blessed."

"And the sisters desire that you take one last sacrament."

"You're kidding."

But he persuaded her in the end and she did it just to get rid of him. And when it was done, he crossed himself and turned abruptly and left. As he strode toward the nave and the side exit of the chapel, he dashed the contents of the sacramental cup on the floor and then wiped it with the sleeve of his red robe.

She was puzzled. Surely the cup should have been returned to its rightful place on the alter. Was he stealing it? Then she heard the clatter of its metal against the stone outside as he discarded it.

She suddenly felt strangely, ridiculously alone, kneeling there, for no reason, and still that very bitter wine taste in her mouth. But when she rose she found her knees unsteady. There was a nausea overcoming her, and a tingling feeling gushing through her bloodstream. She staggered a few steps and then looked back toward the alter. Was this God making one last bid to regather her faith? One last quizzical look passed across her countenance and then the pain gripped her and she screamed out as she doubled up, clutching her midriff, and fell to the floor. Somewhere out there, she could hear voices screaming, or perhaps it was the echo of her own...

*

Then they reached The Congo Republic. A fat man shrugged at them, standing outside the tin shed that was the border post. Behind him, thirty armed men stood in combat postures. Captain Maynard lined his men up in similar postures. In between, Andromeda and the fat man discussed the situation.

"It is impossible to enter The Republic of the Congo," the

man said in poor English.

Andromeda showed him the document Harley had brought her.

"It is a forgery. I must take it away to be examined," the man said and extended his hand. Andromeda put the right of passage behind her back.

At that moment, one of Wagner's C-130s passed overhead and six parachutes popped out. Rather than the usual food containers, six men dangled from the lines. Even the fat man was distracted from eyeing the document greedily.

The plane circled and then came in, to pass by only a hundred yards away, flying at exceedingly low height, so low in fact that it was almost touching the ground. The rear cargo bay was open and from in there, a large dark netted container, half the size of a house, slid out and dropped, skidding along the ground for a time before the lines towing it from the plane dropped. The C-130 lumbered away into the sky.

Spectators from both sides of the argument continued to watch the action pantomime play itself out before them. The six men, loosed from their parachutes, gathered about the container and went to work with heft haste, pulling away the netting, bursting the protective wrapping away. From in there, a Leopard tank emerged.

By then, Maynard had strode down and was speaking to the men. With well-practiced movement, they scrambled aboard, and immediately the gun turret swivelled and the huge barrel came around to point exactly at the fat man. Harley's toy had arrived.

"What is this?" the fat man blubbered, when it was all too plain what it was.

"A present for us from the President of the Republic of The Congo," Andromeda Starlight smiled.

The fat man and his troops immediately fled into the bush. Maynard came striding toward her with a huge smile on his face while the tank crew emerged to sit all over their machine and light jubilant cigarettes.

"Your turn to make a big impression, Captain," Andromeda

laughed.

"Bigger than you think," Maynard chuckled. "The tank needs its batteries charged before has any electrics so the crew had to rotate the turret into position manually. And it can't move it anywhere because it hasn't been fuelled yet. And they couldn't have fired anyway, because the ammunition isn't expected to arrive until sometime tomorrow."

*

When Brian Carrick arrived at the hospital in Salerno, Fabrini was there to meet him, in the company of a tall man, elegant in his dress and manner, white hair and beard immaculately trimmed. Fabrini introduced him as Enzo Severni, who Carrick presumed was a senior doctor or hospital administrator. Joe Solomon could have told him who he really was.

"An appalling tragedy, Mr. Carrick. Such a fine young woman."

They shook hands. Brian wondered how anyone could have such cool hands in so warm a climate.

"What the fuck happened?" Brian demanded.

The first thing he had seen when he arrived at Rome Airport was the smiling, serene image of Chrissie Rice on the television screen, and others of policemen and cardinals, saying things that, although he understood not a word of it, were all too plain. He bullied people until he found someone who spoke English and understood his panicky demands sufficiently to explain. Then the media who were gathering to ambush incoming dignitaries realised who he was and thrust microphones in his face as he pushed his way through to a taxi, abandoning his luggage to its fate.

"Get out of my fuckin' way," he grumbled and physically hurled them aside. The hated paparazzi—he wanted to slug one or two of them, or anyone really.

"The bastards killed her," Fabrini snarled, his eyes as dark as his drooping moustache.

"Now, Mr. Fabrini," Severni was saying. "There has been no post mortem examination at this stage. There is no evidence to support your claim at this stage."

"I don't need any evidence," Fabrini muttered, but to himself.

"Evidence of what?" Brian demanded.

Severni put an arm around Brian's shoulders and turned him to walk along the corridor, speaking in low tones.

"Eyewitnesses reported that the blood that ran from her nose was of a very bright coloration, and that her tongue was a strange shade of blue. My experience of such matters is slight but not to be completely discounted. I believe these symptoms strongly indicate cyanide poisoning."

"Jesus."

"And in such a strong dose that death must have been relatively instantaneous."

"Poor bitch," Brian said, but he was slowly realising that Severni's inexperience might not be so great as he suggested. "Okay, so let's have an autopsy. But why are you bothering?"

"There are many of us who had a very strong regard for that young woman."

"Yeah. It takes a very special sort of bastard to kill someone like her."

"Very special indeed," Severni agreed. "I understand from the nuns that a papal envoy administered her the Holy Sacrament shortly before she died. I have managed to obtain the goblet involved for forensic examination."

"You think the envoy poisoned her? On the orders of the Pope?"

"I doubt any such order could have been given, but perhaps Cardinal Valerno interpreted the Papal will that way," Severni said grimly.

"This Valerno," Fabrini muttered. "Where do I find him?"

"In the Vatican, I assume, Mr. Fabrini," Severni said. "But I believe we can leave that matter to the proper authorities."

"I just can't believe that anyone would kill her," Brian said, shaking his head as if trying to settle the idea into place.

"Christine was a person to whom one always suspected martyrdom would come naturally," Severni said reasonably. "Perhaps the killer believed he was carrying out the will of God."

"So they just hurried the inevitable along a little, huh?"

"Indeed. She had, I understand, become something of an embarrassment to the established order."

"Had she now?"

"I understand it was her wish to remove her flock from this country, and perhaps try to convert them to some new religious order."

"The first part is true. The second is irrelevant."

"Good. Then I believe it would be best if her wishes were carried out."

"I'll have a ship waiting for them in Naples on the 18th. The pilgrimage will carry them in that direction anyway."

"Fine. Mr. Fabrini. You will remain here and lead the pilgrimage. I shall make whatever other arrangements are necessary to ensure they reach Naples."

"I have business in Rome," Fabrini muttered.

"You will remain and lead the pilgrims, Mr. Fabrini," Severni said without adding any severity to his tone. "The people associate you with her. They'll follow you better than anyone else."

Fabrini said nothing. His eyes took on a sulky look that he dared not express.

They had arrived at a room where a nurse and a policeman stood like sentinels either side of the door and two burly individuals sat on chairs opposite.

"And now, Mr. Carrick, if you are able, we would like you to make the formal identification of the body."

"Why me?"

"It would be best if neither myself nor Mr. Fabrini were formally connected to this matter. And perhaps some advantage may be gained if the documentation was made to recognise the project with which you are associated."

"If you say so."

"She will remain in state until the next pilgrimage. Do you

wish to view the body alone?"

"Thanks," Brian said. He had no idea of how to address this man, certainly dared not call him Don, and so offered nothing except his hand.

"A pleasure to be of service. Even in such regrettable circumstances. Good luck, Mr. Carrick."

He turned and walked, taking Fabrini with him. Brian watched him depart for a moment and then turned to the nurse, who silently admitted him to the darkened room.

*

The Orion sat in the shimmering heat haze of the tarmac at Kuwait airport. It made you sweat just to look at it. In the coffee bar in the air-conditioned terminal building, the heat glared at them enviously from outside. Felicity stirred her Earl Grey tea and regarded Harley Thyssen grimly. Thyssen drank coffee, strong and black.

They had talked of Chrissie and of Jami in cold deliberate terms, neither allowing their emotions to show. They had talked of the estimated ten million deaths attributable to the Shastri Events. They maintained cold analytic terms, non-judgmental, unemotional. And now millions more were to die while they sat helplessly. They were dying now, even before the real terror began.

"They were the youngest of us, those two sweet girls," Felicity said, stirring her tea although she took no sugar. "It's so unfair."

"I'm sorry," Thyssen said grimly. "I seem to have grown completely immune to tragedy."

The Zone would be mostly located in the Caspian Sea where there had been little research to determine the presence of underwater volcanoes or fissures, but it would take in the southern coast, penetrating two hundred miles onto the land, engulfing the Elburz Mountains of northern Iran, one of the most populous regions of that country, and might even overwhelm the city of Teheran itself. Fifty miles from that city was one huge volcano—18,000 foot Mt Damavand, which would certainly erupt catastrophically. Another danger area was 500 miles away to the northwest where the borders of Turkey, Armenia and Azerbaijan interlocked—a region of many volcanoes dominated by Mt Ararat.

"Is that why you were able to risk Lorna's life in such a cavalier fashion?" Felicity said, because she was so frustrated and had to lash out at someone.

"I'll probably have to risk all of our lives before this is over," Thyssen said quietly. "In fact, I already am."

Together they had watched it all on the news, CNN by satellite, and it seemed that the news was all about them and yet, strangely, it wasn't. Because it was happening in America, Lorna Simmons came first, along with items concerning President Grayson's budget problems and difficulties with policing the world's trouble spots. A spokesperson expressed a fear that a new Waco, or worse, Jonestown, incident was brewing, based around Lorna's plea to all the Californian pilgrims to proceed to Brazil. An FBI chief assured the nation of his agency's readiness to move in take appropriate action. There was a medical man who declared that the pilgrims were medically normal and that their pilgrim status was almost certainly a mass delusion.

Two items later was a brief mention of Joe Solomon and how a judge had been unable to find any charges against him sustained. However, Mr. Solomon was still in custody, while another line of inquiry was being pursued regard in purchase of properties elsewhere. There were two other crooked billionaires who received similar treatment, and there was no mention of a possible connection between the activities of Lorna and Joe.

"Can they really be that stupid?" Felicity wondered.

"No," Harley Thyssen said. "They know exactly what they're doing."

Deeper in the bulletin, the death of an aging movie star was reported, and then that of Christine Rice, an Italian nun who was being considered by the Vatican for Canonisation, had died under suspicious circumstances. A funeral appropriate to so saintly a person was planned, and a few words from a Cardinal Valerno saying what a great loss to humanity she was. And, toward the end, graphic pictures of the mass migration of the Malawi people from their war-torn homeland across Africa. Professor Daniels of the Smithsonian pointed out that such migrations were common in the history of Africa.

There was discussion of whether the US should send food-aid. Andromeda Starlight appeared in the manner of those movie stars who visit starving regions on behalf of aid agencies. She said regular supplies of food were getting through for the moment. There was no indication that she might be more than a casual observer of the event.

The sports reports took them out of the spotlight for a few minutes, but then they were back again with the weather, unseasonably smoggy due to the high levels of dust in the atmosphere from the volcanic eruptions in Java, displayed against the backdrop of one of the remarkably brilliant sunsets being seen all around the world. There was even a meteorologist there to explain that such periods of excessive vulcanology had been noted throughout Earth's geological history.

"They got through it all without a single mention of either Project Earthshaker, or the Shastri Effect," Felicity said in amazement.

"Nor any suggestion that these matters might in some way be connected," Thyssen pointed out.

"Why are they doing it, Harley?"

"They're still hoping to get away with calling me a crack-pot."

"If only it was true," Felicity said without thinking, and then turned in horror as she realised.

"It's all right," Harley said sadly. "I'd like it to be true myself. Better a padded cell or academic odium than what really lies before us."

What the news broadcast didn't mention was the events

presently taking place in Iran, despite continual footage being shown on the local Kuwaiti network for which you didn't need to understand the language to grasp the essentials. The word had spread of the coming disaster and the population of northern Iran was scattering in all directions, but such was the nature of their history that they found enemies waiting no matter what border the refugees tried to cross. Massacres were taking place everywhere, including inside Iran as the military strove to maintain control. The Islamic Fundamentalist government cursed the Americans for the chaos they were trying to create in their country with their vicious rumours and malignant lies.

And, denied permission to enter Iranian airspace, the Orion waited it out in Kuwait, and Harley and Felicity with it. "I feel so helpless," Felicity said.

"You imagine there is something you can do to prevent this madness?" Thyssen asked her.

"If we can't do anything, what the hell are we doing here?"

"Just in case there's something we can do, that will help a little bit."

Felicity was stirring her tea again. She looked at him from under her brows and spoke very slowly and determinedly.

"Harley, stop being so bloody pragmatic for a moment, and tell me how all this effort is somehow worthwhile."

"You mean the whole project, don't you?"

"Yes. Tell me that Chrissie and Jami died for some decent purpose."

"I can't do that. The most probable outcome is that those people who believe me to be a charlatan have about a ninety percent chance of being proven right."

"Oh, thanks Harley. Thanks very much. So how the hell do you go on?"

"I'm in the ten percent, most of the time."

"Is that the best you can do?"

"On the face of the evidence, yes."

"Well fuck you, Professor Thyssen. Only let's drop the professor charade for a moment and let's have good old Harley, decent human being. What's he think?"

"He doesn't think because he doesn't exist."

"Don't evade me, Harley. I need this. Come on. Tell me about the ten percent. Tell me what you think might happen, or what you hope might happen?"

"I can't do that."

"Bullshit, Harley. You *won't* do it. But you must have some idea because you certainly do have a plan."

"Do I?"

"Yes. You plan to manipulate the Focal Point so it falls inside the Zone of Influence and cram as many pilgrims into the spot as you can. That much I know."

"Fine. I admit that."

"That's why you dumped Lorna in Sulawesi. You needed to be sure a pilgrim could survive a double dose of the Shastri Effect."

"That's right."

"And you got a better result that you expected, because in fact it cured her."

"Actually, we're not sure it did. We have to wait and see if the participants in the next linkage are also cured, not to mention unknown long term effects."

"Rhubarb, rhubarb. You can't tell me you don't believe it, Harley. You've dumped all those Japanese on Joe's Ranchos in Brazil. And I know you planned to move the Italians there as well..."

"Which is probably why they killed Chrissie," Thyssen said coldly.

"Oh no, Harley. You can't have it both ways. There's no evidence that anyone killed her."

"I killed her," Thyssen said. "Just as I also killed Jami."

"There's no proof that Jami is even dead."

"Still my responsibility..."

"Oh no, Harley. You couldn't have known how Jami would behave, and you have no idea how or why Chrissie died. I'm sorry. You just don't get away with blaming yourself all the time."

"I got them into this..."

"They got themselves in. And they both knew the risks. You coerced no one, and it wasn't your fault."

"I was giving the orders. I sent Jami up the mountains. I instructed Chrissie to move the Italians. My orders. My fault."

"One minute you try and tell us you're not in charge of the project, then you take full responsibility when it goes wrong. I'm sorry, Harley. You're being inconsistent."

"I thought you wanted my unscientific opinion."

"I do. But let's drop the maudlin crap and get back to the point. You're piling pilgrims into Brazil. Lorna is busily exporting every Californian she can into the place. Come on, Harley. What do you expect to happen?"

"They'll be cured."

"Cured merely to die three months later when the planet comes apart at the seams?"

"And to see what other effects might take place."

"Like what?"

"Like whatever happens."

"Not convincing, Harley. You aren't interested in curing pilgrims. That was just a fortuitous side-effect. That wasn't why you did it because you didn't know it offered a cure. There was some other reason why you did it."

"Anything we learn might help..."

"Help do what?"

"Whatever we can."

"Don't give me the run around, Harley. Brian told me all about it."

"What did he say?"

"That you're planning to try to kill a black hole. All by yourself. Super-Harley versus a planet-eating singularity."

"If it's a black hole..."

"Which is an interesting way of not denying it."

"Well, if there was some way of stopping that thing, it would be a pity if we didn't try and find it."

"Do you really think you can?"

"No. I definitely think I can't. Neither me nor anyone else."

"Then why are you bothering?"

"Because, if you haven't noticed, its the only chance we have."

"So you believe there's a connection between the Event and the Effect."

"That's the possibility I'm exploring."

"And you hope that somehow you can reverse the Shastri Effect and turn it back against it's source."

"No. I don't think that."

"But that is what you're setting up here."

"I guess."

"Without believing in it."

"Haven't you noticed that it's the only game in town?"

"Thank God for that."

"Felicity. This is no time for believing in miracles."

"Yes it is. You just said so. If a miracle is the only chance you have, then all you can do is go for it."

"Elegantly put."

Felicity drank her tea in a single triumphant gulp. And then leaning back in her chair, she smiled. "You've heard that theory, haven't you, that rocks are actually living things but just with too slow a metabolism for us to be able to recognise it for what it is."

"Yes. I've heard the theory."

"Well, Harley Thyssen. I think we've just seen the living proof of it."

"Oh really? How?"

"Because, in case you didn't notice, I just managed to get some blood out of a stone."

*

It is possible to live in California without a house, but not without a car. Even those who still prevailed in tents on farm properties in the general area between Mexicali and Mojave Desert, and the region around San Francisco, first needed a car to fetch the tent. Detroit's surplus was swallowed at a single gulp, and any caravan for sale anywhere in the United States was snapped up and towed to the increasingly crowded beauty spots on the San Joaquin or the California Aqueduct and all along the San Luiz Canal. All settlements doubled and tripled their populations, all accommodation was devoured and extended and the outskirts were swallowed by enormous shanty towns. Four million refugees were housed wherever it was possible to house a person, everywhere except the one region at the centre.

There was a circle that swung from just south of Bakersfield to just north of Fresno, and from Coalinga on the coast to Coyote Peak in the Sierra Nevadas, around which the National Guard and the US Army had joined forces to throw a cordon and very hurriedly built a cyclone wire fence and barbed wire entanglements. When the sleepers awoke, they found they were prisoners in their own homes. Thousands of aid workers prowled amongst them, keeping them comfortable and maintaining drips until they woke. Then the sleepers were free to go about their lives, provided they stayed within the 440 mile diameter circle that encompassed them. For most, after they had repaired the earthquake damage to their homes, not a lot changed. Except they paid very close attention to the things Lorna Simmons said on television.

"When the time comes," she told them over and over, "get in your car or ask your neighbour for a lift—it'll be okay because you'll all be going the same way. We're heading due north by the compass because the Focal Point is up near the Magnetic North Pole but there's no need to go that far. Head out toward Yosemite National Park where we can have some nice picnics along the road, and then it gets a little complicated but all that volcanic dust in the atmosphere means the snows are melting early and we can get over Tioga Pass and onto US395, heading for Carson City and Reno. You'll know when the time comes. A day and a half later, you'll just turn around and come home again, if you want to. Don't forget to have a nice time."

Just ten miles outside Fresno, the Highway Patrol stopped

them at the road block and refused to let them pass. The stationary convoy built up back beyond Tulare. Lorna watched it all happening from a helicopter as she was flown to the scene. In her mind were sad thoughts of Chrissie as she prepared to lead her own pilgrimage.

"You just stand yourself ahead of them, the people at the front see you and the word spreads like wildfire and they all follow. It's amazing," Chrissie had said. The words gnawed at Lorna's brain as much an anxiety clutched her stomach. It was so much easier doing these things through the filter of a television camera—facing a mob of real people was something else again.

The helicopter banked in toward the twin black belts of the highway. The vast clutter of people, vehicles and trailers piled with belongings obliterating the roadway and spilling off the edges on one side, the clear open road on the other. The Highway Patrol had made a barricade of twenty cars, and they huddled behind them with their guns drawn. Already, the pilgrims had dropped the trailer off a big rig and were positioning the prime mover up to the front to ram their way through. The helicopter was equipped with a loudspeaker and Lorna was shouting into the microphone.

"This is Lorna Simmons. Please stop what you are doing, everybody. I'm coming down. Everyone stay where you are and stop whatever you're doing."

Magically, all of the frenzied movement on the pilgrim side of the line ceased and people and police alike paused to look upward at the helicopter. Lorna smiled. Thank you, Chrissie, she breathed.

The Highway Patrol Captain came down to meet her as the helicopter landed behind the line.

"We got a situation here, ma'am," he said urgently. "Sure appreciate your help or else I don't know what woulda happened."

"Why don't you let them through?" Lorna demanded of him.

"We got orders, ma'am."

"The person who gave you the orders does not understand

the situation," Lorna said. "They have to go. It's compulsive. If your men start shooting, they'll just keep coming until you run out of bullets and then they'll walk right over you. Don't you understand that?"

"I was gettin' that impression."

"Then let them through."

"Can't do it ma'am."

"Look, what on earth do you think is going to happen?"

"Durned if I know."

"Then I'll tell you. They'll just make their way down the highway toward Nevada until sometime tomorrow morning when they'll stop and turn around and come right back again."

"That don't make sense, ma'am."

"Still, that's what will happen. There won't be any problem."

"You can't be so sure of that."

"Captain, what harm are they doing? Just driving on the state highways, minding their own business."

"Waal, to start with, it's a convoy, ma'am, and you gotta have a permit."

"It isn't a convoy. It's just a lot of individuals who all happen to be going the same way."

"I'm sorry, ma'am. I got my orders..."

Lorna stamped her foot with frustration. Her eyes flared and her hair glinted fire in the sunlight. At least, that was what she hoped happened. "Captain, you can't massacre people just because they want to go for a drive. How will you live with yourself, shooting down so many unarmed people?"

"I just can't stand by and let them break the law."

"You mean you can't be seen to back down."

"I mean..."

"Look, Captain, all you have to do is order your men not to shoot. You can explain it to your superiors that on the grounds that you didn't believe the circumstances justified gunning down honest unarmed citizens."

"I guess."

"And then get your men out of the way because we don't

want to hurt any of them either and that rig is coming through."

"We can't let you wreck all them cars, ma'am."

"Then move most of them. We'll just dent a couple so you'll be able to say you stood your ground but we broke through."

The Captain scratched his nose and screwed up his face, looking around in utter discomfort. The rig was roaring its engine. His men where all beginning to shout encouragement to each other as they levelled their weapons. "You ain't bluffin', are you ma'am?"

"I assure you, it's no bluff. These people are under a compulsion to move that they cannot resist and they are not able to back down."

The Captain thought it through again and came up to the same anxiety. "Waal, ma'am. I always enjoyed bein' a patrolman better than this desk job. You got a deal."

"Maybe you could even give us an escort."

"Waal, ma'am. I ain't so sure about that."

"And you can supervise it all from my helicopter."

"Heili-copter, ma'am. Why, in that case, you got a deal."

He hurried back toward the siege, waving his arms and shouting wildly. "Okay, hold your fire. Don't nobody shoot nobody. Get these cars outa here. Leave those. Come on, snap to it. And for God's sake, these are just plain folks so no firin'."

And the rig roared and ploughed through the fenders as the patrol men scattered. As the rig came by, it paused and Lorna swung up onto the tail, beckoning all behind her to follow.

*

Brazil and Sulawesi both straddle the equator and are at exactly opposite sides of the earth, but the Pacific Ocean is wide and along that line is almost the greatest possible distance between them. Moreover, since the part of Sulawesi inhabited by the sleepers there, and the section of the Matto Grasso to which the Japanese pilgrims and many enterprising Californians who wished to go now occupied, are both slightly south of the equator and the Earth being not round but an oblate spheroid, the east-west line placed them even further apart. The shortest way is south, via Antarctica, but of course that placed the European and American pilgrims, along with those few hundred the Kevin Wagner's team relentlessly pursued in Japan, and Andromeda Starlight's hordes, a vast distance away. The next best option, creating a great circle that passed through Sulawesi and Brazil and incorporating the locations of the other groups, was over the Arctic circle. And so the Focal Point moved north again, to locate itself near Prince Patrick Land, by coincidence almost exactly on the Magnetic North Pole.

Harley Thyssen had forgotten to tell Brian Carrick about that until they discussed their plans by satellite telephone just a few days before the linkage. Which, on the whole was rather fortunate, for ignorance allowed Brian to misinform a lot of people of the direction the Italian pilgrimage would go, without having to actually lie to anyone. It might have been the only means by which a man like Brian Carrick could have perpetrated such a deception.

For there were big plans made on the basis of Brian's ignorance. The pilgrimage was to be combined with the state funeral of Christine Rice—Saint Chrissie as the media now always referred to her although no murmuring of beatification had officially emerged from the Vatican—and there would be a great possession. It would begin at the convent and make its way west (following the line of Brian's mistaken belief) through Naples and on to Rome. St Chrissie, lying in state in an open coffin, would lead the pilgrimage for the last time. It was when Thyssen heard these plans on the news—he was busy at the time arranging matters in Brazil—that he had urgently called Brian and put him straight.

"Don't worry about it, mate. We can work around that," Brian told him.

Brian immediately called Severni and they quickly revised their plans. The pilgrims had filed by the body in the first few days after her death as she lay in state in the convent, but immediately that was done, a shop mannequin was substituted with a waxwork face provided by Severni, and the actual corpse was privately interred. The matter was carried off with the greatest secrecy and only three outsiders attended the quiet sad funeral— Felicity Campbell stood by the graveside with Harley Thyssen on one arm and Brian Carrick on the other. They stayed briefly afterwards, before hurrying away to their respective tasks. The secrecy prohibited the attendance of Lorna Simmons.

When the time for the linkage came, the Italian pilgrims set forth, following the shopwindow dummy mounted on a stately carriage and pulled by two white horses. The pilgrims followed in the customary convoy of trucks and wagons and bicycles and motor-scooters and a few crowded cars and only the most acute observer might have noticed that there were twice as many of them as before. Outside Salerno, half the group broke away from the main procession and headed north through the mountains, toward the north coast road where they had travelled so many times before, but this time when the reached the coast, Brian Carrick had a sea-going ferry waiting to carry them away to Brazil.

The fake pilgrims, diligently arranged by Severni, continued to follow the fake body of St Chrissie to Rome, where Cardinal Valerno had made the finest Papal funeral arrangements possible, with all due pageantry, for he, as much as anyone, had cried for Christine Rice. His guilt and shame consumed him and threw him into the work in a frenzy, for he had done what he had to do, what he had been instructed to do, but that did not make it right. When it was over, he had determined, he would quietly take his own life and leave the justifications of his actions to that higher court, to make of it what they might. He was prepared.

As is happened, he need not have bothered, for one evening, just before the linkage was due, as he hurried through the colonnade of St Peter's, where the wind gusted at his robes and scuttled the leaves on the terrazzo, a man stepped into his path. Luigi Valerno frowned, realising he knew the man but the moment that he took to recognise Fabrini was one that he could not spare. Fabrini, his drooping moustache gleaming with sweat, his eyes two spots of black fire, made a single upward thrust that took Valerno just under the breastbone and was firm enough to lift the cardinal onto his toes. The long blade penetrated unerringly into his troubled heart and then Fabrini made a series of jerks and twists with his hand, and the razor point of the blade tore Valerno's heart and lungs to shreds.

Fabrini released the bone handle of the knife and hurried on about his business, not even looking back to watch his victim fall. Valerno's hand replaced the killer's about the handle and, staggering backwards until he hit the wall, he pulled it out and threw it aside. It clattered ringingly on the marble floor. The red robes that they said were so to hide the blood did no such thing and it flowed a great red stain down the front of him. Valerno slid down the wall, his mouth opening and closing like a landed fish, his arms spread, until he sat, understanding what had been done to him fully, wondering how they were going to explain it. Then the pain exploded like a hand grenade within him, and that was what he carried away with him, screaming all the way to eternity.

*

Even the tone with which the airconditioning breathed throughout the building seemed to be whispering conspiracies. People here probably conspired over how much sugar they had in their coffee and whether they read the back page of the newspaper first. It was the US Embassy in Kuwait, where anyone who wasn't a spy was not properly qualified for employment. The Deputy Ambassador, if that was what he was called and who he really was, was flanked by two very handsome young men in very nice suits. They might as well have been wearing armbands with CIA written on them, except Thyssen supposed they were something far more sinister than that.

"It was good of you to come, Professor Thyssen," the Deputy said.

"Did I have a choice?" Thyssen asked flatly.

The biggest earthquake in recorded history, 10.6 on the

moment-magnitude scale, had hit northern Iran. Yet he had left Felicity in the coffee lounge at the airport, waiting for the Orion to be cleared to move.

"I'm afraid that I have to inform you that permission for your team to enter Iran has not been forthcoming."

"I take it the Ayatollah has not yet admitted that the disaster occurred."

"They have called for aid and the United Nations, and indeed the US Government is responding. But the assistance of your team will not be required."

"According to whom?"

"My instructions come direct from the highest level of the Iranian Government."

"Argue with them."

"Professor, your team is not undervalued in this situation, please understand that. But it is their country."

"It's our planet."

"Not all of us are privileged to cross international boundaries as freely as your people seem to, Professor. But in this case, the wishes of the Iranians must be respected."

"And what if I chose to ignore them?"

"Your aircraft will be shot down should it enter Iranian airspace. They aren't kidding. And since your aircraft is unarmed, very slow and the only one of its type in the region, I doubt you'll get very far."

"Have you spoken to President Grayson about this?"

"The President is aware of the matter."

"Get him on the hot line. Let's see if he's willing to say so to me."

"That will not be possible... I hardly think an expression like hot line is meaningful these days anyway."

"Those people are in terrible trouble. The expertise of my team is superior to all other assistance they might be offered."

"With all due respect, Professor, the emergency teams in place have now had considerable experience as a result of working with your people and feel they will be able to cope."

"So we just sit on our asses and let innocent people die."

"We suggest—we strongly suggest—that you return to the United States immediately."

"I intend to. And I'll be hammering on the White House door when I get there."

The Deputy half-turned to the man standing beside him, who immediately removed a long envelope from his inside pocket and presented it to Thyssen. Thyssen was able to ignore it.

"This is a subpoena ordering you to appear at a Senate Inquiry into the activities of one Joseph Solomon, with whom we understand you are an associate."

"Waste of time. I'll take the fifth to all questions."

"You haven't heard the questions..."

"No. But you have heard the answer. But in case I didn't make myself clear, go fuck yourself, and you can stick your subpoena where the sun don't shine."

"These gentlemen have been ordered to remove you to the inquiry by force if necessary."

"It won't be necessary. I'll be there. Somehow I suspect you won't deliver the message with quite the same emphasis that I will."

16
THE JAPANESE PIMPERNEL

Kevin Wagner grimly regarded the rag-tag bunch of people brought before him. Fourteen in number, a cross-section of humanity, Japanese style—men and women, old and young and three children of indiscernible sex. They were dirty and exhausted, dressed in rags, and shuffled as prisoners do when herded by armed soldiers. Captain Tonishu handed him a clipboard on which there was a long list of names, with crosses beside the fourteen that presumably belonged to these folk.

"Where did you find them?" Wagner demanded coarsely of the police captain.

"They were in Hondo's Shrine, on Mount Fuji. They had run out of water and someone saw them when one of them tried to get to the spring."

Wagner nodded grimly. Poor bastards. If they irritated him beyond imagining, still, once confronted with the unfortunate reality of these folk, he shook his head in dismay.

"There are three other groups of similar number, we think, hiding out in shrines. My men are searching them one by one, at this very time," the captain continued.

"Thank you, Captain. And again, thank your men for their efficiency. But once more warn them that time is running out."

"Only sixty-three escapees remain to be found. The locations of at least half of them are known to us. They will be found."

"And only eighteen days left in which to find them. Every last one of them, Captain."

"In time, they will all be found."

"In eighteen days, they will all be found, and on the plane

and gone from here. It's crucial."

"Yes, Mr Wagner. This I try to impress upon my men. But it is hard for them. They have found so many. There are so few remaining to be found. And they do not understand the reason for haste."

"Neither do I," Wagner mumbled and the captain's eyes widened. Wagner inwardly cursed and then strove to cover his error. "What I mean is, those who are not found will miss out on receiving the cure and may remain afflicted for the rest of their lives."

"Yes. So I understand."

"Okay," Wagner said with a dismissive wave. "Leave these to us. Find the rest, and hurry."

The captain bowed obedience and Wagner nodded his head in faint reply. When the policemen were gone, Wagner did not need to do anything. Everyone had been through the procedure enough times to know what to do without being told. The geishas rushed into the room immediately and within a short time, the captives would be washed and dressed and fed. There was a doctor and two nurses to assure their health and administer injections. There were three Japanese officials on the fulltime staff to facilitate identification, passports, visas and other travel arrangements. There were gifts for all, to placate them and assure them that Project Earthquake would generously reward them for their co-operation. Within four hours, they would be processed and at the airport, ready for the next JAL flight to Rio De Janerio. Fifteen thousand, eight hundred and forty-one had travelled thus in the last two months, these fourteen plus sixty-three more and every sleeper would be gone. But the fewer the number became, the harder they were to find.

Yet they all wanted to go, because they were vilified in their own land and Brazil promised a cure and an end to their torment. Those that held out did so for personal reasons—criminals more afraid of the police than the mobs, drug addicts afraid to be separated from their dealers, people who would not leave their dogs or other pets or get too far away from their favourite shrine, old folk who had never left Japan and were determined they never would.

Only they had, since old people were easier to find. All pets were now transported with their owners. Japan's first official heroin dispensary now operated in the *House of the Golden Carp*, there were temporary pardons arranged. It had been a phenomenal feat of administration and it had worked, except for sixty-three people hiding out for sixty-three reasons that no one had thought of yet.

"These people are all of one family," Tamiko, the counsellor, informed him, for all along she had been interviewing them in urgent terms. "The daughter was to be married next month. The family wanted to remain until after the wedding. The groom is not afflicted. It would be a bad omen to postpone the wedding."

"A month will be too late," Wagner told her. "Tell them the wedding need not be postponed. We will fly them back in time for, and meet all added costs for the inconvenience."

"I will tell them so."

With the wisdom of Solomon, so Wagner commanded. Promise them whatever was necessary to assure their co-operation—that was the way forward. He had no idea whether such promises could be kept. That would be up to his underlings. With a sweep of his hand, Wagner made a data bank full of such promises, all of them the easy way out of whatever situation they faced.

"And see it is done," Wagner told her.

The girl bowed and left and the nurses came to lead the captives out. Sixty-three to go. Eighteen days. Wagner's head buzzed. But not so much that he did not take the trouble to give them one last look over.

He wanted to contemplate Miss Tamiko and the secret pleasures that they would share again that evening. Only vaguely did he mentally check the captives off as they filed out the door.

He cursed, and immediately rushed through the doorway. "Keep them here!" he roared at Tamiko. He charged out onto the balcony and leaned out. In the car park below, Captain Tonishu was just climbing into his vehicle.

"Tonishu, you idiot! There's only God-damn thirteen of 'em!"

*

It was probably for the best that Harley Thyssen was not required to appear before the Senate. Clyde Pascoe, the leader of the team of attorneys whom Joe had employed to undertake the case, was able to read a statement from Thyssen and that he wished to take the 5th Amendment and on those grounds did not wish to answer any of the Senator's questions. The gentlemen on the high bench, seated all in a row like bottles on a shelf waiting to be knocked down by whomsoever dared, consulted, protested, but then adjourned. When they convened next morning, it was agreed that it would be sufficient that Professor Thyssen's statement be read into the record.

"How'd you manage that?" Joe asked Pascoe in the next break in proceedings.

"Harley planned to put into the record an accusation that President Grayson knew all about Project Earthshaker's activities and approved the payments himself."

"You mean he wasn't going to take the fifth?"

"Since he's Norwegian, not American, I don't think he can. But anyhow, can you imagine Harley doing something like that?"

"No."

"Nor would he. He planned to get acknowledgment of Earthshaker into the record and then let them fight over it."

"They wouldn't have let him..."

"The important thing about a show trial is you make sure you control what gets shown."

"And where does that leave me?" Joe asked, though cheerfully.

"In the toilet. You're all they've got now. Since you deny all knowledge of the original source of the funds and since you refuse to incriminate Thyssen, that just leaves you out on a limb."

"I can handle that."

"Are you sure? Is he worth protecting like this? After all, he has happily landed you right in it."

"I'm not protecting Harley. I don't really know whether I trust him or even care about him myself. Although I do admire him. It's the project I'm protecting."

"But the project is Thyssen."

"So they would have you believe. And they ridicule him and call him a fake and a liar and therefore discredit the project in the eyes of the public. It seems that no amount of truth and evidence can combat media lies."

"Are you sure he's not really a very charismatic crank?"

"Is that what you think?"

"It's not my role to have such an opinion."

"And the evidence you've seen doesn't convince you otherwise."

"I'm not sure. Maybe it does. But I don't wish to believe what the evidence tells me. *That* doesn't bear thinking about."

"Oh I see. Better to believe the lie than face unpalatable facts."

"Yes, Joe. I think so. If Thyssen and all those other Loony Tunes are right and the planet is about to blow itself up and there isn't a damned thing we can do, why worry yourself to death about it? Better to just ignore it and carry on normally."

"All the other Loony Tunes are Loony Tunes, Clyde. Every fucked-brain fanatic in the world has hopped on this bandwagon. Only Harley is not one of them."

"He seems like one of them."

"They make him seem like one of them."

"In this age of media domination, Joe, it's the same thing."

*

Another family group, seventeen members this time spanning four generations, recumbent about the single room. Wagner would have thought they were sleeping, had he not known they were dead. Outside a clutter of ambulances and police cars stood waiting helplessly, and the paramedics who had been first on the scene now stood back, smoking, and averting their gaze.

"They are waiting for forensic, but I can tell you what happened," Captain Tonishu said bitterly. "They waited until the children were asleep and then burned the candles you see on the table which were laced with a chemical, turned to a poisonous gas by the flame. It is a common enough method in this country, sure and relatively painless."

Wagner, from a distance, gazed upon the faces of two small children that were turned toward him. Pain and fear showed there plainly. The poor kids had wakened in the last moments of life and had known...

"And they were all on our list?" he asked, to be sure of the obvious.

"Oh yes. They left this message."

He held up a scroll with the square of carefully painted characters—the mass suicide note must have taken hours to write.

"How can this happen?" Wagner asked the room in general, ignoring the message.

"It is a common enough occurrence," the captain said in his flat dispassionate tone.

Perhaps, Wagner liked to think, it was the man's unsure command of English that make him sound so heartless. "In Japan, the suicide rate is very high, especially amongst the young. Many of those removed from our list did so by this means. This is only the most shocking case and I thought it would be best if you saw it."

"Thank very much," Wagner said in disgust.

He remembered now, lines drawn through names with the symbol for suicide placed by Tamiko. He had ignored it at the time. Just another one we don't have to find, he thought. And perhaps the Captain knew that, or suspected it, and he brought him to see this to place him more in touch with the reality. Perhaps, just as the captain seemed to lack compassion to him, so did he to the captain.

Three more groups and a number of individuals had been

located and processed and were on their way to Brazil. Before this happened, the list had been reduced to twenty-eight, plus one. Katsumi Sukurai, a young man, had been captured three times and each time escaped—he was on the run again.

He had escaped from the airport when he was found to be missing from the flight manifest, he had escaped while being transported to the police station, he had escaped from the *House of the Golden Carp* when the rest of his family had been brought in. *You can't leave even one behind*, Thyssen had told him, and Wagner knew that and wondered. Katsumi Sukurai was the subject of his worst nightmares—until this.

Wagner turned, leaving the room and its horrors, and walked out into the sunlight.

"Don't you want to know what the message says," the captain asked as he hurried after Wagner.

"No!" Wagner said ruthlessly. "But I guess you better tell me anyhow."

The captain had not brought the document with him. He had carefully replaced it where it was found, for the benefit of the official investigators. But he could recite it.

"It sought many blessings from spirits and friends and asked their forgiveness for the sorrows to follow. It said that they had heard that the American press reported that Professor Thyssen was a mad scientist conducting unnatural experiments on human subjects. It said they wished to take this more honourable path to the cure of their wandering disease."

Mad scientist, Wagner heard an inner voice shriek. Unnatural experiments, it shrieked again. Bastards. The lies were always most dangerous when they paraphrased the truth.

*

For the first time since his arrival in Washington a week ago, Thyssen discovered he was alone. It was hard to credit really. His watchdogs—a rotating roster of indistinguishable Secret Service agents—declared that threats had been made against his life and that he was in protective custody. The difference between that condition and house arrest, which had been his status last time he'd been here and even in the same room—who could forget 3333—at the same hotel, was that arrest meant the guards stayed outside his room and he wasn't allowed to leave whereas protective custody apparently permitted them to be right there in the room with him. But he could go anywhere he liked, with one man before and one after and two more prowling wide on the flanks.

He didn't have anywhere he wanted to go and certainly not with them, but each day they took him someplace else where he was questioned by different people—Treasury, Senate advisers, FBI, tame scientists and someone named Cornelius who didn't seem to belong to any agency at all. They were all very friendly and so he answered all of their questions with absolute honesty.

"Yes, President Grayson knew about the funding. He told me so personally."

"The president denies it."

"It happened in the Oval Office. Am I to assume such conversations are no longer taped?"

"Not since Nixon."

"Very wise."

"Did you know the source of the funding?"

"Of course not. Grayson just said funding would be made available and it suddenly turned up in our bank account."

"And you didn't ask."

"I didn't care."

"And what instructions did you give Mr Solomon in regard to the funds?"

"None."

"Yet he was acting under your orders."

"At no time was he under my orders."

"I don't think the senators will be satisfied with that answer."

"The truth rarely pleases politicians."

"But I thought you were going to take the 5th Amendment?"

"I changed my mind. I'm going to tell them the truth, the

whole truth and every bloody bit of the truth."

"You'll go to jail."

"Bad luck."

"You'll blow your whole damned project right out of the water."

"Yeah, and Grayson and all you bastards along with it."

On the eighth day, they stopped interviewing him and he heard on the news that he had taken the 5th Amendment by proxy. Apparently he was unable to attend the hearing on health grounds. A mental disorder seemed to be the nature of the complaint. Next day they brought him to this nondescript building, not far from the Pentagon, he noticed. They rode and elevator that plainly lied about what floor they were going to and he was escorted down a corridor to an unmarked doorway.

"In there," the secret service man said and Thyssen went through, and his guardians did not. In the dimness, he waited for his eyes to adjust.

The room was huge and might have been the control room at NASA. Rows of computer screens offered the same screen-saver—that of a quietly rotating earth viewed from space. Thyssen thought he must remember to get one of those before he left. There were nine rows of tables, each with ten operator positions, each row stepped below the next so at they all had an unimpeded view of the massive screen facing them. There was a map of the world, with tactical spots marked. The locations of the eruptions were marked in red, the locations of the sleepers were marked in yellow, blue circle indicated the Zones of influence for each event, green indicated individual volcanoes, white the predicted future locations. Which, he could immediately see with a smile, were all wrong. But impressive, nevertheless.

He stepped forward to the nearest monitor and touched the keyboard blindly. The screen immediately offered his own version of the map. Stooping only minimally, Thyssen moved the mouse and clicked on the red dot over Japan. A regional map appeared with about thirty markers. The red one was the *House of the Golden Carp*. Click on that and he got a list, PEO looked promising and he tried it—Project Earthshaker Operative, it meant and a complete dossier on Wagner appeared. Thyssen, bent more severely over the table, refusing to sit in the chair so that he had to reach over to get at the mouse. He backed out and tried OSP. Right on— Outstanding Personnel. It listed the nineteen Japanese sleepers that Wagner was yet to locate.

"Ten bucks says he doesn't make it," a voice said quietly from the far side of the room.

Thyssen raised only his eyes and peered in the direction of the voice. It sounded familiar, slightly, but when he saw the figure, it took him far longer than it should have to realise who it was.

"I don't know you," he said and returned his attention to the screen.

"I thought all teachers remembered all of their students."

"It's an illusion. All students are alike. You can tell the same story about each of them."

"What story is that?"

"First they know nothing. Then you teach them everything they know. Whereby they grab their bit of paper, forget everything you said and sell their asses to big business."

"Some asses buy more than others."

"They're all for sitting and shitting."

From across the room came more laughter than the remark justified. "It is really good to see you again, Harley. You don't know how long I've waited for this."

"It only been six months since you sold us out, Glen."

"I didn't sell you out. I was hi-jacked. But then they offered me this. How could I refuse?"

"Did I forget to give my lecture on loyalty?"

"My option was them or nothing. I took them. They pay well and the work is interesting. And look at this, Harley. Look around you. And it's all mine."

"Yeah. But who owns you?"

"The government. The duly elected government of this country."

"You're using the taxpayer's money to spy on my project and

find out what I would freely have told you anyway."

"Bullshit, Harley. You kept secrets. You didn't tell us everything."

"Sometimes I'm forgetful."

Glen advanced now, three rows down and halfway around the room, but into better lighting. He was nearly unrecognisable. The long hair, moustache and wispy beard were gone, and the hippie duds were traded for silken shirt and snappy trousers. When he stood with his hands in his pockets, he looked like a model in a Calvin Kline advertisement. He was handsome enough to make the cut as well.

"Look at all this, Harley," Glen said again. "All this is yours."

"I wouldn't be happy here, Palenski. It's too orderly. I like it messy."

Glen pushed some papers and files on the desk beside him and let them fall on the floor. "We could mess it up a bit."

"It isn't a matter of messing up. It the notion of things having a right place that I object to."

"Everything has to be somewhere."

"Yeah. And where you last used it is where you're most likely to find it."

"Think of how efficiently you could operate from here," Glen said again. "Go on. Try it."

"I tried it. It's nice. But the price is out of my range."

"Have a try. It's an awesome system..."

Thyssen, standing straight, reached with a minimal finger and touched out keys. He typed a code to open a dialogue box, inserted the user name HORSESHIT after which a row of asterisks appeared as he entered a password. Glen was able to press a single key to bring it up on his own screen.

"It isn't like you to be vulgar, Harley."

Then, after an slight pause, the system jumped to life and encrypted data burst onto the display.

"Shit, what's this?" Glen asked in amazed.

"It's where I stashed a bunch of private files on Val Dennis's system," Thyssen said quietly.

Glen was thrown for only a moment, but it was enough for Thyssen to see the point was lost on him.

"You see. Like I said. We got everything in here."

"You bastards murdered him for this."

"Nobody murdered him..." Glen sighed, but he looked back at the screen, perplexed for an additional instant.

"Oh I see. He stole his own data and gave it to the very people he opposed with every microbe in his body and then he wrecked his own system and beat himself to death."

"It wasn't like that," Glen said, but he needed to sit down to continue. "He was done in a routine drug bust. He resisted and the narks did him over. They showed their usual tidy housekeeping searching for his stash until they found his fake security clearance which they thought was real and panicked. That's how we heard about it. We went over and salvaged what we could of his data. We'd have given it back to him, had he lived."

"I wouldn't have thought it possible for someone to emerge from one of my courses and still be so bloody naive."

"Come on, Harley. I was there at the time and saw it all go down. It's the truth. You gotta believe it."

"I believe that you believe it, Glen. You poor sorry bastard. The drug squad could have busted Val any time they liked from the day he entered high school. But they waited until the moment suited them best. Joe demanded charges be laid but the fuzz couldn't find any record of any such raid. Then they went around there and found a closet full of cocaine. Do you seriously believe they missed it the first time when they went through the place like Typhoid Mary?"

"Well it wasn't done from here..."

"And you reckon I should offer my services to folks who play the game that way."

Glen gathered himself. He stood again and walked away from the incriminating computer screen as if he suddenly feared contamination.

"You don't have any choice, Harley. This is the only game in town."

"I can still operate."

"No you can't. Not when they've got the public thinking you're a blood relative of Fu Manchu."

"You think I haven't been called crazy before?"

"Harley, they'll put you out of business, one way or the other."

"Are you listening to what you're saying?"

"Yes, and I don't like it but its the way it is. This damn thing is too big and too important to leave in the hands of one man. Even a great man, like you, Harley."

"And that's the reason why they want to stop me?"

"The days of renegade individualism are over, Harley. You haven't got a chance."

"There are some things that are too big to be stopped, Palenski."

"They'll stop you, right or wrong. You gotta face reality."

"Fuck reality. Who's going to stop me? You?"

"You've forgotten that you taught me everything you know, Harley. That makes you a superseded model."

"What you gotta worry about, Palenski, are the things I forgot to teach you."

"It doesn't have to be like this, Harley."

"Oh yes it does. In fact, this is the only way it could be."

Harley, while he spoke, touched up Japan again and then straighten with a smile.

"Well, look at that. Kev-baby's found two more of them. You're right. It is a good system."

"It's an unbeatable system, Harley."

"Palenski, now there's one of those things I must have forgot to teach you."

"What was that?"

"It is in the nature of all systems that they will fail in the end."

*

The temple was really only a platform with a few charred stone columns although those columns were massive, more like an Ancient Egyptian temple than something Japanese. The remarkable thing was that the columns still stood, while the rest of the structure had collapsed and its stones had been removed, probably for housing, centuries ago. But now it was just this pile of stones along one of the less used paths up Mt Fuji, about two thirds of the way to the summit. It had been in ruins long before the recent eruption.

The captain had the place surrounded but his men were relaxed, lounging about, smoking and chatting or sleeping, paying little attention to what was supposed to be a siege. Wagner frowned—time was running out and surely these men should have been out there somewhere, hunting down his last remaining fugitives. But he wasn't about to try and tell the captain his job.

These Japanese were like a dog with a bone—once they got their teeth into a captive, they weren't about to let go. Unless his name was Katsumi, who, Wagner had heard although not from the captain, had apparently vanished completely.

But this man was not *The Yellow Pimpernel*. This was an old priest who wasn't going anywhere, not to Brazil, not even out of the temple. The old man, bald and wizened, sat cross-legged on the stone floor before a brazier in which a small fire flickered, silent and seemingly unaware of his surroundings.

Wagner squatted down and tried to speak to the old fellow, but there was not even acknowledgment of his presence. It was another one of those jobs that the captain reckoned Wagner needed to see for himself before he explained. For the moment, Wagner could not understand why they didn't just lay hand to the old bugger and drag him out. But of course, it wasn't so simple.

"It is his lifelong mission to guard these stones," the captain explained.

"Can't we place a guard until he gets back?" Wagner said, knowing that solution would be far too practical to work.

"He must guard them himself. But there is good news."

"I'm always suspicious of your good news, Captain."

"The old priest is dying, Mr. Wagner. He has Leukemia."

"Does he? I don't suppose he's likely to pop off in the next ten days by any chance?"

"Every possibility. He is not expected to last out the month."

"But no guarantee."

"No guarantee."

"Has anyone explained the situation to him?"

"Oh yes. He fully understands. He prays continually that his life be ended before the deadline. Is that the right word?"

"It was never righter. So he wants to die, before the deadline, to help us out."

"That's right. But at present the gods have not obliged."

"I've never met an obliging god yet. Why don't we help him out?"

"He suggested that. He suggested we should shoot him."

"Why don't you?"

"This is another of your honourable jokes?"

"Yeah. You can laugh any time you like."

"It would be murder."

"I know. I don't suppose we can interest him in the idea of suicide?"

"No. This would offend the gods."

"I thought you guys were deeply into bumping yourselves off."

"Only when the alternative is dishonour. Anyway, he must stay and guard the stones."

"Who guards the stones when he dies?"

"The stones will fall when he dies."

"Might I suggest a bomb?"

"Perhaps Professor Thyssen can arrange for Fujiyama to erupt and bring the stones down on the old man."

"I'm sure he would, if he was here."

Wagner walked across the uneven platform and knelt once more beside the old man.

"Die, you old bastard," he said grimly.

The old man turned his kindly eyes upon him and spoke.

There were tears in those eyes. Smoke from the brazier was getting in Wagner's eyes too. The captain, standing over them, translated.

"He promises that he will die before dawn on Monday, as you wish."

"You mean he understood what I said?" Wagner asked in slight shock.

"A dog would have understood what you said."

Wagner bowed his head and raised himself to his feet. Reaching down, he touch the old man's bald head lightly. The old man raised a hand and closed it over his. And then he spoke again.

"There has been too much death," the captain translated. "It hardens every heart. Everyone he ever knew is dead. Every hour, he says to himself exactly what you said to him, in exactly the same tone. Every hour, he prays to die. He will make a special effort now, because it is so important that he be dead."

"Tell him thank you. The lives of many depend on it."

"He knows that. He is sure he will be dead by Monday."

Wagner withdrew his hand. It was tacky with sweat from the old man's diseased scalp. Sickened by that thought, Wagner strode out of the temple.

*

Twenty-four hours had passed since Glen Palenski vanished with a shrug and a smile through a doorway on the far side of the room, and throughout that time, Thyssen was completely alone. A prisoner in fact, in what amounted to a technological torture chamber. All around the room, the virtual planet earth rotated on its screen saver axis, except at those times when temptation had overwhelmed him and he went to work on one of the terminals.

Everything he ever dreamed of and ever needed was in this room as if it had been designed especially for him, which, in an indirect way, it had. No one disturbed him, but he knew in the end someone would. He presumed that his every movement and action was being observed and recorded, by the cameras that peered down from every corner, via the computer system. He assumed he was unable to leave but, after a time, when no one appeared, he checked it out thoroughly. First he went around the room and explored every panel. He went to the toilet and found it windowless. He examined the food dispenser—it·had enough in there to sustain him for months. He sat at a terminal and searched out the plans of the building, the air conditioning system, the ceiling space and cable ducts. There was no way out.

Between times, he kept the monitoring system running. A map of The Congo indicated Andromeda's current position and he went down through the levels until he arrived at a satellite image that showed the fractionally mobile blob of body heat that was her vast legions of pilgrims. There was a list with every name. They had covered 833km since the trek began, four months ago and 117 individuals had died for various reasons since then—mostly aged souls, or children from illness, and three taken by leopards. The map continually calculated their rate of progress and made predictions of where they would be when, at their present rate of progress. Thyssen was carefully not to pay any heed to the final location. He determinedly showed no satisfaction that they were right on schedule.

While he was there, the ship transporting the Italians arrived in Rio de Javier and he could put up the complete passenger manifest, all in alphabetical order except for Brian Carrick who was at the top of the list. A touch of the screen brought up his personal details. It recorded assault charges and classified him as `approach with caution'. Brian would have loved to have know that. While he ran down the manifest, Thyssen was doubly pleased to note the name of *Fabrini, Giacanni*; in its rightful alphabetical place, which was great because Thyssen happened to know Fabrini was not on the ship but already in Brazil, having flown there directly after a not very mysterious detour to Rome.

At times lights flashed and he eventually realised it meant that new data had arrived concerning his team. A news report of the siege of Bakersfield, where the FBI had the pilgrims surrounded and officials warned of a feared massacre or mass suicide. Of Lorna, there was nothing to be seen whereas, you could bet, if they were to permit her to appear on camera, she would certainly do so. Apparently, the news report revolved around the fact that a meeting seemed to be going on in the football stadium and everyone was there. Helicopter shots showed the crowd pouring in. The FBI chiefs thought that portentous. Nobody mentioned the most vital piece of information—whereas last time the Californian pilgrims headed north, this time they would be wanting to go south.

Over by the wall was a couch that was exceedingly comfortable, and there, for a good deal of the time, Thyssen slept. He found he slept more these days, as if he had used up all of his last reserves of energy. He slept, he ate, he eliminated and went back to play more with the computer, and toy with his masters, sensing their frustration growing. Did they really expect that he would be foolish enough to give away his secrets? Did they truly hope temptation would overwhelm him and he would utilise this system to work out his next prediction, thus revealing to them his methods? Actually, if that was their plan, it was a pretty good one. For to sit here, playing with these wonderful toys, seemed to Thyssen to be just a bit childish. Stubborn refusal to give in when his own vision of paradise lay at hand. And what harm could it do anyway? He was beginning to wonder who indeed was the drongo in the end.

*

His disgust was immeasurable. 633 only marginally legal Italian immigrants had passed through the officialdom and entered Brazil, the authorities not raising an eyebrow. Twenty other dubious passengers and crewmen from the ship were admitted with only the merest glance at their documentation. Across the barrier, a hunted murderer—of a cardinal no less—stood with a broad welcoming grin. Of them all, only one individual was stopped—the only one of them all who possessed a completely legal passport and visa.

"Would you be good enough to step in here please, Mr. Carrick."

*

Most days, for most of the day, Andromeda marched at the head of her flock, loping along with the same easy stride they did, dressed in a baggy colourful robes that flowed back from the outline of her body, her hair in a band typical of that which all of the women wore. More often than not, she received visitors who could join her as long as they were willing to walk beside her. Journalists came and did interviews, the camera crews bravely marched backwards over unknown ground for she would permit neither rehearsals nor retakes.

Government officials of all kinds came to discuss documentation or plans. Often Captain Maynard strode beside her in his rolling sailor's gait, making his bi-daily reports and expressing his concerns about the conditions ahead. His job had been made much easier now by the co-operation of the Government of the Republic of The Congo, who saw the pilgrims as a much needed tourist attraction, as well as a bargaining chip in international trade negotiations.

The President of the Republic had taken a personal interest in the food supply chain and had broadened the whole concept to a giant aid program for his entire population, and talked about a democratic election for the near future. The two C-130s carried the supplies into the path of the pilgrims tirelessly but now two dozen similar machines carried out the same operations throughout the vast state of The Congo, although the President was careful to ensure the Earthshaker Project operation was never interfered with. Ahead of and behind the marchers, his troops cleared the road and offered detour routes around the vast swarm of people moving onward, relentlessly onward. The President knew a social miracle when he saw one and most of his people clearly understood that he was fully responsible for it.

Then there were the pilgrims themselves who dared to approach her from behind, usually the most senior female of each family group, to tell her all the gossip concerning the people she marched with, to speak of her kin, and their illnesses and who had lost children in the war and from disease in the bad days and how much better it was now and finally, always finally, where were they going?

"I don't know," Andromeda always answered. "It is you and others like you who will know when we arrive."

The women, flattered beyond imagining, always offered her gifts which she took gracefully, blessed and then handed back. "This gift you have given me, is now my gift to you with my blessing added," she told them. The women retired, thrilled by their newly acquired treasures.

Then there were the headmen, who invariably came with a long list of personal complaints, always against the leaders of their neighbouring tribal groups.

"There will be no fighting," she told them. "Those who fight will return to the old land where there is fighting to be done."

Captain Maynard's men marched back in the mob, pairs of them staying close to the tribal leaders, their weapons always at the ready, and there was never any fighting. Andromeda wondered how they had coped when these men had been needed to cover the flanks.

At the rear of the column was an ever-increasing convoy of trucks which carried those unable to walk, and after them two armoured cars to ensure that any bandits in the vicinity kept their distance.

At the front, the tank creaked and groaned and whirred along, positioning itself to guard the latest payload from the planes against local scavengers. But the bandits and the scavengers too seemed to have understood the same thing as the President—that this was a miracle and they should not interfere.

Often, to the consternation of Captain Maynard, desperadoes with rifles slung, smelling awful and frighteningly skinny the human jackals who were the bandit chiefs marched with Andromeda to assure her that they were taking their band to the hills until the pilgrims had passed for it was death to steal and pillage on the sacred ground upon which they had trod.

But of all her visitors, the most improbable was Joel Tierney. He had arrived in a hired Cessna and she encountered him along the road, sitting on a bale of flourbags, smoking a joint, sweating furiously in his white cotton suit and straw hat. He fell into step beside her.

"We have to talk."

"Talk."

"I can't. Walkin' at this pace."

The pace was slow and easy but Joel had to jog to match her long strides. The conditions were very hot and very humid but then they always were in this part of the world.

"There's commitments, Andy."

"Not anymore."

"Oh come on. I got all sorts of hot deals lined up. Everyone wants in on you, baby."

"Not until this is done, Joel. I'm sorry."

"You can take some time off."

"No Joel. No chance."

"Okay. When? I got CBS. I got Eurovision. I got fucking everybody in the business."

"Except me, Joel. You haven't got me."

"Okay, when?"

"When these people get to where they are going."

"Where's that?"

"We reach the Congo in three weeks."

"Then what?"

"It will take some time to cross. Maybe then. But really, I don't know. First we have to get to the Congo. That's all."

"But why?"

"Because that's where we are going."

"Andy, why are you doing this?"

Really, he asked all the same questions everyone else did. It was just that his motives were different.

"Because it's what I'm doing?"

"It's costing millions."

"I know. But the project has the money and the people must be fed."

"I meant the millions that you're not earnin'."

"I've already made millions. This is what happened as a result. I sang the songs. Now I must lead the people. That's all there is."

"It's because that friend of yours that died, ain't it. Saint Christine. You're tryin' to take her place."

"No. I'm doing the same thing she was doing, with other people, for the same reason."

"But what for?"

"Because this is what we are doing. That's all there is, Joel."

"Jesus, Andy. I spent the best years of my life making you famous, and now you don't want to go on with it."

"We've just passed your plane, Joel. Get in and buzz off."

"You'll pay for this. I'll sue."

"You've already got four breach of contract suits out against me, Joel."

"I dropped 'em."

"Raise them again. At least it'll give you something to do so you'll stop pestering me."

"You'll be sorry. You'll regret this."

"No Joel. No matter what happens, I'll never regret this."

*

On the fifth day of his captivity in this technological paradise, he finally had a visitor. By then he had taken to talking to himself and the machines and the security cameras and Glen, who, he assumed, had security personnel watching and listening, waiting for him to make a slip. No human voice replied but most of the machines did. Of course, he knew they would be monitoring everything, and limited his internet access and email, to prevent him reaching the outside world, but that didn't mean there wasn't plenty to do. On every screen, he had something going on. A chess match with the computer. He took to playing computer games which he hadn't done since the days when *Space Invaders* was new. He set up some wonderful fractals in abysmal motion and was getting close to reproducing the Mandelbrot Set. He reckoned he'd solved Hood's difficulty with Fibonacci but then he lost the solution. He had a whole array of Glen's models running. And he constantly kept track of his colleagues.

He watched Brian Carrick become a separate dot from his Italian pilgrims in Rio—presumably having his usual difficulty with Brazilian Immigration as he did with all officialdom—and saw him move at such a rate that he had to be flying, and land in Washington and then tracked him on a city grid map right to this very building so he knew who his visitor was before he entered.

"Welcome to Harleyworld," he said.

Brian, who showed every sign of having been physically shoved into the room, stood with his mouth open for some time. It crossed Thyssen's mind that most probably, in that instant, Brian's worst suspicions about the leader of Project Earthshaker were confirmed. Perhaps that was why they troubled to drag him across two continents to get him here.

"What's fuckin' goin' on, Harley?"

"Come here and I'll show you."

The guileless Brian Carrick slowly made his way through the rows of computers and sat at the terminal beside Thyssen. Feeling not unlike the villain in a James Bond movie, Thyssen quietly explained everything Brian saw.

"So we're prisoners here?" he said at the end of it.

"Shouldn't bother you, Brian. I understand it's almost your natural state."

"The sort of prisons I frequent don't look like this."

"No," Thyssen said. "What you see is a wonderful, fantastic, glorious, ingenious, state-of-the-art technological bribe."

"They bribed you with this?"

"I'm Eve and everything you see is the apple."

"Where's the snake?"

"The snake is my own self-created Frankensteinian monster, Glen Palenski."

"I never knew him."

"Neither did I," Thyssen said ruefully.

Brian looked around, shaking his head in bewilderment. "Now, you wouldn't bullshit me, would you Harley?"

"I bullshit thee not. All I have to do is press the right buttons and show them how I make my predictions and we'll both be free to walk out of here."

"Simple as that?"

"Simple as that. Isn't that right Glen?" he called over his shoulder.

There was no reply.

"Glen said, simple as that," Thyssen smiled.

"Yeah. I heard him."

"Sadly, that's all it will take."

"So why don't you do it."

It seemed like a silly question, until Thyssen took a moment to think about it. Maybe they chosen wisely indeed, sending Brian Carrick for him to talk to.

"I think you just fulfilled your purpose, Brian."

"You mean, they actually imagine I might talk you into it?"

"That's right. After five humanless days, maybe anyone could talk me into anything."

"So why don't you do it, and we can get out of here and start doing something useful."

Again, Thyssen thought about it. Brian was such a persistent fellow.

"I don't know, Brian. Maybe I'm just pig-headed."

"You're that all right. Look, Harley. Time is running out. Give them what they want. What harm can it do at this stage?"

"I don't know. But I just can't get it out of my head that if I give them what they want, these bastards will take it away from us and make it top secret and then start figuring out how to turn it into a weapon."

"Yeah. They'll do that for sure."

"And I just don't like losing."

"I know how you feel. But I think they got you fucked, mate."

"I really don't want to admit that."

"We gotta have the accurate prediction. We need it now. Where else are you going to find a system that you can do it on except this one?"

"Are you sure you're still on our side, Brian?"

"I'm on our side. It's you who's loyalties are all fucked up. We've done everything we did in spite of these people, regardless of how much they lied and cheated and fiddled and regardless of how much they knew. Now, you can use them to get what you want. So use them."

"I feel too ornery to do that."

"Then be ornery. Let's make them an offer."

Thyssen looked at him in puzzlement. "You lost me. I've only had machines to talk to for five days. Human beings are much harder."

"Since we seem to have no choice but to give them what they want, so we trade. For something we want."

"They don't have anything we want."

"They must have something we want."

*

Negotiators ! Was she sick of them? Almost every day, a committee of some kind came to speak with the infamous Lorna Simmons. They had all sorts of origins, and were led by all sorts of notables—congressmen, senators, movie stars, religious groups, business people, media anchors, mysterious people from the White House—but all of them contained negotiators, siege-breakers from the law enforcement agencies. And it was always the negotiators who did the talking, and what they tried to talk her into was submission.

Which wasn't easy, because there wasn't anything to submit to. They wanted her to say that the sleepers did not exist, that she or Harley or someone had used psychological techniques to cause these people to think they wanted to go walkabout, that there was no such thing as linkage of minds. That Harley Thyssen was a fake and Project Earthshaker was a confidence trick.

"For what purpose?" she demanded.

"You tell us, Miss Simmons."

They wanted to know by what right she spoke of the people of the affected region. She was obliged to hold a popular election and the people, who knew she was the answer to their problems, voted her their representative with a majority of over eighty percent.

"Are you considering running for president?"

"How can I? I'm not a bloody American."

"President of New Zealand then?"

"New Zealand doesn't have a President."

"But just what do you want, Miss Simmons?"

So many times had she explained. On the morning of the eleventh, these people would set off on their journey. The National Guard and the FBI had them hemmed in and they will have nowhere to go. There would be chaos.

"Are you threatening violence, Miss Simmons?"

It didn't help that previously they had gone north, for absolutely no reason whatsoever. This time they would go south, for the same nonexistent reason.

"Why are they going south?"

"Because Professor Thyssen arranged it that way."

"Oh yes, Professor Thyssen."

Again and again, she had tried to get through to them.

"He has arranged the neutral ground in Brazil by moving the Japanese sleepers there. Those people who are in the zone on the 13th will be cured."

"Cured from what?"

"The Shastri Effect."

"But, Miss Simmons. Independent medical examiners have agreed unanimously that there is no such condition as the Shastri Effect."

"The condition only occurs at the time of the linkage."

"Miss Simmons, surely it is obvious, even to you, that such conditions do not and cannot exist."

Around and around they went and it was endless. And then, on the morning of the 6th, without warning, President Grayson appeared on television.

He admitted the existence of the Shastri Effect.

He admitted the validity of Project Earthshaker.

He admitted that Professor Thyssen had been maligned in the media.

He agreed to the transportation of the Bakersfield pilgrims to Brazil.

Anyone who wanted to go could do so. The US Air Force would be providing aircraft, as of that very morning. Lorna watched in awe. Somehow, someway, Harley had talked them into it. She could only wonder what it had cost him in return.

That morning, there were scenes of jubilation in Bakersfield and Fresno and all points in between. Lorna was their hero, although she could not exactly see what she had done. All she wanted was to find one of those bloody negotiators and let them ask their cynical questions again. But they were nowhere to be seen.

*

"So," Thyssen said. "Drongo."

Brian put up his fists pugilistically. "You talkin' to me, buddy?"

Because their bar-room humour went nowhere with Glen and his team, they shrugged at each other. Every seat in the control room had been filled, and the technicians were poised to transfer Thyssen's wisdom into their respective systems.

Thyssen continued. "It begins with an assumption. An object formed in the intense heat of the big bang. It's tiny—no bigger than just a few atoms, maybe. Maybe much smaller than that. But it's dense, very, very dense. The elementary particles of which it's made are compressed so close together that if you could catch it you could weigh it on a butcher's scale. It might weigh a kilogram, probably less. And it travels the universe for 15 million million years or however long you reckon it is since the beginning of time."

"I remember this lecture," Glen said with groan. "It was the one you always gave new students."

"Oh no. This one I'm making up on the spot. It just sounds similar."

"Well how about cutting to the chase."

"No point telling a story if you don't tell it all. I'm just reminding you Glen, of what I taught you but you forgot."

"How do you know I forgot?"

"Because if you hadn't, you'd have figured this out for yourself."

Glen bowed his head and listened with a humble expression. Brian, who thought it all fascinating, was only too well aware that he was hearing the first astrophysics lecture of his life, and from its greatest living exponent, even if he was really a Vulcanologist.

"So it travels throughout the vacuum of space, picks up a few stray particles here and there and absorbs them, maybe doubles in size but increases tenfold or more in weight, until, on the morning of June 30, 1908, it finally hits something— the atmosphere above Tunguska. Food! It is instantly insatiable and begins to devour. As it passes through the atmosphere, it sets off a chain reaction that flattens the surrounding forest and then ploughs into the earth and drops right through to the core. It passes through the centre, but it is captured and slowed by the earth's gravitational pull, loses momentum, and before it can escape the core, it's turned and goes into orbit."

"I did all this," Glen said. "I modelled it, like you said."

But it was Thyssen who pressed the keyboard and brought the images up on the screen.

"Yeah, and your model was right."

"So what are you calling this... this object? Mini black hole? Antimatter? What?"

"I call it death. Doesn't matter what it is, or how theoretically possible and impossible it might be, it exists. Maybe it's made from some kind of elementary particle we haven't discovered yet. There's bound to be more. And this thing is primal. It could only have been created in the first millionth of a second or so of the universe, and never again. It doesn't matter what we call it. The Palenski Particle if you like. But there it is."

Brian could watch it, fascinated. The earth was on screen in cross-section, the core, the mantle, the crust each delineated, and with it the object traced out it course at blinding speed, each orbit about the centre a different course to that before.

"From there, all I needed to do was slip in the recent Shastri events and we had the whole course of its life plotted."

"I did all that. So what?"

"What you forgot was the immense speed at which this thing travelled, and the fact that it was growing in size all the time. It burrowed through the matter in the core, gulping it in, constantly accumulating, and as it gained size and lost momentum, its orbit was always decaying toward the centre of the earth, where, eventually, it would come to rest. But not yet. Something else happened."

Thyssen ran up a new model, one that Glen plainly had not seen before if the way his eyebrows raised was any guide. The model showed the singularity closer, in animation, creating a brief tunnel through the core that the molten rock gradually filled behind it. And as it orbited, it turned back on itself.

"Once it attained a certain size, and its orbit a certain configuration, it went around so fast and so tightly that the tunnel of matter it had created in its wake had not had time to heal yet. And so, suddenly, it hit a vacuum of its own creation as it crossed its own prior course—and the effect would be shattering. Material crushed to elementary particles at the fringe would be blasted off by the impact as it hit the other side, and in an instant those particles, mostly fermions, would radiate outward to the surface of the earth. And that was the Shastri Effect. Out there, on the surface, were living intelligences, us, with brains full of bosons, and when the added fermions hit, those bosons would immediately attack the onslaught. At the point where the particles reached the surface, any available bosons would align in defence and strike back. And that created the mind link."

"You can't prove any of this."

"If you've got a better explanation—that works as well as mine—I'm interested."

Glen's dark eyes glowed. Thyssen continued with cool certainty.

"Following on the heels of the particle burst would be a shock-wave—arriving thirty-three hours later at the point directly ahead of the impact. But, because of the rotation of the earth, that impact would always be at the trailing edge of the planet at the time. Once it hit the surface, it would dissipate over an increasingly wider area, pouring in more fermions creating more boson defences, creating new sleepers. And setting off any volcanoes that happened to be in the vicinity."

Brian, watching it happen, could almost have figured out the rest himself.

"And this is the model you ran?" Glen said grimly. "This is your... your... Drain-o."

"Drongo," Brian corrected. "It means someone who ain't as smart as he oughta be."

"Yes. That's it," Thyssen said grimly.

"But how did you know?"

"I knew because it worked. My early predictions were just guesses and they were all hopelessly wrong. It wasn't until after I theorised on Tunguska that I came up with this and found it got the right answers."

"But how come," Brian asked. "The Shastri Events grew larger and more frequent?"

"Because, despite losing potential material, it was still generally growing larger, travelling shorter orbits, and making a bigger tunnel and therefore a bigger impact, each time."

"It's a great theory, Harley," Brian said. "You think it's true."

"I'm sure it isn't," Thyssen said. "It's just the best anyone can come up with, given the enormous immaturity of our present knowledge. In a few thousand years, maybe, someone will figure out the right answer. Right now, this is the best we can do."

Glen looked forlorn. "I hoped there'd be more. You realise I have to try and explain this to the President."

"You just tell Grayson I sent you," Thyssen grinned.

"You yelled at him, Harley. The President of the United States. Right there in the Oval Office, you yelled at him. They say he still hasn't fully recovered from it."

"I wouldn't like it if everyone loved me," Thyssen grinned.

*

Katsumi Sukurai was the most wanted man in Japan. In the newspapers and public places, his picture smiled at the population, teasing them with his wry grin, challenging them to spot him. He was a young man, a student of accounting, unemployed, the rest of his family was already in Brazil, and Katsumi had escaped from them three times already, and now had gone into smoke. And time was running out.

The final day had dawned and he was not to hand. By midnight, he needed to be on a plane and inside the circle before the link occurred or else everything was wasted.

Kevin Wagner spent most of his time pacing the floor, roaring at the latest group of searchers as they came in, policeman, guardsman, soldiers, volunteers, whoever they were they met with Wagner's rage.

"Fifteen thousand eight hundred and twenty-two people and we found them all and moved them all. Except this one elusive bastard."

"And the old man in the temple," Tamiko said sweetly.

"He said he would die and he'll die."

What bothered Wagner most was that, as he said it, he fingered the imaginary butt of the pistol he wasn't wearing on his hip. Had it really come to this?

Tamiko saw the gesture and frowned at it, because she saw everything he did and frowned at a good deal of it. She was in love with him, Wagner knew, and very efficient and decorative besides. She was completely devoted to his needs.

Wagner realised in that moment that, if it came to that, he found himself unwilling to commit murder to satisfy Harley's needs, Tamiko most certainly would oblige.

He made a fierce effort to calm himself.

"Let's think about it."

"You have done nothing other than think about it, for weeks," Tamiko said. "You must rest now. What is one man, more or less?"

"You don't understand. It's all of them or the whole thing is wasted."

"Why?"

"I don't know why. That's just the way it is. Bring me the file."

"You already have the file. That's it there."

"Oh."

He'd been reading it not an hour before. "Three times we had him and three times he vanished. How? And why?"

"Is why important? Maybe he just doesn't want to go."

"His family has gone. All his friends have gone. Why stay?"

"Maybe he sees it as a challenge."

"Challenge?"

"Yes. It's become a game. Read the file. Each time the escaped, he didn't go anywhere."

Wagner did not want to read the bloody file again. "Explain what you mean?"

Tamiko shrugged her beautiful shoulders and smiled benignly.

"Okay. Please consider. First time, his is in airport, ready to board plane. Then he disappears."

"True."

"He hid in a baggage locker for two days. Then he went to a party at some friend's place."

"We've got all those places covered."

"But don't you see. He didn't really try to escape or else he'd have stayed away from the party. But he was willing to spend what must have been two very uncomfortable days in a baggage locker to do so."

"Must have been a hell of a party."

"It was an ordinary party."

"So?"

"Forget the party. Think about the locker."

"I don't understand how a man can do something like that."

"It was a reasonably large locker and he is a very small man."

"Okay. I don't see what it proves."

Tamiko was pacing, warming to the task. Wagner watched her. Maybe they should just have sex and forget it.

"Next time, he escapes from police during transfer from police station to here."

"He hid in the trunk of the police car."

"That's right. They again search far and wide but he is right under their noses. Still in the car that he was supposed to have escaped from."

"Go on."

"He slips away later, and goes home to his family and is picked up with them. Brought here again, but then vanishes."

Wagner thought about it. He was beginning to get the point.

"Go on."

"He escapes from here. This place is on top of a hill and heavily guarded. There is no way to escape from here. Yet he does..."

"Or did he?"

"Precisely."

"You mean he's been here..."

"Yesterday, the cook is very angry. He accuses us girls of stealing from his kitchen. As if we would..."

Wagner smiled, picking up the telephone. "Captain. I want two dozen men here immediately with jemmies and picks and saws."

He winked at Tamiko while he listened to the usual protests concerning the shortage of available men.

"We're going to demolish this house. He is hiding here somewhere."

*

In a room opposite the Project Earthshaker Control Room, as it had become called, Thyssen slept for fifteen hours and when he awoke the time for the link was drawing near. By then the control room was flooded with people, many of whom Thyssen recognised as former students, all of whom he treated that way. Four major scientists and three military officers, a senator and a number of bureaucratic figures, all bowed to Thyssen's authority with varying degrees of reluctance, as he took them through the procedure before them.

In fact the man in charge of the control room was not Glen Palenski, but a rather dour man named Cornelius, whom Joe Solomon would have immediately recognised. He was a long thin man, bald and white haired, bent in the middle and with a shuffling gait. But despite that there was an elegance about him, and his voice seemed to assume that he would always be obeyed instantly.

He was appointed to command of the project directly by the President, but his actual credentials remained dubious. Certainly, he shut up and listened whenever Thyssen spoke, and if there was doubt, confirmed orders with a slight jerk of his head and silenced protests with a fractional lowering of his eyebrows.

Brian watched all this with growing concern, but that he realised was possibly only because he knew the link was coming on.

"That dude is going to get rid of you, Harley, as soon as he reckons he's got everything he needs from you."

"Yeah, I know. But they're listening to me now. I can't ask more than that."

"Do you know who he is?"

"Nobody knows who he is."

It was time for Brian to be elsewhere. A good testing time. He proposed to Cornelius that he ought to be given a jet and flown to the focal point since that was where he was going anyway. When Brian expected his request to be denied, Cornelius emphatically agreed. But he was reluctant to leave Harley alone here.

"If they were going to dump me, they would have as soon as I gave them Drongo," Harley assessed.

"Maybe they don't trust you still, Harley. Maybe they think you gave them the wrong data."

"It doesn't matter, Brian," Harley said. "It's their problem to get it right from now on. It's possible. I wanted no more than this."

17
THE MARGIN FOR ERROR

On the huge global board, the course of the others was continually plotted. Andromeda's pilgrims would turn west when the link came and they were excellently positioned for it, for before them in that direction was a broad lightly forested plain. A problem in The Congo Republic was the many tributaries of the Congo which had generally kept them to the road—now they would leave it for a time but calculations suggested that they would be able to reach another road before they encountered the next river.

Meanwhile, a vast flood of Americans was flowing into Brazil from Bakersfield, as the Air Force stepped up it operations. Those who could not leave immediately or did not wish to had generally moved northward to Fresno for their journey would be another convoy, heading almost directly south.

Of greater concern were the millions in Indonesia, where all available boats were being provided, under the direction of the US and Indonesia navies. The shortest route to the focal point for them was the south polar one, which was completely impracticable, but the plan was to transport all those that reached the south coast of Sulawesi under their own steam across the Timor Sea to the north coast of Western Australia where camps could be set up in more accessible circumstances than in their own ruined country.

Iran had even greater problems, where little assistance could be offered the pilgrims and their path lay due west, toward Iraq, and Turkey, where they would be most unwelcome, and therefore the less distance they were able to cover, the better. Since their movement would be primarily on foot over rugged mountain terrain, it could be reasonably hoped that they could care for themselves. Information from the region remained slight, but although all three countries had made troop movements to control the pilgrimage, there had been no word of massacres at this stage.

In Russia, the Buryats would do whatever they usually did, for still there was no information and in fact denial of their existence.

The base in Brazil presented its own problems, were a vast tent city was growing up on a huge plain in the middle of nowhere. There were two great Ranchos that they had taken over and one of these possessed a reasonable airstrip, good enough for C-130s but not for jets. The nearest International Airport was Brasilia, over a thousand kilometres away and the pilgrims from America and elsewhere were transferred into smaller aircraft there to complete the trip. Fuel was a continual problem, as was food although there was abundant water, but the promise of a cure for their condition allowed the pilgrims to endure the temporary hardship with a minimum of complaint. The difficulty was getting enough of them to the focal point in time.

But most of the agitation surrounded *The Yellow Pimpernel*, who had been discovered resident under the floorboards of the *House of the Golden Carp* with only hours to spare. Without him, the base camp in Brazil would have been more than a thousand kilometres from the focal point and outside the Zone and Harley's plan would have completely unravelled. Tranquillised and strapped down to a stretcher, the little man was rushed to the airport and into the air. Time was by then so short that, although east was the shortest route to Brazil, they flew west and therefore into the circle formed by the extremities of the linkage, and therefore secured Harley's predicted location.

"Are you sure you got them all?" Harley asked Wagner by radio.

"Yes. There was an old man who said he would die and he died—we don't know how. So there's just me and Katsumi and we passed over Lake Baykal a few minutes ago. So we're inside the circle."

"Thanks Kevin."

"No problem, Harley."

Then the link occurred. At first it seemed as expected, but within half an hour, a message came through by telephone to one of the control room silent numbers.

"Professor Thyssen, there's a call for you... I think."

"You think?"

"The line is terrible and he's very hard to understand."

Thyssen hurried over to the girl who had taken the call and spoke into the receiver.

"Thyssen."

"Ah, Professor. It is Fabrini."

"Yes. What is it?"

"They all want to go. They want to pick up and leave here."

The line was bad and Fabrini's state of agitation didn't help, but Thyssen did not need to ask him to repeat this message, he simply turned and considered the board.

"Which way, Fabrini. Which way are they going?"

He spoke every word individually and clearly and a silence had fallen upon the room.

"West. They want to go west. At least, this is what I think. You want a compass bearing?"

"If you can do it."

"I think, maybe, 240 degree. Maybe more. Is west by south west, I think."

"Shit," Thyssen said.

He stood for a time with his hand over the mouthpiece and his head bowed, deep in thought. Even so, those near him could hear Fabrini chattering. The trance broke after fifteen almost unendurable seconds. Thyssen hit the conference phone button to allow everyone in the room to hear.

"...and they are all here and they say to me, we must go. We must go."

"Okay, Fabrini, listen carefully. What's out there?"

"Many people. Everybody..."

"No. I mean, how is the terrain in the direction they want to go?"

"Ahh... Is flat. I think... I have not been there very far, but I think flat and open for as far as I have seen."

"Okay. Let them go. Tell them to walk. Tell them to take supplies for three days walk. Ask them to go as slowly as they can tolerate. Do you understand?"

"Yes, I think. As slow as they tolerate. I understand."

"It may be just a slight adjustment. But let's be prepared. I want you to let me know if anything changes. Okay."

"Okay, okay. I understand."

The silence continued to hang over the room and the connection was broken, and Thyssen again considered the board. His eyes fell on a single location and he nodded imperceptibly.

"Make contact with Brian, Joe, Andromeda and Wagner. I want to talk to each of them as soon as you raise them."

*

There was a highway under construction running south from Baltimore for about thirty miles and there Joe Solomon was road testing his new motorised wheelchair, escorted by two FBI agents on bicycles.

"I do seem to be wandering off toward the left slightly, Harley," he laughed. "I just thought it was the wheel alignment but maybe you're right."

*

Andromeda marched amid her flock, and when Harley made contact, she paused to discuss the direction with Captain Maynard. Maynard was able to use Omega navigational positioning to pinpoint their line of march exactly.

"No. We don't seem to have any deviation at all, Harley," Andromeda said. "Why? What's the problem?"

*

Lorna, of course, was no longer a sleeper, but all those about her were.

"There seems to be a lot of uncertainty here, Harley. If there is a variation, it can't be much."

"Not at that distance, maybe."

*

In their respective aircraft, Wagner and Brian were able to consult their pilots and determine direction precisely. Wagner, in a JAL 747, was over Turkey by then, and reported there was no variation. But like Andromeda, they too were heading west.

Brian was a different story, He was invited to the cockpit of his commercial flight and directed the pilot onto the exact course. Being over Mexico and heading south, the effect was far more measurable.

"You're right, Harley. We're off to the left by a few degrees."

Harley was already leaning over a woman who could use the computer to plot the data accurately. The focal point had moved, about four hundred kilometres toward the Andes.

"How could this happen, Harley?" Brian wanted to know.

The new position provided its own answer.

"The Buryats. They're gone?"

"How do you mean, gone?" Glen Palenski asked.

"Don't ask me. Ask the Russians."

"You sure they ever existed? They never admitted it."

"We used them to plot the focal point several times in the past. They had to have been there then. Now they aren't."

"What happened to them?"

"Maybe the Ruskies did some quarantine with extreme prejudice."

Cornelius now stepped in, as if finally assuming the command that was always obviously his. "They wouldn't. They aren't that barbaric."

Thyssen paused for a moment to glare at him. "Oh no. Remember that story you bastards spread about the contagion of the Shastri Effect."

"No one here spread any such story."

"No. Of course not. Whatever the reason, 190 Buryats have gone out of existence, and that screws us up completely."

"Maybe we can get Wagner's plane to turn around and go back, and that will drag the focal point back with him," Glen suggested.

Thyssen was impressed. But when they checked, they discovered that by the time the plane landed, refuelled and returned far enough to outflank Andromeda's pilgrims, there would be too little time left to make a significant difference.

"Still, tell them to try," Thyssen said.

"And there's a big storm on their tail that they'll probably have to go around," the operator added, to quell Thyssen's last hopes.

"Naturally," Thyssen breathed.

Cornelius and Glen Palenski exchanged a questioning glance and plainly neither of them was able to provide the other with the answer. Certainly, Thyssen's annoyance was excessive, given the situation.

Cornelius said warily. "I know this means that a lot of them will miss the chance to be cured but I don't see how..."

"No, you wouldn't, would you," Thyssen bit back at him.

But even he could see he was being unreasonable about this. He caught himself, took a breath, and turned back to the board.

"Is the link important for some other reason, Harley?" Glen asked with equal care.

"No. No. I'm just tired, I suppose. And sending all those people all that way—for nothing..."

"You couldn't have known."

"I probably should have guessed."

"And perhaps your Mr. Fabrini will be able to slow them down enough to keep a good proportion of them in the Zone," Glen added.

"Perhaps," Harley sighed.

"Which reminds me," Cornelius said slowly. "I've been wanting to have a word with you about Mr. Fabrini..."

Thyssen turned then, his fury fully restored. The glare he directed at Cornelius was almost enough to strike him a physical blow. "Just who the hell are you, Cornelius?"

"As it happens, I am a Special Adviser to the President on matters of national emergency."

"NCA."

"Classified. However, you can get verification of my credentials from the President any time you feel you need it."

"And what is your capacity here?"

"I am instructed to protect the US tax-payer's investment in Project Earthshaker."

"So you are in charge."

"Technically, in a bureaucratic sense, perhaps. But my orders are specific. I am to do what you tell me, and facilitate to the best of my ability any anything you need. I think that puts you in charge, Professor."

"I think that puts President Grayson in charge, Mr. Cornelius."

"Please, call me John."

"Might as well. Otherwise I'd have to call you Corny."

"You better get some sleep now, Professor. When you wake, we ought to have complete models of the likely effects in Brazil. I'd like you to be able to look them over and offer any suggestions."

Over the following hours, Thyssen considered the outcomes from the models. By that time, Brian had flown over the exact focal point, which proved to be 437 kilometres further away from the Andes from the original anticipated position. The pilgrims were proceeding that way, but there was still a reasonable chance that all of them would be inside the Zone when the event occurred— depending on how close the model was to the actual location. Brian had continued on to take charge of the scene, much to the apparent relief of Cornelius, who undoubtedly was somewhat uncomfortable with the idea of a fugitive from a murder charge being in control.

Once due allowance for error had been made, Thyssen pumped the flight plan into the Orion's onboard computer, and advised Felicity that he had done so.

"How are you bearing up to captivity, Harley?"

"I'm a pretty tame beast, Fee. You know that. They've given me all these nice new toys to play with. That'll keep me pacified."

"Yes. Brian told me all about it. Is it true we lost the Buryats?"

"Looks that way. The western boundary of the link was on Wagner's last Japanese, in midair over Turkey at the time and using that as a base, we've confirmed the position that Brian gave us."

"Bastards. How could they kill all those people?"

"Maybe they all died of natural causes, Felicity. Maybe there were fewer of them than we were told. Or maybe they were all moved to some point further east..."

"Beyond Turkey? Are you kidding?"

"Yeah. I know. Listen, Fee. Once its safe, I want you to get in and sort out the affected pilgrims first, if we have any. If we can use Lorna's experience as a guide, they should only be unconscious for a few minutes. They'll need to be picked up first."

"Yes. I understand. Is the Brazilian Government doing anything about the Indians and peasants in the region?"

"No. They're too remote, and it's too late to organise a proper evacuation."

"So I'm going to have the same sort of mess that I had in Sulawesi to puzzle my way through."

"Well, at least you'll be experienced this time."

"Sure Harley. You take care now."

"You too Fee."

One by one, Thyssen spoke to each of his team, to ensure they were ready. There was plenty of time, and they were all under control, but he found the countdown that was now running was unnerving him. Then the leaders from the various teams in the control room gathered and aired their final concerns.

"Explain, if you will, Professor, the likely effects we can expect in Brazil."

"We anticipate an earthquake at 11.1 on the scale—the greatest magnitude ever known. We cannot be sure what arbitrary effects will arise from it. The Zone we expect to be eight hundred kilometres in diameter, with the epicentre at the base we established in the Mato Grasso. Mato Grasso City is the only large town affected and it will be evacuated. Other smaller places like Frutuoso, Diamantino and Pouso Alegra are all expected to lie just outside the Zone. So, we believe, will the largest town in the region, Cuiaba. There are about nine small settlements inside the Zone that we can do nothing about. Local population figures are not well known but we think there are about 200,000 natives living in the Zone. It's mostly open, sparsely treed country and the damage from the earthquake itself, despite his intensity, might not be very great.

"There was an earthquake in 1994 at 8.3 on the scale just west of the location and only ten people were killed. Mostly, the problem won't be there. The population is too sparse. In the Andes, however, there will be a different problem. The area around La Paz and Lake Titicaca seems the most vulnerable spot. There are dozens of active volcanoes in the region, hundreds of dormant, and the whole range sits on the edge of the Peru-Chile Trench. It's all hopelessly unstable and its possible that we could get a coastal catastrophe twenty or thirty times worse than California. But that's just speculation. We have no idea of what will happen there.

"Between the Andes and the Mato Grasso, in Bolivia, are a series of severe fault lines, and we may get a lava flood similar to the one that occurred at Lake Baikal, only on a much larger scale. That would take the pressure off the Andes and the trench, and its overall effects might not be so great. But everything for a thousand square miles will be utterly destroyed. The faults are so numerous and complex that there is no way of telling which of them is likely to be affected."

The countdown clock ran to zero and started counting

backwards. If the migration of the pilgrims was going as slowly as Thyssen hoped and most of them were still within the anticipated Zone. The countdown clock ran to minus 33 minutes, and then the seismographs went off the scale.

"Give me a reading," Thyssen demanded.

"8.9," came the reply.

"That can't be right."

"We're confirming."

"Get me a fix on the Zone as quick as you can."

"Professor, I'm having trouble raising the Orion."

"Get them. We need their confirmation."

"They're on the air. I just can't raise anybody..."

Thyssen stopped what he was doing, regarded the operator involved for a moment and then looked at the map. The green dot indicated the Orion, flying north-east of the Zone. Thyssen picked up his microphone and said calmly.

"Felicity, can you hear me?"

"They're receiving. They just aren't answering."

Thyssen walk briskly and punched some keys. "Come on, come on. I want that epicentre."

"We're getting it. It's coming... Shit !"

On the screen before him, as well as on the board behind, a blue dotted line indicated the anticipated Zone of Influence. Now more intense blue lines began to map the actually affected area. It was far to the north. At least three hundred kilometres. The epicentre was almost at the edge of the blue circle.

"Oh no," Thyssen said, bowing his head in dismay.

"We still can't raise the Orion, Professor."

"I don't think you will," Thyssen said grimly.

Glen was standing behind him, intently watching the board, and seeing clearly the problem. The green dot was inside the Zone, almost in the middle of it in fact.

"They've been caught."

"What do you mean?" Cornelius had to ask. His voice carried too loudly in the hush that had fallen over the room.

"They're sleepers."

"But the plane's still flying..."

"Automatic pilot. The crew is asleep."

"But isn't Dr Campbell a pilgrim...?"

"No. She never was. No one on the plane was," Thyssen said grimly, to no one in particular. "I'm so stupid. Why didn't I think of that? We needed a pilot who was a pilgrim to keep them safe."

Every eye in the room watched the languid movement of the green dot, as it tracked almost imperceptibly across the board.

"We must be able to do something," Glen insisted in continuing disbelief.

"How much fuel does the Orion have?" Thyssen asked anyone in general.

"About eight hours. I'm confirming..."

"Plot me their exact course."

But he could see the course. It was west, toward Peru.

"One moment... I'm hooked into the onboard computer. Here it comes..."

A red line slowly began to dot its way across the screen, across the vast forest of the headwaters of the Amazon.

"Show me the limit of their range," Thyssen demanded.

A cross was indicated, far out in the Atlantic.

"If they ditch in the sea, we might be able to pick up survivors," Cornelius supposed.

"They'll never make the sea," Thyssen said. "Give me their altitude."

"3000 feet."

"And they have to cross the Andes."

"Jesus."

"Can we tap into the computer and get the automatic pilot to raise the altitude?" Glen asked.

"We can try," the operator said.

Thyssen knew it was hopeless. There were mountains ahead higher than the Orion could fly. And there was no known means of interfering with the automatic pilot of such a vintage aeroplane.

In his mind, he saw the upwardly curved edges of Felicity's lips when she was amused by what she heard but refused to smile.

He saw her habit of brushing her non-existent fringe from her eyes, that suggested she had once had much longer hair. He saw the tears glisten in her eyes as she had looked upon the succeeding tragedies about her.

With a physical thrust of his body, he forced her from his mind. "Take it off the board..." he ordered fiercely.

"But we need..."

"I don't want to see it. Take it off."

The green light disappeared. A shocked silence passed through the room. Thyssen turned and called loudly. "Right, we've got other lives to save. Let's get to it."

*

The Orion flew on through the night. It would not reach Peru and the Andes until dawn. Inside the computers and sensors would be humming out their data dutifully, and in the glow of their pale lights, the domed helmets of the crew would be reflecting their arrays. Each would be sleeping in their positions, their heads bowed forward.

Felicity's helmet would probably take on a bright red glow through the window on the plane, away to the south as if the sun had set too late and in the wrong place. The mighty fires raged in the forest as the lava spewed out of great fissures in the Earth, all along the eastern boundary of the Andes. Some volcanoes near Lake Titicaca had erupted briefly, but the large centres like La Paz had been spared. And the Orion flew on through the fiery night...

Thyssen shook his head to clear the images of horror that continually pervaded his brain, threatening his need to think with any clarity. So far there were no reports of loss of life at all, unless you counted the riders on the Orion as already dead.

Despite the errors of both the focal point and the epicentre, still all of the pilgrims had been within the Zone at the time. There was silence too from them, for about twenty nerve-racking minutes before Brian came on the line.

"Sorry about that. My radio blew out. I had to find another one."

"What's happening there, Brian?"

"We all went down like a sack of spuds. Then we all stood up again. I'm told a few people have been hurt but I've got no reports of deaths at this stage."

"Did you experience any tremors?"

"I was asleep at the time, remember? No, there's no sign of damage here. But it looks like there's a hell of a fire to the south of us."

"Yeah. We think its a lava flood around Santa Cruz in Bolivia. It might be closer than a hundred kilometres to you. Get them moving back toward the base, Brian. Every helicopter in Brazil, Bolivia and Peru is on its way into your area now to start picking up casualties and sleepers."

"Still, it looks like it worked out just the way you said, Harley."

"No, Brian. It didn't."

He explained to Brian what had happened, and then contacted Lorna, Andromeda, Wagner and Joe and told them in formal sober terms. That done, he did a complete round of the operators, discussing the situation with each and gathering as clear a picture of the effects as he could.

"I have to report to the President," Cornelius said. "What will I tell him?"

"Tell him the truth."

"What is the truth?"

"I got it wrong."

"You were still," Glen had to put in, "a damned lot closer than any other prediction."

"But it was still wrong."

"Any idea why?"

"A guess."

"Give me your guess."

"Grayson isn't going to want to hear any guess of mine."

"Give it to me anyway."

"Look at this." He pointed to the map on the board. "The

position of the pilgrims. The predicted position of the epicentre. The actual position of the epicentre. Notice something?"

"A straight line."

"Perfectly aligned. Which might just be a co-incidence, but there's a more likely explanation."

"Which is?"

"Consider too that the magnitude of the earthquake was far less than expected. The pattern has been continual increase and Drongo insists it should have continued to be so."

"If it was right."

"I think it was. But something—some force—diminished the impact and deflected its position."

"What could do that?"

Thyssen allowed a long pause before he said it.

"The pilgrims."

*

Through the night the Orion flew on and with the coming of the dawn, the unbroken green canopy of the Amazonian forest began to emerge out of the mist. And ahead the snowy peaks of the Cordillera de los Andes began to appear ahead. By then it had picked up a tail in the form of a Peruvian Air Force FA18, that sat just below the trail of mist from the four turbo prop engines.

Throughout the night, various schemes had emerged and been discarded of how the problem might be solved. Attempts to externally manipulate the automatic pilot had been utterly unsuccessful, and although the plane was climbing slightly, it had reached only four thousand feet. Directly ahead lay Mt Huascaran, at over 22,000 feet and all the surrounding terrain was 15,000 feet or more. The position at which the Orion would hit had been minutely calculated by then and a rescue helicopter dispatched from Lima to explore the location. There was a long forested ridge in the foothills that the plane might or might not get over, a broad river valley and then a sheer 10,000 foot rock face into which it would plough head on.

"Can we shoot it down?" Glen had asked. "Here, in the valley, make it ditch in the river. There's plenty of open space."

"It would drop like a stone," Captain Munro said. He was a USAF officer brought in to advise on the problem.

They had a detailed map on the monitor by then and stood around it. They were getting video pictures from the rescue helicopter. Thyssen stood in the background, his arms folded. Captain Munro outlined the scenario.

"The best chance of an outcome with survivors is if it clears the body of the ridge but clips the trees, taking out the props. It will then ditch on this down-slope, which is relatively featureless. But it will still be travelling at 400 miles per hour. It will break up and the wreckage will be scattered over a long distance. And it will still be carrying half its fuel capacity. There will be fire. But, with a lot of luck, a miracle might save one or two of them."

"And if it clears the trees?" Glen asked.

"Then the next best option would be for the pilot of the FA18 to shot it down. It will crash in the valley. Survivors, even as a miracle, would be unlikely. But that is better than allowing it to ram into the cliff, where nothing will be recovered whatever."

"Does the pilot know this?" Harley asked.

"Yes. And he has agreed to shoot, on our orders."

"Brave man."

"He understands the realities. He will try to shoot out the props in the right order. Without engines, it may glide for a short distance before the nose goes down and it slips sideways. If it hits the ground when reasonably level, there is a slight chance of survivors."

"Will the chopper be able to stay?" Cornelius asked.

"Oh yes. We ought to have pictures right up to the crash."

"Beautiful," Thyssen murmured, and turned away.

They waited. There was a lot to do and it was a busy time, but they sat and they waited. About the room, there were small areas of activity as other emergencies arose. But mostly they waited and watched. The nose camera of the FA18 provided a grainy but adequate picture of the big prop-jet as it thundered on into the morning. When the pilot dipped the nose, they could see the mountains and everyone gasped.

Thyssen sat far off in a back corner with his head in his hands, not watching, not doing anything, riding the final minutes in sheer silent agony. Then the helicopter reported visual on both aircraft, and he looked up, stood, and advanced toward the large video screen on which it was displayed. People said things, foolish babbling things, words without thought, without sense, without meaning. Over the tree line of the ridge, the two small spots grew bigger, until you to tell which was which. They seemed to be coming on forever, then suddenly they were there.

"Steady, steady," Captain Munro was saying into the microphone, although it was unclear who he was talking to. Probably the fighter pilot.

Then suddenly, after all the anticipation, it happened almost too fast for the eye to see, certainly for the senses to comprehend. The Orion zoomed over the ridge, well above the treetops.

"Shoot out the props, now !" Munro yelled.

In jumpy video, they could see the FA18 seem to hover above the Orion—something flew from the wing and the plane immediately began to tilt sideways. The jet maneuvered deftly and shot out the propeller on the other side, but the Orion continued to slip sideways.

"Take the other starboard engine next!" Munro bellowed, but the pilot reacted so quickly, he had obviously perceived that for himself. This time when the cannon shells hit, there was flame and great chunks of the inner starboard engine could be seen to rip away. It worked, the plane began to level out but then it dipped to starboard. Hastily, the jet pilot was firing at the inner port engine when suddenly he pulled away. Then they saw why, as the ground came into view. At the stage, a full belly view of the banked aircraft was being offered the camera.

Instantly, the wingtip touched, it cart wheeled, and was gone. There was a huge burst of smoke or dust, and flame flashed amid it and everything was lost in the raging billows. Chucks of things, trailing smoke, went ever way, and the cameraman zoomed out to offer a broader view of the circumstances. There were eruptions and smoke and flame and dust everywhere, and absolutely nothing that in any way resembled any part of an aeroplane. Although he whispered, everyone in the room could distinctly hear what Captain Munro said next.

"Yes, we can see that, Lieutenant. Thank you for trying."

18
ATLAS STUMBLES

The small group of people stood apart at all times, isolated from the other mourners, and although everyone was aware of them, no one approached. In the chapel, they had taken the very back row, at the graveside, they stood off a small distance, aloof and insular.

Wendell was able to recognise most of them. The stocky, rugged looking man in a military uniform he did not know but the tall black woman in stately native robes and headband was unmistakably Andromeda Starlight, her arm linked through that of Harley Thyssen, who looked older and greyer than he seemed on television. His other arm was linked by the radiant red-head Lorna Simmons, and then there was Brian Carrick, whom he had met, wearing an ill-fitting black suit.

They lowered the coffin into the grave, but there was nothing of Felicity in there for no part of her had been found. They buried her old teddy-bear, her stethoscope and her favourite picture of herself and a personal gift from each member of the family. The coffin would have been empty anyway since she had promised her entire body to medical research, but that promise remained unkept.

When that was done, Wendell broke away from his weeping children, steering them into the arms of his sisters, moved away from the other mourners, and approached the isolated group. He looked directly into the eyes of Harley Thyssen.

"She always told us that what she was doing was safe."

"There was always great danger," Thyssen said. "She was the bravest woman I ever knew."

"And she knew the risk she was taking?" Wendell had to ask. It was self-torture, but he needed to know.

"She simply ignored it, and trusted me to keep her safe, and I let her down," Thyssen said without emotion. "I made a mistake and she paid the price."

Wendell glanced sideways at the others, and each of them scowled in protest at Thyssen, but only Brian spoke.

"You couldn't have known, Harley."

Thyssen's face remained unflinching. So did that of Wendell Campbell.

"She believed in you, Thyssen. To the exclusion of her family—and I know she loved us with everything she had. To the exclusion of her career, of herself. She never doubted you. And if you're right and she paid the price of that devotion, I doubt that she would have complained about it."

Thyssen bowed his head, no longer able to manage words.

"Her loss to us is immeasurable," Lorna Simmons said. "No one will be able to replace her."

Wendell continued to face Thyssen's bowed head, and finally Thyssen did raise his eyes to meet the challenge.

"Tell me it was worth it, Thyssen. Tell me she died for some good reason."

Thyssen's tormented face could barely contain its pain, but when he spoke it was level and sure. "She saved more than a million lives. And millions more are in grave danger because she is dead. But she's given us a chance to save them too."

Wendell Campbell stepped back a pace. It was his turn to bow his head. But then he extended his hand.

"Don't blame yourself, Professor," he said. "She was always sure of what she was doing."

And they grasped cold hands on that wintry Wellington day, for only an instant, then Wendell turned and walked back to his stricken children.

*

At Auckland airport, they parted company. As they waited in the terminal for their respective flights, they spoke in muted terms of Felicity Campbell. Each of them shed a tear. Each of them hugged the others, even Wagner. Even Thyssen, who looked grey and drawn. Lorna stayed close. Professor Earthshaker was plainly beginning to show the strain.

Thyssen and Lorna would join a flight to Hawaii, where Lorna would remain to do what she could to prepare the islanders for the next event. Thyssen would return to Washington where President Grayson had called an emergency meeting to discuss the crisis.

"It said on the news that they've already started the meeting without you, Harley," Brian informed him unnecessarily.

"There's nothing I can tell them," Thyssen said. "They don't need me any more."

"But can we trust those bastards. Glen and that NCA freak."

"Joe is there. He's in charge of that stuff now. It's politics from here on, and the less I have to do with it, the better it will be for everyone."

This they also knew from the media. Joe Solomon had made what might have been the most meteoric rise in the history of American politics—one day an unemployed lawyer facing all manner of charges before a Senate inquiry; the next day they were facing him as he addressed them in the Senate, as the official Project Earthshaker adviser on the logistics and budgeting of the crisis.

Andromeda would return to her pilgrims, and lead them across the Congo.

"I've done the recalculation on the assumption that I'm right and the singularity has been deflected from its original course. The original anticipated location of the event after next was the Caribbean but the degree of deflection models out to a point in northern Nigeria, and hopefully you and your gang will be there, Andromeda."

"We'll be there, Harley."

Brian was heading for Melbourne to visit his children, and then fly on to Broome and take over organising the pilgrims from

Indonesia, about half of which were now held in a huge camp on the north west Australian coast.

"Are you really just going to hand it all over to them bastards?" Brian still wondered.

"No," Thyssen smiled. "It's you people who are really in control now. They can't do anything without you and they know it. And they don't have time to consider alternatives."

Wagner would fly to Israel to try and do what could be done to assist the trapped pilgrims in Iran.

"There's nothing much we can do in Hawaii," Thyssen had pointed out.   "And not enough time anyway. The hit after will be in Africa and that will be our last best chance."

"You tell me where and I'll clear the space," Wagner grinned.

"You may have a lot of unwanted assistance from the US Army and other such forces."

"I never fight battles before I come to them, Harley," Wagner said. "That's why I always win."

So they parted for what they knew might well be the last time. They were three less than when they last met—who knew how many fewer they would be if they ever met again. They wished each other good luck and parted.

Lorna sat with Harley all the way to Honolulu, flying backwards through the night into the day before. And with the dawn, Lorna ordered breakfast but Thyssen refused to eat. He looked exhausted even though he had snored loudly all the way.

Then he did an odd thing. He lifted his hand from the arm rest and stared at it in puzzlement for a moment. A sort of ironic smile passed over his lips, he gave a brief snort of amusement and closed his eyes and went back to sleep.

As they began descent, she tried to wake him and could not. His breathing was shallow, his skin grey. She called for help. There was a doctor on the flight who was brought by the flight attendant to make an examination.

"This man is very ill," he said. "He will need to be hospitalised as soon as we land. Have the paramedics standing by with a fibulator."

"It's a heart attack?" Lorna asked incredulously.

"I think so, yes," the doctor said. "Does he have a history of heart trouble."

"Not at all."

"Well I'm afraid he does now."

But Lorna knew the truth Harley's heart had not weakened—it had been broken by the terrible deaths of three remarkable women.

*

Joe Solomon watched as Glen Palenski made is way on creaking shoes around behind the seated men and women to whisper in the ear of John Cornelius. The sense of revulsion at the sighting of the young man who had betrayed them was quickly dissipated when he saw the look that passed over the NSA man's face.

Everyone present saw that look and General Marsden, who was droning on about the readiness of the military at the time even faltered and paused.

President Grayson saw it too, and needed only to raise his hand to halt the general completely, and he directed a questioning look at Cornelius, who flinched.

Cornelius sat forward in his armchair, gripping the obviously terrified Palenski by the wrist to keep him in place, and said quietly. "Mr. President, we have just received word that Professor Thyssen will not be joining us. He has suffered a heart attack and is presently under intensive care in Honolulu."

The words crashed about the room like a thunderclap. Joe felt physical pain in his abdomen and the skin on his face and ears seemed to spontaneously combust. Yet he knew it was coming.

Each time he had seen Thyssen, the man looked older, the stress deepening the lines on his face and turning his skin a frightening grey colour. Lately he seemed to be sweating, almost all the time. And who could doubt the enormous weight he carried upon his shoulders, like Atlas, holding up the entire world and weakening under the strain.

He was what, sixty maybe? No one seemed to know really. He was a big man, fleshy, who abused his health continually. Add to that the massive strain of the situation and the disaster was a certainty. Only a powerful sense of immortality seemed to keep him going.

Logical as that all sounded, Joe tried to imagine a felled Harley, broken and beaten and ill, and the image would not come. Harley was a giant, indestructible, his will prodigious, his manner godlike. For all its inevitability, it was an impossible idea to come to grips with.

It was the second day of the conference and they were gathered in armchairs about the fireplace in the Oval Office. Joe was the only member of the Earthshaker group available and had been pulled in at the last minute when it was discovered Thyssen would be delayed by Felicity's funeral. When he had entered, President Grayson had looked at Joe and asked. "I take it then that Professor Thyssen will not be honouring us with his presence today either."

The funeral had been the day before. Thyssen could have been there by then, had he wanted.

"I have no information, sir," Joe had answered, as he had the day before.

The president walked away, shaking his head and saying. "That man. That man."

Now Joe saw the same lines of stress in the face of Eugene Grayson, and the eyes forlorn, the lower lip trembling slightly from the shock of the news. "What is the prognosis, John?" he asked quietly.

"Not good. His condition is critical."

Grayson gave out a massive sigh, and sat back in his armchair, looking around each of the faces present. "Well, we've managed so far without him. But is there any sense in continuing?"

Cornelius leaned forward to tap the lap-top computer on the table before him. "We have all of his data here."

"Data is data. But who can argue his case?" And he looked directly at Joe.

Joe, who had been rarely called upon to speak, found the effort enormous in these powerful circumstances. "If Harley wanted his case argued, he would be here arguing it."

"He seems to be in no position to do so, by no choosing of his own," Grayson said reasonably.

"He went to New Zealand as a personal priority rather than attending these discussions," Joe persisted.

Do not contradict the president, advisers had warned him. The fierce glare in the eyes of Eugene Grayson emphasised the error—those eyes then dismissed Joe and redirected that gaze upon Cornelius, who spoke with comfortable ease. "I believe, Mr. President, that the absence of Professor Thyssen is intentional, and constitutes a demand that his conclusions be accepted as a *fait accompli*, without compromise."

Grayson wobbled his head as he thought about that. "Yes, I think that is a reasonable conclusion. But even if he is right, although we have the data, how are we to interpret it?"

Joe, knowing in part he wished to make amends for his error, now committed the worse sin of interjecting. "It has already been interpreted, by your own people. Isn't that so, John?"

"But there was error..." Cornelius muttered.

"Which has been explained and can be compensated for," Joe argued.

"So you say," Cornelius came back. "Other more reliable and more reputable scientists, with other systems, are now making equally accurate predictions. Several of them predicted the region in Brazil almost as accurately as Thyssen's system."

"Almost..."

Grayson's powerful voice imposed itself over them easily. "Gentlemen, let us not argue. I think it is obvious that we need someone to present Professor Thyssen's position at these talks. The only question is, who?"

Joe, who had only argumentativeness in him, silence himself with some effort.

But Cornelius, a well trained operator, could speak calmly. "If I may be so bold, sir. We have here Dr Glen Palenski, who was for a long time Thyssen's best regarded student. I doubt that there is anyone better equipped to express the Professor's views than he is."

The look of combined terror and astonishment on Glen Palenski's face brought smiles all around the room. Plainly, had Cornelius still not gripped his wrist, he would have bolted for the door.

The President's hooded eyebrows lurched toward Joe. "Your thoughts on this, Mr. Solomon?"

Joe supposed the expression of horror on his own face matched that on Glen's. "It is true that Dr Palenski is the only surviving member of the Earthshaker team who is a trained scientist," Joe heard himself say to his own complete amazement.

"But I sold them out !" wild-eyed Glen Palenski blurted frantically.

"Judas," Joe countered, "was the disciple who loved Christ most."

Every head in the room was in its hands. Some were hiding mirth, some horror, some embarrassment, but all were hiding something. But, because he was President of the United States of America, Eugene Grayson regathered his wits first. He gazed long and hard at the trembling young man across the room, who might have been handcuffed to John Cornelius, so firmly was he gripped. "Dr Palenski, do you believe that Professor Thyssen is right?"

Glen calmed at the question. It was plainly one that was easy to answer. "Yes, sir. I always did. We differed only on matters of loyalty to the state—never on matters concerning Earthshaker."

"And are you willing to present his side of the discussion?"

"Yes sir. I sold him out once. It was a big mistake. I won't do it again."

"Mr. Palenski, I must ask you to confine your statements to those scientific matters in which you are expert."

"Yes sir. Professor Thyssen is right. He was always right. And I can prove it."

"Can you now? Then please, do so."

"Harley believed that the pilgrims deflected and weakened the singularity. Calculations based on his assumptions place the next event in the Pacific Ocean near Hawaii. No one else could arrive at that conclusion without making his assumptions. Therefore, since there will be no pilgrims in the Zone at that event, if his prediction is correct, then his further conclusions will be beyond doubt."

Grayson nodded. "Well, I understood about half of that. If Hawaii comes off as he said, then we are committed to following the Thyssen plan. Is that it?"

"Yes sir."

"John?"

"That's it in a nutshell. And if Hawaii doesn't happen..."

"Then we have to come up with an entirely new plan, isn't that right, John?"

"Yes Mr. President."

"Mr. Solomon?"

"That's how I understand it."

"Mr. Browning? Mr. Walker? General Marsden? Do you have opinions on this specific matter?"

"Not on this specific..."

Grayson again emitted a great sigh. "That man stood in this very office and he argued with me. Me! An eminent scientist and the President of the United States of America, standing toe to toe, hurling insults at each other like two boys in a schoolyard. Can you imagine that? Well, I'm the President and I won that argument as a President should and I have lived to regret that victory. Like Mr. Palenski, I too have no desire to make the same mistake a second time."

*

Brian Carrick flew from Auckland to Melbourne, and was sitting on a bus stop bench outside the school that his kids attended when the panicky call from Lorna told him the news of Harley's collapse. He promised to fly immediately back to Hawaii, and almost rushed straight to the airport, but then he knew he had to continue here first.

Somehow, the sudden awareness of Harley Thyssen's human vulnerability reminded him of his own.

The kids emerged and spied him immediately and made quite a fuss and he took their tiny hands and started to walk, almost from instinct.

"You comin' home soon daddy?" Leo asked him.

It had only been eighteen months but the boy had doubled in size.

"Soon, maybe. If your mum says its okay."

"She's lonely," Sheila said empathically.

"Doesn't Uncle Larry look after you anymore?"

"He comes round sometimes, when somethin' needs fixin'," Leo said diffidently.

"They usta yell at each other all the time," Sheila added helpfully.

They were so busy telling him all the gossip from school and the neighbourhood that they hardly noticed they had reached the house. Judy stood there. She seemed younger somehow. It looked like she had done something with her hair.

"Mummy, mummy, look who we found?" Sheila cried excitedly.

"He was hangin' around outside school," Leo assured her.

Judy ordered them inside but she stayed.

"You in town long, Brian?" she asked as if she was interested.

"I'm flying out tonight. But I'll be back," he said uncertainly. He wasn't at all sure why he was there. When the divorce proceedings had become hung up due to his continual absence, Judy had allowed it all to slip sideways.

"Why don't you stay for dinner," she said. It wasn't a question.

"That'd be fine."

And there it was. So simply done. The accomplishment of something that a virtual army of social workers, psychologists, psychiatrists, marriage counsellors, friends, relatives and legal representatives had comprehensively failed to achieve for eighteen months.

Judy had only one question and she asked it as soon as dinner was done and the kids put to bed. "Do you think things can be put back they way they were, Brian?"

"Are you talking about the planet or us?"

"Both really, but..."

"It's almost over, darl," he said. "It will go one way or the other. For me, for us and for everyone. Maybe it will be okay—there is a chance I think. But after that, it will never be the same."

"I was really referring to us."

"There's a lot to put behind us."

"Larry is just a friend," Judy said determinedly. "I was just trying to make you jealous. You're the only man I ever loved. I just don't have the sense to love anyone else."

"I've had my dalliances too. But you're the only woman I know who can put up with me for more than an hour."

"Well, that's settled then. The kids will be thrilled."

*

The great trek of Andromeda's legions across the breadth of The Congo Republic was ended, and they stopped at Bususulu, where Thyssen's instructions ran out. Before them lay the great rivers that must now be crossed, the Maringa at their feet, the Lulonga further on, and a few miles beyond that, the giant of which those were mere tributaries—the Congo.

Here the road petered out in the marshy land surrounding the rivers. All about the terrain was slightly undulating and covered with dense tropical vegetation. The pilgrims were strung out for miles back along the road, which you couldn't leave at any point. And now there was nowhere to go on to either.

"I'm organising boats," Captain Maynard said, leaning over the map on the bonnet of his land rover. "But really, we have to fly the next leg."

"Next leg?" Andromeda asked.

"The focal point is here, just a little way north west of Lake Chad."

"They said Hawaii…"

"Yeah. We miss that one, but the direction is still okay for us.

Slightly north of west."

"Show me," Andromeda asked, leaning over his shoulder.

Maynard laid the ruler to the map and positioned it carefully from their present location to the Hawaiian Islands. Presently, they were positioned just two degrees above the Equator, and Hawaii was twenty degrees and half the world away. It was only slightly shorter via the Atlantic and Americas than it was back over Asia and the Pacific.

"Straight over Sierra Leone," Andromeda said quietly.

Maynard needed to peer at the map to understand what she meant. Indeed his ruler passed directly over that tiny state of the extreme west coast of Africa.

"So?"

"Oh nothing," Andromeda said awkwardly, and then backed off. "You were saying."

"Well, that's just the direction for the next few days and it will take us that long to get these people across the rivers."

"And then?"

"There's a good airstrip at Mbandaka. Big enough for the C-130s. So we can float the whole shebang downriver and offload them there."

"But that's on this side of the Congo."

"Yes. Then we fly them."

"With two planes?"

"The US Air force is on the way with more. As many as we need. And the destination is N'guigmi, in Niger, near Lake Chad."

Andromeda considered it grimly. "It sounds very complicated, Captain."

"Best we can do."

"Well, we have to get out of this jungle." And then she trailed a casual finger across the map. "What's the terrain like through here."

"Cameroons? Nigeria? Rough. Big mountains. Big jungle. No roads. Hopeless. But that isn't where we're going anyway... Why do you ask?"

"Sierra Leone's that way."

"Sierra Leone?"

"Land of my fathers, Captain."

"I thought you were Jamaican."

"All black Jamaicans came from Africa somewhere, Captain, as slaves under the British. My ancestors came from Sierra Leone."

"I see."

"Do you?"

"You want to go there?"

"It is the way I'm going… The way I've been leading these people all along."

"But you were following Professor Thyssen's plan."

"His plan has run out."

"No. We have new information. Lake Chad…"

"Provided by the American government."

"But they got it from Thyssen…"

"We can't be sure of that. And Harley is hardly in any condition to help us now, even if he is still alive as they say."

"You don't believe it."

"Black people have a funny way of distrusting the American government, Captain. With all due respect to yourself."

"So you think there might be something wrong with the information."

"Harley always told me, personally, which way to go. I distrust any other source."

"I'm sure. Look, why not contact Lorna, or Wagner…"

"With Harley out of the game, we don't know whose instructions they are following."

"Are you sure you aren't just a wee mite paranoid, ma'am?" Maynard said, slowly beginning to realise that she was serious.

"I'm surprised, after the way they've treated you, Captain, that you aren't."

"But… but… if you're not going follow this plan, what are you going to do?"

"I think I should follow my instincts."

"And what do your instincts say?"

"Land of my fathers, Captain."

*

They had offered her a room but she remained by the bedside, dozing from time to time. Beside her a figure barely recognisable as Harley lay with a tube stuck up his nose and the only sign of life the beeping lines of luminescence charting his vital signs across the monitor screen.

Lorna stirred. Her eyes had sunk back into their hollows and showed black rings about them. She looked pale and exhausted. She saw Brian standing in front her without realising he had entered and hugged him for a long time and then told him of the circumstances.

The heart attack was survivable, but there was a lot more wrong with him than that. It was as if every part of him had been hanging on grimly and now that one organ failed, the rest went with it. The nurses were silent and did their work reverently, the doctors merely nodded and kept their distance.

Even now, as the patient slowly began to regain consciousness, there was no excitement or anticipation. "It's all up to his fighting spirit now," the ward doctor had told Lorna when she had made a scene and demanded a response.

"I've seen this before," the Head Nurse murmured. "The only reason he's hanging on is because he refuses to die."

Lorna had remained at the bedside throughout the entire week. Her skin was as grey as Harley's, her hair dishevelled, her clothes unchanged for days. She had spilled small darts of food down the front of herself and didn't care. She had vomited everything she tried to consume. The tranquillisers the nurses had offered had given her only the minimum of sleep. The whites of her eyes were red, her lips were forced into a hard blue line.

"He can't die like this," Lorna said in a broken murmur. "Not now. Not after all he's done."

She sat by the bed, a hunched pathetic figure, and Brian advanced, hunting words that might help when no help was possible.

"Why is he hanging on like this, Brian?" she asked him with calm ruthlessness. "His job is done. He has no life. But he's hanging on."

"I don't know," he said distractedly. ""Maybe it's because of you."

She looked up then, managed a smile and closed her hand over his.

"They're evacuating the hospital," she said grimly. "But he's too ill to move. This place is going to be blown to hell and we can't get him out."

"Maybe he's trying to be ironic," Brian said.

They weren't really making much of an effort to evacuate the Hawaiian islands. People there knew how to live with volcanoes. The epicentre would be far to the north in the Pacific and every caldera could be expected to erupt at maximum force, but the locals knew how to stay away from them. Tidal waves would inundate the islands but most of the population knew to move to the southern areas and high ground where they would be safe. The buildings were designed to withstand earthquakes. All this Lorna knew, based on the idea that Harley's corrected system predicted accurately.

But if the people were hard to move, there was also only a token effort on the part of the government to move them. The entire island group would fall within the Zone and they would add to the numbers of sleepers, ready for the counter attack in Africa next month.

She tried to explain all these things to Brian, but he already knew. And why not, she reasoned. It was probably he who held the clearest picture of these things in his mind. They both could see that the President had meant what he said when he declared they would go with the Thyssen plan. Hawaii would be the dress rehearsal for the final battle.

*

Glen Palenski had prepared himself well. He had diagrams, videos, overheads, the works. He needed to get it right. His audience was the President, the Joint Chiefs of Staff, the heads of Congress and the Senate, the CIA chief, NCA and all those other agencies. And he had ten eminent geologists and astronomers to back him up, seated in a row like targets in a shooting gallery, off to right of stage.

But it was Glen's show, and he would introduce the argument, and then they would debate it. Hardly any of them agreed on any part of it, except on this one point, the one that he was about to make.

"Gentlemen, there is little doubt now that useless the circumstances change dramatically, our planet will be destroyed, and it will happen within a few months. Professor Thyssen offers us a possible solution—no one else does. Therefore the biggest problem that we have is what happens if Thyssen is right. If he is wrong, we are making a great effort for little or no gain, but if he is right, the consequences will be enormous.

"If he is right, several millions of pilgrims will be gathered on the plain near Lake Chad, at this location here. Already, an airstrip is under construction to receive them, on the assumption that Hawaii comes off as Thyssen predicted and we can then assume that his Lake Chad prediction is also right.

"If Thyssen is right, the effect of the presence of these pilgrims will diminish, perhaps even destroy, the singularity. Again, the magnitude and position of the Hawaiian outcome will show us this. If the deflection is as Thyssen has calculated, then the focal point will be here, 270 kilometres northwest of the large island. If the diminishment of the effect is correct, then the impact will be lower on the scale than Iran, and perhaps even than Java.

"In each instance, the scale was increased, 9.6 in California, 10.1 in Java, 10.6 in Iran. But Brazil was only 8.9, and Thyssen proposes that the diminishment was the effect of the presence of the pilgrims.

"Professor Jordan, however, differs and will tell you that it is because the singularity itself is decaying. If so, Hawaii will be less than 8.9. If Thyssen is right, then since there will be no pilgrims present this time, it will increase again, to about 9.5.

"So what of Africa. If Thyssen is wrong, we will have expended a lot of time and energy and money for no gain except perhaps further knowledge. But if he is right, then at Lake Chad we will find all of the pilgrims freed of the Shastri Effect, and the impact will have been further diminished. Perhaps it will be deflected, but if so it will be far smaller. It may even be completely destroyed.

"But if so, it will be at a great cost. At this location, the earth's crust is more even and generally thinner than anywhere else on the planet. There are no nearby volcanic regions, nor tectonic plate boundaries, nor other major faults. But the impact will be bigger that of California, about 10.0. And there will be nowhere for it to let off steam.

"The nearest major volcanic outlets are in Kenya, 1700 miles away, and some in the Cameroons, 600 miles away. We can expect these to erupt, but history has taught us that the Thyssen Bubble will find its own way out. We expect that at the Lake Chad location, the earth will crack open and be swallowed in a lava flood, much as previously happened at Lake Baikal.

"There will be a very great area of devastation. And all of the pilgrims will be, of necessity, at the centre of that area. Right now there are thirteen million pilgrims in total—4 million Americans in Bakersfield or Brazil, 4 million Indonesians mostly gathered in North Australia, 3 million Iranians now in the hands of United Nations forces, and one million others, mostly Africans, some Japanese, Italians, Tahitians and Brazilians, plus we are expecting around one million or more volunteers from around the world who are presently positioning themselves in the Hawaiian Islands with a view to becoming sleepers. We plan to gather all of them, or as many as possible, at the Lake Chad site. If all this is so, then we can expect that all or most of them will die at Lake Chad.

"The danger they face is great, therefore. As these eminent gentlemen will tell you, there is no certainty of the danger. But, I am here to tell you this. If Harley is right in every respect, then the singularity will be destroyed, the earth will be saved, but perhaps at the cost of the lives of all of the pilgrims.

"I believe the strain of that knowledge, and the fact that he needed to keep it secret and carry the burden of it alone, was the reason why Harley Thyssen collapsed. It was too much for one man to carry alone. Now, we must carry it for him."

*

It was a testament to the power of make-up artists that the television persona of Lorna Simmons could be created so perfectly. Only hours ago, Brian had seen the wraith that haunted Green Palms Hospital when he arrived in Honolulu the evening before. It shocked him, rather more than did the comatose figure of Harley Thyssen.

In the studio, as she came by him, Brian was astonished. There was no trance of the distraught and bedraggled person of a few hours earlier. The cosmeticians and hairdressers had been given the opportunity to show their talents to be limitless. Lorna was every bit her radiant self. They must have clipped her ears together behind her head to so completely rid her of the black bags that had been under her eyes.

Still, as she came by, he asked her. "Are you all right?"

"Of course. Come on. Something just came in on the satellite that you ought to see."

They went to the editing suite when the tape was set running immediately. There was the figure of Kevin Wagner, in something more like a safari suit than his usual military garb but the style was still the same. He stood at a rostrum, addressing a room full of people, but it was plainly the television cameras to which his words were directed.

"Man is not the final outcome of evolution. Evolution is a process, ongoing, for all time, and humanity is only the most recent stage of that process. There will be higher beings in the future, evolved from our primitive selves, beings more appropriate to the tasks that lie before us."

"What the hell is this?" Brian asked.

"I thought you might be interested," Lorna said obliquely.

"What tasks lie before us? Once man believed it impossible to sail across the oceans. They believed that the horizon was the edge of the world and if they sailed beyond it, they would fall off. But really, the limitation was that they did not have ships capable of open ocean voyage, and, more importantly, they didn't have sufficient belief in themselves to try."

They talked over the top of him, but that didn't mean they weren't listening to what he said.

"Do we know where he is?" Brian asked, still incredulous.

"He's on my turf. Addressing the pilgrims that still remain in Bakersfield. But I understand he gave the same address to the pilgrims in Brazil two days ago. And it went out to all other pilgrim locations, translated into the appropriate languages."

"Eventually, the ships evolved from the minds of more advanced men and they did conquer the open oceans and find the great continents beyond.

"And now we confront the universe, and the impossibilities of travel to the worlds out there. Voyages in time beyond the span of human life, voyages impossible with our present technology. But if we know anything about science and technology it is that they will find a way. The spaceships that make these voyages possible will be created, just as the unimaginable aeroplane of the time of Columbus would make spanning the continents an everyday event."

"This isn't Wagner. Someone else must have written the speech for him," Lorna said dismissively.

"All very inspirational, isn't it," Brian replied grimly.

"But there are other problems barring our exploration of the universe. The prolonged time periods for such journeys, and the fact that zero gravity and other aspects of that hostile environment inflict deterioration upon the bodies of astronauts to an unacceptable level. After just a few months in space, a man must be taught to walk again, and build up his deteriorated bones and muscles in normal gravity.

"New great star voyaging space ships will evolve, perhaps using the time distortions of near light speed, perhaps seeking out worm holes, but more likely by some means presently unimaginable to us, our ships will sail to the stars. But to do so, new men will have to evolve as well, men better equipped for such journeys. And more."

"I wonder where he got it all from?"

"Yes, Brian. I wonder," Lorna said, eyeing him ironically.

"We will not just voyage to the stars and come back and say, that was fine. No more than Columbus and the other great explorers did. We will go there and inhabit these places permanently, and make our homes there, and live our lives out there. And when, millions of years hence—or perhaps much sooner if the environmentalists are right—the earth is destroyed or rendered uninhabitable for us, it won't matter, for we must by then be denizens of the galaxy, and eventually the entire universe.

"Don't smile and say it won't happen. It is the smile of the flat-earther. It is our nature to go forth and multiply and we will. Of that there is no doubt."

"Now that you mention it," Brian admitted reluctantly. "It does sound familiar at times."

"Men look at this small planet and say, why have we wondrous creatures evolved on this small out of the way place, this tiny speck of dust in the vast cosmos. The answer is because the centre of anywhere in the cosmos is so hot that nothing can evolve. Life can only be nurtured in the quieter corners of the galaxy.

"But all that is to look at it the wrong way around. It doesn't matter where you came from. That's history. That is past. It's where we're going that counts.

"Civilisation did not evolve on Manhattan Island, nor in London nor Paris. That was where we carried it from the insignificant places of our origins. The plains of southern Africa, if the prevailing guesses are correct, is the place where humanity first arose. But those savannas are insignificant in terms of modern civilisation—still the domain of the chimpanzees and baboons that we were there before we evolved. We have moved on, and made our great societies at journey's end, not at the place where we began."

"I knew this would happen," Lorna murmured.

"But of course that lies thousands, maybe millions of years in the future. It won't be humans like us who will do these things, any more than it was a Neanderthal who went to the River Thames and established London. It will be the beings into which we will eventually evolve. Beings appropriate to life in space, on other worlds, adapted to light speed travel, whatever it needs."

"I think he's got a roo loose in the top paddock," Brian declared.

"But it sounds good," Lorna said.

"Too bloody good," Brian replied.

'For that's the way that evolution works. The needs arise, and the creatures that will survive are those that adapt to meet those needs.

'Oh yes, but it all lies in the impossible future and will take care of itself, you say. Evolution doesn't work like that either. Just as the roots of modern humanity and modern civilisation lie millions of years in the past, so the roots of the future lie in the present."

"We really don't need this," Lorna said, looking at Brian as if it was all his fault.

'The evolution of the new humanity of the future does not lie in the future. That's happening now. We see it, here and now, before our very eyes, in ourselves. Evolution occurs not gradually but in sudden leaps and in the Shastri Effect, we see the latest leap of evolution. The link of the subconscious mind—the power of collective intelligence. The next short but vital step along the road to our destiny."

"This bit is his own idea," Brian said, as if washing his hands of it.

Lorna just hissed in reply.

'We have been given a new birthright. For this brief moment, we have been placed face to face with our destiny. Do we hang onto this gift of unity of minds with which we have been fortuitously provided? Or do we go back to where we were by accepting the cure, and so-called normality.

'This is what they are asking of us. Go back to Africa. Return to you primate origins. Take a backward step in evolution. Ignore the benefits of the Shastri Effect. Come here and be made primitive again."

"You have to admit it's a pretty persuasive argument," Brian said lamely.

"And disaster for us," Lorna replied bitterly.

'The next step along the road of evolution has been taken. It is against nature now to turn back. Let us take this gift of greater intelligence and unity and go forward. Do not go to Africa. Stay here and be a part of the future of humanity.

'The Shastri Effect is ours. Don't let them take it away from us."

*

Harley Thyssen was removed from intensive care on the tenth day after his collapse and, being something of a celebrity guest, was placed in a ward on the top floor of the hospital. He found no reason to protest. There Lorna found him when she made a rushed trip to Hawaii.

Lorna had come to shoot some scenes for a television film that would, plainly and simply, explain the whole situation to the world. She prepared the program wisely, offering a full history of the project and the Shastri Effect in a documentary that she hosted and narrated herself. For greater impact, she said, the *top and tail* was filmed in Hawaii, where within days proof of Thyssen's theory would take place. "All that you see around me will be destroyed," she was able to say. No one suggested she had an ulterior motive for being there.

"You shouldn't be here," Thyssen grumped at her. "You have far too much to do to allow this sort of dalliance."

"I've come to rescue you," Lorna said, kissing him firmly on his bloodless lips.

"And take me where?" Thyssen asked skeptically.

"There are plenty of other hospitals."

"I belong here, Lorna. And you know it."

"I'm taking you somewhere safe."

"Nowhere is safe anymore."

"You know what will happen here."

"Yes. And I'll have the best seat in the house."

"You bloody vulcanologists and your death wishes. Wasn't Jami's suicide enough?"

That was going too far. A tear appeared in Thyssen's eye but he managed to keep his voice level. "Lorna. The young and fit and healthy people are having enough trouble getting off the island. I'm staying."

"I've arranged everything."

"Un-arrange it. I'm not the sort of man to accept privileges—you know that. It's hard enough staying alive in my present condition without having to live with the guilt that I took someone else's place on an aeroplane and they got left here and died. It just wouldn't be any good. And with all this medical junk that would have to come with me, you could fit a dozen skinny people in my place."

"Harley, we need you."

"No you don't. It's just like joining the dots from here."

"Oh yes, the great Harley Thyssen master-plan. Everything will just fall into place."

"Anything that happens from here won't happen any better or worse because I'm there."

"Harley, you just don't know…"

But he put his fingers over her lips. "Didn't the nurses tell you that you aren't allow to get me excited by arguing with me?"

Lorna sighed. She backed off immediately, knowing that was true. Obviously she would have to come in on a more subtle tack.

"You knew this was going to happen, didn't you?"

"Which of my many wise or foolish predictions are you referring to now?"

"The heart attack. That was why you arranged for all of us to be able to take over without you."

"No, I didn't. I knew I had health problems and it was a reasonable assumption that the stress would get to me in the end. That's all."

"You can't fool me, Harley. I remember that little experiment of yours when I was the guinea pig. You expected me to die."

"No I didn't. I didn't know what would happen."

"And you kept me on the fringe, as close to the edge of the zone that you could manage."

"The experiment would have been rendered useless if a tree fell on you."

"But you knew that the pilgrims would have to be in the middle of the zone if they are going to kill the black hole. And as many of them at that point as possible. And that, if they succeeded, they would probably all die—not from the depletion of the Shastri Effect but from the effects of the impact."

"I knew that was possible."

"And you've carried this devastating knowledge alone, all along."

"I didn't know any of it for sure. I still don't."

"Oh Harley, you could at least have shared it with me."

"Oh sure, and have two of us worry themselves to death."

"I'm stronger than you."

"Why? Because you're younger? Because you're a woman? You just don't grasp how unbearable it was…"

"It was my right to be a part of it."

"You had, and have, more important things to do. And how could I share what I was never sure of. I've bullshitted my way through this all alone, Lorna. I've never at any time been sure I was right. If someone comes up with a better theory, I'll jump on their bandwagon and dump mine immediately."

"But no one has because no one has, because you're the best, Harley."

"No, Lorna. I didn't get it right because I was a good scientist, but because I was such a very bad one. I guessed. I can't prove a thing. I have no choice but to agree with all those colleagues that call me a fake and a charlatan. I'm full of shit and I always was. I got out there and bullied people, bluffed my way through. I never did good science."

"Once this comes off, Harley, no one is ever going to believe that."

"But I'm so frightened, Lorna. I may be killing millions, just to prop up my own ego."

"The millions will die anyway. But you give millions more the chance to live."

"If I'm right."

"You don't need to be right, Harley. All we needed was a chance. All we wanted was some hope. What was unbearable was the helplessness. We were up against forces that were so enormous, too huge to fight. You cut it down to size so we could see it and get a handle on it. We needed to have at least the illusion that we could fight back. And you have given us that. And all humanity, every your worst opponents, thank you deeply for that."

"You're very kind to say so. I wonder if history will be so kind."

"Without you, there won't be any history."

"Still, it would all have been easier to face if I was dead."

Lorna hesitated. She really didn't want to push him, things being the way they were, but she was desperate to persuade him.

"Will there be enough of them?" she asked quietly.

"Enough what?"

"Pilgrims. At Lake Chad. Enough to kill the singularity?"

"I have no idea, really. The figures are too approximate."

"They always were, Harley. But you always made them work. And that's why we need you."

"I'm afraid that sum is so simple, even you could do it, if you tried. 2.2 million pilgrims deflected the singularity in Brazil, but they also diminished its impact by 20%. 5 times 2.2 is 11 million pilgrims needed to complete the job, in theory. There are 13 million available—if we can get them all there it ought to be enough. But there are so many imponderables, variables, unknowns, approximations and downright guesses to tie into those numbers that no one could seriously suggest it's in any way accurate. But they are all the figures and pilgrims available so we have to go with it and be damned."

"And if you're right and it's enough?"

"We have no knowledge at all as to what will occur when a black hole is eliminated. If there aren't enough pilgrims, there will be a massive earthquake at the site and they will all die. But if there are enough and the plan works, there still might be an even greater explosion. There has never been a time in human experience when something was totally annihilated. Maybe nothing will happen, or maybe it will take the whole planet, or even our very existence, with it. There's no way of knowing."

"But surely, my love," Lorna said, having found the bit of that that she wanted to latch onto, "if something goes out of existence, then it just ceases to exist. Nothing else happens. Not with a bang, but a whimper."

Thyssen laughed. It seemed to give him some pain, but he did it anyway. "Lorna, you sweet child, you really shouldn't take quotations out of context like that. In the circumstances, it's very inappropriate. But anyhow, it's me whose going out with a whimper. As you see, now the sums have become really simple, the theories are all theorised, the guesses have all been made, it's all done and I'm not needed anymore."

That did it. Suddenly Lorna decided to do what she had promised herself she would not do. All the way to Hawaii and even as she came through the doors of the hospital, she kept telling herself not to trouble him with the day-to-day problems that the project was experiencing. But now she knew it was the only way forward. She said. "But you are needed now, Harley. I'm afraid your little ol' master-plan is going off the rails."

"They all do."

"Wagner's gone completely whack-o. He's telling the pilgrims that they are the next great stage of evolution and they should avoid the cure and the focal point."

"I know. I've seen it on the news. How many are swallowing it?"

"Hard to say. In California and Brazil, about half. Less in other places. I'm working my butt off trying to win them back."

"Yes. And that's what you should be doing now, instead of worrying about an old fogey like me."

"And Andromeda wants to take her flock to Sierra Leone instead of Lake Chad."

"It can't be done."

"She's the goddess Gaia. She can do anything she likes."

Thyssen nodded ruefully. "When you elevate someone to a position like that, you must expect delusions of grandeur."

"Is that all you've got to say about it?"

"What makes you think I have some power to persuade her otherwise."

"You invented her."

"And now we reap what we have sown, Lorna. You've got to get her to go the right way. You'd have to do so, whether I was around or not."

"And the Yanks are holding back."

"But at least they're involved now."

"Sure, the Seventh fleet and a huge flotilla of ships is standing by waiting to see what happens here."

"Very wise of them."

"But if they wait too long…"

"I get it. You want to have a heart attack too to put us back on an even footing."

"This isn't a joke, Harley."

"Lorna, just do what you can. Give it your best shot and see how it goes. No one ever expected more of anyone than that."

"And meanwhile you stay here and get blown away."

"For me, it all hangs on what happens here, Lorna. There isn't any place else I should be."

*

A tall man in a cape of many coloured feathers and with a small cap on his bald black head, stood before a group of his fellows on the tarmac. Behind the heat haze made the mountains shimmered. This place was exactly on the equator, and Wagner sweated freely.

They met in open country—a broad plain with trees seen only distantly. The lake was so near you could see the silver mirage rippling. Wagner's three helicopters stood shimmering in the heat haze. His twenty men and the twenty Barak had brought with him stood facing each other with mutual suspicion and weapons levelled. Both groups were in military fatigues and the only real difference was that Wagner's men had M16s and the Fulani soldiers AK47s.

The man of many feathers was tall and black and graceful, wearing a floral frock-like garment with the feathers attached everywhere, but mostly in his hair. The outfit was ceremonial, formal, and meant he was ready to talk.

The man was a Fulani, an emir in fact, and Islamic in the most fundamental way. His greeting to Wagner was to spit at his feet. Wagner spat back.

"I degrade myself to speak to you, American," he said bitterly, but in fine English.

"I don't seek your friendship," Wagner said boldly. "I bring a warning."

"That you Americans are here is a warning to all peace-loving men."

"I do not speak for America. I speak for peace."

"You are American. To you, peace means American dominance."

"Yes. And I warn you that the Americans are coming."

"Are they not already here?"

"As I say, I do not speak for them. But they have done a deal with your enemies, the Hausa, and are coming to occupy this place."

"Why would the Americans wish to occupy this place?"

"For the mineral wealth of the land by the lake."

"Many have come and sought the wealth. None have found it."

"Americans have satellites that can see through the surface of the earth, and they have seen, and like what they saw. And now they will come and join forces with your enemy the Hausa and drive you into the lake."

"There has been peace between the Hausa and the Fulani for fifty years."

"You have heard my warning. Ignore it if you chose."

"What do you want of us?"

"Only that you watch the skies and prepare for war."

"But why do you, who speaks with an American voice, betray America's plans to us."

"I was once an American. Now I have a higher allegiance."

"Are you a son of Allah?"

"No. But I am a friend of his."

*

There was a young nurse who was there every day—she seemed to have made Thyssen her personal responsibility. She was only twenty maybe, with blonde tied back and a face full of freckles, but she had the most delightful smile and wasn't afraid to use it, no matter how badly he behaved. She stood now by the window on this topmost floor of the hospital. The view was fantastic but the nurse seemed to forget that she had other patients.

"You ought to be able to see it all from here," she smiled. Plainly she knew exactly who he was.

"It is a fine view, thank you," he said.

He could see all the way from Kono Head to the mountains west of Pearl. Yep, the best view to be had in all Honolulu.

"Is the world really going to end, Professor?"

"I don't know. But I reckon this place will get a big shake-up. Have you made arrangements to leave?"

"No. We had a meeting. All the staff agreed to stay on. They've evacuated as many people as they could but half the population is still here. They may need us."

"Yes. It's very brave of you."

"I don't think that's what I wanted to hear. What will happen, Professor?"

"Everything that can erupt will. There'll be a tsunami, maybe the biggest ever, but that will hit the north side of the island. It's hard to say just how extensive the damage will be here."

"And everyone here who survives will be one of your… sleepers. Is that what they're called?"

"Yes. We ought to be inside the zone."

"Then we all get to go to Nigeria and kill the monster, isn't that right?"

"Is that what they told you?"

"Well, sort of… The ant-matter or singularity or whatever it is. Anyhow, I volunteered. So did all the other girls."

"Really? It's a terrible risk."

"Sure. But it's my big chance to save the world, Professor. And I don't want to miss it."

"Amazing."

"It's not just me, Professor. All the planes and ships evacuating people to the mainland are coming back full of volunteers wanting to be in on it too."

"Crazy bastards. What if I'm wrong?"

"Then nothing will happen here. Isn't that so?"

"Yes. That's so."

"But we all believe in you, Professor. So it will happen."

"Yes. I think it will."

"So, they wanted me to ask you, where will the safest places be?"

"No place is guaranteed. But the tsunami will loop around the island and there will probably be a secondary wave here. So stay out of basements, and get above ground level. And make sure there's something very solid over your head."

"The usual procedure, huh?"

"Yes. The usual."

When the time came, she returned and he found he welcomed it. He had no regrets when they had been forced to drag Lorna away and send her off to her duties. Plainly she had been convinced that she would never see him again. Maybe she would not.

The nurse sat with him, trying not to make a countdown of it.

"Help me over to the window," Thyssen asked.

"You really aren't allow out of bed yet, Professor."

"What's your name?"

"Debbie."

"Debbie, it hardly matters at this stage. Get this thing out of my arm and help me or I'll do it myself."

She compromised by finding a wheelchair, but he needed to stand to get the view he wanted. She stood by him, holding his hand, and then he put his arm around her.

"Coming on for nightfall," he murmured. "It's late."

But, far out, he could see the glow to the north and knew the big island had roared to life. The building began to shake, and he saw the spurts of flame from Kono Head and at a dozen spots along the eastern side of the island. He even saw the shockwave coming—he grabbed Debbie and dragged her down below the line of the window ledge.

The glass from the windows exploded across the room and the wind, a fiery breath from hell itself, scorched into the room. Thyssen, on the floor, hugged the girl close, in those final seconds, as he felt the sudden nausea, and his vision slip away. He held her as he might have Lorna, had she been there, but who he really thought of was Jami.

"Yes, Jami, I saw it. I felt it. You were right. It was worth it…" was his final thought before blackness swallowed him.

19
THE PLAIN OF CONFRONTATION

He could see they were just in time. As they swept inland from the southern edge of the vast lake, Wagner soon spied the broad area cleared of scrub. Two large prefabricated buildings and a lot of smaller structures and tents had been erected, and the yellow shapes of mechanical monsters dragged long tails of dust as they moved about. The airstrip would be finished in days—they could probably already land a C-130 there.

"Go straight in," Wagner instructed the pilot of his lead helicopter. He had brought with him fifty men, more than enough he could tell. There couldn't be more than a hundred men on the ground and most of those would be native construction workers. All of his own men were trained heliborne assault troops.

"They're asking who we are," the co-pilot responded, his voice crackling inside the helmet Wagner wore.

"Tell them it's Colonel Wagner, come to reinforce the ground troops against rebel attack."

There was a pause while the messages were exchanged. "Keep going right in and land, no matter what," Wagner instructed the pilot in the meantime. "We'll do it the hard way if we have to."

"They're saying they haven't had any trouble with rebels," the co-pilot relayed.

The Black Hawk Assault Helicopters were pulling into a line behind him and on firm descent toward the airstrip below.

"They're moving in on you even as we speak," Wagner said with a smile. It amused him that he was able to speak the truth. In the hills beyond, he knew the Fulani guerillas were making their way up from the south to support his operation. They were because he had arranged it that way. And from the west, Hausa rebels were closing in. That he had arranged as well. Within days this would be the scene of a major battle, and the movement of the pilgrims here would be utterly unsupportable.

"They say they can't let us land without clearance from Captain Maynard," the co-pilot relayed.

"Tell them to get clearance. Maynard takes his orders from me anyway. And by the time he responds we'll be on the ground."

"They've got Captain Maynard on the ground now," the co-pilot said sheepishly.

"Oops," Wagner chuckled, and then. "Patch him through to me."

On the ground, as the Black Hawks ever neared, he could make out the tent that was the command post. A jeep had just pulled up there and a tall figure had strode into the tent.

"Wagner, what in the name of god are you up to?"

"You've got two huge armies of rebels closing in on you. We're the reinforcements."

"Nobody told me about this. I'm sorry, Kev, but you can't land."

"We have to land. We need fuel. And you need us."

"I can't permit this. I have no appropriate instructions from Task Force."

"I don't take orders from Task Force."

"You do now. We all do. This is totally a UN operation, and you are part of us."

"We are one minute from touch-down."

"You can't land, turn back."

"What are you going to do, Maynard. Shoot at us?"

He could almost hear the groan on the other end of the line. In the background, someone said something about another fuck-up.

And then the Black Hawks touched down in a vast cloud of swirling dust. "Go! Go! Go!" Wagner relayed to his men and they spilled from either side of the skittish machines.

The dust from the downdraft of the choppers gave them perfect cover and they deployed as planned, to all parts of the site, invisible in their yellow fatigues and face-masks and goggles until it was too late for any of the ground crew to respond.

Wagner walked out of the man-made yellow fog and saw Maynard coming straight at him. He levelled his M16, and Maynard pulled up short.

"What the hell are you doing?" Maynard shouted, and it cost him a lot to do so in the hostile environment. Wagner was able to walk right up to him while he coughed and spluttered and cleared his watering eyes.

"Call on your men to surrender, Maynard. We got enough troubles without fighting amongst ourselves."

Maynard stared at him. Suddenly, far too late, it was all clear to him. "What are you going to do, Wagner, shoot me?"

"Unlike you, Maynard, I won't make the mistake of hesitating."

Maynard was such an officer and a gentleman that even at this moment of betrayal and defeat, when he swore he did so under his breath. Then he turned to the radio man behind him. "Order all units to stand down."

The order was transmitted. Meanwhile, Wagner had walked past Maynard and they both turned such that their positions were reversed. It was an simple as that.

"Didn't expect you to be here, Maynard. Though you'd have your hands full at the other end."

"To get those people to go somewhere, first you gotta give 'em somewhere to go."

"Last I heard, Andromeda was leading them straight on to Sierra Leone."

"She's got nowhere to go but here."

"Then she's got nowhere to go."

"You won't get away with this, Wagner. You're going to have the whole US air force down on your neck."

"Sure, that is, if Grayson's got the nerve to start a shooting war to defend the Thyssen plan."

"He's committed."

"Sure he is. I'm betting he's as gutless as every politician in all history."

"If you keep us hostage, he'll have to send a rescue mission. My men are mostly US Navy."

"You ain't hostages, buddy. I'm not in the terrorist business. You can leave any time you like. Take our helicopters. I give them to you."

"And how are you going to get out?"

"We ain't going anywhere."

"You can't be serious."

"I sure am. Go. Now. I'm sure your men will squeeze in if they leave all their gear behind. Go with my blessing."

"And what are you going to do when the rebels get here?"

"We'll just have to try and make friends with them."

*

The hospital was built to last, and certainly stand up to more than a distant earthquake and tidal floods surging through its lower floors. The moment Brian entered the building, an illusion was worked on him. Out there was a swamped city, vast pools of mud lay about the rubble, the trees were stripped of branches, everything in sight was damaged. The people toiled in their bright shirts—as if to cheer themselves—with shovels and brooms. There was no power, no water, there were thoughts of evacuating the city if essential services could not soon be restored. Honolulu was paradise turned shambles.

But as the hushed doors of the hospital admitted him into its cool corridors, it was as if nothing had happened. The building was structurally sound, the auxiliary power operating, everything had been cleaned or thrown out—there was a huge heap of carpets and timber furniture in the middle of the car park, as if waiting for bonfire night. Fourth of July was only a week away, Brian supposed.

The white uniforms of the shuffling nurses, implacable as ever with their breezy air of efficiency, were everywhere. Ten days before this building had been flooded up to second floor level and filled with sleepers. When rescue services moved in, it became loaded with casualties to many times its normal capacity. But now no trace of all that remained.

Thyssen was in a room on the top floor. He lay in the bed, pale, looking his age, the rough ruddiness of his pallor and his personality vanquished. Or so it seemed at first.

"Just the man I wanted to see," Thyssen said. His voice was chillingly soft.

"Don't go bungin' the business-as-usual bullshit on me, Harley."

"No, really. I'm getting better every day."

"Yeah. You look it."

"Listen, this is important…"

"Nothing is important. You're a patient. I'm a visitor. That's all there is."

"So where's the flowers?"

"Lorna said you didn't want any."

"Who do you reckon brought these?"

"Actually, you *are* getting better. She said you couldn't hardly speak when she was here. If I'd known you were back in action, I'd have stayed away. I do have a lot of work to do, you know."

Thyssen decided to give up on the banter. Plainly it was tiring him. He charged straight at the point. "You've got to get me to Lake Chad."

"No way. I already checked. Doctors said you're too ill to move."

"Fuck the doctors. I've got to be there. You know that."

"No reason for you to be there at all, that I can see. We have everything under control."

Brian wondered if he ought to say anything about Kevin Wagner's raid, but decided against it. Maybe it didn't matter anymore anyway.

"Come on, Brian. Gimme a break."

"I've got 12 million people to move in there. Do you think we can lay on a plane just for you?"

The argument seemed to defeat Thyssen. The anxiety left him and he breathed for a while. Brian pulled up a chair and sat, regarding him.

"I saw it, Brian. Right out that window. The whole damned thing. Kono Head went up. The wave coming in. I even saw the shock wave go by. The works."

"You'd think you'd be happy now, after that."

"It was worth it, Brian. Really. I think I understand why Jami did what she did. That poor lovely girl. And Felicity. And Chrissie. Three fine women, and I killed them all."

"You killed no one. Stop trying to take all the credit for everything. All three knew the risks they were taking. Nobody forced them to do anything."

"You're not supposed to argue with me and get me excited."

"I didn't come here to argue."

"Then why are you here?" Thyssen finally asked.

"To try and figure out how come you ain't dead. In case I need to know the trick myself."

Thyssen laughed. It seemed to hurt him to do so. "Hard to kill, that's all. Some might say I've been dead for a long time."

"You getting into psycho-babble these days, Harley?"

"No, it's true. You know, I reached a point, when I was about fifty. My wife had died. My kids were gone. I'd done everything in vulcanology that there was to do and it was all boring to me. My life was over and I wasn't dead yet. That's a very awkward position to be in."

"Kids don't come by on Thanksgiving, huh? I thought all Yankee kids did that."

"It was me who didn't turn up for Thanksgiving, for most of their lives. Nor any other time, all that much. I had too much work to do, and just never got home. When I did, I was locked up in my study. They hardly ever saw me. When they left home, they returned the favour. It isn't that they hate me or anything. Less than that. They just don't care about me."

"Why are you telling me this?"

"Same reason I tell you anything else. Because you need to know."

"I've *been* keeping up contact with *my* family."

"I can't help thinking about Felicity. The way that I deprived her family of her for all those last months. It was unforgivable really. Almost as if I did it out of spite."

"I think your heart attack has softened your brain, Harley."

"She wasn't the only GP in the world, you know."

"But she was the best one for the job."

"I can't deny I kept her around for selfish reasons."

"We all liked her, Harley. Loved her, I mean. You can't blame yourself for that."

"I can, and I do. It was all my fault."

"You really think you have that much control, Harley?"

"Well, maybe I am a little deluded on that point."

"Just like the rest of us. We'll all get over it."

Thyssen allowed a pause. He dragged himself further up the pillows, settled, and Brian let all that happen without comment. Finally, Thyssen, arranged to his own satisfaction, eyed his visitor directly.

"Brian, you do realise that I have no idea of what is going to happen at Lake Chad."

"The evidence is good enough for me."

"It's no more than a best guess."

"Harley, you seem to be the only person left in the world who doesn't know that the smart thing to do is go with your guesses. It'll be the right time and place."

"Yes, I think it will, but thinking it will isn't good enough for a scientist."

"You stopped being a scientist a while back, now. You've become a humanitarian instead. Didn't you notice?"

"I wondered what that strange feeling was. But it isn't that. Empirical evidence, circumstantial as it may be, is adequate to suggest I have the time and place right. The hit will be at Lake Chad. What I'm guessing at is what effect the pilgrims will have there and what effect it will have on them."

"As I recall, that was my theory, not yours."

"Okay, but I gave it a scientific basis that in fact it doesn't have. They may all be killed, Brian. I may be sending them all into a trap."

"And every one of them knows that and is willing to take the chance. And thousands of other non-pilgrims are heading there too, because they believe it. It's a matter of faith, Harley."

"But I could be sending 12 million people to their deaths. That makes me a worse monster than Hitler."

"Harley, they aren't doing it for you. They're doing it because they can feel it and it feels right. They all reckon they can beat this thing and they want to be there and give it a go. And you provided them with that chance."

"Still, you must understand why I need to be there. What if they all die and I survive? Think of how unbearable that would be. I have to be there. Whatever happens to them must happen to me."

"It won't happen to you, Harley. The journey will kill you."

"You don't have any choice, Brian," Thyssen smiled. "Didn't they tell you that the zone encompassed this whole island. I'm just another pilgrim now."

*

Sierra Leone. It was the only place to go. Straight on, the way they had been going. Andromeda suddenly discovered that she knew it with a certainty that frightened her. And why? Because her ancestors had been born there. She was going home and taking her people with her.

"You gotta be kidding," Brian said. He had flown in, on his way to Lake Chad to take over, and was stopped because they said he could go no further.

"Why else have we been going this way so relentlessly?" she replied.

"Because its on the way to Lake Chad."

"We can't go to Lake Chad. Wagner's mongrels have taken over there."

"Maynard is gathering an assault force…"

"You expect me to lead my people into a war zone."

"I understand Sierra Leone has a war of its own," Brian said. "And is one of the most impoverished and over-populated places in the region. Hardly the promised land."

"It's home."

"Bullshit! You said yourself you were born in Trinidad."

"Sure I was. But Sierra Leone is my spiritual homeland."

Brian Carrick knew, better than anyone, that when matters

turned spiritual, all reason had failed and there was no point in further argument. "Okay. So how the hell are you going to get there from here?"

"Downriver. We have hundreds of boats, then overland."

"Through the Cameroons? The most rugged place with the steepest mountains in the world. There's no hope."

"Then we'll stay in the boats and sail around…"

"River boats and canoes in the Atlantic? Be realistic, Andromeda. It can't be done."

"Some folks said we couldn't get this far."

"And you have and your people are stuck in the mud and exhausted. They can't go any further."

"It is the only place to go."

"Maynard will be ready to go in the morning."

"I will not lead my people into a war."

"Just hold on."

"Sierra Leone. And it is time to go now."

But the rain poured throughout the night and the pilgrims became increasingly bogged and weary. At dawn, the sky was clearing. Captain Maynard had gathered his forces, and Brian joined him. Maynard's plan was as simple as possible. Refuel, rearm, reinforce, and get back to the airstrip on the Plain of Confrontation as quickly as possible.

"He's only got about fifty men with small arms at the moment. A few rockets and grenade launchers. The longer we delay, the more time he has to build up his troops and his equipment."

He was undoubtedly correct. Already intelligence reports regarding bands of rebels closing in on the airstrip were coming in, and a NATO fighter had forced a Caribou to land after it refused to identify itself. It was loaded with Stinger missiles and other heavy weaponry.

"If he'd got his hands on that lot, it'd have taken months to dig him out."

"Why not wait?" Brian suggested. "The US air force is coming to do this."

"We can't wait for them. It has to be sorted now," Maynard said.

Suddenly everyone was in such a hurry, Brian was thinking. "You might need the extra firepower."

"We have all the fire power we need, and think of the damage that an air strike might do the facility anyway. We have the troops and the guns to do the job—we go in now."

"Not without me you don't," Brian said.

"Nor me," said a quiet voice from the shadows.

"Fabrini! How the hell did you get here?"

"The UN has taken over moving the pilgrims here from Brazil. There was nothing left for me to do there. This seemed to be the place to go."

The Italian, with his drooping moustache, armed to the teeth as always, a one-man army, Brian smiled. "Maybe we got enough firepower after all," he grinned at Maynard.

*

Joe Solomon was a prisoner still, facing an astonishing array of charges relating to his fund raising efforts—he had somehow become one of the worst white collar criminals in history. But he was a prisoner with privileges—presently his cell was a guest room in the White House. Eventually, inevitably, there came a late night visitor—a secret service man knocked on the door, and President Grayson hurried past him and entered the room, closing his guardian outside.

"I wanted a private word with you, Joe," he said, as if he thought he needed permission.

"Certainly, Mr. President," Joe smiled.

"I'd like to be able to say that there's something I can do to help you with your legal problems, but unfortunately such matters lie beyond the scope of my powers."

Grayson moved across the room and stood by the window, gazing through the bars, out into the darkness beyond.

"Perhaps the courts will be lenient when they realise it was all done in a good cause. This situation is so unique, it's hard to say what will happen."

"One of three things will happen, Mr. President. Either nothing will happen at Lake Chad and everyone will go home and I will spend the rest of my life in one of your excellent prisons. Or else everyone at Lake Chad will be killed by the earthquakes caused by the singularity—thus proving its existence—whereby I doubt that any of us will live long enough for my case to make trial. Or else, Thyssen's plan will save us all, which ought to indeed create serious confusion amongst your most experienced legislators. I'm fully prepared to face each possibility."

"In third case, I won't be much of a president if I cannot arrange you some kind of pardon."

"In the light of things, it is a small consideration."

"A fourth possible outcome has arisen, Joe. Right now, there is a fire-fight occurring on the Plain of Confrontation. Intelligence reports are unclear about who is fighting who, but it does raise the possibility that the pilgrims might never get to the focal point. Whereby nothing will be proven."

"A battle, hmm? I'll bet Wagner's cut-throats have something to do with it."

"That is considered likely. Which poses the question of US military intervention."

"It would be wise to figure out which side you are on first."

"That is a luxury a president cannot always afford. The urgency of the situation directs that perhaps we ought to go in and clear the area of all fighters, and get the pilgrimage underway again."

"So where is your dilemma."

"The alternative is to let matters take their course."

"I see. How does that involve me?"

"I needed to speak to someone with absolute and unquestioned faith in Thyssen. Something that, one way or another, all of my advisers lack."

"And you think that might be me?"

"You, with the things you've done, have shown remarkable faith in him."

Joe smiled sadly and shook his head. So it had come down to

this. He wondered if he should have been surprised. All sorts of lies that he might tell occurred to him at that moment, but he firmly decided that he had told his last lie, if indeed he had ever told any. This was the most powerful man in the world, and he needed the truth. "I'm afraid I must disillusion you, sir. I have never liked nor trusted Thyssen. I think him to be the worst scientist on the planet. He proceeds with guesswork and assumptions at all times. He changes his mind and his plan and tells everyone something different. Faith is not possible."

Grayson stared at him for a long time. "Good Grief. Is that what you really think?"

"It is."

"But you stole billions for him!"

"Not for him. I don't know why I did it really. It was there to be done. It was great fun. It was a deathwish. And maybe, just maybe, it might save a great number of lives. But I never believed it and I still don't."

"Joe, I am horrified."

"Would you rather that I had lied to you?"

"No. No, I appreciate your candour. But it doesn't help much with the decision facing me."

"Yes it does. You must do what you believe, Mr. President. Don't do it because you believe in Thyssen, or don't believe. He's not God. He's just a man. You must decide how it feels for you. In your heart, do you think this terrible thing is real, or not. Just like I did. I had the choice between living out life as a cripple with a limited expected lifespan, or else maybe being a hero who saved the world. It was always a very easy choice."

"Mine is not so easy."

"Yes it is. If we survive, you have the choice between trying for a second term as a fair enough president, or else as the greatest of all presidents—the one who made the decisions that saved all humanity. It, too, is an easy choice."

"I begin to see how you persuaded all those people to part with their money, Joe."

"You really don't have any choice, Mr. President. The pilgrims are going to Lake Chad anyway. Either they walk into a war zone or else they don't. It's simple."

"I'm beginning to wish I had never embarked upon this conversation."

"It's what happens when you associate with known criminals, Mr. President."

*

Within hours, Maynard—now aided by Brian Carrick and Fabrini—had thirteen helicopters full of assault troops and five gunships to cover the assault. And in addition, US Marines from a carrier in the Atlantic and UN troops from several locations around Africa were on the way, but they would take a day or two to arrive. Maynard's assault troops would have to take and hold the position until then.

Kevin Wagner, atop the scaffold platform that served as a control tower, knew all that. His computer scanners were picking up messages from all over, for it was all being done in such haste that there was no security. He could listen to the reports flowing back and forth on his own radio and understand their intention. He expected it all anyway. What it lacked in security, it made up for in speed. He had not imagined that Maynard would be able to gather a sufficient force and return the day after he had been evicted. And he did not expect that the US and UN would be willing to commit themselves militarily without the usual diplomatic dithering. But he was ready and confident anyway.

"It's all right," he told Magambo, the rebel leader who was his lieutenant. "My men will be able to hold them off until your main force arrives."

"They will be much outnumbered," Magambo fretted. "And be against superior firepower."

"But we are a superior species and will fight like the supermen we are," Wagner assured him.

In fact his men had little time to prepare any serious defence, and they had only the weapons that they had brought with them.

"It would be against history and against evolution if we were to be defeated," Wagner explained. "Always, the superior being prevails over its fore-runner. To lose would be against nature."

Admittedly, the interception of the Caribou was a bitter blow. Maynard would arrive before any of the extra equipment now.

"Still, we have only to hold them off until your forces arrive," Wagner said assuredly. Magambo shook his head doubtfully.

Soon Maynard's airborne assault force appeared in the southern sky. They were coming straight in, intending to land on the airstrip and assault head on. It was just the sort of fight Wagner was sure he could win.

Almost as soon as Wagner's perimeter forces opened fire, a rocket hit one of the helicopters and it limped toward the ground, trailing smoke. Immediately, all the others took defensive action, and turned away, and soon disappeared back over the horizon.

"See how easy it was," Wagner smiled. But he knew that wasn't true. Maynard would not have given up so easily. Unless, of course, it was the chopper bearing him that was destroyed, the smoke from it's ruins rising out of the plain as the sunset came on.

"Tell the men to stay alert. They may be back," Wagner warned.

He listen to the radio interceptions in the control tower to try and establish what had happened. It had been too easily. Surely they expected that much resistance. It was strangely silent.

"Extinguish all lights. They may try a night assault."

Toward midnight, he heard the first distant gunshot and knew he had been right. Before he could get outside and try to assess the situation, sporadic gunfire was bursting out all around the base. Magambo ran behind Wagner as he hastened to his command post to try and establish the nature of the assault. Tracer rounds sliced through the night all around, along with the dazzling blossoms of explosions. He already guessed what had happened. The heliborne assault had been a feint. In fact they had landed their troops just out of sight of the airstrip and come in overland under cover of darkness.

Already, after the initial onslaught, the firing was diminishing.

In places, it had stopped altogether. Wagner reached his tent and got on the radio, seeking contact with each of his posts in turn. The first two did not reply at all, the third offered only frantic babbling from which the word *Americans* was most prominent.

"You promised that USA would not fight," Magambo fretted.

"Those aren't US troops."

"Who else could they be but American soldiers. You have betrayed us."

"It is not the Americans. It was just Maynard and his men returning. Our troops will be able to fight them off," Wagner seethed.

He kept pressing buttons, shouting call-signs, getting no further response. Maybe the radio was faulty.

He dashed out of the tent, seeking another radio. The control tower—that was the place. He would be able to get the best perspective of what was happening from there. But already, once outside, he could see plainly that the gunfire had all but ceased. Now there was just the occasional flash and detonation amongst the dark buildings. There were no longer voices yelling. The flares were slowly spluttering out. Why weren't his men reporting in?

"What's going on over there?" he bellowed at the nearest post. He could see indistinct images of men moving, close enough to hear him and respond, he was sure. Wagner hurried on. Evolution was irresistible. His men would hold and overcome. The very thought was in his mind when he was thumped in the middle of the back and fell forward, tumbling into the mud at the bottom of a sewage ditch. He tried to right himself, unable to comprehend what had happened. He looked up, and saw Magambo standing at the edge of the ditch with a pistol in his hand. The great stupid black man had not understood, and had cut him down from behind. Straight out of the trees, these dickheads, Wagner muttered in his disbelief as he tried to get to his knees. He'd show the stupid bastard what superman meant. He was about to stand when his boots slipped and he fell again. Then the pain completely enveloped him.

Maybe Magambo had fired again—he wasn't sure what had

happened. It just wasn't right. He was the next stage in evolution and surely it could not end here, in the shit, like this. He fell forward on his face and the last thing he knew was the disgusting taste of the slime that filled his mouth and nostrils...

*

When the soldiers burst in the door, Lorna emerged abruptly from what must have been some sort of trance. She had been raving, saying her stuff, as the crew called it, droning on and on for what must have been hours, lost in her words and herself. She shook her head, trying to shuffle her brain into reality. The autocue that she was supposed to be reading was stalled, and she realised that it had been for some time. She had never really needed it, and *ad libbed* mostly, using the cue to remind herself of where she was up to from time to time. But it had stopped and she went on, completely unaided, robotic, as if she too needed someone to press her off button.

The red light showed the camera too was running, but there was no longer an operator. Vaguely she remembered people leaving, but she had continued, talking and talking, saying her stuff, over and over, every time different but every time the same message.

"Go to the focal point. Leave what you are doing and go. This is our last chance and everyone must be there. Put down what you are doing and go."

And now there were soldiers, breaking in the door, hurling a devastating light into the studio. She saw their silhouettes against the outside world. They had come for her. Still mostly functioning on remote control, she looked up toward the control room as if they could help, could change things. The lights were on and she could see that there was no one there.

"We can't be sure of what will happen. Nothing is guaranteed. But there is the hope that we can make this disaster go away, all of us, all of humanity, and even if you can't go, think of those who are there, be there in spirit if not in fact, be a part. This is the greatest event ever to happen in all history. Don't be the one to miss out."

It was coming back to her vaguely. From time to time, people had approached her; the production assistant to ask if she wanted to take a break; the make-up girl to dab her brow and ask if she was feeling okay; the floor manager to assured himself she wanted to continue. She remembered Louie, her director, saying; "We're going now. Do you want to come with us?" She didn't remember what she answered, if she answered, she supposed that she had just shrugged them off and continued her diatribe. The studio nurse too, telling her she was exhausted. How long had she been at this?

"We are all united in this, the people of the planet earth, regardless of colour, religion or nationality. We are as one, against a singular force. Only our unity can stand against it. All of the pilgrims are there. Anyone who can get there, do so. Anyone who can watch it on television, join us with your thoughts. We are as one today."

She remembered people raving, talking about her as if she wasn't there. "This is the largest television audience ever," they cried jubilantly. "And you, Lorna, are the most popular person to have ever lived." Oddly, she didn't feel any different for that. "And everyone is behind you. They all love you. No person, not Christ nor Buddha nor anyone else, in all history, has ever been loved by so many people as you are today." "You are the queen of the world, Lorna," the PR person babbled. "They'll make you the first President of the Global Republic." Errant nonsense, she was sure. She pressed on, not because of what they said but in spite of it, because she knew Harley had been right and that this gathering of humanity, this unification, was the pure form of love that she had been so desperately seeking. The love of all humanity for all humanity. They could make her President some other day—today she was only Harley's messenger.

"This is love. This is what those emotions and confusions that plague us all have always been about. We are capable of any deed imaginable, good or evil, and any emotion, kind or cruel, that is possible. But most of all we seek love and this is the love we seek.

We, all of us, love one another, totally and selflessly, and for no other reason than because we want to love. It is our greatest right, and it is ours, here and now. Grasp it with both hands and refuse to let go. This is what we have sought for all history. Take it and hold it to your breast. This is why we are honoured with the name *Humanity*."

She remembered there had been crowds, a huge multitude outside the studio and her crew was trapped inside for many hours. The vast throng waited for her to emerge but she stayed and talked and said her stuff. But now they were gone and she was alone. Except for the soldiers.

The officer approached her now, unarmed and unthreateningly. "Miss Simmons? Will you come with us now? Everything is finished here."

"Everyone has gone?" she said, or asked—she wasn't sure which.

"Yes. Everyone has gone. Bakersfield is completely deserted now. Only you are left. I think they forgot that you are not a pilgrim anymore, and would stay on."

"Of course," she smiled. She had forgotten it herself. "Are you sure they are all gone?"

"Every one of them. And we have a plane waiting for you, to take you there if you want to go."

"I have to maintain the broadcast," she said. "I have to keep telling them what to do."

"They all know what to do, Miss Simmons. They are all gathering at the focal point. Everyone who can, from all around the world. They have all heard you, and listened, and believed. There's only you left, and only just time to get you there."

"Of course. I'd forgotten. I get to choose."

"Yes, Miss Simmons. It's up to you."

She paused, but she didn't need to think about it really. It was just that she had been here, immobilised, for so long that she didn't quite know how to leave.

"It's Lorna," she said, giving the soldier a flirtatious flash of her eyes.

He almost fell over backwards in his surprise. "What?"

"My name. It's Lorna. Please call me that."

"If you wish…" the soldier said uncertainly.

"What's your name? You're real name—not the one that goes with your rank and serial number."

"Ryan."

"Okay, Ryan. I'd like to go, but really I must maintain the broadcast, until the event is over."

"We know that. We have a camera crew on the plane. You can continue all the way."

She smiled. The man looked pleased at his own efficiency.

"Then fine. What's holding us up?"

*

All along the southern edge of the mighty Congo River, a vast flotilla had gathered comprising vessels of every kind. There were the huge river ferries looking fearfully top-heavy, and a number of very decrepit wooden tourist boats. There were fishing boats, private boats, row boats and canoes. Anything that could float for miles around was gathered there, compliments of Brian Carrick who had toiled through the tedium of contacting every operator on the whole river system and offering them twice the normal rate. Even police boats and military boats had been turned to the task, amphibians and a gun boat that undoubtably survived from European rule. The presidential barge was there, and a paddle steamer that seemed to have sailed right out of Mark Twain.

Several pontoon jetties had been organised and now onto these flocked Andromeda's legions, making their way to whatever boat was most convenient, and when each was full it pulled away from the pontoons to allow the next vessel to be filled. At this point, the opposite bank of the river was only just visible in the distance, and it had been agreed that the boats wait to travel in convoy for they would tow the pontoons with them —loaded with people—since there was a similar lack of landing facilities on the other side. For the sake of organisation and to appease local officialdom, it had been decided to avoid using any major docks and towns as part of the operation, for they were overcrowded places, shanty towns mostly, and the huge influx people would create more chaos than their meagre docking facilities would solve. More pontoons were on the way and could be expected to be in place by the time the flotilla returned to for their next consignment of humanity, and then they too would be towed across, increasing the landing stage. Even with such maximised organisation, the transportation of the entire group was expected to take several days.

On the far side was mostly a gigantic swamp and the location had been chosen because it was the only bit of dry ground in the region, and just a mile inland from the landing place there was an airstrip which Maynard had commandeered. Here the C130s and other cargo aircraft—mainly DC-3s and similar vintage types from local charter operators, and Caribous and Chinooks provided by the USAF, would be there to immediately begin ferrying the people to Lake Chad. While the large aircraft could make the distance directly, arrangements had been made to refuel the smaller en route.

There was a small white launch that had been gladly provided by friends of the president and it was here that Andromeda positioned herself. Maynard was with her, liaising by radio with his men who directed the loading procedures. The only other occupants of the launch was a local helmsman, and twenty children chosen from the flock as a reward for their bravery on the long march.

"Position me where everyone can see me," Andromeda instructed the helmsman.

Maynard smiled but said nothing. The captains of all the various vessels had their orders. He was on the launch to facilitate getting to any troublespot speedily. He checked the flare pistol he would fire when they gave him the clearance from the land. The helmsman sailed them fifty metres toward the middle of the river, directly away from the fleet. Andromeda stood in the rear of the boat and raised her arms. From the boats, a great roar went up in response.

Maynard offered her a bleak look. "It's hard enough to tell what's going on, Andromeda, without you getting them all over-excited."

"I just wanted to make sure they all knew where I was," Andromeda said determinedly.

Maynard checked his mood. He was a very harried man, and he had left the arrangements at Lake Chad to Brian Carrick, in order to fly down here and supervise this, the most difficult part of the operation. On the Plain of Confrontation, as the Lake Chad base had come to be called—in fact it was officially but less conspicuously the northern extreme of the Plain of Bornu—the airstrips were operating and the pilgrims streaming in and it was all as planned and organised as it would get. But, for the moment, that would have to take care of itself. Getting these people over the river without disaster was the primary concern—the larger scale difficulties he could work on when he got back.

His men were weary from their brief but successful firefight, and should have been rested. But they had the experience in handling these people and anyway, all wanted to be in on the completion of the job. US and UN troops had moved in at Lake Chad. And, best of all, this was a maritime operation when Maynard and his crew had been landlocked for far too long.

The radio signal came through, and Maynard stood in the stern of the launch and fired the flare. Nothing happened for a moment, and then the river began to churn as the innumerable vessels got underway.

As soon as they started to move, Andromeda turned to the helmsman, who had been watching for her signal with some anxiety, and nodded. The launch swerved left with such violence that Maynard was all but thrown into the river. As he recovered himself into a sitting position, Andromeda strode down to the stern and, as before, threw up her arms. From the flotilla, the roar of voices in response could be clearly heard.

Maynard, his head swivelling this way and that, finally regained his footing, but she was so much taller than he that he still seemed to grovel about her feet.

"Where the hell are you going?" he protested frantically.

"Where I said I would go," Andromeda replied blithely.

"You mean Sierra Leone," Maynard said. He was carrying a pistol on his belt and reached for it now. "Mantu. Turn the boat now," he yelled.

"If you pull that gun, Captain," Andromeda said, stepping between the two men. "You'll have to shoot me first. Here. In front of all these children."

Maynard closed his eyes as if not wanting to see that possibility, and then opened them again. "You can't get to Sierra Leone from here. We talked about this."

"We can get there, Captain," Andromeda replied assuredly. "Downriver, where we can find ships and sail to the Land of my Fathers."

Maynard shook his head in dismay. "There aren't those sorts of ships available."

"Captain, after all the hardship we been through together and all the obstacles we've overcome, I'm mighty surprised to hear your negative view."

Maynard, in frustration, gazed away into the distance. He was seriously contemplating overpowering her—if indeed he could—and looked toward the fleet behind them to see what chaos this maneuver was causing. He cocked his head, making sure he was seeing what he saw.

"Not just me, Andromeda. You'll have to persuade them too."

She turned, regarding the vessels back there with a frown. None of them had turned. They were all carrying on straight across the river.

Andromeda threw up her arms in what had become the signal to her flock. When they responded, it was, all of them, to point out the way they should go, for plainly, to all of them, she had missed the turn.

"They aren't following," Andromeda said, in complete horror, to the world in general.

"Apparently not. Maybe they misunderstood your signal."

"But they followed me so far," Andromeda continued in sheer grief. "Why won't they follow me now?"

"Because you are no longer going the right way."

*

When Lorna landed, Brian was there to greet her. Lorna came off the plane with a look of annoyance, spluttering dust and her hand lashing at insects. She would, eternally, hate these hot and fly-blown places.

"Welcome to the end of the world," he grinned at her.

"Am I the last to arrive?"

"Are you kidding? Word is there's millions of people on your tail, coming this way, and more getting ready to leave. This is just the beginning."

"Goodness, Brian. What a organisational nightmare you must be having."

"Done it all before," Brian grinned. "Piece of piss."

He took her on a little guided tour of his operation, after which she realised just exactly how profound his abilities to understate the circumstances were.

By that time, a huge city was beginning to grow on the Plain of Confrontation. Shuttled in from twenty international airports in all directions from the focal point, the biggest fleet of C-130s and similar aircraft in the world landed, disgorged their human cargo and flew away again immediately. The runway was now equipped with landing lights that were rarely extinguished, and they kept coming day and night.

Once landed, the people and their belongings were herded by troops, registered by the Red Cross, and set walking through the rows of tents in various directions until they reached the perimeter where they set up their own camp. Buses and trucks were available only for those who could not walk the distance. So the city continually grew as the able-bodied were given instructions on how to dig latrines and lay water pipes and erect prefabricated structures. Notice boards carried maps of the city that changed daily, indicating food supply areas, hospital facilities, police stations.

It was decided that all materials were brought in by road—all available aircraft were needed to ferry the people. The city grew of its own accord, until the distance to the outskirts could not be walked in a single day, and then not in two days. Able-bodied people removed themselves further out to make room for way-stations and further facilities to be made along each roadway.

It was not the most pleasant place. The heat in the day and extreme cold at night afflicted many, insects plagued everyone all the time. The dust from hundreds of thousands of feet blew about the tent flaps, and if it rained, which was not impossible, the whole place would become a giant quagmire.

Anyone could leave, any time they wanted. They had only to board one of the outgoing aircraft which carried only garbage but otherwise flew back empty. Apart from emergency illnesses, no one did leave.

On the plain most people knew that whatever hardship they faced, it would be over within a week, and that thought seemed to make it bearable for everyone.

They were fortunate that this was a region that the lake flooded annually but which at this time of year was baked hard mud. Once the airfield for the C-130s was completed, the workers immediately began a longer parallel runway, and they had only to smooth out the surface of the baked mud and it was firm enough and long enough to take the severe impact of 747s coming in as direct flights from around the world. The ground was hard enough to withstand them, on a short term basis at least.

Thyssen flew in on one of the first, sleeping all the way. Debbie the nurse awoke him only as they circled the tent city, so that he might see the broad panorama of his work. He grunted and went back to sleep.

For he could finally sleep, for the first time in about a decade. No longer did he need the assistance of alcohol—which was presently denied him by the medical profession anyway—or sedation to bring on sleep. The terror and the remorse had been evicted from his dreams. He no longer had to decide anything. It was out of his hands now and all he had to do was await the results. As such, he was more relaxed than he had ever known himself to be before.

Debbie rolled him off the plane in a wheelchair, into the blazing sun.

"It's very hot," she said.

"It'll get hotter," Thyssen replied

So they gathered, coming from everywhere now, facing possible death but determined to fulfill their belief.

*

Andromeda was the last to leave. Maynard had sent back a long-range helicopter which could fly her in directly and she stepped down onto the airstrip to be swamped by her followers. A great roar went up and they swarmed around her, chanting and cheering despite the heat and dust

"They wouldn't disperse until you got here to lead them," Brian had to shout in her ear. He looked ridiculously calm and unharried when such prodigious chaos reigned all about him.

"Well, I'm here now, Brian. Which way would you like me to go."

"We've reserved a set of prefab huts with a hospital for your lot over there. Most of them are under nourished and need medical attention."

"It was a tough journey, Brian. But here we are."

"The Promised Land?" Brian asked with raised eyebrows.

Andromeda surveyed the scene grimly. "Hardly that! But I guess it'll have to do."

*

On the Plain of Confrontation the great tent city had grown at an astonishing rate. Two days after Maynard's troops cleared the area, it had exceeded the population of Lagos in Nigeria and Addis Abba in Sudan, the largest cities in the region. Two more days and the 1.5 million population of Casablanca had been surpassed. By the end of the first week, the largest city in Central Africa—Kinshasa—was exceeded. Three days before the event, it had passed Cairo and had become the biggest city in Africa.

The Red Cross and UN groups struggled to keep count of the numbers as the city began to double in size, and then doubled again. It was one of the ten most populous cities in the world on the day the sun dawned, perhaps for all of them for the final time. They came and kept on coming, carrying their tents and blankets and food parcels while all around, armies dug pits for hygiene and pumped in water from the lake.

*

In the end it was a small piece of foolish bureaucracy that tripped him up. It was always the way. You could soar to the heights, trade in billions of dollars, chat with presidents and captains of industry, and fool everybody all the time. But all such men fell in the end and it was some little man, faceless and insignificant, who just would not let go on some tiny fragment of the structure, bringing the whole dizzy construct crashing down.

Joe Solomon had no idea who his mentor was, and in the end, did not care. Someone, somewhere, had noticed that they were about to take a man out of the country when he was *sub judice* and refused to sign the appropriate paper or stamp the appropriate stamp. Whatever. Of course Joe tried to explain it.

"But I have to be there. Otherwise it will throw the whole focal point out of position and ruin everything."

No one seemed to know what he was talking about. He wasn't sure he knew himself. I had no idea of what arrangements Thyssen might have made to ensure the focal point stayed right where he wanted it. Maybe every pilgrim in the world was there except him, or perhaps, knowing Thyssen, there were groups positioned precisely around the world to ensure it locked in. Maybe he was within the circle, maybe not. There was no one he was allowed to talk to who could understand the problem.

Of course, as usual, they had arranged to move him when the linkage time came. His guardian agents assured him of this, every time he protested. The usual run in his motorised wheelchair escorted by two agents on bicycles or maybe a stretch limo heading aimlessly in the direction he chose, as had been the options in the past. That the agents understood and were prepared for. The rest was beyond them. They were sure that arrangements would be satisfactory.

"I want to speak to the President!" Joe raged at them.

"Yeah, sure Joe."

Joe sat in his room at the hotel as the linkage came on and his desperation grew, until suddenly he realised he didn't care anymore. He had done enough. All that was needed. He had certainly done Thyssen enough favours. Far too many in fact. He thought it through and realised that he wasn't really thinking anything at all. There was just the pain and the anxiety and who needed that?

He had no thoughts at the end. They found him in his room, overdosed on the painkillers he took constantly. Beside him was a note. *"I have never believed in Thyssen. Whether he is proven right or I am vindicated, I have no wish to be around to see it. Also pressures in Washington have left my run too late, and I am stuck here. This way, I will not distort the position of the pilgrims. No matter what the outcome, I am guilty of fraud on a massive scale. It was all my own idea and all my own guilt. My physical pain, also, has become too much to bear. I am too tired to fight any longer."*

"Do we tell the President?" the secret service agents who found him asked each other. They did not until it was over.

*

In the control room in Washington, the visual display offered a countdown to sunset at Lake Chad, and before it John Cornelius mused on the ironies of life. Here, in the moment of greatest crisis, he found one of his few times of peace. In the next few minutes, fate would decide the future course of his life. One outcome would take him in the direction of the champion of Thyssen's cause, and who was to say that didn't lead all the way to the White House. The opposite outcome would see him as the man who stood up to Thyssen, who tried and failed to save all those unfortunate souls. Where that would lead was less clear, but he was ready for the months and years of inquiries and media attention—all of the documents prepared or shredded, all his speeches to senators or journalists already written.

Cornelius had it covered, whatever the outcome, and now, in these last minutes when there was nothing else to do, he suddenly discovered he had reached the end of his mission. It had all worked out fine, and there was nothing else to be done. He sat in the control room, watching the screens with detached interest. In this one time in his life when there were no more deceptions, there was no more pressure, in that blissful moment between the time when what went before ended, but what followed had not yet begun.

*

Judy Carrick watched it all on television. To her it all looked rather like a country carnival, a barbecue in the bush, with thousands and thousands of people gathered, playing together, talking, drinking, eating, reading, doing all the things that gathered people do amid the random scatter of tents and vehicles and beach umbrellas and director's chairs and rugs laid on the ground. She saw that the sun shone down upon them brilliantly, and if you turned the commentary off, you would have thought there was nothing wrong, that these people were happy to be together, enjoying their day. Only the commentary told her that this was their last day, that these people were facing up to doom.

"There's Daddy," Lou cried.

"Yes, darling. That's Daddy."

There were shots from helicopters but as the sun crept toward the horizon, the camera crews took themselves onto the ground and roamed amongst the public. There seemed to be every kind of human imaginable, and they were interviewed by the crews in every language. But then the reporters hurried away and only stationary, remote cameras remained. The interviews ceased.

We'll stay on the air right to the end, they said, and only those crews who were already pilgrims remained, sticking it out to the last.

"Are you afraid?" was the most common interview question. Most answers were non-committal. *Well maybe a little but I wouldn't be here if I thought.... Do you really think that...? Oh yes, I really believe.*

They stayed and the sun descended and the tension became unbearable. Judy knew that when the moment came, the images would cease, the cameras and communications would go blank, and she couldn't wait for that. She went outside where the children were playing shuttlecock on the lawn. Neighbours, relations, others were watching. They would tell her what happened.

*

Fabrini, the customary Uzi tucked under his arm, stood on a rock, the only high ground for miles around. Away in the distance on the barren plain, he saw what might have been a dust storm. Through binoculars, he studied the cloud. There was no doubt about it—it was a large force of men moving toward them and somehow he could see plainly their menacing intent. The raiders, closing in for the kill. He glanced toward the sun, as it inched toward the horizon. In less than an hour after dark they would be upon these helpless people—heavily armed and with murderous intent.

He hurried down from the rock to where he had parked his jeep. On the radio, he spoke to Captain Maynard, and reported what he had seen.

"We need to get helicopter out there. We must see what they are up to. It don't look no good to me."

Captain Maynard smiled thinly as he listened to Fabrini's garbled report. "All choppers are grounded, Mr. Fabrini. And you better get yourself back here right away."

He was appreciative of Fabrini's warning, but really it only allowed him to feel more secure. When the choppers had been flying earlier, they had already reported the advancing ground-force, and Fabrini only assured him that they would not arrive in time.

In time for what? He had his troops deployed, but Thyssen had instructed him to take no action against them.

"Let them come," Thyssen smiled. "They're within the zone. They add to our strength. The more the merrier."

Maynard shook his head. It was rare enough that an enemy invasion was welcomed. Strange times indeed. His own troops were positioned and ready if needed, but by the minute Maynard was becoming surer that they would not be.

*

When the screens dropped out to static, it hit Glen Palenski like a physical blow. He had expected it, of course, but that didn't make it shock him any less. There in the final frame was Thyssen and the others, positioned on a slight hillock at the centre of their magic city, smiling and happy, and Glen wanted more than anything to be with them. It didn't matter what happened now, whether they lived or died. He knew he should have been there, and that was all.

Because he had to say something, do something, he turned to the operator nearest him and asked: "How long before transmission can be restored?" He asked not for the information—he ready knew that—but out of anxiety, and out of an even more desperate need to show that anxiety—to show he cared, to show he was still human, to himself if no-one else.

"Just as soon as we can get a working camera in there. All those in the zone had burned out circuits and are stuffed. The most likely is camera H3. That one. They could be to the edge of the camp within a few minutes. They'll overfly it and... we'll..."

But the operator didn't want to say what they would see and what they would not see. Nothing, everything, it no longer mattered. The game was played out, and Thyssen had won, whatever happened from here. And Glen knew he was condemned to the role of Judas for eternity.

*

Alone in a roomful of advisers, President Grayson sat on a couch in the oval office, the First Lady at his side, with his head in his hands throughout the entire period of the transmission blackout. At one point, a junior officer, in the next room, could be heard to murmur—"Eleven minutes to estimated restoration of signal..." One of the white house staffers went to tell him to be silent.

*

Brian Carrick sat with the others on the slight rise, comfortable in a director's chair, a bundle of nerves in this place—the focal point—where the anxiety was supposed to end. In a few minutes, they would know and it was the knowledge of that which contented him—the outcome was less important. This would be the beginning of the war of immensities, as Thyssen had termed it. The conflict of mind and matter. If they survived, it would all be plain, not just Thyssen's plan but the whole thing—the very purpose of human existence. It would be a journey to the end of the universe and when they arrived they would be there to stop it from happening. Simple as that. And the journey began here, now, this coming minute.

And now that he knew where he was going, Brian was anxious to get underway. Of course, another possibility was that he might be dead, but who could care about that? For sure he wouldn't be caring about star warriors nor anything else. All that mattered was that they had got here and it was ready to happen. What followed was simply formality.

Andromeda Starlight stood on the mound with her arms uplifted to the horizontal, her great robe billowing even in this slight breeze. Now that she was here, she realised it was her fulfillment. The vast sea of faces before her, to the horizon in every direction, was breathtaking to see, and she responded. Not just to her own supporters, those she had brought so far, but to all of them. This would be the last time, whatever happened. Never again would she have so massive an audience, and she relished it. This was what mattered, where it had all been leading, and tomorrow—if there was a tomorrow—there would be a new dream to pursue, perhaps a new image to evolve. She was beginning to weary of being Gaia anyway. She had played the role to the hilt, to its ultimate point. Now it was time to move on. But this final performance would be the one to remember, for all time to come. And she sang not a word to the biggest audience anyone had ever experienced. All she needed to be was there, and there she was in all her glory.

In the end, Lorna, who had been the eyes through which the world saw these events, could not look. She couldn't stand lest she would fall and there was nowhere to sit, so in the end she knelt beside Thyssen's legs and rested her face in his lap. His great hand closed about her face, caressed her cheek and she felt safe, felt fulfilled, felt it had all been worth it.

Often she had reflected on how far she had come these recent months—from humble Kiwi receptionist-typist to global media superstar and it astonished her and made her proud beyond all reason but somehow it all seemed natural to her as well, as if it would have happened anyway. But now she knew that was not the real journey she had taken, that it was all just life and could be over in a few minutes and she was terrified.

Worst was to think that she didn't need to be here. She was the one pilgrim who had already been cured and who could say what effect a third dose would have on her. But all attempts to get rid of her had failed—this was where she belonged. If it killed her, if it made her a pilgrim again, if it did some other horrible thing to her, it didn't matter. This was where she belonged. Everyone else had come from somewhere else to be here—she was at the centre of her world. She wrapped her arms around Thyssen's legs and hung on with everything she had.

Thyssen was calm. The moment was at hand. There would be the irrevocable posterity, of course, but he didn't care so much about that. In a few seconds, he would be the man who saved the planet, or else the madman who led thirteen million people to their deaths. But really, in the end it didn't make a lot of difference. They could say what they would—all Thyssen really wanted to know was if he was right, if his theory would be vindicated by the facts. For that was the horrible truth—he had never really believed it. All the way as he swept events along before him, he had never completely believed it. In a continual state of doubt, he went forward because forward seemed the only way he could go. But he never believed.

Now, finally, one way or the other, the agony of doubt would end, and he would be at rest.

There was a blinding, devastating flash, an earth swallowing, planet bursting, mind scattering crunch, and then silence.

20
CLASH OF INFINITIES

People lie everywhere. All over the Plain of Confrontation, bodies are strewn. It is like the outcome of a primitive battle—they lie everywhich way, beside each other, across each other, curled in the foetal position, stretched out, twisted. Every way you look there are more and more of them, all still and silent. No primitive battle was ever so great as this.

On for mile after mile, a great carpet of humanity covers the earth, away in all directions to the horizon. Like leaves fallen from the trees in autumn, like the sea weed thrown up along the beach, like the rows and rows of derelict cars in an eternal junkyard. Passing over them for mile upon mile, it is possible, just for a moment, to understand exactly how populous this planet was, to see so many people, from all nations, in all attires, of every age and every kind, all strewn like the litter of civilisation upon the earth.

The wind blows amongst them, flapping this garment, swirling some dust, then darting away as if disturbed by the lack of animation. The sky breathes upon them, as if expecting them to respond as they always have, but not now. Nothing happens.

And still the sea of bodies, reminiscent of those forests flattened by the volcanoes that have roared and thundered in the past. But no volcano roars. There is only the gentle breeze, and the stillness.

The minutes pass, like an eternity and perhaps it is. Perhaps all existence lies between this moment and the next, in the hiatus of existence that has befallen humanity—brave, foolish, inadequate humanity, a species still in its childhood, cut off from all time and memory. They came from nowhere, for no reason, and set out to stamp their mark on the universe but now were struck down, devastated, dashed on the very earth upon which they were forged.

Minutes pass elsewhere, here there is no time. This death of multitudes is beyond conception, beyond measure, beyond time. The sun has now sunk completely below the horizon and the darkness begins to cast a forbidding shadow over the scene. In the half light, child lies with its arm over their still parent, lover face to face with lover, the solitary within the aura of strangers, all still and...

Then there is a voice, but it is a radio voice, that of Professor Harrington in some distant safe location, fading in and becoming louder, a voice over as we fly across the ocean of bodies and tents and belongings, motionless but for the swirling dust and the wind...

"So they came with their hopes and dreams, as so many had come before them—the Seventh Day Adventists, the Children of Allah, and all those other credulous hordes all down through history, to the chosen place at the chosen time, as spoken by the words of their so-called prophets, to meet their maker, to watch the apocalypse... So too came the millions of the children of the false prophet Harley Thyssen, to gather at the end of the world at the place the fire and brimstone would burst forth, where the planet-eating monster of Thyssen's insane nightmares would show its face to them. So they came in their pathetic hopes, like some many before and yet more numerous than all the others put together, to the Plain of Confrontation, in the heat beside the muddy waters of Lake Chad. They came and they waited and the moment of destiny arrived, with the setting of the sun, as their false prophet had told them. They lifted their eyes to heaven, and waited for this the greatest of all miracles, the gullible in their last moment of belief. And what happened, as the moment of judgment passed. Nothing happened.

Nothing happened at all. The moment passed, the sun set on the plain of Chad, and not one thing moved. All around the world, there was not a flicker on the seismographs. There were no great fires in the skies. The earth did not crack with fire and lava, nor did the face of doom emerge from its subterranean lair. Nothing happened.

And they, like all the gulled masses before them, this time knew the truth, that they had been deceived, that they had come all that way and gathered for nothing.

They saw only the falsity of their prophet and knew only the lies they had been told…

Then, Harrington's voice is cut off. Somewhere, there is a cry. Of a bird, perhaps. No, it extends. A continuous, unabating cry that few animals can maintain. Where is it coming from? Where amongst all this scattered, discarded flesh. This desert of human flesh… There.

It is a child, a toddler, sex indeterminate, standing in the wind and the dimness, clutching its mother's arm.

Then others, far across the field of bodies, other older children sit quietly, or play, smiling at each other. Here a man raises himself on his elbows, shakes the dust from his face, and sits up, looking around. There an elderly couple reach out and hug one another. The mother sits up as if summoned, to comfort her crying child.

And now there are people awakening everywhere, all looking around, puzzled, smiling, greeting one another. They are standing, walking, moving to help those still sleeping, always looking around and wondering.

On the hillock at the centre, Lorna was the first awake. She remained with her head resting on Harley's thighs, but her eyes were open and there was a smile on her lips. Then Harley's hand moved to enclose her cheek and run through her hair.

Andromeda Starlight lifted herself, raising herself to her full height, gazing away across the multitude where hundreds of those rose as she did. She lifted her arms and they raised theirs, and a mighty roar of jubilation began to rise from their multitudinous throats…

Brian Carrick shook his head to clear it, and then looked toward Thyssen, his grin firmly fixed on his face. Thyssen pretended not to notice him. Brian reached and punched the old man playfully on the shoulder, but Thyssen rocked exaggeratedly from the blow, and could not avoid the slight flicker of a smile on his face.

The sun had set, satisfied with its day's work, and the first stars began to appear. Thyssen raised his tear-glinted eyes toward them, and his grin broadened.

Barry Klemm enjoyed an array of abandoned careers before resorting to literature. He was a crane jockey, insurance clerk, combat soldier, advertising officer, computer programmer, cleaner, stagehand, postman, sports ground manager, builder's labourer, taxi-driver, film and TV scriptwriter and radio dramatist. He has published two novels for teen-age readers, The Tenth Hero, in 1997, and Last Voyage of the Albatross in 1998 through Addison Wesley Longman and Running Dogs, a novel of the Vietnam war by Black Pepper in 2000.